POSTMARK: MURDER

POSTMARK: MURDER

- *A Caribbean Mystery*
- *Nemesis*
- *Murder in Mesopotamia*
- *Appointment with Death*

by Agatha Christie

Nelson Doubleday, Inc.
Garden City, New York

The characters, places, incidents and situations in this book are imaginary and have no relation to any person, place, or actual happening.

Published by arrangement with Dodd, Mead & Company.

Printed in the United States of America.

ISBN: 1-56865-051-5

©

CONTENTS

A CARIBBEAN MYSTERY

A Miss Marple Murder Mystery

TO
my old friend
John Cruikshank Rose
with happy memories of my visit
to the West Indies

CONTENTS

CAST OF CHARACTERS

MAJOR PALGRAVE—An old soldier with an unfortunate weakness for reliving the past.

MISS JANE MARPLE—She specialized in being a good listener, but when she finally had something to say, even the police sat up and took notice.

TIM KENDAL—The perfect host for a vacation hotel: he charmed the old ladies and made the young ones think he was panting for them.

MOLLY KENDAL—Tim's wife—gay and pretty, but haunted by nightmares—which led her to midnight strolls.

GREG DYSON—He said he was a student of butterflies, and, with his money, who cared if he preferred the young two-legged variety?

"LUCKY" DYSON, GREG'S WIFE—She had married for money and didn't want to miss out on any of the fringe benefits.

EDWARD HILLINGDON—He was so charming to his wife in public, there *had* to be a skeleton in the closet.

EVELYN HILLINGDON—The dark horse in the happy foursome; did fear keep her silent?

CANON PRESCOTT—Round and benevolent, he was just what people expected a man of the cloth to be. Was he too good to be true?

JOAN PRESCOTT, THE CANON'S SISTER—She knew it was unseemly to gossip, but her "innocent" comments about the guests opened Miss Marple's eyes.

MR. RAFIEL—Incredibly old, incredibly rich, he had nothing to do all day but make more money until he decided to join in the island's favorite sport—murder!

ARTHUR JACKSON, RAFIEL'S VALET—Admittedly handsome, but not a gentleman, he was the type Major Palgrave wouldn't have given a second look—unless there was something familiar about him!

ESTHER WALTERS, RAFIEL'S EFFICIENT SECRETARY—She could have been quite glamorous if she tried—Miss Marple wondered why she didn't.

DR. GRAHAM—He was willing to humor Miss Marple and look for the snapshot she said she had lent Major Palgrave.

VICTORIA JOHNSON, MAID AT THE HOTEL—She had the right idea about what killed the Major, but she told it to the wrong people.

1

MAJOR PALGRAVE TELLS A STORY

"Take all this business about Kenya," said Major Palgrave. "Lots of chaps gabbing away who know nothing about the place! Now I spent fourteen years of my life there. Some of the best years of my life, too—"

Old Miss Marple inclined her head.

It was a gentle gesture of courtesy. While Major Palgrave proceeded with the somewhat uninteresting recollections of a lifetime, Miss Marple peacefully pursued her own thoughts. It was a routine with which she was well acquainted. The locale varied. In the past, it had been predominantly India. Majors, colonels, lieutenant-generals—and a familiar series of words: *Simla. Bearers. Tigers. Chota Hazri—Tiffin. Khitmagars,* and so on. With Major Palgrave the terms were slightly different. *Safari. Kikuyu. Elephants. Swahili.* But the pattern was essentially the same. An elderly man who needed a listener so that he could, in memory, relive days in which he had been happy. Days when his back had been straight, his eyesight keen, his hearing acute. Some of these talkers had been handsome soldierly old boys, some again had been regrettably unattractive; and Major Palgrave, purple of face, with a glass eye, and the general appearance of a stuffed frog, belonged in the latter category.

Miss Marple had bestowed on all of them the same gentle charity. She had sat attentively, inclining her head from time to time in gentle agreement, thinking her own thoughts and enjoying what there was to enjoy, in this case the deep blue of a Caribbean Sea.

So kind of dear Raymond, she was thinking gratefully, so really and truly kind. . . . Why he should take so much trouble about his old aunt, she really did not know. Conscience, perhaps; family feeling? Or possibly he was truly fond of her . . .

She thought, on the whole, that he was fond of her—he always had been

—in a slightly exasperated and contemptuous way! Always trying to bring her up to date. Sending her books to read. Modern novels. So difficult—all about such unpleasant people, doing such very odd things and not, apparently, even enjoying them. "Sex" as a word had not been much mentioned in Miss Marple's young days, but there had been plenty of it—not talked about so much—but enjoyed far more than nowadays, or so it seemed to her. Though usually labelled Sin, she couldn't help feeling that that was preferable to what it seemed to be nowadays—a kind of Duty.

Her glance strayed for a moment to the book on her lap lying open at page twenty-three, which was as far as she had got (and indeed as far as she felt like getting!).

"Do you mean that you've had no sexual experience at ALL?" demanded the young man incredulously. "At *nineteen?* But you *must.* It's vital."

The girl hung her head unhappily, her straight greasy hair fell forward over her face.

"I know," she muttered, "I know."

He looked at her, stained old jersey, the bare feet, the dirty toenails, the smell of rancid fat . . . He wondered why he found her so maddeningly attractive.

Miss Marple wondered, too! And really! To have sex experience urged on you exactly as though it was an iron tonic! Poor young things . . .

"My dear Aunt Jane, why must you bury your head in the sand like a very delightful ostrich? All bound up in this idyllic rural life of yours. REAL LIFE—that's what matters."

Thus Raymond—and his Aunt Jane had looked properly abashed and said "Yes," she was afraid she was rather old-fashioned.

Though really rural life was far from idyllic. People like Raymond were so ignorant. In the course of her duties in a country parish, Jane Marple had acquired quite a comprehensive knowledge of the facts of rural life. She had no urge to talk about them, far less to write about them—but she knew them. Plenty of sex, natural and unnatural. Rape, incest, perversions of all kinds. (Some kinds, indeed, that even the clever young men from Oxford who wrote books didn't seem to have heard about.)

Miss Marple came back to the Caribbean and took up the thread of what Major Palgrave was saying. . . .

"A very unusual experience," she said encouragingly. "Most interesting."

"I could tell you a lot more. Some of the things, of course, not fit for a lady's ears—"

With the ease of long practice, Miss Marple dropped her eyelids in a fluttery fashion, and Major Palgrave continued his bowdlerized version of tribal customs while Miss Marple resumed her thoughts of her affectionate nephew.

Raymond West was a very successful novelist and made a large income, and he conscientiously and kindly did all he could to alleviate the life of his elderly aunt. The preceding winter she had had a bad go of pneumonia, and medical opinion had advised sunshine. In lordly fashion Raymond had suggested a trip to the West Indies. Miss Marple had demurred—at the expense, the distance, the difficulties of travel, and at abandoning her house in St. Mary Mead. Raymond had dealt with everything. A friend who was writing a book wanted a quiet place in the country. "He'll look after the house all right. He's very house-proud. He's a queer. I mean—"

He had paused, slightly embarrassed—but surely even dear old Aunt Jane must have heard of queers.

He went on to deal with the next points. Travel was nothing nowadays. She would go by air—another friend, Diana Horrocks, was going out to Trinidad and would see Aunt Jane was all right as far as there, and at St. Honoré she would stay at the Golden Palm Hotel, which was run by the Sandersons. Nicest couple in the world. They'd see she was all right. He'd write to them straightaway.

As it happened the Sandersons had returned to England. But their successors, the Kendals, had been very nice and friendly and had assured Raymond that he need have no qualms about his aunt. There was a very good doctor on the island in case of emergency and they themselves would keep an eye on her and see to her comfort.

They had been as good as their word, too. Molly Kendal was an ingenuous blonde of twenty-odd, always apparently in good spirits. She had greeted the old lady warmly and did everything to make her comfortable. Tim Kendal, her husband—lean, dark and in his thirties—had also been kindness itself.

So there she was, thought Miss Marple, far from the rigours of the English climate, with a nice little bungalow of her own, with friendly smiling West Indian girls to wait on her, Tim Kendal to meet her in the dining-room and crack a joke as he advised her about the day's menu, and an easy path from her bungalow to the sea front and the bathing beach where she could sit in a comfortable basket chair and watch the bathing. There were even a few elderly guests for company. Old Mr. Rafiel, Dr. Graham, Canon Prescott and his sister, and her present cavalier Major Palgrave.

What more could an elderly lady want?

It is deeply to be regretted, and Miss Marple felt guilty even admitting it to herself, but she was not as satisfied as she ought to be.

Lovely and warm, yes—and so good for her rheumatism—and beautiful scenery, though perhaps—a trifle monotonous? So many palm trees. Everything the same every day—never anything happening. Not like St. Mary Mead, where something was always happening. Her nephew had once compared life in St. Mary Mead to scum on a pond, and she had indignantly pointed out that smeared on a slide under the microscope there would be plenty of life to be observed. Yes, indeed, in St. Mary Mead, there was always something going on. Incident after incident flashed through Miss Marple's mind: the mistake in old Mrs. Linnett's cough mixture—that very odd behaviour of young Polegate—the time when Georgy Wood's mother had come down to see him (but was she his mother—?)—the real cause of the quarrel between Joe Arden and his wife. So many interesting human problems—giving rise to endless pleasurable hours of speculation. If only there were something here that she could—well—get her teeth into.

With a start she realized that Major Palgrave had abandoned Kenya for the North West Frontier and was relating his experience as a subaltern. Unfortunately he was asking her with great earnestness: "Now don't you agree?"

Long practice had made Miss Marple quite an adept at dealing with that one.

"I don't really feel that I've got sufficient experience to judge. I'm afraid I've led rather a sheltered life."

"And so you should, dear lady, so you should," cried Major Palgrave gallantly.

"You've had such a very varied life," went on Miss Marple, determined to make amends for her former pleasurable inattention.

"Not bad," said Major Palgrave, complacently. "Not bad at all." He looked round him appreciatively. "Lovely place, this."

"Yes, indeed," said Miss Marple and was then unable to stop herself going on: "Does anything ever happen here, I wonder?"

Major Palgrave stared.

"Oh, rather. Plenty of scandals—eh what? Why, I could tell you—"

But it wasn't really scandals Miss Marple wanted. Nothing to get your teeth into in scandals nowadays. Just men and women changing partners and calling attention to it, instead of trying decently to hush it up and be properly ashamed of themselves.

"There was even a murder here a couple of years ago. Man called Harry Western. Made a big splash in the papers. Dare say you remember it."

Miss Marple nodded without enthusiasm. It had not been her kind of murder. It had made a big splash mainly because everyone concerned had been very rich. It had seemed likely enough that Harry Western had shot the Count de Ferrari, his wife's lover, and equally likely that his well-arranged alibi had been bought and paid for. Everyone seemed to have been drunk, and there was a fine scattering of dope addicts. Not really interesting people, thought Miss Marple—although no doubt very spectacular and attractive to look at. But definitely not her cup of tea.

"And if you ask me, that wasn't the only murder about that time." He nodded and winked. "I had my suspicions—oh, well—"

Miss Marple dropped her ball of wool, and the Major stooped and picked it up for her.

"Talking of murder," he went on, "I once came across a very curious case—not exactly personally."

Miss Marple smiled encouragingly.

"Lots of chaps talking at the club one day, you know, and a chap began telling a story. Medical man he was. One of his cases. Young fellow came and awakened him in the middle of the night. His wife had hanged herself. They hadn't a telephone, so after the chap had cut her down and done what he could, he'd got out his car and hared off looking for a doctor. Well, she wasn't dead but pretty far gone. Anyway, she pulled through. Young fellow seemed devoted to her. Cried like a child. He'd noticed that she'd been odd for some time, fits of depression and all that. Well, that was that. Everything seemed all right. But actually, about a month later, the wife took an overdose of sleeping stuff and passed out. Sad case."

Major Palgrave paused and nodded his head several times. Since there was obviously more to come, Miss Marple waited.

"And that's that, you might say. Nothing there. Neurotic woman, nothing out of the usual. But about a year later, this medical chap was swapping yarns with a fellow medico, and the other chap told him about a woman who'd tried to drown herself, husband got her out, got a doctor, they pulled her round—and then a few weeks later she gassed herself.

"Well, a bit of a coincidence—eh? Same sort of story. My chap said: 'I had a case rather like that. Name of Jones (or whatever the name was).—What was your man's name?' 'Can't remember. Robinson, I think. Certainly not Jones.'

"Well, the chaps looked at each other and said it was pretty odd. And then my chap pulled out a snapshot. He showed it to the second chap. 'That's the fellow,' he said. 'I'd gone along the next day to check up on the particulars, and I noticed a magnificent species of hibiscus just by the front door, a variety I'd never seen before in this country. My camera was in the car and I took a photo. Just as I snapped the shutter, the husband came out of the front door, so I got him as well. Don't think he realized it. I asked him about the hibiscus, but he couldn't tell me its name.' Second medico looked at the snap. He said: 'It's a bit out of focus. But I could swear—at any rate, I'm almost sure—it's the same man.'

"Don't know if they followed it up. But if so, they didn't get anywhere. Expect Mr. Jones or Robinson covered his tracks too well. But queer story, isn't it? Wouldn't think things like that could happen."

"Oh, yes, I would," said Miss Marple placidly. "Practically every day."

"Oh, come, come. That's a bit fantastic."

"If a man gets a formula that works, he won't stop. He'll go on."

"Brides in the bath—eh?"

"That kind of thing, yes."

"Doctor let me have the snap just as a curiosity—"

Major Palgrave began fumbling through an overstuffed wallet, murmuring to himself: "Lots of things in here—don't know why I keep all these things. . . ."

Miss Marple thought she did know. They were part of the Major's stock-in-trade. They illustrated his repertoire of stories. The story he had just told, or so she suspected, had not been originally like that—it had been worked up a good deal in repeated telling.

The Major was still shuffling and muttering: "Forgotten all about *that* business. Good-looking woman she was, you'd never suspect— Now where— Ah—that takes my mind back—what tusks! I must show you—"

He stopped, sorted out a small photographic print and peered down at it.

"Like to see the picture of a murderer?"

He was about to pass it to her when his movement was suddenly arrested. Looking more like a stuffed frog than ever, Major Palgrave appeared to be staring fixedly over her right shoulder—from whence came the sound of approaching footsteps and voices.

"Well, I'm damned—I mean—" He stuffed everything back into his wallet and crammed it into his pocket.

His face went an even deeper shade of purplish red. He exclaimed in a loud, artificial voice: "As I was saying—I'd like to have shown you those elephant tusks— Biggest elephant I've ever shot— Ah, hallo!" His voice took on a somewhat spurious hearty note.

"Look who's here! The great quartette—Flora and Fauna. What luck have you had today—eh?"

The approaching footsteps resolved themselves into four of the hotel guests whom Miss Marple already knew by sight. They consisted of two married couples and though Miss Marple was not as yet acquainted with their surnames, she knew that the big man with the upstanding bush of thick grey hair was addressed as "Greg," that the golden blonde woman, his wife, was known as Lucky—and that the other married couple, the dark lean man and the handsome but rather weather-beaten woman, were Edward and Evelyn.

They were botanists, she understood, and also interested in birds.

"No luck at all," said Greg. "At least no luck in getting what we were after."

"Don't know if you know Miss Marple? Colonel and Mrs. Hillingdon and Greg and Lucky Dyson."

They greeted her pleasantly, and Lucky said loudly that she'd die if she didn't have a drink at once or sooner.

Greg hailed Tim Kendal, who was sitting a little way away with his wife, poring over account books.

"Hi, Tim. Get us some drinks." He addressed the others. "Planter's Punch?"

They agreed.

"Same for you, Miss Marple?"

Miss Marple said Thank you, but she would prefer fresh lime.

"Fresh lime it is," said Tim Kendal, "and five Planter's Punches."

"Join us, Tim?"

"Wish I could. But I've got to fix up these accounts. Can't leave Molly to cope with everything. Steel band tonight, by the way."

"Good," cried Lucky. "Damn it," she winced, "I'm all over thorns. Ouch! Edward deliberately rammed me into a thornbush!"

"Lovely pink flowers," said Hillingdon.

"And lovely long thorns. Sadistic brute, aren't you, Edward?"

"Not like me," said Greg, grinning. "Full of the milk of human kindness."

Evelyn Hillingdon sat down by Miss Marple and started talking to her in an easy, pleasant way.

Miss Marple put her knitting down on her lap. Slowly and with some difficulty, owing to rheumatism in the neck, she turned her head over her right shoulder to look behind her. At some little distance there was the large bungalow occupied by the rich Mr. Rafiel. But it showed no sign of life.

She replied suitably to Evelyn's remarks (really, how kind people were to her!), but her eyes scanned thoughtfully the faces of the two men.

Edward Hillingdon looked like a nice man. Quiet but with a lot of charm. And Greg—big, boisterous, happy-looking. He and Lucky were Canadian or American, she thought.

She looked at Major Palgrave, still acting a bonhomie a little larger than life.

Interesting . . .

2

MISS MARPLE MAKES COMPARISONS

It was very gay that evening at the Golden Palm Hotel.

Seated at her little corner table, Miss Marple looked round her in an interested fashion. The dining-room was a large room open on three sides to the soft warm scented air of the West Indies. There were small table lamps, all softly coloured. Most of the women were in evening dress; light cotton prints out of which bronzed shoulders and arms emerged. Miss Marple herself had been urged by her nephew's wife Joan, in the sweetest way possible, to accept "a small check."

"Because, Aunt Jane, it will be rather hot out there, and I don't expect you have any very thin clothes."

Jane Marple had thanked her and had accepted the check. She came of the age when it was natural for the old to support and finance the young, but also for the middle-aged to look after the old. She could not, however, force herself to buy anything very thin. At her age she seldom felt more than pleasantly warm even in the hottest weather, and the temperature of St. Honoré was not really what is referred to as "tropical heat." This evening she was attired in the best traditions of the provincial gentlewomen of England—grey lace.

Not that she was the only elderly person present. There were representatives of all ages in the room. There were elderly tycoons with young third or fourth wives. There were middle-aged couples from the North of England. There was a gay family from Caracas complete with children. The various countries of South America were well represented, all chattering loudly in Spanish or Portuguese. There was a solid English background of two clergymen, one doctor and one retired judge. There was even a family of Chinese. The dining-room service was mainly done by women, tall black girls of proud carriage, dressed in crisp white; but there was an experienced

Italian headwaiter in charge, and a French wine waiter, and there was the attentive eye of Tim Kendal watching over everything, pausing here and there to have a social word with people at their tables. His wife seconded him ably. She was a good-looking girl. Her hair was a natural golden blonde and she had a wide generous mouth that laughed easily. It was very seldom that Molly Kendal was out of temper. Her staff worked for her enthusiastically, and she adapted her manner carefully to suit her different guests. With the elderly men she laughed and flirted; she congratulated the younger women on their clothes.

"Oh, what a smashing dress you've got on tonight, Mrs. Dyson. I'm so jealous I could tear it off your back." But she looked very well in her own dress, or so Miss Marple thought: a white sheath, with a pale green embroidered silk shawl thrown over her shoulders. Lucky was fingering the shawl. "Lovely colour! I'd like one like it." "You can get them at the shop here," Molly told her and passed on. She did not pause by Miss Marple's table. Elderly ladies she usually left to her husband. "The old dears like a man much better," she used to say.

Tim Kendal came and bent over Miss Marple.

"Nothing special you want, is there?" he asked. "Because you've only got to tell me—and I could get it especially cooked for you. Hotel food, and semitropical at that, isn't quite what you're used to at home, I expect?"

Miss Marple smiled and said that was one of the pleasures of coming abroad.

"That's all right, then. But if there is anything—"

"Such as?"

"Well—" Tim Kendal looked a little doubtful. "Bread and butter pudding?" he hazarded.

Miss Marple smiled and said that she thought she could do without bread and butter pudding very nicely for the present.

She picked up her spoon and began to eat her passion fruit sundae with cheerful appreciation.

Then the steel band began to play. The steel bands were one of the main attractions of the islands. Truth to tell, Miss Marple could have done very well without them. She considered that they made a hideous noise, unnecessarily loud. The pleasure that everyone else took in them was undeniable, however, and Miss Marple, in the true spirit of her youth, decided that as they had to be, she must manage somehow to learn to like them. She could hardly request Tim Kendal to conjure up from somewhere the muted strains of the "Blue Danube." (So graceful—waltzing.) Most peculiar, the way people dance nowadays. Flinging themselves about, seeming quite contorted. Oh, well, young people must enjoy— Her thoughts were arrested.

Because, now she came to think of it, very few of these people were young. Dancing, lights, the music of a band (even a steel band), all that surely was for youth. But where was youth? Studying, she supposed, at universities, or doing a job—with a fortnight's holiday a year. A place like this was too far away and too expensive. This gay and carefree life was all for the thirties and the forties—and the old men who were trying to live up (or down) to their young wives. It seemed, somehow, a pity.

Miss Marple sighed for youth. There was Mrs. Kendal, of course. She wasn't more than twenty-two or three, probably, and she seemed to be enjoying herself—but even so, it was a job she was doing.

At a table nearby Canon Prescott and his sister were sitting. They motioned to Miss Marple to join them for coffee, and she did so. Miss Prescott was a thin severe-looking woman, the Canon was a round, rubicund man, breathing geniality.

Coffee was brought, and chairs were pushed a little way away from the tables. Miss Prescott opened a work bag and took out some frankly hideous table mats that she was hemming. She told Miss Marple all about the day's events. They had visited a new girls' school in the morning. After an afternoon's rest, they had walked through a cane plantation to have tea at a pension where some friends of theirs were staying.

Since the Prescotts had been at the Golden Palm longer than Miss Marple, they were able to enlighten her as to some of her fellow guests.

That very old man, Mr. Rafiel. He came every year. Fantastically rich. Owned an enormous chain of supermarkets in the North of England. The young woman with him was his secretary Esther Walters—a widow. (Quite all right, of course. Nothing improper. After all, he was nearly eighty!)

Miss Marple accepted the propriety of the relationship with an understanding nod, and the Canon remarked: "A very nice young woman; her mother, I understand, is a widow and lives in Chichester."

"Mr. Rafiel has a valet with him, too. Or rather a kind of nurse attendant—he's a qualified masseur, I believe. Jackson, his name is. Poor Mr. Rafiel is practically paralyzed. So sad—with all that money, too."

"A generous and cheerful giver," said Canon Prescott approvingly.

People were regrouping themselves round about, some going farther from the steel band, others crowding up to it. Major Palgrave had joined the Hillingdon-Dyson quartette.

"Now those people—" said Miss Prescott, lowering her voice quite unnecessarily, since the steel band easily drowned it.

"Yes, I was going to ask you about them."

"They were here last year. They spend three months every year in the West Indies, going round the different islands. The tall thin man is Colonel

Hillingdon and the dark woman is his wife—they are botanists. The other two, Mr. and Mrs. Gregory Dyson—they're American. He writes on butterflies, I believe. And all of them are interested in birds."

"So nice for people to have open-air hobbies," said Canon Prescott genially.

"I don't think they'd like to hear you call it hobbies, Jeremy," said his sister. "They have articles printed in the *National Geographic* and in the *Royal Horticultural Journal.* They take themselves very seriously."

A loud outburst of laughter came from the table they had been observing. It was loud enough to overcome the steel band. Gregory Dyson was leaning back in his chair and thumping the table, his wife was protesting, and Major Palgrave emptied his glass and seemed to be applauding.

They hardly qualified for the moment as people who took themselves seriously.

"Major Palgrave should not drink so much," said Miss Prescott acidly. "He has blood pressure."

A fresh supply of Planter's Punches were brought to the table.

"It's so nice to get people sorted out," said Miss Marple. "When I met them this afternoon, I wasn't sure which was married to which."

There was a slight pause. Miss Prescott coughed a small dry cough, and said: "Well, as to that—"

"Joan," said the Canon in an admonitory voice. "Perhaps it would be wise to say no more."

"Really, Jeremy, I wasn't going to say anything. Only that last year, for some reason or other—I really don't know why—we got the idea that Mrs. Dyson was Mrs. Hillingdon until someone told us she wasn't."

"It's odd how one gets impressions, isn't it?" said Miss Marple innocently. Her eyes met Miss Prescott's for a moment. A flash of womanly understanding passed between them.

A more sensitive man than Canon Prescott might have felt that he was *de trop.*

Another signal passed between the women. It said as clearly as if the words had been spoken: *"Some other time . . ."*

"Mr. Dyson calls his wife 'Lucky.' Is that her real name or a nickname?" asked Miss Marple.

"It can hardly be her real name, I should think."

"I happened to ask him," said the Canon. "He said he called her Lucky because she was his good luck piece. If he lost her, he said, he'd lose his luck. Very nicely put, I thought."

"He's very fond of joking," said Miss Prescott.

The Canon looked at his sister doubtfully.

The steel band outdid itself with a wild burst of cacophony, and a troupe of dancers came racing onto the floor.

Miss Marple and the others turned their chairs to watch. Miss Marple enjoyed the dancing better than the music; she liked the shuffling feet and the rhythmic sway of the bodies. It seemed, she thought, very real. It had a kind of power of understatement.

Tonight, for the first time, she began to feel slightly at home in her new environment. Up to now, she had missed what she usually found so easily—points of resemblance in the people she met to various people known to her personally. She had, possibly, been dazzled by the gay clothes and the exotic colouring; but soon, she felt, she would be able to make some interesting comparisons.

Molly Kendal, for instance, was like that nice girl whose name she couldn't remember, but who was a conductress on the Market Basing bus. Helped you in, and never rang the bus on until she was sure you'd sat down safely. Tim Kendal was just a little like the headwaiter at the Royal George in Medchester. Self-confident, and yet, at the same time, worried. (He had had an ulcer, she remembered.) As for Major Palgrave, he was indistinguishable from General Leroy, Captain Flemming, Admiral Wicklow and Commander Richardson. She went on to someone more interesting. Greg, for instance? Greg was difficult because he was American. A dash of Sir George Trollope, perhaps, always so full of jokes at the Civil Defence meetings—or perhaps Mr. Murdoch, the butcher. Mr. Murdoch had had rather a bad reputation, but some people said it was just gossip, and that Mr. Murdoch himself liked to encourage the rumours! "Lucky" now? Well, that was easy—Marleen at the Three Crowns. Evelyn Hillingdon? She couldn't fit Evelyn in precisely. In appearance she fitted many roles—tall, thin, weather-beaten Englishwomen were plentiful. Lady Caroline Wolfe, Peter Wolfe's first wife, who had committed suicide? Or there was Leslie James—that quiet woman who seldom showed what she felt and who had sold her house and left without ever telling anyone she was going. Colonel Hillingdon? No immediate clue there. She'd have to get to know him a little first. One of those quiet men with good manners. You never knew what they were thinking about. Sometimes they surprised you. Major Harper, she remembered, had quietly cut his throat one day. Nobody had ever known why. Miss Marple thought that she did know, but she'd never been quite sure.

Her eyes strayed to Mr. Rafiel's table. The principal thing known about Mr. Rafiel was that he was incredibly rich, he came every year to the West Indies, he was semi-paralyzed and looked like a wrinkled old bird of prey. His clothes hung loosely on his shrunken form. He might have been seventy or eighty, or even ninety. His eyes were shrewd and he was frequently rude, but people seldom took offence, partly because he was so rich, and partly because of his overwhelming personality, which hypnotized you into feeling that somehow, Mr. Rafiel had the right to be rude if he wanted to.

With him sat his secretary Mrs. Walters. She had corn-coloured hair, and a pleasant face. Mr. Rafiel was frequently very rude to her, but she never seemed to notice it. She was not so much subservient, as oblivious. She behaved like a well-trained hospital nurse. Possibly, thought Miss Marple, she had been a hospital nurse.

A young man, tall and good-looking, in a white jacket, came to stand by Mr. Rafiel's chair. The old man looked up at him, nodded, then motioned him to a chair. The young man sat down as bidden. "Mr. Jackson, I presume," said Miss Marple to herself. "His valet-attendant."

She studied Mr. Jackson with some attention.

II

In the bar, Molly Kendal stretched her back and slipped off her high-heeled shoes. Tim came in from the terrace to join her. They had the bar to themselves for the moment.

"Tired, darling?" he asked.

"Just a bit. I seem to be feeling my feet tonight."

"Not too much for you, is it? All this? I know it's hard work." He looked at her anxiously.

She laughed. "Oh, Tim, don't be ridiculous. I love it here. It's gorgeous. The kind of dream I've always had, come true."

"Yes, it would be all right—if one was just a guest. But running the show—that's work."

"Well, you can't have anything for nothing, can you?" said Molly Kendal reasonably.

Tim Kendal frowned.

"You think it's going all right? A success? We're making a go of it?"

"Of course we are."

"You don't think people are saying, 'It's not the same as when the Sandersons were here.'"

"Of course someone will be saying that—they always do! But only some old stick-in-the-mud. I'm sure that we're far better at the job than they were. We're more glamorous. You charm the old pussies and manage to look as though you'd like to make love to the desperate forties and fifties, and I ogle the old gentlemen and make them feel sexy dogs—or play the sweet little daughter the sentimental ones would love to have had. Oh, we've got it all taped splendidly."

Tim's frowned vanished.

"As long as you think so. I get scared. We've risked everything on making a job of this. I chucked my job—"

"And quite right to do so," Molly put in quickly. "It was soul-destroying."

He laughed and kissed the tip of her nose.

"I tell you we've got it taped," she repeated. "Why do you always worry?"

"Made that way, I suppose. I'm always thinking—suppose something should go wrong."

"What sort of thing—"

"Oh, I don't know. Somebody might get drowned."

"Not they. It's one of the safest of all the beaches. And we've got that hulking Swede always on guard."

"I'm a fool," said Tim Kendal. He hesitated—and then said, "You—haven't had any more of those dreams, have you?"

"That was shellfish," said Molly, and laughed.

3

A DEATH IN THE HOTEL

Miss Marple had her breakfast brought to her in bed as usual. Tea, a boiled egg, and a slice of paw-paw.

The fruit on the island, thought Miss Marple, was rather disappointing. It seemed always to be paw-paw. If she could have a nice apple now—but apples seemed to be unknown.

Now that she had been here a week, Miss Marple had cured herself of the impulse to ask what the weather was like. The weather was always the same—fine. No interesting variations.

"The many-splendoured weather of an English day," she murmured to herself and wondered if it was a quotation, or whether she had made it up.

There were, of course, hurricanes, or so she understood. But hurricanes were not weather in Miss Marple's sense of the word. They were more in the nature of an Act of God. There was rain, short violent rainfall that lasted five minutes and stopped abruptly. Everything and everyone was wringing wet, but in another five minutes they were dry again.

The black West Indian girl smiled and said Good morning as she placed the tray on Miss Marple's knees. Such lovely white teeth and so happy and smiling. Nice nature, all these girls, and a pity they were so averse to getting married. It worried Canon Prescott a good deal. Plenty of christenings, he said, trying to console himself, but no weddings.

Miss Marple ate her breakfast and decided how she would spend her day. It didn't really take much deciding. She would get up at her leisure, moving slowly because it was rather hot and her fingers weren't as nimble as they used to be. Then she would rest for ten minutes or so, and she would take her knitting and walk slowly along towards the hotel and decide where she would settle herself. On the terrace overlooking the sea? Or should she go on to the bathing beach to watch the bathers and the children? Usually it was the latter. In the afternoon, after her rest, she might take a drive. It really didn't matter very much.

Today would be a day like any other day, she said to herself.

Only, of course, it wasn't.

Miss Marple carried out her program as planned and was slowly making her way along the path towards the hotel when she met Molly Kendal. For once that sunny young woman was not smiling. Her air of distress was so unlike her that Miss Marple said immediately: "My dear, is anything wrong?"

Molly nodded. She hesitated and then said: "Well, you'll have to know—everyone wll have to know. It's Major Palgrave. He's dead."

"Dead?"

"Yes. He died in the night."

"Oh, dear, I am sorry."

"Yes, it's horrid having a death here. It makes everyone depressed. Of course—he was quite old."

"He seemed quite well and cheerful yesterday," said Miss Marple, slightly resenting this calm assumption that everyone of advanced years was liable to die at any minute.

"He seemed quite healthy," she added.

"He had high blood pressure," said Molly.

"But surely there are things one takes nowadays—some kind of pill. Science is so wonderful."

"Oh, yes, but perhaps he forgot to take his pills, or took too many of them. Like insulin, you know."

Miss Marple did not think that diabetes and high blood pressure were at all the same kind of thing. She asked: "What does the doctor say?"

"Oh, Dr. Graham, who's practically retired now, and lives in the hotel, took a look at him, and the local people came officially, of course, to give a death certificate, but it all seems quite straightforward. This kind of thing is quite liable to happen when you have high blood pressure, especially if you overdo the alcohol, and Major Palgrave was really very naughty that way. Last night, for instance."

"Yes, I noticed," said Miss Marple.

"He probably forgot to take his pills. It is bad luck for the old boy—but people can't live for ever, can they? But it's terribly worrying—for me and Tim, I mean. People might suggest it was something in the food."

"But surely the symptoms of food poisoning and of blood pressure are quite different?"

"Yes. But people do *say* things so easily. And if people decided the food was bad—and left—or told their friends—"

"I really don't think you need worry," said Miss Marple kindly. "As you say, an elderly man like Major Palgrave—he must have been over seventy

—is quite liable to die. To most people it will seem quite an ordinary occurrence—sad, but not out of the way at all."

"If only," said Molly unhappily, "it hadn't been so sudden."

Yes, it had been very sudden, Miss Marple thought as she walked slowly on. There he had been last night, laughing and talking in the best of spirits with the Hillingdons and the Dysons.

The Hillingdons and the Dysons . . . Miss Marple walked more slowly still. Finally she stopped abruptly. Instead of going to the bathing beach, she settled herself in a shady corner of the terrace. She took out her knitting and the needles clicked rapidly as though they were trying to match the speed of her thoughts. She didn't like it—no, she didn't like it. It came so pat.

She went over the occurrences of yesterday in her mind.

Major Palgrave and his stories . . .

That was all as usual and one didn't need to listen very closely. Perhaps, though, it would have been better if she had.

Kenya—he had talked about Kenya and then India—then the North West Frontier—and then—for some reason they had got on to murder. And even then she hadn't really been listening . . .

Some famous case that had taken place out here—that had been in the newspapers.

It was after that—when he picked up her ball of wool—that he had begun telling her about a snapshot. *A snapshot of a murderer*—that is what he had said.

Miss Marple closed her eyes and tried to remember just exactly how that story had gone.

It had been rather a confused story—told to the Major in his club—or in somebody else's club—told him by a doctor—who had heard it from another doctor—and one doctor had taken a snapshot of someone coming through a front door—someone who was a murderer.

Yes, that was it—the various details were coming back to her now.

And he had offered to show her that snapshot. He had got out his wallet and begun hunting through its contents—talking all the time.

And then still talking, he had looked up—had looked—not at her—but at something behind her—behind her right shoulder to be accurate. And he had stopped talking, his face had gone purple—and he had started stuffing back everything into his wallet with slightly shaky hands and had begun talking in a loud unnatural voice about elephant tusks!

A moment or two later the Hillingdons and the Dysons had joined them. . . .

It was then that she had turned her head over her right shoulder to look. . . . But there had been nothing and nobody to see. To her left, some distance away, in the direction of the hotel, there had been Tim Kendal and his wife; and beyond them a family group of Venezuelans. But Major Palgrave had not been looking in that direction. . . .

Miss Marple meditated until lunchtime.

After lunch she did not go for a drive.

Instead she sent a message to say that she was not feeling very well, and to ask if Dr. Graham would be kind enough to come and see her.

4

MISS MARPLE SEEKS MEDICAL ATTENTION

Dr. Graham was a kindly elderly man of about sixty-five. He had practiced in the West Indies for many years, but was now semi-retired, and left most of his work to his West Indian partners. He greeted Miss Marple pleasantly and asked her what the trouble was. Fortunately at Miss Marple's age, there was always some ailment that could be discussed with slight exaggerations on the patient's part. Miss Marple hesitated between "her shoulder" and "her knee," but finally decided upon the knee. Miss Marple's knee, as she would have put it to herself, was always with her.

Dr. Graham was exceedingly kindly but he refrained from putting into words the fact that at her time of life such troubles were only to be expected. He prescribed for her one of the brands of useful little pills that form the basis of a doctor's prescriptions. Since he knew by experience that many elderly people could be lonely when they first came to St. Honoré, he remained for a while gently chatting.

"A very nice man," thought Miss Marple to herself, "and I really feel rather ashamed of having to tell him lies. But I don't quite see what else I can do."

Miss Marple had been brought up to have a proper regard for truth and was indeed by nature a very truthful person. But on certain occasions, when she considered it her duty so to do, she could tell lies with a really astonishing verisimilitude.

She cleared her throat, uttered an apologetic little cough, and said, in an old-ladyish and slightly twittering manner: "There is something, Dr. Graham, I would like to ask you. I don't really like mentioning it—but I don't quite see what else I am to do—although of course it's *quite* unimportant really. But you see, it's important to *me.* And I hope you will understand

and not think what I am asking is tiresome or—or unpardonable in any way."

To this opening Dr. Graham replied kindly: "Something is worrying you? Do let me help."

"It's connected with Major Palgrave. *So* sad about his dying. It was quite a shock when I heard it this morning."

"Yes," said Dr. Graham, "it was very sudden, I'm afraid. He seemed in such good spirits yesterday." He spoke kindly, but conventionally. To him, clearly, Major Palgrave's death was nothing out of the way. Miss Marple wondered whether she was really making something out of nothing. Was this suspicious habit of mind growing on her? Perhaps she could no longer trust her own judgment. Not that it was judgment really, only suspicion. Anyway, she was in for it now! She must go ahead.

"We were sitting talking together yesterday afternoon," she said. "He was telling me about his very varied and interesting life. So many strange parts of the globe."

"Yes, indeed," said Dr. Graham, who had been bored many times by the Major's reminiscences.

"And then he spoke of his family, boyhood rather, and I told him a little about my own nephews and nieces and he listened very sympathetically. And I showed him a snapshot I had with me of one of my nephews. Such a dear boy—at least not exactly a boy now, but always a boy to me, if you understand."

"Quite so," said Dr. Graham, wondering how long it would be before the old lady was going to come to the point.

"I had handed it to him and he was examining it when quite suddenly those people—those very nice people—who collect wild flowers and butterflies, Colonel and Mrs. Hillingdon I think the name is—"

"Oh, yes? The Hillingdons and the Dysons."

"Yes, that's right. They came suddenly along laughing and talking. They sat down and ordered drinks and we all talked together. Very pleasant it was. But without thinking, Major Palgrave must have put back my snapshot into his wallet and returned it to his pocket. I wasn't paying very much attention at the time, but I remembered afterward and I said to myself, 'I mustn't forget to ask the Major to give me back my picture of Denzil.' I *did* think of it last night while the dancing and the band was going on, but I didn't like to interrupt him just then, because they were having such a merry party together and I thought, 'I will remember to ask him for it in the morning.' Only this morning—" Miss Marple paused—out of breath.

"Yes, yes," said Dr. Graham, "I quite understand. And you—well, naturally you want the snapshot back. Is that it?"

Miss Marple nodded her head in eager agreement.

"Yes. That's it. You see, it is the only one I have got and I haven't got the negative. And I would hate to lose that snapshot, because poor Denzil died some five or six years ago and he was my favourite nephew. This is the only picture I have to remind me of him. I wondered—I hoped—it is rather tiresome of me to ask—whether you could possibly manage to get hold of it for me? I don't really know who else to ask, you see. I don't know who'll attend to all his belongings and things like that. It is all so difficult. They would think it such a nuisance of me. You see, they don't understand. Nobody could quite understand what this snapshot means to me."

"Of course, of course," said Dr. Graham. "I quite understand. A most natural feeling on your part. Actually, I am meeting the local authorities shortly—the funeral is tomorrow, and someone will be coming from the Administrator's office to look over his papers and effects before communicating with the next of kin—all that sort of thing. If you could describe this snapshot."

"It was just the front of a house," said Miss Marple. "And someone—Denzil, I mean—was just coming out of the front door. As I say, it was taken by one of my other nephews who is very keen on flower shows—and he was photographing a hibiscus, I think, or one of those beautiful—something like antipasto—lilies. Denzil just happened to come out of the front door at that time. It wasn't a very good photograph of him—just a trifle blurred— But I liked it and have always kept it."

"Well," said Dr. Graham, "that seems clear enough. I think we'll have no difficulty in getting back your picture for you, Miss Marple."

He rose from his chair. Miss Marple smiled up at him.

"You are very kind, Dr. Graham, very kind indeed. You do understand, don't you?"

"Of course I do, of course I do," said Dr. Graham, shaking her warmly by the hand. "Now don't you worry. Exercise that knee every day gently but not too much, and I'll send you round these tablets. Take one three times a day."

5

MISS MARPLE MAKES A DECISION

The funeral service was said over the body of the late Major Palgrave on the following day. Miss Marple attended in company with Miss Prescott. The Canon read the service—after that, life went on as usual.

Major Palgrave's death was already only an incident, a slightly unpleasant incident, but one that was soon forgotten. Life here was sunshine, sea, and social pleasures. A grim visitor had interrupted these activities, casting a momentary shadow, but the shadow was now gone. After all, nobody had known the deceased very well. He had been rather a garrulous elderly man of the club-bore type, always telling you personal reminiscences that you had no particular desire to hear. He had had little to anchor himself to any particular part of the world. His wife had died many years ago. He had had a lonely life and a lonely death. But it had been the kind of loneliness that spends itself in living among people, and in passing the time that way not unpleasantly. Major Palgrave might have been a lonely man, he had also been quite a cheerful one. He had enjoyed himself in his own particular way. And now he was dead, buried, and nobody cared very much, and in another week's time nobody would even remember him or spare him a passing thought.

The only person who could possibly be said to miss him was Miss Marple. Not indeed out of any personal affection, but he represented a kind of life that she knew. As one grew older, so she reflected to herself, one got more and more into the habit of listening; listening possibly without any great interest, but there had been between her and the Major the gentle give and take of two old people. It had had a cheerful, human quality. She did not actually mourn Major Palgrave but she missed him.

On the afternoon of the funeral, as she was sitting knitting in her favourite spot, Dr. Graham came and joined her. She put her needles down and greeted him. He said at once, rather apologetically: "I am afraid I have rather disappointing news, Miss Marple."

"Indeed? About my—"

"Yes. We haven't found that precious snapshot of yours. I'm afraid that will be a disappointment to you."

"Yes. Yes, it is. But of course it does not really matter. It was a sentimentality. I do realize that now. It wasn't in Major Palgrave's wallet?"

"No. Nor anywhere else among his things. There were a few letters and newspaper clippings and odds and ends, and a few old photographs, but no sign of a snapshot such as you mentioned."

"Oh, dear," said Miss Marple. "Well, it can't be helped . . . Thank you very much, Dr. Graham, for the trouble you've taken."

"Oh, it was no trouble, indeed. But I know quite well from my own experience how much family trifles mean to one, especially as one is getting older."

The old lady was really taking it very well, he thought. Major Palgrave, he presumed, had probably come across the snapshot when taking something out of his wallet, and not even realizing how it had come there, had torn it up as something of no importance. But of course it was of great importance to this old lady. Still, she seemed quite cheerful and philosophical about it.

Internally, however, Miss Marple was far from being either cheerful or philosophical. She wanted a little time in which to think things out, but she was also determined to use her present opportunities to the fullest effect.

She engaged Dr. Graham in conversation with an eagerness which she did not attempt to conceal. That kindly man, putting down her flow of talk to the natural loneliness of an old lady, exerted himself to divert her mind from the loss of the snapshot by conversing easily and pleasantly about life in St. Honoré, and the various interesting places perhaps Miss Marple might like to visit. He hardly knew himself how the conversation drifted back to Major Palgrave's decease.

"It seems so sad," said Miss Marple, "to think of anyone dying like this away from home. Though I gather, from what he himself told me, that he had no immediate family. It seems he lived by himself in London."

"He travelled a fair amount, I believe," said Dr. Graham. "At any rate, in the winters. He didn't care for our English winters. Can't say I blame him."

"No, indeed," said Miss Marple. "And perhaps he had some special reason like a weakness of the lungs or something which made it necessary for him to winter abroad?"

"Oh, no, I don't think so."

"He had high blood pressure, I believe. So sad nowadays. One hears so much of it."

"He spoke about it to you, did he?"

"Oh, no. No, *he* never mentioned it. It was somebody else who told me."

"Ah, really."

"I suppose," went on Miss Marple, "that death was to be expected under those circumstances."

"Not necessarily," said Dr. Graham. "There are methods of controlling blood pressure nowadays."

"His death seemed very sudden, but I suppose you weren't surprised."

"Well, I wasn't particularly surprised in a man of that age. But I certainly didn't expect it. Frankly, he always seemed to me in very good form, but I hadn't ever attended him professionally. I'd never taken his blood pressure or anything like that."

"Does one know—I mean, does a doctor know—when a man has high blood pressure just by looking at him?" Miss Marple inquired with a kind of dewy innocence.

"Not just by looking," said the doctor, smiling. "One has to do a bit of testing."

"Oh, I see. That dreadful thing when you put a rubber band round somebody's arm and blow it up—I dislike it so much. But my doctor said that my blood pressure was really very good for my age."

"Well, that's good hearing," said Dr. Graham.

"Of course, the Major was rather fond of Planter's Punch," said Miss Marple thoughtfully.

"Yes. Not the best thing with blood pressure—alcohol."

"One takes tablets, doesn't one, or so I have heard?"

"Yes. There are several on the market. There was a bottle of one of them in his room—Serenite."

"How wonderful science is nowadays," said Miss Marple. "Doctors can do so much, can't they?"

"We all have one great competitor," said Dr. Graham. "Nature, you know. And some of the good old-fashioned home remedies come back from time to time."

"Like putting cobwebs on a cut?" said Miss Marple. "We always used to do that when I was a child."

"Very sensible," said Dr. Graham.

"And a linseed poultice on the chest and rubbing in camphorated oil for a bad cough."

"I see you know it all!" said Dr. Graham, laughing. He got up. "How's the knee? Not been too troublesome?"

"No, it seems much, much better."

"Well, we won't say whether that's Nature or my pills," said Dr. Graham. "Sorry I couldn't have been of more help to you."

"But you have been most kind—I am really ashamed of taking up your time. Did you say that there were no photographs in the Major's wallet?"

"Oh, yes—a very old one of the Major himself as quite a young man on a polo pony—and one of a dead tiger. He was standing with his foot on it. Snaps of that sort—memories of his younger days. But I looked very carefully, I assure you, and the one you describe of your nephew was definitely not there—"

"Oh, I'm sure you looked carefully—I didn't mean that—I was just interested. We all tend to keep such very odd things—"

"Treasures from the past," said the doctor, smiling.

He said good-bye and departed.

Miss Marple remained looking thoughtfully at the palm trees and the sea. She did not pick up her knitting again for some minutes. She had a fact now. She had to think about that fact and what it meant. The snapshot that the Major had brought out of his wallet and replaced so hurriedly was not there after he died. It was not the sort of thing the Major would throw away. He had replaced it in his wallet and it ought to have been in his wallet after his death. Money might have been stolen, but no one would want to steal a snapshot. Unless, that is, they had a special reason for so doing. . . .

Miss Marple's face was grave. She had to make a decision. Was she, or was she not, going to allow Major Palgrave to remain quietly in his grave? Might it not be better to do just that? She quoted under her breath: "Duncan is dead. After Life's fitful fever he sleeps well!" Nothing could hurt Major Palgrave now. He had gone where danger could not touch him. Was it just a coincidence that he should have died on that particular night? Or was it just possibly *not* a coincidence? Doctors accepted the deaths of elderly men so easily. Especially since in his room there had been a bottle of the tablets that people with high blood pressure had to take every day of their lives. But if someone had taken the snapshot from the Major's wallet, that same person could have put that bottle of tablets in the Major's room. She herself never remembered seeing the Major take tablets; he had never spoken about his blood pressure to her. The only thing he had ever said about his health was the admission, "Not as young as I was." He had been occasionally a little short of breath, a trifle asthmatic, nothing else. But someone had mentioned that Major Palgrave had high blood pressure—Molly? Miss Prescott? She couldn't remember.

Miss Marple sighed, then admonished herself in words, though she did not speak those words aloud.

"Now, Jane, what are you suggesting or thinking? Are you, perhaps, just making the whole thing up? Have you really got anything to build on?"

She went over, step by step, as nearly as she could, the conversation between herself and the Major on the subject of murder and murderers.

"Oh, dear," said Miss Marple. "Even if—really, I don't see how I can do anything about it—"

But she knew that she meant to try.

6

IN THE SMALL HOURS

Miss Marple woke early. Like many old people, she slept lightly and had periods of wakefulness which she used for the planning of some action or actions to be carried out on the next or following days. Usually, of course, these were of a wholly private or domestic nature, of little interest to anybody but herself. But this morning Miss Marple lay thinking soberly and constructively of murder, and what, if her suspicions were correct, she could do about it. It wasn't going to be easy. She had one weapon and one weapon only—and that was conversation.

Old ladies were given to a good deal of rambling conversation. People were bored by this, but certainly did not suspect them of ulterior motives. It would not be a case of asking direct questions. (Indeed, she would have found it difficult to know what questions to ask!) It would be a question of finding out a little more about certain people. She reviewed these certain people in her mind.

She could find out, possibly, a little more about Major Palgrave, but would that really help her? She doubted if it would. If Major Palgrave had been killed, it was not because of secrets in his life or to inherit his money or for revenge upon him. In fact, although he was the victim, it was one of those rare cases where a greater knowledge of the victim does not help you or lead you in any way to his murderer. The point, it seemed to her, and the sole point, was that Major Palgrave talked too much!

She had learned one rather interesting fact from Dr. Graham. He had had in his wallet various photographs: one of himself in company with a polo pony, one of a dead tiger, also one or two other shots of the same nature. Now why did Major Palgrave carry these about with him? Obviously, thought Miss Marple, with long experience of old admirals, brigadier-generals and mere majors behind her, because he had certain stories which he enjoyed telling to people. Starting off with "Curious thing happened once when I was out tiger shooting in India . . ." Or a reminiscence of himself and a polo pony. Therefore this story about a suspected murderer would in due course be illustrated by the production of the snapshot from his wallet.

He had been following that pattern in his conversation with her. The subject of murder having come up, and to focus interest on his story, he had done what he no doubt usually did, produced his snapshot and said something in the nature of "Wouldn't think this chap was a murderer, would you?"

The point was that it had been a habit of his. This murderer story was one of his regular repertoire. If any reference to murder came up, then away went the Major, full steam ahead.

In that case, reflected Miss Marple, he might already have told his story to someone else here. Or to more than one person. If that were so, then she herself might learn from that person what the further details of the story had been, possibly what the person in the snapshot had looked like.

She nodded her head in satisfaction. That would be a beginning.

And, of course, there were the people she called in her mind the "Four Suspects." Though really, since Major Palgrave had been talking about a man—there were only two. Colonel Hillingdon or Mr. Dyson, very unlikely looking murderers, but then murderers so often were unlikely. Could there have been anyone else? She had seen no one when she turned her head to look. There was the bungalow, of course. Mr. Rafiel's bungalow. Could somebody have come out of the bungalow and gone in again before she had had time to turn her head? If so, it could only have been the valet-attendant. What was his name? Oh, yes, Jackson. Could it have been Jackson who had come out of the door? That would have been the same pose as the photograph. *A man coming out of a door.* Recognition might have struck suddenly. Up till then, Major Palgrave would not have looked at Arthur Jackson, valet-attendant, with any interest. His roving and curious eye was essentially a snobbish eye—Arthur Jackson was not a *pukka sahib* —Major Palgrave would not have glanced at him twice.

Until, perhaps, he had had the snapshot in his hand, and had looked over Miss Marple's right shoulder and had seen a man coming out of a door . . .?

Miss Marple turned over on her pillow. Program for tomorrow—or rather for today—further investigation of the Hillingdons, the Dysons and Arthur Jackson, valet-attendant.

II

Dr. Graham also woke early. Usually he turned over and went to sleep again. But today he was uneasy and sleep failed to come. This anxiety that made it so difficult to go to sleep again was a thing he had not suffered from for a long time. What was causing this anxiety? Really, he couldn't make it out. He lay there thinking it over. Something to do with—something to do with—yes, Major Palgrave. Major Palgrave's death? He didn't see, though, what there could be to make him uneasy there. Was it something that that twittery old lady had said? Bad luck for her about her snapshot. She'd taken it very well. But now, what was it she had said, what chance word of hers had it been, that had given him this funny feeling of uneasiness? After all, there was nothing *odd* about the Major's death. Nothing at all. At least he supposed there was nothing at all.

It was quite clear that in the Major's state of health—a faint check came in his thought process. Did he really know much about Major Palgrave's state of health? Everybody said that he'd suffered from high blood pressure. But he himself had never had any conversation with the Major about it. But then he'd never had much conversation with Major Palgrave anyway. Palgrave was an old bore and he avoided old bores. Why on earth should he have this idea that perhaps everything mightn't be all right? Was it that old woman? But after all, she hadn't *said* anything. Anyway it was none of his business. The local authorities were quite satisfied. There had been that bottle of Serenite tablets, and the old boy had apparently talked to people about his blood pressure quite freely.

Dr. Graham turned over in bed and soon went to sleep again.

III

Outside the hotel grounds, in one of a row of shanty cabins beside a creek, the girl Victoria Johnson rolled over and sat up in bed. The St. Honoré girl was a magnificent creature with a torso of black marble such as a sculptor would have enjoyed. She ran her fingers through her dark, tightly curling hair. With her foot she nudged her sleeping companion in the ribs.

"Wake up, man."

The man grunted and turned.

"What you want? It's not morning."

"Wake up, man. I want to talk to you."

The man sat up, stretched, showed a wide mouth and beautiful teeth.

"What's worrying you, woman?"

"That Major man who died. Something I don't like. Something wrong about it."

"Ah, what d'you want to worry about that? He was old. He died."

"Listen, man. It's them pills. Them pills the doctor asked me about."

"Well what about them? He took too many maybe."

"No. It's not that. Listen." She leaned toward him, talking vehemently. He yawned and lay down again.

"There's nothing in that. What're you talking about?"

"All the same, I'll speak to Mrs. Kendal about it in the morning. I think there's something wrong there somewhere."

"Shouldn't bother," said the man who, without benefit of ceremony, she considered as her present husband. "Don't let's look for trouble," he said and rolled over on his side yawning.

7

MORNING ON THE BEACH

It was midmorning on the beach below the hotel.

Evelyn Hillingdon came out of the water and dropped on the warm golden sand. She took off her bathing cap and shook her dark head vigorously. The beach was not a very big one. People tended to congregate there in the mornings and about eleven-thirty there was always something of a social reunion. To Evelyn's left in one of the exotic-looking modern basket chairs lay Señora de Caspearo, a handsome woman from Venezuela. Next to her was old Mr. Rafiel, who was by now the doyen of the Golden Palm Hotel and held the sway that only an elderly invalid of great wealth could attain. Esther Walters was in attendance on him. She usually had her shorthand notebook and pencil with her in case Mr. Rafiel should suddenly think of urgent business cables which must be got off at once. Mr. Rafiel, in beach attire, was incredibly desiccated, his bones draped with festoons of dry skin. Though looking like a man on the point of death, he had looked exactly the same for at least the last eight years—or so it was said in the islands. Sharp blue eyes peered out of his wrinkled cheeks, and his principal pleasure in life was denying robustly anything that anyone else said.

Miss Marple was also present. As usual she sat and knitted and listened to what went on, and very occasionally joined in the conversation. When she did so, everyone was surprised because they had usually forgotten that she was there! Evelyn Hillingdon looked at her indulgently and thought that she was a nice old pussy.

Señora de Caspearo rubbed some oil on her long beautiful legs and hummed to herself. She was not a woman who spoke much. She looked discontentedly at the flask of sun oil.

"This is not so good as Frangipanio," she said sadly. "One cannot get it here. A pity." Her eyelids drooped again.

"Are you going in for your dip now, Mr. Rafiel?" asked Esther Walters.

"I'll go in when I'm ready," said Mr. Rafiel snappishly.

"It's half-past eleven," said Mrs. Walters.

"What of it?" said Mr. Rafiel. "Think I'm the kind of man to be tied by the clock? Do this at the hour, do this at twenty minutes past, do that at twenty to—bah!"

Mrs. Walters had been in attendance on Mr. Rafiel long enough to have adopted her own formula for dealing with him. She knew that he liked a good space of time in which to recover from the exertion of bathing and she had therefore reminded him of the time, allowing a good ten minutes for him to rebut her suggestion and then be able to adopt it without seeming to do so.

"I don't like these espadrilles," said Mr. Rafiel, raising a foot and looking at it. "I told that fool Jackson so. The man never pays attention to a word I say."

"I'll fetch you some others, shall I, Mr. Rafiel?"

"No, you won't, you'll sit here and keep quiet. I hate people rushing about like clucking hens."

Evelyn shifted slightly in the warm sand, stretching out her arms.

Miss Marple, intent on her knitting—or so it seemed—stretched out a foot, then hastily she apologized.

"I'm so sorry, so very sorry, Mrs. Hillingdon. I'm afraid I kicked you."

"Oh, it's quite all right," said Evelyn. "This beach gets rather crowded."

"Oh, please don't move. Please. I'll move my chair a little back so that I won't do it again."

As Miss Marple resettled herself, she went on talking in a childish and garrulous manner.

"It still seems so wonderful to be here! I've never been to the West Indies before, you know. I thought it was the kind of place I never should come to, and here I am. All by the kindness of my dear nephew. I suppose you know this part of the world very well, don't you, Mrs. Hillingdon?"

"I have been in this island once or twice before and of course in most of the others."

"Oh, yes. Butterflies, isn't it, and wild flowers? You and your—your friends—or are they relations?"

"Friends. Nothing more."

"And I suppose you go about together a great deal because of your interests being the same?"

"Yes. We've travelled together for some years now."

"I suppose you must have had some rather exciting adventures sometimes?"

"I don't think so," said Evelyn. Her voice was unaccentuated, slightly bored. "Adventures always seem to happen to other people." She yawned.

"No dangerous encounters with snakes or with wild animals or with natives gone berserk?"

"What a fool I sound," thought Miss Marple.

"Nothing worse than insect bites," Evelyn assured her.

"Poor Major Palgrave, you know, was bitten by a snake once," said Miss Marple, making a purely fictitious statement.

"Was he?"

"Did he never tell you about it?"

"Perhaps. I don't remember."

"I suppose you knew him quite well, didn't you?"

"Major Palgrave? No, hardly at all."

"He always had so many interesting stories to tell."

"Ghastly old bore," said Mr. Rafiel. "Silly fool, too. He needn't have died if he'd looked after himself properly."

"Oh, come now, Mr. Rafiel," said Mrs. Walters.

"I know what I'm talking about. If you look after your health properly, you're all right anywhere. Look at me. The doctors gave me up years ago. 'All right,' I said, 'I've got my own rules of health and I shall keep to them. And here I am.' "

He looked round proudly.

It did indeed seem rather a miracle that he should be there.

"Poor Major Palgrave had high blood pressure," said Mrs. Walters.

"Nonsense," said Mr. Rafiel.

"Oh, but he did," said Evelyn Hillingdon. She spoke with sudden, unexpected authority.

"Who says so?" said Mr. Rafiel. "Did he tell you so?"

"Somebody said so."

"He looked very red in the face," Miss Marple contributed.

"Can't go by that," said Mr. Rafiel. "And anyway, he didn't have high blood pressure because he told me so."

"What do you mean, he told you so?" said Mrs. Walters. "I mean, you can't exactly tell people you haven't got a thing."

"Yes you can. I said to him once when he was downing all those Planter's Punches and eating too much, I said, 'You ought to watch your diet and your drink. You've got to think of your blood pressure at your age.' And he said he'd nothing to look out for in that line, that his blood pressure was very good for his age."

"But he took some stuff for it, I believe," said Miss Marple, entering the conversation once more. "Some stuff called—oh, something like—was it Serenite?"

"If you ask me," said Evelyn Hillingdon, "I don't think he ever liked to admit that there could be anything the matter with him or that he could be ill. I think he was one of those people who are afraid of illness and therefore deny there's ever anything wrong with them."

It was a long speech for her. Miss Marple looked thoughtfully down at the top of her dark head.

"The trouble is," said Mr. Rafiel dictatorially, "everybody's too fond of knowing other people's ailments. They think everybody over fifty is going to die of hypertension or coronary thrombosis or one of those things. Poppycock! If a man says there's nothing much wrong with him, I don't suppose there is. A man ought to know about his own health. What's the time? Quarter to twelve? I ought to have had my dip long ago. Why can't you remind me about these things, Esther?"

Mrs. Walters made no protest. She rose to her feet and with some deftness assisted Mr. Rafiel to his. Together they went down the beach, she supporting him carefully. Together they stepped into the sea.

Señora de Caspearo opened her eyes and murmured: "How ugly are old men! Oh, how they are ugly! They should all be put to death at forty, or perhaps thirty-five would be better. Yes?"

Edward Hillingdon and Gregory Dyson came crunching down the beach.

"What's the water like, Evelyn?"

"Just the same as always."

"Never much variation, is there? Where's Lucky?"

"I don't know," said Evelyn.

Again Miss Marple looked down thoughtfully at the dark head.

"Well, now I give my imitation of a whale," said Gregory. He threw off his gaily patterned Bermuda shirt and tore down the beach, flinging himself, puffing and panting, into the sea, doing a fast crawl. Edward Hillingdon sat down on the beach by his wife. Presently he asked, "Coming in again?"

She smiled—put on her cap—and they went down the beach together in a much less spectacular manner.

Señora de Caspearo opened her eyes again.

"I think at first those two they are on their honeymoon, he is so charming to her, but I hear they have been married eight—nine years. It is incredible, is it not?"

"I wonder where Mrs. Dyson is?" said Miss Marple.

"That Lucky? She is with some man."

"You—you think so?"

"It is certain," said Señora de Caspearo. "She is that type. But she is not so young any longer. Her husband—already his eyes go elsewhere. He makes passes—here, there, all the time. I know."

"Yes," said Miss Marple, "I expect you would know."

Señora de Caspearo shot a surprised glance at her. It was clearly not what she had expected from that quarter.

Miss Marple, however, was looking at the waves with an air of gentle innocence.

II

"May I speak to you, ma'am, Mrs. Kendal?"

"Yes, of course," said Molly. She was sitting at her desk in the office.

Victoria Johnson, tall and buoyant in her crisp white uniform, came in farther and shut the door behind her with a somewhat mysterious air.

"I like to tell you something, please, Mrs. Kendal."

"Yes, what is it? Is anything wrong?"

"I don't know that. Not for sure. It's the old gentleman who died. The Major gentleman. He die in his sleep."

"Yes, yes. What about it?"

"There was a bottle of pills in his room. Doctor, he asked me about them."

"Yes?"

"The doctor said, 'Let me see what he has here on the bathroom shelf,' and he looked, you see. He see there was tooth powder and indigestion pills and aspirin and cascara pills, and then these pills in a bottle called Serenite."

"Yes," repeated Molly yet again.

"And the doctor looked at them. He seemed quite satisfied, and nodded his head. But I get to thinking afterwards. Those pills weren't there before. I've not seen them in his bathroom before. The others, yes. The tooth powder and the aspirin and the after-shave lotion and all the rest. But those pills, those Serenite pills, I never noticed them before."

"So you think—" Molly looked puzzled.

"I don't know what to think," said Victoria. "I just think it's not right, so I think I better tell you about it. Perhaps you tell doctor? Perhaps it means something. Perhaps someone put those pills there so he take them and he died."

"Oh, I don't think that's likely at all," said Molly.

Victoria shook her dark head. "You never know. People do bad things."

Molly glanced out of the window. The place looked like an earthly paradise. With its sunshine, its sea, its coral reef, its music, its dancing, it seemed a Garden of Eden. But even in the Garden of Eden, there had been a shadow—the shadow of the Serpent. *Bad things*—how hateful to hear those words.

"I'll make inquiries, Victoria," she said sharply. "Don't worry. And above all, don't go starting a lot of silly rumours."

Tim Kendal came in, just as Victoria was, somewhat unwillingly, leaving.

"Anything wrong, Molly?"

She hesitated—but Victoria might go to him. She told him what the girl had said.

"I don't see what all this rigmarole—what were these pills anyway?"

"Well, I don't really know, Tim. Dr. Robertson when he came said they—were something to do with blood pressure, I think."

"Well, that would be all right, wouldn't it? I mean, he had high blood pressure, and he would be taking things for it, wouldn't he? People do. I've seen them, lots of times."

"Yes," Molly hesitated, "but Victoria seemed to think that he might have taken one of these pills and it would have killed him."

"Oh, darling, that is a bit too melodramatic! You mean that somebody might have changed his blood pressure pills for something else, and that they poisoned him?"

"It does sound absurd," said Molly apologetically, "when you say it like that. But that seemed to be what Victoria thought!"

"Silly girl! We *could* go and ask Dr. Graham about it. I suppose he'd know. But really, it's such nonsense that it's not worth bothering him."

"That's what I think."

"What on earth made the girl think anybody would have changed the pills? You mean, put different pills into the same bottle?"

"I didn't quite gather," said Molly, looking rather helpless. "Victoria seemed to think that was the first time that Serenite bottle had been there."

"Oh, but that's nonsense," said Tim Kendal. "He had to take those pills all the time to keep his blood pressure down." And he went off cheerfully to consult with Fernando the *maître d'hôtel.*

But Molly could not dismiss the matter so lightly. After the stress of lunch was over, she said to her husband: "Tim—I've been thinking— If Victoria is going around talking about this, perhaps we ought just to ask someone about it?"

"My dear girl! Robertson and all the rest of them came and looked at everything and asked all the questions they wanted at the time."

"Yes, but you know how they work themselves up, these girls—"

"Oh, all right! I'll tell you what—we'll go and ask Graham. He'll know."

Dr. Graham was sitting on his loggia with a book. The young couple came in, and Molly plunged into her recital. It was a little incoherent, and Tim took over.

"Sounds rather idiotic," he said apologetically, "but as far as I can make out, this girl has got it into her head that someone put some poison tablets in the—what's the name of the stuff—Sera—something bottle."

"But why should she get this idea into her head?" asked Dr. Graham. "Did she see anything or hear anything or—I mean, why should she think so?"

"I don't know," said Tim rather helplessly. "Was it a different bottle? Was that it, Molly?"

"No," said Molly. "I think what she said was that there was a bottle there labelled—Seven—Seren—"

"Serenite," said the doctor. "That's quite right. A well-known preparation. He'd been taking it regularly."

"Victoria said she'd never seen it in his room before."

"Never seen it in his room before?" said Graham sharply. "What does she mean by that?"

"Well, that's what she said. She said there were all sorts of things on the bathroom shelf. You know, tooth powder, aspirin and after-shave and—oh—she rattled them off gaily. I suppose she's always cleaning them and so she knows them all off by heart. But this one—the Serenite—she hadn't seen it there until the day after he died."

"That's very odd," said Dr. Graham rather sharply. "Is she sure?"

The unusual sharpness of his tone made both of the Kendals look at him. They had not expected Dr. Graham to take quite this attitude.

"She sounded sure," said Molly slowly.

"Perhaps she just wanted to be sensational," suggested Tim.

"I think perhaps," said Dr. Graham, "I'd better have a few words with the girl myself."

Victoria displayed a distinct pleasure at being allowed to tell her story.

"I don't want to get in no trouble," she said. "*I* didn't put that bottle there and I don't know who did."

"But you think it was put there?" asked Graham.

"Well, you see, Doctor, it must have been put there if it wasn't there before."

"Major Palgrave could have kept it in a drawer—or a dispatch-case, something like that."

Victoria shook her head shrewdly.

"Wouldn't do that if he was taking it all the time, would he?"

"No," said Graham reluctantly. "No, it was stuff he would have to take several times a day. You never saw him taking it or anything of that kind?"

"He didn't have it there before. I just thought—word got round as that stuff had something to do with his death, poisoned his blood or something, and I thought maybe he had an enemy put it there so as to kill him."

"Nonsense, my girl," said the doctor robustly. "Sheer nonsense."

Victoria looked shaken.

"You say as this stuff was medicine, good medicine?" she asked doubtfully.

"Good medicine, and what is more, necessary medicine," said Dr. Graham. "So you needn't worry, Victoria. I can assure you there was nothing wrong with that medicine. It was the proper thing for a man to take who had his complaint."

"Surely you've taken a load off my mind," said Victoria. She showed white teeth at him in a cheerful smile.

But the load was not taken off Dr. Graham's mind. That uneasiness of his that had been so nebulous was now becoming tangible.

8

A TALK WITH ESTHER WALTERS

"This place isn't what it used to be," said Mr. Rafiel irritably as he observed Miss Marple approaching the spot where he and his secretary were sitting. "Can't move a step without some old hen getting under your feet. What do old ladies want to come to the West Indies for?"

"Where do you suggest they should go?" asked Esther Walters.

"To Cheltenham," said Mr. Rafiel promptly. "Or Bournemouth," he offered, "or Torquay or Llandrindod Wells. Plenty of choice. They like it there—they're quite happy."

"They can't often afford to come to the West Indies, I suppose," said Esther. "It isn't everyone who is as lucky as you are."

"That's right," said Mr. Rafiel. "Rub it in. Here am I, a mass of aches and pains and disjoints. You grudge me any alleviation! And you don't do any work. Why haven't you typed out those letters yet?"

"I haven't had time."

"Well, get on with it, can't you? I bring you out here to do a bit of work, not to sit about sunning yourself and showing off your figure."

Some people would have considered Mr. Rafiel's remarks quite insupportable, but Esther Walters had worked for him for some years and she knew well enough that Mr. Rafiel's bark was a great deal worse than his bite. He was a man who suffered almost continual pain, and making disagreeable remarks was one of his ways of letting off steam. No matter what he said, she remained quite imperturbable.

"Such a lovely evening, isn't it?" said Miss Marple, pausing beside them.

"Why not?" said Mr. Rafiel. "That's what we're here for, isn't it?"

Miss Marple gave a tinkly little laugh.

"You're so severe—of course the weather *is* a very English subject of conversation—one forgets. Oh, dear—this is the wrong coloured wool." She deposited her knitting bag on the garden table and trotted towards her own bungalow.

"Jackson!" yelled Mr. Rafiel.

Jackson appeared.

"Take me back inside," said Mr. Rafiel. "I'll have my massage now before that chattering hen comes back. Not that massage does me a bit of good," he added. Having said which, he allowed himself to be deftly helped to his feet and went off with the masseur beside him into his bungalow.

Esther Walters looked after them and then turned her head as Miss Marple came back with a ball of wool to sit down near her.

"I hope I'm not disturbing you?" said Miss Marple.

"Of course not," said Esther Walters. "I've got to go off and do some typing in a minute, but I'm going to enjoy another ten minutes of the sunset first."

Miss Marple sat down and in a gentle voice began to talk. As she talked, she summed up Esther Walters. Not at all glamorous, but could be attractive-looking if she tried. Miss Marple wondered why she didn't try. It could be, of course, because Mr. Rafiel would not have liked it, but Miss Marple didn't think Mr. Rafiel would really mind in the least. He was so completely taken up with himself that so long as he was not personally neglected, his secretary might have got herself up like a houri in Paradise without his objecting. Besides, he usually went to bed early and in the evening hours of steel bands and dancing, Esther Walters might easily have —Miss Marple paused to select a word in her mind, at the same time conversing carefully about her visit to Jamestown—ah yes, *blossomed.* Esther Walters might have blossomed in the evening hours.

She led the conversation gently in the direction of Jackson.

On the subject of Jackson, Esther Walters was rather vague.

"He's very competent," she said. "A fully trained masseur."

"I suppose he's been with Mr. Rafiel a long time?"

"Oh, no—about nine months, I think—"

"Is he married?" Miss Marple hazarded.

"Married? I don't think so," said Esther, slightly surprised. "He's never mentioned it if so—

"No," she added. "Definitely *not* married, I should say." And she showed amusement.

Miss Marple interpreted that by adding to it in her own mind the following sentence, "At any rate he doesn't behave as though he were married."

But then, how many married men there were who behaved as though they weren't married! Miss Marple could think of a dozen examples!

"He's quite good-looking," she said thoughtfully.

"Yes—I suppose he is," said Esther without interest.

Miss Marple considered her thoughtfully. Uninterested in men? The kind of woman, perhaps, who was only interested in one man. A widow, they had said.

She asked, "Have you worked for Mr. Rafiel long?"

"Four or five years. After my husband died, I had to take a job again. I've got a daughter at school, and my husband left me very badly off."

"Mr. Rafiel must be a difficult man to work for?" Miss Marple hazarded.

"Not really, when you get to know him. He flies into rages and is very contradictory. I think the real trouble is he gets tired of people. He's had five different valet-attendants in two years. He likes having someone new to bully. But he and I have always got on very well."

"Mr. Jackson seems a very obliging young man?"

"He's very tactful and resourceful," said Esther. "Of course, he's sometimes a little—" she broke off.

Miss Marple considered. "Rather a difficult position sometimes?" she suggested.

"Well, yes. Neither one thing nor the other. However"—she smiled—"I think he manages to have quite a good time."

Miss Marple considered this also. It didn't help her much. She continued her twittering conversation and soon she was hearing a good deal about that nature-loving quartet, the Dysons and the Hillingdons.

"The Hillingdons have been here for the last three or four years at least," said Esther, "but Gregory Dyson has been here much longer than that. He knows the West Indies very well. He came here originally, I believe, with his first wife. She was delicate and had to go abroad in the winters, or go somewhere warm, at any rate."

"And she died? Or was it divorce?"

"No. She died. Out here, I believe. I don't mean this particular island, but one of the West Indies islands. There was some sort of trouble, I believe; some kind of scandal or other. He never talks about her. Somebody else told me about it. They didn't, I gather, get on very well together."

"And then he married this wife 'Lucky.' " Miss Marple said the word with faint dissatisfaction as if to say, "Really, a most incredible name!"

"I believe she was a relation of his first wife."

"Have they known the Hillingdons a great many years?"

"Oh, I think only since the Hillingdons came out here. Three or four years, not more."

"The Hillingdons seem very pleasant," said Miss Marple. "Quiet, of course."

"Yes. They're both quiet."

"Everyone says they're very devoted to each other," said Miss Marple.

The tone of her voice was quite noncommittal, but Esther Walters looked at her sharply.

"But you don't think they are?" she said.

"You don't really think so yourself, do you, my dear?"

"Well, I've wondered sometimes . . ."

"Quiet man like Colonel Hillingdon," said Miss Marple, "are often attracted to flamboyant types." And she added, after a significant pause, "Lucky—such a curious name. Do you think Mr. Dyson has any idea of—of what might be going on?"

"Old scandalmonger," thought Esther Walters. "Really, these old women!"

She said rather coldly, "I've no idea."

Miss Marple shifted to another subject. "It's very sad about poor Major Palgrave, isn't it?" she said.

Esther Walters agreed, though in a somewhat perfunctory fashion.

"The people I'm really sorry for are the Kendals," she said.

"Yes, I suppose it is really rather unfortunate when something of that kind happens in a hotel."

"People come here, you see, to enjoy themselves, don't they?" said Esther. "To forget about illnesses and deaths and income tax and frozen pipes and all the rest of it. They don't like"—she went on, with a sudden flash of an entirely different manner—"any reminders of mortality."

Miss Marple laid down her knitting. "Now that is very well put, my dear," she said; "very well put indeed. Yes, it is as you say."

"And you see they're quite a young couple," went on Esther Walters. "They only just took over from the Sandersons six months ago, and they're terribly worried about whether they're going to succeed or not, because they haven't had much experience."

"And you think this might be really disadvantageous to them?"

"Well, no, I don't frankly," said Esther Walters. "I don't think people remember anything for more than a day or two, not in this atmosphere of 'we've-all-come-out-here-to-enjoy-ourselves-let's-get-on-with it.' I think a death just gives them a jolt for about twenty-four hours or so, and then they don't think of it again once the funeral is over. Not unless they're reminded of it, that is. I've told Molly so, but of course she is a worrier."

"Mrs. Kendal is a worrier? She always seems so carefree."

"I think a lot of that is put on," said Esther slowly. "Actually, I think she's one of those anxious sort of people who can't help worrying all the time that things *may* go wrong."

"I should have thought he worried more than she did."

"No, I don't think so. I think she's the worrier and he worries because she worries, if you know what I mean."

"That is interesting," said Miss Marple.

"I think Molly wants desperately to try and appear very gay and to be enjoying herself. She works at it very hard, but the effort exhausts her. Then she has these odd fits of depression. She's not—well, not really well-balanced."

"Poor child," said Miss Marple. "There certainly are people like that, and very often outsiders don't suspect it."

"No, they put on such a good show, don't they? However," Esther added, "I don't think Molly has really anything to worry about in this case. I mean, people are dying of coronary thrombosis or cerebral hemorrhage or things of that kind all the time nowadays. Far more than they used to, as far as I can see. It's only food poisoning or typhoid or something like that, that makes people get het up."

"Major Palgrave never mentioned to me that he had high blood pressure," said Miss Marple. "Did he to you?"

"He said so to somebody—I don't know who. It may have been to Mr. Rafiel. I know Mr. Rafiel says just the opposite—but then he's like that! Certainly Jackson mentioned it to me once. He said the Major ought to be more careful over the alcohol he took."

"I see," said Miss Marple thoughtfully. She went on: "I expect you found him rather a boring old man? He told a lot of stories and I expect repeated himself a good deal."

"That's the worst of it," said Esther. "You do hear the same story again and again unless you can manage to be quick enough to fend it off."

"Of course I didn't mind so much," said Miss Marple, "because I'm used to that sort of thing. If I get stories told to me rather often, I don't really mind hearing them again, because I've usually forgotten them."

"There is that," said Esther and laughed cheerfully.

"There was one story he was very fond of telling," said Miss Marple, "about a murder. I expect he told you that, didn't he?"

Esther Walters opened her handbag and started searching through it. She drew out her lipstick, saying, "I thought I'd lost it." Then she asked, "I beg your pardon, what did you say?"

"I asked if Major Palgrave told you his favourite murder story?"

"I believe he did, now that I come to think of it. Something about someone who gassed themselves, wasn't it? Only really it was the *wife* who gassed him. I mean she'd given him a sedative of some kind and then stuck his head in the gas oven. Was that it?"

"I don't think that was exactly it," said Miss Marple. She looked at Esther Walters thoughtfully.

"He told such a lot of stories," said Esther Walters apologetically, "and as I said, one didn't always listen."

"He had a snapshot," said Miss Marple, "that he used to show people."

"I believe he did . . . I can't remember what it was now. Did he show it to you?"

"No," said Miss Marple. "He didn't show it to me. We were interrupted—"

9

MISS PRESCOTT AND OTHERS

"The story I heard," began Miss Prescott, lowering her voice and looking carefully around.

Miss Marple drew her chair a little closer. It had been some time before she had been able to get together with Miss Prescott for a heart-to-heart chat. This was owing to the fact that clergymen are very strong family men, so that Miss Prescott was nearly always accompanied by her brother, and there was no doubt that Miss Marple and Miss Prescott found it less easy to take their back hair down in a good gossip when the jovial Canon was of their company.

"It seems," said Miss Prescott, "though of course I don't want to talk any scandal and I really know nothing about it—"

"Oh, I quite understand," said Miss Marple.

"It seems there was some scandal when his first wife was still alive! Apparently this woman, Lucky—such a name!—who I think was a cousin of his first wife, came out here and joined them and I think did some work with him on flowers or butterflies or whatever it was. And people talked a lot because they got on so well together—if you know what I mean."

"People do notice things so much, don't they?" said Miss Marple.

"And then of course, when his wife died rather suddenly—"

"She died here, on this island?"

"No. No, I think they were in Martinique or Tobago at the time."

"I see."

"But I gathered from some other people who were there at the time, and who came on here and talked about things, that the doctor wasn't very satisfied."

"Indeed," said Miss Marple with interest.

"It was only gossip, of course, but—well, Mr. Dyson certainly married again very quickly." She lowered her voice again. "Only a month, I believe."

"Only a month," said Miss Marple.

The two women looked at each other. "It seemed—unfeeling," said Miss Prescott.

"Yes," said Miss Marple. "It certainly did." She added delicately, "Was there—any money?"

"I don't really know. He makes his little joke—perhaps you've heard him—about his wife being his 'lucky piece'—"

"Yes, I've heard him," said Miss Marple.

"And some people think that means that he was lucky to marry a rich wife. Though, of course," said Miss Prescott with the air of one being entirely fair, "she's very good-looking, too, if you care for that type. And I think myself that it was the first wife who had the money."

"Are the Hillingdons well off?"

"Well, I think they're well off. I don't mean fabulously rich; I just mean well off. They have two boys at public school and a very nice place in England, I believe, and they travel most of the winter."

The Canon appearing at this moment to suggest a brisk walk, Miss Prescott rose to join her brother. Miss Marple remained sitting there.

A few minutes later Gregory Dyson passed her, striding along toward the hotel. He waved a cheerful hand as he passed.

"Penny for your thoughts," he called out.

Miss Marple smiled gently, wondering how he would have reacted if she had replied: "I was wondering if you were a murderer."

It really seemed most probable that he was. It all fitted in so nicely—This story about the death of the first Mrs. Dyson. Major Palgrave had certainly been talking about a wife killer—with special reference to the Brides in the Bath Case.

Yes, it fitted—the only objection was that it fitted almost too well. But Miss Marple reproved herself for this thought. Who was she to demand Murders Made to Measure?

A voice made her jump—a somewhat raucous one.

"Seen Greg anyplace, Miss—er—"

Lucky, Miss Marple thought, was not in a good temper.

"He passed by just now—going towards the hotel."

"I'll bet!" Lucky uttered an irritated ejaculation and hurried on.

"Forty, if she's a day, and looks it this morning," thought Miss Marple.

Pity invaded her—Pity for the Luckys of the world, who were so vulnerable to Time.

At the sound of a noise behind her, she turned her chair round.

Mr. Rafiel, supported by Jackson, was making his morning appearance and coming out of his bungalow.

Jackson settled his employer in his wheel chair and fussed round him. Mr. Rafiel waved his attendant away impatiently, and Jackson went off in the direction of the hotel.

Miss Marple lost no time—Mr. Rafiel was never left alone for long. Probably Esther Walters would come and join him. Miss Marple wanted a word alone with Mr. Rafiel and now, she thought, was her chance. She would have to be quick about what she wanted to say. There could be no leading up to things. Mr. Rafiel was not a man who cared for the idle twittering conversation of old ladies. He would probably retreat again into his bungalow, definitely regarding himself the victim of persecution. Miss Marple decided to plump for downrightness.

She made her way to where he was sitting, drew up a chair, sat down, and said: "I want to ask you something, Mr. Rafiel."

"All right, all right," said Mr. Rafiel, "let's have it. What do you want—a subscription, I suppose? Missions in Africa or repairing a church, something of that kind?"

"Yes," said Miss Marple. "I am interested in several objects of that nature, and I shall be delighted if you will give me a subscription for them. But that wasn't actually what I was going to ask you. What I was going to ask you was if Major Palgrave ever told you a story about a murder."

"Oho," said Mr. Rafiel. "So he told it to you too, did he? And I suppose you fell for it, hook, line and sinker."

"I didn't really know what to think," said Miss Marple. "What exactly did he tell you?"

"He prattled on," said Mr. Rafiel, "about a lovely creature, Lucrezia Borgia reincarnated. Beautiful, young, golden-haired, everything."

"Oh," said Miss Marple, slightly taken aback, "and who did she murder?"

"Her husband, of course," said Mr. Rafiel. "Who do you think?"

"Poison?"

"No, I think she gave him a sleeping draught and then stuck him in a gas oven. Resourceful female. Then she said it was suicide. She got off quite lightly. Diminished responsibility or something. That's what it's called nowadays if you're a good-looking woman or some miserable young hooligan whose mother's been too fond of him. Bah!"

"Did the Major show you a snapshot?"

"What—a snapshot of the woman? No. Why should he?"

"Oh—" said Miss Marple.

She sat there, rather taken aback. Apparently Major Palgrave spent his life telling people not only about tigers he had shot and elephants he had hunted but also about murderers he had met. Perhaps he had a whole repertoire of murder stories. One had to face it. She was startled by Mr. Rafiel suddenly giving a roar of "Jackson!" There was no response.

"Shall I find him for you?" said Miss Marple, rising.

"You won't find him. Tom-catting somewhere, that's what he does. No good, that fellow. Bad character. But he suits me all right."

"I'll go and look for him," said Miss Marple.

Miss Marple found Jackson sitting on the far side of the hotel terrace having a drink with Tim Kendal.

"Mr. Rafiel is asking for you," she said.

Jackson made an expressive grimace, drained his glass, and rose to his feet.

"Here we go again," he said. "No peace for the wicked. Two telephone calls and a special diet order—I thought that might give me a quarter of an hour's alibi. Apparently not! Thank you, Miss Marple. Thanks for the drink, Mr. Kendal."

He strode away.

"I feel sorry for that chap," said Tim. "I have to stand him a drink now and then, just to cheer him up. Can I offer you something, Miss Marple? How about fresh lime? I know you're fond of that."

"Not just now, thank you. I suppose looking after someone like Mr. Rafiel must always be rather exacting. Invalids are frequently difficult—"

"I didn't mean only that. It's very well paid and you expect to put up with a good deal of crotchetiness—old Rafiel's not really a bad sort. I meant more that—" He hesitated.

Miss Marple looked inquiring.

"Well—how shall I put it?—it's difficult for him socially. People are so damned snobbish—there's no one here of his class. He's better than a servant and below the average visitor—or they think he is. Rather like the Victorian governess. Even the secretary woman Mrs. Walters feels she's a cut above him. Makes things difficult." Tim paused, then said with feeling: "It's really awful the amount of social problems there are in a place like this."

Dr. Graham passed them. He had a book in his hand. He went and sat at a table overlooking the sea.

"Dr. Graham looks rather worried," remarked Miss Marple.

"Oh! We're all worried."

"You too? Because of Major Palgrave's death?"

"I've left off worrying about that. People seem to have forgotten it—taken it in their stride. No—it's my wife—Molly. Do you know anything about dreams?"

"Dreams?" Miss Marple was surprised.

"Yes—bad dreams—nightmares, I suppose. Oh, we all get that sort of thing sometimes. But Molly—she seems to have them nearly all the time. They frighten her. Is there anything one can do about them? Take for them? She's got some sleeping pills, but she says they make it worse—she struggles to wake up and can't."

"What are the dreams about?"

"Oh, something or someone chasing her. Or watching her and spying on her—she can't shake off the feeling even when she's awake."

"Surely a doctor—"

"She's got a thing against doctors. Won't hear of it. Oh, well—I dare say it will all pass off. But we were so happy. It was all such fun. And now, just lately—Perhaps old Palgrave's death upset her. She seems like a different person since . . ."

He got up.

"Must get on with the daily chores—are you sure you won't have that fresh lime?"

Miss Marple shook her head.

She sat there, thinking. Her face was grave and anxious.

She glanced over at Dr. Graham.

Presently she came to a decision.

She rose and went across to his table.

"I have got to apologize to you, Dr. Graham," she said.

"Indeed?" The doctor looked at her in kindly surprise. He pulled forward a chair and she sat down.

"I am afraid I have done the most disgraceful thing," said Miss Marple. "I told you, Dr. Graham, a deliberate lie."

She looked at him apprehensively.

Dr. Graham did not look at all shattered, but he did look a little surprised.

"Really?" he said. "Ah, well, you mustn't let that worry you too much."

What had the dear old thing been telling lies about, he wondered; her age? Though as far as he could remember, she hadn't mentioned her age. "Well, let's hear about it," he said, since she clearly wished to confess.

"You remember my speaking to you about a snapshot of my nephew, one that I showed to Major Palgrave, and that he didn't give back to me?"

"Yes, yes, of course I remember. Sorry we couldn't find it for you."

"There wasn't any such thing," said Miss Marple in a small, frightened voice.

"I beg your pardon?"

"There wasn't any such thing. I made up that story, I'm afraid."

"You made it up?" Dr. Graham looked slightly annoyed. "Why?"

Miss Marple told him. She told him quite clearly, without twittering. She told him about Major Palgrave's murder story and how he'd been about to show her this particular snapshot and his sudden confusion and then she went on to her own anxiety and to her final decision to try somehow to obtain a view of it.

"And really, I couldn't see any way of doing so without telling you something that was quite untrue," she said. "I do hope you will forgive me."

"You thought that what he had been about to show you was a picture of a murderer?"

"That's what he said it was," said Miss Marple. "At least he said it was given him by this acquaintance who had told him the story about a man who was a murderer."

"Yes, yes. And—excuse me—you believed him?"

"I don't know if I really believed him or not at the time," said Miss Marple. "But then, you see, the next day he died."

"Yes," said Dr. Graham, struck suddenly by the clarity of that one sentence. *The next day he died.* . . .

"And the snapshot had disappeared."

Dr. Graham looked at her. He didn't know quite what to say.

"Excuse me, Miss Marple," he said at last, "but is what you're telling me now—is it really true this time?"

"I don't wonder your doubting me," said Miss Marple. "I should, in your place. Yes, it is true what I am telling you now, but I quite realize that you have only my word for it. Still, even if you don't believe me, I thought I ought to tell you."

"Why?"

"I realized that you ought to have the fullest information possible. In case—"

"In case what?"

"In case you decided to take any steps about it."

10

A DECISION IN JAMESTOWN

Dr. Graham was in Jamestown, in the Administrator's office, sitting at a table opposite his friend Daventry, a grave young man of thirty-five.

"You sounded rather mysterious on the phone, Graham," said Daventry. "Anything special the matter?"

"I don't know," said Dr. Graham, "but I'm worried."

Daventry looked at the other's face, then he nodded as drinks were brought in. He spoke lightly of a fishing expedition he had made lately. Then when the servant had gone away, he sat back in his chair and looked at the other man.

"Now then," he said, "let's have it."

Dr. Graham recounted the facts that had worried him. Daventry gave a slow long whistle.

"I see. You think maybe there's something funny about old Palgrave's death? You're no longer sure that it was just natural causes? Who certified the death? Robertson, I suppose. He didn't have any doubts, did he?"

"No, but I think he may have been influenced in giving the certificate by the fact of the Serenite tablets in the bathroom. He asked me if Palgrave had mentioned that he suffered from hypertension, and I said No, I'd never had any medical conversation with him myself, but apparently he had talked about it to other people in the hotel. The whole thing—the bottle of tablets, and what Palgrave had said to people—it all fitted in—no earthly reason to suspect anything else. It was a perfectly natural inference to make—but I think now it may not have been correct. If it had been my business to give the certificate, I'd have given it without a second thought. The appearances are quite consistent with his having died from that cause. I'd never have thought about it since if it hadn't been for the odd disappearance of that snapshot . . ."

"But look here, Graham," said Daventry, "if you will allow me to say so, aren't you relying a little too much on a rather fanciful story told you by an elderly lady? You know what these elderly ladies are like. They magnify some small detail and work the whole thing up."

"Yes, I know," said Dr. Graham unhappily. "I know that. I've said to myself that it may be so, that it probably is so. But I can't quite convince myself. She was so very clear and detailed in her statement."

"The whole thing seems wildly improbable to me," said Daventry. "Some old lady tells a story about a snapshot that ought not to be there—no, I'm getting mixed myself—I mean the other way about, don't I?—but the only thing you've really got to go on is that a chambermaid says that a bottle of pills which the authorities had relied on for evidence wasn't in the Major's room the day before his death. But there are a hundred explanations for that. He might always have carried those pills about in his pocket."

"It's possible, I suppose, yes."

"Or the chambermaid may have made a mistake and she simply hadn't noticed them before—"

"That's possible, too."

"Well, then."

Graham said slowly: "The girl was very positive."

"Well, the St. Honoré people are very excitable, you know. Emotional. Work themselves up easily. Are you thinking that she knows—a little more than she had said?"

"I think it might be so," said Dr. Graham slowly.

"You'd better try and get it out of her, if so. We don't want to make an unnecessary fuss—unless we've something definite to go on. If he didn't die of blood pressure, what do you think it was?"

"There are too many things it might be nowadays," said Dr. Graham.

"You mean things that don't leave recognizable traces?"

"Not everyone," said Dr. Graham dryly, "is so considerate as to use arsenic."

"Now let's get things quite clear—what's the suggestion? That a bottle of pills was substituted for the real ones? And that Major Palgrave was poisoned in that way?"

"No—it's not like that. That's what the girl—Victoria Something thinks. But she's got it all wrong. If it was decided to get rid of the Major—quickly—he would have been given something—most likely in a drink of some kind. Then to make it appear a natural death, a bottle of the tablets prescribed to relieve blood pressure was put in his room. And the rumour was put about that he suffered from high blood pressure."

"Who put the rumour about?"

"I've tried to find out—with no success. It's been too cleverly done. A says, 'I think B told me.' B, asked, says, 'No, I didn't say so but I do remember C mentioning it one day.' C says, 'Several people talked about it —one of them, I think, was A.' And there we are, back again."

"Someone was clever?"

"Yes. As soon as the death was discovered, everybody seemed to be talking about the Major's high blood pressure and repeating round what other people had said."

"Wouldn't it have been simpler just to poison him and let it go at that?"

"No. That might have meant inquiry—possibly an autopsy. This way, a doctor would accept the death and give a certificate—as he did."

"What do you want me to do? Go to the C.I.D.? Suggest they dig the chap up? It'd make a lot of stink—"

"It could be kept quite quiet."

"Could it? In St. Honoré? Think again! The grapevine would be on to it before it had happened. All the same," Daventry sighed, "I suppose we'll have to do something. But if you ask me, it's all a mare's-nest!"

"I devoutly hope it is," said Dr. Graham.

11

EVENING AT THE GOLDEN PALM

Molly rearranged a few of the table decorations in the dining-room, removed an extra knife, straightened a fork, reset a glass or two, stood back to look at the effect and then walked out on to the terrace outside. There was no one about just at present and she strolled to the far corner and stood by the balustrade. Soon another evening would begin. Chattering, talking, drinking, all so gay and carefree, the sort of life she had longed for and, up to a few days ago, had enjoyed so much. Now even Tim seemed anxious and worried. Natural, perhaps, that he should worry a little. It was important that this venture of theirs should turn out all right. After all, he had sunk all he had in it.

But that, thought Molly, is not really what's worrying him. It's me. But I don't see, said Molly to herself, why he should worry about me. Because he did worry about her. That she was quite sure of. The questions he put, the quick nervous glance he shot at her from time to time. But why? thought Molly. "I've been very careful," she summed up things in her mind. She didn't understand it really herself. She couldn't remember when it had begun. She wasn't even very sure what it was. She'd begun to be frightened of people. She didn't know why. What could they do to her? What should they want to do to her?

She nodded her head, then started violently as a hand touched her arm. She spun round to find Gregory Dyson, slightly taken aback, looking apologetic.

"Ever so sorry. Did I startle you, little girl?"

Molly hated being called "little girl." She said quickly and brightly: "I didn't hear you coming, Mr. Dyson, so it made me jump."

"Mr. Dyson? We're very formal tonight. Aren't we all one great happy family here? Ed and me and Lucky and Evelyn and you and Tim and Esther Walters and old Rafiel. All the lot of us one happy family."

"He's had plenty to drink already," thought Molly. She smiled at him pleasantly.

"Oh, I come over the heavy hostess sometimes," she said lightly. "Tim and I think it's more polite not to be too handy with Christian names."

"Aw, we don't want any of that stuffed-shirt business. Now then, Molly my lovely, have a drink with me."

"Ask me later," said Molly. "I have a few things to get on with."

"Now don't run away." His arms fastened round her arm. "You're a lovely girl, Molly. I hope Tim appreciates his good luck."

"Oh, I see to it that he does," said Molly cheerfully.

"I could go for you, you know, in a big way"—he leered at her—"though I wouldn't let my wife hear me say so."

"Did you have a good trip this afternoon?"

"I suppose so. Between you and me, I get a bit fed up sometimes. You can get tired of the birds and butterflies. What say you and I go for a little picnic on our own one day?"

"We'll have to see about that," said Molly gaily. "I'll be looking forward to it."

With a light laugh she escaped and went back into the bar.

"Hallo, Molly," said Tim, "you seem in a hurry. Who's that you've been with out there?"

He peered out.

"Gregory Dyson."

"What does he want?"

"Wanted to make a pass at me," said Molly.

"Blast him," said Tim.

"Don't worry," said Molly, "I can do all the blasting necessary."

Tim started to answer her, caught sight of Fernando and went over to him, shouting out some directions. Molly slipped away through the kitchen, out through the kitchen door and down the steps to the beach.

Gregory Dyson swore under his breath. Then he walked slowly back in the direction of his bungalow. He had nearly got there when a voice spoke to him from the shadow of one of the bushes. He turned his head, startled. In the gathering dusk he thought for a moment that it was a ghostly figure that stood there. Then he laughed. It had looked like a faceless apparition, but that was because, though the dress was white, the face was black.

Victoria stepped out of the bushes on to the path.

"Mr. Dyson, please?"

"Yes. What is it?"

Ashamed of being startled, he spoke with a touch of impatience.

"I brought you this, sir." She held out her hand. In it was a bottle of tablets. "This belongs to you, doesn't it? Yes?"

"Oh, my bottle of Serenite tablets. Yes, of course. Where did you find it?"

"I found it where it had been put. In the gentleman's room."

"What do you mean—in the gentleman's room?"

"The gentleman who is dead," she added gravely. "I do not think he sleeps very well in his grave."

"Why the devil not?" asked Dyson.

Victoria stood looking at him.

"I still don't know what you're talking about. You mean you found this bottle of tablets in Major Palgrave's bungalow?"

"That is right, yes. After the doctor and the Jamestown people go away, they give me all the things in his bathroom to throw away. The toothpaste and the lotions, and all the other things—including this."

"Well, why didn't you throw it away?"

"Because these are yours. You missed them. You remember, you asked about them?"

"Yes—well—yes, I did. I—I thought I'd just mislaid them."

"No, you did not mislay them. They were taken from your bungalow and put in Major Palgrave's bungalow."

"How do you know?" He spoke roughly.

"I know. I saw." She smiled at him in a sudden flash of white teeth. "Someone put them in the dead gentleman's room. Now I give them back to you."

"Here, wait. What do you mean? What—who did you see?"

She hurried away, back into the darkness of the bushes. Greg made as if to move after her, and then stopped. He stood stroking his chin.

"What's the matter, Greg? Seen a ghost?" asked Mrs. Dyson, as she came along the path from their bungalow.

"Thought I had for a minute or two."

"Who was that you were talking to?"

"The coloured girl who does our place. Victoria, her name is, isn't it?"

"What did she want? Making a pass at you?"

"Don't be stupid, Lucky. That girl's got some idiotic idea into her head."

"Idea about what?"

"You remember I couldn't find my Serenite the other day?"

"You said you couldn't."

"What do you mean, 'I said I couldn't'?"

"Oh, for heck's sake, have you got to take me up on everything?"

"I'm sorry," said Greg. "Everybody goes about being so damn' mysterious." He held out his hand with the bottle in it. "That girl brought them back to me."

"Had she pinched them?"

"No. She—found them somewhere, I think."

"Well, what of it? What's the mystery about?"

"Oh, nothing," said Greg. "She just riled me, that's all."

"Look here, Greg, what is this stuff all about? Come along and have a drink before dinner."

II

Molly had gone down to the beach. She pulled out one of the old basket chairs, one of the more rickety ones that were seldom used. She sat in it for a while looking at the sea, then suddenly she dropped her head in her hands and burst into tears. She sat there sobbing unrestrainedly for some time. Then she heard a rustle close by her and glanced up sharply to see Mrs. Hillingdon looking down at her.

"Hallo, Evelyn, I didn't hear you. I—I'm sorry."

"What's the matter, child?" said Evelyn. "Something gone wrong?" She pulled another chair forward and sat down. "Tell me."

"There's nothing wrong," said Molly. "Nothing at all."

"Of course there is. You wouldn't sit and cry here for nothing. Can't you tell me? Is it—some trouble between you and Tim?"

"Oh, *no.*"

"I'm glad of that. You always look so happy together."

"Not more than you do," said Molly. "Tim and I always think how wonderful it is that you and Edward should seem so happy together after being married so many years."

"Oh, that," said Evelyn. Her voice was sharp as she spoke, but Milly hardly noticed.

"People bicker so," she said, "and have such rows. Even if they're quite fond of each other, they still seem to have rows and not to mind a bit whether they have them in public or not."

"Some people like living that way," said Evelyn. "It doesn't really mean anything."

"Well, I think its horrid," said Molly.

"So do I, really," said Evelyn.

"But to see you and Edward—"

"Oh, it's no good, Molly. I can't let you go on thinking things of that kind. Edward and I—" she paused. "If you want to know the truth, we've hardly said a word to each other in private for the last three years."

"What!" Molly stared at her, appalled. "I—I can't believe it."

"Oh, we both put up quite a good show," said Evelyn. "We're neither of us the kind that like having rows in public. And anyway, there's nothing really to have a row about."

"But what went wrong?" asked Molly.

"Just the usual."

"What do you mean by the usual? Another—"

"Yes, another woman in the case, and I don't suppose it will be difficult for you to guess who the woman is."

"Do you mean Mrs. Dyson—Lucky?"

Evelyn nodded.

"I know they always flirt together a lot," said Molly, "but I thought that was just . . ."

"Just high spirits?" said Evelyn. "Nothing behind it?"

"But why—" Molly paused and tried again. "But didn't you—oh, I mean, well, I suppose I oughtn't to ask."

"Ask anything you like," said Evelyn. "I'm tired of never saying a word, tired of being a well-bred happy wife. Edward just lost his head completely about Lucky. He was stupid enough to come and tell me about it. It made him feel better, I suppose. Truthful. Honourable. All that sort of stuff. It didn't occur to him to think that it wouldn't make me feel better."

"Did he want to leave you?"

Evelyn shook her head. "We've got two children, you know," she said. "Children whom we're both very fond of. They're at school in England. We didn't want to break up the home. And then, of course, Lucky didn't want a divorce either. Greg's a very right man. His first wife left a lot of money. So we agreed to live and let live—Edward and Lucky in happy immorality, Greg in blissful ignorance, and Edward and I just good friends." She spoke with scalding bitterness.

"How—how can you bear it?"

"One gets used to anything. But sometimes—"

"Yes?" said Molly.

"Sometimes I'd like to kill that woman."

The passion behind her voice startled Molly.

"Don't let's talk any more about me," said Evelyn. "Let's talk about you. I want to know what's the matter."

Molly was silent for some moments, and then she said, "It's only—it's only that I think there's something wrong about me."

"Wrong? What do you mean?"

Molly shook her head unhappily. "I'm frightened," she said. "I'm terribly frightened."

"Frightened of what?"

"Everything," said Molly. "It's—growing on me. Voices in the bushes, footsteps—or things that people say. As though someone were watching me all the time, spying on me. Somebody hates me. That's what I keep feeling. Somebody hates me."

"My dear child." Evelyn was shocked and startled. "How long has this been going on?"

"I don't know. It came—it started by degrees. And there have been other things, too."

"What sort of things?"

"There are times," said Molly slowly, "that I can't account for, that I can't remember."

"Do you mean you have blackouts—that sort of thing?"

"I suppose so. I mean sometimes it's— Oh, say, it's five o'clock—and I can't remember anything since about half-past one or two."

"Oh, my dear, but that's just that you've been asleep. Had a doze."

"No," said Molly, "it's not like that at all. Because you see, at the end of the time it's not as though I'd just dozed off. I'm in a different place. Sometimes I'm wearing different clothes and sometimes I seem to have been doing things—even saying things to people, talking to someone, and not remembering that I've done so."

Evelyn looked shocked. "But, Molly, my dear, if this is so, then you ought to see a doctor."

"I won't see a doctor! I don't want to. I wouldn't go near a doctor."

Evelyn looked sharply down into her face, then she took the girl's hand in hers.

"You may be frightening yourself for nothing, Molly. You know there are all kinds of nervous disorders that aren't really serious at all. A doctor would soon reassure you."

"He mightn't. He might say that there was something really wrong with me."

"Why should there be anything wrong with you?"

"Because—" Molly spoke and then was silent. "No reason, I suppose," she said.

"Couldn't your family—haven't you any family, any mother or sisters or someone who could come out here?"

"I don't get on with my mother. I never have. I've got sisters. They're married, but I suppose—I suppose they could come if I wanted them. But I don't want them. I don't want anyone—anyone except Tim."

"Does Tim know about this? Have you told him?"

"Not really," said Molly. "But he's anxious about me and he watches me. It's as though he were trying to—to help me or to shield me. But if he does that, it means I want shielding, doesn't it?"

"I think a lot of it may be imagination, but I still think you ought to see a doctor."

"Old Dr. Graham? He wouldn't be any good."

"There are other doctors on the island."

"It's all right, really," said Molly. "I just—mustn't think of it. I expect, as you say, it's all imagination. Good gracious, it's getting frightfully late. I ought to be on duty now in the dining-room. I—I must go back."

She looked sharply and almost offensively at Evelyn Hillingdon, and then hurried off. Evelyn stared after her.

12

OLD SINS CAST LONG SHADOWS

"I think I am on to something, man."

"What's that you say, Victoria?"

"I think I'm on to something. It may mean money. Big money."

"Now look, girl, you be careful you'll not tangle yourself up in something. Maybe I'd better tackle what it is."

Victoria laughed, a deep rich chuckle.

"You wait and see," she said. "I know how to play this hand. It's money, man; it's big money. Something I see, and something I guess. I think I guess right."

And again the soft rich chuckle rolled out on the night.

II

"Evelyn . . ."

"Yes?"

Evelyn Hillingdon spoke mechanically, without interest. She did not look at her husband.

"Evelyn, would you mind if we chucked all this and went home to England?"

She had been combing her short dark hair. Now her hands came down from her head sharply. She turned towards him.

"You mean—but we've only just come. We've not been out here in the islands for more than three weeks."

"I know. But—would you mind?"

Her eyes searched his incredulously.

"You really want to go back to England? Back home?"

"Yes."

"Leaving—Lucky."

He winced.

"You've known all the time, I suppose, that—that it was still going on?"

"Pretty well. Yes."

"You've never said anything."

"Why should I? We had the whole thing out years ago. Neither of us wanted to make a break. So we agreed to go our separate ways—but keep up the show in public." Then she added before he could speak, "But why are you so set on going back to England now?"

"Because I'm at breaking point. I can't stick at it any longer, Evelyn. I can't." The quiet Edward Hillingdon was transformed. His hands shook, he swallowed, his calm unemotional face seemed distorted by pain.

"For God's sake, Edward, what's the matter?"

"Nothing's the matter except that I want to get out of here—"

"You fell wildly in love with Lucky. And now you've got over it. Is that what you're telling me?"

"Yes. I don't suppose you'll ever feel the same."

"Oh, let's not go into that now! I want to understand what's upsetting you so much, Edward."

"I'm not particularly upset."

"But you are. Why?"

"Isn't it obvious?"

"No, it isn't," said Evelyn. "Let's put it in plain concrete terms. You've had an affair with a woman. That happens often enough. And now it's over. Or isn't it over? Perhaps it isn't over on *her* side. Is that it? Does Greg know about it? I've often wondered."

"I don't know," said Edward. "He's never said anything. He always seems friendly enough."

"Men can be extraordinarily obtuse," said Evelyn thoughtfully. "Or else— Perhaps Greg has got an outside interest of his own!"

"He's made passes at you, hasn't he?" said Edward. "Answer me—I know he has—"

"Oh, yes," said Evelyn carelessly, "but he makes passes at everybody. That's just Greg. It doesn't ever really mean much, I imagine. That's just part of the Greg he-man act."

"Do you care for him, Evelyn? I'd rather know the truth."

"Greg? I'm quite fond of him—he amuses me. He's a good friend."

"And that's all? I wish I could believe you."

"I can't really see how it can possibly matter to you," said Evelyn dryly.

"I suppose I deserve that."

Evelyn walked to the window, looked out across the veranda and came back again.

"I wish you would tell me what's really upsetting you, Edward."

"I've told you."

"I wonder."

"You can't understand, I suppose, how extraordinary a temporary madness of this kind can seem to you after you've got over it."

"I can try, I suppose. But what's worrying me now is that Lucky seems to have got some kind of strange hold upon you. She's not just a discarded mistress. She's a tigress with claws. You must tell me the truth, Edward. It's the only way if you want me to stand by you."

Edward said in a low voice: "If I don't get away from her soon—I shall kill her."

"Kill Lucky? Why?"

"Because of what she made me do . . ."

"What did she make you do?"

"I helped her to commit a murder—"

The words were out. There was silence. Evelyn stared at him.

"Do you know what you are saying?"

"Yes. I didn't know I was doing it. There were things she asked me to get for her—at the chemist's. I didn't know—I hadn't the least idea what she wanted them for. She got me to copy out a prescription she had . . ."

"When was this?"

"Four years ago. When we were in Martinique. When—when Greg's wife—"

"You mean Greg's first wife—Gail? You mean Lucky poisoned her?"

"Yes—and I helped her. Then I realized—"

Evelyn interrupted him.

"When you realized what had happened, Lucky pointed out to you that *you* had written out the prescription, that *you* had got the drugs, that you and she were in it together? Is that right?"

"Yes. She said she had done it out of pity—that Gail was suffering—that she had begged Lucky to get something that would end it all."

"A mercy killing! I see. And you believed that?"

Edward Hillingdon was silent a moment—then he said: "No—I didn't really—not deep down. I accepted it because I wanted to believe it—because I was infatuated with Lucky."

"And afterwards—when she married Greg—did you still believe it?"

"I'd made myself believe it by then."

"And Greg—how much did he know about it all?"

"Nothing at all."

"That I find hard to believe!"

Edward Hillingdon broke out: "Evelyn, I've got to get free of it all! That woman taunts me still with what I did. She knows I don't care for her any longer. Care for her?—I've come to hate her. But she makes me feel I'm tied to her—by the thing we did together—"

Evelyn walked up and down the room—then she stopped and faced him. "The entire trouble with you, Edward, is that you are ridiculously sensitive—and also incredibly suggestible. That devil of a woman has got you just where she wants you by playing on your sense of guilt. And I'll tell you this in plain Bible terms, the guilt that weighs on you is the guilt of adultery—not murder. You were guilt-stricken about your affair with Lucky—and then she made a cat's-paw of you for her murder scheme, and managed to make you feel you shared her guilt. You don't."

"Evelyn . . ." He stepped towards her.

She stepped back a minute—and looked at him searchingly.

"Is this all true, Edward? *Is* it? Or are you making it up?"

"Evelyn! Why on earth should I do such a thing?"

"I don't know," said Evelyn Hillingdon slowly. "It's just perhaps—because I find it hard to trust—anybody. And because— Oh! I don't know. I've got, I suppose, so that I don't know the truth when I hear it."

"Let's chuck all this. Go back home to England."

"Yes. We will. But not now."

"Why not?"

"We must carry on as usual—just for the present. It's important. Do you understand, Edward? Don't let Lucky have an inkling of what we're up to—"

13

EXIT VICTORIA JOHNSON

The evening was drawing to a close. The steel band was at last relaxing its efforts. Tim stood by the dining-room looking over the terrace. He extinguished a few lights on tables that had been vacated.

A voice spoke behind him. "Tim, can I speak to you a moment?"

Tim Kendal started.

"Hallo, Evelyn, is there anything I can do for you?"

Evelyn looked round.

"Come to this table here, and let's sit down a minute."

She led the way to a table at the extreme end of the terrace. There were no other people near them.

"Tim, you must forgive me talking to you, but I'm worried about Molly."

His face changed at once.

"What about Molly?" he said stiffly.

"I don't think she's awfully well. She seems upset."

"Things do seem to upset her rather easily just lately."

"She ought to see a doctor, I think."

"Yes, I know, but she doesn't want to. She'd hate it."

"Why?"

"Eh? What d'you mean?"

"I said why? Why should she hate seeing a doctor?"

"Well," said Tim rather vaguely, "people do sometimes, you know. It's—well, it sort of makes them feel frightened about themselves."

"You're worried about her yourself, aren't you, Tim?"

"Yes. Yes, I am rather."

"Isn't there anyone of her family who could come out here to be with her?"

"No. That'd make things worse—far worse."

"What *is* the trouble—with her family, I mean?"

"Oh, just one of those things. I suppose she's just highly strung and—she didn't get on with them—particularly her mother. She never has. They're—they're rather an odd family in some ways and she cut loose from them. Good thing she did, I think."

Evelyn said hesitantly: "She seems to have had blackouts, from what she told me, and to be frightened of people. Almost like persecution mania."

"Don't say that," said Tim angrily. "Persecution mania! People always say that about people. Just because she—well—maybe she's a bit nervy. Coming out here to the West Indies. You know, people are rather queer, sometimes, about the West Indies and coloured people."

"Surely not girls like Molly?"

"Oh, how does one know the things people are frightened of? There are people who can't be in the room with cats. And other people who faint if a caterpillar drops on them."

"I hate suggesting it—but don't you think perhaps she ought to see a—well, a psychiatrist?"

"No!" said Tim explosively. "I won't have people like that monkeying about with her. I don't believe in them. They make people worse. If her mother had left psychiatrists alone . . ."

"So there was trouble of that kind in her family—was there? I mean a history of"—she chose the word carefully—"instability."

"I don't want to talk about it. I took her away from it all and she was all right, quite all right. She has just got into a nervous state. . . . But these things aren't hereditary. Everybody knows that nowadays. It's an exploded idea. Molly's perfectly sane. It's just that—oh! I believe it was that wretched old Palgrave dying that started it all off."

"I see," said Evelyn thoughtfully. "But there was nothing really to worry anyone in Major Palgrave's death, was there?"

"No, of course there wasn't. But it's a kind of shock when somebody dies suddenly."

He looked so desperate and defeated that Evelyn's heart smote her. She put her hand on his arm.

"Well, I hope you know what you're doing, Tim, but if I could help in any way—I mean if I could go with Molly to New York. I could fly with her there or Miami or somewhere where she could get really first-class medical advice."

"It's very good of you, Evelyn, but Molly's all right. She's getting over it, anyway."

Evelyn shook her head in doubt. She turned away slowly and looked along the line of the terrace. Most people had gone by now to their bungalows. Evelyn was walking towards her table to see if she'd left anything behind there, when she heard Tim give an exclamation. She looked up sharply. He was staring towards the steps at the end of the terrace and she followed his gaze. Then she too caught her breath.

Molly was coming up the steps from the beach. She was breathing with deep, sobbing breaths, her body swayed to and fro as she came, in a curious directionless run. Tim cried: "Molly! What's the matter?"

He ran towards her and Evelyn followed him. Molly was at the top of the steps now and she stood there, both hands behind her back. She said in sobbing breaths: "I found her. . . . She's there in the bushes . . . There in the bushes . . . And look at my hands—look at my *hands.*" She held them out and Evelyn caught her breath as she saw the queer dark stains. They looked dark in the subdued lighting, but she knew well enough that their real colour was red.

"What's happened, Molly?" cried Tim.

"Down there," said Molly. She swayed on her feet. "In the bushes . . ."

Tim hesitated, looked at Evelyn, then shoved Molly a little towards Evelyn and ran down the steps. Evelyn put her arm round the girl.

"Come. Sit down, Molly. Here. You'd better have something to drink."

Molly collapsed in a chair and leaned forward on the table, her forehead on her crossed arms. Evelyn did not question her any more. She thought it better to leave her time to recover.

"It'll be all right, you know," said Evelyn gently. "It'll be all right."

"I don't know," said Molly. "I don't know what happened. I don't know anything. I can't remember. I—" She raised her head suddenly. "What's the matter with me? What's the *matter* with me?"

"It's all right, child. It's all right."

Tim was coming slowly up the steps. His face was ghastly. Evelyn looked up at him, raising her eyebrows in a query.

"It's one of our girls," he said. "What's-her-name—Victoria. Somebody's put a knife in her."

14

INQUIRY

Molly lay on her bed. Dr. Graham and Dr. Robertson, the West Indian police doctor, stood on one side—Tim on the other. Robertson had his hand on Molly's pulse. He nodded to the man at the foot of the bed, a slender dark man in police uniform, Inspector Weston of the St. Honoré Police Force.

"A bare statement—no more," the doctor said.

The other nodded.

"Now, Mrs. Kendal—just tell us how you came to find this girl."

For a moment or two it was as though the figure on the bed had not heard. Then she spoke in a faint, faraway voice.

"In the bushes—white . . ."

"You saw something white—and you looked to see what it was? Is that it?"

"Yes—white—lying there—I tried—tried to lift—she—it—blood—blood all over my hands."

She began to tremble.

Dr. Graham shook his head at them. Robertson whispered, "She can't stand much more."

"What were you doing on the beach path, Mrs. Kendal?"

"Warm—nice—by the sea—"

"You knew who the girl was?"

"Victoria—nice—nice girl—laughs—she used to laugh—oh! and now she won't— She won't ever laugh again. I'll never forget it—I'll never forget it—" Her voice rose hysterically.

"Molly—don't." It was Tim.

"Quiet. Quiet." Dr. Robertson spoke with a soothing authority. "Just relax—relax. Now just a small prick—"

He withdrew the hypodermic.

"She'll be in no fit condition to be questioned for at least twenty-four hours," he said. "I'll let you know when."

II

The big handsome Negro looked from one to the other of the men sitting at the table.

"Ah declare to God," he said. "That's all I know. I don't know anything but what Ah've told you."

The perspiration stood out on his forehead. Daventry sighed. The man presiding at the table, Inspector Weston of the St. Honoré C.I.D., made a gesture of dismissal. Big Jim Ellis shuffled out of the room.

"It's not all he knows, of course," Weston said. He had the soft Island voice. "But it's all we shall learn from him."

"You think he's in the clear himself?" asked Daventry.

"Yes. They seem to have been on good terms together."

"They weren't married?"

A faint smile appeared on Lieutenant Weston's lips. "No," he said, "they weren't married. We don't have so many marriages on the Island. They christen the children, though. He's had two children by Victoria."

"Do you think he was in it, whatever it was, with her?"

"Probably not. I think he'd have been nervous of anything of that kind. And I'd say, too, that what she did know wasn't very much."

"But enough for blackmail?"

"I don't know that I'd even call it that. I doubt if the girl would even understand that word. Payment for being discreet isn't thought of as blackmail. You see, some of the people who stay here are the rich playboy lot, and their morals won't bear much investigation." His voice was slightly scathing.

"We get all kinds, I agree," said Daventry. "A woman, maybe, doesn't want it known that she's sleeping around, so she gives a present to the girl who waits on her. It's tacitly understood that the payment's for discretion."

"Exactly."

"But this," objected Daventry, "wasn't anything of that kind. It was murder."

"I should doubt, though, if the girl knew it was serious. She saw something, some puzzling incident, something to do presumably with this bottle of pills. It belonged to Mr. Dyson, I understand. We'd better see him next."

Gregory came in with his usual hearty air.

"Here I am," he said. "What can I do to help? Too bad about this girl. She was a nice girl. We both liked her. I suppose it was some sort of quarrel or other with a man, but she seemed quite happy and no signs of being in trouble about anything. I was kidding her only last night."

"I believe you take a preparation, Mr. Dyson, called Serenite?"

"Quite right. Little pink tablets."

"You have them on prescription from a physician?"

"Yes. I can show it to you if you like. Suffer a bit from high blood pressure, like so many people do nowadays."

"Very few people seem to be aware of that fact."

"Well, I don't go talking about it. I—well, I've always been well and hearty and I never like people who talk about their ailments all the time."

"How many of the pills do you take?"

"Two, three times a day."

"Do you have a fairly large stock with you?"

"Yes. I've got about half a dozen bottles. But they're locked up, you know, in a suitcase. I only keep out one, the one that's in current use."

"And you missed this bottle a short time ago, so I hear?"

"Quite right."

"And you asked this girl, Victoria Johnson, whether she'd seen it?"

"Yes, I did."

"And what did she say?"

"She said the last time she'd seen it was on the shelf in our bathroom. She said she'd look around."

"And after that?"

"She came and returned the bottle to me some time later. She said, Was this the bottle that was missing?"

"And you said?"

"I said, 'That's it, all right. Where did you find it?' And she said it was in old Major Palgrave's room. I said, 'How on earth did it get there?' "

"And what did she answer to that?"

"She said she didn't know, but—" he hesitated.

"Yes, Mr. Dyson?"

"Well, she gave me the feeling that she did know a little more than she was saying, but I didn't pay much attention. After all, it wasn't very important. As I say, I've got other bottles of the pills with me. I thought perhaps I'd left it around in the restaurant or somewhere, and old Palgrave picked it up for some reason. Perhaps he put it in his pocket meaning to return it to me, then forgot."

"And that's all you know about it, Mr. Dyson?"

"That's all I know. Sorry to be so unhelpful. Is it important? Why?"

Weston shrugged his shoulders. "As things are, anything may be important."

"I don't see where pills come in. I thought you'd want to know about what my movements were when this wretched girl was stabbed. I've written them all down as carefully as I can."

Weston looked at him thoughtfully.

"Indeed? That was very helpful of you, Mr. Dyson."

"Save everybody trouble, I thought," said Greg. He shoved a piece of paper across the table.

Weston studied it, and Daventry drew his chair a little closer and looked over his shoulder.

"That seems very clear," said Weston, after a moment or two. "You and your wife were together changing for dinner in your bungalow until ten minutes to nine. You then went along to the terrace where you had drinks with Señora de Caspearo. At quarter-past nine Colonel and Mrs. Hillingdon joined you and you went in to dine. As far as you can remember, you went off to bed at about half-past eleven."

"Of course," said Greg. "I don't know what time the girl was actually killed—?"

There was a faint semblance of a question in the words. Lieutenant Weston, however, did not appear to notice it.

"Mrs. Kendal found her, I understand? Must have been a very nasty shock for her."

"Yes. Dr. Robertson had to give her a sedative."

"This was quite late, wasn't it, when most people had trundled off to bed?"

"Yes."

"Had she been dead long? When Mrs. Kendal found her, I mean?"

"We're not quite certain of the exact time yet," said Weston smoothly.

"Poor little Molly. It must have been a nasty shock for her. Matter of fact, I didn't notice her about last night. Thought she might have had a headache or something and was lying down."

"When was the last time you did see Mrs. Kendal?"

"Oh, quite early, before I went to change. She was playing about with some of the table decorations and things. Rearranging the knives."

"I see."

"She was quite cheerful then," said Greg. "Kidding and all that. She's a great girl. We're all very fond of her. Tim's a lucky fellow."

"Well, thank you, Mr. Dyson. You can't remember anything more than you've told us about what the girl Victoria said when she returned the tablets?"

"No . . . It was just as I say. Asked me were these the tablets I'd been asking for. Said she'd found them in old Palgrave's room."

"She'd no idea who put them there?"

"Don't think so—can't remember, really."

"Thank you, Mr. Dyson."

Gregory went out.

"Very thoughtful of him," said Weston, gently tapping the paper with his fingernail, "to be so anxious to want us to know for sure exactly where he was last night."

"A little overanxious do you think?" asked Daventry.

"That's very difficult to tell. There are people, you know, who are naturally nervous about their own safety, about being mixed up with anything. It isn't necessarily because they have any guilty knowledge. On the other hand, it might be just that."

"What about opportunity? Nobody's really got much of an alibi, what with the band and the dancing and the coming and going. People are getting up, leaving their tables, coming back. Women go to powder their noses. Men take a stroll. Dyson could have slipped away. Anybody could have slipped away. But he does seem rather anxious to prove that he didn't." He looked thoughtfully down at the paper. "So Mrs. Kendal was rearranging knives on the table," he said. "I rather wonder if he dragged that in on purpose."

"Did it sound like it to you?"

The other considered. "I think it's possible."

Outside the room where the two men were sitting, a noise had arisen. A high voice was demanding admittance shrilly.

"I've got something to tell. I've got something to tell. You take me in to where the gentlemen are. You take me in to where the policeman is."

A uniformed policeman pushed open the door.

"It's one of the cooks here," he said, "very anxious to see you. Says he's got something you ought to know."

A frightened dark man in a cook's cap pushed past him and came into the room. It was one of the minor cooks. A Cuban, not a native of St. Honoré.

"I tell you something. I tell you," he said. "She come through my kitchen, she did, and she had a knife with her. A knife. I tell you. She had a knife in her hand. She come through my kitchen and out the door. Out into the garden. I saw her."

"Now calm down," said Daventry; "calm down. Who are you talking about?"

"I tell you who I'm talking about. I'm talking about the boss's wife, Mrs. Kendal. I'm talking about her. She have a knife in her hand and she go out into the dark. Before dinner that was—and *she didn't come back.*"

15

INQUIRY CONTINUED

"Can we have a word with you, Mr. Kendal?"

"Of course." Tim looked up from his desk. He pushed some papers aside and indicated chairs. His face was drawn and miserable. "How are you getting on? Got any forwarder? There seems to be a doom in this place. People are wanting to leave, you know, asking about air passages. Just when it seemed everything was being a success. Oh, Lord, you don't know what it means, this place, to me and to Molly. We staked everything on it."

"It's very hard on you, I know," said Inspector Weston. "Don't think that we don't sympathize."

"If it all could be cleared up quickly," said Tim. "This wretched girl Victoria—Oh! I oughtn't to talk about her like that. She was quite a good sort, Victoria was. But—but there must be some quite simple reason, some —kind of intrigue, or love affair she had. Perhaps her husband—"

"Jim Ellis wasn't her husband, and they seemed a settled sort of couple."

"If it could only be cleared up quickly," said Tim again. "I'm sorry. You wanted to talk to me about something, ask me something."

"Yes. It was about last night. According to medical evidence Victoria was killed sometime between ten-thirty p.m. and midnight. Alibis, under the circumstances that prevail here, are not very easy to prove. People are moving about, dancing, walking away from the terrace, coming back. It's all very difficult."

"I suppose so. But does that mean that you definitely consider Victoria was killed by one of the guests here?"

"Well, we have to examine that possibility, Mr. Kendal. What I want to ask you particularly about is a statement made by one of your cooks."

"Oh? Which one? What does he say?"

"He's a Cuban, I understand."

"We've got two Cubans and a Puerto Rican."

"This man Enrico states that your wife passed through the kitchen on her way from the dining-room and went out into the garden and that she was carrying a knife."

Tim stared at him.

"Molly, carrying a knife? Well, why shouldn't she? I mean—why—you don't think—what are you trying to suggest?"

"I am talking of the time before people had come into the dining-room. It would be, I suppose, some time about eight-thirty. You yourself were in the dining-room talking to the head waiter, Fernando, I believe."

"Yes." Tim cast his mind back. "Yes, I remember."

"And your wife came in from the terrace?"

"Yes, she did," Tim agreed. "She always went out to look over the tables. Sometimes the boys set things wrong, forgot some of the cutlery, things like that. Very likely that's what it was. She may have been re-arranging cutlery or something. She might have had a spare knife or a spoon, something like that in her hand."

"And she came from the terrace into the dining-room. Did she speak to you?"

"Yes, we had a word or two together."

"What did she say? Can you remember?"

"I think I asked her who she'd been talking to. I heard her voice out there."

"And who did she say she'd been talking to?"

"Gregory Dyson."

"Ah. Yes. That is what *he* said."

Tim went on, "He'd been making a pass at her, I understand. He was a bit given to that kind of thing. It annoyed me and I said 'Blast him' and Molly laughed and said she could do all the blasting that needed to be done. Molly's a very clever girl that way. It's not always an easy position, you know. You can't offend guests, and so an attractive girl like Molly has to pass things off with a laugh and a shrug. Gregory Dyson finds it difficult to keep his hands off any good-looking woman."

"Had there been any altercation between them?"

"No, I don't think so. I think, as I say, she just laughed it off as usual."

"You can't say definitely whether she had a knife in her hand or not?"

"I can't remember—I'm almost sure she didn't. In fact, I'm quite sure she didn't."

"But you said just now . . ."

"Look here, what I meant was that if she was in the dining-room or in the kitchen, it's quite likely she might have picked up a knife or had one in her hand. Matter of fact, I can remember quite well, she came in from the dining-room and she had nothing in her hand. Nothing at all. That's definite."

"I see," said Weston.

Tim looked at him uneasily.

"What on earth is this you're getting at? What did that damn' fool Enrico—Manuel—whichever it was—say?"

"He said your wife came out into the kitchen, that she looked upset, that she had a knife in her hand."

"He's just dramatizing."

"Did you have any further conversation with your wife during dinner or after?"

"No, I don't think I did really. Matter of fact, I was rather busy."

"Was your wife there in the dining-room during the meal?"

"I—oh—yes, we always move about among the guests and things like that. See how things are going on."

"Did you speak to her at all?"

"No, I don't think I did . . . We're usually fairly busy. We don't always notice what the other one's doing, and we certainly haven't got time to talk to each other."

"Actually you don't remember speaking to her until she came up the steps three hours later, after finding the body?"

"It was an awful shock for her. It upset her terribly."

"I know. A very unpleasant experience. How did she come to be walking along the beach path?"

"After the stress of dinner being served, she often does go for a turn. You know, get away from the guests for a minute or two, get a breather."

"When she came back, I understand you were talking to Mrs. Hillingdon."

"Yes. Practically everyone else had gone to bed."

"What was the subject of your conversation with Mrs. Hillingdon?"

"Nothing particular. Why? What's she been saying?"

"So far she hasn't said anything. We haven't asked her."

"We were just talking of this and that. Molly, and hotel running, and one thing and another."

"And then—your wife came up the steps of the terrace and told you what had happened?"

"Yes."

"There was blood on her hands?"

"Of course there was! She'd bent over the girl, tried to lift her, couldn't understand what had happened, what was the matter with her. Of course there was blood on her hands! Look here, what the hell are you suggesting? You *are* suggesting something?"

"Please calm down," said Daventry. "It's all a great strain on you, I know, Tim, but we have to get the facts clear. I understand your wife hasn't been feeling very well lately?"

"Nonsense—she's all right. Major Palgrave's death upset her a bit. Naturally. She's a sensitive girl."

"We shall have to ask her a few questions as soon as she's fit enough," said Weston.

"Well, you can't now. The doctor gave her a sedative and said she wasn't to be disturbed. I won't have her upset and browbeaten, d'you hear?"

"We're not going to do any browbeating," said Weston. "We've just got to get the facts clear. We won't disturb her at present, but as soon as the doctor allows us, we'll have to see her." His voice was gentle—inflexible.

Tim looked at him, opened his mouth, but said nothing.

II

Evelyn Hillingdon, calm and composed as usual, sat down in the chair indicated. She considered the few questions asked her, taking her time over it. Her dark, intelligent eyes looked at Weston thoughtfully.

"Yes," she said, "I was talking to Mr. Kendal on the terrace when his wife came up the steps and told us about the murder."

"Your husband wasn't there?"

"No, he had gone to bed."

"Had you any special reason for your conversation with Mr. Kendal?"

Evelyn raised her finely pencilled eyebrows. It was a definite rebuke.

She said coldly: "What a very odd question. No—there was nothing special about our conversation."

"Did you discuss the matter of his wife's health?"

Again Evelyn took her time.

"I really can't remember," she said at last.

"Are you sure of that?"

"Sure that I can't remember? What a curious way of putting it—one talks about so many things at different times."

"Mrs. Kendal has not been in good health lately, I understand."

"She looked quite all right—a little tired perhaps. Of course running a place like this means a lot of worries, and she is quite inexperienced. Naturally, she gets flustered now and then."

"Flustered." Weston repeated the word. "That was the way you would describe it?"

"It's an old-fashioned word, perhaps, but just as good as the modern jargon we use for everything. A 'virus infection' for a bilious attack—an 'anxiety neurosis' for the minor bothers of daily life—"

Her smile made Weston feel slightly riduculous. He thought to himself that Evelyn Hillingdon was a clever woman. He looked at Daventry, whose face remained unmoved, and wondered what he thought.

"Thank you, Mrs. Hillingdon," said Weston.

III

"We don't want to worry you, Mrs. Kendal, but we have to have your account of just how you came to find this girl. Dr. Graham says you are sufficiently recovered to talk about it now."

"Oh, yes," said Molly, "I'm really quite all right again." She gave them a small nervous smile. "It was just the shock—It *was* rather awful, you know."

"Yes, indeed it must have been. I understand you went for a walk after dinner."

"Yes—I—often do."

Her eyes shifted, Daventry noticed, and the fingers of her hands twined and untwined about each other.

"What time would that have been, Mrs. Kendal?" asked Weston.

"Well, I don't really know—we don't go much by the time."

"The steel band was still playing?"

"Yes—at least—I think so. I can't really remember."

"And you walked—which way?"

"Oh, along the beach path."

"To the left or the right?"

"Oh! First one way—and then the other. I—I—really didn't notice."

"Why didn't you notice, Mrs. Kendal?'

She frowned.

"I suppose I was—well—thinking of things."

"Thinking of anything particular?"

"No. No. Nothing particular. Just things that had to be done—seen to—in the hotel." Again that nervous twining and untwining of fingers. "And then—I noticed something white—in a clump of hibiscus bushes—and I wondered what it was. I stopped and—and pulled—" She swallowed convulsively. "And it was her—Victoria—all huddled up—and I tried to raise her head up and I got—blood—on my hands."

She looked at them and repeated wonderingly as though recalling something impossible: "Blood—on my hands."

"Yes—yes. A very dreadful experience. There is no need for you to tell us more about that part of it. How long had you been walking, do you think, when you found her—"

"I don't know—I have no idea."

"An hour? Half an hour? Or more than an hour—"

"I don't know," Molly repeated.

Daventry asked in a quiet, everyday voice: "Did you take a knife with you on your—walk?"

"A knife?" Molly sounded surprised. "Why should I take a knife?"

"I only ask because one of the kitchen staff mentioned that you had a knife in your hand when you went out of the kitchen into the garden."

Molly frowned.

"But I didn't go out of the kitchen—oh, you mean earlier—before dinner. I—I don't think so—"

"You had been rearranging the cutlery on the tables, perhaps."

"I have to, sometimes. They lay things wrong—not enough knives—or too many. The wrong number of forks and spoons—that sort of thing."

"And did that happen on this particular evening?"

"It may have done—something like that. It's really automatic. One doesn't think, or remember—"

"So you may have gone out of the kitchen that evening carrying a knife in your hand?"

"I don't think I did. I'm sure I didn't—" She added, "Tim was there—he would know. Ask him."

"Did you like this girl—Victoria—was she good at her work?" asked Weston.

"Yes—she was a very nice girl."

"You had had no dispute with her?"

"Dispute? No."

"She had never threatened you—in any way?"

"Threatened me? What do you mean?"

"It doesn't matter. You have no idea of who could have killed her? No idea at all?"

"None." She spoke positively.

"Well, thank you, Mrs. Kendal." He smiled. "It wasn't so terrible, was it?"

"That's all?"

"That's all for now."

Daventry got up, opened the door for her, and watched her go out.

"Tim would know," he quoted as he returned to his chair. "And Tim says definitely that she didn't have a knife."

Weston said gravely: "I think that that is what any husband would feel called upon to say."

"A table knife seems a very poor type of knife to use for murder."

"But it was a *steak* knife, Mr. Daventry. Steaks were on the menu that evening. Steak knives are kept sharp."

"I really can't bring myself to believe that that girl we've just been talking to is a red-handed murderess, Weston."

"It is not necessary to believe it yet. It could be that Mrs. Kendal went out into the garden before dinner, clasping a knife she had taken off one of the tables because it was superfluous. She might not even have noticed she was holding it, and she could have put it down somewhere—or dropped it. It could have been found and used by someone else. I, too, think her an unlikely murderess."

"All the same," said Daventry thoughtfully, "I'm pretty sure she is not telling all she knows. Her vagueness over time is odd. Where was she—what was she doing out there? Nobody, so far, seems to have noticed her in the dining-room that evening."

"The husband was about as usual but not the wife—"

"You think she went to meet someone—Victoria Johnson?"

"Perhaps—or perhaps she saw whoever it was who did go to meet Victoria."

"You're thinking of Gregory Dyson?"

"We know he was talking to Victoria earlier. He may have arranged to meet her again later. Everyone moved around freely on the terrace, remember—dancing, drinking—in and out of the bar."

"No alibi like a steel band," said Daventry wryly.

16

MISS MARPLE SEEKS ASSISTANCE

If anybody had been there to observe the gentle-looking elderly lady who stood meditatively on the loggia outside her bungalow, they would have thought she had nothing more on her mind than deliberation on how to arrange her time that day. An expedition, perhaps, to Castle Cliff—a visit to Jamestown—a nice drive and lunch at Pelican Point—or just a quiet morning on the beach.

But the gentle old lady was deliberating quite other matters—she was in a militant mood.

"Something has got to be done," said Miss Marple to herself.

Moreover, she was convinced that there was no time to be lost. There was urgency.

But who was there that she could convince of that fact? Given time, she thought she could find out the truth by herself.

She had found out a good deal. But not enough—not nearly enough. And time was short.

She realized, bitterly, that here on this paradise of an island, she had none of her usual allies.

She thought regretfully of her friends in England—Sir Henry Chithering—always willing to listen indulgently—his godson Dermot, who in spite of his increased status at Scotland Yard was still ready to believe that when Miss Marple voiced an opinion, there was usually something behind it.

But would that soft-voiced native police officer pay any attention to an old lady's urgency? Dr. Graham? But Dr. Graham was not what she needed—too gentle and hesitant, certainly not a man of quick decisions and rapid actions.

Miss Marple, feeling rather like a humble deputy of the Almighty, almost cried aloud her need in Biblical phrasing.

Who will go for me?
Whom shall I send?

The sound that reached her ears a moment later was not instantly recognized by her as an answer to prayer—far from it. At the back of her mind it registered only as a man possibly calling his dog.

"Hi!"

Miss Marple, lost in perplexity, paid no attention.

"Hi!" The volume thus increased, Miss Marple looked vaguely round.

"Hi!" called Mr. Rafiel impatiently. He added, "You—there—"

Miss Marple had not at first realized that Mr. Rafiel's "Hi, you" was addressed to her. It was not a method that anyone had ever used before to summon her. It was certainly not a gentlemanly mode of address. Miss Marple did not resent it, because people seldom did resent Mr. Rafiel's somewhat arbitrary method of doing things. He was a law unto himself and people accepted him as such. Miss Marple looked across the intervening space between her bungalow and his. Mr. Rafiel was sitting outside on his loggia and he beckoned her.

"You were calling me?" she asked.

"Of course I was calling you," said Mr. Rafiel. "Who did you think I was calling—a cat? Come over here."

Miss Marple looked round for her handbag, picked it up, and crossed the intervening space.

"I can't come to you unless someone helps me," explained Mr. Rafiel, "so you've got to come to me."

"Oh, yes," said Miss Marple, "I quite understand that."

Mr. Rafiel pointed to an adjacent chair. "Sit down," he said, "I want to talk to you. Something damned odd is going on in this island."

"Yes, indeed," agreed Miss Marple, taking the chair as indicated. By sheer habit she drew her knitting out of her bag.

"Don't start knitting again," said Mr. Rafiel. "I can't stand it. I hate women knitting. It irritates me."

Miss Marple returned her knitting to her bag. She did this with no undue air of meekness, rather with the air of one who makes allowances for a fractious patient.

"There's a lot of chit-chat going on," said Mr. Rafiel, "and I bet you're in the forefront of it. You and the parson and his sister."

"It is, perhaps, only natural that there should be chit-chat," said Miss Marple with spirit, "given the circumstances."

"This Island girl gets herself knifed. Found in the bushes. *Might* be ordinary enough. That chap she was living with might have got jealous of another man—or he's got himself another girl and she got jealous and they had a row. Sex in the tropics. That sort of stuff. What do you say?"

"No," said Miss Marple, shaking her head.

"The authorities don't think so, either."

"They would say more to you," pointed out Miss Marple, "than they would say to me."

"All the same, I bet you know more about it than I do. You've listened to the tittle-tattle."

"Certainly I have," said Miss Marple.

"Nothing much else to do, have you, except listen to tittle-tattle?"

"It is often informative and useful."

"D'you know," said Mr. Rafiel, studying her attentively, "I made a mistake about you. I don't often make mistakes about people. There's a lot more to you than I thought there was. All these rumors about Major Palgrave and the stories he told. You think he was bumped off, don't you?"

"I very much fear so," said Miss Marple.

"Well, he was," said Mr. Rafiel.

Miss Marple drew a deep breath. "That is definite, is it?" she asked.

"Yes, it's definite enough. I had it from Daventry. I'm not breaking a confidence, because the facts of the autopsy will have to come out. You told Graham something, he went to Daventry, Daventry went to the administrator, the C.I.D. were informed, and between them they agreed that things looked fishy, so they dug up old Palgrave and had a look."

"And they found?" Miss Marple paused interrogatively.

"They found he'd had a lethal dose of something that only a doctor could pronounce properly. As far as I remember, it sounds vaguely like di-flor, hexagonal-ethylcarbenzol. That's not the right name. But that's roughly what it sounds like. The police doctor put it that way so that nobody should know, I suppose, what it really was. The stuff's probably got some quite simple nice easy name like Evipan or Veronal or Easton's Syrup or something of that kind. This is its official name to baffle laymen with. Anyway, a sizeable dose of it, I gather, would produce death, and the signs would be much the same as those of high blood pressure aggravated by overindulgence in alcohol on a gay evening. In fact, it all looked perfectly natural and nobody questioned it for a moment. Just said 'poor old chap' and buried him quick. Now they wonder if he ever had high blood pressure at all. Did he ever say he had to you?"

"No."

"Exactly! And yet everyone seems to have taken it as a fact."

"Apparently he told people he had."

"It's like seeing ghosts," said Mr. Rafiel. "You never meet the chap who's seen the ghost himself. It's always the second cousin of his aunt, or a friend, or a friend of a friend. But leave that for a moment. They thought he had blood pressure, because there was a bottle of tablets controlling blood pressure found in his room but—and now we're coming to the point—I gather that this girl who was killed went about saying that that bottle was put there by somebody else, and that actually it belonged to that fellow Greg."

"Mr. Dyson has got high blood pressure. His wife mentioned it," said Miss Marple.

"So it was put in Palgrave's room to suggest that he suffered from high blood pressure and to make his death seem natural."

"Exactly," said Miss Marple. "And the story was put about, very cleverly, that he had frequently mentioned to people that he had high blood pressure. But you know, it's very easy to put about a story. Very easy. I've seen a lot of it in my time."

"I bet you have," said Mr. Rafiel.

"It only needs a murmur here and there," said Miss Marple. "You don't say it of your own knowledge, you just say that Mrs. B. told you that Colonel C. told her. It's always at second hand or third hand or fourth hand, and it's very difficult to find out who was the original whisperer. Oh, yes, it can be done. And the people you say it to go on and repeat it to others as if they know it of their own knowledge."

"Somebody's been clever," said Mr. Rafiel thoughtfully.

"Yes," said Miss Marple, "I think somebody's been quite clever."

"This girl saw something, or knew something and tried blackmail, I suppose," said Mr. Rafiel.

"She mayn't have thought of it as blackmail," said Miss Marple. "In these large hotels, there are often things the maids know that some people would rather not have repeated. And so they hand out a larger tip or a little present of money. The girl possibly didn't realize at first the importance of what she knew."

"Still, she got a knife in her back all right," said Mr. Rafiel brutally.

"Yes. Evidently someone couldn't afford to let her talk."

"Well? Let's hear what you think about it all."

Miss Marple looked at him thoughtfully.

"Why should you think I know any more than you do, Mr. Rafiel?"

"Probably you don't," said Mr. Rafiel, "but I'm interested to hear your ideas about what you do know."

"But why?"

"There's not very much to do out here," said Mr. Rafiel, "except make money."

Miss Marple looked slightly surprised.

"Make money? Out here?"

"You can send out half a dozen cables in code every day if you like," said Mr. Rafiel. "That's how I amuse myself."

"Take-over bids?" Miss Marple asked doubtfully, in the tone of one who speaks a foreign language.

"That kind of thing," agreed Mr. Rafiel. "Pitting your wits against other people's wits. The trouble is it doesn't occupy enough time, so I've got interested in this business. It's aroused my curiosity. Palgrave spent a good deal of his time talking to you. Nobody else would be bothered with him, I expect. What did he say?"

"He told me a good many stories," said Miss Marple.

"I know he did. Damn' boring, most of them. And you didn't only have to hear them once. If you got anywhere within range, you heard them three or four times over."

"I know," said Miss Marple. "I'm afraid that does happen when gentlemen get older."

Mr. Rafiel looked at her very sharply.

"I don't tell stories," he said. "Go on. It started with one of Palgrave's stories, did it?"

"He said he knew a murderer," said Miss Marple. "There's nothing really special about that," she added in her gentle voice, "because I suppose it happens to nearly everybody."

"I don't follow you," said Mr. Rafiel.

"I don't mean specifically," said Miss Marple, "but surely, Mr. Rafiel, if you cast over in your mind your recollections of various events in your life, hasn't there nearly always been an occasion when somebody has made some careless reference such as 'Oh, yes, I knew the So-and-So's quite well—he died very suddenly and they always say his wife did him in, but I dare say that's just gossip.' You've heard people say something like that, haven't you?"

"Well, I suppose so—yes, something of the kind. But not—well, not seriously."

"Exactly," said Miss Marple, "but Major Palgrave was a very serious man. I think he enjoyed telling this story. He said he had a snapshot of the murderer. He was going to show it to me but—actually—he didn't."

"Why?"

"Because he saw something," said Miss Marple. "Saw someone, I suspect. His face got very red and he shoved back the snapshot into his wallet and began talking on another subject."

"Who did he see?"

"I've thought about that a good deal," said Miss Marple. "I was sitting outside my bungalow, and he was sitting nearly opposite me and—whatever he saw, he saw over my right shoulder."

"Someone coming along the path then from behind you on the right, the path from the creek and the car park—"

"Yes."

"Was anyone coming along the path?"

"Mr. and Mrs. Dyson and Colonel and Mrs. Hillingdon."

"Anybody else?"

"Not that I can find out. Of course, your bungalow would also be in his line of vision. . . ."

"Ah. Then we include—shall we say—Esther Walters and my chap, Jackson. Is that right? Either of them, I suppose, might have come out of the bungalow and gone back inside again without your seeing them."

"They might have," said Miss Marple. "I didn't turn my head at once."

"The Dysons, the Hillingdons, Esther, Jackson. One of them's a murderer. Or of course, myself," he added, obviously as an afterthought.

Miss Marple smiled faintly.

"And he spoke of the murderer as a man?"

"Yes."

"Right. That cuts out Evelyn Hillingdon, Lucky and Esther Walters. So your murderer, allowing that all this far-fetched nonsense is true, your murderer is Dyson, Hillingdon or my smooth-tongued Jackson."

"Or yourself," said Miss Marple.

Mr. Rafiel ignored this last point.

"Don't say things to irritate me," he said. "I'll tell you the first thing that strikes me, and which you don't seem to have thought of. *If* it's one of those three, why the devil didn't old Palgrave recognize him before? Dash it all, they've all been sitting round looking at each other for the last two weeks. That doesn't seem to make sense."

"I think it could," said Miss Marple.

"Well, tell me how."

"You see, in Major Palgrave's story he hadn't seen this man *himself* at any time. It was a story told to him by a doctor. The doctor gave him the snapshot as a curiosity. Major Palgrave may have looked at the snapshot fairly closely at the time but after that he'd just stack it away in his wallet and keep it as a souvenir. Occasionally, perhaps, he'd take it out and show it to someone he was telling the story to. And another thing, Mr. Rafiel, we don't know how long ago this happened. He didn't give me any indication of that when he was telling the story. I mean this may have been a story he'd been telling to people for years. Five years—ten years—longer still perhaps? Some of his tiger stories go back about twenty years."

"They would!" said Mr. Rafiel.

"So I don't suppose for a moment that Major Palgrave would recognize the face in the snapshot if he came across the man casually. What I think happened, what I'm almost sure must have happened, is that as he told his story he fumbled for the snapshot, took it out, looked down at it, studying the face, and then looked up to see the same face, or one with a strong resemblance coming towards him from a distance of about ten or twelve feet away."

"Yes," said Mr. Rafiel consideringly. "Yes, that's possible."

"He was taken aback," said Miss Marple, "and he shoved it back in his wallet and began to talk loudly about something else."

"He couldn't have been sure," said Mr. Rafiel shrewdly.

"No," said Miss Marple, "he couldn't have been sure. But of course afterwards he would have studied the snapshot very carefully and would have looked at the man and tried to make up his mind whether it was just a likeness or whether it could actually be the same person."

Mr. Rafiel reflected a moment or two, then he shook his head.

"There's something wrong here. The motive's inadequate. Absolutely inadequate. He was speaking to you loudly, was he?"

"Yes," said Miss Marple, "quite loudly. He always did."

"True enough. Yes, he did shout. So whoever was approaching would hear what he said?"

"I should imagine you could hear it for quite a good radius round."

Mr. Rafiel shook his head again. He said, "It's fantastic, too fantastic. Anybody would laugh at such a story. Here's an old booby telling a story about another story somebody told him, and showing a snapshot, and all of it centering round a murder which had taken place years ago! Or at any rate, a year or two. How on earth can *that* worry the man in question? No evidence, just a bit of hearsay, a story at third hand. He could even admit a likeness, he could say: 'Yes, I do look rather like that fellow, don't I! Ha, ha!' Nobody's going to take old Palgrave's identification seriously. Don't tell me so, because I won't believe it. No, the chap, if it was the chap, had nothing to fear—nothing whatever. It's the kind of accusation he can just laugh off. Why on earth should he proceed to murder old Palgrave? It's absolutely unnecessary. You must see that."

"Oh, I do see that," said Miss Marple. "I couldn't agree with you more. That's what makes me uneasy. So very uneasy that I really couldn't sleep last night."

Mr. Rafiel stared at her. "Let's hear what's on your mind," he said quietly.

"I may be entirely wrong," said Miss Marple hesitantly.

"Probably you are," said Mr. Rafiel with his usual lack of courtesy, "but at any rate let's hear what you've thought up in the small hours."

"There could be a very powerful motive if—"

"If what?"

"If there was going to be—quite soon—*another murder.*"

Mr. Rafiel stared at her. He tried to pull himself up a little in his chair.

"Let's get this clear," he said.

"I am so bad at explaining." Miss Marple spoke rapidly and rather incoherently. A pink flush rose to her cheeks. "Supposing there was a murder planned. If you remember, the story Major Palgrave told me concerned a man whose wife died under suspicious circumstances. Then, after a certain lapse of time, there was another murder under exactly the same circumstances. A man of a different name had a wife who died in much the same way and the doctor who was telling it recognized him as the same man, although he'd changed his name. Well, it does look, doesn't it, as though the murderer might be the kind of murderer who made a habit of the thing?"

"You mean like Smith, Brides in the Bath, that kind of thing. Yes."

"As far as I can make out," said Miss Marple, "and from what I have heard and read, a man who does a wicked thing like this and gets away with it the first time, is, alas, encouraged. He thinks it's easy, he thinks he's clever. And so he repeats it. And in the end, as you say, like Smith and the Brides in the Bath, it becomes a habit. Each time in a different place and each time the man changes his name. But the crimes themselves are all very much alike. So it seems to me, although I may be quite wrong—"

"But you don't think you are wrong, do you?" Mr. Rafiel put in shrewdly.

Miss Marple went on without answering, "—that if that were so and if this—this person had got things all lined up for a murder out here, for getting rid of another wife, say, and if this is crime three or four, well then, the Major's story would matter because the murderer couldn't afford to have any similarity pointed out. If you remember, that was exactly the way Smith got caught. The circumstances of a crime attracted the attention of somebody who compared it with a newspaper clipping of some other case. So you do see, don't you, that if this wicked person has got a crime planned, arranged, and shortly about to take place, he couldn't afford to let Major Palgrave go about telling this story and showing that snapshot?"

She stopped and looked appealingly at Mr. Rafiel.

"So you see he had to do something very quickly, as quickly as possible."

Mr. Rafiel spoke, "In fact, that very same night, eh?"

"Yes," said Miss Marple.

"Quick work," said Mr. Rafiel, "but it could be done. Put the tablets in old Palgrave's room, spread the blood pressure rumour about and add a little of our fourteen-syllable drug to a Planter's Punch. Is that it?"

"Yes. But that's all over—we needn't worry about it. It's the future. It's now. With Major Palgrave out of the way and the snapshot destroyed, *this man will go on with his murder as planned.*"

Mr. Rafiel whistled.

"You've got it all worked out, haven't you?"

Miss Marple nodded. She said in a most unaccustomed voice, firm and almost dictatorial, "And we've got to stop it. *You've* got to stop it, Mr. Rafiel."

"Me?" said Mr. Rafiel, astonished. "Why me?"

"Because you're rich and important," said Miss Marple simply. "People will take notice of what you say or suggest. They wouldn't listen to me for a moment. They would say that I was an old lady imagining things."

"They might at that," said Mr. Rafiel. "More fools if they did. I must say, though, that nobody would think you had any brains in your head to hear your usual line of talk. Actually, you've got a logical mind. Very few women have." He shifted himself uncomfortably in his chair. "Where the hell's Esther or Jackson?" he said. "I need resettling. No, it's no good your doing it. You're not strong enough. I don't know what they mean, leaving me alone like this."

"I'll go and find them."

"No, you won't. You'll stay here—and thrash this out. Which of them is it? The egregious Greg? The quiet Edward Hillingdon or my fellow Jackson? It's got to be one of the three, hasn't it?"

17

MR. RAFIEL TAKES CHARGE

"I don't know," said Miss Marple.

"What do you mean? What have we been talking about for the last twenty minutes?"

"It has occurred to me that I may have been wrong."

Mr. Rafiel stared at her.

"Scatty after all!" he said disgustedly. "And you sounded so sure of yourself."

"Oh, I am sure—about the *murder.* It's the *murderer* I'm not sure about. You see, I've found out that Major Palgrave had more than one murder story—you told me yourself he'd told you one about a kind of Lucrezia Borgia—"

"So he did—at that. But that was quite a different kind of story."

"I know. And Mrs. Walters said he had one about someone being gassed in a gas oven—"

"But the story he told you—"

Miss Marple allowed herself to interrupt—a thing that did not often happen to Mr. Rafiel.

She spoke with desperate earnestness and only moderate incoherence.

"Don't you see—it's so difficult to be sure. The whole point in that—so often—one doesn't listen. Ask Mrs. Walters—she said the same thing. You listen to begin with, and then your attention flags—your mind wanders—and suddenly you find you've missed a bit. I just wonder if possibly there may have been a gap—a very small one—between the story he was telling me—about a *man*—and the moment when he was getting out his wallet and saying, 'Like to see a picture of a murderer?' "

"But you thought it was a picture of the man he had been talking about?"

"I thought so—yes. It never occurred to me that it mightn't have been. But now—how can I be sure?"

Mr. Rafiel looked at her very thoughtfully.

"The trouble with you is," he said, "that you're too conscientious. Great mistake. Make up your mind and don't shilly-shally. You didn't shilly-shally to begin with. If you ask me, in all this chit-chat you've been having with the parson's sister and the rest of them, you've got hold of something that's unsettled you."

"Perhaps you're right."

"Well, cut it out for the moment. Let's go ahead with what you had to begin with. Because, nine times out of ten, one's original judgments are right—or so I've found. We've got three suspects. Let's take 'em out and have a good look at them. Any preference?"

"I really haven't," said Miss Marple; "all three of them seem so very unlikely."

"We'll take Greg first," said Mr. Rafiel. "Can't stand the fellow. Doesn't make him a murderer, though. Still, there are one or two points against him. Those blood pressure tablets belonged to him. Nice and handy to make use of."

"That would be a little obvious, wouldn't it?" Miss Marple objected.

"I don't know that it would," said Mr. Rafiel. "After all, the main thing was to do something quickly, and he'd got the tablets. Hadn't much time to go looking round for tablets that somebody else might have. Let's say it's Greg. All right. *If* he wanted to put his dear wife, Lucky, out of the way (Good job, too, I'd say. In fact, I'm in sympathy with him) I can't actually see his motive. From all accounts, he's rich. Inherited money from his first wife, who had pots of it. He qualifies on that as a possible wife murderer, all right. But that's over and done with. He got away with it. But Lucky was his first wife's poor relation. No money there, so if he wants to put *her* out of the way, it must be in order to marry somebody else. Any gossip going around about that?"

Miss Marple shook her head.

"Not that I have heard. He—er—has a very gallant manner with all the ladies."

"Well, that's a nice, old-fashioned way of putting it," said Mr. Rafiel. "All right, he's a stoat. He makes passes. Not enough! We want more than that. Let's go on to Edward Hillingdon. Now there's a dark horse, if ever there was one."

"He is not, I think, a happy man," offered Miss Marple.

Mr. Rafiel looked at her thoughtfully.

"Do you think a murderer ought to be a happy man?"

Miss Marple coughed.

"Well, they usually have been, in my experience."

"I don't suppose your experience has gone very far," said Mr. Rafiel.

In this assumption, as Miss Marple could have told him, he was wrong. But she forbore to contest his statement. Gentlemen, she knew, did not like to be put right in their facts.

"I rather fancy Hillingdon myself," said Mr. Rafiel. "I've an idea that there is something a bit odd going on between him and his wife. You noticed it at all?"

"Oh, yes," said Miss Marple, "I have noticed it. Their behaviour is perfect in public, of course, but that one would expect."

"You probably know more about those sort of people than I would," said Mr. Rafiel. "Very well, then, everything is in perfectly good taste, but it's a probability that, in a gentlemanly way, Edward Hillingdon is contemplating doing away with Evelyn Hillingdon. Do you agree?"

"If so," said Miss Marple, "there must be another woman."

"But what woman?"

Miss Marple shook her head in a dissatisfied manner.

"I can't help feeling—I really can't—that it's not all quite as simple as that."

"Well, who shall we consider next—Jackson? We leave me out of it."

Miss Marple smiled for the first time.

"And why do we leave you out of it, Mr. Rafiel?"

"Because if you want to discuss the possibilities of my being a murderer, you'd have to do it with somebody else. Waste of time talking about it to me. And anyway, I ask you, am I cut out for the part? Helpless, hauled out of bed like a dummy, dressed, wheeled about in a chair, shuffled along for a walk. What earthly chance have *I* of going and murdering anyone?"

"Probably as good a chance as anyone else," said Miss Marple vigorously.

"And how do you make that out?"

"Well, you would agree yourself, I think, that you have brains?"

"Of course I've got brains," declared Mr. Rafiel. "A good deal more than anybody else in this community, I'd say."

"And having brains," went on Miss Marple, "would enable you to overcome the physical difficulties of being a murderer."

"It would take some doing!"

"Yes," said Miss Marple, "it would take some doing. But then, I think, Mr. Rafiel, you would enjoy that."

Mr. Rafiel stared at her for quite a long time and then he suddenly laughed.

"You've got a nerve!" he said. "Not quite the gentle fluffy old lady you look, are you? So you really think I'm a murderer?"

"No," said Miss Marple, "I do not."

"And why?"

"Well, really, I think just because you have got brains. Having brains, you can get most things you want without having recourse to murder. Murder is stupid."

"And anyway, who the devil should I want to murder?"

"That would be a very interesting question," said Miss Marple. "I have not yet had the pleasure of sufficient conversation with you to evolve a theory as to that."

Mr. Rafiel's smile broadened.

"Conversations with you might be dangerous," he said.

"Conversations are always dangerous, if you have something to hide," said Miss Marple.

"You may be right. Let's get on to Jackson. What do you think of Jackson?"

"It is difficult for me to say. I have not had the opportunity really of any conversation with him."

"So you've no views on the subject?"

"He reminds me a little," said Miss Marple reflectively, "of a young man in the Town Clerk's office near where I live, Jonas Parry."

"And?" Mr. Rafiel asked and paused.

"He was not," said Miss Marple, "very satisfactory."

"Jackson's not wholly satisfactory either. He suits me all right. He's first-class at his job, and he doesn't mind being sworn at. He knows he's damn' well paid and so he puts up with things. I wouldn't employ him in a position of trust, but I don't have to trust him. Maybe his past is blameless, maybe it isn't. His references were all right, but I discern—shall I say, a note of reserve. Fortunately, I'm not a man who has any guilty secrets, so I'm not a subject for blackmail."

"No secrets?" said Miss Marple thoughtfully. "Surely, Mr. Rafiel, you have business secrets?"

"Not where Jackson can get at them. No. Jackson is a smooth article, one might say, but I really don't see him as a murderer. I'd say that wasn't his line at all."

He paused a minute and then said suddenly, "Do you know, if one stands back and takes a good look at all this fantastic business, Major Palgrave and his ridiculous stories and all the rest of it, the emphasis is entirely wrong. I'm the person who ought to be murdered."

Miss Marple looked at him in some surprise.

"Proper type casting," explained Mr. Rafiel. "Who's the victim in murder stories? Elderly men with lots of money."

"And lots of people with a good reason for wishing him out of the way, so as to get that money," said Miss Marple. "Is that true also?"

"Well—" Mr. Rafiel considered, "I can count up to five or six men in London who wouldn't burst into tears if they read my obituary in *The Times.* But they wouldn't go so far as to do anything to bring about my demise. After all, why should they? I'm expected to die any day. In fact the bug-blighters are astonished that I've lasted so long. The doctors are surprised too."

"You have, of course, a great will to live," said Miss Marple.

"You think that's odd, I suppose," said Mr. Rafiel.

Miss Marple shook her head.

"Oh, no," she said, "I think it's quite natural. Life is more worth living, more full of interest when you are likely to lose it. It shouldn't be, perhaps, but it is. When you're young and strong and healthy, and life stretches ahead of you, living isn't really important at all. It's young people who commit suicide easily, out of despair from love, sometimes from sheer anxiety and worry. But old people know how valuable life is and how interesting."

"Hah!" said Mr. Rafiel, snorting. "Listen to a couple of old crocks."

"Well, what I said is true, isn't it?" demanded Miss Marple.

"Oh, yes," said Mr. Rafiel, "it's true enough. But don't you think I'm right when I say that I ought to be cast as the victim?"

"It depends on who has reason to gain by your death," said Miss Marple.

"Nobody, really," said Mr. Rafiel. "Apart, as I've said, from my competitors in the business world who, as I have also said, can count comfortably on my being out of it before very long. I'm not such a fool as to leave a lot of money to be divided up among my relations. Precious little they'd get of it after the Government had taken practically the lot. Oh, no, I've attended to all that years ago. Settlements, trusts and all the rest of it."

"Jackson, for instance, wouldn't profit by your death?"

"He wouldn't get a penny," said Mr. Rafiel cheerfully. "I pay him double the salary that he'd get from anyone else. That's because he has to put up with my bad temper; and he knows quite well that he will be the loser when I die."

"And Mrs. Walters?"

"The same goes for Esther. She's a good girl. First-class secretary, intelligent, good-tempered, understands my ways, doesn't turn a hair if I fly off the handle, couldn't care less if I insult her. Behaves like a nice nursery governess in charge of an outrageous and obstreperous child. She irritates me a bit sometimes, but who doesn't? There's nothing outstanding about her. She's rather a commonplace young woman in many ways, but I couldn't have anyone who suited me better. She's had a lot of trouble in her life. Married a man who wasn't much good. I'd say she never had much judgment when it came to men. Some women haven't. They fall for anyone who tells them a hard-luck story. Always convinced that all the man needs is proper female understanding. That, once married to her, he'll pull up his socks and make a go of life! But of course that type of man never does. Anyway, fortunately her unsatisfactory husband died; drank too much at a party one night and stepped in front of a bus. Esther had a daughter to support and she went back to her secretarial job. She's been with me five years. I made it quite clear to her from the start that she need have no expectations from me in the event of my death. I paid her from the start a very large salary, and that salary I've augmented by as much as a quarter as much again each year. However decent and honest people are, one should never trust anybody—that's why I told Esther clearly that she'd nothing to hope for from my death. Every year I live she'll get a bigger salary. If she puts most of that aside every year—and that's what I think she has done—she'll be quite a well-to-do woman by the time I kick the bucket. I've made myself responsible for her daughter's schooling and I've put a sum in trust for the daughter, which she'll get when she comes of age. So Mrs. Esther Walters is very comfortably placed. My death, let me tell you, would mean a serious financial loss to her." He looked very hard at Miss Marple. "She fully realizes all that. She's very sensible, Esther is."

"Do she and Jackson get on?" asked Miss Marple.

Mr. Rafiel shot a quick glance at her.

"Noticed something, have you?" he said. "Yes, I think Jackson's done a bit of tom-catting around, with an eye in her direction, especially lately. He's a good-looking chap, of course, but he hasn't cut any ice in that direction. For one thing, there's class distinction. She's just a cut above him. Not very much. If she was really a cut above him, it wouldn't matter, but the lower middle class—they're very particular. Her mother was a school-teacher and her father a bank clerk. No, she won't make a fool of herself about Jackson. Dare say he's after her little nest egg, but he won't get it."

"Hush—she's coming now!" said Miss Marple.

They both looked at Esther Walters as she came along the hotel path towards them.

"She's quite a good-looking girl, you know," said Mr. Rafiel, "but not an atom of glamour. I don't know why, she's quite nicely turned out."

Miss Marple sighed, a sigh that any woman will give however old at what might be considered wasted opportunities. What was lacking in Esther had been called by so many names during Miss Marple's span of existence. "Not really attractive to men." "No S.A." "Lacks come-hither in her eye." Fair hair, good complexion, hazel, quite a good figure, pleasant smile, but lacking that something that makes a man's head turn when he passes a woman in the street.

"She ought to get married again," said Miss Marple, lowering her voice.

"Of course she ought. She'd make a man a good wife."

Esther Walters joined them, and Mr. Rafiel said, in a slightly artificial voice, "So there you are at last! What's been keeping you?"

"Everyone seemed to be sending cables this morning," said Esther. "What with that, and people trying to check out—"

"Trying to check out, are they? A result of this murder business?"

"I suppose so. Poor Tim Kendal is worried to death."

"And well he might be. Bad luck for that young couple, I must say."

"I know. I gather it was rather a big undertaking for them to take on this place. They've been worried about making a success of it. They were doing very well, too."

"They were doing a good job," agreed Mr. Rafiel.

"He's very capable and a damned hard worker. She's a very nice girl—attractive, too. They've both worked like blacks, though that's an odd term to use out here. Was looking at a fellow shining up a coconut tree to get his breakfast, then he goes to sleep for the rest of the day. Nice life."

He added, "We've been discussing the murder here."

Esther Walters looked slightly startled. She turned her head towards Miss Marple.

"I've been wrong about her," said Mr. Rafiel with characteristic frankness. "Never been much of a one for the old pussies. All knitting wool and tittle-tattle. But this one's got something. Eyes and ears, and she uses them."

Esther Walters looked apologetically at Miss Marple, but Miss Marple did not appear to take offence.

"That's really meant to be a compliment, you know," Esther explained.

"I quite realize that," said Miss Marple. "I realize, too, that Mr. Rafiel is privileged, or thinks he is."

"What do you mean—privileged?" asked Mr. Rafiel.

"To be rude if you want to be rude," said Miss Marple.

"Have I been rude?" said Mr. Rafiel, surprised. "I'm sorry if I've offended you."

"You haven't offended me," said Miss Marple; "I make allowances."

"Now, don't be nasty. Esther, get a chair and bring it here. Maybe you can help."

Esther walked a few steps to the balcony of the bungalow and brought over a light basket chair.

"We'll go on with our consultation," said Mr. Rafiel. "We started with old Palgrave, deceased, and his eternal stories."

"Oh, dear," said Esther. "I'm afraid I used to escape from him whenever I could."

"Miss Marple was more patient," said Mr. Rafiel. "Tell me, Esther, did he ever tell you a story about a murderer?"

"Oh, yes," said Esther. "Several times."

"What was it exactly? Let's have your recollections."

"Well—" Esther paused to think. "The trouble is," she said apologetically, "I didn't really listen very closely. You see, it was rather like that terrible story about the lion in Rhodesia which used to go on and on. One did get rather in the habit of not listening."

"Well, tell us what you do remember."

"I think it arose out of some murder case that had been in the papers. Major Palgrave said that he'd had an experience not every person had had. He'd actually met a murderer face to face."

"Met?" Mr. Rafiel exclaimed. "Did he actually use the word 'met'?"

Esther looked confused.

"I think so." She was doubtful. "Or he may have said, 'I can point you out a murderer.' "

"Well, which was it? There's a difference."

"I can't really be sure. I think he said he'd show me a picture of someone."

"That's better."

"And then he talked a lot about Lucrezia Borgia."

"Never mind Lucrezia Borgia. We know all about her."

"He talked about poisoners and that Lucrezia was very beautiful and had red hair. He said there were probably far more women poisoners going about the world than anyone knew."

"That I fear is quite likely," said Miss Marple.

"And he talked about poison being a woman's weapon."

"Seems to have been wandering from the point a bit," said Mr. Rafiel.

"Well, of course, he always did wander from the point in his stories. And then one used to stop listening and just say 'Yes' and 'Really?' and 'You don't say so.' "

"What about this picture he was going to show you?"

"I don't remember. It may have been something he'd seen in the paper—"

"He didn't actually show you a snapshot?"

"A snapshot? No." She shook her head. "I'm quite sure of that. He did say that she was a good-looking woman, and you'd never think she was a murderer to look at her."

"She?"

"There you are," exclaimed Miss Marple. "It makes it all so confusing."

"He was talking about a woman?" Mr. Rafiel asked.

"Oh, yes."

"The snapshot was a snapshot of a woman?"

"Yes."

"It can't have been!"

"But it was," Esther persisted. "He said, 'She's here in this island. I'll point her out to you, and then I'll tell you the whole story.'"

Mr. Rafiel swore. In saying what he thought of the late Major Palgrave, he did not mince his words.

"The probabilities are," he finished, "that not a word of anything he said was true!"

"One does begin to wonder," Miss Marple murmured.

"So there we are," said Mr. Rafiel. "The old booby started telling you hunting tales. Pig sticking, tiger shooting, elephant hunting, narrow escapes from lions. One or two of them might have happened to somebody else! Then he gets on to the subject of murder and he tells one murder story to cap another murder story. And what's more, he tells them all as if they'd happened to him. Ten to one most of them were a hash-up of what he'd read in the paper, or seen on TV."

He turned accusingly on Esther. "You admit that you weren't listening closely. Perhaps you misunderstood what he was saying."

"I'm certain he was talking about a woman," said Esther obstinately, "because, of course, I wondered who it was."

"Who do you think it was?" asked Miss Marple.

Esther flushed and looked slightly embarrassed.

"Oh, I didn't really—I mean, I wouldn't like to—"

Miss Marple did not insist. The presence of Mr. Rafiel, she thought, was inimical to her finding out exactly what suppositions Esther Walters had made. That could only be cozily brought out in a tête-à-tête between two women. And there was, of course, the possibility that Esther Walters was lying. Naturally, Miss Marple did not suggest this aloud. She registered it as a possibility but she was not inclined to believe in it. For one thing she did not think that Esther Walters was a liar (though one never knew), and for another, she could see no point in such a lie.

"But you say," Mr. Rafiel was now turning upon Miss Marple, "you say that he told you this yarn about a murderer and that he then said he had a picture of him which he was going to show you."

"I thought so, yes."

"You thought so? You were sure enough to begin with!"

Miss Marple retorted with spirit.

"It is never easy to repeat a conversation and be entirely accurate in what the other party to it has said. One is always inclined to jump at what you think they *meant.* Then, afterwards, you put actual words into their mouths. Major Palgrave told me this story, yes. He told me that the man who told it to him, this doctor, had shown him a snapshot of the murderer; but if I am to be quite honest, I must admit that what he actually said to me was 'Would you like to see a snapshot of a murderer?' and naturally I assumed that it was the same snapshot he had been talking about. That it was the snapshot of that particular murderer. But I have to admit that it is possible—only remotely possible, but still possible—that by an association of ideas in his mind he leaped from the snapshot he had been shown in the past to a snapshot he had taken recently of someone here whom he was convinced was a murderer."

"Women!" snorted Mr. Rafiel in exasperation. "You're all the same, the whole blinking lot of you! Can't be accurate. You're never exactly sure of what a thing was. And now," he added irritably, "where does that leave us?" He snorted. "Evelyn Hillingdon, or Greg's wife, Lucky? The whole thing is a mess."

There was a slight apologetic cough. Arthur Jackson was standing at Mr. Rafiel's elbow. He had come so noiselessly that nobody had noticed him.

"Time for your massage, sir," he said.

Mr. Rafiel displayed immediate temper.

"What do you mean by sneaking up on me in that way and making me jump? I never heard you."

"Very sorry, sir."

"I don't think I'll have any massage today. It never does me a damn' bit of good."

"Oh, come, sir, you mustn't say that," Jackson was full of professional cheerfulness. "You'd soon notice it if you left it off."

He wheeled the chair deftly round.

Miss Marple rose to her feet, smiled at Esther and went down to the beach.

18

WITHOUT BENEFIT OF CLERGY

The beach was rather empty this morning. Greg was splashing in the water in his usual noisy style, Lucky was lying on her face on the beach with a sun-tanned back well oiled and her blonde hair splayed over her shoulders. The Hillingdons were not there. Señora de Caspearo, with an assorted bag of gentlemen in attendance, was lying face upwards and talking deep-throated, happy Spanish. Some French and Italian children were playing at the water's edge and laughing. Canon and Miss Prescott were sitting in beach chairs observing the scene. The Canon had his hat tilted forward over his eyes and seemed half asleep. There was a convenient chair next to Miss Prescott and Miss Marple made for it and sat down.

"Oh, dear," she said with a deep sigh.

"I know," said Miss Prescott.

It was their joint tribute to violent death.

"That poor girl," said Miss Marple.

"Very sad," said the Canon. "Most deplorable."

"For a moment or two," said Miss Prescott, "we really thought of leaving, Jeremy and I. But then we decided against it. It would not really be fair, I felt, on the Kendals. After all, it's not *their* fault. It might have happened anywhere."

"In the midst of life we are in death," said the Canon solemnly.

"It's very important, you know," said Miss Prescott, "that they should make a go of this place. They have sunk all their capital in it."

"A very sweet girl," said Miss Marple, "but not looking at all well lately."

"Very nervy," agreed Miss Prescott. "Of course her family—" she shook her head.

"I really think, Joan," said the Canon in mild reproof, "that there are some things—"

"Everybody knows about it," said Miss Prescott. "Her family live in our part of the world. A great-aunt—most peculiar—and one of her uncles took off all his clothes in one of the tube stations. Green Park, I believe it was."

"Joan, that is a thing that should *not* be repeated."

"Very sad," said Miss Marple, shaking her head, "though I believe not an uncommon form of madness. I know when we were working for the Armenian relief, a most respectable elderly clergyman was afflicted the same way. They telephoned his wife and she came along at once and took him home in a cab, wrapped in a blanket."

"Of course, Molly's immediate family's all right," said Miss Prescott. "She never got on very well with her mother, but then so few girls seem to get on with their mothers nowadays."

"Such a pity," said Miss Marple, shaking her head, "because, really, a young girl needs her mother's knowledge of the world and experience."

"Exactly," said Miss Prescott with emphasis. "Molly, you know, took up with some man—quite unsuitable, I understand."

"It so often happens," said Miss Marple.

"Her family disapproved, naturally. She didn't tell them about it. They heard about it from a complete outsider. Of course her mother said she must bring him along so that they met him properly. This, I understand, the girl refused to do. She said it was humiliating to him. Most insulting to be made to come and meet her family and be looked over. Just as though you were a horse, she said."

Miss Marple sighed. "One does need so much tact when dealing with the young," she murmured.

"Anyway, there it was! They forbade her to see him."

"But you can't do that nowadays," said Miss Marple. "Girls have jobs and they meet people whether anyone forbids them or not."

"But then, very fortunately," went on Miss Prescott, "she met Tim Kendal, and the other man sort of faded out of the picture. I can't tell you how relieved the family was."

"I hope they didn't show it too plainly," said Miss Marple. "That so often puts girls off from forming suitable attachments."

"Yes, indeed."

"One remembers oneself—" murmured Miss Marple, her mind going back to the past. A young man she had met at a croquet party. He had seemed so nice—rather gay, almost Bohemian in his views. And then he had been unexpectedly warmly welcomed by her father. He had been suitable, eligible; he had been asked freely to the house more than once, and Miss Marple had found that, after all, he was *dull.* Very dull.

The Canon seemed safely comatose and Miss Marple advanced tentatively to the subject she was anxious to pursue.

"Of course you know so much about this place," she murmured. "You have been here several years running, have you not?"

"Well, last year and two years before that. We like St. Honoré very much. Always such nice people here. Not the flashy, ultra-rich set."

"So I suppose you know the Hillingdons and the Dysons well!"

"Yes, fairly well."

Miss Marple coughed and lowered her voice slightly.

"Major Palgrave told me such an interesting story," she said.

"He had a great repertoire of stories, hadn't he? Of course he had travelled very widely. Africa, India, even China, I believe."

"Yes indeed," said Miss Marple. "But I didn't mean one of *those* stories. This was a story concerned with—well, with one of the people I have just mentioned."

"Oh!" said Miss Prescott. Her voice held meaning.

"Yes. Now I wonder—" Miss Marple allowed her eyes to travel gently round the beach to where Lucky lay sunning her back. "Very beautifully tanned, isn't she?" remarked Miss Marple. "And her hair. Most attractive. Practically the same colour as Molly Kendal's, isn't it?"

"The only difference," said Miss Prescott, "is that Molly's is natural and Lucky's comes out of a bottle!"

"Really, Joan," the Canon protested, unexpectedly awake again. "Don't you think that is rather an uncharitable thing to say?"

"It's not uncharitable," said Miss Prescott acidly. "Merely a fact."

"It looks very nice to me," said the Canon.

"Of course. That's why she does it. But I assure you, my dear Jeremy, it wouldn't deceive any woman for a moment. Would it?" She appealed to Miss Marple.

"Well, I'm afraid—" said Miss Marple, "of course I haven't the experience that you have—but I'm afraid—yes, I should say definitely not natural. The appearance at the roots every fifth or sixth day—" She looked at Miss Prescott and they both nodded with quiet female assurance.

The Canon appeared to be dropping off again.

"Major Palgrave told me a really extraordinary story," murmured Miss Marple, "about—well, I couldn't quite make out. I am a little deaf sometimes. He appeared to be saying or hinting—" she paused.

"I know what you mean. There was a great deal of talk at the time—"

"You mean at the time that—"

"When the first Mrs. Dyson died. Her death was quite unexpected. In fact, everybody thought she was a *malade imaginaire*—a hypochondriac.

So when she had this attack and died so unexpectedly, well, of course, people did talk."

"There wasn't—any—trouble at the time?"

"The doctor was puzzled. He was quite a young man and he hadn't had much experience. He was what I call one of those antibiotics-for-all men. You know, the kind that doesn't bother to look at the patient much, or worry what's the matter with him. They just give them some kind of pill out of a bottle and if they don't get better, then they try a different pill. Yes, I believe he *was* puzzled, but it seemed she had had gastric trouble before. At least her husband said so, and there seemed no reason for believing anything was wrong."

"But you yourself think—"

"Well, I always try to keep an open mind, but one does wonder, you know. And what with various things people said—"

"Joan!" The Canon sat up. He looked belligerent.

"I don't like—I really don't like to hear this kind of ill-natured gossip being repeated. We've always set our faces against that kind of thing. See no evil, hear no evil, speak no evil—and what is more, think no evil! That should be the motto of every Christian man and woman."

The two women sat in silence. They were rebuked, and in deference to their training, they deferred to the criticism of a man. But inwardly they were frustrated, irritated and quite unrepentant. Miss Prescott threw a frank glance of irritation towards her brother. Miss Marple took out her knitting and looked at it. Fortunately for them Chance was on their side.

"Mon père," said a small shrill voice. It was one of the French children who had been playing at the water's edge. She had come up unnoticed, and was standing by Canon Prescott's chair.

"Mon père," she fluted.

"Eh? Yes, my dear? *Oui, qu'est-ce qu'il y a, ma petite?"*

The child explained. There had been a dispute about who should have the water-wings next and also other matters of seaside etiquette. Canon Prescott was extremely fond of children, especially small girls. He was always delighted to be summoned to act as arbiter in their disputes. He rose willingly now and acompanied the child to the water's edge. Miss Marple and Miss Prescott breathed deep sighs and turned avidly towards each other.

"Jeremy, of course rightly, is very against ill-natured gossip," said Miss Prescott, "but one cannot really ignore what people are saying. And there was, as I say, a great deal of talk at the time."

"Yes?" Miss Marple's tone urged her forward.

"This young woman, you see, Miss Greatorex I think her name was then, I can't remember now, was a kind of cousin and she looked after Mrs. Dyson. Gave her all her medicines and things like that." There was a short, meaningful pause. "And of course there had, I understand"—Miss Prescott's voice was lowered—"been goings-on between Mr. Dyson and Miss Greatorex. A lot of people had noticed them. I mean things like that are quickly observed in a place like this. Then there was some curious story about some stuff that Edward Hillingdon got for her at a chemist."

"Oh, Edward Hillingdon came into it?"

"Oh, yes, he was very much attracted. People noticed it. And Lucky—Miss Greatorex—played them off against each other. Gregory Dyson and Edward Hillingdon. One has to face it, she has always been an attractive woman."

"Though not as young as she was," Miss Marple replied.

"Exactly. But she was always very well turned out and made up. Of course not so flamboyant when she was just the poor relation. She always seemed very devoted to the invalid. But, well, you see how it was."

"What was this story about the chemist—how did that get known?"

"Well, it wasn't in Jamestown. I think it was when they were in Martinique. The French, I believe, are more lax than we are in the matter of drugs. This chemist talked to someone, and the story got around. Well, you know how these things happen."

Miss Marple did. None better.

"He said something about Colonel Hillingdon asking for something and not seeming to know what it was he was asking for. Consulting a piece of paper, you know, on which it was written down. Anyway, as I say, there was talk."

"But I don't see quite why Colonel Hillingdon—" Miss Marple frowned in perplexity.

"I suppose he was just being used as a cat's-paw. Anyway, Gregory Dyson married again in an almost indecently short time. Barely a month later, I understand."

They looked at each other.

"But there was no real suspicion?" Miss Marple asked.

"Oh, no, it was just—well, talk. Of course there may have been absolutely nothing in it."

"Major Palgrave thought there was."

"Did he say so to you?"

"I wasn't really listening very closely," confessed Miss Marple. "I just wondered if—er—well, if he'd said the same things to you?"

"He did point her out to me one day," said Miss Prescott.

"Really? He actually pointed her out?"

"Yes. As a matter of fact, I thought at first it was Mrs. Hillingdon he was pointing out. He wheezed and chuckled a bit and said, 'Look at that woman over there. In my opinion that's a woman who's done murder and got away with it.' I was very shocked, of course. I said, 'Surely you're joking, Major Palgrave,' and he said, 'Yes, yes, dear lady, let's call it joking.' The Dysons and the Hillingdons were sitting at a table quite near to us, and I was afraid they'd overhear. He chuckled and said, 'Wouldn't care to go to a drink party and have a certain person mix me a cocktail. Too much like supper with the Borgias.' "

"How very interesting," said Miss Marple. "Did he mention a—a photograph?"

"I don't remember. . . . Was it some newspaper cutting?"

Miss Marple, about to speak, shut her lips. The sun was momentarily obscured by a shadow. Evelyn Hillingdon paused beside them.

"Good morning," she said.

"I was wondering where you were," said Miss Prescott, looking up brightly.

"I've been to Jamestown, shopping."

"Oh, I see."

Miss Prescott looked round vaguely and Evelyn Hillingdon said: "Oh, I didn't take Edward with me. Men hate shopping."

"Did you find anything of interest?"

"It wasn't that sort of shopping. I just had to go to the chemist."

With a smile and a slight nod she went on down the beach.

"Such nice people, the Hillingdons," said Miss Prescott, "though she's not really very easy to know, is she? I mean, she's always very pleasant and all that, but one never seems to get to know her any better."

Miss Marple agreed thoughtfully.

"One never knows what she is thinking," said Miss Prescott.

"Perhaps that is just as well," said Miss Marple.

"I beg your pardon?"

"Oh, nothing really, only that I've always had the feeling that perhaps her thoughts might be rather disconcerting."

"Oh," said Miss Prescott, looking puzzled. "I see what you mean." She went on with a slight change of subject. "I believe they have a very charming place in Hampshire, and a boy—or is it two boys—who have just gone—or one of them—to Winchester."

"Do you know Hampshire well?"

"No. Hardly at all. I believe their house is somewhere near Alton."

"I see." Miss Marple paused and then said, "And where do the Dysons live?"

"California," said Miss Prescott. "When they are at home, that is. They are great travellers."

"One really knows so little about the people one meets when one is travelling," said Miss Marple. "I mean—how shall I put it— One only knows, doesn't one, what they choose to tell you about themselves. For instance, you don't really know that the Dysons live in California."

Miss Prescott looked startled.

"I'm sure Mr. Dyson mentioned it."

"Yes. Yes, exactly. That's what I mean. And the same thing perhaps with the Hillingdons. I mean when you say that they live in Hampshire, you're really repeating what they told you, aren't you?"

Miss Prescott looked slightly alarmed. "Do you mean that they don't live in Hampshire?" she asked.

"No, no, not for one moment," said Miss Marple, quickly apologetic. "I was only using them as an instance as to what one knows or doesn't know about people." She added, "*I* have told you that I live at St. Mary Mead, which is a place no doubt, of which you have never heard. But you don't, if I may say so, know it of your own knowledge, do you?"

Miss Prescott forbore from saying that she really couldn't care less where Miss Marple lived. It was somewhere in the country and in the south of England and that was all she knew. "Oh, I do see what you mean," she agreed hastily, "and I know that one can't possibly be too careful when one is abroad."

"I didn't exactly mean that," said Miss Marple.

There were some odd thoughts going through Miss Marple's mind. Did she really know, she was asking herself, that Canon Prescott and Miss Prescott were really Canon Prescott and Miss Prescott? They said so. There was no evidence to contradict them. It would really be easy, would it not, to put on a dog-collar, to wear the appropriate clothes, to make the appropriate conversation. If there was a motive . . .

Miss Marple was fairly knowledgeable about the clergy in her part of the world, but the Prescotts came from the north. Durham, wasn't it? She had no doubt they were the Prescotts, but still, it came back to the same thing —one believed what people said to one.

Perhaps one ought to be on one's guard against that. Perhaps . . . She shook her head thoughtfully.

19

USES OF A SHOE

Canon Prescott came back from the water's edge slightly short of breath (playing with children is always exhausting).

Presently he and his sister went back to the hotel, finding the beach a little too hot.

"But," said Señora de Caspearo scornfully as they walked away, "how can a beach be too hot? It is nonsense, that. And look what she wears—her arms and her neck are all covered up. Perhaps it is as well, that. Her skin it is hideous, like a plucked chicken!"

Miss Marple drew a deep breath. Now or never was the time for conversation with Señora de Caspearo. Unfortunately she did not know what to say. There seemed to be no common ground on which they could meet.

"You have children, Señora?" she inquired.

"I have three angels," said Señora de Caspearo, kissing her fingertips.

Miss Marple was rather uncertain as to whether this meant that Señora de Caspearo's offspring were in heaven or whether it merely referred to their characters.

One of the gentlemen in attendance made a remark in Spanish, and Señora de Caspearo flung back her head appreciatively and laughed loudly and melodiously.

"You understand what he said?" she inquired of Miss Marple.

"I'm afraid not," said Miss Marple apologetically.

"It is just as well. He is a wicked man."

A rapid and spirited interchange of Spanish badinage followed.

"It is infamous—infamous," said Señora de Caspearo, reverting to English with sudden gravity, "that the police do not let us go from this island. I storm, I scream, I stamp my foot—but all they say is No—No. You know how it will end—we shall all be killed."

Her bodyguard attempted to reassure her.

"But, yes—I tell you it is unlucky here. I knew it from the first— That old Major, the ugly one—he had the Evil Eye—you remember? His eyes, they crossed. It is bad, that! I make the Sign of the Horns every time when he looks my way." She made it in illustration. "Though since he is cross-eyed, I am not always sure when he does look my way—"

"He had a glass eye," said Miss Marple in an explanatory voice. "An accident, I understand, when he was quite young. It was not his fault."

"I tell you he brought bad luck. I say it is the evil eye he had."

Her hand shot out again in the well-known Latin gesture—the first finger and the little finger sticking out, the two middle ones doubled in. "Anyway," she said cheerfully, "he is dead—I do not have to look at him any more. I do not like to look at things that are ugly."

It was, Miss Marple thought, a somewhat cruel epitaph on Major Palgrave.

Farther down the beach Gregory Dyson had come out of the sea. Lucky had turned herself over on the sand. Evelyn Hillingdon was looking at Lucky, and her expression, for some reason, made Miss Marple shiver.

"Surely I can't be cold—in this hot sun," she thought.

What was the old phrase—*"A goose walking over your grave—"*

She got up and went slowly back to her bungalow.

On the way she passed Mr. Rafiel and Esther Walters coming down the beach. Mr. Rafiel winked at her. Miss Marple did not wink back. She looked disapproving.

She went into her bungalow and lay down on her bed. She felt old and tired and worried.

She was quite certain that there was no time to be lost—no time—to—be lost. . . . It was getting late. The sun was going to set—the sun—one must always look at the sun through smoked glass. Where was that piece of smoked glass that someone had given her? . . .

No, she wouldn't need it, after all. A shadow had come over the sun, blotting it out. A shadow. Evelyn Hillingdon's shadow— No, not Evelyn Hillingdon—The shadow (what were the words?) the *Shadow of the Valley of Death.* That was it. She must—what was it? Make the Sign of the Horns—to avert the Evil Eye—Major Palgrave's Evil Eye.

Her eyelids flickered open. She had been asleep. But there was a shadow—someone peering in at her window.

The shadow moved away—and Miss Marple saw who it was. It was Jackson.

"Impertinence—peering in like that," she thought—and added parenthetically, "Just like Jonas Parry."

The comparison reflected no credit on Jackson.

Then she wondered why Jackson had been peering into her bedroom. To see if she was there? Or to note that she was there, but was asleep.

She got up, went into the bathroom and peered cautiously through the window.

Arthur Jackson was standing by the door of the bungalow next door—Mr. Rafiel's bungalow. She saw him give a rapid glance round and then slip quickly inside. Interesting, thought Miss Marple. Why did he have to look round in that furtive manner? Nothing in the world could have been more natural than his going into Mr. Rafiel's bungalow, since he himself had a room at the back of it. He was always going in and out of it on some errand or other. So why that quick, guilty glance round? "Only one reason," said Miss Marple, answering her own question, "he wanted to be sure that nobody was observing him enter at this particular moment because of something he was going to do in there."

Everybody, of course, was on the beach at this moment except those who had gone for expeditions. In about twenty minutes or so, Jackson himself would arrive on the beach in the course of his duties to aid Mr. Rafiel to take his sea dip. If he wanted to do anything in the bungalow unobserved, now was a very good time. He had satisfied himself that Miss Marple was asleep on her bed, he had satisfied himself that there was nobody near at hand to observe his movements. Well, she must do her best to do exactly that.

Sitting down on her bed, Miss Marple removed her neat sandal shoes and replaced them with a pair of sneakers. Then she shook her head, removed the sneakers, burrowed in her suitcase and took out a pair of shoes the heel on one of which she had recently caught on a hook by the door. It was now in a slightly precarious state and Miss Marple adroitly rendered it even more precarious by attention with a nail file. Then she emerged with due precaution from her door, walking in stockinged feet. With all the care of a big game hunter approaching upwind of a herd of antelope, Miss Marple gently circumnavigated Mr. Rafiel's bungalow.

Cautiously she manoeuvred her way around the corner of the house. She put on one of the shoes she was carrying, gave a final wrench to the heel of the other, sank gently to her knees and lay prone under the window. If Jackson heard anything, if he came to the window to look out, an old lady would have had a fall owing to the heel coming off her shoe. But evidently Jackson had heard nothing.

Very, very gently Miss Marple raised her head. The windows of the bungalow were low. Shielding herself slightly with a festoon of creeper, she peered inside. . . .

Jackson was on his knees before a suitcase. The lid of the suitcase was up and Miss Marple could see that it was a specially fitted affair containing compartments filled with various kinds of papers. Jackson was looking through the papers, occasionally drawing documents out of long envelopes. Miss Marple did not remain at her observation post for long. All she wanted was to know what Jackson was doing. She knew now. Jackson was snooping. Whether he was looking for something in particular or whether he was just indulging his natural instincts, she had no means of judging. But it confirmed her in her belief that Arthur Jackson and Jonas Parry had strong affinities in other things than facial resemblance.

Her problem was now to withdraw. Very carefully she dropped down again and crept along the flower-bed until she was clear of the window. She returned to her bungalow and carefully put away the shoe and the heel that she had detached from it. She looked at them with affection—a good device which she could use on another day if necessary. She resumed her own sandal shoes, and went thoughtfully down to the beach again.

Choosing a moment when Esther Walters was in the water, Miss Marple moved into the chair Esther had vacated.

Greg and Lucky were laughing and talking with Señora de Caspearo and making a good deal of noise.

Miss Marple spoke very quietly, almost under her breath, without looking at Mr. Rafiel.

"Do you know that Jackson snoops?"

"Doesn't surprise me," said Mr. Rafiel. "Caught him at it, did you?"

"I managed to observe him through a window. He had one of your suitcases open and was looking through your papers."

"Must have managed to get hold of a key to it. Resourceful fellow. He'll be disappointed though. Nothing he gets hold of in that way will do him a mite of good."

"He's coming down now," said Miss Marple, glancing up towards the hotel.

"Time for that idiotic sea dip of mine."

He spoke again—very quietly.

"As for you—don't be too enterprising. We don't want to be attending your funeral next. Remember your age, and be careful. There's somebody about who isn't too scrupulous, remember."

20

NIGHT ALARM

Evening came. The lights came up on the terrace. People dined and talked and laughed, albeit less loudly and merrily than they had a day or two ago. The steel band played.

But the dancing ended early. People yawned—went off to bed. The lights went out. There was darkness and stillness. The Golden Palm Tree slept. . . .

"Evelyn, Evelyn!" The whisper came sharp and urgent.

Evelyn Hillingdon stirred and turned on her pillow.

"Evelyn. Please wake up."

Evelyn Hillingdon sat up abruptly. Tim Kendal was standing in the doorway. She stared at him in surprise.

"Evelyn, please, could you come? It's—Molly. She's ill. I don't know what's the matter with her. I think she must have taken something."

Evelyn was quick, decisive.

"All right, Tim. I'll come. You go back to her. I'll be with you in a moment."

Tim Kendal disappeared. Evelyn slipped out of bed, threw on a dressing-gown and looked across at the other bed. Her husband, it seemed, had not been awakened. He lay there, his head turned away, breathing quietly. Evelyn hesitated for a moment, then decided not to disturb him. She went out of the door and walked rapidly to the main building and beyond it to the Kendals' bungalow. She caught up with Tim in the doorway.

Molly lay in bed. Her eyes were closed and her breathing was clearly not natural. Evelyn bent over her, rolled up an eyelid, felt her pulse and then looked at the bedside table. There was a glass there which had been used. Beside it was an empty phial of tablets. She picked it up.

"They were her sleeping pills," said Tim, "but that bottle was half full yesterday or the day before. I think she—must have taken the lot."

"Go and get Dr. Graham," said Evelyn, "and on the way waken one of the cooks and tell him to make strong coffee. Strong as possible. Hurry."

Tim dashed off. Just outside the doorway he collided with Edward Hillingdon.

"Oh, sorry, Edward."

"What's happening here?" demanded Hillingdon. "What's going on?"

"It's Molly. Evelyn's with her. I must get hold of the doctor. I suppose I ought've gone to him first, but I—I wasn't sure and I thought Evelyn would know. Molly would have hated it if I'd fetched a doctor when it wasn't necessary."

He went off, running. Edward Hillingdon looked after him for a moment and then he walked into the bedroom.

"What's happening?" he said. "Is it serious?"

"Oh, there you are, Edward. I wondered if you'd woken up. This silly child has been taking things."

"Is it bad?"

"One can't tell without knowing how much she's taken. I shouldn't think it was too bad if we get going in time. I've sent for coffee. If we can get some of that down her—"

"But why should she do such a thing? You don't think—" He stopped.

"What don't I think?" asked Evelyn.

"You don't think it's because of the inquiry—the police—all that?"

"It's possible, of course. That sort of thing could be very alarming to a nervous type."

"Molly never used to seem a nervous type."

"One can't really tell," said Evelyn. "It's the most unlikely people sometimes who lose their nerve."

"Yes, I remember . . ." Again he stopped.

"The truth is," said Evelyn, "that one doesn't really know anything about anybody." She added, "Not even the people who are nearest to you. . . ."

"Isn't that going a little too far, Evelyn—exaggerating too much?"

"I don't think it is. When you think of people, it is in the image you have made of them for yourself."

"I know you," said Edward Hillingdon quietly.

"You think you do."

"No. I'm sure." He added, "And you're sure of me."

Evelyn looked at him, then turned back to the bed. She took Molly by the shoulders and shook her.

"We ought to be doing something, but I suppose it's better to wait until Dr. Graham comes. Oh, I think I hear them."

II

"She'll do now." Dr. Graham stepped back, wiped his forehead with a handkerchief and breathed a sigh of relief.

"You think she'll be all right, sir?" Tim demanded, anxiously.

"Yes, yes. We got to her in good time. Anyway, she probably didn't take enough to kill her. A couple of days and she'll be as right as rain, but she'll have a rather nasty day or two first." He picked up the empty bottle. "Who gave her these things anyway?"

"A doctor in New York. She wasn't sleeping well."

"Well, well. I know all we medicos hand these things out freely nowadays. Nobody tells young women who can't sleep to count sheep, or get up and eat a biscuit, or write a couple of letters and then go back to bed. Instant remedies, that's what people demand nowadays. Sometimes I think it's a pity we give them to them. You've got to learn to put up with things in life. All very well to stuff a comforter into a baby's mouth to stop it crying. Can't go on doing that all a person's life." He gave a small chuckle. "I bet you, if you asked Miss Marple what she does if she can't sleep, she'd tell you she counted sheep going under a gate." He turned back to the bed where Molly was stirring. Her eyes were open now. She looked at them without interest or recognition. Dr. Graham took her hand.

"Well, well, my dear, and what have you been doing to yourself?"

She blinked but did not reply.

"Why did you do it, Molly, why? Tell me why?" Tim took her other hand.

Still her eyes did not move. If they rested on anyone, it was on Evelyn Hillingdon. There might have been even a faint question in them, but it was hard to tell. Evelyn spoke as though there had been the question.

"Tim came and fetched me," she said.

Her eyes went to Tim, then shifted to Dr. Graham.

"You're going to be all right now," said Dr. Graham, "but don't do it again."

"She didn't mean to do it," said Tim quietly. "I'm sure she didn't mean to do it. She just wanted a good night's rest. Perhaps the pills didn't work at first and so she took more of them. Is that it, Molly?"

Her head moved very faintly in a negative motion.

"You mean—you took them on purpose?" said Tim.

Molly spoke then. "Yes," she said.

"But why, Molly, why?"

The eyelids faltered. "Afraid." The word was just heard.

"Afraid? Of what?"

But her eyelids closed down.

"Better let her be," said Dr. Graham. Tim spoke impetuously.

"Afraid of what? The police? Because they've been hounding you, asking you questions? I don't wonder. Anyone might feel frightened. But it's just their way, that's all. Nobody thinks for one moment—" he broke off.

Dr. Graham made him a decisive gesture.

"I want to go to sleep," said Molly.

"The best thing for you," said Dr. Graham.

He moved to the door and the others followed him.

"She'll sleep all right," said Graham.

"Is there anything I ought to do?" asked Tim. He had the usual slightly apprehensive attitude of a man in illness.

"I'll stay if you like," said Evelyn kindly.

"Oh, no. No, that's quite all right," said Tim.

Evelyn went back towards the bed. "Shall I stay with you, Molly?"

Molly's eyes opened again. She said, "No," and then after a pause, "just Tim."

Tim came back and sat down by the bed.

"I'm here, Molly," he said and took her hand. "Just go to sleep. I won't leave you."

She sighed faintly and her eyes closed.

The doctor paused outside the bungalow and the Hillingdons stood with him.

"You're sure there's nothing more I can do?" asked Evelyn.

"I don't think so, thank you, Mrs. Hillingdon. She'll be better with her husband now. But possibly tomorrow—after all, he's got this hotel to run—I think someone should be with her."

"D'you think she might—try again?" asked Hillingdon.

Graham rubbed his forehead irritably.

"One never knows in these cases. Actually, it's most unlikely. As you've seen for yourselves, the restorative treatment is extremely unpleasant. But of course one can never be absolutely certain. She may have more of this stuff hidden away somewhere."

"I should never have thought of suicide in connection with a girl like Molly," said Hillingdon.

Graham said dryly, "It's not the people who are always talking of killing themselves, threatening to do so, who do it. They dramatize themselves that way and let off steam."

"Molly always seemed such a happy girl. I think perhaps"—Evelyn hesitated—"I ought to tell you, Dr. Graham."

She told him then about her interview with Molly on the beach the night that Victoria had been killed. Graham's face was very grave when she had finished.

"I'm glad you've told me, Mrs. Hillingdon. There are very definite indications there of some kind of deep-rooted trouble. Yes. I'll have a word with her husband in the morning."

III

"I want to talk to you seriously, Kendal, about your wife."

They were sitting in Tim's office. Evelyn Hillingdon had taken his place by Molly's bedside and Lucky had promised to come and, as she expressed it, "spell her" later. Miss Marple had also offered her services. Poor Tim was torn between his hotel commitments and his wife's condition.

"I can't understand it," said Tim. "I can't understand Molly any longer. She's changed. Changed out of all seeming."

"I understand she's been having bad dreams?"

"Yes. Yes, she complained about them a good deal."

"For how long?"

"Oh, I don't know. About—oh, I suppose a month—perhaps longer. She—we—thought they were just—well, nightmares, you know."

"Yes, yes, I quite understand. But what's a much more serious sign is the fact that she seems to have felt afraid of someone. Did she complain about that to you?"

"Well, yes. She said once or twice that—oh, people were following her."

"Ah! Spying on her?"

"Yes, she did use that term once. She said they were her enemies and they'd followed her here."

"Did she have enemies, Mr. Kendal?"

"No. Of course she didn't."

"No incident in England, anything you know about before you were married?"

"Oh, no, nothing of that kind. She didn't get on with her family very well, that was all. Her mother was rather an eccentric woman, difficult to live with perhaps, but . . ."

"Any signs of mental instability in her family?"

Tim opened his mouth impulsively, then shut it again. He pushed a fountain pen about on the desk in front of him.

The doctor said: "I must stress the fact that it would be better to tell me, Tim, if that is the case."

"Well, yes, I believe so. Nothing serious, but I believe there was an aunt or something who was a bit batty. But that's nothing. I mean—well, you get that in almost any family."

"Oh, yes, yes, that's quite true. I'm not trying to alarm you about that, but it just might show a tendency to—well, to break down or imagine things if any stress arose."

"I don't really know very much," said Tim. "After all, people don't pour out all their family histories to you, do they?"

"No, no. Quite so. She had no former friend—she was not engaged to anyone, anyone who might have threatened her or made jealous threats? That sort of thing?"

"I don't know. I don't think so. Molly *was* engaged to some other man before I came along. Her parents were against it, I understand, and I think she really stuck to the chap more out of opposition and defiance than anything else." He gave a sudden half-grin. "You know what it is when you're young. If people cut up a fuss, it makes you much keener on whoever it is."

Dr. Graham smiled, too. "Ah, yes, one often sees that. One should never take exception to one's children's objectionable friends. Usually they grow out of them naturally. This man, whoever he was, didn't make threats of any kind against Molly?"

"No, I'm sure he didn't. She would have told me. She said herself she just had a silly adolescent craze on him, mainly because he had such a bad reputation."

"Yes, yes. Well, that doesn't sound serious. Now there's another thing. Apparently your wife has had what she describes as blackouts. Brief passages of time during which she can't account for her actions. Did you know about that, Tim?"

"No," said Tim slowly. "No. I didn't. She never told me. I did notice, you know, now you mention it, that she seemed rather vague sometimes and . . ." He paused, thinking. "Yes, that explains it. I couldn't understand how she seemed to have forgotten the simplest things, or sometimes seemed not to know what time of day it was. I just thought she was absent-minded, I suppose."

"What it amounts to, Tim, is just this. I advise you most strongly to take your wife to see a good specialist."

Tim flushed angrily.

"You mean a mental specialist, I suppose?"

"Now, now, don't be upset by labels. A neurologist, a psychologist, someone who specializes in what the layman calls nervous breakdowns. There's a good man in Kingston. Or there's New York, of course. There is something that is causing these nervous terrors of your wife's. Something perhaps for which she hardly knows the reason herself. Get advice about her, Tim. Get advice as soon as possible."

He clapped his hand on the young man's shoulder and got up.

"There's no immediate worry. Your wife has good friends and we'll all be keeping an eye on her."

"She won't—you don't think she'll try it again?"

"I think it most unlikely," said Dr. Graham.

"You can't be sure," said Tim.

"One can never be sure," said Dr. Graham; "that's one of the first things you learn in my profession." Again he laid a hand on Tim's shoulder. "Don't worry too much."

"That's easy to say," said Tim as the doctor went out of the door. "Don't worry, indeed! What does he think I'm made of?"

21

JACKSON ON COSMETICS

"You're sure you don't mind, Miss Marple?" said Evelyn Hillingdon.

"No, indeed, my dear," said Miss Marple. "I'm only too delighted to be of use in any way. At my age, you know, one feels very useless in the world. Especially when I am in a place like this, just enjoying myself. No duties of any kind. No, I'll be delighted to sit with Molly. You go along on your expedition. Pelican Point, wasn't it?"

"Yes," said Evelyn. "Both Edward and I love it. I never get tired of seeing the birds diving down, catching up the fish. Tim's with Molly now. But he's got things to do and he doesn't seem to like her being left alone."

"He's quite right," said Miss Marple. "I wouldn't in his place. One never knows, does one? when anyone has attempted anything of that kind—Well, go along, my dear."

Evelyn went off to join a little group that was waiting for her—her husband, the Dysons and three or four other people. Miss Marple checked her knitting requirements, saw that she had all she wanted with her, and walked over towards the Kendals' bungalow.

As she came up to the loggia, she heard Tim's voice through the half-open French window.

"If you'd only tell me why you did it, Molly. What made you? Was it anything I did? There must be some reason. If you'd only tell me."

Miss Marple paused. There was a little pause inside before Molly spoke. Her voice was flat and tired.

"I don't know, Tim; I really don't know. I suppose—something came over me."

Miss Marple tapped on the window and walked in.

"Oh, there you are, Miss Marple. It is very good of you."

"Not at all," said Miss Marple. "I'm delighted to be of any help. Shall I sit here in this chair? You're looking much better, Molly. I'm so glad."

"I'm all right," said Molly. "Quite all right. Just—oh, just sleepy."

"I shan't talk," said Miss Marple. "You just lie quiet and rest. I'll get on with my knitting."

Tim Kendal threw her a grateful glance and went out. Miss Marple established herself in her chair.

Molly was lying on her left side. She had a half-stupefied, exhausted look. She said in a voice that was almost a whisper: "It's very kind of you, Miss Marple. I—I think I'll go to sleep."

She half turned away on her pillows and closed her eyes. Her breathing grew more regular, though it was still far from normal. Long experience of nursing made Miss Marple almost automatically straighten the sheet and tuck it under the mattress on her side of the bed. As she did so, her hand encountered something hard and rectangular under the mattress. Rather surprised, she took hold of this and pulled it out. It was a book. Miss Marple threw a quick glance at the girl in the bed, but she lay there utterly quiescent. She was evidently asleep. Miss Marple opened the book. It was, she saw, a current work on nervous diseases. It came open naturally at a certain place which gave a description of the onset of persecution mania and various other manifestations of schizophrenia and allied complaints.

It was not a highly technical book, but one that could be easily understood by a layman. Miss Marple's face grew very grave as she read. After a minute or two she closed the book and stayed thinking. Then she bent forward and with some care replaced the book where she had found it, under the mattress.

She shook her head in some perplexity. Noiselessly she rose from her chair. She walked the few steps towards the window, then turned her head sharply over her shoulder. Molly's eyes were open, but even as Miss Marple turned, the eyes shut again. For a minute or two Miss Marple was not quite certain whether she might not have imagined that quick, sharp glance. Was Molly then only pretending to be asleep? That might be natural enough. She might feel that Miss Marple would start talking to her if she showed herself awake. Yes, that could be all it was.

Was she reading into that glance of Molly's a kind of slyness that was somehow innately disagreeable? One doesn't know, Miss Marple thought to herself; one really doesn't know.

She decided that she would try to manage a little talk with Dr. Graham as soon as it could be managed. She came back to her chair by the bed. She decided after about five minutes or so that Molly was really asleep. No one could have lain so still, could have breathed so evenly. Miss Marple got up again. She was wearing her sneakers today. Not perhaps very elegant, but admirably suited to this climate and comfortable and roomy for the feet.

She moved gently round the bedroom, pausing at both of the windows, which gave out in two different directions.

The hotel grounds seemed quiet and deserted. Miss Marple came back and was standing a little uncertainly before regaining her seat, when she thought she heard a faint sound outside. Like the scrape of a shoe on the loggia? She hesitated a moment, then she went to the window, pushed it a little farther open, stepped out and turned her head back into the room as she spoke.

"I shall be gone only a very short time, dear," she said, "just back to my bungalow to see where I could possibly have put that pattern. I was so sure I had brought it with me. You'll be quite all right till I come back, won't you?" Then turning her head back, she nodded to herself. "Asleep, poor child. A good thing."

She went quietly along the loggia, down the steps and turned sharp right to the path there. Passing along between the screen of some hibiscus bushes, an observer might have been curious to see that Miss Marple veered sharply on to the flower-bed, passed round to the back of the bungalow and entered it again through the second door there. This led directly into a small room that Tim sometimes used as an unofficial office, and from that into the sitting-room.

Here there were wide curtains semi-drawn to keep the room cool. Miss Marple slipped behind one of them. Then she waited. From the window here she had a good view of anyone who approached Molly's bedroom. It was some few minutes, four or five, before she saw anything.

The neat figure of Jackson in his white uniform went up the steps of the loggia. He paused for a minute at the balcony there, and then appeared to be giving a tiny discreet tap on the door of the window that was ajar. There was no response that Miss Marple could hear. Jackson looked around him, a quick furtive glance, then he slipped inside the open doors. Miss Marple moved to the door which led directly into the bedroom. She did not go through it, but applied her eyes to the hinge.

Jackson had walked into the room. He approached the bed and looked down for a minute on the sleeping girl. Then he turned away and walked not to the sitting-room door, but to the far door which led into the adjoining bathroom. Miss Marple's eyebrows rose in slight surprise. She reflected a minute or two, then walked out into the passageway and into the bathroom by the other door.

Jackson spun round from examining the shelf over the wash-basin. He looked taken aback, which was not surprising.

"Oh," he said, "I—I didn't . . ."

"Mr. Jackson," said Miss Marple, in great surprise.

"I thought you'd be here somewhere," said Jackson.

"Did you want anything?" inquired Miss Marple.

"Actually," said Jackson, "I was just looking at Mrs. Kendal's brand of face cream."

Miss Marple appreciated the fact that as Jackson was standing with a jar of face cream in his hand he had been adroit in mentioning the fact at once.

"Nice smell," he said, wrinkling up his nose. "Fairly good stuff, as these preparations go. The cheaper brands don't suit every skin. Bring it out in a rash as likely as not. The same thing with face powders sometimes."

"You seem to be very knowledgeable on the subject," said Miss Marple.

"Worked in the pharmaceutical line for a bit," said Jackson. "One learns to know a good deal about cosmetics there. Put stuff in a fancy jar, package it expensively, and it's astonishing what you could rook women for."

"Is that what you—?" Miss Marple broke off deliberately.

"Well, no, I didn't come in here to talk about cosmetics," Jackson agreed.

"You've not had much time to think up a lie," thought Miss Marple to herself. "Let's see what you'll come out with."

"Matter of fact," said Jackson, "Mrs. Walters lent her lipstick to Mrs. Kendal the other day. I came in to get it back for her. I tapped on the window and then I saw Mrs. Kendal was fast asleep, so I thought it would be quite all right if I just walked across into the bathroom and looked for it."

"I see," said Miss Marple. "And did you find it?"

Jackson shook his head. "Probably in one of her handbags," he said lightly. "I won't bother. Mrs. Walters didn't make a point of it. She only just mentioned it casually." He went on, surveying the toilet preparations: "Doesn't have very much, does she? Ah, well, doesn't need it at her age. Good natural skin."

"You must look at women with quite a different eye from ordinary men," said Miss Marple, smiling pleasantly.

"Yes. I suppose various jobs do alter one's angle."

"You know a good deal about drugs?"

"Oh, yes. Good working acquaintance with them. If you ask me, there are too many of them about nowadays. Too many tranquillizers and pep pills and miracle drugs and all the rest of it. All right if they're given on prescription, but there are too many of them you can get without prescription. Some of them can be dangerous."

"I suppose so," said Miss Marple. "Yes, I suppose so."

"They have a great effect, you know, on behaviour. A lot of this teen-age hysteria you get from time to time. It's not natural causes. The kids've been taking things. Oh, there's nothing new about it. It's been known for ages. Out in the East—not that I've ever been there—all sorts of funny things used to happen. You'd be surprised at some of the things women gave their husbands. In India, for example, in the bad old days, a young wife who married an old husband. Didn't what to get rid of him, I suppose, because she'd have been burnt on the funeral pyre, or if she wasn't burnt she'd have been treated as an outcast by the family. No catch to have been a widow in India in those days. But she could keep an elderly husband under drugs, make him semi-imbecile, give him hallucinations, drive him more or less off his head." He shook his head. "Yes, lot of dirty work."

He went on: "And witches, you know. There's a lot of interesting things known now about witches. Why did they always confess, why did they admit so readily that they *were* witches, that they had flown on broomsticks to the Witches' Sabbath?"

"Torture," said Miss Marple.

"Not always," said Jackson. "Oh, yes, torture accounted for a lot of it, but they came out with some of those confessions almost before torture was mentioned. They didn't so much confess as boast about it. Well, they rubbed themselves with ointments, you know. Anointing they used to call it. Some of the preparations, belladonna, atropine, all that sort of thing; if you rub them on the skin they give you hallucinations of levitation, of flying through the air. They thought it all was genuine, poor devils. And look at the Assassins—medieval people, out in Syria, the Lebanon, somewhere like that. They fed them Indian hemp, gave them hallucinations of paradise and houris, and endless time. They were told that that was what would happen to them after death, but to attain it they had to go and do a ritual killing. Oh, I'm not putting it in fancy language, but that's what it came to."

"What it came to," said Miss Marple, "is in essence the fact that people are highly credulous."

"Well, yes, I suppose you could put it like that."

"They believe what they are told," said Miss Marple. "Yes, indeed, we're all inclined to do that," she added. Then she said, "Who told you these stories about India, about the doping of husbands with datura?" and she added sharply, before he could answer, "Was it Major Palgrave?"

Jackson looked slightly surprised. "Well—yes, as a matter of fact, it was. He told me a lot of stories like that. Of course most of it must have been before his time, but he seemed to know all about it."

"Major Palgrave was under the impression that he knew a lot about everything," said Miss Marple. "He was often inaccurate in what he told people." She shook her head thoughtfully. "Major Palgrave," she said, "has a lot to answer for."

There was a slight sound from the adjoining bedroom. Miss Marple turned her head sharply. She went quickly out of the bathroom into the bedroom. Lucky Dyson was standing just inside the window.

"I—oh! I didn't think you were here, Miss Marple."

"I just stepped into the bathroom for a moment," said Miss Marple with dignity and a faint air of Victorian reserve.

In the bathroom, Jackson grinned broadly. Victorian modesty always amused him.

"I just wondered if you'd like me to sit with Molly for a bit," said Lucky. She looked over towards the bed. "She's asleep, isn't she?"

"I think so," said Miss Marple. "But it's really quite all right. You go and amuse yourself, my dear. I thought you'd gone on that expedition?"

"I was going," said Lucky, "but I had such a filthy headache that at the last moment I cried off. So I thought I might as well make myself useful."

"That was very nice of you," said Miss Marple. She reseated herself by the bed and resumed her knitting. "But I'm quite happy here."

Lucky hesitated for a moment or two and then turned away and went out. Miss Marple waited a moment, then tiptoed back into the bathroom, but Jackson had departed, no doubt through the other door. Miss Marple picked up the jar of face cream he had been holding and slipped it into her pocket.

22

A MAN IN HER LIFE?

Getting a little chat in a natural manner with Dr. Graham was not so easy as Miss Marple had hoped. She was particularly anxious not to approach him directly, since she did not want to lend undue importance to the questions that she was going to ask him.

Tim was back, looking after Molly, and Miss Marple had arranged that she should relieve him there during the time that dinner was served and he was needed in the dining-room. He had assured her that Mrs. Dyson was quite willing to take that on, or even Mrs. Hillingdon, but Miss Marple said firmly that they were both young women who liked enjoying themselves and that she herself preferred a light meal early and so that would suit everybody. Tim once again thanked her warmly. Hovering rather uncertainly round the hotel and on the pathway which connected with various bungalows, among them Dr. Graham's, Miss Marple tried to plan what she was going to do next.

She had a lot of confused and contradictory ideas in her head, and if there was one thing that Miss Marple did not like, it was to have confused and contradictory ideas. This whole business had started out clearly enough. Major Palgrave with his regrettable capacity for telling stories, his indiscretion that had obviously been overheard, and the corollary, his death within twenty-four hours. Nothing difficult about *that,* thought Miss Marple.

But afterwards, she was forced to admit, there was nothing but difficulty. Everything pointed in too many different directions at once. Once admit that you didn't believe a word that anybody had said to you, that nobody could be trusted, and that many of the persons with whom she conversed here had had regrettable resemblances to certain persons at St. Mary Mead, and where did that lead you?

Her mind was increasingly focused on the victim. Someone was going to be killed, and she had the increasing feeling that she ought to know quite well who that someone was. There had been *something*. Something she had heard? Noticed? Seen?

Something someone had told her that had a bearing on the case. Joan Prescott? Joan Prescott had said a lot of things about a lot of people. Scandal? Gossip? What exactly had Joan Prescott said?

Gregory Dyson, Lucky—Miss Marple's mind hovered over Lucky. Lucky, she was convinced with a certainty born of her natural suspicions, had been actively concerned in the death of Gregory Dyson's first wife. Everything pointed to it. Could it be that the predestined victim over whom she was worrying was Gregory Dyson? That Lucky intended to try her luck again with another husband, and for that reason wanted not only freedom but the handsome inheritance that she would get as Gregory Dyson's widow?

"But really," said Miss Marple to herself, "this is all pure conjecture. I'm being stupid. I know I'm being stupid. The truth must be quite plain, if one could just clear away the litter. Too much litter, that's what's the matter."

"Talking to yourself?" said Mr. Rafiel.

Miss Marple jumped. She had not noticed his approach. Esther Walters was supporting him and he was coming slowly down from his bungalow to the terrace.

"I really didn't notice you, Mr. Rafiel."

"Your lips were moving. What's become of all this urgency of yours?"

"It's still urgent," said Miss Marple, "only I can't just see what must be perfectly plain—"

"I'm glad it's as simple as that. Well, if you want any help, count on me."

He turned his head as Jackson approached them along the path.

"So there you are, Jackson. Where the devil have you been? Never about when I want you."

"Sorry, Mr. Rafiel."

Dexterously he slipped his shoulder under Mr. Rafiel's. "Down to the terrace, sir?"

"You can take me to the bar," said Mr. Rafiel. "All right, Esther, you can go now and change into your evening togs. Meet me on the terrace in half an hour."

He and Jackson went off together. Mrs. Walters dropped into the chair by Miss Marple. She rubbed her arm gently.

"He seems a very light weight," she observed, "but at the moment my arm feels quite numb. I haven't seen you this afternoon at all, Miss Marple."

"No, I've been sitting with Molly Kendall," Miss Marple explained. "She seems really very much better."

"If you ask me, there was never very much wrong with her," said Esther Walters.

Miss Marple raised her eyebrows. Esther Walters' tone had been decidedly dry.

"You mean—you think her suicide attempt . . ."

"I don't think there was any suicide attempt," said Esther Walters. "I don't believe for a moment she took a real overdose, and I think Dr. Graham knows that perfectly well."

"Now you interest me very much," said Miss Marple. "I wonder why you say that?"

"Because I'm almost certain that it's the case. Oh, it's a thing that happens very often. It's a way, I suppose, of calling attention to oneself," went on Esther Walters.

" 'You'll be sorry when I'm dead?' " quoted Miss Marple.

"That sort of thing," agreed Esther Walters, "though I don't think that was the motive in this particular instance. That's the sort of thing you feel like when your husband's playing you up and you're terribly fond of him."

"You don't think Molly Kendal is fond of her husband?"

"Well," said Esther Walters, "do you?"

Miss Marple considered. "I have," she said, "more or less assumed it." She paused a moment before adding, "perhaps wrongly."

Esther was smiling her rather wry smile.

"I've heard a little about her, you know. About the whole business."

"From Miss Prescott?"

"Oh," said Esther, "from one or two people. There's a man in the case. Someone she was keen on. Her people were dead against him."

"Yes," said Miss Marple, "I did hear that."

"And then she married Tim. Perhaps she was fond of him in a way. But the other man didn't give up. I've wondered once or twice if he didn't actually follow her out here."

"Indeed. But—who?"

"I've no idea who," said Esther, "and I should imagine that they've been very careful."

"You think she cares for this other man?"

Esther shrugged her shoulders. "I dare say he's a bad lot," she said, "but that's very often the kind who knows how to get under a woman's skin and stay there."

"You never heard what kind of a man—what he did—anything like that?"

Esther shook her head. "No. People hazard guesses, but you can't go by that type of thing. He may have been a married man. That may have been why her people disliked him, or he may have been a real bad lot. Perhaps he drank. Perhaps he tangled with the law—I don't know. But she cares for him still. That I know positively."

"You've seen something, heard something?" Miss Marple hazarded.

"I know what I'm talking about," said Esther. Her voice was harsh and unfriendly.

"These murders—" began Miss Marple.

"Can't you forget murders?" said Esther. "You've got Mr. Rafiel now all tangled up in them. Can't you just—let them be? You'll never find out any more, I'm sure of that."

Miss Marple looked at her.

"You think you know, don't you?" she said.

"I think I do, yes. I'm fairly sure."

"Then oughtn't you to tell what you know—do something about it?"

"Why should I? What good would it do? I couldn't prove anything. What would happen anyway? People get let off nowadays so easily. They call it diminished responsibility and things like that. A few years in prison and you're out again, as right as rain."

"Supposing, because you don't tell what you know, somebody else gets killed—another victim?"

Esther shook her head with confidence. "That won't happen," she said.

"You can't be sure of it."

"I am sure. And in any case, I don't see who—" She frowned. "Anyway," she added, almost inconsequently, "perhaps it is—diminished responsibility. Perhaps you can't help it—not if you are really mentally unbalanced. Oh, I don't know. By far the best thing would be if she went off with whoever it is, then we could all forget about things."

She glanced at her watch, gave an exclamation of dismay and got up.

"I must go and change."

Miss Marple sat looking at her. Pronouns, she thought, were always puzzling, and women like Esther Walters were particularly prone to strew them about haphazard. Was Esther Walters for some reason convinced that a woman had been responsible for the deaths of Major Palgrave and Victoria? It sounded like it. Miss Marple considered.

"Ah, Miss Marple, sitting here all alone—and not even knitting?"

It was Dr. Graham, for whom she had sought so long and so unsuccessfully. And here he was prepared of his own accord to sit down for a few minutes' chat. He wouldn't stay long, Miss Marple thought, because he too was bent on changing for dinner, and he usually dined fairly early. She explained that she had been sitting by Molly Kendal's bedside that afternoon.

"One can hardly believe she has made such a good recovery so quickly," she said.

"Oh, well," said Dr. Graham, "it's not very surprising. She didn't take a very heavy overdose, you know."

"Oh, I understood she'd taken quite a half-bottle full of tablets."

Dr. Graham was smiling indulgently.

"No," he said, "I don't think she took that amount. I dare say she meant to take them, then probably at the last moment she threw half of them away. People, even when they think they want to commit suicide, often don't really want to do it. They manage not to take a full overdose. It's not always deliberate deceit, it's just the subconscious looking after itself."

"Or, I suppose it might be deliberate. I mean, wanting it to appear that . . ." Miss Marple paused.

"It's possible," said Dr. Graham.

"If she and Tim had had a row, for instance?"

"They don't have rows, you know. They seem very fond of each other. Still, I suppose it can always happen once. No, I don't think there's very much wrong with her now. She could really get up and go about as usual. Still, it's safer to keep her where she is for a day or two—"

He got up, nodded cheerfully and went off towards the hotel. Miss Marple sat where she was a little while longer.

Various thoughts passed through her mind. The book under Molly's mattress— The way Molly had feigned sleep—

Things Joan Prescott and, later, Esther Walters, had said . . .

And then she went back to the beginning of it all—to Major Palgrave.

Something struggled in her mind. Something about Major Palgrave.

Something that if she could only remember—

23

THE LAST DAY

"And the evening and the morning were the last day," said Miss Marple to herself.

Then, slightly confused, she sat upright again in her chair. She had dozed off, an incredible thing to do because the steel band was playing and anyone who could doze off during the steel band— Well, it showed, thought Miss Marple, that she was getting used to this place! What was it she had been saying? Some quotation that she'd got wrong. Last day? *First* day. That's what it ought to be. This wasn't the first day. Presumably it wasn't the last day either.

She sat upright again. The fact was that she was extremely tired. All this anxiety, this feeling of having been shamefully inadequate in some way . . . She remembered unpleasantly once more that queer sly look that Molly had given her from under her half-closed eyelids. What had been going on in that girl's head? How different, thought Miss Marple, everything had seemed at first. Tim Kendal and Molly, such a natural, happy young couple. The Hillingdons so pleasant, so well-bred, such what is called "nice" people. The gay hearty extrovert, Greg Dyson, and the gay strident Lucky, talking nineteen to the dozen, pleased with herself and the world . . . A quartet of people getting on so well together. Canon Prescott that genial kindly man. Joan Prescott, an acid streak in her, but a very nice woman, and nice women have their gossipy distractions. They have to know what is going on, to know when two and two make four, and when it is possible to stretch them to five! There was no harm in such women. Their tongues wagged but they were kind if you were in misfortune. Mr. Rafiel, a personality, a man of character, a man that you would never by any chance forget. But Miss Marple thought she knew something else about Mr. Rafiel.

The doctors had often given him up, so he had said, but this time, she thought, they had been more certain in their pronouncements. Mr. Rafiel knew that his days were numbered.

Knowing this with certainty, was there any action he might have been likely to take?

Miss Marple considered the question.

It might, she thought, be important.

What was it exactly he had said, his voice a little too loud, a little too sure? Miss Marple was very skillful in tones of voice. She had done so much listening in her life.

Mr. Rafiel had been telling her something that wasn't true.

Miss Marple looked around her. The night air, the soft fragrance of flowers, the tables with their little lights, the women with their pretty dresses, Evelyn in a dark indigo and white print, Lucky in a white sheath, her golden hair shining. Everybody seemed gay and full of life tonight. Even Tim Kendal was smiling. He passed her table and said: "Can't thank you enough for all you've done. Molly's practically herself again. The doc says she can get up tomorrow."

Miss Marple smiled at him and said that that was good hearing. She found it, however, quite an effort to smile. Decidedly, she was tired. . . .

She got up and walked slowly back to her bungalow. She would have liked to go on thinking, puzzling, trying to remember, trying to assemble various facts and words and glances. But she wasn't able to do it. The tired mind rebelled. It said "Sleep! You've got to go to sleep!"

Miss Marple undressed, got into bed, read a few verses of the Thomas à Kempis which she kept by her bed, then she turned out the light. In the darkness she sent up a prayer. One couldn't do everything oneself. One had to have help. "Nothing will happen tonight," she murmured hopefully.

II

Miss Marple woke suddenly and sat up in bed. Her heart was beating. She switched on the light and looked at the little clock by her bedside. Two a.m. Two a.m. and outside activity of some kind was going on. She got up, put on her dressing-gown and slippers, and a woollen scarf round her head and went out to reconnoitre. There were people moving about with torches. Among them she saw Canon Prescott and went to him.

"What's happening?"

"Oh, Miss Marple? It's Mrs. Kendal. Her husband woke up, found she'd slipped out of bed and gone out. We're looking for her."

He hurried on. Miss Marple walked more slowly after him. Where had

Molly gone? Why? Had she planned this deliberately, planned to slip away as soon as the guard on her was relaxed, and while her husband was deep in sleep? Miss Marple thought it was probable. But why? What was the reason? Was there, as Esther Walters had so strongly hinted, some other man? If so, who could that man be? Or was there some more sinister reason?

Miss Marple walked on, looking around her, peering under bushes. Then suddenly she heard a faint call: "Here. . . . This way. . . ."

The cry had come from some little distance beyond the hotel grounds. It must be, thought Miss Marple, near the creek of water that ran down to the sea. She went in that direction as briskly as she could.

There were not really so many searchers as it had seemed to her at first. Most people must still be asleep in their bungalows. She saw a place on the creek bank where there were people standing. Someone pushed past her, almost knocking her down, running in that direction. It was Tim Kendal. A minute or two later she heard his voice cry out: "Molly! My God, Molly!"

It was a minute or two before Miss Marple was able to join the little group. It consisted of one of the Cuban waiters, Evelyn Hillingdon, and two of the native girls. They had parted to let Tim through. Miss Marple arrived as he was bending over to look.

"Molly . . ." He slowly dropped on to his knees. Miss Marple saw the girl's body clearly, lying there in the creek, her face below the level of the water, her golden hair spread over the pale green embroidered shawl that covered her shoulders. With the leaves and rushes of the creek, it seemed almost like a scene from *Hamlet,* with Molly as the dead Ophelia. . . .

As Tim stretched out a hand to touch her, the quiet, common-sense Miss Marple took charge and spoke sharply and authoritatively.

"Don't move her, Mr. Kendal," she said. "She mustn't be moved."

Tim turned a dazed face up to her.

"But—I must—it's Molly. I must . . ."

Evelyn Hillingdon touched his shoulder.

"She's dead, Tim. I didn't move her, but I did feel her pulse."

"Dead?" said Tim unbelievingly. "Dead? You mean she's—drowned herself?"

"I'm afraid so. It looks like it."

"But why?" A great cry burst from the young man. "Why? She was so happy this evening. Talking about what we'd do tomorrow. Why should this terrible death wish come over her again? Why should she steal away as she did—rush out into the night, come down here and drown herself?

What despair did she have—what misery—why couldn't she tell me anything?"

"I don't know, my dear," said Evelyn gently. "I don't know."

Miss Marple said: "Somebody had better get Dr. Graham. And someone will have to telephone the police."

"The police?" Tim uttered a bitter laugh. "What good will they be?"

"The police have to be notified in a case of suicide," said Miss Marple.

Tim rose slowly to his feet.

"I'll get Graham," he said heavily. "Perhaps—even now—he could—do something."

He stumbled away in the direction of the hotel.

Evelyn Hillingdon and Miss Marple stood side by side looking down at the dead girl.

Evelyn shook her head. "It's too late. She's quite cold. She must have been dead at least an hour—perhaps more. What a tragedy it all is. Those two always seemed so happy. I suppose she was always unbalanced."

"No," said Miss Marple. "I don't think she was unbalanced."

Evelyn looked at her curiously. "What do you mean?"

The moon had been behind a cloud, but now it came out into the open. It shone with a luminous silvery brightness on Molly's outspread hair . . .

Miss Marple gave a sudden ejaculation. She bent down, peering, then stretched out her hand and touched the golden head. She spoke to Evelyn Hillingdon, and her voice sounded quite different.

"I think," she said, "that we had better make sure."

Evelyn Hillingdon stared at her in astonishment.

"But you yourself told Tim we mustn't touch anything?"

"I know. But the moon wasn't out. I hadn't seen—"

Her finger pointed. Then, very gently, she touched the blonde hair and parted it so that the roots were exposed . . .

Evelyn gave a sharp ejaculation.

"Lucky!"

And then after a moment she repeated: "Not Molly. . . . Lucky."

Miss Marple nodded. "Their hair was of much the same colour—but hers, of course, was dark at the roots because it was dyed."

"But she's wearing Molly's shawl?"

"She admired it. I heard her say she was going to get one like it. Evidently she did."

"So that's why we were—deceived. . . ."

Evelyn broke off as she met Miss Marple's eyes watching her.

"Someone," said Miss Marple, "will have to tell her husband."

There was a moment's pause, then Evelyn said: "All right. I'll do it."

She turned and walked away through the palm trees.

Miss Marple remained for a moment motionless, then she turned her head very slightly and said. "Yes, Colonel Hillingdon?"

Edward Hillingdon came from the trees behind her to stand by her side.

"You knew I was there?"

"You cast a shadow," said Miss Marple.

They stood a moment in silence.

He said, more as though he were speaking to himself: "So, in the end, she played her luck too far. . . ."

"You are, I think, glad that she is dead?"

"And that shocks you? Well, I will not deny it. I am glad she is dead."

"Death is often a solution to problems."

Edward Hillingdon turned his head slowly. Miss Marple met his eyes calmly and steadfastly.

"If you think—" He took a sharp step towards her.

There was a sudden menace in his tone.

Miss Marple said quietly: "Your wife will be back with Mr. Dyson in a moment. Or Mr. Kendal will be here with Dr. Graham."

Edward Hillingdon relaxed. He turned back to look down at the dead woman.

Miss Marple slipped away quietly. Presently her pace quickened.

Just before reaching her own bungalow, she paused. It was here that she had sat that day talking to Major Palgrave. It was here that he had fumbled in his wallet looking for the snapshot of a murderer. . . .

She remembered how he had looked up, and how his face had gone purple and red. . . . "So ugly," as Señora de Caspearo had said. "He has the Evil Eye."

The Evil Eye . . . Eye . . . *Eye.* . . .

24

NEMESIS

Whatever the alarms and excursions of the night, Mr. Rafiel had not heard them.

He was fast asleep in bed, a faint thin snore coming from his nostrils, when he was taken by the shoulders and shaken violently.

"Eh—what—what the devil's this?"

"It's me," said Miss Marple, for once ungrammatical, "though I should put it a little more strongly than that. The Greeks, I believe, had a word for it. Nemesis, if I am not wrong."

Mr. Rafiel raised himself on his pillows as far as he could. He stared at her. Miss Marple, standing there in the moonlight, her head encased in a fluffy scarf of pale pink wool, looking as unlike a figure of Nemesis as it was possible to imagine.

"So you're Nemesis, are you?" said Mr. Rafiel after a momentary pause.

"I hope to be—with your help."

"Do you mind telling me quite plainly what you're talking about like this in the middle of the night?"

"I think we may have to act quickly. Very quickly. I have been foolish. Extremely foolish. I ought to have known from the very beginning what all this was about. It was so simple."

"What was simple, and what are you talking about?"

"You slept through a good deal," said Miss Marple. "A body was found. We thought at first it was the body of Molly Kendal. It wasn't; it was Lucky Dyson. Drowned in the creek."

"Lucky, eh?" said Mr. Rafiel. "And drowned? In the creek. Did she drown herself or did somebody drown her?"

"Somebody drowned her," said Miss Marple.

"I see. At least I think I see. That's what you mean by saying it's so simple, is it? Greg Dyson was always the first possibility, and he's the right one. Is that it? Is that what you're thinking? And what you're afraid of is that he may get away with it."

Miss Marple took a deep breath.

"Mr. Rafiel, will you trust me? We have got to stop a murder being committed."

"I thought you said it had been committed."

"That murder was committed in error. Another murder may be committed any moment now. There's no time to lose. We must prevent it happening. We must go at once."

"It's all very well to talk like that," said Mr. Rafiel. "We, you say? What do you think *I* can do about it? I can't even walk without help. How can you and I set about preventing a murder? You're about a hundred and I'm a broken-up old crock."

"I was thinking of Jackson," said Miss Marple. "Jackson will do what you tell him, won't he?"

"He will indeed," said Mr. Rafiel, "especially if I add that I'll make it worth his while. Is that what you want?"

"Yes. Tell him to come with me and tell him to obey any orders I give him."

Mr. Rafiel looked at her for about six seconds. Then he said: "Done. I expect I'm taking the biggest risk of my life. Well, it won't be the first one." He raised his voice. "Jackson." At the same time he picked up the electric bell that lay beside his hand and pressed the button.

Hardly thirty seconds passed before Jackson appeared through the connecting door to the adjoining room.

"You called and rang, sir? Anything wrong?" He broke off, staring at Miss Marple.

"Now, Jackson, do as I tell you. You will go with this lady, Miss Marple. You'll go where she takes you and you'll do exactly as she says. You'll obey every order she gives you. Is that understood?"

"I—"

"Is that understood?"

"Yes, sir."

"And for doing that," said Mr. Rafiel, "you won't be the loser. I'll make it worth your while."

"Thank you, sir."

"Come along, Mr. Jackson," said Miss Marple. She spoke over her shoulder to Mr. Rafiel. "We'll tell Mrs. Walters to come to you on our way. Get her to get you out of bed and bring you along."

"Bring me along where?"

"To the Kendals' bungalow," said Miss Marple. "I think Molly will be coming back there."

II

Molly came up the path from the sea. Her eyes stared fixedly ahead of her. Occasionally, under her breath, she gave a little whimper.

She went up the steps of the loggia, paused a moment, then pushed open the window and walked into the bedroom. The lights were on, but the room itself was empty. Molly went across to the bed and sat down. She sat for some minutes, now and again passing her hand over her forehead and frowning.

Then, after a quick surreptitious glance round, she slipped her hand under the mattress and brought out the book that was hidden there. She bent over it, turning the pages to find what she wanted.

Then she raised her head as the sound of running foot-steps came from outside. With a quick guilty movement she pushed the book behind her back.

Tim Kendal, panting and out of breath, came in and uttered a great sigh of relief at the sight of her.

"Thank God. Where have you been, Molly? I've been searching everywhere for you."

"I went to the creek."

"You went—" he stopped.

"Yes. I went to the creek. But I couldn't wait there. I couldn't. There was someone in the water—and she was dead."

"You mean— Do you know I thought it was you? I've only just found out it was Lucky."

"I didn't kill her. Really, Tim, I didn't kill her. I'm sure I didn't. I mean —I'd remember if I did, wouldn't I?"

Tim sank slowly down on the end of the bed.

"You didn't— Are you sure of that—? No. No, of course you didn't!" He fairly shouted the words. "Don't start thinking like that, Molly. Lucky drowned herself. Of course she drowned herself. Hillingdon was through with her. She went and lay down with her face in the water—"

"Lucky wouldn't do that. She'd never do that. But *I* didn't kill her. I swear I didn't."

"Darling, of course you didn't!" He put his arms round her, but she pulled herself away.

"I hate this place. It ought to be all sunlight. It seemed to be all sunlight.

But it isn't. Instead there's a shadow—a big black shadow. And I'm in it—and I can't get out—"

Her voice had risen to a shout.

"Hush, Molly. For God's sake, hush!" He went into the bathroom, came back with a glass.

"Look. Drink this. It'll steady you."

"I—I can't drink anything. My teeth are chattering so."

"Yes you can, darling. Sit down. Here, on the bed." He put his arm round her. He approached the glass to her lips. "There you are now. Drink it."

A voice spoke from the window.

"Jackson," said Miss Marple clearly. "Go over. Take that glass from him and hold it tightly. Be careful. He's strong and he may be pretty desperate."

There were certain points about Jackson. He was a man of training, trained to obey orders. He was a man with a great love for money, and money had been promised him by his employer, that employer being a man of stature and authority. He was also a man of extreme muscular development heightened by his training. His not to reason why, his but to do.

Swift as a flash he had crossed the room. His hand went over the glass that Tim was holding to Molly's lips, his other arm had fastened round Tim. A quick flick of the wrist and he had the glass. Tim turned on him wildly, but Jackson held him firmly.

"What the devil—let go of me. Let go of me. Have you gone mad? What are you doing?"

Tim struggled violently.

"Hold him, Jackson," said Miss Marple.

"What's going on? What's the matter here?"

Supported by Esther Walters, Mr. Rafiel, came through the window.

"You asked what's the matter?" shouted Tim. "Your man's gone mad—stark, staring mad, that's what's the matter. Tell him to let go of me."

"No," said Miss Marple.

Mr. Rafiel turned to her.

"Speak up, Nemesis," he said. "We've got to have chapter and verse of some kind."

"I've been stupid and a fool," said Miss Marple, "but I'm not being a fool now. When the contents of that glass that he was trying to make his wife drink have been analyzed, I'll wager—yes, I'll wager my immortal soul that you'll find it's got a lethal dose of narcotic in it. It's the same pattern, you see, the same pattern as in Major Palgrave's story. A wife in a depressed state, and she tries to do away with herself, husband saves her in time. Then the second time she succeeds. Yes, it's the right pattern. Major Palgrave told me the story and he took out a snapshot and then he looked up and saw—"

"Over your right shoulder—" continued Mr. Rafiel.

"No," said Miss Marple, shaking her head. "He didn't see anything over my right shoulder."

"What are you talking about? You told me . . ."

"I told you wrong. I was completely wrong. I was stupid beyond belief. Major Palgrave appeared to me to be looking over my right shoulder, glaring, in fact, at something— But he couldn't have seen anything, because he was looking through his left eye, and his left eye was his glass eye."

"I remember—he had a glass eye," said Mr. Rafiel. "I'd forgotten—or I took it for granted. You mean he couldn't see anything?"

"Of course he could see," said Miss Marple. "He could see all right, but he could only see with one eye. The eye he could see with was his right eye. And so, you see, he must have been looking at something or someone not to the right of me but to the left of me."

"Was there anyone on the left of you?"

"Yes," said Miss Marple. "Tim Kendal and his wife were sitting not far off. Sitting at a table just by a big hibiscus bush. They were doing accounts there. So you see the Major looked up. His glass left eye was glaring over my shoulder, but what he saw with his other eye was a man sitting by a hibiscus bush and the face was the same, only rather older, as the face in the snapshot. Also by a hibiscus bush. Tim Kendal had heard the story the Major had been telling and he saw that the Major had recognized him. So, of course, he had to kill him. Later, he had to kill the girl Victoria because she'd seen him putting a bottle of tablets in the Major's room. She didn't think anything of it at first because of course it was quite natural on various occasions for Tim Kendal to go into the guests' bungalows. He might have just been returning something that had been left on a restaurant table. But she thought about it and then she asked him questions and so he had to get rid of her. But this is the real murder, the murder he's been planning all along. He's a wife-killer, you see."

"What damned nonsense, what—" Tim Kendal shouted.

There was a sudden cry, a wild angry cry. Esther Walters detached herself from Mr. Rafiel, almost flinging him down, and rushed across the room. She pulled vainly at Jackson.

"Let go of him—let go of him. It's not true. Not a word of it's true. Tim —Tim darling, it's not true. You could never kill anyone, I know you couldn't. I know you wouldn't. It's that horrible girl you married. She's been telling lies about you. They're not true. None of them are true. I believe in you. I love you and trust in you. I'll never believe a word anyone says. I'll—"

Then Tim Kendal lost control of himself.

"For God's sake, you damned bitch," he said, "shut up, can't you? D'you want to get me hanged? Shut up, I tell you. Shut that big, ugly mouth of yours."

"Poor silly creature," said Mr. Rafiel slowly. "So that's what's been going on, is it?"

25

MISS MARPLE USES HER IMAGINATION

"So that's what had been going on?" said Mr. Rafiel.

He and Miss Marple were sitting together in a confidential manner.

"She'd been having an affair with Tim Kendal, had she?"

"Hardly an affair, I imagine," said Miss Marple primly. "It was, I think, a romantic attachment with the prospect of marriage in the future."

"What—after his wife was dead?"

"I don't think poor Esther Walters knew that Molly was going to die," said Miss Marple. "I just think she believed the story Tim Kendal told her about Molly having been in love with another man, and the man having followed her here, and I think she counted on Tim's getting a divorce. I think it was all quite proper and respectable. But she was very much in love with him."

"Well, that's easily understood. He was an attractive chap. But what made him go for her—d'you know that too?"

"You know, don't you?" said Miss Marple.

"I dare say I've got a pretty fair idea, but I don't know how you should know about it. As far as that goes, I don't see how Tim Kendal could know about it."

"Well, I really think I could explain all that with a little imagination, though it would be simpler if you told me."

"I'm not going to tell you," said Mr. Rafiel. "You tell me, since you're being so clever."

"Well, it seems to me possible," said Miss Marple, "that as I have already hinted to you, your man Jackson was in the habit of taking a good snoop through your various business papers from time to time."

"Perfectly possible," said Mr. Rafiel, "but I shouldn't have said there was anything there that could do him much good. I took care of that."

"I imagine," said Miss Marple, "he read your will."

"Oh, I see. Yes, yes, I did have a copy of my will along."

"You told me," said Miss Marple, "you told me (as Humpty Dumpty said—very loud and clear) that you had not left anything to Esther Walters in your will. You had impressed that fact upon her, and also upon Jackson. It was true in Jackson's case, I should imagine. You have not left him anything, but you had left Esther Walters money, though you weren't going to let her have any inkling of the fact. Isn't that right?"

"Yes, it's quite right, but I don't know how you knew."

"Well, it's the way you insisted on the point," said Miss Marple. "I have a certain experience of the way people tell lies."

"I give in," said Mr. Rafiel. "All right. I left Esther fifty thousand pounds. It would come as a nice surprise to her when I died. I suppose that, knowing this, Tim Kendal decided to exterminate his present wife with a nice dose of something or other and marry fifty thousand pounds and Esther Walters. Possibly to dispose of her also in good time. But how did he know she was going to have fifty thousand pounds?"

"Jackson told him, of course," said Miss Marple. "They were very friendly, those two. Tim Kendal was nice to Jackson and, quite, I should imagine, without ulterior motive. But among the bits of gossip that Jackson let slip, I think Jackson told him that unbeknownst to herself, Esther Walters was going to inherit a fat lot of money, and he may have said that he himself hoped to induce Esther Walters to marry him, though he hadn't had much success so far in taking her fancy. Yes, I think that's how it happened."

"The things you imagine always seem perfectly plausible," said Mr. Rafiel.

"But I was stupid," said Miss Marple, "very stupid. Everything fitted in really, you see. Tim Kendal was a very clever man as well as being a very wicked one. He was particularly good at putting about rumours. Half the things I've been told here came from him originally, I imagine. There were stories going around about Molly wanting to marry an undesirable young man, but I rather fancy that the undesirable young man was actually Tim Kendal himself, though that wasn't the name he was using then. Her people had heard something, perhaps that his background was rather fishy. So he put on a high indignation act, refused to be taken by Molly to be 'shown off' to her people, and then he brewed up a little scheme with her which they both thought great fun. She pretended to sulk and pine for him. Then a Mr. Tim Kendal turned up, primed with the names of various old friends of Molly's people, and they welcomed him with open arms as being the sort of young man who would put the former delinquent one out of Molly's head. I am afraid Molly and he must have laughed over it a good deal. Anyway, he married her, and with her money he bought out the people who ran this place, and they came out here. I should imagine that he ran through her money at a pretty fair rate. Then he came across Esther Walters and he saw a nice prospect of more money."

"Why didn't he bump me off?" said Mr. Rafiel.

Miss Marple coughed.

"I expect he wanted to be fairly sure of Mrs. Walters first. Besides—I mean . . ." She stopped, a little confused.

"Besides, he realized he wouldn't have to wait long," said Mr. Rafiel, "and it would clearly be better for me to die a natural death. Being so rich. Deaths of millionaires are scrutinized rather carefully, aren't they, unlike mere wives?"

"Yes, you're quite right. Such a lot of lies as he told," said Miss Marple. "Look at the lies he got Molly herself to believe—putting that book on mental disorders in her way. Giving her drugs which would give her dreams and hallucinations. You know, your Jackson was rather clever over that. I think he recognized certain of Molly's symptoms as being the result of drugs. And he came into the bungalow that day to potter about a bit in the bathroom. That face cream he examined. He might have got some idea from the old tales of witches rubbing themselves with ointments that had belladonna in them. Belladonna in face cream could have produced just that result. Molly would have blackouts. Times she couldn't account for, dreams of flying through the air. No wonder she got frightened about herself. She had all the signs of mental illness. Jackson was on the right track. Maybe he got the idea from Major Palgrave's stories about the use of datura by Indian women on their husbands."

"Major Palgrave!" said Mr. Rafiel. "Really, that man!"

"He brought about his own murder," said Miss Marple, "and that poor girl Victoria's murder, and he nearly brought about Molly's murder. But he recognized a murderer, all right."

"What made you suddenly remember about his glass eye?" asked Mr. Rafiel curiously.

"Something that Señora de Caspearo said. She talked some nonsense about his being ugly, and having the Evil Eye; and I said it was only a glass eye, and he couldn't help that, poor man, and she said his eyes looked different ways, they were cross-eyes—which, of course, they were. And she said it brought bad luck. I knew—I *knew* that I had heard something that day that was important. Last night, just after Lucky's death, it came to me what it was! And then I realized there was no time to waste . . ."

"How did Tim Kendal come to kill the wrong woman?"

"Sheer chance. I think his plan was this: Having convinced everybody—and that included Molly herself—that she was mentally unbalanced, and after giving her a sizable dose of the drug he was using, he told her that between them they were going to clear up all these murder puzzles. But she had got to help him. After everyone was asleep, they would go separately and meet at an agreed spot by the creek.

"He said he had a very good idea who the murderer was, and they would trap him. Molly went off obediently—but she was confused and stupefied with the drug she had been given, and it slowed her up. Tim arrived there first and saw what he thought was Molly. Golden hair and pale green shawl. He came up behind her, put his hand over her mouth, and forced her down into the water and held her there."

"Nice fellow! But wouldn't it have been easier just to give her an overdose of narcotic?"

"Much easier, of course. But that might have given rise to suspicion. All narcotics and sedatives had been very carefully removed from Molly's reach, remember. And if she had got hold of a fresh supply, who was more likely to have supplied it than her husband? But if, in a fit of despair, she went out and drowned herself while her innocent husband slept, the whole thing would be a romantic tragedy, and no one would be likely to suggest that she had been drowned deliberately. Besides," added Miss Marple, "murderers always find it difficult to keep things simple. They can't keep themselves from elaborating."

"You seem convinced you know all there is to be known about murderers! So you believe Tim didn't know he had killed the wrong woman?"

Miss Marple shook her head.

"He didn't even look at her face, just hurried off as quickly as he could, let an hour elapse, then started to organize a search for her, playing the part of a distracted husband."

"But what the devil was Lucky doing hanging about the creek in the middle of the night?"

Miss Marple gave an embarrassed little cough.

"It is possible, I think, that she was—er—waiting to meet someone."

"Edward Hillingdon?"

"Oh, *no,*" said Miss Marple. "That's all over. I wondered whether—just possibly—she might have been waiting for Jackson?"

"Waiting for Jackson?"

"I've noticed her—look at him once or twice," murmured Miss Marple, averting her eyes.

Mr. Rafiel whistled.

"My Tomcat Jackson! I wouldn't put it past him! Tim must have had a shock later when he found he'd killed the wrong woman."

"Yes, indeed. He must have felt quite desperate. Here was Molly alive and wandering about. And the story he'd circulated so carefully about her mental condition wouldn't stand up for a moment once she got into the hands of competent mental specialists. And once she told her damning story of his having asked her to meet him at the creek, where would Tim Kendal be? He'd only one hope—to finish off Molly as quickly as possible. Then there was a very good chance that everyone would believe that Molly, in a fit of mania, had drowned Lucky, and had then, horrified by what she had done, taken her own life."

"And it was then," said Mr. Rafiel, "that you decided to play Nemesis, eh?"

He leaned back suddenly and roared with laughter. "It's a damned good joke," he said. "If you knew what you looked like that night with that fluffy pink wool all round your head, standing there and saying you were Nemesis! I'll never forget it!"

EPILOGUE

The time had come and Miss Marple was waiting at the airport for her plane. Quite a lot of people had come to see her off. The Hillingdons had left already. Gregory Dyson had flown to one of the other islands and the rumour had come that he was devoting himself to an Argentinian widow. Señora de Caspearo had returned to South America.

Molly had come to see Miss Marple off. She was pale and thin, but she had weathered the shock of her discovery bravely, and with the help of one of Mr. Rafiel's nominees whom he had wired for to England, she was carrying on with the running of the hotel.

"Do you good to be busy," Mr. Rafiel observed. "Keep you from thinking. Got a good thing here."

"You don't think the murders—"

"People love murders when they're all cleared up," Mr. Rafiel had assured her. "You carry on, girl, and keep your heart up. Don't distrust all men because you've met one bad lot."

"You sound like Miss Marple," Molly had said, "she's always telling me Mr. Right will come along one day."

Mr. Rafiel grinned at this sentiment. So Molly was there and the two Prescotts and Mr. Rafiel, of course, and Esther—an Esther who looked older and sadder and to whom Mr. Rafiel was quite often unexpectedly kind. Jackson also was very much to the fore, pretending to be looking after Miss Marple's baggage. He was all smiles these days and let it be known that he had come into money.

There was a hum in the sky. The plane was arriving. Things were somewhat informal here. There was no "taking your place by Channel 8" or Channel 9. You just walked out from the little flower-covered pavilion on to the tarmac.

"Good-bye, darling Miss Marple." Molly kissed her.

"Good-bye. Do try and come and visit us." Miss Prescott shook her warmly by the hand.

"It has been a great pleasure to know you," said the Canon. "I second my sister's invitation most warmly."

"All the best, Madam," said Jackson, "and remember any time you want any massage free, just you send me a line and we'll make an appointment."

Only Esther Walters turned slightly away when the time came for good-byes. Miss Marple did not force one upon her. Mr. Rafiel came last. He took her hand.

"Ave Caesar, nos morituri te salutamus," he said.

"I'm afraid," said Miss Marple, "I don't know very much Latin."

"But you understand that?"

"Yes." She said no more. She knew quite well what he was telling her.

"It has been a great pleasure to know you," she said.

Then she walked across the tarmac and got into the plane.

NEMESIS

A Miss Marple Murder Mystery

to daphne honeybone

CONTENTS

1

OVERTURE

In the afternoons it was the custom of Miss Jane Marple to unfold her second newspaper. Two newspapers were delivered at her house every morning. The first one Miss Marple read while sipping her early morning tea, that is, if it was delivered in time. The boy who delivered the papers was notably erratic in his management of time. Frequently, too, there was either a new boy or a boy who was acting temporarily as a stand-in for the first one. And each one would have ideas of his own as to the geographical route that he should take in delivering. Perhaps it varied monotony for him. But those customers who were used to reading their paper early so that they could snap up the more saucy items in the day's news before departing for their bus, train or other means of progress to the day's work were annoyed if the papers were late, though the middle-aged and elderly ladies who resided peacefully in St. Mary Mead often preferred to read a newspaper propped up on their breakfast table.

Today, Miss Marple had absorbed the front page and a few other items in the daily paper that she had nicknamed "The Daily All-Sorts," this being a slightly satirical allusion to the fact that her paper, the *Daily Newsgiver,* owing to a change of proprietor, to her own and to other of her friends' great annoyance, now provided articles on men's tailoring, women's dress, female heartthrobs, competitions for children, and complaining letters from women and had managed pretty well to shove any real news off any part of it but the front page, or to some obscure corner where it was impossible to find it. Miss Marple, being old-fashioned, preferred her newspapers to *be* newspapers and give you news.

In the afternoon, having finished her luncheon, treated herself to twenty minutes' nap in a specially purchased, upright armchair which catered for the demands of her rheumatic back, she had opened *The Times,* which lent itself still to a more leisurely perusal. Not that *The Times* was what it used to be. The maddening thing about *The Times* was that you couldn't find anything any more. Instead of going through from the front page and knowing where everything else was so that you passed easily to any special articles on subjects in which you were interested, there were now extraordinary interruptions to this time-honoured program. Two pages were suddenly devoted to travel in Capri with illustrations. Sport appeared with far more prominence than it had ever had in the old days. Court news and obituaries were a little more faithful to routine. The births, marriages and details which had at one time occupied Miss Marple's attention first of all owing to their prominent position had migrated to a different part of *The Times,* though of late, Miss Marple noted, they had come almost permanently to rest on the back page.

Miss Marple gave her attention first to the main news on the front page. She did not linger long on that because it was equivalent to what she had already read this morning, though possibly couched in a slightly more dignified manner. She cast her eye down the table of contents. Articles, comments, science, sport; then she pursued her usual plan, turned the paper over and had a quick run down the births, marriages and deaths, after which she proposed to turn to the page given to correspondence, where she nearly always found something to enjoy; from that she passed on to the Court Circular, on which page today's news from the sale rooms could also be found. A short article on science was often placed there, but she did not propose to read that. It seldom made sense for her.

Having turned the paper over as usual to the births, marriages and deaths, Miss Marple thought to herself, as so often before:

"It's sad really, but nowadays one is only interested in the deaths!"

People had babies, but the people who had babies were not likely to be even known by name to Miss Marple. If there had been a column dealing with babies labelled as grandchildren, there might have been some chance of a pleasurable recognition. She might have thought to herself:

"Really, Mary Prendergast has had a *third* granddaughter!" though even that perhaps might have been a bit remote.

She skimmed down Marriages, also with not a very close survey, because most of her old friends' daughters or sons had married some years ago already. She came to the Deaths column and gave that her more serious attention. Gave it enough, in fact, so as to be sure she would not miss a name. Alloway, Angopastro, Arden, Barton, Bedshaw, Burgoweisser (dear me, what a *German* name, but he seemed to be late of Leeds). Camperdown, Carpenter, Clegg. Clegg? Now was that one of the Cleggs she knew? No, it didn't seem to be Janet Clegg. Somewhere in Yorkshire. McDonald, McKenzie, Nicholson. Nicholson? No. Again not a Nicholson she knew. Ogg, Ormerod—that must be one of the aunts, she thought. Yes, probably so. Linda Ormerod. No, she hadn't known her. Quantril? Dear me, that must be Elizabeth Quantril. Eighty-five. Well, really! She had thought Elizabeth Quantril had died some years ago. Fancy her having lived so long! So delicate she'd always been, too. Nobody had expected *her* to make old bones. Race, Radley, Rafiel. Rafiel? Something stirred. That name was familiar. Rafiel. Belford Park, Maidstone. Belford Park, Maidstone. No, she couldn't recall that address. No flowers. Jason Rafiel. Oh, well, an unusual name. She supposed she'd just heard it somewhere. Ross-Perkins. Now that might be—no, it wasn't. Ryland? Emily Ryland. No. No, she'd never known an Emily Ryland. *Deeply loved by her husband and children.* Well, very nice or very sad, whichever way you liked to look at it.

Miss Marple laid down her paper, glancing idly through the crossword while she puzzled to remember why the name Rafiel was familiar to her.

"It will come to me," said Miss Marple, knowing from long experience the way old people's memories worked.

"It'll come to me, I have no doubt."

She glanced out of the window towards the garden, withdrew her gaze and tried to put the garden out of her mind. Her garden had been the source of great pleasure and also a great deal of hard work to Miss Marple for many, many years. And now, owing to the fussiness of doctors, working in the garden was forbidden to her. She'd once tried to fight this ban, but had come to the conclusion that she had, after all, better do as she was told. She had arranged her chair at such an angle as not to be easy to look out in the garden unless she definitely and clearly wished to see something in particular. She sighed, picked up her knitting bag and took out a small child's wooly jacket in process of coming to a conclusion. The back was done and the front. Now she would have to get on with the sleeves. Sleeves were always boring. Two sleeves, both alike. Yes, very boring. Pretty coloured pink wool, however. Pink wool. Now wait a minute—where did that fit in? Yes—Yes—it fitted in with that name she'd just read in the paper. Pink wool. A blue sea. A Caribbean sea. A sandy beach. Sunshine. Herself knitting and—why, of course, Mr. Rafiel. That trip she had made to the Caribbean. The island of St. Honoré. A treat from her nephew Raymond. And she remembered Joan, her niece-in-law, Raymond's wife, saying:

"Don't get mixed up in any more murders, Aunt Jane. It isn't good for you."

Well, she hadn't wished to get mixed up in any murders, but it just happened. That was all. Simply because of an elderly major with a glass eye who had insisted on telling her some very long and boring stories. Poor Major—now what was *his* name? She'd forgotten that now. Mr. Rafiel and his secretary, Mrs.—Mrs. Walters, yes, Esther Walters, and his masseur-attendant, Jackson. It all came back. Well, well. Poor Mr. Rafiel. So Mr. Rafiel was dead. He had known he was going to die before very long. He had practically told her so. It seemed as though he had lasted longer than the doctors had thought. He was a strong man, an obstinate man—a very rich man.

Miss Marple remained in thought, her knitting needles working regularly, but her mind not really on her knitting. Her mind was on the late Mr. Rafiel, and remembering what she could remember about him. Not an easy man to forget, really. She could conjure his appearance up mentally quite well. Yes, a very definite personality, a difficult man, an irritable man, shockingly rude sometimes. Nobody ever resented his being rude, though. She remembered that also. They didn't resent his being rude because he was so rich. Yes, he had been very rich. He had had his secretary with him and a valet attendant, a qualified masseur. He had not been able to get about very well without help.

Rather a doubtful character that nurse-attendant had been, Miss Marple thought. Mr. Rafiel had been very rude to him sometimes. He had never seemed to mind. And that, again, of course was because Mr. Rafiel was so rich.

"Nobody else would pay him half what I do," Mr. Rafiel had said, "and he knows it. He's good at his job, though."

Miss Marple wondered whether Jackson?—Johnson?—had stayed on with Mr. Rafiel. Stayed on for what must have been—another year? A year and three or four months. She thought probably not. Mr. Rafiel was one who liked a change. He got tired of people, tired of their ways, tired of their faces, tired of their voices.

Miss Marple understood that. She had felt the same sometimes. That companion of hers, that nice, attentive, maddening woman with her cooing voice.

"Ah," said Miss Marple, "what a change for the better since—" oh, dear, she'd forgotten *her* name now—Miss—Miss Bishop?—no, not Miss Bishop; of course not. Why had she thought of the name Bishop? Oh, dear, how difficult it was.

Her mind went back to Mr. Rafiel and to—no, it wasn't Johnson, it had been Jackson, Arthur Jackson.

"Oh, dear," said Miss Marple again, "I always get *all* the names wrong. And of course, it was Miss *Knight* I was thinking of. Not Miss *Bishop.* Why do I think of her as Miss Bishop?" The answer came to her. Chess, of course. A chess piece. A knight. A bishop.

"I shall be calling her Miss Castle next time I think of her, I suppose, or Miss Rook. Though, really, she's not the sort of person who would ever rook anybody. No, indeed. And what was the name of that nice secretary that Mr. Rafiel had? Oh, yes, Esther Walters. That was right. I wonder what has happened to Esther Walters? She'd inherited money? She would probably inherit money now."

Mr. Rafiel, she remembered, had told her something about that, or she had—oh, dear, what a muddle things were when you tried to remember with any kind of exactitude. Esther Walters. It had hit her badly, that business in the Caribbean, but she would have got over it. She'd been a widow, hadn't she? Miss Marple hoped that Esther Walters had married again some nice, kindly, reliable man. It seemed faintly unlikely. Esther Walters, she thought, had had rather a genius for liking the wrong kind of men to marry.

Miss Marple went back to thinking about Mr. Rafiel. No flowers, it had said. Not that she herself would have dreamed of sending flowers to Mr. Rafiel. He could buy up all the nurseries in England if he'd wanted to. And anyway, they hadn't been on those terms. They hadn't been—friends, or on terms of affection. They had been—what was the word she wanted?—allies. Yes, they had been allies for a very short time. A very exciting time. And he had been an ally worth having. She had known so. She'd known it as she had gone running through a dark, tropical night in the Caribbean and had come to him. Yes, she remembered, she'd been wearing that pink wool—what used they to call them when she was young?—a fascinator. That nice pink wool kind of shawl-scarf that she'd put round her head, and he had looked at her and laughed and later, when she had said —she smiled at the remembrance—one word she had used and he had laughed, but he hadn't laughed in the end. No, he'd done what she asked him and therefore—"Ah!" Miss Marple sighed, it had been, she had to admit it, all very exciting. And she'd never told her nephew or dear Joan about it because, after all, it was what they'd told her not to do, wasn't it? Miss Marple nodded her head. Then she murmured softly:

"Poor Mr. Rafiel, I hope he didn't—suffer."

Probably not. Probably he'd been kept by expensive doctors under sedatives, easing the end. He had suffered a great deal in those weeks in the Caribbean. He'd nearly always been in pain. A brave man.

A brave man. She was sorry he was dead because she thought that though he'd been elderly and an invalid and ill, the world had lost something through his going. She had no idea what he could have been like in business. Ruthless, she thought, and rude and overmastering and aggressive. A great attacker. But—but a good friend, she thought. And somewhere in him a deep kind of kindness that he was very careful never to show on the surface. A man she admired and respected. Well, she was sorry he was gone and she hoped he hadn't minded too much and that his passing had been easy. And now he would be cremated no doubt and put in some large, handsome marble vault. She didn't even know if he'd been married. He had never mentioned a wife, never mentioned children. A lonely man? Or had his life been so full that he hadn't needed to feel lonely? She wondered.

She sat there quite a long time that afternoon, wondering about Mr. Rafiel. She had never expected to see him again after she had returned to England and she never had seen him again. Yet in some queer way she could at any moment have felt she was in touch with him. If he had approached her or had suggested that they meet again, feeling perhaps a bond because of a life that had been saved between them, or of some other bond. A bond—

"Surely," said Miss Marple, aghast at an idea that had come into her mind, "there can't be a bond of *ruthlessness* between us?" Was she, Jane Marple—could she ever be—ruthless? "D'you know," said Miss Marple to herself, "it's extraordinary I never thought about it before. I believe, you know, I *could* be ruthless . . ."

The door opened and a dark, curly head was popped in. It was Cherry, the welcome successor to Miss Bishop—Miss Knight.

"Did you say something?" said Cherry.

"I was speaking to myself," said Miss Marple; "I just wondered if I could ever be ruthless."

"What, you?" said Cherry. "Never! You're kindness itself."

"All the same," said Miss Marple, "I believe I *could* be ruthless if there was due cause."

"What would you call due cause?"

"In the cause of justice," said Miss Marple.

"You did have it in for little Gary Hopkins, I must say," said Cherry. "When you caught him torturing his cat that day. Never knew you had it in you to go for anyone like that! Scared him stiff, you did. He's never forgotten it."

"I hope he hasn't tortured any more cats."

"Well, he's made sure you weren't about if he did," said Cherry. "In fact I'm not at all sure as there isn't other boys as got scared. Seeing you with your wool and the pretty things you knits and all that—anyone would think you were gentle as a lamb. But there's times I could say you'd behave like a lion if you was goaded into it."

Miss Marple looked a little doubtful. She could not quite see herself in the role in which Cherry was now casting her. Had she ever—she paused on the reflection, recalling various moments—there had been intense irritation with Miss Bishop—Knight. (Really, she must *not* forget names in this way.) But her irritation had shown itself in more or less ironical remarks. Lions, presumably, did not use irony. There was nothing ironical about a lion. It sprang. It roared. It used its claws; presumably it took large bites at its prey.

"Really," said Miss Marple, "I don't think I have ever behaved quite like that."

Walking slowly along her garden that evening with the usual feelings of vexation rising in her, Miss Marple considered the point again. Possibly the sight of a plant of snap-dragons recalled it to her mind. Really, she had told old George again and again that she only wanted sulphur-colored antirrhinums, not that rather ugly purple shade that gardeners always seemed so fond of. "Sulphur yellow," said Miss Marple aloud.

Someone the other side of the railing that abutted on the lane past her house turned her head and spoke.

"I beg your pardon? You said something?"

"I was talking to myself, I'm afraid," said Miss Marple, turning to look over the railing.

This was someone she did not know, and she knew most people in St. Mary Mead. Knew them by sight even if not personally. It was a thick-set woman in a shabby but tough tweed skirt, and wearing good country shoes. She wore an emerald pullover and a knitted woolen scarf.

"I'm afraid one does at my age," added Miss Marple.

"Nice garden you've got here," said the other woman.

"Not particularly nice now," said Miss Marple. "When I could attend to it myself—"

"Oh, I know. I understand just what you feel. I suppose you've got one of those—I have a lot of names for them, mostly very rude—elderly chaps who say they know all about gardening. Sometimes they do, sometimes they don't know a thing about it. They come and have a lot of cups of tea and do a little very mild weeding. They're quite nice, some of them, but all the same it does make one's temper rise." She added, "I'm quite a keen gardener myself."

"Do you live here?" asked Miss Marple with some interest.

"Well, I'm boarding with a Mrs. Hastings. I think I've heard her speak of you. You're Miss Marple, aren't you?"

"Oh, yes."

"I've come as a sort of companion-gardener. My name is Bartlett, by the way. Miss Bartlett. There's not really much to do there," said Miss Bartlett. "She goes in for annuals and all that. Nothing you can really get your teeth into." She opened her mouth and showed her teeth when making this remark. "Of course I do a few odd jobs as well. Shopping, you know, and things like that. Anyway, if you want any time put in here, I could put in an hour or two for you. I'd say I might be better than any chap you've got now."

"That would be easy," said Miss Marple. "I like flowers best. Don't care so much for vegetables."

"I do vegetables for Mrs. Hastings. Dull but necessary. Well, I'll be getting along." Her eyes swept over Miss Marple from head to foot, as though memorizing her, then she nodded cheerfully and tramped off.

Mrs. Hastings? Miss Marple couldn't remember the name of any Mrs. Hastings. Certainly Mrs. Hastings was not an old friend. She had certainly never been a gardening chum. Ah, of course, it was probably those newly built houses at the end of Gibraltar Road. Several families had moved in in the last year. Miss Marple sighed, looked again with annoyance at the antirrhinums, saw several weeds which she yearned to root up, one or two exuberant suckers she would like to attack with her secateurs, and finally, sighing and manfully resisting temptation, she made a detour round by the lane and returned to her house. Her mind recurred again to Mr. Rafiel. They had been, he and she——what was the title of that book they used to quote so much when she was young? *Ships that pass in the night.* Rather apt it was, really, when she came to think of it. Ships that pass in the night . . . It was in the night that she had gone to him to ask—no, to demand—help. To insist, to say no time must be lost. And he had agreed, and put things in train at once! Perhaps she *had* been rather lionlike on that occasion? No. No, that was quite wrong. It had not been anger she had felt. It had been insistence on something that was absolutely imperative to be put in hand at once. And he'd understood.

Poor Mr. Rafiel. The ship that had passed in the night had been an interesting ship. Once you got so used to his being rude, he might have been quite an agreeable man. No! She shook her head. Mr. Rafiel could never have been an agreeable man. Well, she must put Mr. Rafiel out of her head.

> Ships that pass in the night, and speak each other in passing,
> Only a signal shown and a distant voice in the darkness.

She would probably never think of him again. She would look out perhaps to see if there was an obituary of him in *The Times.* But she did not think it was very likely. He was not a very well-known character, she thought. Not famous. He had just been very rich. Of course, many people did have obituaries in the paper just because they were very rich; but she thought that Mr. Rafiel's richness would possibly not have been of that kind. He had not been prominent in any great industry; he had not been a great financial genius or a noteworthy banker. He had just all his life made enormous amounts of money. . . .

2

CODE WORD NEMESIS

It was about a week or so after Mr. Rafiel's death that Miss Marple picked up a letter from her breakfast tray and looked at it for a moment before opening it. The other two letters that had come by this morning's post were bills, or just possibly receipts for bills. In either case they were not of any particular interest. This letter might be.

A London postmark, typewritten address, a long, good quality envelope. Miss Marple slit it neatly with the paper knife she always kept handy on her tray. It was headed Messrs. Broadribb and Schuster, Solicitors and Notaries Public, with an address in Bloomsbury. It asked her, in suitable courteous and legal phraseology, to call upon them one day in the following week, at their office, to discuss a proposition that might be to her advantage. Thursday, the twenty-fourth, was suggested. If that date was not convenient, perhaps she would let them know what date she would be likely to be in London in the near future. They added that they were the solicitors to the late Mr. Rafiel, with whom they understood that she had been acquainted.

Miss Marple frowned in some slight puzzlement. She got up rather more slowly than usual thinking about the letter she had received. She was escorted downstairs by Cherry, who was meticulous in hanging about in the hall so as to make sure that Miss Marple did not come to grief walking by herself down the staircase, which was of the old-fashioned kind that turned a sharp corner in the middle of its run.

"You take very good care of me, Cherry," said Miss Marple.

"Got to," said Cherry, in her usual idiom. "Good people are scarce."

"Well, thank you for the compliment," said Miss Marple, arriving safely with her last foot on the ground floor.

"Nothing the matter, is there?" asked Cherry. "You look a bit rattled like, if you know what I mean."

"No, nothing's the matter," said Miss Marple. "I had rather an unusual letter from a firm of solicitors."

"Nobody is suing you for anything, are they?" said Cherry, who was inclined to regard solicitors' letters as invariably associated with disaster of some kind.

"Oh, no, I don't think so," said Miss Marple. "Nothing of that kind. They just asked me to call upon them next week in London."

"Perhaps you've been left a fortune," said Cherry hopefully.

"That, I think, is very unlikely," said Miss Marple.

"Well, you never know," said Cherry.

Settling herself in her chair and taking her knitting out of its embroidered knitting bag, Miss Marple considered the possibility of Mr. Rafiel having left her a fortune. It seemed even more unlikely than when Cherry had suggested it. Mr. Rafiel, she thought, was not that kind of man.

It was not possible for her to go on the date suggested. She was attending a meeting of the Women's Institute to discuss the raising of a sum for building a small additional couple of rooms. But she wrote, naming a day in the following week. In due course her letter was answered and the appointment definitely confirmed. She wondered what Messrs. Broadribb and Schuster were like. The letter had been signed by J. R. Broadribb, who was, apparently, the senior partner. It was possible, Miss Marple thought, that Mr. Rafiel might have left her some small memoir or souvenir in his will. Perhaps some book on rare flowers that had been in his library and which he thought would please an old lady who was keen on gardening. Or perhaps a cameo brooch which had belonged to some great-aunt of his. She amused herself by these fancies. They were only fancies, she thought, because in either case it would merely be a case of the executors'—if these lawyers were the executors—forwarding her by post any such object. They would not have wanted an interview.

"Oh, well," said Miss Marple, "I shall know next Tuesday."

II

"Wonder what she'll be like," said Mr. Broadribb to Mr. Schuster, glancing at the clock as he did so.

"She's due in a quarter of an hour," said Mr. Schuster. "Wonder if she'll be punctual?"

"Oh, I should think so. She's elderly, I gather, and much more punctilious than the young scatterbrains of today."

"Fat or thin, I wonder?" said Mr. Schuster.

Mr. Broadribb shook his head.

"Didn't Rafiel ever describe her to you?" asked Mr. Schuster.

"He was extraordinarily cagey in everything he said about her."

"The whole thing seems very odd to me," said Mr. Schuster. "If we only knew a bit more about what it all meant . . ."

"It might be," said Mr. Broadribb thoughtfully, "something to do with Michael."

"What? After all these years? Couldn't be. What put that into your head? Did he mention—?"

"No, he didn't mention anything. Gave me no clue at all as to what was in his mind. Just gave me instructions."

"Think he was getting a bit eccentric and all that towards the end?"

"Not in the least. Mentally he was as brilliant as ever. His physical ill-health never affected his brain, anyway. In the last two months of his life he made an extra two hundred thousand pounds. Just like that."

"He had a flair," said Mr. Schuster with due reverence. "Certainly, he always had a flair."

"A great financial brain," said Mr. Broadribb, also in a tone of reverence suitable to the sentiment. "Not many like him, more's the pity."

A buzzer went on the table. Mr. Schuster picked up the receiver. A female voice said:

"Miss Jane Marple is here to see Mr. Broadribb by appointment."

Mr. Schuster looked at his partner, raising an eyebrow for an affirmative or a negative. Mr. Broadribb nodded.

"Show her up," said Mr. Schuster. And he added, "Now we'll see."

Miss Marple entered a room where a middle-aged gentleman with a thin, spare body and a long rather melancholy face rose to greet her. This apparently was Mr. Broadribb, whose appearance somewhat contradicted his name. With him was a rather younger middle-aged gentleman of definitely more ample proportions. He had black hair, small keen eyes and a tendency to a double chin.

"My partner, Mr. Schuster," Mr. Broadribb presented.

"I hope you didn't feel the stairs too much," said Mr. Schuster. "Seventy if she is a day—nearer eighty perhaps," he was thinking in his own mind.

"I always get a little breathless going upstairs."

"An old-fashioned building this," said Mr. Broadribb apologetically. "No lift. Ah, well, we are a very long-established firm and we don't go in for as many of the modern gadgets as perhaps our clients expect of us."

"This room has very pleasant proportions," said Miss Marple politely.

She accepted the chair that Mr. Broadribb drew forward for her. Mr. Schuster, in an unobtrusive sort of way, left the room.

"I hope that chair is comfortable," said Mr. Broadribb. "I'll pull that curtain slightly, shall I? You may feel the sun a little too much in your eyes."

"Thank you," said Miss Marple gratefully.

She sat there upright, as was her habit. She wore a light tweed suit, a string of pearls and a small velvet toque. To himself Mr. Broadribb was saying, "The Provincial Lady. A good type. Fluffy old girl. May be scatty—may not. Quite a shrewd eye. I wonder where Rafiel came across her? Somebody's aunt, perhaps, up from the country?" While these thoughts passed through his head, he was making the kind of introductory small talk relating to the weather, the unfortunate effects of late frosts early in the year and such other remarks as he considered suitable.

Miss Marple made the necessary responses and sat placidly awaiting the opening of preliminaries to the meeting.

"You will be wondering what all this is about," said Mr. Broadribb, shifting a few papers in front of him and giving her a suitable smile. "You've heard, no doubt, of Mr. Rafiel's death, or perhaps you saw it in the paper."

"I saw it in the paper," said Miss Marple.

"He was, I understand, a friend of yours."

"I met him first just over a year ago," said Miss Marple. "In the West Indies," she added.

"Ah. I remember. He went out there, I believe, for his health. It did him some good, perhaps, but he was already a very ill man, badly crippled, as you know."

"Yes," said Miss Marple.

"You knew him well?"

"No," said Miss Marple, "I would not say that. We were fellow visitors in a hotel. We had occasional conversations. I never saw him again after my return to England. I live very quietly in the country, you see, and I gather that he was completely absorbed in business."

"He continued transacting business right up—well, I could almost say right up to the day of his death," said Mr. Broadribb. "A very fine financial brain."

"I am sure that was so," said Miss Marple. "I realized quite soon that he was a—well, a very remarkable character altogether."

"I don't know if you have any idea—whether you've been given any idea at some time by Mr. Rafiel—as to what this proposition is that I have been instructed to put up to you?"

"I cannot imagine," said Miss Marple, "what possible kind of proposition Mr. Rafiel might have wanted to put up to me. It seems most unlikely."

"He had a very high opinion of you."

"That is kind of him, but hardly justified," said Miss Marple. "I am a very simple person."

"As you no doubt realize, he died a very rich man. The provisions of his will are on the whole fairly simple. He had already made dispositions of his fortune some time before his death. Trusts and other beneficiary arrangements."

"That is, I believe, very usual procedure nowadays," said Miss Marple, "though I am not at all cognizant of financial matters myself."

"The purpose of this appointment," said Mr. Broadribb, "is that I am instructed to tell you that a sum of money has been laid aside to become yours absolutely at the end of one year, but conditional on your accepting a certain proposition, with which I am to make you acquainted."

He took from the table in front of him a long envelope. It was sealed. He passed it across the table to her.

"It would be better, I think, that you should read for yourself of what this consists. There is no hurry. Take your time."

Miss Marple took her time. She availed herself of a small paper knife which Mr. Broadribb handed to her, slit up the envelope, took out the enclosure, one sheet of typewriting, and read it. She folded it up again, then reread it and looked at Mr. Broadribb.

"This is hardly very definite. Is there no more definite elucidation of any kind?"

"Not so far as I am concerned. I was to hand you this and tell you the amount of the legacy. The sum in question is twenty thousand pounds free of legacy duty."

Miss Marple sat looking at him. Surprise had rendered her speechless. Mr. Broadribb said no more for the moment. He was watching her closely. There was no doubt of her surprise. It was obviously the last thing Miss Marple had expected to hear. Mr. Broadribb wondered what her first words would be. She looked at him with the directness, the severity that one of his own aunts might have done. When she spoke, it was almost accusingly.

"That is a very large sum of money," said Miss Marple.

"Not quite so large as it used to be," said Mr. Broadribb (and just restrained himself from saying, "Mere chicken feed nowadays").

"I must admit," said Miss Marple, "that I am amazed. Frankly, quite amazed."

She picked up the document and read it carefully through again.

"I gather you know the terms of this?" she said.

"Yes. It was dictated to me personally by Mr. Rafiel."

"Did he not give you any explanation of it?"

"No, he did not."

"You suggested, I suppose, that it might be better if he did," said Miss Marple. There was a slight acidity in her voice now.

Mr. Broadribb smiled faintly.

"You are quite right. That is what I did. I said that you might find it difficult to—oh, to understand exactly what he was driving at."

"Very remarkable," said Miss Marple.

"There is no need, of course," said Mr. Broadribb, "for you to give me an answer now."

"No," said Miss Marple, "I should have to reflect upon this."

"It is, as you have pointed out, quite a substantial sum of money."

"I am old," said Miss Marple. "Elderly, we say, but old is a better word. Definitely old. It is both possible and indeed probable that I might not live as long as a year to earn this money, in the rather doubtful case that I *was* able to earn it."

"Money is not to be despised at any age," said Mr. Broadribb.

"I could benefit certain charities in which I have an interest," said Miss Marple, "and there are always people. People whom one wishes one could do a little something for but one's own funds do not admit of it. And then I will not pretend that there are not pleasures and desires—things that one has not been able to indulge in or to afford—I think Mr. Rafiel knew quite well that to be able to do so quite unexpectedly would give an elderly person a great deal of pleasure."

"Yes, indeed," said Mr. Broadribb. "A cruise abroad, perhaps? One of these excellent tours as arranged nowadays. Theatres, concerts—the ability to replenish one's cellars."

"My tastes would be a little more moderate than that," said Miss Marple. "Partridges," she said thoughtfully, "it is very difficult to get partridges nowadays, and they're very expensive. I should enjoy a partridge—a whole partridge—to myself, very much. A box of *marrons glacés* are an expensive taste which I cannot often gratify. Possibly a visit to the opera. It means a car to take one to Covent Garden and back, and the expense of a night in a hotel. But I must not indulge in idle chat," she said. "I will take this back with me and reflect upon it. Really, what on earth made Mr. Rafiel—you have no idea why he should have suggested this particular proposition, and why he should think that I could be of service to him in any way? He must have known that it was over a year, nearly two years since he had seen me and that I might have got much more feeble than I have, and much more unable to exercise such small talents as I might have. He was taking a risk. There are other people surely much better qualified to undertake an investigation of this nature?"

"Frankly, one would think so," said Mr. Broadribb, "but he selected you, Miss Marple. Forgive me if this is idle curiosity, but have you had—oh, how shall I put it?—any connection with crime or the investigation of crime?"

"Strictly speaking I should say no," said Miss Marple. "Nothing professional, that is to say. I have never been a probation officer or indeed sat as a magistrate on a bench or been connected in any way with a detective agency. To explain to you, Mr. Broadribb, which I think is only fair for me to do and which I think Mr. Rafiel ought to have done, to explain it in any way all I can say is that during our stay in the West Indies, we both, Mr. Rafiel and myself, had a certain connection with a crime that took place there. A rather unlikely and perplexing murder."

"And you and Mr. Rafiel solved it?"

"I should not put it quite like that," said Miss Marple. "Mr. Rafiel, by the force of his personality, and I, by putting together one or two obvious indications that came to my notice, were successful in preventing a second murder just as it was about to take place. I could not have done it alone; I was physically far too feeble. Mr. Rafiel could not have done it alone; he was a cripple. We acted as allies, however."

"Just one other question I should like to ask you, Miss Marple. Does the word 'Nemesis' mean anything to you?"

"Nemesis," said Miss Marple. It was not a question. A very slow and unexpected smile dawned on her face. "Yes," she said, "it does mean something to me. It meant something to me and it meant something to Mr. Rafiel. I said it to him, and he was much amused by my describing myself by that name."

Whatever Mr. Broadribb had expected, it was not that. He looked at Miss Marple with something of the same astonished surprise that Mr. Rafiel had once felt in a bedroom by the Caribbean sea. A nice and quite intelligent old lady. But really—Nemesis!

"You feel the same, I am sure," said Miss Marple.

She rose to her feet.

"If you should find or receive any further instructions in this matter, you will perhaps let me know, Mr. Broadribb. It seems to me extraordinary that there should not be something of that kind. This leaves me entirely in the dark really as to what Mr. Rafiel is asking me to do or try to do."

"You are not acquainted with his family, his friends, his—"

"No. I told you. He was a fellow traveller in a foreign part of the world.

We had a certain association as allies in a very mystifying matter. That is all." As she was about to go to the door, she turned suddenly and asked: "He had a secretary, Mrs. Esther Walters. Would it be infringing etiquette if I asked if Mr. Rafiel left her fifty thousand pounds?"

"His bequests will appear in the press," said Mr. Broadribb. "I can answer your question in the affirmative. Mrs. Walters' name is now Mrs. Anderson, by the way. She has remarried."

"I am glad to hear that. She was a widow with one daughter, and she was a very adequate secretary, it appears. She understood Mr. Rafiel very well. A nice woman. I am glad she has benefited."

That evening, Miss Marple, sitting in her straight-backed chair, her feet stretched out to the fireplace where a small wood fire was burning owing to the sudden cold spell which, as is its habit, can always descend on England at any moment selected by itself, took once more from the long envelope the document delivered to her that morning. Still in a state of partial unbelief, she read, murmuring the words here and there below her breath as though to impress them on her mind:

To Miss Jane Marple, resident in the village of St. Mary Mead.

This will be delivered to you after my death by the good offices of my solicitor, James Broadribb. He is the man I employ for dealing with such legal matters as fall in the field of my private affairs, not my business activities. He is a sound and trustworthy lawyer. Like the majority of the human race, he is susceptible to the sin of curiosity. I have not satisfied his curiosity. In some respects this matter will remain between you and myself. Our code word, my dear lady, is Nemesis. I don't think you will have forgotten in what place and in what circumstances you first spoke that word to me. In the course of my business activities over what is now quite a long life, I have learnt one thing about a man whom I wish to employ. He has to have a flair. A flair for the particular job I want him to do. It is not knowledge, it is not experience. The only word that describes it is *flair.* A natural gift for doing a certain thing.

You, my dear, if I may call you that, have a natural flair for justice, and that has led to your having a natural flair for crime. I want you to investigate a certain crime. I have ordered a certain sum to be placed so that if you accept this request and as a result of your investigation this crime is properly elucidated, the money will become yours absolutely. I have set aside a year for you to engage on this mission. You are not young, but you are, if I may say so, tough. I think I can trust a reasonable fate to keep you alive for a year at least.

I think the work involved will not be distasteful to you. You have a natural genius, I should say, for investigation. The necessary funds for what I may describe as working capital for making this investigation will be remitted to you during that period whenever necessary. I offer this to you as an alternative to what may be your life at present.

I envisage you sitting in a chair, a chair that is agreeable and comfortable for whatever kind or form of rheumatism from which you may suffer. All persons of your age, I consider, are likely to suffer from some form of rheumatism. If this ailment affects your knees or your back, it will not be easy for you to get about much and you will spend your time mainly in knitting. I see you, as I saw you once one night as I rose from sleep disturbed by your urgency, in a cloud of pink wool.

I envisage you knitting more jackets, head scarves and a good many other things of which I do not know the names. If you prefer to continue knitting, that is your decision. If you prefer to serve the cause of justice, I hope that you may at least find it interesting.

Let justice roll down like waters
And righteousness like an everlasting stream.

Amos.

3

MISS MARPLE TAKES ACTION

Miss Marple read this letter three times—then she laid it aside and sat frowning slightly while she considered the letter and its implications.

The first thought that came to her was that she was left with a surprising lack of definite information. Would there be any further information coming to her from Mr. Broadribb? Almost certainly she felt that there would be no such thing. That would not have fitted in with Mr. Rafiel's plan. Yet how on earth could Mr. Rafiel expect her to do anything, to take any course of action in a matter about which she knew nothing? It was intriguing. After a few minutes more for consideration, she decided that Mr. Rafiel had meant it to be intriguing. Her thoughts went back to him, for the brief time that she had known him. His disability, his bad temper, his flashes of brilliance, of occasional humour. He'd enjoy, she thought, teasing people. He had been enjoying, she felt, and this letter made it almost certain, baffling the natural curiosity of Mr. Broadribb.

There was nothing in the letter he had written her to give her the slightest clue as to what this business was all about. It was no help to her whatsoever. Mr. Rafiel, she thought, had very definitely not meant it to be of any help. He had had—how could she put it?—other ideas. All the same, she could not start out into the blue knowing nothing. This could almost be described as a crossword puzzle with no clues given. There would *have* to be clues. She would *have* to know what she was wanted to do, where she was wanted to go, whether she was to solve some problem sitting in her armchair and laying aside her knitting needles in order to concentrate better. Or did Mr. Rafiel intend her to take a plane or a boat to the West Indies or to South America or to some other specially directed spot? She would either have to find out for herself what it was she was meant to do, or else she would have to receive definite instructions. He might think she had sufficient ingenuity to guess at things, to ask questions, to find out that way. No, she couldn't quite believe that.

"If he does think that," said Miss Marple aloud, "he's gaga. I mean, he was gaga before he died."

But she didn't think Mr. Rafiel would have been gaga.

"I shall receive instructions," said Miss Marple. "But what instructions and when?"

It was only then that it occurred to her suddenly that without noticing it she had definitely accepted the mandate. She spoke aloud again, addressing the atmosphere.

"I believe in eternal life," said Miss Marple. "I don't know exactly where you are, Mr. Rafiel, but I have no doubt that you are *somewhere*—I will do my best to fulfill your wishes."

II

It was three days later when Miss Marple wrote to Mr. Broadribb. It was a very short letter, keeping strictly to the point.

Dear Mr. Broadribb,

I have considered the suggestion you made to me and I am letting you know that I have decided to accept the proposal made to me by the late Mr. Rafiel. I shall do my best to comply with his wishes, though I am not at all assured of success. Indeed, I hardly see how it is possible for me to be successful. I have been given no direct instructions in his letter and have not been—I think the term is briefed—in any way. If you have any further communication you are holding for me which sets out definite instructions, I should be glad if you will send it to me, but I imagine that as you have not done so, that is not the case.

I presume that Mr. Rafiel was of sound mind and disposition when he died? I think I am justified in asking if there has been recently in his life any criminal affair in which he might possibly have been interested, either in the course of his business or in his personal relations. Has he ever expressed to you any anger or dissatisfaction with some notable miscarriage of justice about which he felt strongly? If so, I think I should be justified in asking you to let me know about it. Has any relation or connection of his suffered some hardship, lately been the victim of some unjust dealing, or what might be considered as such?

I am sure you will understand my reasons for asking these things. Indeed, Mr. Rafiel himself may have expected me to do so.

III

Mr. Broadribb showed this to Mr. Schuster, who leaned back in his chair and whistled.

"She's going to take it on, is she? Sporting old bean," he said. Then he added, "I suppose she knows something of what it's all about, does she?"

"Apparently not," said Mr. Broadribb.

"I wish we did," said Mr. Schuster. "He was an odd cuss."

"A difficult man," said Mr. Broadribb.

"I haven't got the least idea," said Mr. Schuster, "have you?"

"No, I haven't," said Mr. Broadribb. He added, "He didn't want me to have, I suppose."

"Well, he's made things a lot more difficult by doing that. I don't see the least chance that some old girl from the country can interpret a dead man's brain and know what fantasy was plaguing him. You don't think he was leading her up the garden path? Having her on? Sort of joke, you know. Perhaps he thinks that she thinks she's the cat's whiskers at solving village problems, but he's going to teach her a sharp lesson—"

"No," said Mr. Broadribb, "I don't quite think that. Rafiel wasn't that type of man."

"He was a mischievous devil sometimes," said Mr. Schuster.

"Yes, but not—I think he was serious over this. *Something* was worrying him. In fact I'm quite sure something was worrying him."

"And he didn't tell you what it was or give you the least idea?"

"No, he didn't."

"Then how the devil can he expect—?" Schuster broke off.

"He can't really have expected anything to come of this," said Mr. Broadribb. "I mean, how is she going to set about it?"

"A practical joke, if you ask me."

"Twenty thousand pounds is a lot of money."

"Yes, but if he knows she can't do it?"

"No," said Mr. Broadribb. "He wouldn't have been as unsporting as all that. He must think she's got a chance of doing or finding out whatever it is."

"And what do we do?"

"Wait," said Mr. Broadribb. "Wait and see what happens next. After all, there has to be some development."

"Got some sealed orders somewhere, have you?"

"My dear Schuster," said Mr. Broadribb, "Mr. Rafiel had implicit trust in my discretion and in my ethical conduct as a lawyer. Those sealed instructions are to be opened only under certain circumstances, none of which has yet arisen."

"And never will," said Mr. Schuster.

That ended the subject.

IV

Mr. Broadribb and Mr. Schuster were lucky in so much as they had a full professional life to lead. Miss Marple was not so fortunate. She knitted and she reflected and she also went out for walks, occasionally remonstrated with by Cherry for so doing.

"You know what the doctor said. You weren't to take too much exercise."

"I walk very slowly," said Miss Marple, "and I am not doing anything. Digging, I mean, or weeding. I just—well, I just put one foot in front of the other and wonder about things."

"What things?" asked Cherry with some interest.

"I wish I knew," said Miss Marple, and asked Cherry to bring her an extra scarf as there was a chilly wind.

"What's fidgeting her, that's what I would like to know," said Cherry to her husband as she set before him a Chinese plate of rice and a concoction of kidneys. "Chinese dinner," she said.

Her husband nodded approval.

"You get a better cook every day," he said.

"I'm worried about her," said Cherry. "I'm worried because she's worried a bit. She had a letter and it stirred her all up."

"What she needs is to sit quiet," said Cherry's husband. "Sit quiet, take it easy, get herself new books from the library, get a friend or two to come and see her."

"She's thinking out something," said Cherry. "Sort of plan. Thinking out how to tackle something, that's how I look at it."

She broke off the conversation at this stage and took in the coffee tray and put it down by Miss Marple's side.

"Do you know a woman who lives in a new house somewhere here, she's called Mrs. Hastings?" asked Miss Marple. "And someone called Miss Bartlett, I think it is, who lives with her—?"

"What—do you mean the house that's been all done up and repainted at the end of the village? The people there haven't been there very long. I don't know what their names are. Why do you want to know? They're not very interesting. At least I shouldn't say they were."

"Are they related?" asked Miss Marple.

"No. Just friends, I think."

"I wonder why—" said Miss Marple, and broke off.

"You wondered why what?"

"Nothing," said Miss Marple. "Clear my little hand desk, will you, and give me my pen and the notepaper. I'm going to write a letter."

"Who to?" said Cherry with the natural curiosity of her kind.

"To a clergyman's sister," said Miss Marple. "His name is Canon Prescott."

"That's the one you met abroad in the West Indies, isn't it? You showed me his photo in your album."

"Yes."

"Not feeling bad, are you? Wanting to write to a clergyman and all that?"

"I'm feeling extremely well," said Miss Marple, "and I am anxious to get busy on something. It's just possible Miss Prescott might help."

Dear Miss Prescott, [wrote Miss Marple]

I hope you have not forgotten me. I met you and your brother in the West Indies, if you remember, at St. Honoré. I hope the dear Canon is well and did not suffer much with his asthma in the cold weather last winter.

I am writing to ask you if you can possibly let me have the address of Mrs. Walters—Esther Walters—whom you may remember from the Caribbean days. She was secretary to old Mr. Rafiel. She did give me her address at the time, but unfortuantely I have mislaid it. I was anxious to write to her, as I have some horticultural information which she asked me about but which I was not able to tell her at the time. I heard in a roundabout way the other day that she had married again, but I don't think my informant was very certain of these facts. Perhaps you know more about her than I do.

I hope this is not troubling you too much. With kind regards to your brother and best wishes to yourself,

Yours sincerely,
Jane Marple.

Miss Marple felt better when she had dispatched this missive.

"At least," she said, "I've started doing something. Not that I hope much for this, but still it might help."

Miss Prescott answered the letter almost by return of post. She was a most efficient woman. She wrote a pleasant letter and enclosed the address in question.

> I have not heard anything directly about Esther Walters, [she said] but like you I heard from a friend that they had seen a notice of her remarriage. Her name now is, I believe, Mrs. Alderson or Anderson. Her address in Winslow Lodge, near Alton, Hants. My brother sends his best wishes to you. It is sad that we live so far apart. We in the north of England and you south of London. I hope that we may meet on some occasion in the future.
>
> Yours sincerely,
> Joan Prescott.

"Winslow Lodge, Alton," said Miss Marple, writing it down. "Not so far away from here, really. No. Not so far away. I could—I don't know what would be the best method—possibly one of Inch's taxis. Slightly extravagant, but if anything results from it, it could be charged as expenses quite legitimately. Now do I write to her beforehand or do I leave it to chance? I think it would be better, really, to leave it to chance. Poor Esther. She could hardly remember me with any affection or kindliness."

Miss Marple lost herself in a train of thought that arose from her memories. It was quite possible that her actions in the Caribbean had saved Esther Walters from being murdered in the not-far-distant future. At any rate, that was Miss Marple's belief, but probably Esther Walters had not believed any such thing. "A nice woman," said Miss Marple, uttering the words in a soft tone aloud; "a very nice woman. The kind that would so easily marry a bad lot. In fact, the sort of woman that would marry a murderer if she were ever given half a chance. I still consider," continued Miss Marple thoughtfully, sinking her voice still lower, "that I probably saved her life. In fact, I am almost sure of it, but I don't think she would agree with that point of view. She probably dislikes me very much. Which makes it more difficult to use her as a source of information. Still, one can but try. It's better than sitting here waiting, waiting, waiting."

Was Mr. Rafiel perhaps making fun of her when he had written that letter? He was not always a particularly kindly man—he could be very careless of people's feelings.

"Anyway," said Miss Marple, glancing at the clock and deciding that she would have an early night in bed, "when one thinks of things just before going to sleep, quite often ideas come. It may work out that way."

"Sleep well?" asked Cherry as she put down an early morning tea tray on the table at Miss Marple's elbow.

"I had a curious dream," said Miss Marple.

"Nightmare?"

"No, no, nothing of that kind. I was talking to someone, not anyone I knew very well. Just talking. Then when I looked, I saw it wasn't that person at all I was talking to. It was somebody else. Very odd."

"Bit of a mixup," said Cherry helpfully.

"It just reminded me of something," said Miss Marple, "or rather of someone I once knew. Order Inch for me, will you? To come here about half-past eleven."

Inch was part of Miss Marple's past. Originally the proprietor of a cab, Mr. Inch had died, been succeeded by his son "Young Inch," then aged forty-four, who had turned the family business into a garage and acquired two aged cars. On his decease the garage acquired a new owner. There had been since then Pip's Cars, James's Taxis, and Arthur's Car Hire. Old inhabitants still spoke of Inch.

"Not going to London, are you?"

"No, I'm not going to London. I shall have lunch perhaps in Haslemere."

"Now what are you up to now?" said Cherry, looking at her suspiciously.

"Endeavouring to meet someone by accident and make it seem purely natural," said Miss Marple. "Not really very easy, but I hope that I can manage it."

At half-past eleven the taxi waited. Miss Marple instructed Cherry.

"Ring up this number, will you, Cherry? Ask if Mrs. Anderson is at home. If Mrs. Anderson answers or if she is going to come to the telephone, say a Mr. Broadribb wants to speak to her. You," said Miss Marple, "are Mr. Broadribb's secretary. If she's out, find out what time she will be in."

"And if she is in and I get her?"

"Ask what day she could arrange to meet Mr. Broadribb at his office in London next week. When she tells you make a note of it and ring off."

"The things you think of! Why all this? Why do you want me to do it?"

"Memory is a curious thing," said Miss Marple. "Sometimes one remembers a voice even if one hasn't heard it for over a year."

"Well Mrs. What's-a-name won't have heard mine at any time will she?"

"No," said Miss Marple. "That is why *you* are making the call."

Cherry fulfilled her instruction. Mrs. Anderson was out shopping she learned, but would be in for lunch and all the afternoon.

"Well, that makes things easier," said Miss Marple. "Is Inch here? Ah, yes. Good morning, Edward," she said to the present driver of Arthur's taxis, whose actual name was George. "Now this is where I want you to go. It ought not to take, I think, more than an hour and a half."

The expedition set off.

4

ESTHER WALTERS

Esther Walters came out of the supermarket and went towards where she had parked her car. Parking grew more difficult every day, she thought. She collided with somebody, an elderly woman limping a little who was walking towards her. She apologized, and the other woman made an exclamation.

"Why, indeed, it's—surely—it's Mrs. Walters, isn't it? Esther Walters? You don't remember me, I expect. Jane Marple. We met in the hotel in St. Honoré oh—quite a long time ago. A year and a half."

"Miss Marple? So it is, of course. Fancy seeing you!"

"How very nice to see you. I am lunching with some friends near here, but I have to pass back through Alton later. Will you be at home this afternoon? I should so like to have a nice chat with you. It's so nice to see an old friend."

"Yes, of course. Any time after three o'clock."

The arrangement was ratified.

"Old Jane Marple," said Esther Anderson, smiling to herself. "Fancy her turning up. I thought she'd died a long time ago."

Miss Marple rang the bell of Winslow Lodge at three-thirty precisely. Esther opened the door to her and brought her in.

Miss Marple sat down in the chair indicated to her, fluttering a little in the restless manner that she adopted when slightly flustered—or at any rate, when she was seeming to be slightly flustered. In this case it was misleading, since things had happened exactly as she had hoped they would happen.

"It's so nice to see you," she said to Esther. "So very nice to see you again. You know, I do think things are so very odd in this world. You hope you'll meet people again and you're quite sure you will. And then time passes and suddenly it's all such a surprise."

"And then," said Esther, "one says it's a small world, doesn't one?"

"Yes, indeed, and I think there is something in that. I mean, it does seem a very large world and the West Indies are such a very long way away from England. Well, I mean, of course I might have met you anywhere. In London or at Harrods. On a railway station or in a bus. There are so many possibilities."

"Yes, there are a lot of possibilities," said Esther. "I certainly shouldn't have expected to meet you just here, because this isn't really quite your part of the world, is it?"

"No. No, it isn't. Not that you're really so very far from St. Mary Mead where I live. Actually, I think it's only about twenty-five miles. But twenty-five miles in the country, when one hasn't got a car—and of course I couldn't afford a car, and anyway, I mean, I can't drive a car—so it wouldn't be much to the point, so one really only does see one's neighbours on the bus route, or else one goes by a taxi from the village."

"You're looking wonderfully well," said Esther.

"I was just going to say *you* were looking wonderfully well, my dear. I had no idea you lived in this part of the world."

"I have only done so for a short time. Since my marriage, actually."

"Oh, I didn't know. How interesting. I suppose I must have missed it. I always do look down the marriages."

"I've been married four or five months," said Esther. "My name is Anderson now."

"Mrs. Anderson," said Miss Marple. "Yes, I must try and remember that. And your husband?"

It would be unnatural, she thought, if she did not ask about the husband. Old maids were notoriously inquisitive.

"He is an engineer," said Esther. "He runs the Time and Motion Branch. He is"—she hesitated—"a little younger than I am."

"Much better," said Miss Marple immediately. "Oh, much better, my dear. In these days men age so much quicker than women. I know it used not to be said so, but actually it's true. I mean, they get more things the matter with them. I think, perhaps, they worry and work too much. And then they get high blood pressure or low blood pressure or sometimes a little heart trouble. They're rather prone to gastric ulcers, too. I don't think *we* worry so much, you know. I think we're a tougher sex."

"Perhaps we are," said Esther.

She smiled now at Miss Marple, and Miss Marple felt reassured. The last time she had seen Esther, Esther had looked as though she hated her, and probably she had hated her at that moment. But now, well, now perhaps she might even feel slightly grateful. She might have realized that she herself might even have been under a stone slab in a respectable churchyard instead of living a presumably happy life with Mr. Anderson.

"You look very well," she said, "and very gay."

"So do you, Miss Marple."

"Well, of course, I am rather older now. And one has so many ailments. I mean, not desperate ones, nothing of that kind, but I mean one has always some kind of rheumatism or some kind of ache and pain somewhere. One's feet are not what one would like feet to be. And there's usually one's back or a shoulder or painful hands. Oh, dear, one shouldn't talk about these things. What a very nice house you have."

"Yes, we haven't been in it very long. We moved in about four months ago."

Miss Marple looked round. She had rather thought that that was the case. She thought, too, that when they had moved in they had moved in on quite a handsome scale. The furniture was expensive, it was comfortable—comfortable and just this side of luxury. Good curtains, good covers, no particular artistic taste displayed, but then she would not have expected that. She thought she knew the reason for this appearance of prosperity. She thought it had come about on the strength of the late Mr. Rafiel's handsome legacy to Esther. She was glad to think that Mr. Rafiel had not changed his mind.

"I expect you saw the notice of Mr. Rafiel's death," said Esther, speaking almost as if she knew what was in Miss Marple's mind.

"Yes. Yes, indeed I did. It was about a month ago now, wasn't it? I was so sorry. Very distressed really, although, well, I suppose one knew—he almost admitted it himself, didn't he? He hinted several times that it wouldn't be very long. I think he was quite a brave man about it all, don't you?"

"Yes, he was a very brave man, and a very kind one really," said Esther. "He told me, you know, when I first worked for him, that he was going to give me a very good salary but that I would have to save out of it because I needn't expect to have anything more from him. Well, I certainly didn't expect to have anything more from him. He was very much a man of his word, wasn't he? But apparently he changed his mind."

"Yes," said Miss Marple. "Yes, I am very glad of that. I thought perhaps—not that he, of course, said anything—but I wondered."

"He left me a very big legacy," said Esther. "A surprisingly large sum of money. It came as a very great surprise. I could hardly believe it at first."

"I think he wanted it to be a surprise to you. I think he was perhaps that kind of man," said Miss Marple. She added: "Did he leave anything to—oh, what was his name?—the man attendant, the nurse-attendant?"

"Oh, you mean Jackson? No, he didn't leave anything to Jackson, but I believed he made him some handsome presents in the last year."

"Have you ever seen anything more of Jackson?"

"No. No, I don't think I've met him once since the time out in the islands. He didn't stay with Mr. Rafiel after they got back to England. I think he went to Lord Somebody who lives in Jersey or Guernsey."

"I would like to have seen Mr. Rafiel again," said Miss Marple. "It seems odd after we'd all been mixed up so. He and you and I and some others. And then, later, when I'd come home, when six months had passed—it occurred to me one day how closely associated we had been in our time of stress, and yet how little I really knew about Mr. Rafiel. I was thinking it only the other day, after I'd seen the notice of his death. I wished I could know a little more. Where he was born, you know, and his parents. What they were like. Whether he had any children or nephews or cousins or any family. I would so like to know."

Esther Anderson smiled slightly. She looked at Miss Marple and her expression seemed to say "Yes, I'm sure you always want to know everything of that kind about everyone you meet." But she merely said:

"No, there was really only one thing that everyone did know about him."

"That he was very rich," said Miss Marple immediately. "That's what you mean, isn't it? When you know that someone is very rich, somehow, well, you don't ask any more. I mean you don't ask to know any more. You say 'He is very rich' or you say 'He is enormously rich,' and your voice just goes down a little because it's so impressive, isn't it, when you meet someone who is immensely rich?"

Esther laughed slightly.

"He wasn't married, was he?" asked Miss Marple. "He never mentioned a wife."

"He lost his wife many years ago. About four or five years after they were married, I believe. I believe she was much younger than he was—I think she died of cancer. Very sad."

"Had he children?"

"Oh, yes, two daughters and a son. One daughter is married and lives in America. The other daughter died young, I believe. I met the American one once. She wasn't at all like her father. Rather a quiet, depressed-looking young woman." She added, "Mr. Rafiel never spoke about the son. I rather think that there had been trouble there. A scandal or something of that kind. I believe he died some years ago. Anyway, his father never mentioned him."

"Oh, dear. That was very sad."

"I think it happened quite a long time ago. I believe he took off for somewhere or other abroad and never came back—died out there, wherever it was."

"Was Mr. Rafiel very upset about it?"

"One wouldn't know with him," said Esther. "He was the kind of man who would always decide to cut his losses. If his son turned out to be unsatisfactory, a burden instead of a blessing, I think he would just shrug the whole thing off. Do what was necessary perhaps in the way of sending him money for support, but never thinking of him again."

"One wonders," said Miss Marple. "He never spoke of him or said anything?"

"If you remember, he was a man who never said anything much about personal feelings or his own life."

"No. No, of course not. But I thought perhaps, you having been—well, his secretary for so many years, that he might have confided any troubles to you."

"He was not a man for confiding troubles," said Esther. "If he had any, which I rather doubt. He was wedded to his business, one might say. He was father to his business and his business was the only kind of son or daughter that he had that mattered, I think. He enjoyed it all, investment, making money. Business coups—"

"Call no man happy until he is dead," murmured Miss Marple, repeating the words in the manner of one pronouncing them as a kind of slogan, which indeed they appeared to be in these days, or so she would have said.

"So there was nothing especially worrying him, was there, before his death?"

"No. Why should you think so?" Esther sounded surprised.

"Well, I didn't actually think so," said Miss Marple, "I just wondered because things do worry people more when they are—I won't say getting old—because he really wasn't old, but I mean things worry you more when you are laid up and can't do as much as you did and have to take things easy. Then worries just come into your mind and make themselves felt."

"Yes, I know what you mean," said Esther. "But I don't think Mr. Rafiel was like that. Anyway," she added, "I ceased being his secretary some time ago. Two or three months after I met Edmund."

"Ah, yes. Your husband. Mr. Rafiel must have been very upset at losing you."

"Oh, I don't think so," said Esther lightly. "He was not one who would be upset over that sort of thing. He'd immediately get another secretary—which he did. And then if she didn't suit him, he'd just get rid of her with a kindly golden handshake and get somebody else, till he found somebody who suited him. He was an intensely sensible man always."

"Yes. Yes, I can see that. Though he could lose his temper very easily."

"Oh, he enjoyed losing his temper," said Esther. "It made a bit of drama for him, I think."

"Drama," said Miss Marple thoughtfully. "Do you think—I have often wondered—do you think that Mr. Rafiel had any particular interest in criminology, the study of it, I mean? He—well, I don't know . . ."

"You mean because of what happened in the Caribbean?" Esther's voice had gone suddenly hard.

Miss Marple felt doubtful of going on and yet she must somehow or other try to get a little helpful knowledge.

"Well, no, not because of that, but afterwards, perhaps, he wondered about the psychology of these things. Or he got interested in the cases where justice had not been administered properly or—oh, well . . ."

She sounded more scatterbrained every minute.

"Why should he take the least interest in anything of that kind? And don't let's talk about that horrible business in St. Honoré."

"Oh, no, I think you are quite right. I'm sure I'm very sorry. I was just thinking of some of the things that Mr. Rafiel sometimes said. Queer turns of phrase, sometimes, and I just wondered if he had any theories, you know . . . about the causes of crime?"

"His interests were always entirely financial," said Esther shortly. "A really clever swindle of a criminal kind might have interested him, nothing else—"

She was looking coldly still at Miss Marple.

"I am sorry," said Miss Marple apologetically. "I—I shouldn't have talked about distressing matters that are fortunately past. And I must be getting on my way," she added. "I have got my train to catch and I shall only just have time. Oh, dear, what did I do with my bag? Oh, yes, here it is."

She collected her bag, umbrella and a few other things, fussing away until the tension had slightly abated. As she went out the door, she turned to Esther, who was urging her to stay and have a cup of tea.

"No, thank you, my dear, I'm so short of time. I'm very pleased to have seen you again and I do offer my best congratulations and hopes for a very happy life. I don't suppose you will be taking up any post again now, will you?"

"Oh, some people do. They find it interesting, they say. They get bored when they have nothing to do. But I think I shall rather enjoy living a life of leisure. I shall enjoy the legacy, too, that Mr. Rafiel left me. It was very kind of him and I think he'd want me—well, to enjoy it even if I spent it in what he'd think of perhaps as a rather silly, female way! Expensive clothes and a new hair-do and all that. He'd have thought that sort of thing very silly." She added suddenly, "I was fond of him, you know. Yes, I was quite fond of him. I think it was because he was a sort of challenge to me. He was difficult to get on with, and therefore I enjoyed managing it."

"And managing him?"

"Well, not quite managing him, but perhaps a little more than he knew I was."

Miss Marple trotted away down the road. She looked back once and waved her hand—Esther Anderson was still standing on the doorstep, and she waved back cheerfully.

"I thought this might have been something to do with her or something she knew about," said Miss Marple to herself. "I think I'm wrong. No. I don't think she's concerned in the business, whatever it is, in any way. Oh, dear, I feel Mr. Rafiel expected me to be much cleverer than I am being. I think he expected me to put things together—but what things? And what do I do next, I wonder?" She shook her head.

She had to think over things very carefully. This business had been, as it were, left to her. Left to her to refuse, to accept, to understand what it was all about? Or not to understand anything, but to go forward and hope that some kind of guidance might be given to her. Occasionally she closed her eyes and tried to picture Mr. Rafiel's face. Sitting in the garden of the hotel in the West Indies, in his tropical suit; his bad-tempered corrugated face, his flashes of occasional humour. What she really wanted to know was what had been in his mind when he worked up this scheme, when he set out to bring it about. To lure her into accepting it, to persuade her to accept it, to—well, perhaps one should say—to bully her into accepting it. The third was much the most likely, knowing Mr. Rafiel. And yet, take it that he had wanted something done and he had chosen her, settled upon her to do it. Why? Because she had suddenly come into his mind? But why should she have come into his mind?

She thought back to Mr. Rafiel and the things that had occurred at St. Honoré. Had perhaps the problems he had been considering at the time of his death sent his mind back to that visit to the West Indies? Was it in some way connected with someone who had been out there, who had taken part or been an onlooker there and was that what had put Miss Marple into his mind? Was there some link or some connection? If not, why should he suddenly think of her? What was it about her that could make her useful to him, in any way at all? She was an elderly, rather scatterbrained, quite ordinary person, physically not very strong, mentally not nearly as alert as she used to be. What had been her special qualifications, if any? She couldn't think of any. Could it possibly have been a bit of fun on Mr. Rafiel's part? Even if Mr. Rafiel had been on the point of death he might have wanted to have some kind of joke that suited his peculiar sense of humour.

She could not deny that Mr. Rafiel could quite possibly wish to have a joke, even on his deathbed. Some ironical humour of his might be satisfied.

"I must," said Miss Marple to herself firmly, "I must have some qualification for something." After all, since Mr. Rafiel was no longer in this world, he could not enjoy his joke at first hand. What qualifications had she got? "What qualities have I got that could be useful to anyone for *anything?"* said Miss Marple.

She considered herself with proper humility. She was inquisitive, she asked questions, she was the sort of age and type that could be expected to ask questions. That was one point, a possible point. You could send a private detective round to ask questions, or some psychological investigator, but it was true that you could much more easily send an elderly lady with a habit of snooping and being inquisitive, of talking too much, of wanting to find out about things, and it would seem perfectly natural.

"An old tabby," said Miss Marple to herself. "Yes, I can see I'm quite recognizable as an old tabby. There are so many old tabbies, and they're all so much alike. And, of course, yes, I'm very ordinary. An ordinary rather scatterbrained old lady. And that of course is very good camouflage. Dear me. I wonder if I'm thinking on the right lines? I do, sometimes, know what people are like. I mean, I know what people are like, because they remind me of certain other people I have known. So I know some of their faults and some of their virtues. I know what kind of people they are. There's that."

She thought again of St. Honoré and the Hotel of the Golden Palm. She had made one attempt to inquire into the possibilities of a link by her visit to Esther Walters. That had been definitely nonproductive, Miss Marple decided. There didn't seem any further link leading from there. Nothing that would tie up with his request that Miss Marple should busy herself with something, the nature of which she still had no idea!

"Dear me," said Miss Marple, "what a tiresome man you are, Mr. Rafiel!" She said it aloud and there was definite reproach in her voice.

Later, however, as she climbed into bed and applied her cozy hot water bottle to the most painful portion of her rheumatic back, she spoke again—in what might be taken as a semi-apology.

"I've done the best I could," she said.

She spoke aloud with the air of addressing one who might easily be in the room. It is true he might be anywhere, but even then there might be some telepathic or telephonic communication, and if so, she was going to speak definitely and to the point.

"I've done all I could. The best according to my limitations, and I must now leave it up to you."

With that she settled herself more comfortably, stretched out a hand, switched off the electric light, and went to sleep.

5

INSTRUCTIONS FROM BEYOND

It was some three or four days later that a communication arrived by the second post. Miss Marple picked up the letter, did what she usually did to letters, turned it over, looked at the stamp, looked at the handwriting, decided that it wasn't a bill and opened it. It was typewritten.

Dear Miss Marple,

By the time you read this, I shall be dead and also buried. Not cremated, I am glad to think. It has always seemed to me unlikely that one would manage to rise up from one's handsome bronze vase full of ashes and haunt anyone if one wanted so to do! Whereas the idea of rising from one's grave and haunting anyone is quite possible. Shall I want to do that? Who knows? I might even want to communicate with you.

By now my solicitors will have communicated with you and will have put a certain proposition before you. I hope you will have accepted it. If you have not accepted it, don't feel in the least remorseful. It will be your choice.

This should reach you, if my solicitors have done what they were told to do and if the posts have done the duty they are expected to perform, on the eleventh of the month. In two days from now you will receive a communication from a travel bureau in London. I hope what it proposes will not be distasteful to you. I needn't say more. I want you to have an open mind. Take care of yourself. I think you will manage to do that. You are a very shrewd person. The best of luck and may your guardian angel be at your side looking after you. You may need one.

The best of luck.

Your affectionate friend,
J. B. Rafiel

"Two days!" said Miss Marple.

She found it difficult to pass the time. The post office did their duty and so did the Famous Houses and Gardens of Great Britain.

Dear Miss Jane Marple,

Obeying instructions given us by the late Mr. Rafiel, we send you particulars of our Tour No. 37 of the Famous Houses and Gardens of Great Britain which starts from London on Thursday next—the seventeenth.

If it should be possible for you to come to our office in London, our Mrs. Sandbourne, who is to accompany the tour, will be very glad to give you all particulars and to answer all questions.

Our tours last for a period of two to three weeks. This particular tour, Mr. Rafiel thinks, will be particularly acceptable to you as it will visit a part of England which as far as he knows you have not yet visited, and takes in some really very attractive scenery and gardens. He has arranged for you to have the best accommodation and all the luxury available that we can provide.

Perhaps you will let us know which day would suit you to visit our office in Berkeley Street?

Miss Marple folded up the letter, put it in her bag, noted the telephone number, thought of a few friends whom she knew, rang up two of them, one of whom had been for tours with the Famous Houses and Gardens, and spoke highly of them, the other one had not been personally on a tour but had friends who had travelled with this particular firm and who said everything was very well done, though rather expensive, and not too exhausting for the elderly. She then rang up the Berkeley Street number and said she would call upon them on the following Tuesday.

The next day she spoke to Cherry on the subject.

"I may be going away, Cherry," she said. "On a tour."

"A tour?" said Cherry. "One of these travel tours? You mean a package tour abroad?"

"Not abroad. In this country," said Miss Marple. "Mainly visiting historic buildings and gardens."

"Do you think it's all right to do that at your age? These things can be very tiring, you know. You have to walk miles sometimes."

"My health is really very good," said Miss Marple, "and I have always heard that in these tours they are careful to provide restful intervals for people who are not particularly strong."

"Well, be careful of yourself, that's all," said Cherry. "We don't want you falling down with a heart attack, even if you are looking at a particularly sumptuous fountain or something. You're a bit old, you know, to do this sort of thing. Excuse me saying it, it sounds rude, but I don't like to think of you passing out because you've done too much or anything like that."

"I can take care of myself," said Miss Marple with some dignity.

"All right, but you just be careful," said Cherry.

Miss Marple packed a suitable bag, went to London, booked a room at a modest hotel. ("Ah, Bertram's Hotel," she thought in her mind, "what a wonderful hotel *that* was! Oh, dear, I must forget all those things; the St. George is quite a pleasant place.") At the appointed time she was in Berkeley Street and was shown into the office where a pleasant woman of about thirty-five rose to meet her, explained that her name was Mrs. Sandbourne and that she would be in personal charge of this particular tour.

"Am I to understand," said Miss Marple, "that this trip is in my case—?" She hesitated.

Mrs. Sandbourne, sensing slight embarrassment, said:

"Oh, yes, I ought to have explained perhaps better in the letter we sent you. Mr. Rafiel had paid all expenses."

"You do know that he is dead?" said Miss Marple.

"Oh, yes, but this was arranged before his death. He mentioned that he was in ill-health but wanted to provide a treat for a very old friend of his who had not had the opportunity of travelling as much as she could have wished."

II

Two days later, Miss Marple, carrying her small overnight bag, her new and smart suitcase surrendered to the driver, had boarded a most comfortable and luxurious coach which was taking a northwesterly route out of London. She studied the passenger list which was attached to the inside of a handsome brochure giving details of the daily itinerary of the coach, and various information as to hotels and meals, places to be seen, and occasional alternatives on some days which, although the fact was not stressed, actually intimated that one choice of itinerary was for the young and active and that the other would be peculiarly suitable for the elderly, those whose feet hurt them, who suffered from arthritis or rheumatism and who would prefer to sit about and not walk long distances or up too many hills. It was all very tactful and well arranged.

Miss Marple read the passenger list and surveyed her fellow passengers.

There was no difficulty about doing this because the other fellow passengers were doing much the same themselves. They were surveying her, among others, but nobody as far as Miss Marple could notice was taking any particular interest in her.

Mrs. Riseley-Porter
Miss Joanna Crawford
Colonel and Mrs. Walker
Mr. and Mrs. H. T. Butler
Miss Elizabeth Temple
Professor Wanstead
Mr. Richard Jameson
Miss Lumley
Miss Bentham
Mr. Caspar
Miss Cooke
Miss Barrow
Mr. Emlyn Price
Miss Jane Marple

There were four elderly ladies. Miss Marple took note of them first so, as it were, to clear them out of the way. Two were travelling together. Miss Marple put them down as about seventy. They could roughly be considered as contemporaries of her own. One of them was very definitely the complaining type, one who would want to have seats at the front of the coach or else would make a point of having them at the back of the coach. Would wish to sit on the sunny side or could only bear to sit on the shady side. Who would want more fresh air or less fresh air. They had with them travelling rugs and knitted scarves and quite an assortment of guidebooks. They were slightly crippled and often in pain from feet or backs or knees, but were nevertheless of those whom age and ailments could not prevent from enjoying life while they still had it. Old girls, but definitely not stay-at-home old girls. Miss Marple made an entry in the little book she carried.

Fifteen passengers not including herself or Mrs. Sandbourne. And since she had been sent on this coach tour, one at least of those fifteen passengers must be of importance in some way. Either as a source of information or someone concerned with the law or a law case, or it might even be a murderer—a murderer who might have already killed or one who might be preparing to kill. Anything was possible, Miss Marple thought, with Mr. Rafiel! Anyway, she must make notes of these people.

On the right-hand page of her notebook she would note down who might be worthy of attention from Mr. Rafiel's point of view and on the left she would note down or cross off those who could only be of any interest if they could produce some useful information for her—information, it might be, that they did not even know they possessed. Or rather that even if they possessed it, they did not know it could possibly be useful to her or to Mr. Rafiel or to the law or to Justice with a capital "J." At the back of her little book, she might this evening make a note or two as to whether anyone had reminded her of characters she had known in the past at St. Mary Mead and other places. Any similarities might make a useful pointer. It had done so on other occasions.

The other two elderly ladies were apparently separate travellers. Both of them were about sixty. One was a well-preserved, well-dressed woman of obvious social importance in her own mind, but probably in other people's minds as well. Her voice was loud and dictatorial. She appeared to have in tow a niece, a girl of about eighteen or nineteen who addressed her as Aunt Geraldine. The niece, Miss Marple noted, was obviously well accustomed to coping with Aunt Geraldine's bossiness. She was a competent girl as well as being an attractive one.

Across the aisle from Miss Marple was a big man with square shoulders and a clumsy-looking body, looking as though he had been carelessly assembled by an ambitious child out of chunky bricks. His face looked as though nature had planned it to be round but the face had rebelled at this and decided to achieve a square effect by developing a powerful jaw. He had a thick head of greyish hair and enormous bushy eyebrows which moved up and down to give point to what he was saying. His remarks seemed mainly to come out in a series of barks as though he was a talkative sheep dog. He shared his seat with a tall dark foreigner who moved restlessly in his seat and gesticulated freely. He spoke a most peculiar English, making occasional remarks in French and German. The bulky man seemed quite capable of meeting these onslaughts of foreign languages, and shifted obligingly to either French or German. Taking a quick glance at them again, Miss Marple decided that the bushy eyebrows must be Professor Wanstead and the excitable foreigner was Mr. Caspar.

She wondered what it was they were discussing with such animation, but was baffled by the rapidity and force of Mr. Caspar's delivery.

The seat in front of them was occupied by the other woman of about sixty, a tall woman, possibly over sixty, but a woman who would have stood out in a crowd anywhere. She was still a very handsome woman with dark grey hair coiled high on her head, drawn back from a fine forehead. She had a low, clear, incisive voice. A personality, Miss Marple thought. Someone! Yes, she was decidedly someone. "Reminds me," she thought to herself, "of Dame Emily Waldron." Dame Emily Waldron had been the principal of an Oxford college and a notable scientist, and Miss Marple, having once met her in her nephew's company, had never quite forgotten her.

Miss Marple resumed her survey of the passengers. There were two married couples, one American, middle-aged, amiable, a talkative wife and a placidly agreeing husband. They were obviously dedicated travellers and sightseers. There was also an English middle-aged couple whom Miss Marple noted down without hesitation as a retired military man and wife. She ticked them off from the list as Colonel and Mrs. Walker.

In the seat behind her was a tall, thin man of about thirty with a highly technical vocabulary, clearly an architect. There were also two middle-aged ladies travelling together rather further up the coach. They were discussing the brochure and deciding what the tour was going to hold for them in the way of attractions. One was dark and thin and the other was fair and sturdily built and the latter's face seemed faintly familiar to Miss Marple. She wondered where she had seen or met her before. However, she could not recall the occasion to mind. Possibly someone she had met at a cocktail party or sat opposite to in a train. There was nothing very special about her to remember.

Only one more passenger remained for her to appraise, and this was a young man, possibly of about nineteen or twenty. He wore the appropriate clothes for his age and sex: tight black jeans, a polo-necked purple sweater and his head was an outsize rich mop of undisciplined black hair. He was looking with an air of interest at the bossy woman's niece, and the bossy woman's niece also, Miss Marple thought, was looking with some interest at him. In spite of the preponderance of old girls and middle-aged females there were, at any rate, two young people among the passengers.

They stopped for lunch at a pleasant riverside hotel, and the afternoon sightseeing was given over to Blenheim. Miss Marple had already visited Blenheim twice before, so she saved her feet by limiting the amount of sightseeing indoors and coming fairly soon to the enjoyment of the gardens and the beautiful view.

By the time they arrived at the hotel where they were to stay the night, the passengers were getting to know each other. The efficient Mrs. Sandbourne, still brisk and unwearied by her duties in directing the sightseeing, did her part very well; creating little groups by adding anyone who looked as if he or she were left out to one or other of them, murmuring, "You must make Colonel Walker describe his garden to you. Such a wonderful collection of fuchsias he has." With such little sentences she drew people together.

Miss Marple was now able to attach names to all the passengers. Bushy eyebrows turned out to be Professor Wanstead, as she had thought, and the foreigner was Mr. Caspar. The bossy woman was Mrs. Riseley-Porter and her neice was called Joanna Crawford. The young man with the hair was Emlyn Price, and he and Joanna Crawford appeared to be finding out that certain things in life, such as decided opinions, they had in common, on economics, art, general dislikes, politics and such topics.

The two eldest ladies graduated naturally to Miss Marple as a kindred old girl. They discussed happily arthritis, rheumatism, diets, new doctors, remedies both professional, patent, and reminiscences of old wives' treatments which had had success where all else failed. They discussed the many tours they had been on to foreign places in Europe; hotels, travel agencies and finally the County of Somerset where Miss Lumley and Miss Bentham lived, and where the difficulties of getting suitable gardeners could hardly be believed.

The two middle-aged ladies travelling together turned out to be Miss Cooke and Miss Barrow. Miss Marple still felt that one of these two, the fair one, Miss Cooke, was faintly familiar to her, but she still could not remember where she had seen her before. Probably it was only her fancy. It might also be just fancy, but she could not help feeling that Miss Barrow and Miss Cooke appeared to be avoiding her. They seemed rather anxious to move away if she approached. That, of course, might be entirely her imagination.

Fifteen people, one of whom at least must matter in some way. In casual conversation that evening she introduced the name of Mr. Rafiel, so as to note if anyone reacted in any way. Nobody did.

The handsome woman was identified as Miss Elizabeth Temple, who was the retired headmistress of a famous girls' school. Nobody appeared to Miss Marple likely to be a murderer, except possibly Mr. Caspar, and that was probably foreign prejudice. The thin young man was Richard Jameson, an architect.

"Perhaps I shall do better tomorrow," said Miss Marple to herself.

III

Miss Marple went to bed definitely tired out. Sightseeing was pleasant but exhausting, and trying to study fifteen or sixteen people at once and wondering as you did so which of them could possibly be connected with a murder was even more exhausting. It had a touch of such unreality about it that one could not, Miss Marple felt, take it seriously. These seemed to be all perfectly nice people, the sort of people who go on cruises and on tours and all the rest of it. However, she took another quick and cursory glance at the passenger list, making a few little entries in her notebook.

Mrs. Riseley-Porter? Not connected with crime. Too social and self-centred.

Niece, Joanna Crawford? The same? But very efficient.

Mrs. Riseley-Porter, however, might have information of some kind which Miss Marple might find had a bearing on matters. She must keep on agreeable terms with Mrs. Riseley-Porter.

Miss Elizabeth Temple? A personality. Interesting. She did not remind Miss Marple of any murderer she'd ever known. "In fact," said Miss Marple to herself, "she really radiates integrity. *If* she had committed a murder, it would be a very popular murder. Perhaps for some noble reason or for some reason that she thought noble." But that wasn't satisfactory either. Miss Temple, she thought, would always know what she was doing and why she was doing it and would not have any silly ideas about nobility when merely evil existed. "All the same," said Miss Marple, "she's *someone* and she might—she just might be a person Mr. Rafiel wanted me to meet for some reason." She jotted down these thoughts on the right-hand side of her notebook.

She shifted her point of view. She had been considering a possible murderer—what about a prospective victim? Who was a possible victim? No one very likely. Perhaps Mrs. Riseley-Porter might qualify—rich—rather disagreeable. The efficient niece might inherit. She and the anarchistic Emlyn Price might combine in the cause of anti-capitalism. Not a very credible idea, but no other feasible murderee seemed to offer.

Professor Wanstead? An interesting man, she was sure. Kindly, too. Was he a scientist or was he medical? She was not as yet sure, but she put him down on the side of science. She herself knew nothing of science, but it seemed not at all unlikely.

Mr. and Mrs. Butler? She wrote them off. Nice Americans. No connections with anyone in the West Indies or anyone she had known. No, she didn't think that the Butlers could be relevant.

Richard Jameson? That was the thin architect. Miss Marple didn't see how architecture could come into it, though it might, she supposed. A priest's hole, perhaps? One of the houses they were going to visit might have a priest's hole which would contain a skeleton. And Mr. Jameson, being an architect, would know just where the priest's hole was. He might aid her to discover it, or she might aid him to discover it and then they would find a body. "Oh, really," said Miss Marple, "what nonsense I am talking and thinking."

Miss Cooke and Miss Barrow? A perfectly ordinary pair. And yet she'd certainly seen one of them before. At least she'd seen Miss Cooke before. Oh, well, it would come to her, she supposed.

Colonel and Mrs. Walker? Nice people. Retired army folk. Served abroad mostly. Nice to talk to, but she didn't think there'd be anything for her there.

Miss Bentham and Miss Lumley? The old girls. Unlikely to be criminals, but, being elderly, they might know plenty of gossip, or have some information, or might make some illuminating remark even if it happened to come about in connection with rheumatism, arthritis or patent medicine.

Mr. Caspar? Possibly a dangerous character. Very excitable. She would keep him on the list for the present.

Emlyn Price? A student presumably. Students were very violent. Would Mr. Rafiel have sent her on the track of a student? Well, it would perhaps depend on what the student had done or wished to do or was going to do. A dedicated anarchist, perhaps.

"Oh, dear," said Miss Marple, suddenly exhausted, "I must go to bed."

Her feet ached, her back ached and her mental reactions were not, she thought, at their best. She slept at once. Her sleep was enlivened by several dreams.

One where Professor Wanstead's bushy eyebrows fell off because they were not his own eyebrows, but false ones. As she woke again, her first impression was that which so often follows dreams—a belief that the dream in question had solved everything—"Of course," she thought, "of *course!*" His eyebrows were false and that solved the whole thing. He was the criminal.

Sadly, it came to her that nothing was solved. Professor Wanstead's eyebrows coming off was of no help at all.

Unfortunately now she was no longer sleepy. She sat up in bed with some determination.

She sighed and slipped on her dressing gown, moved from her bed to an upright chair, took a slightly larger notebook from her suitcase and started work.

"The project I have undertaken," she wrote, "is connected certainly with crime of some kind. Mr. Rafiel has distinctly stated that in his letter. He said I had a flair for justice and that necessarily included a flair for crime. So crime is involved, and it is presumably not espionage or fraud or robbery, because such things have never come my way and I have no connection with such things, or knowledge of them, or special skills. What Mr. Rafiel knows of me is only what he knew during the period of time when we were both in St. Honoré. We were connected there with a murder.

Murders as reported in the press have never claimed any attention. I have never read books on criminology as a subject or really been interested in such a thing. No, it has just happened that I have found myself in the vicinity of murder rather more often than would seem normal. My attention had been directed to murders involving friends or acquaintances. These curious coincidences of connections with special subjects seem to happen to people in life. One of my aunts, I remember, was on five occasions shipwrecked and a friend of mine was what I believe is officially called accident-prone. I know some of her friends refused to ride in a taxi with her. She had been in four taxi accidents and three car accidents and two railway accidents. Things like this seem to happen to certain people for no appreciable reason. I do not like to write it down, but it does appear that murders seem to happen in my vicinity."

Miss Marple paused, changed her position, put a cushion in her back, and continued:

"I must try to make as logical a survey as I can of this project which I have undertaken. My instructions, or my 'briefing,' as naval friends of mine put it, are so far quite inadequate. Practically nonexistent. So I must ask myself one clear question. What is all this *about?* Answer! *I do not know.* Curious and interesting. An odd way for a man like Mr. Rafiel to go about things, especially when he was a successful business and financial operator. He wants me to guess, to employ my instinct, to observe and to obey such directions as are given to me or are hinted to me.

"So: Point 1. Direction will be given me. Direction from a dead man. Point 2. What is involved in my problem is *justice.* Either to set right an injustice or to avenge evil by bringing it to justice. This is in accord with the code word Nemesis given to me by Mr. Rafiel.

"After explanations of the principle involved, I received my first factual directive. It was arranged by Mr. Rafiel before his death that I was to go on Tour No. 37 of Famous Houses and Gardens. Why? That is what I have to ask myself. Is it for some geographical or territorial reason? A correction or a clue? Some particular famous house? Or something involving some particular garden or landscape connected? This seems unlikely. The more likely explanation lies in the *people* or one of the people on this particular coach party. None of them is known to me personally, but one of them at least must be connected with the riddle I have to solve. Somebody among our group is connected or concerned with a murder. Somebody has information or a special link with the victim of a crime, or someone personally is himself or herself a murderer—a murderer as yet unsuspected."

Miss Marple stopped here suddenly. She nodded her head. She was satisfied now with her analysis so far as it went.

And so to bed.

Miss Marple added to her notebook:

"Here endeth the First Day."

6

LOVE

The following morning they visited a small Queen Anne manor house. The drive there had not been very long or tiring. It was a very charming-looking house and had an interesting history as well as a very beautiful and unusually laid-out garden.

Richard Jameson, the architect, was full of admiration for the structural beauty of the house and being the kind of young man who is fond of hearing his own voice, he slowed down in nearly every room that they went through, pointing out very special moulding or fireplace, and giving historical dates and references. Some of the group, appreciative at first, began to get slightly restive, as the somewhat monotonous lecturing went on. Some of them began to edge carefully away and fall behind the party. The local caretaker, who was in charge, was not himself too pleased by having his occupation usurped by one of the sightseers. He made a few efforts to get matters back into his own hands, but Mr. Jameson was unyielding. The caretaker made a last try.

"In this room, ladies and gentlemen, the White Parlour, folks call it, is where they found a body. A young man it was, stabbed with a dagger, lying on the hearth-rug. Way back in seventeen hundred and something it was. It was said that the Lady Moffatt of that day had a lover. He came through a small side door and up a steep staircase to this room through a loose panel there was to the left of the fireplace. Sir Richard Moffatt, her husband, you see, was said to be across the seas in the Low Countries. But he came home, and in he came unexpectedly and caught 'em there together."

He paused proudly. He was pleased at the response from his audience, glad of a respite from the architectural details which they had been having forced down their throats.

"Why, isn't that just too romantic, Henry?" said Mrs. Butler in her resonant trans-Atlantic tones. "Why, you know, there's quite an atmosphere in this room. I feel it. I certainly can feel it."

"Mamie is very sensitive to atmospheres," said her husband proudly to those around him. "Why, once when we were in an old house down in Louisiana . . ."

The narrative of Mamie's special sensitivity got into its swing, and Miss Marple and one or two others seized their opportunity to edge gently out of the room and down the exquisitely moulded staircase to the ground floor.

"A friend of mine," said Miss Marple to Miss Cooke and Miss Barrow, who were next to her, "had a most nerve-racking experience only a few years ago. A dead body on their library floor one morning."

"One of the family?" asked Miss Barrow. "An epileptic fit?"

"Oh, no, it was murder. A strange girl in evening dress. A blonde. But her hair was dyed. She was really a brunette; and—oh . . ." Miss Marple broke off, her eyes fixed on Miss Cooke's yellow hair where it escaped from her headscarf.

It had come to her suddenly. She knew why Miss Cooke's face was familiar and she knew where she had seen her before. But when she had seen her then, Miss Cooke's hair had been dark—almost black. And now it was bright yellow.

Mrs. Riseley-Porter, coming down the stairs, spoke decisively as she pushed past them and completed the staircase and turned into the hall.

"I really cannot go up and down any more of those stairs," she declared, "and standing around in these rooms is very tiring. I believe the gardens here, although not extensive, are quite celebrated in horticultural circles. I suggest we go there without loss of time. It looks as though it might cloud over before long. I think we shall get rain before the morning is out."

The authority with which Mrs. Riseley-Porter could enforce her remarks had its usual result. All those near at hand or within hearing followed her obediently out through French doors in the dining room into the garden. The gardens had indeed all that Mrs. Riseley-Porter had claimed for them. She herself took possession firmly of Colonel Walker and set off briskly. Some of the others followed them; others took paths in the opposite direction.

Miss Marple herself made a determined beeline for a garden seat which appeared to be of comfortable proportions as well as of artistic merit. She sank down on it with relief, and a sigh matching her own was emitted by Miss Elizabeth Temple as she followed Miss Marple and came to sit beside her on the seat.

"Going over houses is always tiring," said Miss Temple. "The most tiring thing in the world. Especially if you have to listen to an exhaustive lecture in each room."

"Of course all that we were told is very interesting," said Miss Marple rather doubtfully.

"Oh, do you think so?" said Miss Temple. Her head turned slightly and her eyes met those of Miss Marple. Something passed between the two women, a kind of rapport—of understanding tinged with mirth.

"Don't you?" asked Miss Marple.

"No," said Miss Temple.

This time the understanding was definitely established between them. They sat there companionably in silence. Presently Elizabeth Temple began to talk about gardens, and this garden in particular. "It was designed by Holman," she said, "somewhere about eighteen hundred or seventeen ninety-eight. He died young. A pity. He had great genius."

"It is so sad when anyone dies young," said Miss Marple.

"I wonder," said Elizabeth Temple.

She said it in a curious, meditative way.

"But they miss so much," said Miss Marple. "So many things."

"Or escape so much," said Miss Temple.

"Being as old as I am now," said Miss Marple, "I suppose I can't help feeling that early death means missing things."

"And I," said Elizabeth Temple, "having spent nearly all my life among the young, look at life as a period in time complete in itself. What did T. S. Eliot say: *The moment of the rose and the moment of the yew tree are of equal duration.*"

Miss Marple said, "I see what you mean . . . A life of whatever length is a complete experience. But don't you"—she hesitated—"ever feel that a life could be incomplete because it has been cut unduly short?"

"Yes, that is so."

Miss Marple said, looking at the flowers near her, "How beautiful peonies are. That long border of them—so proud and yet so beautifully fragile."

Elizabeth Temple turned her head towards her.

"Did you come on this trip to see the houses or to see gardens?" she asked.

"I suppose really to see the houses," said Miss Marple. "I shall enjoy the gardens most, though, but the houses—they will be a new experience for me. Their variety and their history, and the beautiful old furniture and the pictures." She added: "A kind friend gave me this trip as a gift. I am very grateful. I have not seen very many big and famous houses in my life."

"A kind thought," said Miss Temple.

"Do you often go on these sightseeing tours?" asked Miss Marple.

"No. This is not for me exactly a sightseeing tour."

Miss Marple looked at her with interest. She half opened her lips to speak but refrained from putting a question. Miss Temple smiled at her.

"You wonder why I am here, what my motive is, my reason. Well, why don't you make a guess?"

"Oh, I wouldn't like to do that," said Miss Marple.

"Yes, do do so." Elizabeth Temple was urgent. "It would interest me. Yes, really interest me. Make a guess."

Miss Marple was silent for quite a few moments. Her eyes looked at Elizabeth Temple steadily, ranging over her thoughtfully in her appraisement. She said:

"This is not from what I know about you or what I have been told about you. I know that you are quite a famous person and that your school is a very famous one. No. I am only making my guess from what you look like. I should write you down as a pilgrim. You have the look of one who is on a pilgrimage."

There was a silence and then Elizabeth said:

"That describes it very well. Yes. I am on a pilgrimage."

Miss Marple said after a moment or two:

"The friend who sent me on this tour and paid all my expenses is now dead. He was a Mr. Rafiel, a very rich man. Did you by any chance know him?"

"Jason Rafiel? I know him by name, of course. I never knew him personally, or met him. He gave a large endowment once to an educational project in which I was interested. I was very grateful. As you say, he was a very wealthy man. I saw the notice of his death in the papers a few weeks ago. So he was an old friend of yours?"

"No," said Miss Marple. "I had met him just over a year ago abroad. In the West Indies. I never knew much about him. His life or his family or any personal friends that he had. He was a great financier but otherwise, or so people always said, he was a man who was very reserved about himself. Did you know his family or anyone . . ." Miss Marple paused. "I often wondered, but one does not like to ask questions and seem inquisitive."

Elizabeth was silent for a minute—then she said:

"I knew a girl once—a girl who had been a pupil of mine at Fallowfield, my school. She was no actual relation to Mr. Rafiel, but she was at one time engaged to marry Mr. Rafiel's son."

"But she didn't marry him?" Miss Marple asked.

"No."

"Why not?"

Miss Temple said:

"One might hope to say—like to say—because she had too much sense.

He was not the type of a young man one would want anyone one was fond of to marry. She was a very lovely girl and a very sweet girl. I don't know why she didn't marry him. Nobody has ever told me." She sighed and then said, "Anyway, she died . . ."

"Why did she die?" said Miss Marple.

Elizabeth Temple stared at the peonies for some minutes. When she spoke, she uttered one word. It echoed like the tone of a deep bell—so much so that it was startling.

"Love!" she said.

Miss Marple queried the word sharply. "Love?"

"One of the most frightening words there is in the world," said Elizabeth Temple.

Again her voice was bitter and tragic

"Love . . ."

7

AN INVITATION

Miss Marple decided to miss out on that afternoon's sightseeing. She admitted to being somewhat tired and would perhaps give a miss to an ancient church and its fourteenth-century glass. She would rest for a while and join them at the tearoom which had been pointed out to her on the main street. Mrs. Sandbourne agreed that she was being very sensible.

Miss Marple, resting on a comfortable bench outside the tearoom, reflected on what she planned to do next and whether it would be wise to do it or not.

When the others joined her at teatime, it was easy for her to attach herself unobtrusively to Miss Cooke and Miss Barrow and sit with them at a table for four. The fourth chair was occupied by Mr. Caspar, whom Miss Marple considered as not sufficiently conversant with the English language to matter.

Leaning across the table as she nibbled a slice of Swiss roll, Miss Marple said to Miss Cooke:

"You know, I am quite sure we have met before. I have been wondering and wondering about it—I'm not as good as I was at remembering faces, but I'm sure I have met you somewhere."

Miss Cooke looked kindly but doubtful. Her eyes went to her friend, Miss Barrow. So did Miss Marple's. Miss Barrow showed no signs of helping to probe the mystery.

"I don't know if you've ever stayed in my part of the world," went on Miss Marple. "I live in St. Mary Mead. Quite a small village, you know. At least, not so small nowadays, there is so much building going on everywhere. Not very far from Much Benham and only twelve miles from the coast at Loomouth."

"Oh," said Miss Cooke, "let me see. Well, I know Loomouth quite well and perhaps—"

Suddenly Miss Marple made a pleased exclamation.

"Why, of course! I was in my garden one day at St. Mary Mead and you spoke to me as you were passing by on the footpath. You said you were staying down there, I remember, with a friend—"

"Of course," said Miss Cooke. "How stupid of me. I do remember you now. We spoke of how difficult it was nowadays to get anyone—to do job gardening, I mean—anyone who was any *use.*"

"Yes. You were not living there, I think? You were staying with someonc."

"Yes, I was staying with . . . with . . ." For a moment Miss Cooke hesitated, with the air of one who hardly knows or remembers a name.

"With a Mrs. Sutherland, was it?" suggested Miss Marple.

"No, no, it was . . . er . . . Mrs.—"

"Hastings," said Miss Barrow firmly as she took a piece of chocolate cake.

"Oh, yes, in one of the new houses," said Miss Marple.

"Hastings," said Mr. Caspar unexpectedly. He beamed. "I have been to Hastings—I have been to Eastbourne, too." He beamed again. "Very nice —by the sea."

"Such a coincidence," said Miss Marple, "meeting again so soon—such a small world, isn't it?"

"Oh, well, we are all so fond of gardens," said Miss Cooke vaguely.

"Flowers very pretty," said Mr. Caspar. "I like very much—" He beamed again.

"So many rare and beautiful shrubs," said Miss Cooke.

Miss Marple went full speed ahead with a gardening conversation of some technicality—Miss Cooke responded. Miss Barrow put in an occasional remark.

Mr. Caspar relapsed into smiling silence.

Later, as Miss Marple took her usual rest before dinner, she conned over what she had collected. Miss Cooke had admitted being in St. Mary Mead. She had admitted walking past Miss Marple's house. Had agreed it was quite a coincidence. Coincidence? thought Miss Marple meditatively, turning the word over in her mouth rather as a child might do to a certain lollipop to decide its flavour. Was it a coincidence? Or had she had some reason to come there? Had she been sent there? Sent there—for what reason? Was that a ridiculous thing to imagine?

"Any coincidence," said Miss Marple to herself, "is always worth noticing. You can throw it away later if it *is* only a coincidence."

Miss Cooke and Miss Barrow appeared to be a perfectly normal pair of friends doing the kind of tour which, according to them, they did every year. They had been on an Hellenic cruise last year and a tour of bulbs in

Holland the year before, and Northern Ireland the year before that. They seemed perfectly pleasant and ordinary people. But Miss Cooke, she thought, had for a moment looked as though she were about to disclaim her visit to St. Mary Mead. She had looked at her friend Miss Barrow rather as though she were seeking instruction as to what to say. Miss Barrow was presumably the senior partner.

"Of course, really, I may have been imaginging all these things," thought Miss Marple. "They may have no significance whatever."

The word *danger* came unexpectedly into her mind. Used by Mr. Rafiel in his first letter—and there had been some reference to her needing a guardian angel in his second letter. Was she going into danger in this business?—and why? From whom?

Surely not from Miss Cooke and Miss Barrow. Such an ordinary-looking couple.

All the same Miss Cook *had* dyed her hair and altered her style of hairdressing. Disguised her appearance as much as she could, in fact. Which was odd, to say the least of it! She considered once more her fellow travellers.

Mr. Caspar, now, it would have been much easier to imagine that *he* might be dangerous. Did he understand more English than he pretended to do? She began to wonder about Mr. Caspar.

Miss Marple had never quite succeeded in abandoning her Victorian view of foreigners. One never *knew* with foreigners. Quite absurd, of course, to feel like that—she had many friends from various foreign countries. All the same . . . Miss Cooke, Miss Barrow, Mr. Caspar, that young man with the wild hair—Emlyn Something—a revolutionary—a practising anarchist? Mr. and Mrs. Butler—such nice Americans—but perhaps too good to be true?

"Really," said Miss Marple, "I must pull myself together."

She turned her attention to the itinerary of their trip. Tomorrow, she thought, was going to be rather strenuous. A morning's sightseeing drive, starting rather early; a long, rather athletic walk on a coastal path in the afternoon. Certain interesting marine flowering plants. It would be tiring. A tactful suggestion was appended. Anyone who felt like a rest could stay behind in their hotel, the Golden Boar, which had a very pleasant garden, or could do a short excursion which would only take an hour to a beauty spot nearby. She thought perhaps that she would do that.

But though she did not know it then, her plans were to be suddenly altered.

As Miss Marple came down from her room in the Golden Boar the next day after washing her hands before luncheon, a woman in a tweed coat and skirt came forward rather nervously and spoke to her.

"Excuse me, are you Miss Marple—Miss Jane Marple?"

"Yes, that is my name," said Miss Marple, slightly surprised.

"My name is Mrs. Glynne. Lavinia Glynne. I and my two sisters live near here and—well, we heard you were coming, you see—"

"You heard I was coming?" said Miss Marple with some slight surprise.

"Yes. A very old friend of ours wrote to us—oh, quite some time ago, it must have been three weeks ago, but he asked us to make a note of this date. The date of the Famous Houses and Gardens Tour. He said that a great friend of his—or a relation, I'm not quite sure which would be on that tour."

Miss Marple continued to look surprised.

"I'm speaking of a Mr. Rafiel," said Mrs. Glynne.

"Oh! Mr. Rafiel," said Miss Marple. "You—you know that—?"

"That he died? Yes. So sad. Just after his letter came. I think it must have been certainly very soon after he wrote to us. But we felt a special urgency to try to do what he had asked. He suggested, you know, that perhaps you would like to come and stay with us for a couple of nights. This part of the tour is rather strenuous. I mean, it's all right for the young people but it is very trying for anyone older. It involves several miles of walking and a certain amount of climbing up difficult cliff paths and places. My sisters and I would be so very pleased if you could come and stay in our house here. It is only ten minutes' walk from the hotel and I'm sure we could show you many interesting things locally."

Miss Marple hesitated a minute. She liked the look of Mrs. Glynne, plump, good-natured, and friendly though a little shy. Besides—here again must be Mr. Rafiel's instructions—the next step for her to take? Yes, it must be so.

She wondered why she felt nervous. Perhaps because she was now at home with the people in the tour, felt part of the group although as yet she had only known them for three days.

She turned to where Mrs. Glynne was standing, looking up at her anxiously.

"Thank you—it is most kind of you. I shall be very pleased to come."

8

THE THREE SISTERS

Miss Marple stood looking out of a window. Behind her, on the bed, was her suitcase. She looked out over the garden with unseeing eyes. It was not often that she failed to see a garden she was looking at in either a mood of admiration or a mood of criticism. In this case it would presumably have been criticism. It was a neglected garden, a garden on which little money had been spent possibly for some years, and on which very little work had been done. The house, too, had been neglected. It was well proportioned, the furniture in it had been good furniture once, but had had little in late years of polishing or attention. It was not a house, she thought, that had been, at any rate of late years, loved in any way. It lived up to its name: The Old Manor House—a house, built with grace and a certain amount of beauty, lived in once, cherished. The daughters and sons had married and left and now it was lived in by Mrs. Glynne who, from a word she had let fall when she showed Miss Marple up to the bedroom appointed to her, had inherited it with her sisters from an uncle and had come here to live with her sisters after her husband had died. They had all grown older, their incomes had dwindled, labour had been more difficult to get.

The other sisters, presumably, had remained unmarried, one older, one younger than Mrs. Glynne, two Miss Bradbury-Scotts.

There was no sign of anything which belonged to a child in the house. No discarded ball, no old perambulator, no little chair or a table. This was just a house with three sisters.

"Sounds very Russian," murmured Miss Marple to herself. She did mean the Three Sisters, didn't she? Chekhov, was it? or Dostoevski? Really, she couldn't remember. Three sisters. But these would certainly not be the kind of three sisters who were yearning to go to Moscow. These three sisters were presumably, she was almost sure they were, content to remain where they were. She had been introduced to the other two who had come, one out of the kitchen and one down a flight of stairs to welcome her. Their manners were well bred and gracious. They were what Miss Marple would have called in her youth by the now obsolete term "ladies"—and what she once recalled calling "decayed ladies." Her father had said to her: "No, dear Jane, not *decayed*. Distressed gentlewomen."

Gentlewomen nowadays were not so liable to be distressed. They were aided by government or by societies or by a rich relation. Or, perhaps—by someone like Mr. Rafiel. Because, after all, that was the whole point, the whole reason for her being here, wasn't it? Mr. Rafiel had arranged all this. He had taken, Miss Marple thought, a good deal of trouble about it. He had known presumably, some four or five weeks before his death, just when that death was likely to be, give and take a little, since doctors were usually moderately optimistic, knowing from experience that patients who ought to die within a certain period very often took an unexpected lease of life and lingered on, still doomed, but obstinately declining to take the final step. On the other hand, hospital nurses when in charge of patients had, Miss Marple thought from her experience, always expected the patients to be dead the next day, and were much surprised when they were not. But in voicing their gloomy views to Doctor, when he came, they were apt to receive in reply as the doctor went out of the hall door a private aside of "Linger a few weeks yet, I shouldn't wonder." Very nice of Doctor to be so optimistic, Nurse would think, but surely Doctor was wrong. Doctor very often wasn't wrong. He knew that people who were in pain, helpless, crippled, even unhappy, still liked living and wanted to live. They would take one of Doctor's pills to help them pass the night, but they had no intention of taking a few more than necessary of Doctor's pills just in order to pass the threshold to a world that they did not as yet know anything about!

Mr. Rafiel. That was the person Miss Marple was thinking about as she looked across the garden with unseeing eyes. Mr. Rafiel? She felt now that she was getting a little closer to understanding the task laid upon her, the project suggested to her. Mr. Rafiel was a man who made plans. Made them in the same way that he planned financial deals and takeovers. In the words of her servant Cherry, he had had a problem. When Cherry had a problem, she often came and consulted Miss Marple about it.

"This was a problem that Mr. Rafiel could not deal with himself, which must have annoyed him very much," Miss Marple thought, "because he could usually deal with any problem himself and insisted on doing so. But he was bedridden and dying. He could arrange his financial affairs, communicate with his lawyers, with his employees and with such friends and relations as he had, but there was something or someone that he had not arranged for. A problem he had not solved, a problem he still wanted to solve, a project he still wanted to bring about. And apparently it was not one that could be settled by financial aid, by business dealings, by the services of a lawyer.

"So he thought of me," said Miss Marple.

It still surprised her very much. Very much indeed. However, in the sense she was now thinking of it, his letter had been quite explicit. He had thought she had certain qualifications for doing something. It had to do, she thought once again, with something in the nature of crime or affected by crime. The only other thing he knew about Miss Marple was that she was devoted to gardens. Well, it could hardly be a gardening problem that he wanted her to solve. But he might think of her in connection with crime—crime in the West Indies and crimes in her own neighbourhood at home. A crime—where?

Mr. Rafiel had made arrangements. Arrangements, to begin with, with his lawyers. They had done their part. At the right interval of time they had forwarded to her his letter. It had been, she thought, a well-considered and well-thought-out letter. It would have been simpler, certainly, to tell her exactly what he wanted her to do and why he wanted it done. She was surprised in a way that he had not, before his death, sent for her, probably in a somewhat peremptory way and more or less lying on what he would have assured her was his deathbed, and would then have bullied her until she consented to do what he was asking her. But no, that would not really have been Mr. Rafiel's way, she thought. He could bully people, none better, but this was not a case for bullying, and he did not wish either, she was sure, to appeal to her, to beg her to do him a favour, to urge her to redress a wrong. No. That again would not have been Mr. Rafiel's way. He wanted, she thought, as he had probably wanted all his life, to pay for what he required. He wanted to pay her and therefore he wanted to interest her enough to enjoy doing certain work. The pay was offered to intrigue her, not really to tempt her. It was to arouse her interest. She did not think that he had said to himself, "Offer enough money and she'll leap at it," because, as she knew very well herself, the money sounded very agreeable but she was not in urgent need of money. She had her dear and affectionate nephew who, if she was in straits for money of any kind, if she needed repairs to her house or visits to a specialist or special treats, dear Raymond would always provide them. No. The sum he offered was to be exciting. It was to be exciting in the same way as it was exciting when you had a ticket for the Irish Sweep. It was a fine big sum of money that you could never achieve by any other means except luck.

But all the same, Miss Marple thought to herself, she would need some luck as well as hard work, she would require a lot of thought and pondering and possibly what she was doing might involve a certain amount of danger. But she'd got to find out herself what it was all about, he wasn't going to tell her, partly perhaps because he did not want to influence her? It is hard to tell anyone about something without letting slip your own point of view about it. It could be that Mr. Rafiel had thought that his own point of view might be wrong. It was not very like him to think such a thing, but it could be possible. He might suspect that his judgment, impaired by illness, was not quite as good as it used to be. So she, Miss Marple, his agent, his employee, was to make her own guesses, come to her own conclusions. Well, it was time she came to a few conclusions now. In other words, back to the old question, *What was all this about?*

She had been directed. Let her take that first. She had been directed by a man who was now dead. She had been directed away from St. Mary Mead. Therefore, the task, whatever it must be, could not be attacked from there. It was not a neighbourhood problem, it was not a problem that you could solve just by looking through newspaper cuttings or making inquiries, not, that is, until you found what you had to make inquiries about. She had been directed, first to the lawyer's office, then to read a letter—two letters—in her home, then to be sent on a pleasant and well-run tour round some of the Famous Houses and Gardens of Great Britain. From that she had come to the next stepping-stone—the house she was in at this moment. The old Manor House, Jocelyn St. Mary, where lived Miss Clotilde Bradbury-Scott, Mrs. Glynne and Miss Anthea Bradbury-Scott. Mr. Rafiel had arranged that, arranged it beforehand—some weeks before he died. Probably it was the next thing he had done after instructing his lawyers and after booking a seat on the tour in her name. Therefore, she was in this house for a purpose. It might be for only two nights, it might be for longer. There might be certain things arranged which would lead her to stay longer or she would be asked to stay longer. That brought her back to where she stood now.

Mrs. Glynne and her two sisters. They must be concerned, implicated in whatever this was. She would have to find out what it was. The time was short. That was the only trouble. Miss Marple had no doubt for one moment that she had the capacity to find out things. She was one of those chatty, fluffy old ladies whom other people expect to talk, to ask questions that were, on the face of it, merely gossipy questions. She would talk about her childhood and that would lead to one of the sisters talking about theirs. She'd talk about food she had eaten, servants she had had, daughters and cousins and relations, travel, marriages, births and—yes—deaths. There must be no show of special interest in her eyes when she heard about a death. Not at all. Almost automatically she was sure she could come up with the right response such as, "Oh, dear me, how *very* sad!" She would have to find out relationships, incidents, life stories, see if any suggestive incidents would pop up, so to speak. It might be some incidents in the neighbourhood, not directly concerned with these three people. Something they could know about, or were pretty sure to talk about. Anyway, there would be *something* here, some clue, some pointer. The second day from now she would rejoin the tour. Her mind swept from the house to the coach and the people who had sat in it. It might be that what she was seeking had been there in the coach, and would be there again when she rejoined it. One person, several people, some innocent (some not so innocent), some long past story. She frowned a little, trying to remember something—something that had flashed in her mind that she had thought: Really, I am sure—of what had she been sure?

Her mind went back to the three sisters. She must not be too long up here. She must unpack a few modest needs for two nights, something to change into this evening, nightclothes, sponge bag, and then go down and rejoin her hostesses and make pleasant talk. A main point had to be decided. Were the three sisters to be her allies or were the three sisters enemies? They might fall into either category. She must think about that carefully.

There was a tap on the door and Mrs. Glynne entered.

"I do hope you will be quite comfortable here. Can I help you unpack? We have a very nice woman, Janet, who comes in, but she is only here in the morning. But she'll help you with anything."

"Oh, no, thank you," said Miss Marple. "I only took out just a few necessities."

"I thought I'd show you the way downstairs again. It's rather a rambling house, you know. There are two staircases and it does make it a little difficult. Sometimes people lose their way."

"Oh, it's very kind of you," said Miss Marple.

"I hope then you will come downstairs and we will have a glass of sherry before lunch."

Miss Marple accepted gratefully and followed her guide down the stairs. Mrs. Glynne, she judged, was a good many years younger than she herself was. Fifty, perhaps. Not much more. Miss Marple negotiated the stairs carefully; her left knee was always a little uncertain. There was, however, a banister at one side of the stairs. Very beautiful stairs they were, and she remarked on them.

"It is really a very lovely house," she said. "Built I suppose in the seventeen hundreds. Am I right?"

"Seventeen eighty," said Mrs. Glynne.

She seemed pleased with Miss Marple's appreciation. She took Miss

Marple into the drawing room, a large graceful room. There were one or two rather beautiful pieces of furniture. A Queen Anne desk and a William and Mary oystershell bureau. There were also some rather cumbrous Victorian settees and cabinets. The curtains were of chintz, faded and somewhat worn, the carpet was, Miss Marple thought, Irish. Possibly a Limerick Aubusson type. The sofa was ponderous and the velvet of it much worn. The other two sisters were already sitting there. They rose as Miss Marple came in and approached her, one with a glass of sherry, the other directing her to a chair.

"I don't know whether you like sitting rather high? So many people do."

"I do," said Miss Marple. "It's so much easier. One's back, you know."

The sisters appeared to know about the difficulties of backs. The eldest of the sisters was a tall, handsome woman, dark with a black coil of hair. The other one might have been a good deal younger. She was thin, with grey hair that had once been fair hanging untidily on her shoulders and a faintly wraithlike appearance. She could be cast successfully as a mature Ophelia, Miss Marple thought.

Clotilde, Miss Marple thought, was certainly no Ophelia, but she would have made a magnificent Clytemnestra—she could have stabbed a husband in his bath with exultation. But since she had never had a husband, that solution wouldn't do. Miss Marple could not see her murdering anyone else but a husband—there had been no Agamemnon in this house.

Clotilde Bradbury-Scott, Anthea Bradbury-Scott, Lavinia Glynne. Clotilde was handsome, Lavinia was plain but pleasant-looking, Anthea had one eyelid which twitched from time to time. Her eyes were large and grey and had an odd way of glancing round to right and then to left, and then suddenly in a rather strange manner, behind her over her shoulder. It was as though she felt someone was watching her all the time. Odd, thought Miss Marple. She wondered a little about Anthea.

They sat down and conversation ensued. Mrs. Glynne left the room apparently for the kitchen. She was, it seemed, the active domestic one of the three. The conversation took a usual course. Clotilde Bradbury-Scott explained that the house was a family one. It had belonged to her great-uncle and then to her uncle, and when he had died it was left to her and her two sisters, who had joined her there.

"He only had one son you see," explained Miss Bradbury-Scott, "and he was killed in the war. We are really the last of the family, except for some very distant cousins."

"A beautifully proportioned house," said Miss Marple. "Your sister tells me it was built about seventeen eighty."

"Yes, I believe so. One could wish, you know, it was not quite so large and rambling."

"Repairs, too," said Miss Marple, "come very heavy nowadays."

"Oh, yes, indeed," Clotilde sighed. "And in many ways we have had to let a lot of it just fall down. Sad, but there it is. A lot of the outhouses, for instance, and a greenhouse. We had a very beautiful big greenhouse."

"Lovely muscat grapevine in it," said Anthea. "And cherry pie used to grow all along the walls inside. Yes, I really regret that very much. Of course, during the war one could not get any gardeners. We had a very young gardener and then he was called up. One does not of course grudge that, but all the same it was impossible to get things repaired and so the whole greenhouse fell down."

"So did the little conservatory near the house."

Both sisters sighed with the sighing of those who have noted time passing and times changing—but not for the better.

There was a melancholy here in this house, thought Miss Marple. It was impregnated somehow with sorrow—a sorrow that could not be dispersed or removed since it had penetrated too deep. It had sunk in. . . . She shivered suddenly.

9

POLLYGONUM BALDSCHUANICUM

The meal was conventional. A small joint of mutton, roast potatoes, followed by a plum tart with a small jug of cream and rather indifferent pastry. There were a few pictures round the dining-room wall, family pictures, Miss Marple presumed, Victorian portraits without any particular merit, the sideboard was large and heavy, a handsome piece of plum-coloured mahogany. The curtains were of dark crimson damask and at the big mahogany table ten people could easily have been seated.

Miss Marple chatted about the incidents of the tour in so far as she had been on it. As this, however, had only been three days, there was not very much to say.

"Mr. Rafiel, I suppose, was an old friend of yours?" said the eldest Miss Bradbury-Scott.

"Not really," said Miss Marple. "I met him first when I was on a cruise to the West Indies. He was out there for his health, I imagine."

"Yes, he had been very crippled for some years," said Anthea.

"Very sad," said Miss Marple. "Very sad indeed. I really admired his fortitude. He seemed to manage to do so much work. Every day, you know, he dictated to his secretary and was continually sending off cables. He did not seem to give in at all kindly to being an invalid."

"Oh, no, he wouldn't," said Anthea.

"We have not seen much of him of late years," said Mrs. Glynne. "He was a busy man, of course. He always remembered us at Christmas very kindly."

"Do you live in London, Miss Marple?" asked Anthea.

"Oh, no," said Miss Marple. "I live in the country. A very small place halfway between Loomouth and Market Basing. About twenty-five miles from London. It used to be a very pretty Old-world village but of course like everything else, it is becoming what they call developed nowadays." She added, "Mr. Rafiel, I suppose, lived in London? At least I noticed that in the St. Honoré hotel register his address was somewhere in Eaton Square, I think, or was it Belgrave Square?"

"He had a country house in Kent," said Clotilde. "He used to entertain there, I think, sometimes. Business friends, mostly, you know, or people from abroad. I don't think any of us ever visited him there. He nearly always entertained us in London on the rare occasions when we happened to meet."

"It was very kind of him," said Miss Marple, "to suggest to you that you should invite me here during the course of this tour. Very thoughtful. One wouldn't really have expected a busy man such as he must have been to have had such kindly thoughts."

"We have invited before friends of his who have been on these tours. On the whole they are very considerate the way they arrange these things. It is impossible, of course, to suit everybody's taste. The young ones naturally wish to walk, to make long excursions, to ascend hills for a view, and all that sort of thing. And the older ones who are not up to it, remain in the hotels, but hotels round here are not really at all luxurious. I am sure you would have found today's trip and the one to St. Bonaventure tomorrow, also, very fatiguing. Tomorrow I believe there's a visit to an island, you know, in a boat, and sometimes it can be very rough."

"Even going round houses can be very tiring," said Mrs. Glynne.

"Oh, I know," said Miss Marple. "So much walking and standing about. One's feet get very tired. I suppose, really, I ought not to take these expeditions, but it is such a temptation to see beautiful buildings and fine rooms and furniture. All these things. And of course some splendid pictures."

"And the gardens," said Anthea. "You like gardens, don't you?"

"Oh, yes," said Miss Marple, "specially the gardens. From the description in the prospectus I am really looking forward very much to seeing some of the finely kept gardens of the historic houses we have still to visit." She beamed round the table.

It was all very pleasant, very natural, and yet she wondered why for some reason she had a feeling of strain—a feeling that there was something unnatural here. But what did she mean by unnatural? The conversation was ordinary enough, consisting mainly of platitudes. She herself was making conventional remarks and so were the three sisters.

The Three Sisters, thought Miss Marple, once again considering that phrase. Why did anything thought of in threes somehow seem to suggest a sinister atmosphere? The Three Sisters. The Three Witches of Macbeth. Well, one could hardly compare these three sisters to the three witches.

Although Miss Marple had always thought at the back of her mind that the theatrical producers made a mistake in the way in which they produced the three witches. One production which she had seen, indeed, seemed to her quite absurd. The witches had looked more like pantomime creatures with flapping wings and ridiculously spectacular steeple hats. They had danced and slithered about. Miss Marple remembered saying to her nephew, who was standing her this Shakespearean treat, "You know, Raymond, my dear, if *I* were ever producing this splendid play, I would make the three witches *quite* different. I would have them three ordinary, normal old women. Old Scottish women. They wouldn't dance or caper. They would look at each other rather slyly and you would feel a sort of menace just behind the ordinariness of them."

Miss Marple helped herself to the last mouthful of plum tart and looked across the table at Anthea. Ordinary, untidy, very vague-looking, a bit scatterbrained. Why should she feel that Anthea was sinister?

"I am imagining things," said Miss Marple to herself. "I mustn't do that."

After luncheon she was taken on a tour of the garden. It was Anthea who was deputed to accompany her. It was, Miss Marple thought, rather a sad progress. Here, there had once been a well-kept though certainly not in any way an outstanding or remarkable garden. It had had the elements of an ordinary Victorian garden. A shrubbery, a drive of speckled laurels, no doubt there had once been a well-kept lawn and paths, a kitchen garden of about an acre and a half, too big evidently for the three sisters who lived here now. Part of it was unplanted and had gone largely to weeds. Ground elder had taken over most of the flower beds and Miss Marple's hands could hardly restrain themselves from pulling up the vagrant bindweed asserting its superiority.

Miss Anthea's long hair flapped in the wind, shedding from time to time a vague hairpin on the path or the grass. She talked rather jerkily.

"You have a very nice garden, I expect," she said.

"Oh, it's a very small one," said Miss Marple.

They had come along a grass path and were pausing in front of a kind of hillock that rested against the wall at one end of it.

"Our greenhouse," said Miss Anthea mournfully.

"Oh, yes, where you had such a delightful grapevine."

"Three vines," said Anthea. "A black Hamburg and one of those small white grapes, very sweet, you know. And a third one of beautiful muscats."

"And a heliotrope, you said."

"Cherry pie," said Anthea.

"Ah, yes, cherry pie. Such a lovely smell. Was there any bomb trouble round here? Did that—er—knock the greenhouse down?"

"Oh, no, we never suffered from anything of that kind. This neighbourhood was quite free of bombs. No, I'm afraid it just fell down from decay. We hadn't been here so very long and we had no money to repair it or to build it up again. And, in fact, it wouldn't have been worth it, really, because we couldn't have kept it up even if we did. I'm afraid we just let it fall down. There was nothing else we could do. And now you see, it's all grown over."

"Ah, that, completely covered by—what it that flowering creeper just coming into bloom?"

"Oh, yes. It's quite a common one," said Anthea. "It begins with a P. Now what is the name of it," she said doubtfully. "Poly something, something like that."

"Oh, yes. I think I do know the name. Polygonum Baldschuanicum. Very quick-growing, I think, isn't it? Very useful, really, if one wants to hide any tumble-down building or anything ugly of that kind."

The mound in front of her was certainly thickly covered with the all-enveloping green and white flowering plant. It was, as Miss Marple well knew, a kind of menace to anything else that wanted to grow. Polygonum covered everything, and covered it in a remarkably short time.

"The greenhouse must have been quite a big one," she said.

"Oh, yes—we had peaches in it, too—and nectarines." Anthea looked miserable.

"It looks really very pretty now," said Miss Marple in a consoling tone. "Very pretty little white flowers, aren't they?"

"We have a very nice magnolia tree down this path to the left," said Anthea. "Once I believe there used to be a very find border here—a herbaceous border. But that again one cannot keep up. It is too difficult. Everything is too difficult. Nothing is like it used to be—it's all spoilt—everywhere."

She led the way quickly down a path at right angles which ran along a side wall. Her pace had increased. Miss Marple could hardly keep up with her. It was, thought Miss Marple, as though she were deliberately being steered away from the polygonum mound by her hostess—steered away as from some ugly or displeasing spot. Was she ashamed perhaps that the past glories no longer remained? The polygonum certainly was growing with extraordinary abandonment. It was not even being clipped or kept to reasonable proportions. It made a kind of flowery wilderness of that bit of the garden.

She almost looks as though she was running away from it, thought Miss

Marple, as she followed her hostess. Presently her attention was diverted to a broken-down pigsty which had a few rose tendrils round it.

"My great-uncle used to keep a few pigs," explained Anthea, "but of course one would never dream of doing anything of that kind nowadays, would one? Rather too noisome, I am afraid. We save a few floribunda roses near the house. I really think floribundas are such a great answer to difficulties."

"Oh, I know," said Miss Marple.

She mentioned the names of a few recent productions in the rose line. All the names, she thought, were entirely strange to Miss Anthea.

"Do you often come on these tours?"

The question came suddenly.

"You mean the tours of houses and of gardens?"

"Yes. Some people do it every year."

"Oh, I couldn't hope to do that. They're rather expensive, you see. A friend very kindly gave me a present of this to celebrate my next birthday. So kind."

"Oh. I wondered. I wondered why you came. I mean—it's bound to be rather tiring, isn't it? Still, if you usually go to the West Indies, and places like that . . ."

"Oh, the West Indies was the result of kindness, too. On the part of a nephew, that time. A dear boy. So very thoughtful for his old aunt."

"Oh, I see. Yes, I see."

"I don't know what one would do without the younger generation," said Miss Marple. "They are so kind, are they not?"

"I—I suppose so I don't really know. I we haven't—any young relations."

"Does your sister, Mrs. Glynne, have any children? She did not mention any. One never likes to ask."

"No. She and her husband never had any children. It's as well perhaps."

"And what do you mean by that?" Miss Marple wondered as they returned to the house.

10

"OH! FOND, OH! FAIR, THE DAYS THAT WERE"

At half-past eight the next morning there was a smart tap on the door, and in answer to Miss Marple's "Come in" the door was opened and an elderly woman entered, bearing a tray with a teapot, a cup and a milk jug and a small plate of bread and butter.

"Early morning tea, ma'am," she said cheerfully. "It's a nice day, it is. I see you've got your curtains drawn back already. You've slept well then?"

"Very well indeed," said Miss Marple, laying aside a small devotional book which she had been reading.

"Well, it's a lovely day, it is. They'll have it nice for going to the Bonaventure Rocks. It's just as well you're not doing it. It's cruel hard on the legs, it is."

"I'm really very happy to be here," said Miss Marple. "So kind of Miss Bradbury-Scott and Mrs. Glynne to issue this invitation."

"Ah, well, it's nice for them, too. It cheers them up to have a bit of company to the house. Ah, it's a sad place nowadays, so it is."

She pulled the curtains at the window rather more fully, pushed back a chair and deposited a can of hot water in the china basin.

"There's a bathroom on the next floor," she said, "but we think it's better always for someone elderly to have their hot water here, so they don't have to climb the stairs."

"It's very kind of you, Janet, I'm sure—you know this house well?"

"I was here as a girl—I was the housemaid then. Three servants they had—a cook, a housemaid—a parlourmaid—kitchenmaid, too, at one time. That was in the old Colonel's time. Horses he kept, too, and a groom. Ah, those were the days. Sad it is when things happen the way they do. He lost his wife young, the Colonel did. His son was killed in the war and his only daughter went away to live on the other side of the world. Married a

New Zealander, she did. Died having a baby and the baby died, too. He was a sad man living alone here, and he let the house go—it wasn't kept up as it should have been. When he died, he left the place to his niece Miss Clotilde and her two sisters, and she and Miss Anthea came here to live—and later Miss Lavinia lost her husband and came to join them—" she sighed and shook her head. "They never did much to the house—couldn't afford it—and they let the garden go as well—"

"It all seems a great pity," said Miss Marple.

"And such nice ladies as they all are, too. Miss Anthea is the scatty one, but Miss Clotilde went to university and is very brainy—she talks three languages—and Mrs. Glynne, she's a very nice lady indeed. I thought when she came to join them as things might go better. But you never know, do you, what the future holds? I feel sometimes as though there was a doom on this house."

Miss Marple looked inquiring.

"First one thing and then another. The dreadful plane accident—in Spain it was—and everybody killed. Nasty things, aeroplanes—I'd never go in one of them. Miss Clotilde's friends were both killed, they were, husband and wife—the daughter was still at school luckily—and escaped, but Miss Clotilde brought her here to live and did everything for her. Took her abroad for trips—to Italy and France, treated her like a daughter. She was such a happy girl—and a very sweet nature. You'd never dream that such an awful thing could happen."

"An awful thing. What was it? Did it happen here?"

"No, not here, thank God. Though in a way you might say it *did* happen here. It was here that she met him. He was in the neighbourhood—and the ladies knew his father, who was a very rich man, so he came here to visit—that was the beginning—"

"They fell in love?"

"Yes, she fell in love with him right away. He was an attractive-looking boy with a nice way of talking and passing the time of day. You'd never think—you'd never think for one moment—" She broke off.

"There was a love affair? And it went wrong? And the girl committed suicide?"

"Suicide?" the old woman stared at Miss Marple with startled eyes.

"Whoever now told you *that?* Murder it was—barefaced murder. Strangled and her head beaten to pulp. Miss Clotilde had to go and identify her—she's never been quite the same since. They found her body a good thirty miles from here—in the scrub of a disused quarry. And it's believed that it wasn't the first murder he'd done. There had been other girls. Six months she'd been missing and the police searching far and wide. Oh! A wicked devil he was—a bad lot from the day he was born, or so it seems. They say nowadays as there are those as can't help what they do—not right in the head, and they can't be held responsible. I don't believe a word of it! Killers are killers. And they won't even hang them nowadays. I know as there's often madness as runs in old families—there was the Derwents over to Brassington—every second generation one or other of them died in the loony bin—and there was old Mrs. Paulett—walked about the lanes in her diamond tiara saying she was Marie Antoinette until they shut her up. But there wasn't anything really wrong with her—just sillylike. But this boy. Yes, he was a devil right enough."

"What did they do to him?"

"They abolished hanging by then—or else he was too young. I can't remember it all now. They found him guilty. It may have been Bostol or Broadsand—one of those places beginning with 'B' as they sent him to."

"What was the name of the boy?"

"Michael—can't remember his last name. It's ten years ago that it happened—one forgets. Italian sort of name—like a picture. Someone who paints pictures—Raffle, that's it—"

"Michael Rafiel?"

"That's right! There was a rumour as went about that his father being so rich got him wangled out of prison. An escape like the bank robbers. But I think as that was just talk—"

So it had not been suicide. It had been murder. "Love!" Elizabeth Temple had named as the cause of a girl's death. In a way she was right. A young girl had fallen in love with a killer—and for love of him had gone unsuspecting to an ugly death.

Miss Marple gave a little shudder. On her way along the village street yesterday she had passed a newspaper placard: EPSOM DOWNS MURDER, SECOND GIRL'S BODY DISCOVERED, YOUTH ASKED TO ASSIST POLICE.

So history repeated itself. An old pattern—an ugly pattern. Some lines of forgotten verse came haltingly into her brain:

> Rose white youth, passionate, pale,
> A singing stream in a silent vale,
> A fairy prince in a prosy tale,
> Oh, there's nothing in life so finely frail
> As rose white youth.

Who was there to guard youth from pain and death—youth who could not, who had never been able to, guard itself? Did they know too little? Or was it that they knew too much, and therefore thought they knew it all?

II

Miss Marple, coming down the stairs that morning, probably rather earlier than she had been expected, found no immediate sign of her hostesses. She let herself out at the front door and wandered once round the garden. It was not because she'd really enjoyed this particular garden. It was some vague feeling that there was something here that she ought to notice, something that would give her some idea, or that had given her some idea only she had not—well, frankly, she had not been bright enough to realize just what the bright idea had been. Something she ought to take note of, something that had a bearing.

She was not at the moment anxious to see any of the three sisters. She wanted to turn a few things over in her mind—the new facts that had come to her through Janet's early tea chat.

A side gate stood open and she went through it to the village street and along a line of small shops to where a steeple poked up announcing the site of the church and its churchyard. She pushed open the lych gate and wandered about among the graves, some dating from quite a while back, some by the far well later ones, and one or two beyond the wall in what was obviously a new enclosure. There was nothing of great interest among the older tombs. Certain names recurred as they do in villages. A good many Princes of village origin had been buried. Jasper Prince, deeply regretted. Margery Prince, Edgar and Walter Prince, Melanie Prince, 4 years old. A family record. Hiram Broad—Ellen Jane Broad, Eliza Broad, 91 years.

She was turning away from the latter when she observed an elderly man moving in slow motion among the graves, tidying up as he walked. He gave her a salute and a "good morning."

"Good morning," said Miss Marple. "A very pleasant day."

"It'll turn to rain later," said the old man.

He spoke with the utmost certainty.

"There seem to be a lot of Princes and Broads buried here," said Miss Marple.

"Ah, yes, there've always been Princes here. Used to own quite a bit of land once. There have been Broads a good many years, too."

"I see a child is buried here. Very sad when one sees a child's grave."

"Ah, that'll be little Melanie that was. Mellie, we called her. Yes, it was a sad death. Run over, she was. Ran out into the street, went to get sweets at the sweetshop. Happens a lot nowadays with cars going through at the pace they do."

"It is sad to think," said Miss Marple, "that there are so many deaths all the time. And one doesn't really notice it until one looks at the inscriptions in the churchyard. Sickness, old age, children run over, sometimes even more dreadful things. Young girls killed. Crimes, I mean."

"Ah, yes, there's a lot of that about. Silly girls, I call most of 'em. And their mums haven't got time to look after them properly nowadays—what with going out to work so much."

Miss Marple rather agreed with his criticism, but had no wish to waste time in agreement on the trend of the day.

"Staying at The Old Manor House, aren't you?" the old man asked. "Come here on the coach tour I saw. But it got too much for you, I suppose. Some of those that are gettin' on can't always take it."

"I did find it a little exhausting," confessed Miss Marple, "and a very kind friend of mine, a Mr. Rafiel, wrote to some friends of his here and they invited me to stay for a couple of nights."

The name Rafiel clearly meant nothing to the elderly gardener.

"Mrs. Glynne and her two sisters have been very kind," said Miss Marple. "I suppose they've lived here a long time?"

"Not so long as that. Twenty years maybe. Belonged to old Colonel Bradbury-Scott. The Old Manor House did. Close on seventy he was when he died."

"Did he have any children?"

"A son what was killed in the war. That's why he left the place to his nieces. Nobody else to leave it to."

He went back to his work among the graves.

Miss Marple went into the church. It had felt the hand of a Victorian restorer, and had bright Victorian glass in the windows. One or two brasses and some tablets on the walls were all that was left of the past.

Miss Marple sat down in an uncomfortable pew and wondered about things.

Was she on the right track now? Things were connecting up—but the connections were far from clear.

A girl had been murdered (actually several girls had been murdered)—suspected young men (or "youths," as they were usually called nowadays) had been rounded up by the police, to "assist them in their inquiries." A common pattern. But this was all old history, dating back ten or twelve years. There was nothing to find out—now, no problems to solve. A tragedy labelled Finis.

What could be done by her? What could Mr. Rafiel possibly want her to do?

Elizabeth Temple . . . She must get Elizabeth Temple to tell her more.

Elizabeth had spoken of a girl who had been engaged to be married to Michael Rafiel. But was that really so? That fact did not seem to be known to those in The Old Manor House.

A more familiar version came into Miss Marple's mind—the kind of story that had been reasonably frequent in her own village. Starting as always, "Boy meets girl." Developing in the usual way—

"And then the girl finds she is pregnant," said Miss Marple to herself, "and she tells the boy and she wants him to marry her. But he, perhaps, doesn't want to marry her—he has never had any idea of marrying her. But things may be made difficult for him in this case. His father, perhaps, won't hear of such a thing. Her relations will insist that he 'does the right thing.' And by now he is tired of the girl—he's got another girl perhaps. And so he takes a quick brutal way out—strangles her, beats her head to a pulp to avoid identification. It fits with his record—a brutal, sordid crime—but forgotten and done with."

She looked round the church in which she was sitting. It looked so peaceful. The reality of evil was hard to believe in. A flair for evil—that was what Mr. Rafiel had attributed to her. She rose and walked out of the church and stood looking round the churchyard again. Here, among the gravestones and their worn inscriptions no sense of evil moved in her.

Was it evil she had sensed yesterday at The Old Manor House? The deep depression of despair, that dark desperate grief? Anthea Bradbury-Scott, her eyes gazing fearfully back over one shoulder, as though fearing some presence that stood there—always stood there—behind her.

They knew something, those three sisters, but what was it that they knew?

Elizabeth Temple, she thought again. She pictured Elizabeth Temple with the rest of the coach party, striding across the downs at this moment, climbing up a steep path and gazing over the cliffs out to sea.

Tomorrow, when she rejoined the tour, she would get Elizabeth Temple to tell her more.

Miss Marple retraced her steps to The Old Manor House, walking rather slowly because she was by now tired. She could not really feel that her morning had been productive in any way. So far The Old Manor House had given her no distinctive ideas of any kind, a tale of a past tragedy told by Janet, but there were always past tragedies treasured in the memories of domestic workers and which were remembered quite as clearly as all the happy events such as spectacular weddings, big entertainments and successful operations or accidents from which people had recovered in a miraculous manner.

As she drew near the gate, she saw two female figures standing there. One of them detached itself and came to meet her. It was Mrs. Glynne.

"Oh, there you are," she said. "We wondered, you know. I thought you must have gone out for a walk somewhere and I did so hope you wouldn't overtire yourself. If I had known you had come downstairs and gone out, I would have come with you to show anything there is to show. Not that there is very much."

"Oh, I just wandered around," said Miss Marple. "The churchyard, you know, and the church. I'm always very interested in churches. Sometimes there are very curious epitaphs. Things like that. I make quite a collection of them. I suppose the church here was restored in Victorian times?"

"Yes, they did put in some rather ugly pews, I think. You know, good quality wood, and strong and all that, but not very artistic."

"I hope they didn't take away anything of particular interest."

"No, I don't think so. It's not really a very old church."

"There did not seem to be many tablets or brasses or anything of that kind," agreed Miss Marple.

"You are quite interested in ecclesiastical architecture?"

"Oh, I don't make a study of it or anything like that, but of course in my own village, St. Mary Mead, things do rather revolve round the church. I mean, they always have. In my younger days, that was so. Nowadays of course it's rather different. Were you brought up in this neighbourhood?"

"Oh, not really. We lived not very far away, about thirty miles or so. At Little Herdsley. My father was a retired serviceman—a major in the artillery. We came over here occasionally to seek my uncle—indeed to see my great-uncle before him. No. I've not even been here very much of late years. My other two sisters moved in after my uncle's death, but at that time I was still abroad with my husband. He only died about four or five years ago."

"Oh, I see."

"They were anxious I should come and join them here and really, it seemed the best thing to do. We had lived in India for some years. My husband was still stationed there at the time of his death. It was very difficult nowadays to know where one would wish to—should I say, put one's roots down."

"Yes, indeed. I can quite see that. And you felt, of course, that you had roots here since your family had been here for a long time."

"Yes. Yes, one did feel that. Of course, I'd always kept up with my sisters, had been to visit them. But things are always very different from what one thinks they will be. I have bought a small cottage near London, near Hampton Court, where I spend a good deal of my time, and I do a little occasional work for one or two charities in London."

"So your time is fully occupied. How wise of you."

"I have felt of late that I should spend more time here perhaps. I've been a little worried about my sisters."

"Their health?" suggested Miss Marple. "One is rather worried nowadays, especially as there is not really anyone competent whom one can employ to look after people as they become rather feebler or have certain ailments. So much rheumatism and arthritis about. One is always so afraid of people falling down in the bath or an accident coming down stairs. Something of that kind."

"Clotilde has always been very strong," said Mrs. Glynne. "Tough, I should describe her. But I am rather worried sometimes about Anthea. She is vague, you know—very vague indeed. And she wanders off sometimes—and doesn't seem to know where she is."

"Yes, it is sad when people worry. There is so much to worry one."

"I don't really think there is much to worry Anthea."

"She worries about income tax, perhaps, money affairs," suggested Miss Marple.

"No, no, not that so much but—oh, she worries so much about the garden. She remembers the garden as it used to be, and she's very anxious, you know, to—well, to spend money in putting things right again. Clotilde has had to tell her that really one can't afford that nowadays. But she keeps talking of the hothouses, the peaches that used to be there. The grapes—and all that."

"And the cherry pie on the walls?" suggested Miss Marple, remembering a remark.

"Fancy your remembering that. Yes. Yes, it's one of the things one does remember. Such a charming smell, heliotrope. And such a nice name for it, cherry pie. One always remembers that. And the grapevine. The little, small, early sweet grapes. Ah, well, one must not remember the past too much."

"And the flower borders too, I suppose," said Miss Marple.

"Yes. Yes, Anthea would like to have a big well-kept herbaceous border again. Really not feasible now. It is as much as one can do to get local people who will come and mow the lawns every fortnight. Every year one seems to employ a different firm. And Anthea would like pampas grass planted again. And the Mrs. Simpkin pinks. White, you know. All long the stone edge border. And a fig tree that grew just outside the greenhouse. She remembers all these and talks about them."

"It must be difficult for you."

"Well, yes. Arguments, you see, hardly appeal in any way. Clotilde, of course, is very downright about things. She just refuses point-blank and says she doesn't want to hear another word about it."

"It is difficult," said Miss Marple, "to know how to take things. Whether one should be firm. Rather authoritative. Perhaps, even, well, just a little—a little *fierce,* you know, or whether one should be sympathetic. Listen to things and perhaps hold out hopes which one knows are not justified. Yes, it's difficult."

"But it's easier for me because you see I go away again, and then come back now and then to stay. So it's easy for me to pretend things may be easier soon and that something may be done. But really, the other day when I came home and I found that Anthea had tried to engage a most expensive firm of landscape gardeners to renovate the garden, to build up the greenhouses again—which is quite absurd because even if you put vines in they would not bear for another two or three years. Clotilde knew nothing about it and she was extremely angry when she discovered the estimate for this work on Anthea's desk. She was really quite unkind."

"So many things are difficult," said Miss Marple.

It was a useful phrase which she used often.

"I shall have to go rather early tomorrow morning, I think," said Miss Marple. "I was making inquiries at the Golden Boar where I understand the coach party assembles tomorrow morning. They are making quite an early start. Nine o'clock, I understand."

"Oh, dear. I hope you will not find it too fatiguing."

"Oh, I don't think so. I gather we are going to a place called—now wait a minute, what was it called?—Stirling St. Mary. Something like that. And it does not seem to be very far away. There's an interesting church to see on the way and a castle. In the afternoon there is a quite pleasant garden, not too many acres, but some special flowers. I feel sure that after this very nice rest that I have had here, I shall be quite all right. I understand now that I would have been very tired if I had had these two days of climbing up cliffsides and all the rest of it."

"Well, you must rest this afternoon, so as to be fresh for tomorrow," said Mrs. Glynne, as they went into the house. "Miss Marple has been to visit the church," said Mrs. Glynne to Clotilde.

"I'm afraid there is not very much to see," said Clotilde. "Victorian glass of a most hideous kind, I think myself. No expense spared. I'm afraid my uncle was partly to blame. He was very pleased with those rather crude reds and blues."

"Very crude. Very vulgar, I always think," said Lavinia Glynne.

Miss Marple settled down after lunch to have a nap, and she did not join her hostesses until nearly dinnertime. After dinner a good deal of chat went on until it was bed-time. Miss Marple set the tone in remembrances—remembrances of her own youth, her early days, places she had visited, travels or tours she had made, occasional people she had known.

She went to bed tired, with a sense of failure. She had learned nothing more, possibly because there was nothing more to learn. A fishing expedition where the fish did not rise—possibly because there were no fish there. Or it could be that she did not know the right bait to use.

11

ACCIDENT

Miss Marple's tea was brought at seven-thirty the following morning so as to allow her plenty of time to get up and pack her few belongings. She was just closing her small suitcase when there was a rather hurried tap on the door and Clotilde came in, looking upset.

"Oh, dear, Miss Marple, there is a young man downstairs who has called to see you. Emlyn Price. He is on the tour with you and they sent him here."

"Of course, I remember him. Yes. Quite young?"

"Oh, yes. Very modern-looking, and a lot of hair and all that, but he has really come to—well, to break some bad news to you. There has been, I am sorry to say, an accident."

"An accident?" Miss Marple stared. "You mean—to the coach? There has been an accident on the road? Someone has been hurt?"

"No. No, it was not the coach. There was no trouble there. It was in the course of the expedition yesterday afternoon. There was a great deal of wind, you may remember, though I don't think that had anything to do with it. People strayed about a bit, I think. There is a regular path, but you can also climb up and go across the downs. Both ways lead to the Memorial Tower on the top of Bonaventure—where they were all making for. People got separated a bit and I suppose, really, there was no one actually guiding them or looking after them which, perhaps, there ought to have been. People aren't very sure-footed always and the slope overhanging the gorge is very steep. There was a bad fall of stones or rocks which came crashing down the hillside and knocked someone out on the path below."

"Oh, dear," said Miss Marple, "I am sorry. I am most terribly sorry. Who was it who was hurt?"

"A Miss Temple or Tenderdon, I understand."

"Elizabeth Temple," said Miss Marple. "Oh, dear, I am sorry. I talked to her a good deal. I sat in the next seat to her on the coach. She is, I believe, a retired schoolmistress, a very well-known one."

"Of course," said Clotilde, "I know her quite well. She was headmistress of Fallowfield, quite a famous school. I'd no idea she was on this tour. She retired as headmistress, I think a year or two ago, and there is a new, rather young headmistress there now with rather advanced progressive ideas. But Miss Temple is not very old, really; she's about sixty, I should think, and very active, fond of climbing and walking and all the rest of it. This really seems most unfortunate. I hope she's not badly hurt. I haven't heard any details yet."

"This is quite ready now," said Miss Marple, snapping down the lid of her suitcase. "I will come down at once and see Mr. Price."

Clotilde seized the suitcase.

"Let me. I can carry this perfectly. Come down with me, and be careful of the stairs."

Miss Marple came down. Emlyn Price was waiting for her. His hair was looking even wilder than usual and he was wearing a splendid array of fancy boots and a leather jerkin and brilliant emerald green trousers.

"Such an unfortunate business," he said, seizing Miss Marple's hand. "I thought I'd come along myself and—well, break it to you about the accident. I expect Miss Bradbury-Scott has told you. It's Miss Temple. You know. The school dame. I don't know quite what she was doing or what happened, but some stones, or rather boulders, rolled down from above. It's rather a precipitous slope and it knocked her out and they had to take her off to hospital with concussion last night. I gather she's rather bad. Anyway, the tour for today is cancelled and we are stopping on here tonight."

"Oh, dear," said Miss Marple, "I am sorry. I'm very sorry."

"I think they've decided not to go on today because they really have to wait and see what the medical report is, so we are proposing to spend one more night here at the Golden Boar and to rearrange the tour a little, so that perhaps we shall miss out altogether going to Grangmering, which we were going to do tomorrow, and which is not very interesting, really, or so they say. Mrs. Sandbourne has gone off early to the hospital to see how things are this morning. She's going to join us at the Golden Boar for coffee at eleven o'clock. I thought perhaps you'd like to come along and hear the latest news."

"I'll certainly come along with you," said Miss Marple. "Of course. At once."

She turned to say good-bye to Clotilde and Mrs. Glynne, who had joined her.

"I must thank you so much," she said. "You have been so kind and it has been so delightful to have these two nights here. I feel so rested and everything. Most unfortunate this has occurred."

"If you would like to spend another night," said Mrs. Glynne, "I am sure—" She looked at Clotilde.

It occurred to Miss Marple, who had as sharp a sideways glance as anyone could desire, that Clotilde had a slightly disapproving look. She almost shook her head, though it was such a small movement that it was hardly noticeable. But she was, Miss Marple thought, hushing down the suggestion that Mrs. Glynne was making.

". . . although of course I expect it would be nicer for you to be with the others and to—"

"Oh, yes, I think it would be better," said Miss Marple. "I shall know then what the plans are and what to do about things, and perhaps I could be of help in some way. One never knows. So thank you again very much. It will not be difficult, I expect, to get a room at the Golden Boar." She looked at Emlyn, who said reassuringly:

"That'll be all right. Several rooms have been vacated today. They won't be full at all. Mrs. Sandbourne, I think, has booked for all the party to stay there tonight, and tomorrow we shall see—well, we shall see how this all goes on."

Good-byes were said again and thanks. Emlyn Price took Miss Marple's belongings and started out at a good striding pace.

"It's really only just round the corner, and then the first street to the left," he said.

"Yes, I passed it yesterday, I think. Poor Miss Temple. I do hope she's not badly hurt."

"I think she is rather," said Emlyn Price. "Of course, you know what doctors are, and hospital people. They say the same thing always: 'as well as can be expected.' There's no local hospital—they had to take her to Carristown, which is about eight miles away. Anyway, Mrs. Sandbourne will be back with the news by the time we've fixed you up at the hotel."

They got there to find the tour assembled in the coffee room and coffee and morning buns and pastries were being served. Mr. and Mrs. Butler were talking at the moment.

"Oh, it's just too, too tragic this happening," said Mrs. Butler. "Just too upsetting, isn't it? Just when we were all so happy and enjoying everything so much. Poor Miss Temple. And I always thought she was very sure-footed. But there, you know, you never can never tell, can you, Henry?"

"No, indeed," said Henry. "No, indeed. I am wondering really—yes, our time's very short, you know—whether we hadn't better—well, give up this tour at this point here. Not continue with it. It seems to me that there's bound to be a bit of difficulty resuming things until we know definitely. If this was—well—I mean, if this should be so serious that it could prove fatal, there might—well—I mean there might have to be an inquest or something of that kind."

"Oh, Henry, don't say dreadful things like that!"

"I'm sure," said Miss Cooke, "that you are being a little too pessimistic, Mr. Butler. I am sure that things couldn't be as serious as that."

In his foreign voice Mr. Caspar said: "But yes, they are serious. I hear yesterday. When Mrs. Sandbourne talk on telephone to doctor. It is very, very serious. They say she has concussion bad—very bad. A special doctor he is coming to look at her and see if he can operate or if impossible. Yes—it is all very bad."

"Oh, dear," said Miss Lumley. "If there's any doubt, perhaps we ought to go home, Mildred. I must look up the trains, I think." She turned to Mrs. Butler. "You see, I have made arrangements about my cats with the neighbours, and if I was delayed a day or two it might make great difficulties for everyone."

"Well, it's no good our working ourselves up too much," said Mrs. Riseley-Porter in her deep, authoritative voice. "Joanna, put this bun in the wastepaper basket, will you? It is really quite uneatable. Most unpleasant jam. But I don't want to leave it on my plate. It might make for bad feeling."

Joanna got rid of the bun. She said:

"Do you think it would be all right if Emlyn and I went out for a walk? I mean, just saw something of the town? It's not much good our sitting about here, making gloomy remarks, is it? We can't do anything."

"I think you'd be very wise to go out," said Miss Cooke.

"Yes, you go along," said Miss Barrow before Mrs. Riseley-Porter could speak.

Miss Cooke and Miss Barrow looked at each other and sighed, shaking their heads.

"The grass was very slippery," said Miss Barrow. "I slid once or twice myself, you know, on that very short turf."

"And the stones, too," said Miss Cooke. "Quite a shower of small stones fell down just as I was turning a corner on the path. Yes, one struck me on the shoulder quite sharply."

Tea, coffee, biscuits and cakes dispatched, everyone seemed somewhat dissociated and ill at ease. When a catastrophe has occurred, it is very difficult to know what is the proper way to meet it. Everyone had given their view, had expressed surprise and distress. They were now awaiting news and at the same time had a slight hankering after some form of sightseeing, some interest to carry them through the morning. Lunch would not be served until one o'clock and they really felt that to sit around and repeat their same remarks would be rather a gloomy business.

Miss Cooke and Miss Barrow rose as one woman and explained that it was necessary for them to do a little shopping. One or two things they needed, and they also wished to go to the post office and buy stamps.

"I want to send off one or two postcards. And I want to inquire about postal dues on a letter to China," said Miss Barrow.

"And I want to match some wools," said Miss Cooke. "And also it seemed to me there was rather an interesting building on the other side of the market square."

"I think it would do us all good to get out," said Miss Barrow.

Colonel and Mrs. Walker also rose and suggested to Mr. and Mrs. Butler that they, too, might go out and see what there was to see. Mrs. Butler expressed hopes of an antique shop.

"Only I don't really mean a real antique shop. More what you would call a junk shop. Sometimes you can pick up some really interesting things there."

They all trooped out. Emlyn Price had already sidled to the door and disappeared in pursuit of Joanna without troubling to use conversation to explain his departure. Mrs. Riseley-Porter, having made a belated attempt to call her niece back, said she thought that at least the lounge would be rather more pleasant to sit in. Miss Lumley agreed—Mr. Caspar escorted the ladies with the air of a foreign equerry.

Professor Wanstead and Miss Marple remained.

"I think myself," said Professor Wanstead, addressing Miss Marple, "that it would be pleasant to sit outside the hotel. There is a small terrace giving on the street. If I might persuade you?"

Miss Marple thanked him and rose to her feet. She had hardly exchanged a word so far with Professor Wanstead. He had several learned-looking books with him, one of which he was usually perusing; even in the coach he continued to try to read.

"But perhaps you, too, want to shop," he said. "For myself, I would prefer to wait somewhere peacefully for the return of Mrs. Sandbourne. It is important, I think, that we should know exactly what we are in for."

"I quite agree with you as to that," said Miss Marple. "I did a certain amount of walking round the town yesterday and I don't feel any necessity to do so again today. I'd rather wait here in case there is anything I can do to help. Not that I suppose there is, but one never knows."

They moved together through the hotel door and round the corner to where there was a little square of garden with a raised stone walk close to the wall of the hotel and on which there were various forms of basket chairs. There was no one there at the moment, so they sat down. Miss Marple looked thoughtfully at her vis-à-vis—at his corrugated and wrinkled face, his bushy brows, his luxuriant head of grey hair. He walked with a slight stoop. He had an interesting face, Miss Marple decided. His voice was dry and caustic, a professional man of some kind, she thought.

"I am not wrong, am I?" said Professor Wanstead. "You *are* Miss Jane Marple?"

"Yes, I am Jane Marple."

She was slightly surprised, though for no particular reason. They had not been long enough together for people to be identified by the other travellers. The last two nights she had not been with the rest of the party. It was quite natural.

"I thought so," said Professor Wanstead, "from a description I have had of you."

"A description of me?" Miss Marple was again slightly surprised.

"Yes, I had a description of you"—he paused for a moment; his voice was not exactly lowered, but it lost volume, although she could still hear it quite easily—"from Mr. Rafiel."

"Oh," said Miss Marple, startled. "From Mr. Rafiel."

"You are surprised?"

"Well, yes, I am rather."

"I don't know that you should be."

"I didn't expect—" began Miss Marple, and then stopped.

Professor Wanstead did not speak. He was merely sitting, looking at her intently. In a minute or two, thought Miss Marple to herself, he will say to me, "What symptoms exactly, dear lady? Any discomfort in swallowing? And lack of sleep? Digestion in good order?" She was almost sure now that he was a doctor.

"When did he describe me to you? That must have been—"

"You were going to say some time ago—some weeks ago. Before his death—that is so. He told me that you would be on this tour."

"And he knew that you would be on it, too—that you were going on it."

"You can put it that way," said Professor Wanstead. "He said," he continued, "that you would be travelling on this tour, that he had, in fact, arranged for you to be travelling on this tour."

"It was very kind of him," said Miss Marple. "Very kind indeed. I was most surprised when I found he'd booked me. Such a treat. Which I could not have afforded for myself."

"Yes," said Professor Wanstead. "Very well put." He nodded his head as one who applauds a good performance by a pupil.

"It is sad that it has been interrupted in this fashion," said Miss Marple. "Very sad indeed. When I am sure we were all enjoying ourselves so much."

"Yes," said Professor Wanstead. "Yes, very sad. And unexpected, do you think, or not unexpected?"

"Now what do you mean by that, Professor Wanstead?"

His lips curled in a slight smile as he met her challenging look.

"Mr. Rafiel," he said, "spoke to me about you at some length, Miss Marple. He suggested that I should be on this tour with you. I should in due course almost certainly make your acquaintance, since members in a tour inevitably make each other's acquaintance, though it usually takes a day or two for them to split up, as it were, into possible groupings led by similar tastes or interests. And he further suggested to me, that I should, shall we say, keep an eye on you."

"Keep an eye on me?" said Miss Marple, showing some slight displeasure. "And for what reason?"

"I think reasons of protection. He wanted to be quite sure that nothing should happen to you."

"Happen to me? What should happen to me, I should like to know?"

"Possibly what happened to Miss Elizabeth Temple," said Professor Wanstead.

Joanna Crawford came round the corner of the hotel. She was carrying a shopping basket. She passed them, nodding a little, she looked towards them with slight curiosity and went on down the street. Professor Wanstead did not speak until she had gone out of sight.

"A nice girl," he said; "at least I think so. Content at present to be a beast of burden to an autocratic aunt, but I have no doubt will reach the age of rebellion fairly soon."

"What did you mean by what you said just now?" said Miss Marple, uninterested for the moment in Joanna's possible rebellion.

"That is a question which, perhaps, owing to what has happened, we shall have to discuss."

"You mean because of the accident?"

"Yes. If it was an accident."

"Do you think it wasn't an accident?"

"Well, I think it's just possible. That's all."

"I don't of course know anything about it," said Miss Marple, hesitating.

"No. You were absent from the scene. You were—shall I put it this way—were you just possibly on duty elsewhere?"

Miss Marple was silent for a moment. She looked at Professor Wanstead once or twice and then she said:

"I don't think I know exactly what you mean."

"You are being careful. You are quite right to be careful."

"I have made it a habit," said Miss Marple.

"To be careful?"

"I should not put it exactly like that, but I have made a point of being always ready to disbelieve as well as believe anything that is told to me."

"Yes, and you are quite right, too. You don't know anything about me. You know my name from the passenger list of a very agreeable tour visiting castles and historic houses and splendid gardens. Possibly the gardens are what will interest you most."

"Possibly."

"There are other people here, too, who are interested in gardens."

"Or profess to be interested in gardens."

"Ah," said Professor Wanstead. "You have noticed that."

He went on, "Well, it was my part, or at any rate to begin with, to observe you, to watch what you were doing, to be near at hand in case there was any possibility of—well, we might call it roughly—dirty work of any kind. But things are slightly altered now. You must make up your mind if I am your enemy or your ally."

"Perhaps you are right," said Miss Marple. "You put it very clearly but you have not given me any information about yourself on which to judge. You were a friend, I presume, of the late Mr. Rafiel?"

"No," said Professor Wanstead, "I was not a friend of Mr. Rafiel. I had met him once or twice. Once on a committee of a hospital, once at some other public event. I knew about him. He, I gather, also knew about me. If I say to you, Miss Marple, that I am a man of some eminence in my own profession, you may think me a man of bounding conceit."

"I don't think so," said Miss Marple. "I should say, if you say that about yourself, that you are probably speaking the truth. You are, perhaps, a medical man."

"Ah. You are perceptive, Miss Marple. Yes, you are quite perceptive. I have a medical degree, but I have a specialty, too. I am a pathologist and psychologist. I don't carry credentials about with me. You will probably have to take my word up to a certain point, though I can show you letters addressed to me, and possibly official documents that might convince you. I undertake mainly specialist work in connection with medical jurisprudence. To put it in perfectly plain everyday language, I am interested in the different types of criminal brain. That has been a study of mine for many years. I have written books on the subject, some of them violently disputed, some of them which have attracted adherence to my ideas. I do not do very arduous work nowadays. I spend my time mainly writing up my subject, stressing certain points that have appealed to me. From time to time I come across things that strike me as interesting—things that I want to study more closely. This I am afraid must seem rather tedious to you."

"Not at all," said Miss Marple. "I am hoping, perhaps, from what you are saying now that you will be able to explain to me certain things which Mr. Rafiel did not see fit to explain to me. He asked me to embark upon a certain project but he gave me no useful information on which to work. He left me to accept it and to proceed, as it were, completely in the dark. It seemed to me extremely foolish of him to treat the matter in that way."

"But you accepted it?"

"I accepted it. I will be quite honest with you. I had a financial incentive."

"Did that weigh with you?"

Miss Marple was silent for a moment and then she said slowly:

"You may not believe it, but my answer to that is, 'Not really.' "

"I am not surprised. But your interest was aroused. That is what you are trying to tell me."

"Yes. My interest was aroused. I had known Mr. Rafiel not well, casually, but for a certain period of time—some weeks, in fact—in the West Indies. I see you know about it, more or less."

"I know that that was where Mr. Rafiel met you and where—shall I say—you two collaborated."

Miss Marple looked at him rather doubtfully. "Oh," she said, "he said that, did he?" She shook her head.

"Yes, he did," said Professor Wanstead. "He said you had a remarkable flair for criminal matters."

Miss Marple raised her eyebrows as she looked at him.

"And I suppose that seems to you most unlikely," she said. "It surprises you."

"I seldom allow myself to be surprised at what happens," said Professor Wanstead. "Mr. Rafiel was a very shrewd and astute man, a good judge of people. He thought that you, too, were a good judge of people."

"I would not set myself up as a good judge of people," said Miss Marple. "I would only say that certain people remind me of certain other people that I have known, and that therefore I can presuppose a certain likeness between the way they would act. If you think I know all about what I am supposed to be doing here, you are wrong."

"By accident more than design," said Professor Wanstead, "we seem to have settled here in a particularly suitable spot for discussion of certain matters. We do not appear to be overlooked, we cannot easily be overheard, we are not near a window or a door and there is no balcony or window overhead. In fact, we can talk."

"I should appreciate that," said Miss Marple. "I am stressing the fact that I am myself completely in the dark as to what I am doing or supposed to be doing. I don't know why Mr. Rafiel wanted it that way."

"I think I can guess that. He wanted you to approach a certain set of facts, of happenings, unbiased by what anyone would tell you first."

"So you are not going to tell me anything either?" Miss Marple sounded irritated. "Really!" she said. "There are limits."

"Yes," said Professor Wanstead. He smiled suddenly. "I agree with you. We must do away with some of these limits. I am going to tell you certain facts that will make certain things fairly clear to you. You in turn may be able to tell me certain facts."

"I rather doubt it," said Miss Marple. "One or two rather peculiar indications, perhaps, but indications are not facts."

"Therefore—" said Professor Wanstead, and paused.

"For goodness' sake, tell me something," said Miss Marple.

12

A CONSULTATION

"I'm not going to make a long story of things. I'll explain quite simply how I came into this matter. I act as confidential adviser from time to time for the Home Office. I am also in touch with certain institutions. There are certain establishments which, in the event of crime, provide board and lodging for certain types of criminals who have been found guilty of certain acts. They remain there at what is termed Her Majesty's pleasure, sometimes for a definite length of time and in direct association with their age. If they are below a certain age, they have to be received in some place of detention specially indicated. You understand that, no doubt."

"Yes, I understand quite well what you mean."

"Usually I am consulted fairly soon after whatever the—shall we call it—crime has happened, to judge such matters as treatment, possibilities in the case, prognosis favourable or unfavourable, all the various words. They do not mean much and I will not go into them. But occasionally also I am consulted by a responsible head of such an institution for a particular reason. In this matter I received a communication from a certain department which was passed to me through the Home Office. I went to visit the head of this institution—in fact, the governor responsible for the prisoners or patients or whatever you like to call them. He was by way of being a friend of mine—a friend of fairly long standing though not one with whom I was on terms of great intimacy. I went down to the institution in question and the governor laid his troubles before me. They referred to one particular inmate. He was not satisfied about this inmate. He had certain doubts. This was the case of a young man or one who had been a young man, in fact little more than a boy, when he came here. That was now several years ago. As time went on, and after the present governor had taken up his own residence there (he had not been there at the original arrival of this prisoner), he became worried. Not because he himself was a professional man, but because he was a man of experience of criminal patients and prisoners.

To put it quite simply, this had been a boy who from his early youth had been completely unsatisfactory. You can call it by what term you like. A young delinquent, a young thug, a bad lot, a person of diminished responsibility. There are many terms. Some of them fit, some of them don't fit, some of them are merely puzzling. He was a criminal type. That was certain. He had joined gangs, he had beaten up people, he was a thief, he had stolen, he had embezzled, he had taken part in swindles, he had initiated certain frauds. In fact, he was a son who would be any father's despair."

"Oh, I see," said Miss Marple.

"And what do you see, Miss Marple?"

"Well, what I think I see is that you are talking of Mr. Rafiel's son."

"You are quite right. I am talking of Mr. Rafiel's son. What do you know about him?"

"Nothing," said Miss Marple. "I only heard—and that was yesterday—that Mr. Rafiel had a delinquent, or unsatisfactory, if we like to put it mildly, son. A son with a criminal record. I know very little about him. Was he Mr. Rafiel's only son?"

"Yes, he was Mr. Rafiel's only son. But Mr. Rafiel also had two daughters. One of them died when she was fourteen, the elder daughter married quite happily but had no children."

"Very sad for him."

"Possibly," said Professor Wanstead. "One never knows. His wife died young and I think it possible that her death saddened him very much, though he was never willing to show it. How much he cared for his son and daughters, I don't know. He provided for them. He did his best for them. He did his best for this son, but what his feelings were, one cannot say. He was not an easy man to read that way. I think his whole life and interest lay in his profession of making money. It was the making of it, like all great financiers, that interested him—not the actual money which he secured by it. That, as you might say, was sent out like a good servant to earn more money in more interesting and unexpected ways. He enjoyed finance. He loved finance. He thought of very little else.

"I think he did all that was possible for his son. He got him out of scrapes at school, he employed good lawyers to get him released from court proceedings whenever possible, but the final blow came, perhaps presaged by some earlier happenings. The boy was taken to court on a charge of assault against a young girl. It was said to be assault and rape and he suffered a term of imprisonment for it with some leniency shown because of his youth. But later, a second and really serious charge was brought against him."

"He killed a girl," said Miss Marple. "Is that right? That's what I heard."

"He lured a girl away from her home. It was some months before her body was found. She had been strangled. And afterward her face and head had been disfigured by some heavy stones or rocks, presumably to prevent her identity being made known."

"Not a very nice business," said Miss Marple in her most old-ladylike tone.

Professor Wanstead looked at her for a moment or two.

"You describe it that way?"

"It is how it seems to me," said Miss Marple. "I don't like that sort of thing, I never have. If you expect me to feel sympathy, regret, urge an unhappy childhood, blame bad environment; if you expect me in fact to weep over him, this young murderer of yours, I do not feel inclined so to do. I do not like evil beings who do evil things."

"I am delighted to hear it," said Professor Wanstead. "What I suffer in the course of my profession from people weeping and gnashing their teeth and blaming everything on some happening in the past, you would hardly believe. If people knew the bad environments that people have had, the unkindness, the difficulties of their lives and the fact that nevertheless they can come through unscathed, I don't think they would so often take the opposite point of view. The misfits are to be pitied, yes, they are to be pitied if I may say so for the genes with which they are born and over which they have no control themselves. I pity epileptics in the same way. If you know what genes are—"

"I know, more or less," said Miss Marple. "It's common knowledge nowadays, though naturally I have no exact chemical or technical knowledge."

"The governor, a man of experience, told me exactly why he was so anxious to have my verdict. He had felt increasingly in his experience of this particular inmate that, in plain words, the boy was not a killer. He didn't think he was the type of a killer, he was like no killer he had ever seen before, he was of the opinion that the boy was the kind of criminal type who would never go straight no matter what treatment was given to him, would never reform himself; and for whom nothing in one sense of the word could be done, but at the same time he felt increasingly certain that the verdict upon him had been a wrong one. He did not believe that the boy had killed a girl, first strangled her and then disfigured her after rolling her body into a ditch. He just couldn't bring himself to believe it. He'd look over the facts of the case, which seemed to be fully proved. This boy had known the girl, he had been seen with her on several different occasions before the crime. They had presumably slept together and there were other points. His car had been seen in the neighbourhood. He himself had been recognized and all the rest of it. A perfectly fair case. But my friend was unhappy about it, he said. He was a man who had a very strong feeling for justice. He wanted a different opinion. He wanted, in fact, not the police side which he knew, he wanted a professional medical view. That was my field, he said. My line of country entirely. He wanted me to see this young man and talk with him, visit him, make a professional appraisal of him and give him my opinion."

"Very interesting," said Miss Marple. "Yes, I call that very interesting. After all, your friend—I mean your governor—was a man of experience, a man who loved justice. He was a man whom you'd be willing to listen to. Presumably, then, you did listen to him."

"Yes," said Professor Wanstead, "I was deeply interested. I saw the subject, as I will call him. I approached him from several different attitudes. I talked to him, I discussed various changes likely to occur in the law. I told him it might be possible to bring down a lawyer, a Queen's Counsel, to see what points there might be in his favour, and other things. I approached him as a friend but also as an enemy so that I could see how he responded to different approaches, and I also made a good many physical tests, such as we use very frequently nowadays. I will not go into those with you because they are wholly technical."

"Then what did you think in the end?"

"I thought," said Professor Wanstead, "I thought my friend was likely to be right. I did not think that Michael Rafiel was a murderer."

"What about the earlier case you mentioned?"

"That told against him, of course. Not in the jury's mind, because of course they did not hear about that until after the judge's summing up, but certainly in the judge's mind. It told against him, but I made a few inquiries myself afterwards. He had assaulted a girl. He had conceivably raped her, but he had not attempted to strangle her and in my opinion—I have seen a great many cases which come before the assizes—it seemed to me highly unlikely that there was a very definite case of rape. Girls, you must remember, are far more ready to be raped nowadays than they used to be. Their mothers insist, very often, that they should call it rape. The girl in question had had several boy friends who had gone further than friendship. I did not think it counted very greatly as evidence against him. The actual murder case—yes, that was undoubtedly murder—but I continued to feel by all tests—physical tests, mental tests, psychological tests—none of them accorded with this particular crime."

"Then what did you do?"

"I communicated with Mr. Rafiel. I told him that I would like an interview with him on a certain matter concerning his son. I went to him. I told him what I thought, what the governor thought, that we had no evidence, that there were no grounds of appeal at present, but that we both believed that a miscarriage of justice had been committed. I said I thought possibly an inquiry might be held, it might be an expensive business, it might bring out certain facts that could be laid before the Home Office, it might be successful, it might not. There might be something there, some evidence if you looked for it. I said it would be expensive to look for it, but I presumed that would make no difference to anyone in his position. I had realized by that time that he was a sick man, a very ill man. He told me so himself. He told me that he had been in expectation of an early death, that he'd been warned two years ago that death could not be delayed for what they first thought was about a year, but later they realized he would last rather longer because of his unusual physical strength. I asked him what he felt about his son."

"And what did he feel about his son?" said Miss Marple.

"Ah, you want to know that. So did I. He was, I think, extremely honest with me even if—"

"—even if rather ruthless?" said Miss Marple.

"Yes, Miss Marple. You are using the right word. He was a ruthless man, but he was a just man and an honest man. He said, 'I've known what my son was like for many years. I have not tried to change him because I don't believe that anyone could change him. He is made a certain way. He is crooked. He's a bad lot. He'll always be in trouble. He's dishonest. Nobody, nothing could make him go straight. I am well assured of that. I have in a sense washed my hands of him. Though not legally or outwardly; he has always had money if he required it. Help, legal or otherwise, if he gets into trouble. I have done always what I could do. Well, let us say if I had a son who was a spastic, who was sick, who was epileptic, I would do what I could for him. If I have a son who is sick morally, shall we say, and for whom there is no cure, I'd have done what I could also. No more and no less. What can I do for him now?' I told him that it depended what he wanted to do. 'There's no difficulty about that,' he said. 'I am handicapped but I can see quite clearly what I want to do. I want to get him vindicated. I want to get him released from confinement. I want to get him free to continue to lead his own life as best he can lead it. If he must lead it in further dishonesties, then he must lead it that way. I will leave provision for him, to do for him everything that can be done. I don't want him suffering, imprisoned, cut off from his life because of a perfectly natural and unfortunate mistake. If somebody else, some other man killed that girl,

I want the fact brought to light and recognized. I want justice for Michael. But I am handicapped. I am a very ill man. My time is measured now not in years or months but in weeks.'

"Lawyers, I suggested—I know a firm— He cut me short. 'Your lawyers will be useless. You can employ them but they will be useless. I must arrange what I can arrange in such a limited time.' He offered me a large fee to undertake the search for the truth and to undertake everything possible with no expense spared. 'I can do next to nothing myself. Death may come at any moment. I empower you as my chief help, and to assist you at my request I will try to find a certain person.' He wrote down a name for me. Miss Jane Marple. He said, 'I don't want to give you her address. I want you to meet her in surroundings of my own choosing,' and he then told me of this tour, this charming, harmless, innocent tour of historic houses, castles and gardens. He would provide me with a reservation on it ahead for a certain date. 'Miss Jane Marple,' he said, 'will also be on that tour. You will meet her there, you will encounter her casually, and thus it will be seen clearly to be a casual meeting.'

"I was to choose my own time and moment to make myself known to you, if I thought it advisable; or not to make myself known to you if I thought that that would be the better way. You have already asked me if I or my friend the governor had any reason to suspect or know of any other person who might have been guilty of the murder. My friend the governor certainly suggested nothing of the kind, and he had already taken up the matter with the police officer who had been in charge of the case a most reliable detective-superintendent with very good experience in these matters."

"No other man was suggested? No other friend of the girl's? No other former friend who might have been supplanted?"

"There was nothing of that kind to find. I asked Mr. Rafiel to tell me a little about you. He did not however consent to do so. He told me you were elderly. He told me that you were a person who knew about people. He told me one other thing." He paused.

"What's the other thing?" said Miss Marple. "I have some natural curiosity, you know. I really can't think of any other advantage I conceivably could have. I am slightly deaf. My eyesight is not quite as good as it used to be. I cannot really think that I have any advantages beyond the fact that I may, I suppose, seem rather foolish and simple, and am, in fact, what used to be called in rather earlier days an 'old tabby.' I *am* an old tabby. Is that the sort of thing he said?"

"No," said Professor Wanstead. "What he said was he thought you had a very fine sense of evil."

"Oh," said Miss Marple. She was taken aback.

Professor Wanstead was watching her.

"Would you say that was true?" he said.

Miss Marple was quiet for quite a long time. At last she said:

"Perhaps it is. Yes, perhaps. I have at several different times in my life been apprehensive, have recognized that there was evil in the neighbourhood, the surroundings, that the environment of someone who was evil was near me, connected with what was happening."

She looked at him suddenly and smiled.

"It's rather, you know," she said, "like being born with a very keen sense of smell. You can smell a leak of gas when other people can't do so. You can distinguish one perfume from another very easily. I had an aunt once," continued Miss Marple thoughtfully, "who said she could smell when people told a lie. She said there was quite a distinctive odour came to her. Their noses twitched, she said, and then the smell came. I don't know if it was true or not, but—well, on several occasions she was quite remarkable. She said to my uncle once, 'Don't, Jack, engage that young man you were talking to this morning. He was telling you lies the whole time he was talking.' That turned out to be quite true."

"A sense of evil," said Professor Wanstead. "Well, if you do sense evil, tell me. I shall be glad to know. I don't think I have a particular sense of evil myself. Ill-health, yes, but not—not evil up here." He tapped his forehead.

"I'd better tell you briefly how I came into things now," said Miss Marple. "Mr. Rafiel, as you know, died. His lawyers asked me to come and see them, apprised me of his proposition. I received a letter from him which explained nothing. After that I heard nothing more for some little time. Then I got a letter from the company who run these tours saying that Mr. Rafiel before his death had made a reservation for me knowing that I should enjoy a trip very much, and wanting to give it to me as a surprise present. I was very astonished but took it as an indication of the first step that I was to undertake. I was to go on this tour and presumably in the course of the tour some other indication or hint or clue or direction would come to me. I think it did. Yesterday, no, the day before, I was received on my arrival here by three ladies who live at an old manor house and who very kindly extended an invitation to me. They had heard from Mr. Rafiel, they said, who had written some time before his death saying that a very old friend of his would be coming on this tour and would they be kind enough to put her up for two or three days as he thought she was not fit to attempt the particular ascent of this rather difficult climb up the headland to where there was a memorial tower which was the principal event of yesterday's tour."

"And you took that also as an indication of what you were to do?"

"Of course," said Miss Marple. "There can be no other reason for it. He was not a man to shower benefits for nothing, out of compassion for an old lady who wasn't good at walking up hills. No. He *wanted* me to go there."

"And you went there? And what then?"

"Nothing," said Miss Marple. "Three sisters."

"Three weird sisters?"

"They ought to have been," said Miss Marple, "but I don't think they were. They didn't seem to be, anyway. I don't know yet. I suppose they may have been—they may be, I mean. They seem ordinary enough. They didn't belong to this house. It had belonged to an uncle of theirs and they'd come here to live some years ago. They are in rather poor circumstances, they are amiable, not particularly interesting. All slightly different in type. They do not appear to have been well acquainted with Mr. Rafiel. Any conversation I have had with them appears to yield nothing."

"So you learnt nothing during your stay?"

"I learnt the facts of the case you've just told me. Not from them. From an elderly servant, who started her reminiscences dating back to the time of the uncle. She knew of Mr. Rafiel only as a name. But she was eloquent on the theme of the murder. It had all started with the visit here of a son of Mr. Rafiel's who was a bad lot, of how the girl had fallen in love with him and that he'd strangled the girl, and how sad and tragic and terrible it all was. 'With bells on, as you might say,' " said Miss Marple, using a phrase of her youth. "Plenty of exaggeration, but it was a nasty story, and she seemed to believe that the police view was that this hadn't been his only murder."

"It didn't seem to you to connect up with the three weird sisters?"

"No, only that they'd been the guardians of the girl—and had loved her dearly. No more than that."

"They might know something—something about another man?"

"Yes—that's what we want, isn't it? The other man—a man of brutality, who wouldn't hesitate to bash in a girl's head after he'd killed her. The kind of man who could be driven frantic with jealousy. There are men like that."

"No other curious things happened at The Old Manor?"

"Not really. One of the sisters, the youngest, I think, kept talking about the garden. She sounded as though she was a very keen gardener, but she couldn't be because she didn't know the names of half the things. I laid a trap or two for her, mentioning special rare shrubs and saying did she know it? and yes, she said, wasn't it a wonderful plant? I said it was not very hardy and she agreed. But she didn't know anything about plants. That reminds me—"

"Reminds you of what?"

"Well, you'll think I'm just silly about gardens and plants, but I mean one does *know* things about them. I mean, I know a few things about birds and I know some things about gardens."

"And I gather that it's not birds but gardens that are troubling you."

"Yes. Have you noticed two middle-aged women on this tour? Miss Barrow and Miss Cooke."

"Yes. I've noticed them. Pair of middle-aged spinsters travelling together."

"That's right. Well, I've found out something odd about Miss Cooke. That is her name, isn't it? I mean it's her name on the tour."

"Why—has she got another name?"

"I think so. She's the same person who visited me—I won't say visited me exactly, but she was outside my garden fence in St. Mary Mead, the village where I live. She expressed pleasure at my garden and talked about gardening with me. Told me she was living in the village and working in somebody's garden who'd moved into a new house there. I rather think," said Miss Marple, "yes, I rather think that the whole thing was lies. There again, she knew nothing about gardening. She pretended to, but it wasn't true."

"Why do you think she came there?"

"I'd no idea at the time. She said her name was Bartlett—and the name of the woman she said she was living with began with 'H,' though I can't remember it for the moment. Her hair was not only differently done but it was a different colour and her clothes were of a different style. I didn't recognize her at first on this trip. Just wondered why her face was vaguely familiar. And then suddenly it came to me—because of the dyed hair. I said where I had seen her before. She admitted that she'd been there—but pretended that she, too, hadn't recognized *me.* All lies."

"And what's your opinion about all that?"

"Well, one thing certainly—Miss Cooke (to give her her present name) came to St. Mary Mead just to have a look at me—so that she'd be quite sure to be able to recognize me when we met again—"

"And why was that felt to be necessary?"

"I don't know. There are two possibilities. I'm not sure that I like one of them very much."

"I don't know," said Professor Wanstead, "that I like it very much either."

They were both silent for a minute or two, and then Professor Wanstead said:

"I don't like what happened to Elizabeth Temple. You've talked to her during this trip?"

"Yes, I have. When she's better I'd like to talk to her again—she could tell me—us—things about the girl who was murdered. She spoke to me of this girl—who had been at her school, who had been going to marry Mr. Rafiel's son—but didn't marry him. Instead she died. I asked how or why she died—and she answered with the word 'love.' I took it as meaning a suicide—but it was murder. Murder through jealousy would fit. Another man. Some other man we've got to find. Miss Temple may be able to tell us who he was."

"No other sinister possibilities?"

"I think, really, it is casual information we need. I see no reason to believe that there is any sinister suggestion in any of the coach passengers—or any sinister suggestion about the people living in The Old Manor House. But one of those three sisters may have known or remembered something that the girl or Michael once said. Clotilde used to take the girl abroad. Therefore, she may know of something that occurred on some foreign trip perhaps. Something that the girl said or mentioned or did on some trip. Some man that the girl met. Something which has nothing to do with The Old Manor House here. It is difficult because only by talking, by casual information, can you get any clue. The second sister, Mrs. Glynne, married fairly early, has spent time, I gather, in India and Africa. She may have heard of something through her husband, or through her husband's relations, through various things that are unconnected with The Old Manor House here although she has visited it from time to time. She knew the murdered girl presumably, but I should think she knew her much less well than the other two. But that does not mean that she may not know some significant facts about the girl. The third sister is more scatterbrained, more localized, does not seem to have known the girl as well. But still she, too, may have information about possible lovers—or boy friends—seen the girl with an unknown man. That's her, by the way, passing the hotel now."

Miss Marple, however occupied by her tête-à-tête, had not relinquished the habits of a lifetime. A public thoroughfare was always to her an observation post. All the passers-by, either loitering or hurrying, had been noticed automatically.

"Anthea Bradbury-Scott—the one with the big parcel. She's going to the post office, I suppose. It's just round the corner, isn't it?"

"Looks a bit daft to me," said Professor Wanstead, "all that floating hair—grey hair, too—a kind of Ophelia of fifty."

"I thought of Ophelia, too, when I first saw her. Oh, dear, I wish I knew what I ought to do next. Stay here at the Golden Boar for a day or two, or go on with the coach tour. It's like looking for a needle in a haystack. If you stick your fingers in it long enough, you ought to come up with something—even if you do get pricked in the process."

13

BLACK AND RED CHECK

Mrs. Sandbourne returned just as the party was sitting down to lunch. Her news was not good. Miss Temple was still unconscious. She certainly could not be moved for several days.

Having given the bulletin, Mrs. Sandbourne turned the conversation to practical matters. She produced suitable timetables of trains for those who wished to return to London and proposed suitable plans for the resumption of the tour on the morrow or the next day. She had a list of suitable short expeditions in the near neighbourhood for this afternoon—small groups in hired cars.

Professor Wanstead drew Miss Marple aside as they went out of the dining room.

"You may want to rest this afternoon. If not, I will call for you here in an hour's time. There is an interesting church you might care to see."

"That would be very nice," said Miss Marple.

II

Miss Marple sat quite still in the car that had come to fetch her. Professor Wanstead was sitting beside her. He had called for her at the time he had said.

"I thought you might enjoy seeing this particular church. And a very pretty village, too," he explained. "There's no reason, really, why one should not enjoy the local sights when one can."

"It's very kind of you, I'm sure," Miss Marple had said.

She had looked at him with that slightly fluttery gaze of hers.

"Very kind," she said. "It just seems—well, I don't want to say it seems heartless, but, well, you know what I mean."

"My dear lady, Miss Temple is not an old friend of yours or anything like that. Sad as this accident has been."

"Well," said Miss Marple again, "this is very kind of you."

The car was, she presumed, a hired one. A kindly thought to take an elderly lady to see one of the sights of the neighbourhood. Professor Wanstead might have taken somebody younger, more interesting and certainly better-looking. Miss Marple looked at him thoughtfully once or twice as they drove through the village. He was not looking at her. He was gazing out of his own window.

When they had left the village behind and were on a second-class country road twisting round the hillside, he turned his head and said to her:

"We are not going to a church, I am afraid."

"No," said Miss Marple, "I thought perhaps we weren't."

"Yes, the idea would have come to you."

"Where are we going, may I ask?"

"We are going to a hospital in Carristown."

"Ah, yes, that was where Miss Temple was taken?"

It was a question, though it hardly needed to be one.

"Yes," he said. "Mrs. Sandbourne saw her and brought me back a letter from the hospital authorities. I have just finished talking to them on the telephone."

"Is she going on well?"

"No. Not going on very well."

"I see. At least—I hope I don't see," said Miss Marple.

"Her recovery is very problematical, but there is nothing that can be done. She may not recover consciousness again. On the other hand she may have a few lucid intervals."

"And you are taking me there? Why? I am not a friend of hers, you know. I only just met her for the first time on this trip."

"Yes, I realized that. I'm taking you there because in one of the lucid intervals she has had, she asked for you."

"I see," said Miss Marple. "I wonder why she should ask for me, why she should have thought that I—that I could be useful in any way to her, or do anything. She is a woman of perception. In her way, you know, a great woman. As headmistress of Fallowfield she occupied a prominent position in the educational world."

"The best girls' school there is, I suppose?"

"Yes. She was a great personality. She was herself a woman of considerable scholarship. Mathematics were her specialty, but she was an 'all-around'—what I should call an educator. Was interested in education, what girls were fitted for, how to encourage them. Oh, many other things.

It is sad and very cruel if she dies," said Miss Marple. "It will seem such a waste of a life. Although she had retired from her headmistress-ship, she still exercised a lot of power. This accident—" She stopped. "Perhaps you do not want us to discuss the accident?"

"I think it is better that we should do so. A big boulder crashed down the hillside. It has been known to happen before, though only at very long divided intervals of time. However, somebody came and spoke to me about it," said Professor Wanstead.

"Came and spoke to you about the accident? Who was it?"

"The two young people. Joanna Crawford and Emlyn Price."

"What did they say?"

"Joanna told me that she had the impression there was someone on the hillside. Rather high up. She and Emlyn were climbing up from the lower main path, following a rough track that wound round the curve of the hill. As they turned a corner, she definitely saw, outlined against the skyline, a man or a woman who was trying to roll a big boulder forward along the ground. The boulder was rocking—and finally it started to roll, at first slowly and then gathering speed down the hillside. Miss Temple was walking along the main path below, and had come to a point just underneath it when the boulder hit her. If it was done deliberately, it might not, of course, have succeeded; it might have missed her—but it did succeed. If what was being attempted was a deliberate attack on the woman walking below, it succeeded only too well."

"Was it a man or a woman they saw?" asked Miss Marple.

"Unfortunately, Joanna Crawford could not say. Whoever it was was wearing jeans or trousers, and had on a lurid polo neck pullover in red and black checks. The figure turned and moved out of sight almost immediately. She is inclined to think it was a man, but cannot be certain."

"And she thinks, or you think, that it was a deliberate attempt on Miss Temple's life?"

"The more she mulls it over, the more she thinks that that was exactly what it was. The boy agrees."

"You have no idea who it might have been?"

"No idea whatever. No more have they. It might be one of our fellow-travellers, someone who went for a stroll that afternoon. It might be someone completely unknown who knew that the coach was making a halt here and chose this place to make an attack on one of the passengers. Some youthful lover of violence for violence's sake. Or it might have been an enemy."

"It seems very melodramatic if one says 'a secret enemy,' " said Miss Marple.

"Yes, it does. Who would want to kill a retired and respected headmistress? That is a question we want answered. It is possible, faintly possible, that Miss Temple herself might be able to tell us. She might have recognized the figure above her or she might more likely have known of someone who bore her ill-will for some special reason."

"It still seems unlikely."

"I agree with you," said Professor Wanstead. "She seems a totally unlikely person to be a fit victim of attack, but yet when one reflects, a headmistress knows a great many people. A great many people, shall we put it this way, have passed through her hands."

"A lot of girls, you mean, have passed through her hands."

"Yes. Yes, that is what I meant. Girls and their families. A headmistress must have knowledge of many things. Romances, for instance, that girls might indulge in, unknown to their parents. It happens, you know. It happens very often. Especially in the last ten or twenty years. Girls are said to mature earlier. That is physically true, though in a deeper sense of the word, they mature late. They remain childish longer—childish in the clothes they like to wear, childish with their floating hair. Even their mini skirts represent a worship of childishness. Their baby doll nightdresses, their gym slips and shorts—all children's fashions. They wish not to become adult—not to have to accept our kind of responsibility. And yet like all children, they want to be thought grown-up and free to do what they think are grown-up things. And that leads sometimes to tragedy and sometimes to the aftermath of tragedy."

"Are you thinking of some particular case?"

"No. No, not really. I'm only thinking—well, shall we say letting possibilities pass through my mind? I cannot believe that Elizabeth Temple had a *personal* enemy—an enemy ruthless enough to wish to take an opportunity of killing her. What I do think—" He looked at Miss Marple. "Would you like to make a suggestion?"

"Of a possibility? Well, I think I know or guess what you are suggesting. You are suggesting that Miss Temple knew something, knew some fact or had some knowledge that would be inconvenient or even dangerous to somebody if it was known."

"Yes, I do feel exactly that."

"In that case," said Miss Marple, "it seems indicated that there is someone on our coach tour who recognized Miss Temple or knew who she was, but who perhaps after the passage of some years was not remembered or might even not have been recognized by Miss Temple. It seems to throw it back on our passengers, does it not?" She paused. "That pullover you mentioned—red and black checks, you said?"

"Oh, yes? The pullover—" He looked at her curiously. "What was it that struck you about that?"

"It was very noticeable," said Miss Marple. "That is what your words led me to infer. It was very mentionable. So much so that the girl Joanna mentioned it specifically."

"Yes. And what does that suggest to you?"

"The trailing of flags," said Miss Marple thoughtfully. "Something that will be seen, remembered, observed, recognized."

"Yes." Professor Wanstead looked at her with encouragement.

"When you describe a person you have seen—seen not close at hand but from a distance—the first thing you will describe will be their clothes. Not their faces, not their walk, not their hands, not their feet. A scarlet tam-o'-shanter, a purple cloak, a bizarre leather jacket, a pullover of brilliant reds and blacks. Something very recognizable, very noticeable. The object of it being that when that person removes that garment, gets rid of it, sends it by post in a parcel to some address, say, about a hundred miles away, or thrusts it in a rubbish bin in a city or burns it or tears it up or destroys it, she or he will be the one person modestly and rather drably attired who will not be suspected or looked at or thought of. It must have been *meant,* that scarlet and black check jersey. Meant so that it will be recognized again though actually it will never again be seen on that particular person."

"A very sound idea," said Professor Wanstead. "As I have told you," continued the professor, "Fallowfield is situated not very far from here. Sixteen miles, I think. So this is Elizabeth Temple's part of the world—a part she knows well, with people in it that she also might know well."

"Yes. It widens the possibilities," said Miss Marple. "I agree with you," she said presently, "that the attacker is more likely to have been a man than a woman. That boulder, if it was done with intent, was sent on its course very accurately. Accuracy is more a male quality than a female one. On the other hand there might easily have been someone on our coach, or possibly in the neighbourhood, who saw Miss Temple in the street, a former pupil of hers in past years—someone whom she herself might not recognize after a period of time. But the girl or woman would have recognized her, because a headmaster or headmistress of over sixty is not unlike the same headmaster or headmistress at the age of fifty. She is recognizable. Some woman who recognized her former headmistress and also knew that her headmistress knew something damaging about her. Someone who might in some way prove a danger to her." She sighed. "I myself do not know this part of the world at all. Have you any particular knowledge of it?"

"No," said Professor Wanstead. "I could not claim a personal knowledge of this part of the country. I know something, however, of various things that have happened in this part of the world entirely because of what you have told me. If it had not been for my acquaintanceship with you and the things you have told me I should have been more at sea than I am.

"What are you yourself actually doing here? You do not know. Yet you were sent here. It was deliberately arranged by Rafiel that you should come here, that you should take this coach tour, that you and I should meet. There have been other places where we have stopped or through which we have passed, but special arrangements here were made so that you should actually stay for a couple of nights here. You were put up with former friends of his who would not have refused any request he made. Was there a reason for that?"

"So that I could learn certain facts that I had to know," said Miss Marple.

"A series of murders that took place a good many years ago?" Professor Wanstead looked doubtful. "There is nothing unusual in that. You can say the same of many places in England and Wales. These things seem always to go in a series. First a girl found assaulted and murdered. Then another girl not very far away. Then something of the same kind perhaps twenty miles away. The same pattern of death.

"Two girls were reported missing from Jocelyn St. Mary itself, the one that we have been discussing whose body was found six months later, many miles away and who was last seen in the company of Michael Rafiel—"

"And the other?"

"A girl called Nora Broad. Not a 'quiet girl with no boy friends.' Possibly with one boy friend too many. Her body was never found. It will be—one day. There have been cases when twenty years have passed," said Wanstead. He slowed down. "We have arrived. This is Carristown, and here is the hospital."

Shepherded by Professor Wanstead, Miss Marple entered. The professor was obviously expected. He was ushered into a small room where a woman rose from a desk.

"Oh, yes," she said, "Professor Wanstead. And—er—this is—er—" She hesitated slightly.

"Miss Jane Marple," said Professor Wanstead. "I talked to Sister Barker on the telephone."

"Oh, yes. Sister Barker said that she would be accompanying you."

"How is Miss Temple?"

"Much the same, I think. I am afraid there is not much improvement to report." She rose. "I will take you to Sister Barker."

Sister Barker was a tall, thin woman. She had a low, decisive voice and dark grey eyes that had a habit of looking at you and looking away almost immediately, leaving you with the feeling that you had been inspected in a very short space of time and judgment pronounced upon you.

"I don't know what arrangements you have in mind," said Professor Wanstead.

"Well, I had better tell Miss Marple just what we have arranged. First I must make it clear to you that the patient, Miss Temple, is still in a coma with very rare lucid intervals. She appears to come to occasionally, to recognize her surroundings and to be able to say a few words. But there is nothing one can do to stimulate her. It has to be left to the utmost patience. I expect Professor Wanstead has already told you that in one of her intervals of consciousness she uttered quite distinctly the words 'Miss Jane Marple.' And then: *'I want to speak to her. Miss Jane Marple.'* After that she relapsed into unconsciousness. Doctor thought it advisable to get in touch with the other occupants of the coach. Professor Wanstead came to see us and explained various matters and said he would bring you over. I am afraid that all we can ask you to do is to sit in the private ward where Miss Temple is, and perhaps be ready to make a note of any words she should say if she does regain consciousness. I am afraid the prognosis is not very hopeful. To be quite frank, which is better, I think, since you are not a near relative and are unlikely to be disturbed by this information, Doctor thinks that she is sinking fast, that she may die without recovering consciousness. There is nothing one can do to relieve the concussion. It is important that someone should hear what she says, and Doctor thinks it advisable that she should not see too many people round her if she regains consciousness. If Miss Marple is not worried at the thought of sitting there alone, there will be a nurse in the room, though not obviously so. That is, she will not be noticed from the bed, and will not move unless she's asked for. She will sit in a corner of the room shielded by a screen." She added, "We have a police official there also, ready to take down anything. The doctor thinks it advisable that he also should not be noticed by Miss Temple. One person alone, and that possibly a person she expects to see, will not alarm her or make her lose knowledge of what she wants to say to you. I hope this will not be too difficult a thing to ask you?"

"Oh, no," said Miss Marple. "I'm quite prepared to do that. I have a small notebook with me and a biro pen that will not be in evidence. I can remember things by heart for a very short time, so I need not appear to be obviously taking notes of what she says. You can trust my memory and I am not deaf—not deaf in the real sense of the word. I don't think my hearing is quite as good as it used to be, but if I am sitting near a bedside, I ought to be able to hear anything she says quite easily even if it is whispered. I am used to sick people. I have had a good deal to do with them in my time."

Again the lightning glance of Sister Barker went over Miss Marple. This time a faint inclination of the head showed satisfaction.

"It is kind of you," she said, "and I am sure that if there is any help you can give, we can rely on you to give it. If Professor Wanstead likes to sit in the waiting room downstairs, we can call him at any moment if it should be necessary. Now, Miss Marple, perhaps you will accompany me."

Miss Marple followed Sister along a passage and into a small, well-appointed single room. In the bed there, in a dimly lighted room, since the blinds were half drawn, lay Elizabeth Temple. She lay there like a statue, yet she did not give the impression of being asleep. Her breath came uncertainly in slight gasps. Sister Barker bent to examine her patient, motioned Miss Marple into a chair beside the bed. She then crossed the room to the door again. A young man with a notebook in his hand came from behind the screen there.

"Doctor's orders, Mr. Reckitt," said Sister Barker.

A nurse also appeared. She had been sitting in the opposite corner of the room.

"Call me if necessary, Nurse Edmonds," said Sister Barker, "and get Miss Marple anything she may need."

Miss Marple loosened her coat. The room was warm. The nurse approached and took it from her. Then she retired to her former position. Miss Marple sat down in the chair. She looked at Elizabeth Temple thinking, as she had thought before when looking at her in the coach, what a fine-shaped head she had. Her grey hair drawn back from it fitted her face in a perfect caplike effect. A handsome woman, and a woman of personality. Yes, a thousand pities, Miss Marple thought, a thousand pities if the world was going to lose Elizabeth Temple.

Miss Marple eased the cushion at her back, moved the chair a fraction of an inch and sat quietly to wait. Whether to wait in vain or to some point, she had no idea. Time passed. Ten minutes, twenty minutes, half an hour, thirty-five minutes. Then suddenly, quite unexpectedly, as it were, a voice came. Low, but distinct, slightly husky, with none of the resonance it had once held: "Miss Marple."

Elizabeth Temple's eyes were open now. They were looking at Miss Marple. They looked competent, perfectly sensible. She was studying the face of the woman who was sitting by her bed, studying her without any sign of emotion, of surprise—only, one would say, of scrutiny—fully conscious scrutiny. And the voice spoke again:

"Miss Marple. You are Jane Marple?"

"That is right. Yes," said Miss Marple, "Jane Marple."

"Henry often spoke of you. He said things about you."

The voice stopped. Miss Marple said with a slight query in her voice: "Henry?"

"Henry Clithering, an old friend of mine—very old friend."

"An old friend of mine, too," said Miss Marple. "Henry Clithering."

Her mind went back to the many years she had known him, Sir Henry Clithering, the things he had said to her, the assistance he had asked from her sometimes, and the assistance that she had asked from him. A very old friend.

"I remembered your name. On the passenger list. I thought it must be you. You could help. That's what he—Henry, yes—would say if he were here. You might be able to help. To find out. It's important—very important, although—it's a long time ago now—a—long—time—ago."

Her voice faltered a little, her eyes half closed. Nurse got up, came across the room, picked up a small glass and held it to Elizabeth Temple's lips. Miss Temple took a sip, nodded her head dismissively. Nurse put down the glass and went back to her chair.

"If I can help, I will," said Miss Marple. She asked no further questions.

Miss Temple said, "Good," and after a minute or two, again, "Good."

For two or three minutes she lay with her eyes closed. She might have been asleep or unconscious. Then her eyes opened again suddenly.

"Which," she said, "which of them? That's what one has got to know. Do you know what I am talking about?"

"I think so. A girl who died—Nora Broad?" A frown came quickly to Elizabeth Temple's forehead.

"No, no, no. The other girl. Verity Hunt."

There was a pause and then, "Jane Marple. You're old—older than when he talked about you. You're older, but you can still find out things, can't you?"

Her voice became slightly higher, more insistent.

"You can, can't you? Say you can. I've not much time. I know that. I know it quite well. One of them, but which? Find out. Henry would have said you can. It may be dangerous for you—but you'll find out, won't you?"

"With God's help, I will," said Miss Marple. It was a vow.

"Ah."

The eyes closed, then opened again. Something like a smile seemed to try to twitch the lips.

"The big stone from above. The stone of death."

"Who rolled that stone down?"

"Don't know. No matter—only—Verity. Find out about Verity. Truth. Another name for truth, Verity."

Miss Marple saw the faint relaxation of the body on the bed. There was a faintly whispered "Good-bye. Do your best . . ."

Her body relaxed, the eyes closed. The nurse came again to the bedside. This time she took up the pulse, felt it, and beckoned to Miss Marple. Miss Marple rose obediently and followed her out of the room.

"That's been a big effort for her," said the nurse. "She won't regain consciousness again for some time. Perhaps not at all. I hope you learnt something?"

"I don't think I did," said Miss Marple, "But one never knows, does one?"

"Did you get anything?" asked Professor Wanstead as they went out to the car.

"A name," said Miss Marple. "Verity. Was that the girl's name?"

"Yes. Verity Hunt."

Elizabeth Temple died an hour and a half later. She died without regaining consciousness.

14

MR. BROADRIBB WONDERS

"See *The Times* this morning?" said Mr. Broadribb to his partner, Mr. Schuster.

Mr. Schuster said he couldn't afford *The Times,* he took the *Telegraph.*

"Well, it may be in that, too," said Mr. Broadribb. "In the deaths, Miss Elizabeth Temple, D.Sc."

Mr. Schuster looked faintly puzzled.

"Headmistress of Fallowfield. You've heard of Fallowfield, haven't you?"

"Of course," said Schuster. "Girls' school. Been going for fifty years or so. First-class, fantastically expensive. So she was the headmistress of it, was she? I thought the headmistress had resigned some time ago. Six months at least. I'm sure I read about it in the paper. That is to say there was a bit about the new headmistress. Married woman. Youngish. Thirty-five to forty. Modern ideas. Give the girls lessons in cosmetics, let 'em wear trouser suits. Something of that kind."

"Hum," said Mr. Broadribb, making the noise that solicitors of his age are likely to make when they hear something which elicits criticism based on long experience. "Don't think she'll ever make the name that Elizabeth Temple did. Quite someone, she was. Been there a long time, too."

"Yes," said Mr. Schuster, somewhat uninterested. He wondered why Broadribb was so interested in defunct schoolmistresses.

Schools were not really of particular interest to either of the two gentlemen. Their own offspring were now more or less disposed of. Mr. Broadribb's two sons were respectively in the Civil Service and in an oil firm, and Mr. Schuster's rather younger progeny were at different universities where both of them respectively were making as much trouble for those in authority as they possibly could do. He said:

"What about her?"

"She was on a coach tour," said Mr. Broadribb.

"Those coaches," said Mr. Schuster. "I wouldn't let any of my relations go on one of those. One went off a precipice in Switzerland last week, and two months ago one had a crash and twenty were killed. Don't know who drives these things nowadays."

"It was one of those Country Houses and Gardens and Objects of Interest in Britain—or whatever they call it—tours," said Mr. Broadribb. "That's not quite the right name, but you know what I mean."

"Oh, yes, I know. Oh, the—er—yes, that's the one we sent Miss What's-a-name on. The one old Rafiel booked."

"Miss Jane Marple was on it."

"She didn't get killed too, did she?" asked Mr. Schuster.

"Not so far as I know," said Mr. Broadribb. "I just wondered a bit, though."

"Was it a road accident?"

"No. It was at one of the beauty spot places. They were walking on a path up a hill. It was a stiff walk—up a rather steep hill with boulders and things on it. Some of the boulders got loose and came rushing down the mountainside. Miss Temple was knocked out and taken to hospital with concussion and died—"

"Bad luck," said Mr. Schuster, and waited for more.

"I only wondered," said Mr. Broadribb, "because I happened to remember that—well, that Fallowfield was the school where the girl was at."

"What girl? I don't really know what you're talking about, Broadribb."

"The girl who was done in by young Michael Rafiel. I was just recalling a few things which might seem to have some slight connection with this curious Jane Marple business that old Rafiel was so keen on. Wish he'd told us more."

"What's the connection?" said Mr. Schuster.

He looked more interested now. His legal wits were in process of being sharpened, to give a sound opinion on whatever it was that Mr. Broadribb was about to confide to him.

"That girl. Can't remember her last name now. Christian name was Hope or Faith or something like that. Verity, that was her name. Verity Hunter, I think it was. She was one of that series of murdered girls. Found her body in a ditch about thirty miles away from where she'd gone missing. Been dead six months. Strangled, apparently, and her head and face had been bashed in—to delay recognition, they thought, but she was recognized all right. Clothes, handbag, jewellery nearby—some mole or scar. Oh, yes, she was identified quite easily—"

"Actually, she was the one the trial was all about, wasn't she?"

"Yes. Suspected of having done away with perhaps three other girls during the past year, Michael was. But evidence wasn't so good in the other deaths—so the police went all-out on this one—plenty of evidence—bad record. Earlier cases of assault and rape. Well, we all know what rape is nowadays. Mum tells the girl she's got to accuse the young man of rape even if the young man hasn't had much chance, with the girl at him all the time to come to the house while Mum's away at work or Dad's gone on holiday. Doesn't stop badgering him until she's forced him to sleep with her. Then, as I say, Mum tells the girl to call it rape. However, that's not the point," said Mr. Broadribb. "I wondered if things mightn't tie up a bit, you know. I thought this Jane Marple business with Rafiel might have something to do with Michael."

"Found guilty, wasn't he? And given a life sentence?"

"I can't remember now—it's so long ago. Or did they get away with a verdict of diminished responsibility?"

"And Verity Hunter or Hunt was educated at that school. Miss Temple's school. She wasn't still a schoolgirl, though, was she, when she was killed? Not that I can remember."

"Oh, no. She was eighteen or nineteen, living with relations or friends of her parents, or something like that. Nice house, nice people, nice girl, by all accounts—the sort of girl whose relations always say 'she was a very quiet girl, rather shy, didn't go about with strange people and had no boy friends.' Relations never know what boy friends a girl has. The girls take mighty good care of that. And young Rafiel was said to be very attractive to girls."

"Never been any doubt that he did it?" asked Mr. Schuster.

"Not a scrap. Told a lot of lies in the witness box, anyway. His counsel would have done better not to have let him give evidence. A lot of his friends gave him an alibi that didn't stand up, if you know what I mean. All his friends seemed to be fluent liars."

"What's your feeling about it, Broadribb?"

"Oh, I haven't got any feelings," said Mr. Broadribb, "I was just wondering if this woman's death might tie up."

"In what way?"

"Well, you know—about these boulders that fall down cliffsides and drop on top of someone. It's not always in the course of nature. Boulders usually stay where they are, in my experience."

15

VERITY

"Verity," said Miss Marple.

Elizabeth Margaret Temple had died the evening before. It had been a peaceful death. Miss Marple, sitting once more amid the faded chintz of the drawing room in The Old Manor House, had laid aside the baby's pink coat which she had previously been engaged in knitting and had substituted a crocheted purple scarf. This half-mourning touch went with Miss Marple's early-Victorian ideas of tactfulness in face of tragedy.

An inquest was to be held on the following day. The vicar had been approached and had agreed to hold a brief memorial service in the church as soon as arrangements could be made. Undertakers suitably attired, with proper mourning faces, took general charge of things in liaison with the police. The inquest was to take place on the following morning at 11 o'clock. Members of the coach tour had agreed to attend the inquest. And several of them had chosen to remain on so as to attend the church service also.

Mrs. Glynne had come to the Golden Boar and urged Miss Marple to return to The Old Manor House until she finally returned to the tour.

"You will get away from all the reporters."

Miss Marple had thanked all three sisters warmly and had accepted.

The coach tour would be resumed after the memorial service, driving first to South Bedestone, thirty-five miles away, where there was a good hotel which had been originally chosen for a stopping place. After that the tour would go on as usual.

There were, however, as Miss Marple had considered likely, certain persons who were disengaging themselves and returning home, or were going in other directions and not continuing on the tour. There was something to be said in favour of either decision. To leave what would become a journey of painful memories, or to continue with the sightseeing that had already been paid for and which had been interrupted only by one of those painful accidents that may happen on any sightseeing expedition. A lot would depend, Miss Marple thought, on the outcome of the inquest.

Miss Marple, after exchanging various conventional remarks proper to the occasion with her three hostesses, had devoted herself to her purple wool and had sat considering her next line of investigation. And so it was that with her fingers still busy, she had uttered the one word "Verity"—throwing it as one throws a pebble into a stream, solely to observe what the result—if any—would be. Would it mean something to her hostesses? It might or it might not. Otherwise, when she joined the members of the tour at their hotel meal this evening, which had been arranged, she would try the effect of it there. It had been, she thought to herself, the last word or almost the last word that Elizabeth Temple had spoken. So therefore, thought Miss Marple (her fingers still busy because she did not need to look at her crocheting, she could read a book or conduct a conversation while her fingers, though slightly crippled with rheumatism, would proceed correctly through their appointed movements). So therefore, "Verity."

Like a stone into a pool, causing ripples, a splash, something? Or nothing. Surely there would be a reaction of one sort or another. Yes, she had not been mistaken. Although her face registered nothing, the keen eyes behind her glasses had watched three people in a simultaneous manner as she had trained herself to do for many years now, when wishing to observe her neighbours either in church, mother's meeting, or at other public functions in St. Mary Mead when she had been on the track of some interesting piece of news or gossip.

Mrs. Glynne had dropped the book she was holding and had looked across toward Miss Marple with slight surprise—surprise, it seemed, at the particular word coming from Miss Marple, but not surprise really to hear it.

Clotilde reacted differently. Her head shot up, she leant forward a little, then she looked not at Miss Marple but across the room in the direction of the window. Her hands clenched themselves, she kept very still. Miss Marple, although dropping her head slightly as though she was not looking any more, noted that her eyes were filling with tears. Clotilde sat quite still and let the tears roll down her cheeks. She made no attempt to take out a handkerchief, she uttered no word. Miss Marple was impressed by the aura of grief that came from her.

Anthea's reaction was different. It was quick, excited, almost pleasurable.

"Verity? Verity, did you say? Did you know her? I'd no idea. It is Verity Hunt you mean?"

Lavinia Glynne said, "It's a Christian name?"

"*I* never knew anyone of that name," said Miss Marple, "but I did mean a Christian name. Yes. It is rather unusual, I think. Verity." She repeated it thoughtfully.

She let her purple wool ball fall and looked round with the slightly apologetic and embarrassed look of one who realizes she had made a serious faux pas, but not sure why.

"I—I am so sorry. Have I said something I shouldn't? It was only because . . ."

"No, of course not," said Mrs. Glynne. "It was just that it is—it is a name we know, a name with which we have—associations."

"It just came into my mind," said Miss Marple, still apologetic, "because, you know, it was poor Miss Temple who said it. I went to see her, you know, yesterday afternoon. Professor Wanstead took me. He seemed to think that I might be able to—to—I don't know if it's the proper word—to *rouse* her, in some way. She was in a coma and they thought—not that I was a friend of hers at any time, but we had chatted together on the tour and we often sat beside each other, as you know, on some of the days and we had talked. And he thought perhaps I might be of some use. I'm afraid I wasn't, though. Not at all. I just sat there and waited and then she did say one or two words, but they didn't seem to mean anything. But finally, just when it was time for me to go, she did open her eyes and looked at me—I don't know if she was mistaking me for someone—but she did say that word. Verity! And, well, of course it stuck in my mind, especially with her passing away yesterday evening. It must have been someone or something that she had in her mind. But of course it might just mean—well, of course it might just mean truth. That's what verity means, doesn't it?"

She looked from Clotilde to Lavinia to Anthea.

"It was the Christian name of a girl we knew," said Lavinia Glynne. "That is why it startled us."

"Especially because of the awful way she died," said Anthea.

Clotilde said in her deep voice, "Anthea! There's no need to go into these details."

"But after all, everyone knows quite well about her," said Anthea. She looked towards Miss Marple. "I thought perhaps you might have known about her because you knew Mr. Rafiel, didn't you? Well, I mean, he wrote to us about you, so you must have known him. And I thought perhaps—well, he'd mentioned the whole thing to you."

"I'm so sorry," said Miss Marple. "I'm afraid I don't quite understand what you're talking about."

"They found her body in a ditch," said Anthea.

There was never any holding Anthea, Miss Marple thought, not once she got going. But she thought that Anthea's vociferous talk was putting additional strain on Clotilde. She had taken out a handkerchief now in a quiet, noncommittal way. She brushed tears from her eyes and then sat upright, her back very straight, her eyes deep and tragic.

"Verity," she said, "was a girl we cared for very much. She lived here for a while. I was very fond of her—"

"And she was very fond of you," said Lavinia.

"Her parents were friends of mine," said Clotilde. "They were killed in a plane accident."

"She was at school at Fallowfield," explained Lavinia. "I suppose that was how Miss Temple came to remember her."

"Oh, I see," said Miss Marple. "Where Miss Temple was headmistress, is that it? I have heard of Fallowfield often, of course. It's a very fine school, isn't it?"

"Yes," said Clotilde. "Verity was a pupil there. After her parents died she came to stay with us for a time while she decided what she wanted to do with the future. She was eighteen or nineteen. A very sweet girl and a very affectionate and loving one. She thought perhaps of training for nursing, but she had very good brains and Miss Temple was insistent that she ought to go to university. So she was studying and having coaching for that when—when this terrible thing happened."

She turned her face away.

"I—do you mind if we don't talk about it any more just now?"

"Oh, of course not," said Miss Marple. "I'm so sorry to have impinged on some tragedy. I didn't know. I—I haven't heard . . . I thought—well, I mean . . ." She became more and more incoherent.

That evening she heard a little more. Mrs. Glynne came to her bedroom when she was changing her dress to go out and join the others at the hotel.

"I thought I ought to come and explain a little to you," said Mrs. Glynne, "about—the girl Verity Hunt. Of course you couldn't know that our sister Clotilde was particularly fond of her and that her really horrible death was a terrible shock. We never mention her if we can help it, but—I think it would be easier if I told you the facts completely and you will understand. Apparently Verity had, without our knowledge, made friends with an undesirable—a more than undesirable—it turned out to be a dangerous—young man who already had a criminal record. He came here to visit us when he was passing through once. We knew his father very well." She paused. "I think I'd better tell you the whole truth if you don't know, and you don't seem to. He was actually Mr. Rafiel's son Michael—"

"Oh, dear," said Miss Marple, "not—not—I can't remember his name, but I do remember hearing that there was a son—and that he hadn't been very satisfactory."

"A little more than that," said Mrs. Glynne. "He'd always given trouble. He'd been had up in court once or twice for various things. Once assaulting a teenager—other things of that type. Of course I consider myself that the magistrates are too lenient with that kind of thing. They don't want to upset a young man's university career. And so they let them off with a—I forget what they call it—a suspended sentence, something of that kind. If these boys were sent to jail at once, it would perhaps warn them off that type of life. He was a thief, too. He had forged checks, he pinched things. He was a thoroughly bad lot. We were friends of his mother's. It was lucky for her, I think, that she died young before she had time to be upset by the way her son was turning out. Mr. Rafiel did all he could, I think. Tried to find suitable jobs for the boy, paid fines for him and things like that. But I think it was a great blow to him, though he pretended to be more or less indifferent and to write it off as one of those things that happen. We had, as probably people here in the village will tell you, we had a bad outbreak of murders and violence in this district. Not only here. They were in different parts of the country, twenty miles away, sometimes fifty miles away. One or two, it's suspected by the police, were nearly a hundred miles away. But they seemed to centre more or less on this part of the world. Anyway, Verity one day went out to visit a friend and—well, she didn't come back. We went to the police about it, the police sought for her, searched the whole countryside, but they couldn't find any trace of her. We advertised, they advertised, and they suggested that she'd gone off with a boy friend. Then word began to get round that she had been seen with Michael Rafiel. By now the police had their eye on Michael as a possibility for certain crimes that had occurred, although they couldn't find any direct evidence. Verity was said to have been seen, described by her clothing and other things, with a young man of Michael's appearance and in a car that corresponded to a description of his car. But there was no further evidence until her body was discovered six months later—thirty miles from here in a rather wild part of wooded country, in a ditch covered with stones and piled earth. Clotilde had to go to identify it. It was Verity, all right. She'd been strangled and her head beaten in. Clotilde has never quite got over the shock. There were certain marks, a mole and an old scar and of course her clothes and the contents of her handbag. Miss Temple was very fond of Verity. She must have thought of her just before she died."

"I'm sorry," said Miss Marple, "I'm really very, very sorry. Please tell your sister that I didn't know. I had no idea."

16

THE INQUEST

Miss Marple walked slowly along the village street on her way towards the market place where the inquest was to take place in the old-fashioned Georgian building which had been known for a hundred years as the Curfew Arms. She glanced at her watch. There was still a good twenty minutes before she need be there. She looked into the shops. She paused before the shop that sold wool and babies' jackets, and peered inside for a few moments. A girl in the shop was serving. Small wooly coats were being tried on two children. Further along the counter there was an elderly woman.

Miss Marple went into the shop, went along the counter to a seat opposite the elderly woman, and produced a sample of pink wool. She had run out, she explained, of this particular brand of wool and had a little jacket she needed to finish. The match was soon made, some more samples of wool that Miss Marple had admired were brought out for her to look at, and soon she was in conversation, starting with the sadness of the accident which had just taken place. Mrs. Merrypit, if her name was identical with that which was written up outside the shop, was full of the importance of the accident and the general difficulties of getting local governments to do anything about the dangers of footpaths and public rights of way.

"After the rain, you see, you get all the soil washed off and then the boulders get loose and then down they come. I remember one year they had three falls—three accidents there was. One boy nearly killed, he was, and then later that year, oh, six months later, I think, there was a man got his arm broken, and the third time it was poor old Mrs. Walker. Blind she was and pretty well deaf, too. She never heard nothing or she could have got out of the way, they say. Somebody saw it and they called out to her, but they was too far away to reach her or to run to get her. And so she was killed."

"Oh, how sad," said Miss Marple; "how tragic. The sort of thing that's not easily forgotten, is it?"

"No, indeed. I expect the coroner'll mention it today."

"I expect he will," said Miss Marple. "In a terrible way it seems quite a natural thing to happen, doesn't it, though of course there are accidents sometimes by pushing things about, you know. Just pushing, making stones rock. That sort of thing."

"Ah, well, there's boys as be up to anything. But I don't think I've ever seen them up that way fooling about."

Miss Marple went on to the subject of pullovers, bright-coloured pullovers.

"It's not for myself," she said, "it's for one of my great-nephews. You know, he wants a polo-necked pullover and very bright colours he'd like."

"Yes, they do like bright colours nowadays, don't they?" agreed Mrs. Merrypit. "Not in jeans. Black jeans they like. Black or dark blue. But they like a bit of brightness up above."

Miss Marple described a pullover of check design in bright colours. There appeared to be quite a good stock of pullovers and jerseys, but anything in red and black did not seem to be on display, nor even was anything like it mentioned as having been lately in stock. After looking at a few samples, Miss Marple prepared to take her departure, chatting first about the former murders she had heard about which had happened in this part of the world.

"They got the fellow in the end," said Mrs. Merrypit. "Nice-looking boy, hardly have thought it of him. He'd been well-brought-up, you know. Been to university and all that. Father was very rich, they say. Touched in the head, I suppose. Not that they sent him to Broadway, or whatever the place is. No, they didn't do that, but I think myself he must have been a mental case—there was five or six other girls, so they said. The police had one after another of the young men round hereabouts to help them. Geoffrey Grant they had up. They were pretty sure it was him to begin with. He was always a bit queer ever since he was a boy. Interfered with little girls going to school, you know. He used to offer them sweets and get them to come down the lanes with him and see the primroses, or something like that. Yes, they had very strong suspicions about him. But it wasn't him. And then there was another one. Bert Williams, but he'd been far away on two occasions at least—what they call an alibi, so it couldn't be him. And then at last it came to this—what's-'is-name, I can't remember him now. Luke I think his name was—no, Mike something. Very nice-looking, as I say, but he had a bad record. Yes, stealing, forging checks, all sort of things like that. And two what you call 'em paternity cases. No, I don't mean that, but you know what I mean. When a girl's going to have a baby. You know and they make an order and make the fellow pay. He'd got two girls in the family way before this."

"Was this girl in the family way?"

"Oh, yes, she was. At first we thought when the body was found it might have been Nora Broad. That was Mrs. Broad's niece, down at the mill shop. Great one for going with the boys, she was. She'd gone away missing from home in the same way. Nobody knew where she was. So when this body turned up six months later, they thought at first it was her."

"But it wasn't?"

"No—someone quite different."

"Did her body ever turn up?"

"No. I suppose it might someday, but they think on the whole it was pushed into the river. Ah, well, you never know, do you? You never know what you may dig up off a ploughed field or something like that. I was taken once to see all that treasure. Luton Loo was it—some name like that. Somewhere in the East Counties. Under a ploughed field it was. Beautiful. Gold ships and Viking ships and gold plate, enormous great platters. Well, you never know. Any day you may turn up a dead body or you may turn up a gold platter. And it may be hundreds of years old like that gold plate was, or it may be a three- or four-years-old body, like Mary Lucas, who'd been missing for four years, they say. Somewhere near Reigate she was found. Ah, well, all these things! It's a sad life. Yes, it's a very sad life. You never know what's coming."

"There was another girl who'd lived here, wasn't there," said Miss Marple, "who was killed?"

"You mean the body they thought was Nora Broad's but it wasn't? Yes. I've forgotten her name now. Hope, it was, I think. Hope or Charity. One of those sort of names, if you know what I mean. Used to be used a lot in Victorian times, but you don't hear them so much nowadays. Lived at the Manor House, she did. She'd been there for some time after her parents were killed."

"Her parents died in an accident, didn't they?"

"That's right. In a plane going to Spain or Italy, one of those places."

"And you say she came to live here? Were they relations of hers?"

"I don't know if they were relations, but Mrs. Glynne, as she is now, was, I think, a great friend of her mother's or something that way. Mrs. Glynne, of course, was married and gone abroad, but Miss Clotilde—that's the eldest one, the dark one—she was very fond of the girl. She took her abroad, to Italy and France and all sorts of places, and she had her trained —a bit of typewriting and shorthand and that sort of thing, and art classes, too. She's very arty, Miss Clotilde is. Oh, she was mighty fond of the girl.

Broken hearted she was when she disappeared. Quite different to Miss Anthea—"

"Miss Anthea is the youngest one, isn't she?"

"Yes. Not quite all there, some people say. Scattylike, you know, in her mind. Sometimes you see her walking along talking to herself, you know, and tossing her head in a very queer way. Children get frightened of her sometimes. They say she's a bit queer about things. I don't know. You hear everything in a village, don't you? The great-uncle who lived here before, he was a bit peculiar, too. Used to practice revolver shooting in the garden. For no reason at all so far as anyone could see. Proud of his marksmanship, he said he was, whatever marksmanship is."

"But Miss Clotilde is not peculiar?"

"Oh, no, she's clever, she is. Knows Latin and Greek, I believe. Would have liked to go to university, but she had to look after her mother, who was an invalid for a long time. But she was very fond of Miss—now, what was her name?—Faith, perhaps. She was very fond of her and treated her like a daughter. And then along comes this young what's-his-name, Michael, I think it was—and then one day the girl just goes off without saying a word to anyone. I don't know if Miss Clotilde knew as she was in the family way."

"But you knew," said Miss Marple.

"Ah, well, I've got a lot of experience. I usually know when a girl's that way. It's plain enough to the eye. It's not only the shape, as you might say, you can tell by the look in their eyes and the way they walk and sit, and the sort of giddy fits they get and sick turns now and again. Oh, yes, I thought to myself. Here's another one of them. Miss Clotilde had to go and identify the body. Nearly broke her up, it did. She was like a different woman for weeks afterwards. Fairly loved that girl, she did."

"And the other one—Miss Anthea?"

"Funnily enough, you know, I thought she had a kind of pleased look as though she was—yes, just pleased. Not nice, eh? Farmer Plummer's daughter used to look like that. Always used to go and see pigs killed. Enjoyed it. Funny things goes on in families."

Miss Marple said good-bye, saw she had another ten minutes to go and passed on to the post office. The post office and general store of Jocelyn St. Mary was just off the Market Square.

Miss Marple went into the post office, bought some stamps, looked at some of the postcards and then turned her attention to various paperback books. A middle-aged woman with rather a vinegary face presided behind the postal counter. She assisted Miss Marple to free a book from the wire support in which the books were.

"Stick a bit sometimes, they do. People don't put them back straight, you see."

There was by now no one else in the shop. Miss Marple looked with distaste at the jacket of the book, a naked girl with bloodstained markings on her face and a sinister-looking killer bending over her with a blood-stained knife in his hand.

"Really," she said, "I don't like these horrors nowadays."

"Gone a bit too far with some of their jackets, haven't they?" said Mrs. Vinegar. "Not everyone as likes them. Too fond of violence in every way, I'd say nowadays."

Miss Marple detached a second book. *"Whatever Happened to Baby Jane?"* she read. "Oh, dear, it's a sad world one lives in."

"Oh, yes, I know. Saw in yesterday's paper, I did, some woman left her baby outside a supermarket and then someone else comes along and wheels it away. And all for no reason as far as one can see. The police found her, all right. They all seem to say the same things, whether they steal from a supermarket or take away a baby. Don't know what came over them, they say."

"Perhaps they really don't," suggested Miss Marple.

Mrs. Vinegar looked even more like vinegar.

"Take me a lot to believe that, it would."

Miss Marple looked round—the post office was still empty. She advanced to the window.

"If you are not too busy, I wonder if you could answer a question of mine," said Miss Marple. "I have done something extremely stupid. Of late years I make so many mistakes. This was a parcel addressed to a charity. I send them clothes—pullovers and children's woolies, and I did it up and addressed it and it was sent off—and only this morning it came to me suddenly that I'd made a mistake and written the wrong address. I don't suppose any list is kept of the addresses of parcels—but I thought someone might have just happened to remember it. The address I meant to put was The Dockyard and Thames Side Welfare Association."

Mrs. Vinegar was looking quite kindly now, touched by Miss Marple's patent incapacity and general state of senility and dither.

"Did you bring it yourself?"

"No, I didn't—I'm staying at The Old Manor House—and one of them—Mrs. Glynne, I think—said she or her sister would post it. Very kind of her—"

"Let me see now. It would have been on Tuesday, would it? It wasn't Mrs. Glynne who brought it in, it was the youngest one, Miss Anthea."

"Yes, yes, I think that was the day—"

"I remember it quite well. In a good-sized dress box—and moderately heavy, I think. But not what you said. Dockyard Association—I can't recall anything like that. It was the Reverend Mathews—the East Ham Women and Children's Woollen Clothing Appeal."

"Oh, yes." Miss Marple clasped her hands in an ecstasy of relief. "How clever of you—I see now how I came to do it. At Christmas I *did* send things to the East Ham Society in answer to a special appeal for knitted things, so I must have copied down the wrong address. Can you just repeat it?" She entered it carefully in a small notebook.

"I'm afraid the parcel's gone off, though—"

"Oh, yes, but I can write, explaining the mistake and ask them to forward the parcel to the Dockyard Association instead. Thank you so much."

Miss Marple trotted out.

Mrs. Vinegar produced stamps for her next customer, remarking in an aside to a colleague—"Flighty as they make them, poor old creature. Expect she's always doing that sort of thing."

Miss Marple went out of the post office and ran into Emlyn Price and Joanna Crawford.

Joanna, she noticed, was very pale and looked upset.

"I've got to give evidence," she said. "I don't know—what will they ask me? I'm so afraid. I—I don't like it. I told the police sergeant, I told him what I thought we saw."

"Don't you worry, Joanna," said Emlyn Price. "This is just a coroner's inquest, you know. He's a nice man, a doctor, I believe. He'll just ask you a few questions and you'll say what you saw."

"You saw it, too," said Joanna.

"Yes, I did," said Emlyn. "At least I saw there was someone up there. Near the boulders and things. Now come on, Joanna."

"They came and searched our rooms in the hotel," said Joanna. "They asked our permission, but they had a search warrant. They looked in our rooms and among the things in our luggage."

"I think they wanted to find that check pullover you described. Anyway, there's nothing for you to worry about. If you'd had a black and scarlet pullover yourself, you wouldn't have talked about it, would you? It was black and scarlet, wasn't it?"

"I don't know," said Emlyn Price. "I don't really know the colours of things very well. I think it was a sort of bright colour. That's all I know."

"They didn't find one," said Joanna. "After all, none of us have very many things with us. You don't when you go on a coach travel. There wasn't anything like that among anybody's things. I've never seen anyone —of our lot, I mean, wearing anything like that. Not so far. Have you?"

"No, I haven't, but I suppose—I don't know that I should know if I had seen it," said Emlyn Price. "I don't always know red from green."

"No, you're a bit colour-blind, aren't you?" said Joanna. "I noticed that the other day."

"What do you mean, you noticed it?"

"My red scarf. I asked if you'd seen it. You said you'd seen a green one somewhere and you brought me the red one. I'd left it in the dining room. But you didn't really know it was red."

"Well, don't go about saying I'm colour-blind. I don't like it. Puts people off in some way."

"Men are more often colour-blind than women," said Joanna. "It's one of those sex-link things," she added with an air of erudition. "You know, it passes through the female and comes out in the male."

"You make it sound as though it was measles," said Emlyn Price. "Well, here we are."

"You don't seem to mind," said Joanna as they walked up the steps.

"Well, I don't really. I've never been to an inquest. Things are rather interesting when you do them for the first time."

II

Dr. Stokes was a middle-aged man with greying hair and spectacles. Police evidence was given first, then the medical evidence, with technical details of the concussion injuries which had caused death. Mrs. Sandbourne gave particulars of the coach tour, the expedition as arranged for that particular afternoon, and the particulars of how the fatality had occurred. Miss Temple, she said, although not young, was a very brisk walker. The party were going along a well-known footpath which led round the curve of a hill which slowly mounted to the old Moorland Church originally built in Elizabethan times, though repaired and added to later. On an adjoining crest was what was called the Bonaventure Memorial. It was a fairly steep ascent and people usually climbed it at a different pace from each other. The younger ones very often ran or walked ahead and reached their destination much earlier than the others. The elderly ones took it slowly. She herself usually kept at the rear of the party so that she could, if necessary, suggest to people who were tired that they could, if they liked, go back. Miss Temple, she said, had been talking to a Mr. and Mrs. Butler. Miss Temple, though she was over sixty, had been slightly impatient at their slow pace and had outdistanced them, had turned a corner and gone on ahead rather rapidly, which she had done often before. She was inclined to get impatient if waiting for people to catch up for too long, and preferred to make her own pace. They had heard a cry ahead, and she and the others had run on, turned a curve of the pathway and found Miss Temple lying on the ground. A large boulder detached from the hillside above where there were several others of the same kind, must, they had thought, have rolled down the hillside and struck Miss Temple as she was going along the path below. A most unfortunate and tragic accident.

"You had no idea there was anything but an accident?"

"No, indeed. I can hardly see how it could have been anything but an accident."

"You saw no one above you on the hillside?"

"No. This is the main path round the hill but of course people do wander about over the top. I did not see anyone that particular afternoon."

Then Joanna Crawford was called. After particulars of her name and age Dr. Stokes asked:

"You were not walking with the remainder of the party?"

"No, we had left the path. We'd gone round the hill a little higher up the slope."

"You were walking with a companion?"

"Yes. With Mr. Emlyn Price."

"There was no one else actually walking with you?"

"No. We were talking and we were looking at one or two of the flowers. They seemed of rather an uncommon kind. Emlyn's interested in botany."

"Were you out of sight of the rest of the party?"

"Not all the time. They were walking along the main path—some way below us, that is."

"Did you see Miss Temple?"

"I think so. She was walking ahead of the others, and I think I saw her turn a corner of the path ahead of them. We didn't see her after this because the contour of the hill hid her."

"Did you see someone walking above you on the hillside?"

"Yes. Up among a good many boulders. There's a sort of great patch of boulders on the side of the hill."

"Yes," said Dr. Stokes, "I know exactly the place you mean. Large granite boulders. People call them the Wethers, or the Grey Wethers sometimes."

"I suppose they might look like sheep from a distance, but we weren't so very far away from them."

"And you saw someone up there?"

"Yes. Someone was more or less in the middle of the boulders, leaning over them."

"Pushing them, do you think?"

"Yes. I thought so, and wondered why. He seemed to be pushing at one on the outside of the group near the edge. They were so big and so heavy I would have thought it was impossible to push them. But the one he or she was pushing seemed to be balanced rather like a rocking stone."

"You said first he, now you say *he* or *she,* Miss Crawford. Which do you think it was?"

"Well, I thought—I suppose—I suppose I thought it was a man, but I wasn't actually thinking at the time. It was—he or she was—wearing trousers and a pullover, a sort of man's pullover with a polo neck."

"What colour was the pullover?"

"Rather a bright red and black in checks. And there was longish hair at the back of a kind of beret, rather like a woman's hair, but then it might just as well have been a man's."

"It certainly might," said Dr. Stokes rather drily. "Identifying a male or female figure by their hair is certainly not easy these days." He went on: "What happened next?"

"Well, the stone began to roll over. It sort of toppled over the edge and then it began to gain speed. I said to Emlyn, 'Oh, it's going to go right over down the hill.' Then we heard a sort of crash as it fell. And I think I heard a cry from below, but I might have imagined it."

"And then?"

"Oh, we ran on up a bit and round the corner of the hill to see what had happened to the stone."

"And what did you see?"

"We saw the boulder below on the path with a body underneath it—and people coming running round the corner."

"Was it Miss Temple who uttered the cry?"

"I think it must have been. It might have been one of the others who was catching up and turned the corner. Oh! It was—it was horrible."

"Yes, I'm sure it was. What had happened to the figure you'd seen above? The man or woman in the red and black pullover? Was that figure still there among the stones?"

"I don't know. I never looked up there. I was—I was busy looking at the accident and running down the hill to see if one could do anything. I did just look up, I think, but there wasn't anyone in sight. Only the stones. There were a lot of contours and you could lose anyone quite easily from view."

"Could it have been one of your party?"

"Oh, no. I'm sure it wasn't one of us. I would have known because, I mean, one would have known by their clothes. I'm sure nobody was wearing a scarlet and black pullover."

"Thank you, Miss Crawford."

Emlyn Price was called next. His story was practically a replica of Joanna's.

There was a little more evidence which did not amount to much.

The coroner brought in that there was not sufficient evidence to show how Elizabeth Temple had come to her death, and adjourned the inquest for a fortnight.

17

MISS MARPLE MAKES A VISIT

As they walked back from the inquest to the Golden Boar, hardly anyone spoke. Professor Wanstead walked beside Miss Marple, and since she was not a very fast walker, they fell slightly behind the others.

"What will happen next?" Miss Marple asked at last.

"Do you mean legally or to us?"

"I suppose both," said Miss Marple, "because one will surely affect the other."

"It will be presumably a case of the police making further inquiries arising out of the evidence given by those two young people."

"Yes."

"Further inquiry will be necessary. The inquest was bound to be adjourned. One can hardly expect the coroner to give a verdict of accidental death."

"No. I understand that." She said, "What did you think of their evidence?"

Professor Wanstead directed a sharp glance from under his beetling eyebrows.

"Have you any ideas on the subject, Miss Marple?" His voice was suggestive. "Of course," said Professor Wanstead, "we knew beforehand what they were going to say."

"Yes."

"What you mean is that you are asking what I thought about them themselves, their feelings about it."

"It was interesting," said Miss Marple. "Very interesting. The red and black check pullover. Rather important, I think, don't you? Rather striking?"

"Yes, exactly that."

He shot again that look at her under his eyebrows. "What does it suggest to you exactly?"

"I think," said Miss Marple, "I think the description of that might give us a valuable clue."

They came to the Golden Boar. It was only about half-past twelve and Mrs. Sandbourne suggested a little refreshment before going in to luncheon. As sherry and tomato juice and other liquors were being consumed, Mrs. Sandbourne proceeded to make certain announcements.

"I have taken advice," she said, "both from the coroner and Inspector Douglas. Since the medical evidence has been taken fully, there will be at the church a funeral memorial service tomorrow at eleven o'clock. I'm going to make arrangements with Mr. Courtney, the local vicar, about it. On the following day it will be best, I think, to resume our tour. The program will be slightly altered, since we have lost three days, but I think it can be reorganized on rather simpler lines. I have heard from one or two members of our party that they would prefer to return to London, presumably by rail. I can quite understand the feelings lying behind this, and would not like to try to influence you in any way. This death has been a very sad occurrence. I still cannot help but believe that Miss Temple's death was the result of an accident. Such a thing has happened before on that particular pathway, though there do not appear in this case to have been any geological or atmospherical conditions causing it. I think a further investigation will have to be made. Of course, some hiker on a walking tour—that kind of thing—may have been pushing about boulders quite innocently, not realizing that there was a danger for someone walking below in what he or she was doing. If so, if that person comes forward, the whole thing may be cleared up quite quickly, but I agree one cannot take that for granted at present. It seems unlikely that the late Miss Temple could have had any enemy or anyone who wished her harm of any kind. What I should suggest is that we do not discuss the accident any further. Investigations will be made by the local authorities whose business it is. I think we will probably all like to attend the memorial service in the church tomorrow. And after that, on continuing the tour, I hope that it may distract our minds from the shock we have had. There are still some very interesting and famous houses to see and some very beautiful scenery also."

Luncheon being announced shortly after that, the subject was not discussed any further. That is to say, not openly. After lunch, as they took coffee in the lounge, people were prone to get together in little groups, discussing their further arrangements.

"Are you continuing on the tour?" asked Professor Wanstead of Miss Marple.

"No," said Miss Marple. She spoke thoughtfully. "No. I think—I think that what has happened inclines me to remain here a little longer."

"At the Golden Boar or at The Old Manor House?"

"That rather depends as to whether I receive any further invitation to go back to The Old Manor House. I would not like to suggest it myself, because my original invitation was for the two nights that the tour was to have stayed here originally. I think possibly it would be better for me to remain at the Golden Boar."

"You don't feel like returning to St. Mary Mead?"

"Not yet," said Miss Marple. "There are one or two things I could do here, I think. One thing I have done already." She met his inquiring gaze. "If you are going on," she said, "with the rest of the party, I will tell you what I have put in hand, and suggest a small sideline of inquiry that might be helpful. The other reason that I wish to stay here I will tell you later. There are certain inquiries—local inquiries—that I want to make. They may not lead anywhere, so I think it as well not to mention them now. And you?"

"I should like to return to London. I have work there waiting to be done. Unless, that is, I can be helpful to you here?"

"No," said Miss Marple, "I do not think so at present. I expect you have various inquiries of your own that you wish to put in hand."

"I came on the tour to meet you, Miss Marple."

"And now you have met me and know what I know, or practically all that I know, you have other inquiries to put in hand. I understand that. But before you leave here, I think there are one or two things—well, that might be helpful, might give a result."

"I see. You have ideas."

"I am remembering what you said."

"You have perhaps pinned down the smell of evil?"

"It is difficult," said Miss Marple, "to know exactly what something wrong in the atmosphere really means."

"But you do feel that there is something wrong in the atmosphere?"

"Oh, yes. Very clearly."

"And especially since Miss Temple's death which, of course, was not an accident, no matter what Mrs. Sandbourne hopes."

"No," said Miss Marple, "it was not an accident. What I don't think I have told you is that Miss Temple said to me once that she was on a pilgrimage."

"Interesting," said the Professor. "Yes, interesting. She didn't tell you what the pilgrimage was, to where or to whom?"

"No," said Miss Marple, "if she'd lived just a little longer and not been so weak, she might have told me. But unfortunately, death came a little too soon."

"So that you have not any further ideas on that subject."

"No. Only a feeling of assurance that her pilgrimage was put an end to by malign design. Someone wanted to stop her going wherever she was going, or stop her going to whomever she was going to. One can only hope that chance or Providence may throw light on that."

"That's why you're staying here?"

"Not only that," said Miss Marple. "I want to find out something more about a girl called Nora Broad."

"Nora Broad." He looked faintly puzzled.

"The other girl who disappeared about the same time as Verity Hunt did. You remember you mentioned her to me. A girl who had boy friends and was, I understand, very ready to have boy friends. A foolish girl, but attractive apparently to the male sex. I think," said Miss Marple, "that to learn a little more about her might help me in my inquiries."

"Have it your own way, Detective-Inspector Marple," said Professor Wanstead.

The service took place on the following morning. All the members of the tour were there. Miss Marple looked round the church. Several of the locals were there also—Mrs. Glynne was there and her sister Clotilde. The youngest one, Anthea, did not attend. There were one or two people from the village also, she thought. Probably not acquainted with Miss Temple but there out of a rather morbid curiosity in regard to what was now spoken of by the term "foul play." There was, too, an elderly clergyman—in gaiters, well over seventy, Miss Marple thought, a broadshouldered old man with a noble mane of white hair. He was slightly crippled and found it difficult both to kneel and to stand. It was a fine face, Miss Marple thought, and she wondered who he was. Some old friend of Elizabeth Temple, she presumed, who might perhaps have come from quite a long distance to attend the service?

As they came out of the church, Miss Marple exchanged a few words with her fellow travellers. She knew now pretty well who was doing what. The Butlers were returning to London.

"I told Henry I just couldn't go on with it," said Mrs. Butler. "You know—I feel all the time that any minute just as we might be walking round a corner, someone, you know, might shoot us or throw a stone at us—someone who has got a down perhaps on the Famous Houses of England."

"Now then, Mamie, now then," said Mr. Butler, "don't you let your imagination go as far as that!"

"Well, you just don't know nowadays. What with hijackers about and kidnapping and all the rest of it, I don't feel really protected anywhere."

Old Miss Lumley and Miss Bentham were continuing with the tour, their anxieties allayed.

"We've paid very highly for this tour and it seems a pity to miss anything just because this very sad accident has happened. We rang up a very good neighbour of ours last night, and they are going to see to the cats, so we don't need to worry."

It was going to remain an accident for Miss Lumley and Miss Bentham. They had decided it was more comfortable that way.

Mrs. Risely-Porter was also continuing on the tour. Colonel and Mrs. Walker were resolved that nothing would make them miss seeing a particularly rare collection of fuchsias in the garden due to be visited the day after tomorrow. The architect, Jameson, was also guided by his wish to see various buildings of special interest for him. Mr. Caspar, however, was departing by rail, he said. Miss Cooke and Miss Barrow seemed undecided.

"Pretty good walks round here," said Miss Cooke. "I think we'll stay at the Golden Boar for a little. That's what you're going to do, isn't it, Miss Marple?"

"I really think so," said Miss Marple. "I don't feel quite equal to going on travelling and all that. I think a day or two's rest would be helpful to me after what's happened."

As the little crowd dispersed, Miss Marple took an unostentatious route of her own. From her handbag she took out a leaf torn from her notebook on which she had entered two addresses. The first, a Mrs. Blackett, lived in a neat little house and garden just by the end of the road where it sloped down towards the valley. A small neat woman opened the door.

"Mrs. Blackett?"

"Yes, yes, ma'am, that's my name."

"I wonder if I might just come in and speak to you for a minute or two. I have just been to the service and I am feeling a little giddy. If I could just sit down for a minute or two?"

"Dear me, now, dear me. Oh, I'm sorry for that. Come right in, ma'am, come right in. That's right. You sit down here. Now I'll get you a glass of water—or maybe you'd like a pot of tea?"

"No, thank you," said Miss Marple, "a glass of water would put me right."

Mrs. Blackett returned with a glass of water and a pleasurable prospect of talking about ailments and giddiness and other things.

"You know, I've got a nephew like that. He oughtn't to be at his age, he's not much over fifty, but now and then he'll come over giddy all of a sudden and unless he sits down at once—why, you know, sometimes he'll pass out right on the floor. Terrible, it is. Terrible. And doctors, they don't seem able to do anything about it. Here's your glass of water."

"Ah," said Miss Marple, sipping, "I feel much better."

"Been to the service, have you, for the poor lady as got done in, as some say, or accident as others. I'd say it's accident every time. But these inquests and coroners, they always want to make things look criminal, they do."

"Oh, yes," said Miss Marple. "I've been so sorry to hear of a lot of things like that in the past. I was hearing a great deal about a girl called Nora. Nora Broad, I think."

"Ah, Nora, yes. Well, she was my cousin's daughter. Yes. A long while ago, that was. Went off and never come back. These girls, there's no holding them. I said often, I did, to Nancy Broad—that's my cousin—I said to her, 'You're out working all day' and I said 'what's Nora doing? You know she's the kind that likes the boys. Well,' I said, 'there'll be trouble. You see if there isn't.' And sure enough, I was quite right."

"You mean—?"

"Ah, the usual trouble. Yes, in the family way. Mind you, I don't think as my cousin Nancy knew about it yet. But of course, I'm sixty-five and I know what's what and I know the way a girl looks and I think I know who it was, but I'm not sure. I might have been wrong because he went on living in the place and he was real cut up when Nora was missing."

"She went off, did she?"

"Well, she accepted a lift from someone—a stranger. That's the last time she was seen. I forget the make of the car now. Some funny name it had. An Audit or something like that. Anyway, she'd been seen once or twice in that car. And off she went in it. And it was said it was that same car that the poor girl what got herself murdered used to go riding in. But I don't think as that happened to Nora. If Nora'd been murdered, the body would have come to light by now. Don't you think so?"

"It certainly seems likely," said Miss Marple. "Was she a girl who did well at school and all that?"

"Ah, no, she wasn't. She was idle and she wasn't too clever at her books either. No. She was all for the boys from the time she was twelve years old onwards. I think in the end she must have gone off with someone or other for good. But she never let anyone know. She never sent as much as a postcard. Went off, I think, with someone as promised her things. You know. Another girl I knew—but that was when I was young—went off with one of them Africans. He told her as his father was a shake. Funny sort of word, but a shake, I think it was. Anyway it was somewhere in

Africa or in Algiers. Yes, in Algiers it was. Somewhere there. And she was going to have all sorts of wonderful things. He had six camels, the boy's father, she said, and a whole troop of horses and she was going to live in a wonderful house, she was, with carpets hanging up all over the wall, which seems a funny place to put carpets. And off she went. She come back again three years later. Yes. Terrible time she'd had. Terrible. They lived in a nasty little house made of earth. Yes, it was. And nothing much to eat except what they call cos-cos, which I always thought was lettuce, but it seems it isn't. Something more like semolina pudding. Oh, terrible it was. And in the end he said she was no good to him and he'd divorce her. He said he'd only got to say 'I divorce you,' three times, and he did and walked out and somehow or other some kind of society out there took charge of her and paid her fare home to England. And there she was. Ah, but that was about thirty to forty years ago, that was. Now Nora, that was only about seven or eight years ago. But I expect she'll be back one of these days, having learnt her lesson and finding out that all these fine promises didn't come to much."

"Had she anyone to go to here except her—her mother—your cousin, I mean? Anyone who—"

"Well, there's many as was kind to her. There was the people at The Old Manor House, you know. Mrs. Glynne wasn't there then, but Miss Clotilde, she was always one to be good to the girls from school. Yes, many a nice present she's given Nora. She gave her a very nice scarf and a pretty dress once. Very nice, it was. A summer frock, a sort of foulard silk. Ah, she was very kind, Miss Clotilde was. Tried to make Nora take more interest in her schooling. Lots of things like that. Advised her against the way she was going on because, you see—well I wouldn't like to say it, not when she's my cousin's child though, mark you, my cousin is only one who married my boy cousin, that is to say—but I mean it was something terrible the way she went on with all the boys. Anyone could pick her up. Real sad it is. I'd say she'll go on the streets in the end. I don't believe she has any future but that. I don't like to say these things, but there it is. Anyway, perhaps it's better than getting herself murdered like Miss Hunt did, what lived at The Old Manor House. Cruel, that was. They thought she'd gone off with someone, and the police, they was busy. Always asking questions and having the young men who'd been with the girl up to help them with their inquiries and all that. Geoffrey Grant there was, Billy Thompson, and the Langfords' Harry. All unemployed—with plenty of jobs going if they'd wanted to take them. Things usedn't to be like that when I was young. Girls behaved proper. And the boys knew they'd got to work if they wanted to get anywhere."

Miss Marple talked a little more, said that she was now quite restored, thanked Mrs. Blackett, and went out.

Her next visit was to a girl who was planting out lettuces.

"Nora Broad? Oh, *she* hasn't been in the village for years. Went off with someone, she did. She was a great one for boys. I always wondered where she'd end up. Did you want to see her for any particular reason?"

"I had a letter from a friend abroad," said Miss Marple untruthfully. "A very nice family and they were thinking of engaging a Miss Nora Broad. She'd been in some trouble, I think. Married someone who was rather a bad lot and had left her and gone off with another woman, and she wanted to get a job looking after children. My friend knew nothing about her, but I gathered she came from this village. So I wondered if there was anyone here who could—well, tell me something about her. You went to school with her, I understand?"

"Oh, yes, we were in the same class, we were. Mind you, I didn't approve of all Nora's goings-on. She was boy-mad, she was. Well, I had a nice boy friend myself that I was going steady with at the time, and I told her she'd do herself no good going off with every Tom, Dick and Harry that offered her a lift in a car or took her along to a pub where she told lies about her age, as likely or not. She was a good mature girl as looked a lot older than she was."

"Dark or fair?"

"Oh, she had dark hair. Pretty hair, it was. Always looselike, you know, as girls do."

"Were the police worried about her when she disappeared?"

"Yes. You see, she didn't leave no word behind. She just went out one night and didn't come back. She was seen getting into a car, and nobody saw the car again and nobody saw her. Just at that time there'd been a good many murders, you know. Not specially round here, but all over the country. The police, they were rounding up a lot of young men and boys. Thought as Nora might be a body at the time, we did. But not she. She was all right. I'd say as likely as not she's making a bit of money still in London or one of these big towns doing a striptease, something of that kind. That's the kind she was."

"I don't think," said Miss Marple, "if it's the same person, that she'd be very suitable for my friend."

"She'd have to change a bit if she was to be suitable," said the girl.

18

ARCHDEACON BRABAZON

When Miss Marple, slightly out of breath and rather tired, got back to the Golden Boar, the receptionist came out from her pen and across to greet her.

"Oh, Miss Marple, there is someone here who wants to speak to you, Archdeacon Brabazon."

"Archdeacon Brabazon?" Miss Marple looked puzzled.

"Yes. He's been trying to find you. He had heard you were with this tour and he wanted to talk to you before you might have left or gone to London. I told him that some of them were going back to London by the later train this afternoon, but he is very, very anxious to speak to you before you go. I have put him in the television lounge. It is quieter there. The other is very noisy just at this moment."

Slightly surprised, Miss Marple went to the room indicated. Archdeacon Brabazon turned out to be the elderly cleric whom she had noticed at the memorial service. He rose and came towards her.

"Miss Marple. Miss Jane Marple?"

"Yes, that is my name. You wanted—"

"I am Archdeacon Brabazon. I came here this morning to attend the service for a very old friend of mine, Miss Elizabeth Temple."

"Oh, yes?" said Miss Marple. "Do sit down."

"Thank you, I will. I am not quite as strong as I was." He lowered himself carefully into a chair.

"And you—"

Miss Marple sat down beside him.

"Yes," she said, "you wanted to see me?"

"Well, I must explain how that comes about. I'm quite aware that I am a complete stranger to you. As a matter of fact I made a short visit to the hospital at Carristown, talking to the matron before going on to the church here. It was she who told me that before she died Elizabeth had asked to see a fellow member of the tour. Miss Jane Marple. And that Miss Jane Marple had visited her and sat with her just a very, very short time before Elizabeth died."

He looked at her anxiously.

"Yes," said Miss Marple, "that is so. It surprised me to be sent for."

"You are an old friend of hers?"

"No," said Miss Marple. "I only met her on this tour. That's why I was surprised. We had expressed ideas to each other, occasionally sat next to each other in the coach, and had struck up quite an acquaintanceship. But I was surprised that she should have expressed a wish to see me when she was so ill."

"Yes. Yes, I can quite imagine that. She was, as I have said, a very old friend of mine. In fact, she was coming to see me, to visit me. I live in Fillminster, which is where your coach tour will be stopping the day after tomorrow. And by arrangement she was coming to visit me there; she wanted to talk to me about various matters about which she thought I could help her."

"I see," said Miss Marple. "May I ask you a question? I hope it is not too intimate a question."

"Of course, Miss Marple. Ask me anything you like."

"One of the things Miss Temple said to me was that her presence on the tour was not merely because she wished to visit historic homes and gardens. She described it by a rather unusual word to use, as a pilgrimage."

"Did she," said Archdeacon Brabazon. "Did she indeed now? Yes, that's interesting. Interesting and perhaps significant."

"So what I am asking you is, do you think that the pilgrimage she spoke of was her visit to you?"

"I think it must have been," said the Archdeacon. "Yes, I think so."

"We had been talking," said Miss Marple, "about a young girl. A girl called Verity."

"Ah, yes. Verity Hunt."

"I did not know her surname. Miss Temple, I think, mentioned her only as Verity."

"Verity Hunt is dead," said the Archdeacon. "She died quite a number of years ago. Did you know that?"

"Yes," said Miss Marple. "I knew it. Miss Temple and I were talking about her. Miss Temple told me something that I did not know. She said she had been engaged to be married to the son of a Mr. Rafiel. Mr. Rafiel is, or again I must say was, a friend of mine. Mr. Rafiel has paid the expenses of this tour out of his kindness. I think, though, that possibly he wanted—indeed, intended—me to meet Miss Temple on this tour. I think he thought she could give me certain information."

"Certain information about Verity?"

"Yes."

"That is why she was coming to me. She wanted to know certain facts."

"She wanted to know," said Miss Marple, "why Verity broke off her engagement to marry Mr. Rafiel's son."

"Verity," said Archdeacon Brabazon," did not break off her engagement. I am certain of that. As certain as one can be of anything."

"Miss Temple did not know that, did she?"

"No. I think she was puzzled and unhappy about what happened and was coming to me to ask me why the marriage did not take place."

"And why did it not take place?" asked Miss Marple. "Please do not think that I am unduly curious. It's not idle curiosity that is driving me. I, too, am on—not a pilgrimage—but what I should call a mission. I, too, want to know why Michael Rafiel and Verity Hunt did not marry."

The Archdeacon studied her for a moment or two.

"You are involved in some way," he said. "I see that."

"I am involved," said Miss Marple, "by the dying wishes of Michael Rafiel's father. He asked me to do this for him."

"I have no reason not to tell you all I know," said the Archdeacon slowly. "You are asking me what Elizabeth Temple would have been asking me, you are asking me something I do not know myself. Those two young people, Miss Marple, intended to marry. They had made arrangements to marry. I was going to marry them. It was a marriage, I gather, which was being kept secret. I knew both these young people. I knew that dear child Verity from a long way back. I prepared her for confirmation, I used to hold services in Lent, for Easter, on other occasions, in Elizabeth Temple's school. A very fine school it was, too. A very fine woman she was. A wonderful teacher with a great sense of each girl's capabilities—for what she was best fitted for in studies. She urged careers on girls she thought would relish careers, and did not force girls that she felt were not really suited to them. She was a great woman and a very dear friend. Verity was one of the most beautiful children—girls, rather—that I have come across. Beautiful in mind, in heart, as well as in appearance. She had the great misfortune to lose her parents before she was truly adult. They were both killed in a charter plane going on a holiday to Italy. Verity went to live when she left school with a Miss Clotilde Bradbury-Scott, whom you know, probably, as living here. She had been a close friend of Verity's mother. There are three sisters, though the second one was married and living abroad, so there were only two of them living here. Clotilde, the eldest one, became extremely attached to Verity. She did everything possible to give her a happy life. She took her abroad once or twice, gave her art lessons in Italy and loved and cared for her dearly in every way. Verity, too, came to love her probably as much as she could have loved her own mother. She depended on Clotilde. Clotilde herself was an intellectual and well-educated woman. She did not urge a university career on Verity, but this I gather was really because Verity did not really yearn after one. She preferred to study art and music and such subjects. She lived at The Old Manor House and had, I think, a very happy life. She always seemed to be happy. Naturally, I did not see her after she came here, since Fillminster, where I was in the cathedral, is nearly sixty miles from here. I wrote to her at Christmas and other festivals, and she remembered me always with a Christmas card. But I saw nothing of her until the day came when she suddenly turned up, a very beautiful and fully grown young woman by then, with an attractive young man whom I also happened to know slightly, Mr. Rafiel's son Michael. They came to me because they were in love with each other and wanted to get married."

"And you agreed to marry them?"

"Yes, I did. Perhaps, Miss Marple, you may think that I should not have done so. They had come to me in secret. It was obvious. Clotilde Bradbury-Scott, I should imagine, had tried to discourage the romance between them. She was well within her rights in doing so. Michael Rafiel, I will tell you frankly, was not the kind of husband you would want for any daughter or relation of yours. She was too young, really, to make up her mind, and Michael had been a source of trouble ever since his very young days. He had been had up before junior courts, he had had unsuitable friends, he had been drawn into various gangster activities, he'd sabotaged buildings and telephone boxes. He had been on intimate terms with various girls, had maintenance claims which he had had to meet. Yes, he was a bad lot with the girls as well as in other ways, yet he was extremely attractive and they fell for him and behaved in a silly fashion. He had served two short jail sentences. Frankly, he had a criminal record. I was acquainted with his father, though I did not know him well, and I think that his father did all that he could—all that a man of his character could—to help his son. He came to the rescue, he got him jobs in which he might have succeeded. He paid up his debts, paid out damages. He did all this. I don't know—"

"But he could have done more, you think?"

"No," said the Archdeacon, "I've come to an age now when I know that one must accept one's fellow human beings as being the kind of people and having the kind of, shall we say in modern terms, genetic make-up which gives them the characters they have. I don't think that Mr. Rafiel had affection for his son, a great affection at any time. To say he was reasonably fond of him would be the most you could say. He gave him no love. Whether it would have been better for Michael if he had had love from his father, I do not know. Perhaps it would have made no difference. As it was, it was sad. The boy was not stupid. He had a certain amount of intellect and talent. He could have done well if he had wished to do well and had taken the trouble. But he was by nature—let us admit it frankly—a delinquent. He had certain qualities one appreciated. He had a sense of humour, he was in various ways generous and kindly. He would stand by a friend, help a friend out of a scrape. He treated his girl friends badly, got them into trouble, as the local saying is, and then more or less abandoned them and took up with somebody else. So there I was faced with those two and—yes—I agreed to marry them. I told Verity, I told her quite frankly the kind of boy she wanted to marry. I found that he had not tried to deceive her in any way. He'd told her that he'd always been in trouble both with the police, and in every other way. He told her that he was going, when he married her, to turn over a new leaf. Everything would be changed. People do not change. He might mean to change. Verity, I think, knew it. She said, 'I know what Mike is like. I know he'll probably always be like it, but I love him. I may be able to help him and I may not. But I'll take that risk.'

"And I will tell you this, Miss Marple. I know—none better, I have done a lot with young people, I have married a lot of young people and I have seen them come to grief, I have seen them unexpectedly turn out well—but I know this and recognize it. I know when a couple are really in love with each other. And by that I do not mean just sexually attracted. There is too much talk about sex, too much attention is paid to it. I do not mean that anything about sex is wrong. That is nonsense. But sex cannot take the place of love, it goes with love, but it cannot succeed by itself. To love means the words of the marriage service. For better, for worse, for richer, for poorer, in sickness and in health. That is what you take on if you love and wish to marry. Those two loved each other. To love and to cherish until death do us apart. And that," said the Archdeacon, "is where my story ends. I cannot go on because I do not know what happened. I only know that I agreed to do as they asked, that I made the necessary arrangements; we settled a day, an hour, a time, a place. I think perhaps that I was to blame for agreeing to the secrecy."

"They didn't want anyone to know?" said Miss Marple.

"No. Verity did not want anyone to know, and I should say most certainly Mike did not want anyone to know. They were afraid of being stopped. To Verity, I think, besides love, there was also a feeling of escape. Natural, I think, owing to the circumstances of her life. She had lost her real guardians, her parents, she had entered on her new life after their death, at an age when a schoolgirl arrives at having a 'crush' on someone. An attractive mistress. Anything from the games mistress to the mathematics mistress, or a prefect or an older girl. A state that does not last for very long, is merely a natural part of life. Then from that you go on to the next stage when you realize that what you want in your life is what complements yourself—a relationship between a man and a woman. You start then to look about you for a mate—the mate you want in life. And if you are wise, you take your time, you have friends, but you are looking, as the old nurses used to say to children, for Mr. Right to come along. Clotilde Bradbury-Scott was exceptionally good to Verity, and Verity, I think, gave her what I should call hero-worship. She was a personality as a woman—handsome, accomplished, interesting. I think Verity adored her in an almost romantic way and I think Clotilde came to love Verity as though she were her own daughter. And so Verity grew to maturity in an atmosphere of adoration, lived an interesting life with interesting subjects to stimulate her intellect. It was a happy life, but I think little by little she was conscious, shall we say—of a wish to escape. Escape from being loved. To escape, she didn't know into what or where. But she did know after she met Michael. She wanted to escape to a life where male and female come together to create the next stage of living in this world. But she knew that it was impossible to make Clotilde understand how she felt. She knew that Clotilde would be bitterly opposed to her taking her love for Michael seriously. And Clotilde, I fear, was right in her belief . . . I know that now. He was not a husband that Verity ought to have taken or had. The road that she started out on led not to life, not to increased living and happiness. It led to shock, pain, death. You see, Miss Marple, that I have a grave feeling of guilt. My motives were good, but I didn't know what I ought to have known. I knew Verity, but I didn't know Michael. I understood Verity's wish for secrecy because I knew what a strong personality Clotilde Bradbury-Scott had. She might have had a strong enough influence over Verity to persuade her to give up the marriage."

"You think then that that was what she did do? You think Clotilde told her enough about Michael to persuade her to give up the idea of marrying him?"

"No, I do not believe that. I still do not. Verity would have told me if so. She would have got word to me."

"What did actually happen on that day?"

"I haven't told you that yet. The day was fixed. The time, the hour and the place, and I waited. Waited for a bride and bridegroom who didn't come, who sent no word, no excuse, *nothing*. I didn't know why! I never have known why. It still seems to me unbelievable. Unbelievable, I mean, not that they did not come, that could be explicable easily enough, but that they sent no word. Some scrawled line of writing. And that is why I wondered and hoped that Elizabeth Temple, before she died, might have told you something. Given you some message perhaps for me. If she knew or had any idea that she was dying, she might have wanted to get a message to me."

"She wanted information *from* you," said Miss Marple. "That, I am sure, was the reason she was coming to you."

"Yes. Yes, that is probably true. It seemed to me, you see, that Verity would have said nothing to the people who could have stopped her, Clotilde and Anthea Bradbury-Scott, but because she had always been very devoted to Elizabeth Temple—and Elizabeth Temple had had great influence over her—it seems to me that she would have written and given her information of some kind."

"I think she did," said Miss Marple.

"Information, you think?"

"The information she gave to Elizabeth Temple," said Miss Marple, "was this. That she was going to marry Michael Rafiel. Miss Temple knew that. It was one of the things she said to me. She said: 'I knew a girl called Verity who was going to marry Michael Rafiel' and the only person who could have told her that was Verity herself. Verity must have written to her or sent some word to her. And then when I said: 'Why didn't she marry him?' she said, 'She died.' "

"Then we come to a full stop," said Archdeacon Brabazon. He sighed. "Elizabeth and I knew no more than those two facts. Elizabeth, that Verity was going to marry Michael. And I that those two were going to marry, that they had arranged it and that they were coming on a settled day and time. And I waited for them, but there was no marriage. No bride, no bridegroom, no word."

"And you have no idea what happened?" said Miss Marple.

"I do not for one minute believe that Verity or Michael definitely parted, broke off."

"But *something* must have happened between them? Something that opened Verity's eyes perhaps to certain aspects of Michael's character and personality that she had not realized or known before."

"That is not a satisfying answer because still she would have let me know. She would not have left me waiting to join them together in holy matrimony. To put the most ridiculous side of it, she was a girl with beautiful manners, well-brought-up. She would have sent word. No. I'm afraid that only one thing could have happened."

"Death?" said Miss Marple. She was remembering that one word that Elizabeth Temple had said which had sounded like the deep tone of a bell.

"Yes." Archdeacon Brabazon sighed. "Death."

"Love," said Miss Marple thoughtfully.

"By that you mean—" he hesitated.

"It's what Miss Temple said to me. I said: 'What killed her?' and she said: 'Love,' and that love was the most frightening word in the world."

"I see," said the Archdeacon. "I see—or I think I see."

"What is your solution?"

"Split personality." He sighed. "Something that is not apparent to other people unless they are technically qualified to observe it. Jekyll and Hyde are real, you know. They were not Stevenson's invention as such. Michael Rafiel was a—must have been schizophrenic. He had a dual personality. I have no medical knowledge, no psychoanalytic experience. But there must have been in him the two parts of two identities. One, a well-meaning, almost lovable boy, a boy perhaps whose principal attraction was his wish for happiness. But there was also a second personality, someone who was forced by some mental deformation perhaps—something we as yet are not sure of—to kill—not an enemy, but the person he loved, and so he killed Verity. Not knowing perhaps *why* he had to or *what* it meant. There are very frightening things in this world of ours, mental quirks, mental disease or deformity of a brain. One of my parishioners was a very sad case in point. Two elderly women living together, pensioned. They had been friends in service together somewhere. They appeared to be a happy couple. And yet one day one of them killed the other. She sent for an old friend of hers, the vicar of her parish, and said: 'I have killed Louisa. It is very sad,' she said, 'but I saw the devil looking out of her eye and I knew I was being commanded to kill her.' Things like that make one sometimes despair of living. One says Why? and How? and yet one day knowledge will come. Doctors will find out or learn about some small deformity of a chromosome or gene—some gland that overworks or leaves off working."

"So you think that's what happened?" said Miss Marple.

"It did happen. The body was not found, I know, for some time afterwards. Verity just disappeared. She went away from home and was not seen again . . ."

"But it must have happened *then*—that very day—"

"But surely at the trial—"

"You mean after the body was found, when the police finally arrested Michael?"

"He had been one of the first, you know, to be asked to come and give assistance to the police. He had been seen about with the girl, she had been noticed in his car. They were sure all along that he was the man they wanted. He was their first suspect, and they never stopped suspecting him. The other young men who had known Verity were questioned, and one and all had alibis or lack of evidence. The police continued to suspect Michael, and finally the body was found. Strangled and the head and face disfigured with heavy blows. A mad frenzied attack. He wasn't sane when he struck those blows. Mr. Hyde, let us say, had taken over."

Miss Marple shivered.

The Archdeacon went on, his voice low and sad. "And yet, even now, sometimes, I hope and feel that it was some other young man who killed her—someone who was definitely mentally deranged, though no one had any idea of it. Some stranger, perhaps, whom she had met in the neighbourhood. Someone whom she had met by chance, who had given her a lift in a car, and then—" He shook his head.

"I suppose that could have been true," said Miss Marple.

"Mike made a bad impression in court," said the Archdeacon. "Told foolish and senseless lies. Lied as to where his car had been. Got his friends to give him impossible alibis. He was frightened. He said nothing of his plan to marry. I believe his counsel was of the opinion that that would tell against him—that she might have been forcing him to marry her and that he didn't want to. It's so long ago now, I remember no details. But the evidence was dead against him. He was guilty—and he looked guilty.

"So you see, do you not, Miss Marple, that I'm a very sad and unhappy man? I made the wrong judgment, I encouraged a very sweet and lovely girl to go to her death because I did not know enough of human nature. I was ignorant of the danger she was running. I believed that if she had had any fear of him, and sudden knowledge of something evil in him, she would have broken her pledge to marry him and have come to me and told me of her fear, of her new knowledge of him. But nothing of that ever happened. Why did he kill her? Did he kill her because perhaps he knew she was going to have a child? Because by now, he had formed a tie with some other girl and did not want to be forced to marry Verity? I can't believe it. Or was it some entirely different reason? Because *she* had suddenly felt a fear of him, a knowledge of danger from him, and had broken off her association with him? Did that rouse his anger, his fury, and did that lead him to violence and to killing her? One does not know."

"You do not know," said Miss Marple, "but you do still know and believe one thing, don't you?"

"What do you mean exactly by 'believe'? Are you talking from the religious point of view?"

"Oh, no," said Miss Marple, "I didn't mean that. I mean, there seems to be in you, or so I feel it, a very strong belief that those two loved each other, that they meant to marry, but that *something* happened that prevented it—something that ended in her death, but you still really believe that they *were* coming to you to get married that day?"

"You are quite right, my dear. Yes, I cannot help still believing in two lovers who wished to get married, who were ready to take each other on for better, for worse, for richer, for poorer, in sickness and in health. She loved him and she would have taken him for better or for worse. As far as she had gone, she took him for worse. It brought about her death."

"You must go on believing as you do," said Miss Marple. "I think, you know, that *I* believe it, too."

"But then what?"

"I don't know yet," said Miss Marple. "I'm not sure, but I think Elizabeth Temple did know or was beginning to know what happened. A frightening word, she said. *Love.* I thought when she spoke that what she meant was that because of a love affair the girl had committed suicide. Because she found out something about Michael, or because something about Michael suddenly upset her and revolted her. But it couldn't have been suicide."

"No," said the Archdeacon, "that couldn't be so. The injuries were described very fully at the trial. You don't commit suicide by beating in your own head."

"Horrible!" said Miss Marple. "Horrible! And you couldn't do that to anyone you loved even if you had to kill 'for love,' could you? If he'd killed her, he couldn't have done it that way. Strangling—perhaps, but you wouldn't beat in the face and the head that you loved." She murmured, "Love, love—a frightening word."

19

GOOD-BYES ARE SAID

The coach was drawn up in front of the Golden Boar on the following morning. Miss Marple had come down and was saying good-bye to various friends. She found Mrs. Riseley-Porter in a state of high indignation.

"Really, girls nowadays," she said. "No vigour. No stamina."

Miss Marple looked at her inquiringly.

"Joanna, I mean. My niece."

"Oh, dear. Is she not well?"

"Well, she says not. I can't see anything much the matter with her. She says she's got a sore throat, she feels she might have a temperature coming on. All nonsense, I think."

"Oh, I'm very sorry," said Miss Marple. "Is there anything I can do? Look after her?"

"I should leave her alone, if I were you," said Mrs. Riseley-Porter. "If you ask me, it's all an excuse."

Miss Marple looked inquiringly at her once more.

"Girls are so silly. Always falling in love."

"Emlyn Price?" said Miss Marple.

"Oh, so you've noticed it, too. Yes, they're really getting to a stage of spooning about together. I don't much care for him anyway. One of these long-haired students, you know. Always going on demos or something like that. Why can't they say demonstrations properly? I hate abbreviations. And how am *I* going to get along? Nobody to look after me, collect my luggage, take it in, take it out. Really. I'm paying for this complete trip and everything."

"I thought she seemed so attentive to you," said Miss Marple.

"Well, not the last day or two. Girls don't understand that people have to have a little assistance when they get to middle age. They seem to have some absurd idea—she and the Price boy—of going to visit some mountain or some landmark. About a seven- or eight-mile walk there and back."

"But surely if she has a sore throat and a temperature—?"

"You'll see, as soon as the coach is gone, the sore throat will get better and the temperature will go down," said Mrs. Riseley-Porter. "Oh, dear, we've got to get on board now. Oh, good-bye, Miss Marple. It's nice to have met you. I'm sorry you're not coming with us."

"I'm very sorry myself," said Miss Marple, "but really, you know, I'm not so young and vigorous as you are, Mrs. Riseley-Porter, and I really feel after all the—well, shock and everything else the last few days, I really must have a complete twenty-four hours' rest."

"Well, hope to see you somewhere in the future."

They shook hands. Mrs. Riseley-Porter climbed into the coach.

A voice behind Miss Marple's shoulder said:

"Bon voyage and good riddance."

She turned to see Emlyn Price. He was grinning.

"Was that addressed to Mrs. Riseley-Porter?"

"Yes. Who else?"

"I'm sorry to hear that Joanna is under the weather this morning."

Emlyn Price grinned at Miss Marple again.

"She'll be all right," he said, "as soon as that coach is gone."

"Oh, really!" said Miss Marple. "Do you mean—?"

"Yes, I do mean," said Emlyn Price. "Joanna's had enough of that aunt of hers bossing her around all the time."

"Then you are not going in the coach either?"

"No. I'm staying on here for a couple of days. I'm going to get around a bit and do a few excursions. Don't look so disapproving, Miss Marple. You're not really as disapproving as all that, are you?"

"Well," said Miss Marple, "I have known such things happen in my own youth. The excuses may have been different, and I think we had less chance of getting away with things than you do now."

Colonel and Mrs. Walker came up and shook Miss Marple warmly by the hand.

"So nice to have known you and had all those delightful horticultural talks," said the Colonel. "I believe the day after tomorrow we're going to have a real treat, if nothing else happens. Really, it's too sad, this very unfortunate accident. I must say I think myself it is an accident. I really think the coroner was going beyond everything in his feelings about this."

"It seems very odd," said Miss Marple, "that nobody has come forward, if they were up on top there, pushing about rocks and boulders and things, that they haven't come forward to say so."

"Think they'll be blamed, of course," said Colonel Walker. "They're going to keep jolly quiet, that's what they're going to so. Well, good-bye.

I'll send you a cutting of that Magnolia highdownensis and one of the Mahonia japonica, too. Though I'm not quite sure if it would do as well where you live."

They in turn got into the coach. Miss Marple turned away. She turned to see Professor Wanstead waving to the departing coach. Mrs. Sandbourne came out, said good-bye to Miss Marple and got in the coach and Miss Marple took Professor Wanstead by the arm.

"I want you," she said. "Can we go somewhere where we can talk?"

"Yes. What about the place where we sat the other day?"

"Round here there's a very nice verandah place, I think."

They walked round the corner of the hotel. There was some gay horn blowing, and the coach departed.

"I wish, in a way, you know," said Professor Wanstead, "that you weren't staying behind. I'd rather have seen you safely on your way in the coach." He looked at her sharply. "Why are you staying here? Nervous exhaustion or something else?"

"Something else," said Miss Marple. "I'm not particularly exhausted, though it makes a perfectly natural excuse for somebody of my age."

"I feel, really, I ought to stay here and keep an eye on you."

"No," said Miss Marple, "there's no need to do that. There are other things you ought to be doing."

"What things?" He looked at her. "Have you got ideas or knowledge?"

"I think I have knowledge, but I'll have to verify it. There are certain things that I can't do myself. I think you will help to do them because you're in touch with what I refer to as the authorities."

"Meaning Scotland Yard, chief constables and the governors of Her Majesty's Prisons?"

"Yes. One or other or all of them. You might have the Home Secretary in your pocket, too."

"You certainly do have ideas! Well, what do you want me to do?"

"First of all I want to give you this address."

She took out a notebook and tore out one page and handed it to him.

"What's this? Oh, yes, well-known charity, isn't it?"

"One of the better ones, I believe. They do a lot of good. You send them clothes," said Miss Marple, "children's clothes and women's clothes. Coats. Pullovers, all those sort of things."

"Well, do you want me to contribute to this?"

"No, it's an appeal for charity, it's a bit of what belongs to what we're doing—what you and I are doing."

"In what way?"

"I want you to make inquiries there about a parcel which was sent from here two days ago, posted from this post office."

"Who posted it? Did you?"

"No," said Miss Marple. "No. But I assumed responsibility for it."

"What does that mean?"

"It means," said Miss Marple, smiling slightly, "that I went into the post office here and I explained rather incoherently and—well, like the old girl I am—that I had very foolishly asked someone to take a parcel for me and post it, and I had put the wrong address on it. I was very upset by this. The postmistress very kindly said she remembered the parcel, but the address on it was not the one I was mentioning. It was this one, the one I have just given to you. I explained that I had been very foolish and written the wrong address on it, confusing it with another one I sometimes send things to. She told me it was too late to do anything about it now because the parcel, naturally, had gone off. I said it was quite all right, that I would send a letter to the particular charity to which the parcel had been sent and explain that it had been addressed to them by mistake. Would they very kindly forward it on to the charity that I had meant to receive it."

"It seems rather a roundabout way."

"Well," said Miss Marple, "one has to say something. I'm not going to do that at all. You are going to deal with the matter. We've got to know what's inside that parcel! I have no doubt you can get means."

"Will there be anything inside the parcel to say who actually sent it?"

"I rather think not. It may have a slip of paper saying 'from friends' or it may have a fictitious name and address—something like Mrs. Pippin, Fourteen Westbourne Grove, and if anyone made inquiries there, there'd be no person of such a name living there."

"Oh. Any other alternatives?"

"It might possibly, most unlikely but possible, have a slip saying 'From Miss Anthea Bradbury-Scott'—"

"Did she—?"

"She took it to the post," said Miss Marple.

"And you had asked her to take it there?"

"Oh, no," said Miss Marple. "I hadn't asked anyone to post anything. The first I saw of the parcel was when Anthea passed the garden of the Golden Boar where you and I were sitting talking, carrying it."

"But you went to the post office and represented that the parcel was yours."

"Yes," said Miss Marple, "which was quite untrue. But post offices are careful. And, you see, I wanted to find out where it had been sent."

"You wanted to find out if such a parcel had been sent, and if it had been sent by one of the Bradbury-Scotts—or especially Miss Anthea?"

"I knew it would be Anthea," said Miss Marple, "because we'd seen her."

"Well?" He took the paper from her hand. "Yes, I can set this in motion. You think this parcel will be interesting?"

"I think the contents of it might be quite important."

"You like keeping your secrets, don't you?" said Professor Wanstead.

"Not exactly secrets," said Miss Marple; "they are only probabilities that I am exploring. One does not like to make definite assertions unless one has a little more definite knowledge."

"Anything else?"

"I think—I think that whoever's in charge of these things ought to be warned that there might be a second body to be found."

"Do you mean a second body connected with the particular crime that we have been considering? A crime that took place ten years ago?"

"Yes," said Miss Marple. "I'm quite sure of it, as a matter of fact."

"Another body. Whose body?"

"Well," said Miss Marple, "it's only my idea so far."

"Any idea where this body is?"

"Oh, yes!" said Miss Marple. "I'm quite sure I know where it is, but I have to have a little more time before I can tell you that."

"What kind of a body? Man's? Woman's? Child's? Girl's?"

"There's another girl who is missing," said Miss Marple. "A girl called Nora Broad. She disappeared from here and she's never been heard any more of. I think her body might be in a particular place."

Professor Wanstead looked at her.

"You know, the more you say, the less I like leaving you here," he said. "Having all these ideas—and possibly doing something foolish—either—" He stopped.

"Either it's all nonsense—" said Miss Marple.

"No, no, I didn't mean that. But either you know too much—which might be dangerous . . . I think I am going to stay here to keep an eye on you."

"No, you're not," said Miss Marple. "You've got to go to London and set certain things moving."

"You spoke as though you knew a good deal, Miss Marple."

"I think I do know a good deal now. But I have got to be sure."

"Yes, but if you make sure, that may be the last thing you do make sure of! We don't want a third body—yours."

"Oh, I'm not expecting anything like that," said Miss Marple.

"There might be danger, you know, if any of your ideas are right. Have you suspicions of any one particular person?"

"I think I have certain knowledge as to one person. I have got to find out—I have got to stay here. You asked me once if I felt an atmosphere of evil. Well, that atmosphere is here, all right—an atmosphere of evil, of danger, if you like—of great unhappiness, of fear . . . I've got to do something about that. The best I can do. But an old woman like me can't do very much."

Professor Wanstead counted under his breath. "One—two—three—four—"

"What are you counting?" asked Miss Marple.

"The people who left in the coach. Presumably you're not interested in them, since you've let them go off and you're staying here."

"Why should I be interested in them?"

"Because you said Mr. Rafiel had sent you in the coach for a particular reason and sent you on this tour for a particular reason and sent you to The Old Manor House for a particular reason. Very well, then. The death of Elizabeth Temple ties up with someone in the coach. Your remaining here ties up with The Old Manor House."

"You're not quite right," said Miss Marple. "There are connections between the two. I want someone to tell me things."

"Do you think you can make anyone tell you things?"

"I think I might. You'll miss your train if you don't go soon."

"Take care of yourself," said Professor Wanstead.

"I mean to take care of myself."

The door into the lounge opened and two people came out—Miss Cooke and Miss Barrow.

"Hullo," said Professor Wanstead. "I thought you'd gone off with the coach."

"Well, we changed our minds at the last moment," said Miss Cooke cheerfully. "You know we've just discovered that there are some very agreeable walks near here, and there are one or two places I'm very anxious to see. A church with a very unusual Saxon front. Only four or five miles away and quite easily reached by the local bus, I think. You see, it's not only houses and gardens. I'm very interested in church architecture."

"So am I," said Miss Barrow. "There's also Finley Park, which is a very fine piece of horticultural planting not far from here. We really thought that it would be much pleasanter to stay here for a day or two."

"You're staying here at the Golden Boar?"

"Yes. We were fortunate enough to be able to get a very nice double room—really a better one than the one we have had for the last two days."

"You will miss your train," said Miss Marple again.

"I wish," said Professor Wanstead, "that you—"

"I shall be quite all right," said Miss Marple urgently. "Such a kind man," she said as he disappeared round the side of the house, "who really takes so much care of me—I might be a great-aunt of his or something like that."

"It's all been a great shock, hasn't it?" said Miss Cooke. "Perhaps you may like to come with us when we go to visit St. Martins in the Grove."

"You're very kind," said Miss Marple, "but I don't think today I feel quite strong enough for expeditions. Perhaps tomorrow if there is anything interesting to see."

"Well, we must leave you, then."

Miss Marple smiled at them both and went into the hotel

20

MISS MARPLE HAS IDEAS

Having had lunch in the dining room, Miss Marple went out on the terrace to drink her coffee. She was just sipping her second cup when a tall, thin figure came striding up the steps and approached her, speaking rather breathlessly. She saw that it was Anthea Bradbury-Scott.

"Oh, Miss Marple, we've only just heard, you know, that you didn't go with the coach after all. We thought you were going on with the tour. We had no idea you were staying on here. Both Clotilde and Lavinia sent me here to say we do so hope you will come back to The Old Manor House and stay with us. I'm sure it will be nicer for you to be there. There are so many people coming and going here always, especially over a weekend and things like that. So we'd be very, very glad—we really would—if you would come back to us."

"Oh, that's very kind of you," said Miss Marple. "Really very kind, but I'm sure—I mean, you know it was just a two-day visit. I meant originally to go off with the coach. I mean, after the two days. If it hadn't been for this very, very tragic accident but—well, I really felt I couldn't go on any longer. I thought I must have at least, well, at least one night's rest."

"But I mean it would be so much better if you came to us. We'd try and make you comfortable."

"Oh, there's no question of that," said Miss Marple. "I was extremely comfortable staying with you. Oh, yes, I did enjoy it very much. Such a beautiful house. And all your things are so nice. You know, your china and glass and furniture. It's such a pleasure to be in a home and not a hotel."

"Then you must come with me now. Yes, you really must. I could go and pack your things for you."

"Oh—well, that's very kind of you. I can do that myself."

"Well, shall I come and help you?"

"That would be very kind," said Miss Marple.

They repaired to her bedroom where Anthea, in a somewhat slapdash manner, packed Miss Marple's belongings together. Miss Marple, who had her own ways of folding things, had to bite her lip to keep an air of complacency on her face. Really, she thought, she can't fold *anything* properly.

Anthea got hold of a porter from the hotel and he carried the suitcase round the corner and down the street to The Old Manor House. Miss Marple tipped him adequately and, still uttering fussy little speeches of thanks and pleasure, rejoined the sisters.

"The three sisters!" she was thinking. "Here we are again." She sat down in the drawing room and closed her eyes for a minute, breathing rather fast. She appeared to be somewhat out of breath. It was only natural, she felt, at her age, and after Anthea and the hotel porter had set a fast pace. But really she was trying to acquire through her closed eyes what the feeling was she had on coming into this house again. Was something in it sinister? No, not so much sinister as unhappy. Deep unhappiness. So much so it was almost frightening.

She opened her eyes again and looked at the two other occupants of the room. Mrs. Glynne had just come in from the kitchen, bearing an afternoon tea tray. She looked as she had looked all along—comfortable, no particular emotions or feelings. Perhaps almost too devoid of them, Miss Marple thought. Had she accustomed herself through perhaps a life of some stress and difficulty to show nothing to the outer world, to keep a reserve and let no one know what her inner feelings were?

She looked from her to Clotilde. She had a Clytemnestra look, as she had thought before. She had certainly not murdered her husband, for she had never had a husband to murder, and it seemed unlikely that she had murdered the girl to whom she was said to have been extremely attached. That, Miss Marple was quite sure, was true. She had seen before how the tears had welled from Clotilde's eyes when the death of Verity had been mentioned.

And what about Anthea? Anthea had taken that cardboard box to the post office. Anthea had come to fetch her. Anthea—she was very doubtful about Anthea. Scatterbrained? Too scatterbrained for her age. Eyes that wandered and came back to you. Eyes that seemed to see things that other people might not see, over your shoulder. She's frightened, thought Miss Marple. Frightened of something. What was she frightened of? Was she perhaps frightened of going back to some institution or establishment where she might have spent part of her life? Frightened of those two sisters of hers feeling that it was unwise for her to remain at liberty? Were they uncertain, those two, what their sister Anthea might do or say?

There was *some* atmosphere here. She wondered, as she sipped the last of her tea, what Miss Cooke and Miss Barrow were doing. Had they gone to visit that church or was that all talk, meaningless talk? It was odd. Odd the way they had come and looked at her at St. Mary Mead so as to know her again on the coach, but not to acknowledge that they had ever seen or met her before.

There were quite a lot of difficult things going on. Presently Mrs. Glynne removed the tea tray, Anthea went out into the garden and Miss Marple was left alone with Clotilde.

"I think," said Miss Marple, "that you know an Archdeacon Brabazon, do you not?"

"Oh, yes," said Clotilde, "he was in church yesterday at the service. Do you know him?"

"Oh, no," said Miss Marple, "but he did come to the Golden Boar and he came and spoke to me there. I gather he had been to the hospital and was inquiring about poor Miss Temple's death. He wondered if Miss Temple had sent any message to him. I gather she was thinking of paying him a visit. But of course I told him that although I did go there in case I could do anything, there was nothing that could be done except sit by poor Miss Temple's bed. She was unconscious, you know. I could have done nothing to help her."

"She didn't say—say anything—any explanation of what had happened?" asked Clotilde.

She asked without much interest. Miss Marple wondered if she felt more interest than she expressed, but on the whole she thought not. She thought Coltilde was busy with thoughts of something quite different.

"Do you think it was an accident?" Miss Marple asked, "or do you think there is something in that story that Mrs. Riseley-Porter's niece told about seeing someone pushing a boulder?"

"Well, I suppose if those two said so, they must have seen it."

"Yes. They both said so, didn't they," said Miss Marple, "though not quite in the same terms. But perhaps that's quite natural."

Clotilde looked at her curiously.

"You seem to be intrigued by that."

"Well, it seems so very unlikely," said Miss Marple, "an unlikely story, unless—"

"Unless what?"

"Well, I just wondered," said Miss Marple.

Mrs. Glynne came into the room again.

"You just wondered what?" she asked.

"We're talking about the accident, or the nonaccident," said Clotilde. "But who—?"

"It seems a very odd story that they told," said Miss Marple again.

"There's something about this place," said Clotilde suddenly. "Something about this atmosphere. We never got over it here. Never. Never since —since Verity died. It's years, but it doesn't go away. A shadow's here." She looked at Miss Marple. "Don't you think so, too? Don't you feel a shadow here?"

"Well, I'm a stranger," said Miss Marple. "It's different for you and your sisters who've lived here and who knew the dead girl. She was, I gather, as Archdeacon Brabazon was saying—a very charming and beautiful girl."

"She was a lovely girl. A dear child, too," said Clotilde.

"I wish I'd known her better," said Mrs. Glynne. "Of course I was living abroad at that time. My husband and I came home on leave once, but we were mostly in London. We didn't come down here often."

Anthea came in from the garden. She was carrying in her hand a great bunch of lilies.

"Funeral flowers," she said. "That's what we ought to have here today, isn't it? I'll put them in a great jar. Funeral flowers," and she laughed suddenly—a queer, hysterical little giggle.

"Anthea," said Clotilde, "don't—don't do that. It's not—it's not right."

"I'll go and put them in water," said Anthea cheerfully. She went out of the room.

"Really," said Mrs. Glynne, "Anthea! I do think she's—"

"She's getting worse," said Clotilde.

Miss Marple adopted an attitude of not listening or hearing. She picked up a small enamel box and looked at it with admiring eyes.

"She'll probably break a vase now," said Lavinia.

She went out of the room. Miss Marple said:

"You are worried about your sister, about Anthea?"

"Well, yes, she's always been rather unbalanced. She's the youngest and she was rather delicate as a girl. But lately, I think, she's got definitely worse. She hasn't got any idea, I think, of the gravity of things. She has these silly fits of hysteria—hysterical laughter at things one ought to be serious about. We don't want to—well, to send her anywhere or—you know. She ought to have treatment, I think, but I don't think she would like to go away from home. This is her home, after all. Though sometimes it's—it's very difficult."

"All life is difficult sometimes," said Miss Marple.

"Lavinia talks of going away," said Clotilde. "She talks of going to live abroad again. At Taormina, I think. She was there with her husband a lot and they were very happy. She's been at home with us now for many years, but she seems to have this longing to get away and to travel. Sometimes I think—sometimes I think she doesn't like being in the same house as Anthea."

"Oh, dear," said Miss Marple. "Yes, I have heard of cases like that where these difficulties do arise."

"She's afraid of Anthea," said Clotilde. "Definitely afraid of her. And, really, I keep telling her there's nothing to be afraid of. Anthea's just rather silly at times. You know, has queer ideas and says queer things. But I don't think there's any danger of her—well, I mean of—oh, I don't know what I mean. Doing anything dangerous or strange or queer."

"There's never been any trouble of that kind?" inquired Miss Marple.

"Oh, no. There's never been anything. She gets nervous fits of temper sometimes and she takes rather sudden dislikes to people. She's very jealous, you know, over things. Very jealous of a lot of—well, fuss being made over different people. I don't know. Sometimes I think we'd better sell this house and leave it altogether."

"It is sad for you, isn't it?" said Miss Marple. "I think I can understand that it must be very sad for you living here with the memory of the past."

"You understand that, do you? Yes, I can see that you do. One cannot help it. One's mind goes back to that dear, lovable child. She was like a daughter to me. She was the daughter, anyway, of one of my best friends. She was very intelligent, too. She was a clever girl. She was a good artist. She was doing very well with her art training and designing. She was taking up a good deal of designing. I was very proud of her. And then—this wretched attachment, this terrible mentally afflicted boy."

"You mean Mr. Rafiel's son, Michael Rafiel?"

"Yes. If only he'd never come here. It just happened that he was staying in this part of the world and his father suggested he might look us up and he came and had a meal with us. He could be very charming, you know. But he always had been a sad delinquent, a bad record. He'd been in prison twice, and had a very bad history with girls. But I never thought that Verity . . . just a case of infatuation. I suppose it happens to girls of that age. She was infatuated with him. Thought of nothing else, wouldn't hear a word against him. Insisted that everything that had happened to him had not been his fault. You know the things girls say. 'Everyone is against him,' that's what they always say. Everyone's against him. Nobody made allowances for him. Oh, one gets tired of hearing these things said. Can't one put a little sense into girls?"

"They have not usually very much sense, I agree," said Miss Marple.

"She wouldn't listen. I—I tried to keep him away from the house. I told him he was not to come here any more. That, of course, was stupid. I realized that afterwards. It only meant that she went and met him outside the house. I don't know where. They had various meeting places. He used to call for her in his car at an agreed spot and bring her home late at night. Once or twice he didn't bring her home until the next day. I tried to tell them it must stop, that it must all cease, but they wouldn't listen. Verity wouldn't listen. I didn't expect him to, of course."

"She intended to marry him?" asked Miss Marple.

"Well, I don't think it ever got as far as that. I don't think he ever wanted to marry her or thought of such a thing."

"I am very sorry for you," said Miss Marple. "You must have suffered a lot."

"Yes. The worst was having to go and identify the body. That was some time after—after she'd disappeared from here. We thought, of course, that she'd run away with him and we thought that we'd get news of them some time. I knew the police seemed to be taking it rather seriously. They asked Michael to go to the police station and help them with inquiries, and his account of himself didn't seem to agree with what local people were saying.

"Then they found her. A long way from here. About thirty miles away. In a kind of ditch, a hedgy spot down an unfrequented lane where anyone hardly ever went. Yes, I had to go and view the body in the mortuary. A terrible sight. The cruelty, the force that had been used. What did he want to do that to her for? Wasn't it enough that he strangled her? He strangled her with her own scarf. I can't—I can't talk about it any more. I can't bear it, I can't bear it."

Tears rained suddenly down her face.

"I'm sorry for you," said Miss Marple. "I'm very, very sorry."

"I believe you are." Clotilde looked at her suddenly. "And even you don't know the worst of it."

"In what way?"

"I don't know—I don't know about Anthea."

"What do you mean about Anthea?"

"She was so queer at that time. She was—she was very jealous. She suddenly seemed to turn against Verity—to look at her as though she hated her. Sometimes I thought—I thought perhaps—oh, no, it's an awful thing to think, you can't think that about your own sister—she did once attack someone. You know, she used to get these storms of rage. I wondered if it *could* have been—oh, I mustn't say such things. There's no question of any such thing. Please forget what I've said. There's nothing in it, nothing at all. But—but—well, she's not quite normal. I've got to face that. When she was quite young, queer things happened once or twice—with animals. We had a parrot—a parrot that said things, silly things that parrots do say, and she wrung its neck and I've never felt the same since. I've near felt that I could trust her. I've never felt *sure.* I've never felt—oh, goodness, I'm getting hysterical, too."

"Come, come," said Miss Marple, "don't think of these things."

"No. It's bad enough to know—to know that Verity died—died in that horrible way. At any rate, other girls are safe from that boy. Life sentence he got. He's still in prison. They won't let him out to do anything to anyone else. Though why they couldn't bring it in as some mental trouble—diminished responsibility—one of these things they use nowadays. He ought to have gone to Broadmoor. I'm sure he wasn't responsible for anything that he did."

She got up and went out of the room. Mrs. Glynne had come back and passed her sister in the doorway.

"You mustn't pay any attention to Clotilde," she said. "She's never quite recovered from that ghastly business years ago. She loved Verity very much."

"She seems to be worried about your other sister."

"About Anthea? Anthea's all right. She's—er—well, she flighty, you know. She's a bit—hysterical. Apt to get to worked up about things, and she has queer fancies, imagination sometimes. But I don't think there's any need for Clotilde to worry so much. Dear me, who's that passing the window?"

Two apologetic figures suddenly showed themselves in the French window.

"Oh, do excuse us," said Miss Barrow. "We were just walking round the house to see if we could find Miss Marple. We had heard she'd come here with you and I wonder—oh, there you are, my dear Miss Marple. I wanted to tell you that we didn't get to that church after all this afternoon. Apparently it's closed for cleaning, so I think we shall have to give up any other expedition today and go on one tomorrow. I do hope you don't mind us coming in this way. I did ring at the front doorbell but it didn't seem to be ringing."

"I'm afraid it doesn't sometimes," said Mrs. Glynne. "You know, it's rather temperamental. Sometimes it rings and sometimes it doesn't. But do sit down and talk to us a little. I'd no idea that you hadn't gone with the coach."

"No, we thought we would do a little sightseeing round here, as we had got so far, and going with the coach would really be rather—well, rather painful after what has happened just a day or two ago."

"You must have some sherry," said Mrs. Glynne.

She went out of the room and presently returned. Anthea was with her, quite calm now, bringing glasses and a decanter of sherry, and they sat down together.

"I can't help wanting to know," said Mrs. Glynne, "what really is going to happen in this business. I mean of poor Miss Temple. It seems so very impossible to know what the police think. They still seem to be in charge, and I mean the inquest being adjourned, so obviously they are not satisfied. I don't know if there's anything in the nature of the wound."

"I shouldn't think so," said Miss Barrow. "I mean a blow on the head, bad concussion—well, I mean that came from the boulder. The only point is, Miss Marple, if the boulder rolled itself down or somebody rolled it."

"Oh," said Miss Cooke, "but surely you can't think that—who on earth would want to roll a boulder down, do that sort of thing? I suppose there are always hooligans about. You know, some young foreigners or students. I really wonder, you know, whether—well—"

"You mean," said Miss Marple, "you wondered if that someone was one of our fellow travellers."

"Well, I—I didn't say that," said Miss Cooke.

"But surely," said Miss Marple, "we can't help—well, thinking about that sort of thing. I mean, there must be some explanation. If the police seem sure it wasn't an accident, well, then it must have been done by somebody and—well, Miss Temple was a stranger to this place here. It doesn't seem as if anyone could have done it—anyone local, I mean. So it really comes back to—well, to all of us who were in the coach, doesn't it?"

She gave a faint, rather whinnying old lady's laugh.

"Oh, surely!"

"No, I suppose I ought not to say such things. But you know, really, crimes are very interesting. Sometimes the most extraordinary things have happened."

"Have you any definite feeling yourself, Miss Marple? I should be interested to hear," said Clotilde.

"Well, one does think of possibilities."

"Mr. Caspar," said Miss Cooke. "You know, I didn't like the look of that man from the first. He looked to me—well, I thought he might have something to do with espionage or something. You know, perhaps come to this country to look for atomic secrets or something."

"I don't think we've got any atomic secrets round here," said Mrs. Glynne.

"Of course we haven't," said Anthea. "Perhaps it was someone who was following her. Perhaps it was someone who was tracking her because she was a criminal of some kind."

"Nonsense," said Clotilde. "She was the headmistress, retired, of a very well-known school, she was a very fine scholar. Why should anyone be trying to track *her* down?"

"Oh, I don't know. She might have gone peculiar or something."

"I'm sure," said Mrs. Glynne, "that Miss Marple has some ideas."

"Well, I have some ideas," said Miss Marple. "It seems to me that—well the only people that could be . . . Oh, dear, this is so difficult to say. But I mean there are two people who just spring into one's mind as possibilities logically. I don't think that it's really so at all, because I'm sure they're both very nice people, but there's nobody else really logically who could be suspected, should I say."

"Who do you mean? This is very interesting."

"Well, I don't think I ought to say such things. It's only a—a sort of wild conjecture."

"Who do you think might have rolled the boulder down? Who do you think could have been the person that Joanna and Emlyn Price saw?"

"Well, what I did think was that—that perhaps they hadn't seen anybody."

"I don't quite understand," said Anthea. "They hadn't seen anybody?"

"Well, perhaps they might have made it all up."

"What—about seeing someone?"

"Well, it's possible, isn't it?"

"Do you mean as a sort of joke or a sort of unkind idea? What *do* you mean?"

"Well, I suppose—one does hear of young people doing very extraordinary things nowadays," said Miss Marple. "You know, putting things in horses' eyes, smashing legation windows and attacking people. Throwing stones at people, and it's usually being done by somebody young, isn't it? And they were the only young people, weren't they?"

"You mean Emlyn Price and Joanna might have rolled over that boulder?"

"Well, they're the only sort of obvious people, aren't they?" said Miss Marple.

"Fancy!" said Clotilde. "Oh, I should never have thought of that. But I see—yes, I just see that there could be something in what you say. Of course, I don't know what those two were like. I haven't been travelling with them."

"Oh, they were very nice," said Miss Marple. "Joanna seemed to me a particularly—you know, capable girl."

"Capable of doing anything?" asked Anthea.

"Anthea," said Clotilde, "do be quiet."

"Yes. Quite capable," said Miss Marple. "After all, if you're going to do what may result in murder, you'd have to be rather capable so as to manage not to be seen or anything."

"They must have been in it together, though," suggested Miss Barrow.

"Oh, yes," said Miss Marple. "They were in it together and they told roughly the same story. They are the—well, they are the obvious suspects, that's all I can say. They were out of sight of the others. All the other people were on the lower path. They could have gone up to the top of the hill, they could have rocked the boulder. Perhaps they didn't mean to kill Miss Temple specially. They may have meant it just as a—well, just as a piece of anarchy or smashing something or someone—anyone, in fact. They rolled it over. And then, of course, they told the story of seeing someone there. Some rather peculiar costume or other which also sounds very unlikely and—well, I oughtn't to say these things, but I *have* been thinking about it."

"It seems to me a very interesting thought," said Mrs. Glynne. "What do you think, Clotilde?"

"I think it's a possibility. I shouldn't have thought of it myself."

"Well," said Miss Cooke, rising to her feet, "we must be going back to the Golden Boar now. Are you coming with us, Miss Marple?"

"Oh, no," said Miss Marple. "I suppose you don't know. I've forgotten to tell you. Miss Bradbury-Scott very kindly asked me to come back and stay another night—or two nights—here."

"Oh, I see. Well, I'm sure that'll be very nice for you. Much more comfortable. They seem rather a noisy lot that have arrived at the Golden Boar this evening."

"Won't you come round and have some coffee with us after dinner?" suggested Clotilde. "It's quite a warm evening. We can't offer you dinner because I'm afraid we haven't got enough in the house, but if you'll come in and have some coffee with us . . ."

"That would be very nice," said Miss Cooke. "Yes, we will certainly avail ourselves of your hospitality."

21

THE CLOCK STRIKES THREE

Miss Cooke and Miss Barrow arrived very promptly at eight forty-five. One wore beige lace and the other one a shade of olive green. During dinner, Anthea had asked Miss Marple about these two ladies.

"It seems very funny of them," she said, "to want to stay behind."

"Oh, I don't think so," said Miss Marple. "I think it is really quite natural. They have a rather exact plan, I imagine."

"What do you mean by a plan?" asked Mrs. Glynne.

"Well, I should think they are always prepared for various eventualities and had a plan for dealing with them."

"Do you mean," said Anthea with some interest, "do you mean that they had a plan for dealing with murder?"

"I wish," said Mrs. Glynne, "that you wouldn't talk of poor Miss Temple's death as murder."

"But of course it's murder," said Anthea. "All I wonder is who wanted to murder her? I should think probably some pupil of hers at the school who always hated her and had it in for her."

"Do you think hate can last as long as that?" asked Miss Marple.

"Oh, I should think so. I should think you could hate anyone for years."

"No," said Miss Marple, "I think hate would die out. You could try and keep it up artificially, but I think you would fail. It's not as strong a force as love," she added.

"Don't you think that Miss Cooke or Miss Barrow or both of them might have done the murder?"

"Why should they?" said Mrs. Glynne. "Really, Anthea! They seemed very nice women to me."

"I think there's something rather mysterious about them," said Anthea. "Don't you, Clotilde?"

"I think perhaps you're right," said Clotilde. "They seemed to me to be slightly artificial, if you know what I mean."

"I think there's something very sinister about them," said Anthea.

"You've got such an imagination always," said Mrs. Glynne. "Anyway, they were walking along the bottom path, weren't they? You saw them there, didn't you?" she said to Miss Marple.

"I can't say that I noticed them particularly," said Miss Marple. "In fact, I had no opportunity of doing so."

"You mean—?"

"She wasn't there," said Clotilde. "She was here in our garden."

"Oh, of course. I forgot."

"A very nice, peaceful day it was," said Miss Marple. "I enjoyed it very much. Tomorrow morning I would like to go out and look again at that mass of white flowers coming into bloom at the end of the garden near that raised-up mound. It was just beginning to come out the other day. It must be a mass of bloom now. I shall always remember that as part of my visit here, you know."

"I hate it," said Anthea. "I want it taken away. I want to build up a greenhouse again there. Surely if we save enough money we can do that, Clotilde?"

"We'll leave that alone," said Clotilde. "I don't want that touched. What use is a greenhouse to us now? It would be years before grapes would bear fruit again."

"Come," said Mrs. Glynne, "we can't go on arguing over that. Let us go into the drawing room. Our guests will be coming shortly for coffee."

It was then that the guests had arrived. Clotilde brought in the tray of coffee. She poured out the cups and distributed them. She placed one before each guest and then brought one to Miss Marple. Miss Cooke leaned forward.

"Oh, do forgive me, Miss Marple, but, really, do you know, I shouldn't drink that if I were you. Coffee, I mean, at this time of night. You won't sleep properly."

"Oh, do you think so?" said Miss Marple. "I am quite used to coffee in the evening."

"Yes, but this is very strong, good coffee. I should advise you not to drink it."

Miss Marple looked at Miss Cooke. Miss Cooke's face was very earnest. Her fair, unnatural-looking hair flopped over one eye. The other eye blinked slightly.

"I see what you mean," said Miss Marple. "Perhaps you are right. You know something, I gather, about diet."

"Oh, yes, I made quite a study of it. I had some training in nursing, you know, and one thing and another."

"Indeed." Miss Marple pushed the cup away slightly. "I suppose there is no photograph of this girl?" she asked. "Verity Hunt, or whatever her name was? The Archdeacon was talking about her. He seemed to have been very fond of her."

"I think he was. He was fond of all young people," said Clotilde.

She got up, went across the room and lifted the lid of a desk. From that she took a photograph and brought it over for Miss Marple to see.

"That was Verity," she said.

"A beautiful face," said Miss Marple. "Yes, a very beautiful and unusual face. Poor child."

"It's dreadful nowadays," said Anthea, "these things seem happening the whole time. Girls going out with every kind of young man. Nobody taking any trouble to look after them."

"They have to look after themselves nowadays," said Clotilde, "and they've no idea of how to do it, heaven help them!"

She stretched out a hand to take back the photograph from Miss Marple. As she did so, her sleeve caught the coffee cup and knocked it to the floor.

"Oh, dear!" said Miss Marple. "Was that my fault? Did I jog your arm?"

"No," said Clotilde, "it was my sleeve. It's rather a floating sleeve. Perhaps you would like some hot milk, if you are afraid to take coffee?"

"That would be very kind," said Miss Marple. "A glass of hot milk when I went to bed would be very soothing indeed, and always gives one a good night."

After a little more desultory conversation, Miss Cooke and Miss Barrow took their departure—a rather fussy departure in which first one and then the other came back to collect some article they'd left behind—a scarf, a handbag and a pocket handkerchief.

"Fuss, fuss, fuss," said Anthea, when they had departed.

"Somehow," said Mrs. Glynne, "I agree with Clotilde that those two don't seem real, if you know what I mean," she said to Miss Marple.

"Yes," said Miss Marple, "I do rather agree with you. They don't seem very real. I have wondered about them a good deal. Wondered, I mean, why they came on this tour and if they were really enjoying it. And what was their reason for coming."

"And have you discovered the answers to all those things?" asked Clotilde.

"I think so," said Miss Marple. She sighed. "I've discovered the answers to a lot of things," she said.

"Up to now I hope you've enjoyed yourself," said Clotilde.

"I am glad to have left the tour now," said Miss Marple. "I don't think I should have enjoyed much more of it."

"No. I can quite understand that."

Clotilde fetched a glass of hot milk from the kitchen and accompanied Miss Marple up to her room.

"Is there anything else I can get you?" she asked. "Anything at all?"

"No, thank you," said Miss Marple. "I have everything I want. I have my little night bag here, you see, so I need not do any more unpacking. Thank you," she said, "it is very kind of you and your sisters to put me up again tonight."

"Well, we couldn't do much less, having had Mr. Rafiel's letter. He was a very thoughtful man."

"Yes," said Miss Marple, "the kind of man who—well, thinks of everything. A good brain, I should think."

"I believe he was a very noted financier."

"Financially and otherwise, he thought of a lot of things," said Miss Marple. "Ah, well, I shall be glad to get to bed. Good night, Miss Bradbury-Scott."

"Shall I send you breakfast up in the morning? You'd like to have it in bed?"

"No, no, I wouldn't put you out for the world. No, no, I would rather come down. A cup of tea, perhaps, would be very nice, but I want to go out in the garden. I particularly want to see that mound all covered with white flowers, so beautiful and so triumphant—"

"Good night," said Clotilde; "sleep well."

II

In the hall of The Old Manor House the grandfather clock at the bottom of the stairs struck two o'clock. The clocks in the house did not all strike in unison and some of them, indeed, did not strike at all. To keep a house full of antique clocks in working order was not easy. At three o'clock the clock on the first floor landing struck a soft-chimed three o'clock. A faint chink of light showed through the hinge of the door.

Miss Marple sat up in bed and put her fingers on the switch of the electric lamp by her bed. The door opened very softly. There was no light outside now, but the soft footstep came through the door into the room. Miss Marple switched the light on.

"Oh," she said, "it's you, Miss Bradbury-Scott. Is there anything special?"

"I just came to see if you wanted anything," said Miss Bradbury-Scott.

Miss Marple looked at her. Clotilde had on a long purple robe. What a handsome woman she was, thought Miss Marple. Her hair framing her forehead, a tragic figure, a figure of drama. Again Miss Marple thought of Greek plays. Clytemnestra again.

"You're sure there is nothing I can bring you?"

"No, thank you," said Miss Marple. "I'm afraid," she said apologetically, "that I have not drunk my milk."

"Oh, dear, why not?"

"I did not think it would be very good for me," said Miss Marple.

Clotilde stood there at the foot of the bed, looking at her.

"Not wholesome, you know," said Miss Marple.

"Just what do you mean by that?" Clotilde's voice was harsh now.

"I think you know what I mean," said Miss Marple. "I think you've known all the evening. Perhaps before that."

"I have no idea what you are talking about."

"No?" There was a faint satirical note to the questioning monosyllable.

"I am afraid the milk is cold now. I will take it away and get you some hot."

Clotilde stretched out a hand and took the glass of milk from the bedside.

"Don't trouble yourself," said Miss Marple. "Even if you brought it to me, I should not drink it."

"I really cannot understand the point of what you're saying. Really," said Clotilde, looking at her. "What a very extraordinary person you are. What sort of a woman are you? Why are you talking like this? Who are you?"

Miss Marple pulled down the mass of pink wool that encircled her head, a pink wool scarf of the same kind that she had once worn in the West Indies.

"One of my names," she said, "is Nemesis."

"Nemesis? And what does that mean?"

"I think you know," said Miss Marple. "You are a very well-educated woman. Nemesis is long delayed sometimes, but it comes in the end."

"What are you talking about?"

"About a very beautiful girl whom you killed," said Miss Marple.

"Whom I killed? What do you mean?"

"I mean the girl Verity."

"And why should I kill her?"

"Because you loved her," said Miss Marple.

"Of course I loved her. I was devoted to her. And she loved me."

"Somebody said to me not very long ago that love was a very frightening word. It *is* a frightening word. You loved Verity too much. She meant everything in the world to you. She was devoted to you until something else came into her life. A different kind of love came into her life. She fell in love with a boy, a young man. Not a very suitable one, not a very good specimen, not anyone with a good record, but she loved him and he loved her and she wanted to escape—to escape from the burden of the bondage of love she was living in with you. She wanted a normal woman's life. To live with the man of her choice, to have children by him. She wanted marriage and the happiness of normality."

Clotilde moved. She came to a chair and sat down in it, staring at Miss Marple.

"So," she said, "you seem to understand very well."

"Yes, I do understand."

"What you say is quite true. I shan't deny it. It doesn't matter if I do or do not deny it."

"No," said Miss Marple, "you are quite right there. It will not matter."

"Do you know at all—can you imagine—how I have suffered?"

"Yes," said Miss Marple, "I can imagine it. I've always been able to imagine things."

"Did you imagine the agony, the agony of thinking, of knowing you are going to lose the thing you love best in the world? And was losing it to a miserable, depraved delinquent—a man unworthy of my beautiful, splendid girl. I had to stop it. I had to—I had to."

"Yes," said Miss Marple. "Sooner than let the girl go, you killed her. Because you loved her, you killed her."

"Do you think I could ever do a thing like that? Do you think I could strangle the girl I loved? Do you think I could bash her face in, crush her head to a pulp? Nothing but a vicious, depraved man would do a thing like that."

"No," said Miss Marple, "you wouldn't do that. You loved her and you would not be able to do that."

"Well, then, you see, you are talking nonsense."

"You didn't do that to her. The girl that happened to was not the girl you loved. Verity's here still, isn't she? She's here in the garden. I don't think you strangled her. I think you gave her a drink of coffee or of milk, you gave her a painless overdose of sleeping stuff. And then when she was dead, you took her out into the garden, you pulled aside the fallen bricks of the greenhouse, and you made a vault for her there, under the floor with the bricks, and covered it over. And then the polygonum was planted there and has flowered ever since, growing bigger and stronger every year. Verity has remained here with you. You never let her go."

"You fool! You crazy old fool! Do you think you are ever going to get away to tell this story?"

"I think so," said Miss Marple. "I'm not quite sure of it. You are a strong woman, a great deal stronger than I am."

"I'm glad you appreciate that."

"And you wouldn't have any scruples," said Miss Marple. "You know one doesn't stop at one murder. I have noticed that in the course of my life and in what I have observed of crime. You killed two girls, didn't you? You killed the girl you loved and you killed a different girl."

"I killed a silly little tramp, an adolescent tart, Nora Broad. How did you know about her?"

"I wondered," said Miss Marple. "I didn't think from what I saw of you that you could have borne to strangle and disfigure the girl you loved. But another girl disappeared also about that time, a girl whose body has never been found. But I thought that the body *had* been found, only they hadn't known that body was Nora Broad's. It was dressed in Verity's clothes, it was identified as Verity by the person who would be the first applied to, the person who knew her better than anyone else. You had to go and say if the body found was the body of Verity. You recognized it. You said that that dead body was Verity's."

"And why should I do that?"

"Because you wanted the boy who had taken Verity away from you, the boy whom Verity had loved and who had loved Verity, you wanted him tried for murder. And so you hid that second body in a place where it would not be too easily discovered. When it was discovered, it would be thought to be the wrong girl. You would make sure that it was identified in the way you wanted. You dressed it in Verity's clothes, put her handbag there, a letter or two, a bangle, a little cross on a chain—you disfigured her face.

"A week ago you committed a third murder, the murder of Elizabeth Temple. You killed her because she was coming to this part of the world, and you were afraid of what she might have known, from what Verity might have written to her or told her. You thought that if Elizabeth Temple got together with Archdeacon Brabazon, they might with what they both knew come at some appraisal of the truth. Elizabeth Temple must not be allowed to meet the Archdeacon. You are a very powerful woman. You could have rolled that boulder down the hillside. It must have taken some doing, but you are very strong."

"Strong enough to deal with you," said Clotilde.

"I don't think," said Miss Marple, "that you will be allowed to do that."

"What do you mean, you miserable, shrivelled-up old woman?"

"Yes," said Miss Marple, "I'm old and I have very little strength in my arms or my legs. Very little strength anywhere. But I am in my own way an emissary of justice."

Clotilde laughed. "And who'll stop me from putting an end to you?"

"I think," said Miss Marple, "my guardian angel."

"Trusting to your guardian angel, are you?" said Clotilde, and laughed again.

She advanced towards the bed.

"Possibly two guardian angels," said Miss Marple. "Mr. Rafiel always did things on a lavish scale."

Her hand slipped under the pillow and out again. In it was a whistle which she put to her lips. It was something of a sensation in whistles. It had the shrill fury that would attract a policeman from the end of a street. Two things happened almost simultaneously. The door of the room opened. Clotilde turned. Miss Barrow was standing in the doorway. At the same moment the large wardrobe hanging cupboard opened and Miss Cooke stepped out of it. There was a grim air of professionalism about them both which was very noticeable in contrast to their pleasant social behavior a little earlier in the evening.

"Two guardian angels," said Miss Marple happily. "Mr. Rafiel has done me very proud, as one used to say!"

22

MISS MARPLE TELLS HER STORY

"When did you find out," asked Professor Wanstead, "that those two women were private agents accompanying you for your protection?"

He leaned forward in his chair, looking thoughtfully at the white-haired old lady who sat in an upright position in the chair opposite him. They were in an official government building in London, and there were four other persons present.

An official from the Public Prosecutor's Office; the Assistant Commissioner of Scotland Yard, Sir James Lloyd; the Governor of Manstone Prison, Sir Andrew McNeil. The fourth person was the Home Secretary.

"Not until the last evening," said Miss Marple. "I wasn't actually sure until then. Miss Cooke had come to St. Mary Mead and I found out fairly quickly that she was not what she represented herself to be, which was a woman knowledgeable in gardening who had come there to help a friend with her garden. So I was left with the choice of deciding what her real object had been, once she had acquainted herself with my appearance, which was obviously the only thing she could have come for. When I recognized her again on the coach, I had to make up my mind if she was accompanying the tour in the role of guardianship, or whether those two women were enemies enlisted by what I might call the other side.

"I was only really sure that last evening when Miss Cooke prevented me, by very distinct words of warning, from drinking the cup of coffee that Clotilde Bradbury-Scott had just set down in front of me. She phrased it very cleverly, but the warning was clearly there. Later, when I was wishing those two good night, one of them took my hand in both of hers, giving me a particularly friendly and affectionate handshake. And in doing so she passed something into my hand, which, when I examined it later, I found to be a high-powered whistle. I took it to bed with me, accepted the glass of milk which was urged upon me by my hostess, and wished her good night, being careful not to change my simple and friendly attitude."

"You didn't drink the milk?"

"Of course not," said Miss Marple. "What do you take me for?"

"I beg your pardon," said Professor Wanstead. "It surprises me that you didn't lock your door."

"That would have been quite the wrong thing to do," said Miss Marple. "I wanted Clotilde Bradbury-Scott to come in. I wanted to see what she would say or do. I thought it was almost certain that she *would* come in, when sufficient time had elapsed, to make sure that I had drunk the milk and was in an unconscious sleep from which presumably I would not have woken up again."

"Did you help Miss Cooke to conceal herself in the wardrobe?"

"No. It was a complete surprise when she came out of that suddenly. I suppose," said Miss Marple thoughtfully, thinking it over, "I suppose she slipped in there just when I had gone down the passage to the—er—to the bathroom."

"You knew the two women were in the house?"

"I thought they would be at hand somewhere after they'd given me the whistle. I do not think it was a difficult house to which to gain access, there were no shuttered windows or burglar alarms or anything of that kind. One of them came back on the pretext of having left a handbag and a scarf. Between them they probably managed to leave a window unfastened, and I should imagine they came back into the house almost as soon as they left it, while the inhabitants inside were going up to bed."

"You took a big risk, Miss Marple."

"I hoped for the best," said Miss Marple. "One cannot go through life without attracting certain risks if they are necessary."

"Your tip about the parcel dispatched to that charity, by the way, was entirely successful. It contained a brand-new brightly coloured man's polo-necked pullover in scarlet and black checks. Most noticeable. What made you think of that?"

"Well," said Miss Marple, "that was really very simple. The description that Emlyn and Joanna gave of the figure they had seen made it seem almost certain that these very bright-coloured and noticeable clothes were *meant* to be noticed, and that therefore it would be very important that they should not be hidden locally or kept among the person's own belongings. They must be got out of the way as soon as could be. And really there is only one way successfully of disposing of something. That is through the general post. Anything in the nature of clothes can be very easily dispatched to charities. Think how pleased the people who collect winter garments for Unemployed Mothers, or whatever the name of the charity, would be to find a nearly brand-new woollen pullover. All I had to do was to find out the address where it had been sent."

"And you *asked* them that at the post office?" The Home Secretary looked slightly shocked.

"Not directly, of course. I mean, I had to be a little flustered and explain how I'd put the wrong address on some clothes that I was sending to a charity and could they by any chance tell me if the parcel one of my kind hostesses had brought up there had been sent off? And a very nice woman there did her best and remembered that it was *not* the address I was hoping it had been sent to, and she gave me the address that she *had* noted. She had no suspicion, I think, that I had any wish for the information apart from being—well, rather muddle-headed, elderly, and very worried about where my parcel of worn clothes had gone."

"Ah," said Professor Wanstead, "I see you are an actress, Miss Marple, as well as an avenger." Then he said, "When did you first begin to discover what had happened ten years ago?"

"To begin with," said Miss Marple, "I found things very difficult, almost impossible. In my mind I was blaming Mr. Rafiel for not having made things clear to me. But I see now that he'd been very wise not to do so. Really, you know, he was extraordinarily clever. I can see why he was such a big financier and made so much money so easily. He laid his plans so well. He gave me just enough information in small packets each time. I was, as it were, directed. First my guardian angels were alerted to note what I looked like. Then I was directed on the tour and to the people on it."

"Did you suspect, if I may use that word, anyone on the tour at first?"

"Only as possibilities."

"No feeling of evil?"

"Ah, you have remembered that. No, I did not think there was any definite atmosphere of evil. I was not told who my contact was there, but *she* made herself known to *me.*"

"Elizabeth Temple?"

"Yes. It was like a searchlight," said Miss Marple, "illuminating things on a dark night. So far, you see, I had been in the dark. There were certain things that must be, must logically be, I mean, because of what Mr. Rafiel had indicated. There must be somewhere a victim and somewhere a murderer. Yes, a killer was indicated because that was the only liaison that had existed between Mr. Rafiel and myself. There had been a murder in the West Indies. Both he and I had been involved in it and all he knew of me was my connection with that. So it could not be any other type of crime.

And it could not, either, be a casual crime. It must be, and show itself definitely to be, the handiwork of someone who had accepted evil—evil instead of good. There seemed to be two victims indicated. There must be someone who had been killed and there must be clearly a victim of injustice—a victim who had been accused of a crime he or she had not committed. So now, while I pondered these things, I had no light upon them until I talked to Miss Temple. She was very intense, very compelling. There came the first link which I had with Mr. Rafiel. She spoke of a girl she had known, a girl who had once been engaged to Mr. Rafiel's son. Here then was my first ray of light. Presently she also told me that the girl had not married him. I asked why not and she said: 'Because she died.' I asked then how she had died, what had killed her, and she said very strongly, very compellingly—I can hear her voice still, it was like the sound of a deep bell—she said *Love.* And she said after that: 'The most frightening word there can be is love.' I did not know then exactly what she meant. In fact the first idea that came to me was that the girl had committed suicide as a result of an unhappy love affair. It can happen often enough, and a very sad tragedy it is when it does happen. That was the most I knew then—that and the fact that the journey she herself was engaged upon was no mere pleasure tour. She was going, she told me, on a pilgrimage. She was going to some place or to some person. I did not learn then who the person was; that only came later."

"Archdeacon Brabazon?"

"Yes. I had no idea then of his existence. But from then on I felt that the chief characters—the chief actors—in the drama, whichever way you like to put it, were not on the tour. They were not members of the coach party. I hesitated just for a short time, hesitated over some particular persons. I hesitated, considering Joanna Crawford and Emlyn Price."

"Why fix on them?"

"Because of their youth," said Miss Marple. "Because youth is so often associated with suicide, with violence, with intense jealousy and tragic love. A man kills his girl—it happens. Yes, my mind went to them, but it did not seem to me there was any association there. No shadow of evil, of despair, of misery. I used the idea of them later as a kind of false pointer when we were drinking sherry at The Old Manor House that last evening. I pointed out how they could be the most easy suspects in the death of Elizabeth Temple. When I see them again," said Miss Marple punctiliously, "I shall apologize to them for having used them as useful characters to distract attention from my real ideas."

"And the next thing was the death of Elizabeth Temple?"

"No," said Miss Marple. "Actually the next thing was my arrival at The

Old Manor House—the kindness of my reception and taking up my stay there under their hospitable roof. That again had been arranged by Mr. Rafiel. So I knew that I must go there, but not for what reason I was to go there. It might be merely a place where more information would come to me to lead me onwards in my quest. I am sorry," Miss Marple said suddenly, becoming her normal apologetic and slightly fussy self, "I am talking at much too great a length. I really must not inflict on you all that I thought and . . ."

"Please go on," said Professor Wanstead. "You may not know it, but what you are telling me is particularly interesting to me. It ties up with so much I have known and seen in the work I do. Go on giving me what you felt."

"Yes, go on," said Sir Andrew McNeil.

"It *was* feeling," said Miss Marple. "It wasn't really, you know, logical deduction. It was based on a kind of emotional reaction or susceptibility to —well, I can only call it atmosphere."

"Yes," said Wanstead, "there is atmosphere—atmosphere in houses, atmosphere in places, in the garden, in the forest, in a public house, in a cottage."

"The three sisters. That is what I thought and felt and said to myself when I went in to The Old Manor House. I was so kindly received by Lavinia Glynne. There's something about the phrase—the three sisters— that springs up in your mind as sinister. It combines with the three sisters in Russian literature, the three witches on Macbeth's heath. It seemed to me that there was an atmosphere there of sorrow, of deep-felt unhappiness, also an atmosphere of fear and a kind of struggling different atmosphere which I can only describe as an atmosphere of normality."

"Your last word interests me," said Wanstead.

"It was due, I think, to Mrs. Glynne. She was the one who came to meet me when the coach arrived and explained the invitation. She was an entirely normal and pleasant woman, a widow. She was not very happy, but when I say she was not very happy, it was nothing to do with sorrow or deep unhappiness, it was just that she had the wrong atmosphere for her own character. She took me back with her and I met the other two sisters. The next morning I was to hear from an aged housemaid who brought my early-morning tea a story of past tragedy, of a girl who had been killed by her boy friend—of several other girls in the neighbourhood who'd fallen victims to violence or sexual assault. I had to make my second appraisal. I had dismissed the people in the coach as not being personally concerned in my search. Somewhere still there was a killer. I had to ask myself if one of the killers could be here—here in this house where I had been sent. Clotilde, Lavinia, Anthea. Three names of three weird sisters, three happy—unhappy—suffering—frightened—what were they? My attention was caught first by Clotilde. A tall, handsome woman. A personality. Just as Elizabeth Temple had been a personality. I felt that here where the field was limited, I must at least sum up what I could about the three sisters. Three Fates. Who could be a killer? What kind of a killer? What kind of a killing? I could feel then rising up rather slowly, like a miasma does, an atmosphere. I don't think there is any other word that expresses it except evil. Not necessarily that any one of these three was evil, but they were certainly living in an atmosphere where evil had happened, had left its shadow or was still threatening them. Clotilde, the eldest, was the first one I considered. She was handsome, she was strong, she was, I thought, a woman of intense emotional feeling. I saw her, I will admit, as a possible Clytemnestra. I had recently," Miss Marple dropped into her everyday tones, "been taken very kindly to a Greek play performed at a well-known boys' public school not far from my home. I had been very, very impressed by the acting of the Agamemnon and particularly the performance of the boy who had played Clytemnestra. A very remarkable performance. It seemed to me that in Clotilde I could imagine a woman who could plan and carry out the killing of a husband in his bath."

For a moment Professor Wanstead had all he could do to repress a laugh. It was the seriousness of Miss Marple's tone. She gave him a slight twinkle from her eyes.

"Yes, it sounds rather silly, does it not, said like that? But I could *see* her that way, playing that part, that is to say. Very unfortunately, she had no husband. She had never had a husband, and therefore did not kill a husband. Then I considered my guide to the house—Lavinia Glynne. She seemed an extremely nice, wholesome and pleasant woman. But alas, certain people who have killed have produced much that effect on the world round them. They have been charming people. Many murderers have been delightful and pleasant men, and people have been astonished. They are what I call the respectable killers—the ones who would commit murder from entirely utilitarian motives—without emotion, but to gain a required end. I didn't think it was very likely and I should be highly surprised if it was so, but I could not leave out Mrs. Glynne. She had had a husband. She was a widow and had been a widow for some years. It could be. I left it at that. And then I came to the third sister—Anthea. She was a disquieting personality—badly coordinated, it seemed to me, scatterbrained, and in a condition of some emotion which I thought on the whole was fear. She was frightened of something. Intensely frightened of something. Well, that could fit in, too. If she had committed a crime of some kind, a crime which she had thought was finished with and past, there might have been some recrudescence, some raising up of old problems, something perhaps connected with the Elizabeth Temple inquiries; she might have felt fear that an old crime would be revived or discovered. She had a curious way of looking at you, and then looking sharply from side to side over one shoulder as though she saw something standing behind her—something that made her afraid. So she, too, was a possible answer, a possibly slightly mentally unhinged killer who could have killed because she considered herself persecuted—because she was afraid. These were only ideas. They were only a rather more pronounced assessment of possibilities that I had already gone through on the coach. But the atmosphere of the house was on me more than ever. That next day I walked in the garden with Anthea. At the end of the principal grass path was a mound—a mound created by the falling down of a former greenhouse. Owing to a lack of repairs and of gardeners at the end of the war, it had fallen into disuse, come to pieces, bricks had been piled up surmounted with earth and turf, and had been planted with a certain creeper—a creeper well known when you want to hide or cover some rather ugly piece of building in your garden. Polygonum it is called. One of the quickest flowering shrubs which swallows and kills and dries up and gets rid of everything it grows over. It grows over everything. It is in a way a rather frightening plant. It has beautiful white flowers so it can look very lovely. It was just coming into bloom. I stood there with Anthea, and she seemed to be desperately unhappy over the loss of the greenhouse. She said it had had such lovely grapes, it seemed to be the thing she remembered most about the garden when she had been a child there. And she wanted, she wanted desperately to have enough money so as to dig up the mound, level the ground and rebuild the greenhouse and stock it with muscat grapes and peaches as the old greenhouse had been. It was a terrible nostalgia for the past she was feeling. It was more than that. Again, very clearly, I felt an atmosphere of fear. Something about the mound made her frightened. I couldn't then think what it was. You know the next thing that happened. It was Elizabeth Temple's death, and there was no doubt, from the story told by Emlyn Price and Joanna Crawford, that there could be only one conclusion. It was not an accident. It was deliberate murder.

"I think it was from then on," said Miss Marple, "that I knew. I came to the conclusion there had been three killings. I heard the full story of Mr. Rafiel's son, the delinquent boy, the ex-jailbird, and I thought that he was all those things, but none of them showed him as being a killer or likely to be a killer. All the evidence was against him. There was no doubt in anyone's mind that he had killed the girl whose name I had now learned as being Verity Hunt. But Archdeacon Brabazon put the final crown on the business, as it were. He had known those two young people. They had come to him with their story of wanting to get married and he had taken it upon himself to decide that they should get married. He thought that it was not perhaps a wise marriage, but it was a marriage that was justified by the fact that they both loved each other. The girl loved the boy with what he called a true love—a love as true as her name. And he thought that the boy, for all his bad sexual reputation, had truly loved the girl and had every intention of being faithful to her and trying to reform some of his evil tendencies. The Archdeacon was not optimistic. He did not, I think, believe it would be a thoroughly happy marriage, but it was to his mind what he called a necessary marriage—necessary because if you love enough you will pay the price, even if the price is disappointment and a certain amount of unhappiness. But one thing I was quite sure of. That disfigured face, that battered-in head could not have been the action of a boy who really loved the girl. This was not a story of sexual assault. In this love affair the love was rooted in tenderness. I was ready to take the Archdeacon's word for that. But I knew, too, that I'd got the right clue, the clue that was given me by Elizabeth Temple. She had said that the cause of Verity's death was love—one of the most frightening words there is.

"It was quite clear then," said Miss Marple. "I think I'd known for some time, really. It was just the small things that hadn't fitted in, but now they did. They fitted in with what Elizabeth Temple had said. The cause of Verity's death. She had said first the one word 'love' and then that 'love could be the most frightening word there was.' It was all mapped out so plainly then—the overwhelming love that Clotilde had had for this girl. The girl's hero-worship of her, dependency on her, and then as she grew a little older, her normal instincts came into play. She wanted love. She wanted to be free to love, to marry, to have children. And along came the boy that she could love. She knew that he was unreliable, she knew he was what was technically called a bad lot, but that," said Miss Marple in a more ordinary tone of voice, "is not what puts any girl off a boy. No. Young women like bad lots. They always have. They fall in love with bad lots. They are quite sure they can change them. And the nice, kind, steady, reliable husbands got the answer, in my young days, that one would be 'a sister to them,' which never satisfied them at all. Verity fell in love with Michael Rafiel, and Michael Rafiel was prepared to turn over a new leaf and marry this girl and was sure he would never wish to look at another girl again. I don't say this would have been a happy-ever-after thing, but it was, as the Archdeacon said quite surely, it *was* real love. And so they planned to get married. And I think Verity wrote to Elizabeth and told her that she was going to marry Michael Rafiel. It was arranged in secret because I think Verity did realize that what she was doing was essentially an escape. She was escaping from a life that she didn't want to live any longer, from someone whom she loved very much but not in the way she loved Michael. And she would not be allowed to do so. Permission would not be willingly given, every obstacle would be put in their way. So, like other young people, they were going to elope. There was no need for them to fly off to Gretna Green, they were of sufficiently mature age to marry. So she appealed to Archdeacon Brabazon, her old friend who had confirmed her—who was a real friend. And the wedding was arranged—the day, the time, probably even she bought secretly some garment in which to be married. They were to meet somewhere, no doubt. They were to come to the rendezvous separately. I think he came there, but she did not come. He waited, perhaps—waited and then tried to find out why she didn't come. I think then a message may have been given him, even a letter sent him, possibly in a forged handwriting, saying she had changed her mind. It was all over and she was going away for a time to get over it. I don't know. But I don't think he ever dreamt of the real reason of why she hadn't come, of why she had sent no word. He hadn't thought for one moment that she had been deliberately, cruelly, almost madly, perhaps, destroyed. Clotilde was not going to lose the person she loved. She was not going to let her escape, she was not going to let her go to the young man whom she herself hated and loathed. She would keep Verity, keep her in her own way. But what I could not believe was—I did not believe that she'd strangled the girl and had then disfigured her face. I don't think she could have borne to do that. I think that she had rearranged the bricks of the fallen greenhouse and piled up earth and turf over most of it. The girl had already been given a drink, an overdose of sleeping draught, probably. Grecian, as it were, in tradition. One cup of hemlock—even if it wasn't hemlock. And she buried the girl there in the garden, piled the bricks over her and the earth and the turf—"

"Did neither of the other sisters suspect it?"

"Mrs. Glynne was not there then. Her husband had not died and she was still abroad. But Anthea was there. I think Anthea did know *something* of what went on. I don't know that she suspected death at first, but she knew that Clotilde had been occupying herself with the raising up of a mound at the end of the garden to be covered with flowering shrubs, to be a place of beauty. I think perhaps the truth came to her little by little. And then Clotilde, having accepted evil, done evil, surrendered to evil, had no qualms about what she would do next. I think she enjoyed planning it. She had a certain amount of influence over a sly, sexy little village girl who came to her cadging for benefits now and then. I think it was easy for her to arrange one day to take the girl on a picnic or an expedition a good long way away—thirty or forty miles. She'd chosen the place before-hand, I think. She strangled the girl, disfigured her, hid her under turned earth, leaves and branches. Why should anyone ever suspect her of doing any such thing? She put Verity's handbag there and a little chain Verity used to wear round her neck and possibly dressed her in clothes belonging to Verity. She hoped the crime would not be found out for some time, but in the meantime she spread abroad rumours of Nora Broad having been seen about in Michael's car, going about with Michael. Possibly she spread a story that Verity had broken off the engagement to be married because of his infidelity with this girl. She may have said anything and I think everything she said she enjoyed, poor lost soul."

"Why do you say 'poor lost soul,' Miss Marple?"

"Because," said Miss Marple, "I don't suppose there can be any agony so great as what Clotilde has suffered all this time—ten years now—living in eternal sorrow. Living, you see, with the thing she *had* to live with. She had kept Verity, kept her there at The Old Manor House, in the garden, kept her there forever. She didn't realize at first what that meant—her passionate longing for the girl to be alive again. I don't think she ever suffered from remorse. I don't think she had even that consolation. She just suffered—went on suffering year after year. And I know now what Elizabeth Temple meant—better perhaps than she herself did. Love *is* a very terrible thing. It is alive to evil, it can be one of the most evil things there can be. And Clotilde had to live with that day after day, year after year. I think, you know, that Anthea was frightened of that. I think she knew more clearly the whole time what Clotilde had done and she thought that Clotilde knew that she knew. And she was afraid of what Clotilde might do. Clotilde gave that parcel to Anthea to post, the one with the pullover. She said things to me about Anthea, that she was mentally disturbed, that if she suffered from persecution or jealousy, Anthea might do anything. I think—yes—that in the not-so-distant future—something might have happened to Anthea—an arranged suicide because of a guilty conscience—"

"And yet you are sorry for that woman?" asked Sir Andrew. "Malignant evil is like cancer—a malignant tumor. It brings suffering."

"Of course," said Miss Marple.

"I suppose you have been told what happened that night," said Professor Wanstead, "after your guardian angels had removed you?"

"You mean Clotilde? She had picked up my glass of milk, I remember. She was still holding it when Miss Cooke took me out of the room. I suppose she—drank it, did she?"

"Yes. Did you know that might happen?"

"I didn't think of it, no, not at the moment. I suppose I could have known it if I'd thought about it."

"Nobody could have stopped her. She was so quick about it, and nobody quite realized there was anything wrong with the milk."

"So she drank it."

"Does that surprise you?"

"No, it would have seemed to her the natural thing to do, one can't really wonder. It had come by this time that she wanted to escape—from all the things she was having to live with. Just as Verity had wanted to escape from the life she was living there. Very odd, isn't it, that the retribution one brings on oneself fits so closely with what has caused it?"

"You sound sorrier for her than you were for the girl who died."

"No," said Miss Marple, "it's a different kind of being sorry. I'm sorry for Verity because of all that she missed, all that she was so near to obtaining—a life of love and devotion and service to the man she had chosen, and whom she truly loved—truly and in all verity. She missed all that and nothing can give that back to her. I'm sorry for her because of what she *didn't* have. But she escaped what Clotilde had to suffer—sorrow, misery, fear and a growing cultivation and imbibing of evil. Clotilde had to live with all those. Sorrow, frustrated love which she could never get back, she had to live with the two sisters who suspected, who were afraid of her, and she had to live with the girl she had kept there."

"You mean Verity?"

"Yes. Buried in the garden, buried in the tomb that Clotilde had prepared. She was *there* in The Old Manor House and I think Clotilde *knew* she was there. It might be that she even saw her or thought she saw her sometimes when she went to pick a spray of polygonum blossom. She must have felt very close to Verity then. Nothing worse could happen to her, could it, than that? Nothing worse . . ."

23

END PIECES

"That old lady gives me the creeps," said Sir Andrew McNeil when he had said good-bye and thanks to Miss Marple.

"So gentle—and so ruthless," said the Assistant Commissioner.

Professor Wanstead took Miss Marple down to his car, which was waiting, and then returned for a few final words.

"What do you think of her, Edmund?"

"The most frightening woman I ever met," said the Home Secretary.

"Ruthless?" asked Professor Wanstead.

"No, no, I don't mean that but—well, a very frightening woman."

"Nemesis," said Professor Wanstead thoughtfully.

"Those two women," said the P.P.D. man, "you know, the security agents who were looking after her, they gave a most extraordinary description of her that night. They got into the house quite easily, hid themselves in a small downstairs room until everyone went upstairs, then one went into the bedroom and into the wardrobe and the other stayed outside the room to watch. The one in the bedroom said that when she threw open the door of the wardrobe and came out, there was the old lady sitting up in bed with a pink fluffy shawl round her neck and a perfectly placid face, twittering away and talking like an elderly schoolmarm. They said she gave them quite a turn."

"A pink fluffy shawl," said Professor Wanstead. "Yes, yes, I do remember—"

"What do you remember?"

"Old Rafiel. He told me about her, you know, and then he laughed. He said one thing he'd never forget in all his life. He said it was when one of the funniest scatterbrained old ladies he'd ever met came marching into his bedroom out in the West Indies, with a fluffy pink scarf round her neck, telling him he was to get up and do something to prevent a murder. And he said: 'What on earth do you think you're doing?' And she said she was

Nemesis. Nemesis! He could not imagine anything less like it, he said. I like the touch of the pink woolly scarf," said Professor Wanstead thoughtfully. "I like that very much."

II

"Michael," said Professor Wanstead, "I want to introduce you to Miss Jane Marple, who's been very active on your behalf."

The young man of thirty-two looked at the white-haired, rather dicky old lady with a slightly doubtful expression.

"Oh—er—" he said, "well, I guess I have heard about it. Thanks very much."

He looked at Wanstead.

"It's true, is it, they're going to give me a free pardon or something silly like that?"

"Yes. A release will be put through quite soon. You'll be a free man in a very short time."

"Oh." Michael sounded slightly doubtful.

"It will take a little getting used to, I expect," said Miss Marple kindly.

She looked at him thoughtfully, seeing him in retrospect as he might have been ten years or so ago. Still quite attractive—though he showed all the signs of strain. Attractive, yes. Very attractive, she thought he would have been once. A gaiety about him then, there would have been, and a charm. He'd lost that now, but it would come back perhaps. A weak mouth and attractively shaped eyes that could look you straight in the face, and probably had been always extremely useful for telling lies that you really wanted to believe. Very like—who was it?—she dived into past memories—Jonathan Birkin, of course. He had sung in the choir. A really delightful baritone voice. And how fond the girls had been of him! Quite a good job he'd had as clerk in Messrs. Gabriels' firm. A pity there had been that little matter of the checks.

"Oh," said Michael. He said, with even more embarrassment: "It's been very kind of you, I'm sure, to take so much trouble."

"I've enjoyed it," said Miss Marple. "Well, I'm glad to have met you. Good-bye. I hope you've got a very good time coming to you. Our country is in rather a bad way just now, but you'll probably find some job or other that you might quite enjoy doing."

"Oh, yes. Thanks, thanks very much. I—I really am very grateful, you know."

His tone sounded still extremely unsure about it.

"It's not me you ought to be grateful to," said Miss Marple. "You ought to be grateful to your father."

"Dad? Dad never thought much of me."

"Your father when he was a dying man was determined to see that you got justice."

"Justice." Michael Rafiel considered it.

"Yes, your father thought justice was important. He was, I think, a very just man himself. In the letter he wrote me asking me to undertake this proposition, he directed me to a quotation:

> "Let justice roll down like waters
> And righteousness like an everlasting stream."

"Oh! What's it mean? Shakespeare?"

"No, the Bible—one has to think about it—I had to."

Miss Marple unwrapped a parcel she had been carrying.

"They gave me this," she said. "They thought I might like to have it—because I had helped to find out the truth of what had really happened. I think, though, that you are the person who should have first claim on it—that is if you really want it. But maybe you do not want it—"

She handed him the photograph of Verity Hunt that Clotilde Bradbury-Scott had shown her once in the drawing room of The Old Manor House. He took it—and stood with it, staring down on it. His face changed, the lines of it softened, then hardened. Miss Marple watched him without speaking. The silence went on for some little time. Professor Wanstead also watched them both, the old lady and the boy.

It came to him that this was in some way a crisis—a moment that might affect a whole new way of life.

Michael Rafiel sighed—he stretched out and gave the photograph back to Miss Marple.

"No, you are right, I do not want it. All that life is gone. She's gone—I can't keep her with me. Anything I do now has got to be new—going forward. You—" he hesitated, looking at her—"you understand?"

"Yes," said Miss Marple. "I understand. I think you are right. I wish you good luck in the life you are now going to begin."

He said good-bye and went out.

"Well," said Professor Wanstead, "not an enthusiastic young man. He could have thanked you a bit more for what you did for him."

"Oh, that's quite all right," said Miss Marple. "I didn't expect him to do so. It would have embarrassed him even more. It is, you know," she added, "very embarrassing when one has to thank people and start life again and see everything from a different angle and all that. I think he might do well. He's not bitter. That's the great thing. I understand quite well why that girl loved him—"

"Well, perhaps he'll go straight this time."

"One rather doubts that," said Miss Marple. "I don't know that he'd be able to help himself unless—of course," she said, "the great thing to hope for is that he'll meet a really nice girl."

"What I like about you," said Professor Wanstead, "is your delightfully practical mind."

III

"She'll be here presently," said Mr. Broadribb to Mr. Schuster.

"Yes. The whole thing's pretty extraordinary, isn't it?"

"I couldn't believe it at first," said Broadribb. "You know, when poor old Rafiel was dying, I thought this whole thing was—well, senility or something. Not that he was old enough for that."

The buzzer went. Mr. Schuster picked up the phone.

"Oh, she's here, is she? Bring her up," he said. "She's come," he said. "I wonder now. You know, it's the oddest thing I ever heard in my life. Getting an old lady to go racketing round the countryside looking for she doesn't know what. The police think, you know, that that woman committed not just one murder but three. Three! I ask you! Verity Hunt's body was under the mound in the garden, just as the old lady said it was. She hadn't been strangled and the face was not disfigured."

"I wonder the old lady herself didn't get done in," said Mr. Broadribb. "Far too old to be able to take care of herself."

"She had a couple of detectives, apparently, looking after her."

"What, *two* of them?"

"Yes, I didn't know that."

Miss Marple was ushered into their room.

"Congratulations, Miss Marple," said Mr. Broadribb, rising to greet her.

"Very best wishes. Splendid job," said Mr. Schuster, shaking hands.

Miss Marple sat down composedly on the other side of the desk.

"As I told you in my letter," she said, "I think I have fulfilled the terms of the proposition that was made to me. I have succeeded in what I was asked to do."

"Oh, I know. Yes, we've heard already. We've heard from Professor Wanstead and from the legal department and from the police authorities. Yes, it's been a splendid job, Miss Marple. We congratulate you."

"I was afraid," said Miss Marple, "that I would not be able to do what was required of me. It seemed so very difficult, almost impossible at first."

"Yes, indeed. It seems quite impossible to me. I don't know how you did it, Miss Marple."

"Oh, well," said Miss Marple, "it's just perseverance, isn't it, that leads to things?"

"Now about the sum of money we are holding. It's at your disposal at any time now. I don't know whether you would like us to pay it into your bank or whether you would like to consult us possibly as to the investment of it? It's quite a large sum."

"Twenty thousand pounds," said Miss Marple. "Yes, it is a very large sum by my way of thinking. Quite extraordinary," she added.

"If you would like an introduction to our brokers, they could give you possibly some ideas about investing."

"Oh, I don't want to invest any of it."

"But surely it would be—"

"There's no point in saving at my age," said Miss Marple. "I mean the point of this money—I'm sure Mr. Rafiel meant it that way—is to enjoy a few things that one thought one never would have the money to enjoy."

"Well, I see your point of view," said Mr. Broadribb. "Then your instructions would be that we pay this sum of money into your bank?"

"Middleton's Bank, One thirty-two High Street, St. Mary Mead," said Miss Marple.

"You have a deposit account, I expect. We will place it to your deposit account?"

"Certainly not," said Miss Marple. "Put it into my current account."

"You don't think—"

"I do think," said Miss Marple. "I want it in my current account."

She got up and shook hands.

"You could ask your bank manager's advice, you know, Miss Marple. It really is—one never knows when one wants something for a rainy day."

"The only thing I shall want for a rainy day will be my umbrella," said Miss Marple.

She shook hands with them both again.

"Thank you so much, Mr. Broadribb. And you, too, Mr. Schuster. You've been so kind to me, giving me all the information I needed."

"You really want that money put into your current account?"

"Yes," said Miss Marple. "I'm going to spend it, you know. I'm going to have some fun with it."

She looked back from the door and she laughed. Just for one moment Mr. Schuster, who was a man of more imagination than Mr. Broadribb, had a vague impression of a young and pretty girl shaking hands with the vicar at a garden party in the country. It was, as he realized a moment later, a recollection of his own youth. But Miss Marple had, for a minute, reminded him of that particular girl, young, happy, going to enjoy herself.

"Mr. Rafiel would have liked me to have fun," said Miss Marple.

She went out of the door.

"Nemesis," said Mr. Broadribb. "That's what Rafiel called her. Nemesis! Never seen anybody less like Nemesis, have you?"

Mr. Schuster shook his head.

"It must have been another of Mr. Rafiel's little jokes," said Mr. Broadribb.

MURDER IN MESOPOTAMIA

A Hercule Poirot Mystery

Dedicated to my many
archaeological friends
in Iraq and Syria

CONTENTS

FOREWORD
BY
GILES REILLY, M.D.

The events chronicled in this narrative took place some four years ago. Circumstances have rendered it necessary, in my opinion, that a straightforward account of them should be given to the public. There have been the wildest and most ridiculous rumors suggesting that important evidence was suppressed and other nonsense of that kind. Those misconstructions have appeared more especially in the American press.

For obvious reasons it was desirable that the account should not come from the pen of one of the expedition staff, who might reasonably be supposed to be prejudiced.

I therefore suggested to Miss Amy Leatheran that she should undertake the task. She is obviously the person to do it. She has a professional character of the highest, she is not biased by having any previous connection with the University of Pittstown Expedition to Iraq, and she was an observant and intelligent eyewitness.

It was not very easy to persuade Miss Leatheran to undertake this task—in fact, persuading her was one of the hardest jobs of my professional career—and even after it was completed she displayed a curious reluctance to let me see the manuscript. I discovered that this was partly due to some critical remarks she had made concerning my daughter Sheila. I soon disposed of that, assuring her that as children criticize their parents freely in print nowadays, parents are only too delighted when their offspring come in for their share of abuse! Her other objection was extreme modesty about her literary style. She hoped I would "put the grammar right and all that." I have, on the contrary, refused to alter so much as a single word. Miss Leatheran's style in my opinion is vigorous, individual, and entirely apposite. If she calls Hercule Poirot "Poirot" in one paragraph and "Mr. Poirot" in the next, such a variation is both interesting and suggestive. At one moment she is, so to speak, "remembering her manners" (and hospital nurses are great sticklers for etiquette) and at the next her interest in what she is telling is that of a pure human being—cap and cuffs forgotten!

The only thing I have done is to take the liberty of writing a first chapter—aided by a letter kindly supplied by one of Miss Leatheran's friends. It is intended to be in the nature of a frontispiece—that is, it gives a rough sketch of the narrator.

CHAPTER I

FOREWORD

In the hall of the Tigris Palace Hotel in Baghdad a hospital nurse was finishing a letter. Her fountain pen drove briskly over the paper.

. . . Well, dear, I think that's really all my news. I must say it's been nice to see a bit of the world—though England for me every time, thank you! The dirt *and the* mess *in Baghdad you wouldn't believe—and not romantic at all like you'd think from the Arabian Nights! Of course, it's pretty just on the river, but the town itself is just awful—and no proper shops at all. Major Kelsey took me through the bazaars, and of course there's no denying they're* quaint*—but just a lot of rubbish and hammering away at copper pans till they make your head ache—and not what I'd like to use myself unless I was sure about the cleaning. You've got to be so careful of verdigris with copper pans.*

I'll write and let you know if anything comes of the job that Dr. Reilly spoke about. He said this American gentleman was in Baghdad now and might come and see me this afternoon. It's for his wife—she has "fancies," so Dr. Reilly said. He didn't say any more than that, and of course, dear, one knows what that usually means *(but I hope not actually D.T.'s!). Of course, Dr. Reilly didn't* say *anything—but he had a look—if you know what I mean. This Dr. Leidner is an archaeologist and is digging up a mound out in the desert somewhere for some American museum.*

Well, dear, I will close now. I thought what you told me about little Stubbins was simply killing! *Whatever did Matron say?*

No more now.

Yours ever,
Amy Leatheran.

Enclosing the letter in an envelope, she addressed it to Sister Curshaw, St. Christopher's Hospital, London.

As she put the cap on her fountain pen, one of the native boys approached her.

"A gentleman come see you. Doctor Leidner."

Nurse Leatheran turned. She saw a man of middle height with slightly stooping shoulders, a brown beard, and gentle, tired eyes.

Dr. Leidner saw a woman of thirty-two of erect, confident bearing. He saw a good humored face with slightly prominent blue eyes and glossy brown hair. She looked, he thought, just what a hospital nurse for a nervous case ought to look. Cheerful, robust, shrewd, and matter-of-fact.

Nurse Leatheran, he thought, would do.

CHAPTER II

INTRODUCING AMY LEATHERAN

I don't pretend to be an author or to know anything about writing. I'm doing this simply because Dr. Reilly asked me to, and somehow when Dr. Reilly asks you to do a thing you don't like to refuse.

"Oh, but, doctor," I said, "I'm not literary—not literary at all."

"Nonsense!" he said. "Treat it as case notes, if you like."

Well, of course, you *can* look at it that way.

Dr. Reilly went on. He said that an unvarnished plain account of the Tell Yarimjah business was badly needed.

"If one of the interested parties writes it, it won't carry conviction. They'll say it's biased one way or another."

And, of course, that was true, too. I was in it all and yet an outsider, so to speak.

"Why don't you write it yourself, doctor?" I asked.

"I wasn't on the spot—you were. Besides," he added with a sigh, "my daughter won't let me."

The way he knuckles under to that chit of a girl of his is downright disgraceful. I had half a mind to say so, when I saw that his eyes were twinkling. That was the worst of Dr. Reilly. You never knew whether he was joking or not. He always said things in the same slow, melancholy way—but half the time there was a twinkle underneath it.

"Well," I said doubtfully, "I suppose I *could.*"

"Of course you could."

"Only I don't quite know how to set about it."

"There's a good precedent for that. Begin at the beginning, go on to the end, and then leave off."

"I don't even know quite where and what the beginning was," I said doubtfully.

"Believe me, nurse, the difficulty of beginning will be nothing to the difficulty of knowing how to stop. At least that's the way it is with me when I have to make a speech. Someone's got to catch hold of my coattails and pull me down by main force."

"Oh, you're joking, doctor."

"It's profoundly serious I am. Now what about it?"

Another thing was worrying me. After hesitating a moment or two I said, "You know, doctor, I'm afraid I might tend to be—well, a little *personal* sometimes."

"God bless my soul, woman, the more personal you are the better! This is a story of human beings—not dummies! Be personal—be prejudiced—be catty—be anything you please! Write the thing your own way. We can always prune out the bits that are libelous afterward! You go ahead. You're a sensible woman, and you'll give a sensible common-sense account of the business."

So that was that, and I promised to do my best.

And here I am beginning, but as I said to the doctor, it's difficult to know just where to start.

I suppose I ought to say a word or two about myself. I'm thirty-two and my name is Amy Leatheran. I took my training at St. Christopher's and after that did two years' maternity. I did a certain amount of private work and I was for four years at Miss Bendix's Nursing Home in Devonshire Place. I came out to Iraq with a Mrs. Kelsey. I'd attended her when her baby was born. She was coming out to Baghdad with her husband and had already got a children's nurse booked who had been for some years with friends of hers out there. Their children were coming home and going to school, and the nurse had agreed to go to Mrs. Kelsey when they left. Mrs. Kelsey was delicate and nervous about the journey out with so young a child, so Major Kelsey arranged that I should come out with her and look after her and the baby. They would pay my passage home unless we found someone needing a nurse for the return journey.

Well, there is no need to describe the Kelseys—the baby was a little love and Mrs. Kelsey quite nice, though rather the fretting kind. I enjoyed the voyage very much. I'd never been a long trip on the sea before.

Dr. Reilly was on board the boat. He was a black-haired, long-faced man who said all sorts of funny things in a low, sad voice. I think he enjoyed pulling my leg and used to make the most extraordinary statements to see if I would swallow them. He was the civil surgeon at a place called Hassanieh—a day and a half's journey from Baghdad.

I had been about a week in Baghdad when I ran across him and he asked when I was leaving the Kelseys. I said that it was funny his asking that because as a matter of fact the Wrights (the other people I mentioned) were going home earlier than they had meant to and their nurse was free to come straightaway.

He said that he had heard about the Wrights and that that was why he had asked me.

"As a matter of fact, nurse, I've got a possible job for you."

"A case?"

He screwed his face up as though considering.

"You could hardly call it a case. It's just a lady who has—shall we say—fancies?"

"Oh!" I said.

(One usually knows what *that* means—drink or drugs!)

Dr. Reilly didn't explain further. He was very discreet.

"Yes," he said. "A Mrs. Leidner. Husband's an American—an American Swede to be exact. He's the head of a large American dig."

And he explained how this expedition was excavating the site of a big Assyrian city something like Nineveh. The expedition house was not actually very far from Hassanieh, but it was a lonely spot and Dr. Leidner had been worried for some time about his wife's health.

"He's not been very explicit about it, but it seems she has these fits of recurring nervous terrors."

"Is she left alone all day among natives?" I asked.

"Oh, no, there's quite a crowd—seven or eight. I don't fancy she's ever alone in the house. But there seems to be no doubt that she's worked herself up into a queer state. Leidner has any amount of work on his shoulders, but he's crazy about his wife and it worries him to know she's in this state. He felt he'd be happier if he knew that some responsible person with expert knowledge was keeping an eye on her."

"And what does Mrs. Leidner herself think about it?"

Dr. Reilly answered gravely. "Mrs. Leidner is a very lovely lady. She's seldom of the same mind about anything two days on end. But on the whole she favors the idea." He added, "She's an odd woman. A mass of affectation and, I should fancy, a champion liar—but Leidner seems honestly to believe that she is scared out of her life by something or other."

"What did she herself say to you, doctor?"

"Oh, she hasn't consulted me! She doesn't like me, anyway—for several reasons. It was Leidner who came to me and propounded this plan. Well, nurse, what do you think of the idea? You'd see something of the country before you go home—they'll be digging for another two months. And excavation is quite interesting work."

After a moment's hesitation while I turned the matter over in my mind: "Well," I said. "I really think I might try it."

"Splendid," said Dr. Reilly, rising. "Leidner's in Baghdad now. I'll tell him to come round and see if he can fix things up with you."

Dr. Leidner came to the hotel that afternoon. He was a middle-aged man with a rather nervous, hesitating manner. There was something gentle and kindly and rather helpless about him.

He sounded very devoted to his wife, but he was very vague about what was the matter with her.

"You see," he said, tugging at his beard in a rather perplexed manner that I later came to know to be characteristic of him, "my wife is really in a very nervous state. I—I'm quite worried about her."

"She is in good physical health?" I asked.

"Yes—oh, yes, I think so. No, I should not think there was anything the matter with her physically. But she—well—imagines things, you know."

"What kind of things?" I asked.

But he shied off from the point, merely murmuring perplexedly, "She works herself up over nothing at all. I really can see no foundations for these fears."

"Fears of what, Doctor Leidner?"

He said vaguely, "Oh, just—nervous terrors, you know."

Ten to one, I thought to myself, *it's drugs. And he doesn't realize it!* Lots of men don't. Just wonder why their wives are so jumpy and have such extraordinary changes of mood.

I asked whether Mrs. Leidner herself approved of the idea of my coming. His face lighted up.

"Yes. I was surprised. Most pleasurably surprised. She said it was a very good idea. She said she would feel very much safer."

The word struck me oddly. *Safer.* A very queer word to use. I began to surmise that Mrs. Leidner might be a mental case. He went on with a kind of boyish eagerness.

"I'm sure you'll get on very well with her. She's really a very charming woman." He smiled disarmingly. "She feels you'll be the greatest comfort to her. I felt the same as soon as I saw you. You look, if you will allow me to say so, so splendidly healthy and full of common sense. I'm sure you're just the person for Louise."

"Well, we can but try, Doctor Leidner," I said cheerfully. "I'm sure I hope I can be of use to your wife. Perhaps she's nervous of natives and colored people?"

"Oh, dear me, no." He shook his head, amused at the idea. "My wife likes Arabs very much—she appreciates their simplicity and their sense of humor. This is only her second season—we have been married less than two years—but she already speaks quite a fair amount of Arabic."

I was silent for a moment or two, then I had one more try.

"Can't you tell me at all what it is your wife is afraid of, Doctor Leidner?" I asked.

He hesitated. Then he said slowly, "I hope—I believe—that she will tell you that herself."

And that's all I could get out of him.

CHAPTER III

GOSSIP

It was arranged that I should go to Tell Yarimjah the following week. Mrs. Kelsey was settling into her house at Alwiyah, and I was glad to be able to take a few things off her shoulders.

During that time I heard one or two allusions to the Leidner expedition. A friend of Mrs. Kelsey's, a young squadron leader, pursed his lips in surprise as he exclaimed, "Lovely Louise. So that's her latest!" He turned to me. "That's our nickname for her, nurse. She's always known as Lovely Louise."

"Is she so very handsome, then?" I asked.

"It's taking her at her own valuation. *She* thinks she is!"

"Now don't be spiteful, John," said Mrs. Kelsey. "You know it's not only she who thinks so! Lots of people have been very smitten by her."

"Perhaps you're right. She's a bit long in the tooth, but she has a certain attraction."

"You were completely bowled over yourself," said Mrs. Kelsey, laughing.

The squadron leader blushed and admitted rather shamefacedly, "Well, she has a way with her. As for Leidner himself, he worships the ground she walks on—and all the rest of the expedition has to worship, too! It's expected of them!"

"How many are there altogether?" I asked.

"All sorts and nationalities, nurse," said the squadron leader cheerfully. "An English architect, a French father from Carthage—he does the inscriptions—tablets and things, you know. And then there's Miss Johnson. She's English, too—sort of general bottle washer. And a little plump man who does the photography—he's an American. And the Mercados. Heaven knows what nationality they are. She's quite young—a snaky-looking creature—and, oh!—doesn't she hate Lovely Louise! And there are a couple of youngsters, and that's the lot. A few odd fish, but nice on the whole—don't you agree, Pennyman?"

He was appealing to an elderly man who was sitting thoughtfully twirling a pair of pince-nez.

The latter started and looked up.

"Yes—yes—very nice indeed. Taken individually, that is. Of course, Mercado is rather a queer fish—"

"He has such a very *odd* beard," put in Mrs. Kelsey. "A queer limp kind."

Major Pennyman went on without noticing her interruption.

"The young 'uns are both nice. The American's rather silent, and the English boy talks a bit too much. Funny, it's usually the other way round. Leidner himself is a delightful fellow—so modest and unassuming. Yes, individually they are all pleasant people. But somehow or other, I may have been fanciful, but the last time I went to see them I got a queer impression of something being wrong. I don't know what it was exactly. Nobody seemed quite natural. There was a queer atmosphere of tension. I can explain best what I mean by saying that they all passed the butter to each other too politely."

Blushing a little, because I don't like airing my own opinions too much, I said, "If people are too much cooped up together it's got a way of getting on their nerves. I know that myself from experience in hospital."

"That's true," said Major Kelsey, "but it's early in the season, hardly time for that particular irritation to have set in."

"An expedition is probably like our life here in miniature," said Major Pennyman. "It has its cliques and rivalries and jealousies."

"It sounds as though they'd got a good many newcomers this year," said Major Kelsey.

"Let me see." The squadron leader counted them off on his fingers. "Young Coleman is new, so is Reiter. Emmott was out last year and so were the Mercados. Father Lavigny is a newcomer. He's come in place of Doctor Byrd, who was ill this year and couldn't come out. Carey, of course, is an old hand. He's been out ever since the beginning, five years ago. Miss Johnson's been out nearly as many years as Carey."

"I always thought they got on so well together at Tell Yarimjah," remarked Major Kelsey. "They seemed like a happy family—which is really surprising when one considers what human nature is! I'm sure Nurse Leatheran agrees with me."

"Well," I said. "I don't know that you're not right! The rows I've known in hospital and starting often from nothing more than a dispute about a pot of tea."

"Yes, one tends to get petty in close communities," said Major Pennyman. "All the same I feel there must be something more to it in this case.

Leidner is such a gentle, unassuming man, with really a remarkable amount of tact. He's always managed to keep his expedition happy and on good terms with each other. And yet I *did* notice that feeling of tension the other day."

Mrs. Kelsey laughed.

"And you don't see the explanation? Why, it leaps to the eye!"

"What do you mean?"

"*Mrs.* Leidner, of course."

"Oh, come, Mary," said her husband, "she's a charming woman—not at all the quarrelsome kind."

"I didn't say she was quarrelsome. She *causes* quarrels!"

"In what way? And why should she?"

"Why? Why? Because she's bored. She's not an archaeologist, only the wife of one. She's bored, shut away from any excitements and so she provides her own drama. She amuses herself by setting other people by the ears."

"Mary, you don't know in the least. You're merely imagining."

"Of course I'm imagining! But you'll find I'm right. Lovely Louise doesn't look like the Mona Lisa for nothing! She mayn't mean any harm, but she likes to see what will happen."

"She's devoted to Leidner."

"Oh! I dare say. I'm not suggesting vulgar intrigues. But she's an *allumeuse,* that woman."

"Women are so sweet to each other," said Major Kelsey.

"I know. Cat, cat, cat, that's what you men say. But we're usually right about our own sex."

"All the same," said Major Pennyman thoughtfully, "assuming all Mrs. Kelsey's uncharitable surmises to be true, I don't think it would quite account for that curious sense of tension—rather like the feeling there is before a thunderstorm. I had the impression very strongly that the storm might break any minute."

"Now don't frighten nurse," said Mrs. Kelsey. "She's going there in three days' time and you'll put her right off."

"Oh, you won't frighten me," I said, laughing.

All the same I thought a good deal about what had been said. Dr. Leidner's curious use of the word *safer* recurred to me. Was it his wife's secret fear, unacknowledged or expressed perhaps, that was reacting on the rest of the party? Or was it the actual tension (or perhaps the unknown cause of it) that was reacting on *her* nerves?

I looked up the word *allumeuse* that Mrs. Kelsey had used in a dictionary, but couldn't get any sense out of it.

Well, I thought to myself, *I must wait and see.*

CHAPTER IV

I ARRIVE IN HASSANIEH

Three days later I left Baghdad.

I was sorry to leave Mrs. Kelsey and the baby, who was a little love and was thriving splendidly, gaining her proper number of ounces every week. Major Kelsey took me to the station and saw me off. I should arrive at Kirkuk the following morning, and there someone was to meet me.

I slept badly. I never sleep very well in a train and I was troubled by dreams.

The next morning, however, when I looked out of the window it was a lovely day and I felt interested and curious about the people I was going to see.

As I stood on the platform hesitating and looking about me I saw a young man coming toward me. He had a round pink face, and really, in all my life, I have never seen anyone who seemed so exactly like a young man out of one of Mr. P. G. Wodehouse's books.

"Hallo, 'allo, 'allo," he said. "Are you Nurse Leatheran? Well, I mean you must be—I can see that. Ha ha! My name's Coleman. Doctor Leidner sent me along. How are you feeling? Beastly journey and all that? Don't I know these trains! Well, here we are—had any breakfast? This your kit? I say, awfully modest, aren't you? Mrs. Leidner has four suitcases and a trunk—to say nothing of a hatbox and a patent pillow, and this, that, and the other. Am I talking too much? Come along to the old bus."

There was what I heard called later a station wagon waiting outside. It was a little like a wagonette, a little like a lorry and a little like a car. Mr. Coleman helped me in, explaining that I had better sit next to the driver so as to get less jolting.

Jolting! I wonder the whole contraption didn't fall to pieces! And nothing like a road—just a sort of track all ruts and holes. Glorious East indeed! When I thought of our splendid arterial roads in England it made me quite homesick.

Mr. Coleman leaned forward from his seat behind me and yelled in my ear a good deal.

"Track's in pretty good condition," he shouted just after we had all been thrown up in our seats till we nearly touched the roof.

And apparently he was speaking quite seriously.

"Very good for you—jogs the liver," he said. "You ought to know that, nurse."

"A stimulated liver won't be much good to me if my head's split open," I observed tartly.

"You should come along here after it's rained! The skids are glorious. Most of the time one's going sideways."

To this I did not respond.

Presently we had to cross the river, which we did on the craziest ferry-boat you can imagine. To my mind it was a mercy we ever got across, but everyone seemed to think it was quite usual.

It took us about four hours to get to Hassanieh, which, to my surprise, was quite a big place. Very pretty it looked, too, before we got there from the other side of the river—standing up quite white and fairylike with minarets. It was a bit different, though, when one had crossed the bridge and come right into it. Such a smell, and everything ramshackle and tumble-down, and mud and mess everywhere.

Mr. Coleman took me to Dr. Reilly's house, where, he said, the doctor was expecting me to lunch.

Dr. Reilly was just as nice as ever, and his house was nice, too, with a bathroom and everything spick and span. I had a nice bath, and by the time I got back into my uniform and came down I was feeling fine.

Lunch was just ready and we went in, the doctor apologizing for his daughter, who he said was always late.

We'd just had a very good dish of eggs in sauce when she came in and Dr. Reilly said, "Nurse, this is my daughter Sheila."

She shook hands, hoped I'd had a good journey, tossed off her hat, gave a cool nod to Mr. Coleman, and sat down.

"Well, Bill," she said. "How's everything?"

He began to talk to her about some party or other that was to come off at the club, and I took stock of her.

I can't say I took to her much. A thought too cool for my liking. An offhand sort of girl, though good-looking. Black hair and blue eyes—a pale sort of face and the usual lipsticked mouth. She'd a cool, sarcastic way of talking that rather annoyed me. I had a probationer like her under me once—a girl who worked well, I'll admit, but whose manner always riled me.

It looked to me rather as though Mr. Coleman was gone on her. He stammered a bit, and his conversation became slightly more idiotic than it was before, if that was possible! He reminded me of a large stupid dog wagging its tail and trying to please.

After lunch Dr. Reilly went off to the hospital, and Mr. Coleman had some things to get in the town, and Miss Reilly asked me whether I'd like to see round the town a bit or whether I'd rather stop in the house. Mr. Coleman, she said, would be back to fetch me in about an hour.

"Is there anything to see?" I asked.

"There are some picturesque corners," said Miss Reilly. "But I don't know that you'd care for them. They're extremely dirty."

The way she said it rather nettled me. I've never been able to see that picturesqueness excuses dirt.

In the end she took me to the club, which was pleasant enough, overlooking the river, and there were English papers and magazines there.

When we got back to the house Mr. Coleman wasn't there yet, so we sat down and talked a bit. It wasn't easy, somehow.

She asked me if I'd met Mrs. Leidner yet.

"No," I said. "Only her husband."

"Oh," she said. "I wonder what you'll think of her?"

I didn't say anything to that. And she went on. "I like Doctor Leidner very much. Everybody likes him."

That's as good as saying, I thought, *that you don't like his wife.*

I still didn't say anything and presently she asked abruptly, "What's the matter with her? Did Doctor Leidner tell you?"

I wasn't going to start gossiping about a patient before I got there even, so I said evasively, "I understand she's a bit run down and wants looking after."

She laughed—a nasty sort of laugh—hard and abrupt.

"Good God," she said. "Aren't nine people looking after her already enough?"

"I suppose they've all got their work to do," I said.

"Work to do? Of course they've got work to do. But Louise comes first—she sees to that, all right."

No, I said to myself. *You* don't *like her.*

"All the same," went on Miss Reilly, "I don't see what she wants with a professional hospital nurse. I should have thought amateur assistance was more in her line; not someone who'll jam a thermometer in her mouth, and count her pulse and bring everything down to hard facts."

Well, I must admit it, I was curious.

"You think there's nothing the matter with her?" I asked.

"Of course there's nothing the matter with her! The woman's as strong as an ox. 'Dear Louise hasn't slept.' 'She's got black circles under her eyes.' Yes—put there with a blue pencil! Anything to get attention, to have everybody hovering round her, making a fuss of her!"

There was something in that, of course. I had (what nurse hasn't?) come across many cases of hypochondriacs whose delight it is to keep a whole household dancing attendance. And if a doctor or a nurse were to say to them, "There's nothing on earth the matter with you!" well, to begin with, they wouldn't believe it, and their indignation would be as genuine as indignation can be.

Of course, it was quite possible that Mrs. Leidner might be a case of this kind. The husband, naturally, would be the first to be deceived. Husbands, I've found, are a credulous lot where illness is concerned. But all the same, it didn't quite square with what I'd heard. It didn't, for instance, fit in with that word *safer.*

Funny how that word had got kind of stuck in my mind.

Reflecting on it, I asked, "Is Mrs. Leidner a nervous woman? Is she nervous, for instance, of living out far from anywhere?"

"What is there to be nervous of? Good heavens, there are ten of them! And they've got guards, too—because of the antiquities. Oh, no, she's not nervous—at least—"

She seemed struck by some thought and stopped—going on slowly after a minute or two.

"It's odd your saying that."

"Why?"

"Flight Lieutenant Jervis and I rode over the other day. It was in the morning. Most of them were up on the dig. She was sitting writing a letter and I suppose she didn't hear us coming. The boy who brings you in wasn't about for once, and we came straight up onto the verandah. Apparently she saw Flight Lieutenant Jervis's shadow thrown on the wall—and she fairly screamed! Apologized, of course. Said she thought it was a strange man. A bit odd, that. I mean, even if it was a strange man, why get the wind up?"

I nodded thoughtfully.

Miss Reilly was silent, then burst out suddenly, "I don't know what's the matter with them there this year. They've all got the jumps. Johnson goes about so glum she can't open her mouth. David never speaks if he can help it. Bill, of course, never stops, and somehow his chatter seems to make the others worse. Carey goes about looking as though something would snap any minute. And they all watch each other as though—as though— Oh, I don't know, but it's *queer."*

It was odd, I thought, that two such dissimilar people as Miss Reilly and Major Pennyman should have been struck in the same manner.

Just then Mr. Coleman came bustling in. Bustling was just the word for it. If his tongue had hung out and he had suddenly produced a tail to wag you wouldn't have been surprised.

"Hallo-allo," he said. "Absolutely the world's best shopper—that's me. Have you shown nurse all the beauties of the town?"

"She wasn't impressed," said Miss Reilly dryly.

"I don't blame her," said Mr. Coleman heartily. "Of all the one-horse tumble-down places!"

"Not a lover of the picturesque or the antique, are you, Bill? I can't think why you are an archaeologist."

"Don't blame me for that. Blame my guardian. He's a learned bird—fellow of his college—browses among books in bedroom slippers—that kind of man. Bit of a shock for him to have a ward like me."

"I think it's frightfully stupid of you to be forced into a profession you don't care for," said the girl sharply.

"Not forced, Sheila, old girl, not forced. The old man asked if I had any special profession in mind, and I said I hadn't and so he wangled a season out here for me."

"But haven't you any idea really what you'd *like* to do? You *must* have!"

"Of course I have. My idea would be to give work a miss altogether. What I'd like to do is to have plenty of money and go in for motor-racing."

"You're absurd!" said Miss Reilly.

She sounded quite angry.

"Oh, I realize that it's quite out of the question," said Mr. Coleman cheerfully. "So, if I've got to do something, I don't much care what it is so long as it isn't mugging in an office all day long. I was quite agreeable to seeing a bit of the world. 'Here goes,' I said, and along I came."

"And a fat lot of use you must be, I expect!"

"There you're wrong. I can stand up on the dig and shout '*Y'Allah*' with anybody! And as a matter of fact I'm not so dusty at drawing. Imitating handwriting used to be my specialty at school. I'd have made a first-class forger. Oh, well, I may come to that yet. If my Rolls-Royce splashes you with mud as you're waiting for a bus, you'll know that I've taken to crime."

Miss Reilly said coldly, "Don't you think it's about time you started instead of talking so much?"

"Hospitable, aren't we, nurse?"

"I'm sure Nurse Leatheran is anxious to get settled in."

"You're always sure of everything," retorted Mr. Coleman with a grin.

That was true enough, I thought. Cocksure little minx.

I said dryly, "Perhaps we'd better start, Mr. Coleman."

"Right you are, nurse."

I shook hands with Miss Reilly and thanked her, and we set off.

"Damned attractive girl, Sheila," said Mr. Coleman. "But always ticking a fellow off."

We drove out of the town and presently took a kind of track between green crops. It was very bumpy and full of ruts.

After about half an hour Mr. Coleman pointed to a big mound by the river bank ahead of us and said, "Tell Yarimjah."

I could see little black figures moving about it like ants.

As I was looking they suddenly began to run all together down the side of the mound.

"Fidos," said Mr. Coleman. "Knocking-off time. We knock off an hour before sunset."

The expedition house lay a little way back from the river.

The driver rounded a corner, bumped through an extremely narrow arch, and there we were.

The house was built round a courtyard. Originally it had occupied only the south side of the courtyard with a few unimportant outbuildings on the east. The expedition had continued the building on the other two sides. As the plan of the house was to prove of special interest later, I append a rough sketch of it.

All the rooms opened onto the courtyard, and most of the windows—the exception being in the original south building where there were windows giving on the outside country as well. These windows, however, were barred on the outside. In the southwest corner a staircase ran up to a long flat roof with a parapet running the length of the south side of the building which was higher than the other three sides.

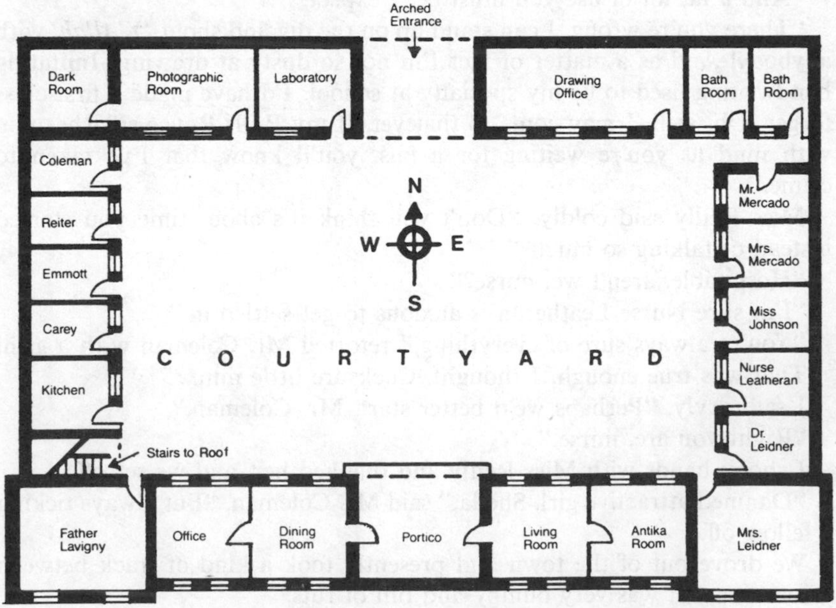

Mr. Coleman led me along the east side of the courtyard and round to where a big open verandah occupied the center of the south side. He pushed open a door at one side of it and we entered a room where several people were sitting round a tea table.

"Toodle-oodle-oo!" said Mr. Coleman. "Here's Sairey Gamp."

The lady who was sitting at the head of the table rose and came to greet me.

I had my first glimpse of Louise Leidner.

CHAPTER V

TELL YARIMJAH

I don't mind admitting that my first impression on seeing Mrs. Leidner was one of downright surprise. One gets into the way of imagining a person when one hears them talked about. I'd got it firmly into my head that Mrs. Leidner was a dark, discontented kind of woman. The nervy kind, all on edge. And then, too, I'd expected her to be—well, to put it frankly—a bit vulgar.

She wasn't a bit like what I'd imagined her! To begin with, she was very fair. She wasn't a Swede, like her husband, but she might have been as far as looks went. She had that blond Scandinavian fairness that you don't very often see. She wasn't a young woman. Midway between thirty and forty, I should say. Her face was rather haggard, and there was some gray hair mingled with the fairness. Her eyes, though, were lovely. They were the only eyes I've ever come across that you might truly describe as violet. They were very large, and there were faint shadows underneath them. She was very thin and fragile-looking, and if I say that she had an air of intense weariness and was at the same time very much alive, it sounds like nonsense—but that's the feeling I got. I felt, too, that she was a lady through and through. And that means something—even nowadays.

She put out her hand and smiled. Her voice was low and soft with an American drawl in it.

"I'm so glad you've come, nurse. Will you have some tea? Or would you like to go to your room first?"

I said I'd have tea, and she introduced me to the people sitting round the table.

"This is Miss Johnson—and Mr. Reiter. Mrs. Mercado. Mr. Emmott. Father Lavigny. My husband will be in presently. Sit down here between Father Lavigny and Miss Johnson."

I did as I was bid, and Miss Johnson began talking to me, asking about my journey and so on.

I liked her. She reminded me of a matron I'd had in my probationer days whom we had all admired and worked hard for.

She was getting on for fifty, I should judge, and rather mannish in appearance, with iron-gray hair cropped short. She had an abrupt, pleasant voice, rather deep in tone. She had an ugly, rugged face with an almost laughably turned-up nose which she was in the habit of rubbing irritably when anything troubled or perplexed her. She wore a tweed coat and skirt made rather like a man's. She told me presently that she was a native of Yorkshire.

Father Lavigny I found just a bit alarming. He was a tall man with a great black beard and pince-nez. I had heard Mrs. Kelsey say that there was a French monk there, and I now saw that Father Lavigny was wearing a monk's robe of some white woolen material. It surprised me rather, because I always understood that monks went into monasteries and didn't come out again.

Mrs. Leidner talked to him mostly in French, but he spoke to me in quite fair English. I noticed that he had shrewd, observant eyes which darted about from face to face.

Opposite me were the other three. Mr. Reiter was a stout, fair young man with glasses. His hair was rather long and curly, and he had very round blue eyes. I should think he must have been a lovely baby, but he wasn't much to look at now! In fact he was just a little like a pig. The other young man had very short hair cropped close to his head. He had a long, rather humorous face and very good teeth, and he looked very attractive when he smiled. He said very little, though, just nodded if spoken to or answered in monosyllables. He, like Mr. Reiter, was an American. The last person was Mrs. Mercado, and I couldn't have a good look at her because whenever I glanced in her direction I always found her staring at me with a kind of hungry stare that was a bit disconcerting to say the least of it. You might have thought a hospital nurse was a strange animal the way she was looking at me. No manners at all!

She was quite young—not more than about twenty-five—and sort of dark and slinky-looking, if you know what I mean. Quite nice looking in a kind of way, but rather as though she might have what my mother used to call "a touch of the tar brush." She had on a very vivid pullover, and her nails matched it in color. She had a thin, birdlike, eager face with big eyes and rather a tight, suspicious mouth.

The tea was very good—a nice strong blend—not like the weak China stuff that Mrs. Kelsey always had and that had been a sore trial to me.

There was toast and jam and a plate of rock buns and a cutting cake. Mr.

Emmott was very polite passing me things. Quiet as he was he always seemed to notice when my plate was empty.

Presently Mr. Coleman bustled in and took the place beyond Miss Johnson. There didn't seem to be anything the matter with *his* nerves. He talked away nineteen to the dozen.

Mrs. Leidner sighed once and cast a wearied look in his direction but it didn't have any effect. Nor did the fact that Mrs. Mercado, to whom he was addressing most of his conversation, was far too busy watching me to do more than make perfunctory replies.

Just as we were finishing, Dr. Leidner and Mr. Mercado came in from the dig.

Dr. Leidner greeted me in his nice, kind manner. I saw his eyes go quickly and anxiously to his wife's face and he seemed to be relieved by what he saw there. Then he sat down at the other end of the table, and Mr. Mercado sat down in the vacant place by Mrs. Leidner. He was a tall, thin, melancholy man, a good deal older than his wife, with a sallow complexion and a queer, soft, shapeless-looking beard. I was glad when he came in, for his wife stopped staring at me and transferred her attention to him, watching him with a kind of anxious impatience that I found rather odd. He himself stirred his tea dreamily and said nothing at all. A piece of cake lay untasted on his plate.

There was still one vacant place, and presently the door opened and a man came in.

The moment I saw Richard Carey I felt he was one of the handsomest men I'd seen for a long time—and yet I doubt if that were really so. To say a man is handsome and at the same time to say he looks like a death's head sounds a rank contradiction, and yet it was true. His head gave the effect of having the skin stretched unusually tightly over the bones—but they were beautiful bones. The lean line of jaw and temple and forehead was so sharply outlined that he reminded me of a bronze statue. Out of this lean brown face looked two of the brightest and most intensely blue eyes I have ever seen. He stood about six foot and was, I should imagine, a little under forty years of age.

Dr. Leidner said, "This is Mr. Carey, our architect, nurse."

He murmured something in a pleasant, inaudible English voice and sat down by Mrs. Mercado.

Mrs. Leidner said, "I'm afraid the tea is a little cold, Mr. Carey."

He said, "Oh, that's quite all right, Mrs. Leidner. My fault for being late. I wanted to finish plotting those walls."

Mrs. Mercado said, "Jam, Mr. Carey?"

Mr. Reiter pushed forward the toast.

And I remembered Major Pennyman saying, *"I can explain best what I mean by saying that they all passed the butter to each other a shade too politely."*

Yes, there was something a little odd about it. A shade formal. You'd have said it was a party of strangers—not people who had known each other—some of them—for quite a number of years.

CHAPTER VI

FIRST EVENING

After tea Mrs. Leidner took me to show me my room.

Perhaps here I had better give a short description of the arrangement of the rooms. This was very simple and can easily be understood by a reference to the plan.

On either side of the big open porch were doors leading into the two principal rooms. That on the right led into the dining-room, where we had had tea. The one on the other side led into an exactly similar room (I have called it the living-room) which was used as a sitting-room and kind of informal workroom—that is, a certain amount of drawing (other than the strictly architectural) was done there, and the more delicate pieces of pottery were brought there to be pieced together. Through the living-room one passed into the antiquities room where all the finds from the dig were brought in and stored on shelves and in pigeonholes, and also laid out on big benches and tables. From the antika room there was no exit save through the living-room.

Beyond the antika room, but reached through a door which gave on the courtyard, was Mrs. Leidner's bedroom. This, like the other rooms on that side of the house, had a couple of barred windows looking out over the plowed countryside. Round the corner next to Mrs. Leidner's room, but with no actual communicating door, was Dr. Leidner's room. This was the first of the rooms on the east side of the building. Next to it was the room that was to be mine. Next to me was Miss Johnson's, with Mr. and Mrs. Mercado's beyond. After that came two so-called bathrooms.

(When I once used that last term in the hearing of Dr. Reilly he laughed at me and said a bathroom was either a bathroom or not a bathroom! All the same, when you've got used to taps and proper plumbing, it seems strange to call a couple of mud rooms with a tin hip bath in each of them, and muddy water brought in kerosene tins, *bathrooms!)*

All this side of the building had been added by Dr. Leidner to the original Arab house. The bedrooms were all the same, each with a window and a door giving onto the courtyard.

Along the north side were the drawing-office, the laboratory, and the photographic rooms.

To return to the verandah, the arrangement of rooms was much the same on the other side. There was the dining-room leading into the office where the files were kept and the cataloguing and typing was done. Corresponding to Mrs. Leidner's room was that of Father Lavigny, who was given the largest bedroom; he used it also for the decoding—or whatever you call it—of tablets.

In the southwest corner was the staircase running up to the roof. On the west side were first the kitchen quarters and then four small bedrooms used by the young men—Carey, Emmott, Reiter, and Coleman.

At the northwest corner was the photographic room with the darkroom leading out of it. Next to that the laboratory. Then came the only entrance—the big arched doorway through which we had entered. Outside were sleeping-quarters for the native servants, the guardhouse for the soldiers, and stables, etc., for the water horses. The drawing-office was to the right of the archway occupying the rest of the north side.

I have gone into the arrangements of the house rather fully here because I don't want to have to go over them again later.

As I say, Mrs. Leidner herself took me around the building and finally established me in my bedroom, hoping that I should be comfortable and have everything I wanted.

The room was nicely though plainly furnished—a bed, a chest of drawers, a washstand, and a chair.

"The boys will bring you hot water before lunch and dinner—and in the morning, of course. If you want it any other time, go outside and clap your hands, and when the boy comes say, *'Jib mai' har.'* Do you think you can remember that?"

I said I thought so and repeated it a little haltingly.

"That's right. And be sure and shout it. Arabs don't understand anything said in an ordinary 'English' voice."

"Languages are funny things," I said. "It seems odd there should be such a lot of different ones."

Mrs. Leidner smiled.

"There is a church in Palestine in which the Lord's Prayer is written up in—ninety, I think it is—different languages."

"Well!" I said. "I must write and tell my old aunt that. She *will* be interested."

Mrs. Leidner fingered the jug and basin absently and shifted the soap dish an inch or two.

"I do hope you'll be happy here," she said. "And not get too bored."

"I'm not often bored," I assured her. "Life's not long enough for that."

She did not answer. She continued to toy with the washstand as though abstractedly.

Suddenly she fixed her dark-violet eyes on my face.

"What exactly did my husband tell you, nurse?"

Well, one usually says the same thing to a question of that kind.

"I gathered you were a bit run-down and all that, Mrs. Leidner," I said glibly. "And that you just wanted someone to look after you and take any worries off your hands."

She bent her head slowly and thoughtfully.

"Yes," she said. "Yes—that will do very well."

That was just a little bit enigmatic, but I wasn't going to question it. Instead I said, "I hope you'll let me help you with anything there is to do in the house. You mustn't let me be idle."

She smiled a little. "Thank you, nurse."

Then she sat down on the bed and, rather to my surprise, began to cross-question me rather closely. I say rather to my surprise because, from the moment I set eyes on her, I felt sure that Mrs. Leidner was a lady. And a lady, in my experience, very seldom displays curiosity about one's private affairs.

But Mrs. Leidner seemed anxious to know everything there was to know about me. Where I'd trained and how long ago. What had brought me out to the East. How it had come about that Dr. Reilly had recommended me. She even asked me if I had ever been in America or had any relations in America. One or two other questions she asked me that seemed quite purposeless at the time, but of which I saw the significance later.

Then, suddenly, her manner changed. She smiled—a warm, sunny smile—and she said, very sweetly, that she was very glad I had come and that she was sure I was going to be a comfort to her.

She got up from the bed and said, "Would you like to come up to the roof and see the sunset? It's usually very lovely about this time."

I agreed willingly.

As we went out of the room she asked, "Were there many other people on the train from Baghdad? Any men?"

I said that I hadn't noticed anybody in particular. There had been two Frenchmen in the restaurant car the night before. And a party of three men whom I gathered from their conversation had to do with the pipeline.

She nodded and a faint sound escaped her. It sounded like a small sigh of relief.

We went up to the roof together.

Mrs. Mercado was there, sitting on the parapet, and Dr. Leidner was bending over looking at a lot of stones and broken pottery that were laid out in rows. There were big things he called querns, and pestles and celts and stone axes, and more broken bits of pottery with queer patterns on them than I've ever seen all at once.

"Come over here," called out Mrs. Mercado. "Isn't it *too,* too beautiful?"

It certainly was a beautiful sunset. Hassanieh in the distance looked quite fairylike with the setting sun behind it, and the River Tigris flowing between its wide banks looked like a dream river rather than a real one.

"Isn't it lovely, Eric?" said Mrs. Leidner.

The doctor looked up with abstracted eyes, murmured, "Lovely, lovely," perfunctorily and went on sorting potsherds.

Mrs. Leidner smiled and said, "Archaeologists only look at what lies beneath their feet. The sky and the heavens don't exist for them."

Mrs. Mercado giggled.

"Oh, they're very queer people—you'll soon find *that* out, nurse," she said. She paused and then added, "We are all *so* glad you've come. We've been so very worried about our dear Mrs. Leidner, haven't we, Louise?"

"Have you?" Her voice was not encouraging.

"Oh, yes. She really has been *very* bad, nurse. All sorts of alarms and excursions. You know when anybody says to me of someone, 'It's just nerves,' I always say, 'But what could be *worse?*' Nerves are the core and center of one's being, aren't they?"

Puss, puss, I thought to myself.

Mrs. Leidner said dryly, "Well, you needn't be worried about me any more, Marie. Nurse is going to look after me."

"Certainly I am," I said cheerfully.

"I'm sure that will make all the difference," said Mrs. Mercado. "We've all felt that she ought to see a doctor or do *something.* Her nerves have really been all to pieces, haven't they, Louise dear?"

"So much so that I seem to have got on *your* nerves with them," said Mrs. Leidner. "Shall we talk about something more interesting than my wretched ailments?"

I understood then that Mrs. Leidner was the sort of woman who could easily make enemies. There was a cool rudeness in her tone (not that I blamed her for it) which brought a flush to Mrs. Mercado's rather sallow cheeks. She stammered out something, but Mrs. Leidner had risen and had joined her husband at the other end of the roof. I doubt if he heard her coming till she laid her hand on his shoulder, then he looked up quickly. There was affection and a kind of eager questioning in his face.

Mrs. Leidner nodded her head gently. Presently, her arm through his, they wandered to the far parapet and finally down the steps together.

"He's devoted to her, isn't he?" said Mrs. Mercado.

"Yes," I said. "It's very nice to see."

She was looking at me with a queer, rather eager sidelong glance. "What do you think is really the matter with her, nurse?" she asked, lowering her voice a little.

"Oh, I don't suppose it's much," I said cheerfully. "Just a bit run-down, I expect."

Her eyes still bored into me as they had done at tea. She said abruptly, "Are you a mental nurse?"

"Oh, dear, no!" I said. "What made you think that?"

She was silent for a moment, then she said, "Do you know how queer she's been? Did Doctor Leidner tell you?"

I don't hold with gossiping about my cases. On the other hand, it's my experience that it's often very hard to get the truth out of the relatives, and until you know the truth you're often working in the dark and doing no good. Of course, when there's a doctor in charge, it's different. He tells you what it's necessary for you to know. But in this case there wasn't a doctor in charge. Dr. Reilly had never been called in professionally. And in my own mind I wasn't at all sure that Dr. Leidner had told me all he could have done. It's often the husband's instinct to be reticent—and more honor to him, I say. But all the same, the more I knew the better I could tell which line to take. Mrs. Mercado (whom I put down in my own mind as a thoroughly spiteful little cat) was clearly dying to talk. And frankly, on the human side as well as the professional, I wanted to hear what she had to say. You can put it that I was just every-day curious if you like.

I said, "I gather Mrs. Leidner's not been quite her normal self lately?"

Mrs. Mercado laughed disagreeably.

"Normal? I should say not. Frightening us to death. One night it was fingers tapping on her window. And then it was a hand without an arm attached. But when it came to a yellow face pressed against the window—and when she rushed to the window there was nothing there—well, I ask you, it *is* a bit creepy for all of us."

"Perhaps somebody was playing a trick on her," I suggested.

"Oh, no, she fancied it all. And only three days ago at dinner they were firing off shots in the village—nearly a mile away—and she jumped up and screamed out—it scared us all to death. As for Doctor Leidner, he rushed to her and behaved in the most ridiculous way. 'It's nothing, darling, it's nothing at all,' he kept saying. I think, you know, nurse, men sometimes *encourage* women in these hysterical fancies. It's a pity because it's a bad thing. Delusions shouldn't be encouraged."

"Not if they *are* delusions," I said dryly.

"What else could they be?"

I didn't answer because I didn't know what to say. It was a funny business. The shots and the screaming were natural enough—for anyone in a nervous condition, that is. But this queer story of a spectral face and hand was different. It looked to me like one of two things—either Mrs. Leidner had made the story up (exactly as a child shows off by telling lies about something that never happened in order to make herself the center of attraction) or else it was, as I had suggested, a deliberate practical joke. It was the sort of thing, I reflected, that an unimaginative hearty sort of young fellow like Mr. Coleman might think very funny. I decided to keep a close watch on him. Nervous patients can be scared nearly out of their minds by a silly joke.

Mrs. Mercado said with a sideways glance at me, "She's very romantic-looking, nurse, don't you think so? The sort of woman things *happen* to."

"Have many things happened to her?" I asked.

"Well, her first husband was killed in the war when she was only twenty. I think that's very pathetic and romantic, don't you?"

"It's one way of calling a goose a swan," I said dryly.

"Oh, nurse. What an extraordinary remark!"

It was really a very true one. The amount of women you hear say, "If Donald—or Arthur—or whatever his name was—had *only* lived." And I sometimes think but if he had, he'd have been a stout, unromantic, short-tempered, middle-aged husband as likely as not.

It was getting dark and I suggested that we should go down. Mrs. Mercado agreed and asked if I would like to see the laboratory. "My husband will be there—working."

I said I would like to very much and we made our way there. The place was lighted by a lamp but it was empty. Mrs. Mercado showed me some of the apparatus and some copper ornaments that were being treated, and also some bones coated with wax.

"Where can Joseph be?" said Mrs. Mercado.

She looked into the drawing-office, where Carey was at work. He hardly looked up as we entered, and I was struck by the extraordinary look of strain on his face. It came to me suddenly: *This man is at the end of his tether. Very soon, something will snap.* And I remembered somebody else had noticed that same tenseness about him.

As we went out again I turned my head for one last look at him. He was bent over his paper, his lips pressed very closely together, and that "death's head" suggestion of his bones very strongly marked. Perhaps it was fanciful, but I thought that he looked like a knight of old who was going into battle and knew he was going to be killed.

And again I felt what an extraordinary and quite unconscious power of attraction he had.

We found Mr. Mercado in the living-room. He was explaining the idea of some new process to Mrs. Leidner. She was sitting on a straight wooden chair, embroidering flowers in fine silks, and I was struck anew by her strange, fragile, unearthly appearance. She looked a fairy creature more than flesh and blood.

Mrs. Mercado said, her voice high and shrill, "Oh, *there* you are, Joseph. We thought we'd find you in the lab."

He jumped up looking startled and confused, as though her entrance had broken a spell. He said stammeringly, "I—I must go now. I'm in the middle of—the middle of—" He didn't complete the sentence but turned toward the door.

Mrs. Leidner said in her soft, drawling voice, "You must finish telling me some other time. It was very interesting."

She looked up at us, smiled rather sweetly but in a faraway manner, and bent over her embroidery again. In a minute or two she said, "There are some books over there, nurse. We've got quite a good selection. Choose one and sit down."

I went over to the bookshelf. Mrs. Mercado stayed for a minute or two, then, turning abruptly, she went out. As she passed me I saw her face and I didn't like the look of it. She looked wild with fury.

In spite of myself I remembered some of the things Mrs. Kelsey had said and hinted about Mrs. Leidner. I didn't like to think they were true because I liked Mrs. Leidner, but I wondered, nevertheless, if there mightn't perhaps be a grain of truth behind them.

I didn't think it was all her fault, but the fact remained that dear, ugly Miss Johnson, and that common little spitfire, Mrs. Mercado, couldn't hold a candle to her in looks or in attraction. And, after all, men are men all over the world. You soon see a lot of that in my profession.

Mercado was a poor fish, and I don't suppose Mrs. Leidner really cared two hoots for his admiration—but his wife cared. If I wasn't mistaken, she minded badly and would be quite willing to do Mrs. Leidner a bad turn if she could.

I looked at Mrs. Leidner sitting there and sewing at her pretty flowers, so remote and far away and aloof. I felt somehow I ought to warn her. I felt that perhaps she didn't know how stupid and unreasoning and violent jealousy and hate can be—and how little it takes to set them smoldering.

And then I said to myself, "Amy Leatheran, you're a fool. Mrs. Leidner's no chicken. She's close on forty if she's a day, and she must know all about life there is to know."

But I felt that all the same perhaps she didn't.

She had such a queer untouched look.

I began to wonder what her life had been. I knew she'd only married Dr. Leidner two years ago. And according to Mrs. Mercado her first husband had died nearly twenty years ago.

I came and sat down near her with a book, and presently I went and washed my hands for supper. It was a good meal—some really excellent curry. They all went to bed early and I was glad for I was tired.

Dr. Leidner came with me to my room to see I had all I wanted.

He gave me a warm handclasp and said eagerly, "She likes you, nurse. She's taken to you at once. I'm so glad. I feel everything's going to be all right now."

His eagerness was almost boyish.

I felt, too, that Mrs. Leidner had taken a liking to me, and I was pleased it should be so.

But I didn't quite share his confidence. I felt, somehow, that there was more to it all than he himself might know.

There was *something*—something I couldn't get at. But I felt it in the air.

My bed was comfortable, but I didn't sleep well for all that. I dreamed too much.

The words of a poem by Keats, that I'd had to learn as a child, kept running through my head. I kept getting them wrong and it worried me. It was a poem I'd always hated—I suppose because I'd had to learn it whether I wanted to or not. But somehow when I woke up in the dark I saw a sort of beauty in it for the first time.

"Oh, say what ails thee, knight at arms, alone and—what was it?—*palely loitering—"* I saw the knight's face in my mind for the first time—and it was Mr. Carey's face—a grim, tense, bronzed face like some of those poor young men I remembered as a girl during the war. And I felt sorry for him—and then I fell off to sleep again and I saw that the Belle Dame sans Merci was Mrs. Leidner and she was leaning sideways on a horse with an embroidery of flowers in her hands—and then the horse stumbled and everywhere there were bones coated in wax, and I woke up all goose flesh and shivering, and told myself that curry never *had* agreed with me at night.

CHAPTER VII

THE MAN AT THE WINDOW

I think I'd better make it clear right away that there isn't going to be any local color in this story. I don't know anything about archaeology and I don't know that I very much want to. Messing about with people and places that are buried and done with doesn't make sense to me. Mr. Carey used to tell me that I hadn't got the archaeological temperament and I've no doubt he was quite right.

The very first morning after my arrival Mr. Carey asked if I'd like to come and see the palace he was—*planning* I think he called it. Though how you can plan for a thing that's happened long ago I'm sure I don't know! Well, I said I'd like to, and to tell the truth, I was a bit excited about it. Nearly three thousand years old that palace was, it appeared. I wondered what sort of palaces they had in those days, and if it would be like the pictures I'd seen of Tutankhamen's tomb furniture. But would you believe it, there was nothing to see but *mud!* Dirty mud walls about two feet high—and that's all there was to it. Mr. Carey took me here and there telling me things—how this was the great court, and there were some chambers here and an upper story and various other rooms that opened off the central court. And all I thought was, *But how does he* know? though, of course, I was too polite to say so. I can tell you it *was* a disappointment! The whole excavation looked like nothing but mud to me—no marble or gold or anything handsome—my aunt's house in Cricklewood would have made a much more imposing ruin! And those old Assyrians or whatever they were called themselves *kings.* When Mr. Carey had shown me his old "palace," he handed me over to Father Lavigny, who showed me the rest of the mound. I was a little afraid of Father Lavigny, being a monk and a foreigner and having such a deep voice and all, but he was very kind—though rather vague. Sometimes I felt it wasn't much more real to him than it was to me.

Mrs. Leidner explained that later. She said that Father Lavigny was only interested in "written documents"—as she called them. They wrote everything on clay, these people, queer heathenish-looking marks, too, but quite sensible. There were even school tablets—the teacher's lesson on one side and the pupil's effort on the back of it. I confess that that did interest me rather—it seemed so human, if you know what I mean.

Father Lavigny walked round the work with me and showed me what were temples or palaces and what were private houses, and also a place which he said was an early Akkadian cemetery. He spoke in a funny jerky way, just throwing in a scrap of information and then reverting to other subjects.

He said, "It is strange that you have come here. Is Mrs. Leidner really ill, then?"

"Not exactly ill," I said cautiously.

He said, "She is an odd woman. A dangerous woman, I think."

"Now what do you mean by that?" I said. "Dangerous? How dangerous?"

He shook his head thoughtfully.

"I think she is ruthless," he said. "Yes, I think she could be absolutely ruthless."

"If you'll excuse me," I said, "I think you're talking nonsense."

He shook his head.

"You do not know women as I do," he said.

And that was a funny thing, I thought, for a monk to say. But, of course, I suppose he might have heard a lot of things in confession. But that rather puzzled me, because I wasn't sure if monks heard confessions or if it was only priests. I supposed he *was* a monk with that long woolen robe—all sweeping up the dirt—and the rosary and all!

"Yes, she could be ruthless," he said musingly. "I am quite sure of that. And yet—though she is so hard—like stone, like marble—yet she is afraid. What is she afraid of?"

That, I thought, *is what we should all like to know!*

At least it was possible that her husband did know, but I didn't think anyone else did.

He fixed me with a sudden bright, dark eye.

"It is odd here? You find it odd? Or quite natural?"

"Not quite natural," I said, considering. "It's comfortable enough as far as the arrangements go—but there isn't quite a comfortable feeling."

"It makes *me* uncomfortable. I have the idea"—he became suddenly a little more foreign—"that something prepares itself. Doctor Leidner, too, he is not quite himself. Something is worrying him, also."

"His wife's health?"

"That perhaps. But there is more. There is—how shall I say it—an uneasiness."

And that was just it, there was an uneasiness.

We didn't say any more just then, for Dr. Leidner came toward us. He showed me a child's grave that had just been uncovered. Rather pathetic it was—the little bones—and a pot or two and some little specks that Dr. Leidner told me were a bead necklace.

It was the workmen that made me laugh. You never saw such a lot of scarecrows—all in long petticoats and rags, and their heads tied up as though they had toothache. And every now and then, as they went to and fro carrying away baskets of earth, they began to sing—at least I suppose it was meant to be singing—a queer sort of monotonous chant that went on and on over and over again. I noticed that most of their eyes were terrible—all covered with discharge, and one or two looked half blind. I was just thinking what a miserable lot they were when Dr. Leidner said, "Rather a fine-looking lot of men, aren't they?" and I thought what a queer world it was and how two different people could see the same thing each of them the other way round. I haven't put that very well, but you can guess what I mean.

After a bit Dr. Leidner said he was going back to the house for a mid-morning cup of tea. So he and I walked back together and he told me things. When *he* explained, it was all quite different. I sort of *saw* it all—how it used to be—the streets and the houses, and he showed me ovens where they baked bread and said the Arabs used much the same kind of ovens nowadays.

We got back to the house and found Mrs. Leidner had got up. She was looking better today, not so thin and worn. Tea came in almost at once, and Dr. Leidner told her what had turned up during the morning on the dig. Then he went back to work and Mrs. Leidner asked me if I would like to see some of the finds they had made up to date. Of course I said yes, so she took me through into the antika room. There was a lot of stuff lying about—mostly broken pots it seemed to me—or else ones that were all mended and stuck together. The whole lot might have been thrown away, I thought.

"Dear, dear," I said, "it's a pity they're all so broken, isn't it? Are they really worth keeping?"

Mrs. Leidner smiled a little and she said, "You mustn't let Eric hear you. Pots interest him more than anything else, and some of these are the oldest things we have—perhaps as much as seven thousand years old." And she explained how some of them came from a very deep cut on the mound down toward the bottom, and how, thousands of years ago, they had been broken and mended with bitumen, showing people prized their things just as much then as they do nowadays.

"And now," she said, "we'll show you something more exciting."

And she took down a box from the shelf and showed me a beautiful gold dagger with dark-blue stones in the handle.

I exclaimed with pleasure.

Mrs. Leidner laughed.

"Yes, everybody likes gold! Except my husband."

"Why doesn't Doctor Leidner like it?"

"Well, for one thing, it comes expensive. You have to pay the workmen who find it the weight of the object in gold."

"Good gracious!" I exclaimed. "But why?"

"Oh, it's a custom. For one thing it prevents them from stealing. You see, if they *did* steal it wouldn't be for the archaeological value but for the intrinsic value. They could melt it down. So we make it easy for them to be honest."

She took down another tray and showed me a really beautiful gold drinking-cup with a design of rams' heads on it.

Again I exclaimed.

"Yes, it is beautiful, isn't it? These came from a prince's grave. We found other royal graves but most of them had been plundered. This cup is our best find. It is one of the most lovely ever found anywhere. Early Akkadian. Unique."

Suddenly, with a frown, Mrs. Leidner brought the cup up close to her eyes and scratched at it delicately with her nail.

"How extraordinary! There's actually wax on it. Someone must have been in here with a candle."

She detached the little flake and replaced the cup in its place.

After that she showed me some queer little terra-cotta figurines—but most of them were just rude. Nasty minds those old people had, I say.

When we went back to the porch Mrs. Mercado was sitting polishing her nails. She was holding them out in front of her admiring the effect. I thought myself that anything more hideous than that orange-red could hardly have been imagined.

Mrs. Leidner had brought with her from the antika room a very delicate little saucer broken in several pieces, and this she now proceeded to join together. I watched her for a minute or two and then asked if I could help.

"Oh, yes, there are plenty more." She fetched quite a supply of broken pottery and we set to work. I soon got into the hang of it and she praised my ability. I suppose most nurses are handy with their fingers.

"How busy everybody is," said Mrs. Mercado. "It makes me feel dreadfully idle. Of course, I *am* idle."

"Why shouldn't you be if you like?" said Mrs. Leidner.

Her voice was quite uninterested.

At twelve we had lunch. Afterward Dr. Leidner and Mr. Mercado cleaned some pottery, pouring a solution of hydrochloric acid over it. One pot went a lovely plum color and a pattern of bulls' horns came out on another one. It was really quite magical. All the dried mud that no washing would remove sort of foamed and boiled away.

Mr. Carey and Mr. Coleman went out on the dig, and Mr. Reiter went off to the photographic room.

"What will you do, Louise?" Dr. Leidner asked his wife. "I suppose you'll rest for a bit?"

I gathered that Mrs. Leidner usually lay down every afternoon.

"I'll rest for about an hour. Then perhaps I'll go out for a short stroll."

"Good. Nurse will go with you, won't you?"

"Of course," I said.

"No, no," said Mrs. Leidner. "I like going alone. Nurse isn't to feel so much on duty that I'm not allowed out of her sight."

"Oh, but I'd like to come," I said.

"No, really, I'd rather you didn't." She was quite firm—almost peremptory. "I must be by myself every now and then. It's necessary to me."

I didn't insist, of course. But as I went off for a short sleep myself it struck me as odd that Mrs. Leidner, with her nervous terrors, should be quite content to walk by herself without any kind of protection.

When I came out of my room at half past three the courtyard was deserted save for a little boy with a large copper bath who was washing pottery, and Mr. Emmott, who was sorting and arranging it. As I went toward them Mrs. Leidner came in through the archway. She looked more alive than I had seen her yet. Her eyes shone and she looked uplifted and almost gay.

Dr. Leidner came out from the laboratory and joined her. He was showing her a big dish with bulls' horns on it.

"The prehistoric levels are being extraordinarily productive," he said. "It's been a good season so far. Finding that tomb right at the beginning was a real piece of luck. The only person who might complain is Father Lavigny. We've had hardly any tablets so far."

"He doesn't seem to have done very much with the few we have had," said Mrs. Leidner dryly. "He may be a very fine epigraphist but he's a remarkably lazy one. He spends all his afternoons sleeping."

"We miss Byrd," said Dr. Leidner. "This man strikes me as slightly unorthodox—though, of course, I'm not competent to judge. But one or two of his translations have been surprising to say the least of it. I can hardly believe, for instance, that he's right about that inscribed brick, and yet he must know."

After tea Mrs. Leidner asked me if I would like to stroll down to the river. I thought that perhaps she feared that her refusal to let me accompany her earlier in the afternoon might have hurt my feelings.

I wanted her to know that I wasn't the touchy kind, so I accepted at once.

It was a lovely evening. A path led between barley fields and then through some flowering fruit trees. Finally we came to the edge of the Tigris. Immediately on our left was the Tell with the workmen singing in their queer monotonous chant. A little to our right was a big water wheel which made a queer groaning noise. It used to set my teeth on edge at first. But in the end I got fond of it and it had a queer soothing effect on me. Beyond the water wheel was the village from which most of the workmen came.

"It's rather beautiful, isn't it?" said Mrs. Leidner.

"It's very peaceful," I said. "It seems funny to me to be so far away from everywhere."

"Far from everywhere," repeated Mrs. Leidner. "Yes. Here at least one might expect to be safe."

I glanced at her sharply, but I think she was speaking more to herself than to me, and I don't think she realized that her words had been revealing.

We began to walk back to the house.

Suddenly Mrs. Leidner clutched my arm so violently that I nearly cried out.

"Who's that, nurse? What's he doing?"

Some little distance ahead of us, just where the path ran near the expedition house, a man was standing. He wore European clothes and he seemed to be standing on tiptoe and trying to look in at one of the windows.

As we watched he glanced round, caught sight of us, and immediately continued on the path toward us. I felt Mrs. Leidner's clutch tighten.

"Nurse," she whispered. "Nurse—"

"It's all right, my dear, it's all right," I said reassuringly.

The man came along and passed us. He was an Iraqi, and as soon as she saw him near to, Mrs. Leidner relaxed with a sigh.

"He's only an Iraqi, after all," she said.

We went on our way. I glanced up at the windows as I passed. Not only were they barred, but they were too high from the ground to permit of anyone seeing in, for the level of the ground was lower here than on the inside of the courtyard.

"It must have been just curiosity," I said.

Mrs. Leidner nodded.

"That's all. But just for a minute I thought—"

She broke off.

I thought to myself, "You thought *what?* That's what I'd like to know? *What* did you think?"

But I knew one thing now—that Mrs. Leidner was afraid of a definite flesh-and-blood person.

CHAPTER VIII

NIGHT ALARM

It's a little difficult to know exactly what to note in the week that followed my arrival at Tell Yarimjah.

Looking back as I do from my present standpoint of knowledge I can see a good many little signs and indications that I was quite blind to at the time.

To tell the story properly, however, I think I ought to try and recapture the point of view that I actually held—puzzled, uneasy, and increasingly conscious of *something* wrong.

For one thing *was* certain, that curious sense of strain and constraint was *not* imagined. It was genuine. Even Bill Coleman, the insensitive, commented upon it.

"This place gets under my skin," I heard him say. "Are they always such a glum lot?"

It was David Emmott to whom he spoke, the other assistant. I had taken rather a fancy to Mr. Emmott; his taciturnity was not, I felt sure, unfriendly. There was something about him that seemed very steadfast and reassuring in an atmosphere where one was uncertain what anyone was feeling or thinking.

"No," he said in answer to Mr. Coleman. "It wasn't like this last year."

But he didn't enlarge on the theme, or say any more.

"What I can't make out is what it's all about," said Mr. Coleman in an aggrieved voice.

Emmott shrugged his shoulders but didn't answer.

I had a rather enlightening conversation with Miss Johnson. I liked her very much. She was capable, practical, and intelligent. She had, it was quite obvious, a distinct hero worship for Dr. Leidner.

On this occasion she told me the story of his life since his young days. She knew every site he had dug, and the results of the dig. I would almost dare swear she could quote from every lecture he had ever delivered. She considered him, she told me, quite the finest field archaeologist living.

"And he's so simple. So completely unworldly. He doesn't know the meaning of the word 'conceit.' Only a really great man could be so simple."

"That's true enough," I said. "Big people don't need to throw their weight about."

"And he's so lighthearted, too. I can't tell you what fun we used to have—he and Richard Carey and I—the first years we were out here. We were such a happy party. Richard Carey worked with him in Palestine, of course. Theirs is a friendship of ten years or so. Oh, well, I've known him for seven."

"What a handsome man Mr. Carey is," I said.

"Yes—I suppose he is."

She said it rather curtly.

"But he's just a little bit quiet, don't you think?"

"He usedn't to be like that," said Miss Johnson quickly. "It's only since—"

She stopped abruptly.

"Only since—" I prompted.

"Oh, well." Miss Johnson gave a characteristic motion of her shoulders. "A good many things are changed nowadays."

I didn't answer. I hoped she would go on—and she did—prefacing her remarks with a little laugh as though to detract from their importance.

"I'm afraid I'm rather a conservative old fogy. I sometimes think that if an archaeologist's wife isn't really interested, it would be wiser for her not to accompany the expedition. It often leads to friction."

"Mrs. Mercado?" I suggested.

"Oh, her!" Miss Johnson brushed the suggestion aside. "I was really thinking of Mrs. Leidner. She's a very charming woman—and one can quite understand why Doctor Leidner 'fell for her'—to use a slang term. But I can't help feeling she's out of place here. She—it unsettles things."

So Miss Johnson agreed with Mrs. Kelsey that it was Mrs. Leidner who was responsible for the strained atmosphere. But then where did Mrs. Leidner's own nervous fears come in?

"It unsettles *him,*" said Miss Johnson earnestly. "Of course, I'm—well, I'm like a faithful but jealous old dog. I don't like to see him so worn out and worried. His whole mind ought to be on the work—not taken up with his wife and her silly fears! If she's nervous of coming to out-of-the-way places, she ought to have stayed in America. I've no patience with people who come to a place and then do nothing but grouse about it!"

And then, a little fearful of having said more than she meant to say, she went on. "Of course I admire her very much. She's a lovely woman and she's got great charm of manner when she chooses."

And there the subject dropped.

I thought to myself that it was always the same way—wherever women are cooped up together, there's bound to be jealousy. Miss Johnson clearly didn't like her chief's wife (that was perhaps natural) and unless I was much mistaken Mrs. Mercado fairly hated her.

Another person who didn't like Mrs. Leidner was Sheila Reilly. She came out once or twice to the dig, once in a car and twice with some young man on a horse—on two horses I mean, of course. It was at the back of my mind that she had a weakness for the silent young American, Emmott. When he was on duty at the dig she used to stay talking to him, and I thought, too, that *he* admired *her*.

One day, rather injudiciously, I thought, Mrs. Leidner commented upon it at lunch.

"The Reilly girl is still hunting David down," she said with a little laugh. "Poor David, she chases you up on the dig, even! How foolish girls are!"

Mr. Emmott didn't answer, but under his tan his face got rather red. He raised his eyes and looked right into hers with a very curious expression—a straight, steady glance with something of a challenge in it.

She smiled very faintly and looked away.

I heard Father Lavigny murmur something, but when I said "Pardon?" he merely shook his head and did not repeat his remark.

That afternoon Mr. Coleman said to me, "Matter of fact I didn't like Mrs. L. any too much at first. She used to jump down my throat every time I opened my mouth. But I've begun to understand her better now. She's one of the kindest women I've ever met. You find yourself telling her all the foolish scrapes you ever got into before you know where you are. She's got her knife into Sheila Reilly, I know, but then Sheila's been damned rude to her once or twice. That's the worst of Sheila—she's got no manners. And a temper like the devil!"

That I could well believe. Dr. Reilly spoiled her.

"Of course she's bound to get a bit full of herself, being the only young woman in the place. But that doesn't excuse her talking to Mrs. Leidner as though Mrs. Leidner were her great-aunt. Mrs. L's not exactly a chicken, but she's a damned good looking woman. Rather like those fairy women who come out of marshes with lights and lure you away." He added bitterly, "You wouldn't find Sheila luring anyone. All she does is to tick a fellow off."

I only remember two other incidents of any kind of significance.

One was when I went to the laboratory to fetch some acetone to get the stickiness off my fingers from mending the pottery. Mr. Mercado was sitting in a corner, his head was laid down on his arms and I fancied he was asleep. I took the bottle I wanted and went off with it.

That evening, to my great surprise, Mrs. Mercado tackled me.

"Did you take a bottle of acetone from the lab?"

"Yes," I said. "I did."

"You know perfectly well that there's a small bottle always kept in the antika room."

She spoke quite angrily.

"Is there? I didn't know."

"I think you did! You just wanted to come spying round. I know what hospital nurses are."

I stared at her.

"I don't know what you're talking about, Mrs. Mercado," I said with dignity. "I'm sure I don't want to spy on anyone."

"Oh, no! Of course not. Do you think I don't know what you're here for?"

Really, for a minute or two I thought she must have been drinking. I went away without saying any more. But I thought it was very odd.

The other thing was nothing very much. I was trying to entice a pi dog pup with a piece of bread. It was very timid, however, like all Arab dogs—and was convinced I meant no good. It slunk away and I followed it—out through the archway and round the corner of the house. I came round so sharply that before I knew, I had cannoned into Father Lavigny and another man who were standing together—and in a minute I realized that the second man was the same one Mrs. Leidner and I had noticed that day trying to peer through the window.

I apologized and Father Lavigny smiled, and with a word of farewell greeting to the other man he returned to the house with me.

"You know," he said, "I am very ashamed. I am a student of Oriental languages and none of the men on the work can understand me! It is humiliating, do you not think? I was trying my Arabic on that man, who is a townsman, to see if I got on better—but it still wasn't very successful. Leidner says my Arabic is too pure."

That was all. But it just passed through my head that it was odd the same man should still be hanging round the house.

That night we had a scare.

It must have been about two in the morning. I'm a light sleeper, as most nurses have to be. I was awake and sitting up in bed by the time that my door opened.

"Nurse, nurse!"

It was Mrs. Leidner's voice, low and urgent.

I struck a match and lighted the candle.

She was standing by the door in a long blue dressing-gown. She was looking petrified with terror.

"There's someone—someone—in the room next to mine. I heard him—scratching on the wall."

I jumped out of bed and came to her.

"It's all right," I said. "I'm here. Don't be afraid, my dear."

She whispered, "Get Eric."

I nodded and ran out and knocked on his door. In a minute he was with us. Mrs. Leidner was sitting on my bed, her breath coming in great gasps.

"I heard him," she said. "I heard him—scratching on the wall."

"Someone in the antika room?" cried Dr. Leidner.

He ran out quickly—and it just flashed across my mind how differently these two had reacted. Mrs. Leidner's fear was entirely personal, but Dr. Leidner's mind leaped at once to his precious treasures.

"The antika room!" breathed Mrs. Leidner. "Of course! How stupid of me."

And rising and pulling her gown round her, she bade me come with her. All traces of her panic-stricken fear had vanished.

We arrived in the antika room to find Dr. Leidner and Father Lavigny. The latter had also heard a noise, had risen to investigate, and had fancied he saw a light in the antika room. He had delayed to put on slippers and snatch up a torch and had found no one by the time he got there. The door, moreover, was duly locked, as it was supposed to be at night.

While he was assuring himself that nothing had been taken, Dr. Leidner had joined him.

Nothing more was to be learned. The outside archway door was locked. The guard swore nobody could have got in from outside, but as they had probably been fast asleep this was not conclusive. There were no marks or traces of an intruder and nothing had been taken.

It was possible that what had alarmed Mrs. Leidner was the noise made by Father Lavigny taking down boxes from the shelves to assure himself that all was in order.

On the other hand, Father Lavigny himself was positive that he had *(a)* heard footsteps passing his window and *(b)* seen the flicker of a light, possibly a torch, in the antika room.

Nobody else had heard or seen anything.

The incident is of value in my narrative because it led to Mrs. Leidner's unburdening herself to me on the following day.

CHAPTER IX

MRS. LEIDNER'S STORY

We had just finished lunch. Mrs. Leidner went to her room to rest as usual. I settled her on her bed with plenty of pillows and her book, and was leaving the room when she called me back.

"Don't go, nurse, there's something I want to say to you."

I came back into the room.

"Shut the door."

I obeyed.

She got up from the bed and began to walk up and down the room. I could see that she was making up her mind to something and I didn't like to interrupt her. She was clearly in great indecision of mind.

At last she seemed to have nerved herself to the required point. She turned to me and said abruptly, "Sit down."

I sat down by the table very quietly. She began nervously. "You must have wondered what all this is about?"

I just nodded without saying anything.

"I've made up my mind to tell you—everything! I must tell someone or I shall go mad."

"Well," I said. "I think really it would be just as well. It's not easy to know the best thing to do when one's kept in the dark."

She stopped in her uneasy walk and faced me.

"Do you know what I'm frightened of?"

"Some man," I said.

"Yes—but I didn't say whom—I said what."

I waited.

She said, *"I'm afraid of being killed!"*

Well, it was out now. I wasn't going to show any particular concern. She was near enough hysterics as it was.

"Dear me," I said. "So that's it, is it?"

Then she began to laugh. She laughed and she laughed—and the tears ran down her face.

"The way you said that!" she gasped. "The way you said it—"

"Now, now," I said. "This won't do." I spoke sharply. I pushed her into a chair, went over to the washstand, and got a cold sponge and bathed her forehead and wrists.

"No more nonsense," I said. "Tell me calmly and sensibly all about it."

That stopped her. She sat up and spoke in her natural voice.

"You're a treasure, nurse," she said. "You make me feel as though I'm six. I'm going to tell you."

"That's right," I said. "Take your time and don't hurry."

She began to speak, slowly and deliberately. "When I was a girl of twenty I married. A young man in one of our state departments. It was in 1918."

"I know," I said. "Mrs. Mercado told me. He was killed in the war."

But Mrs. Leidner shook her head.

"That's what she thinks. That's what everybody thinks. The truth is something quite different. I was a queer patriotic, enthusiastic girl, nurse, full of idealism. When I'd been married a few months I discovered—by a quite unforeseeable accident—that my husband was a spy in German pay. I learned that the information supplied by him had led directly to the sinking of an American transport and the loss of hundreds of lives. I don't know what most people would have done, but I'll tell you what I did. I went straight to my father, who was in the War Department, and told him the truth. Frederick *was* killed in the war—but he was killed in America—shot as a spy."

"Oh, dear, dear!" I ejaculated. "How terrible!"

"Yes," she said. "It was terrible. He was so kind, too—so gentle. And all the time— But I never hesitated. Perhaps I was wrong."

"It's difficult to say," I said. "I'm sure I don't know what one would do."

"What I'm telling you was never generally known outside the state departments. Ostensibly my husband had gone to the front and had been killed. I had a lot of sympathy and kindness shown me as a war widow."

Her voice was bitter, and I nodded comprehendingly.

"Lots of people wanted to marry me, but I always refused. I'd had too bad a shock. I didn't feel I could ever *trust* anyone again."

"Yes, I can imagine feeling like that."

"And then I became very fond of a certain young man. I wavered. An amazing thing happened! I got an anonymous letter—from Frederick—saying that if I ever married another man, he'd kill me!"

"From Frederick? From your dead husband?"

"Yes. Of course, I thought at first I was mad or dreaming. At last I went to my father. He told me the truth. My husband hadn't been shot, after all. He'd escaped—but his escape did him no good. He was involved in a train wreck a few weeks later and his dead body was found among others. My father had kept the fact of his escape from me, and since the man had died anyway he had seen no reason to tell me anything until now.

"But the letter I received opened up entirely new possibilities. Was it perhaps a fact that my husband was still alive?

"My father went into the matter as carefully as possible. And he declared that as far as one could humanly be sure the body that was buried as Frederick's *was* Frederick's. There had been a certain amount of disfiguration, so that he could not speak with absolute cast-iron certainty, but he reiterated his solemn belief that Frederick was dead and that this letter was a cruel and malicious hoax.

"The same thing happened more than once. If I seemed to be on intimate terms with any man, I would receive a threatening letter."

"In your husband's handwriting?"

She said slowly, "That is difficult to say. I had no letters of his. I had only my memory to go by."

"There was no allusion or special form of words used that could make you sure?"

"No. There *were* certain terms—nicknames, for instance—private between us—if one of those had been used or quoted, then I should have been quite sure."

"Yes," I said thoughtfully. "That is odd. It looks as though it *wasn't* your husband. But is there anyone else it could be?"

"There is a possibility. Frederick had a younger brother—a boy of ten or twelve at the time of our marriage. He worshiped Frederick, and Frederick was devoted to him. What happened to this boy, William his name was, I don't know. It seems to me possible that, adoring his brother as fanatically as he did, he may have grown up regarding me as directly responsible for his death. He had always been jealous of me and may have invented this scheme by way of punishment."

"It's possible," I said. "It's amazing the way children do remember if they've had a shock."

"I know. This boy may have dedicated his life to revenge."

"Please go on."

"There isn't very much more to tell. I met Eric three years ago. I meant never to marry. Eric made me change my mind. Right up to our wedding day I waited for another threatening letter. None came. I decided that whoever the writer might be, he was either dead, or tired of his cruel sport. *Two days after our marriage I got this.*"

Drawing a small attaché case which was on the table toward her, she unlocked it, took out a letter, and handed it to me.

The ink was slightly faded. It was written in a rather womanish hand with a forward slant.

You have disobeyed. Now you cannot escape. You must be Frederick Bosner's wife only! You have got to die.

"I was frightened—but not so much as I might have been to begin with. Being with Eric made me feel safe. Then, a month later, I got a second letter."

I have not forgotten. I am making my plans. You have got to die. Why did you disobey?

"Does your husband know about this?"

Mrs. Leidner answered slowly. "He knows that I am threatened. I showed him both letters when the second one came. He was inclined to think the whole thing a hoax. He thought, also, that it might be someone who wanted to blackmail me by pretending my first husband was alive."

She paused and then went on.

"A few days after I received the second letter we had a narrow escape from death by gas poisoning. Somebody entered our apartment after we were asleep and turned on the gas. Luckily I woke and smelled the gas in time. Then I lost my nerve. I told Eric how I had been persecuted for years, and I told him that I was sure this madman, whoever he might be, did really mean to kill me. I think that for the first time I really did think it *was* Frederick. There was always something a little ruthless behind his gentleness.

"Eric was still, I think, less alarmed than I was. He wanted to go to the police. Naturally I wouldn't hear of that. In the end we agreed that I should accompany him here, and that it might be wise if I didn't return to America in the summer but stayed in London and Paris.

"We carried out our plan and all went well. I felt sure that now everything would be all right. After all, we had put half the globe between ourselves and my enemy.

"And then—a little over three weeks ago—I received a letter—with an Iraq stamp on it."

She handed me a third letter.

You thought you could escape. You were wrong. You shall not be false to me and live. I have always told you so. Death is coming very soon.

"And a week ago—*this!* Just lying on the table here. It had not even gone through the post."

I took the sheet of paper from her. There was just one phrase scrawled across it.

I have arrived.

She stared at me.

"You see? You understand? He's going to kill me. It may be Frederick—it may be little William—*but he's going to kill me.*"

Her voice rose shudderingly. I caught her wrist.

"Now—now," I said warningly. "Don't give way. We'll look after you. Have you got any sal volatile?"

She nodded toward the washstand, and I gave her a good dose.

"That's better," I said, as the color returned to her cheeks.

"Yes, I'm better now. But, oh, nurse, do you see why I'm in this state? When I saw that man looking in through my window, I thought: *He's come!* Even when *you* arrived I was suspicious. I thought you might be a man in disguise—"

"The idea!"

"Oh, I know it sounds absurd. But you might have been in league with him perhaps—not a hospital nurse at all."

"But that's nonsense!"

"Yes, perhaps. But I've got beyond sense."

Struck by a sudden idea, I said, "You'd *recognize* your husband, I suppose?"

She answered slowly. "I don't even know that. It's over fifteen years ago. I mightn't recognize his face."

Then she shivered.

"I saw it one night—but it was a *dead* face. There was a tap, tap, tap on the window. And then I saw a face, a dead face, ghastly and grinning against the pane. I screamed and screamed. And they said there wasn't anything there!"

I remembered Mrs. Mercado's story.

"You don't think," I said hesitatingly, "that you *dreamed* that?"

"I'm sure I didn't!"

I wasn't so sure. It was the kind of nightmare that was quite likely under the circumstances and that easily might be taken for a waking occurrence. However, I never contradict a patient. I soothed Mrs. Leidner as best I could and pointed out that if any stranger arrived in the neighborhood it was pretty sure to be known.

I left her, I think, a little comforted, and I went in search of Dr. Leidner and told him of our conversation.

"I'm glad she's told you," he said simply. "It has worried me dreadfully. I feel sure that all those faces and tappings on the windowpane have been sheer imagination on her part. I haven't known what to do for the best. What do you think of the whole thing?"

I didn't quite understand the tone in his voice, but I answered promptly enough.

"It's possible," I said, "that these letters may be just a cruel and malicious hoax."

"Yes, that is quite likely. But what are we to *do?* They are driving her mad. I don't know what to think."

I didn't, either. It had occurred to me that possibly a woman might be concerned. Those letters had a feminine note about them. Mrs. Mercado was at the back of my mind.

Supposing that by some chance she had learned the facts of Mrs. Leidner's first marriage. She might be indulging her spite by terrorizing the other woman.

I didn't quite like to suggest such a thing to Dr. Leidner. It's so difficult to know how people are going to take things.

"Oh, well," I said cheerfully, "we must hope for the best. I think Mrs. Leidner seems happier already from just talking about it. That's always a help, you know. It's bottling things up that makes them get on your nerves."

"I'm very glad she has told you," he repeated. "It's a good sign. It shows she likes and trusts you. I've been at my wit's end to know what to do for the best."

It was on the tip of my tongue to ask him whether he'd thought of giving a discreet hint to the local police, but afterward I was glad I hadn't done so.

What happened was this. On the following day Mr. Coleman was going in to Hassanieh to get the workmen's pay. He was also taking in all our letters to catch the air mail.

The letters, as written, were dropped into a wooden box on the dining-room window sill. Last thing that night Mr. Coleman took them out and was sorting them out into bundles and putting rubber bands round them.

Suddenly he gave a shout.

"What is it?" I asked.

He held out a letter with a grin.

"It's our Lovely Louise—she really *is* going balmy. She's addressed a letter to someone at Forty-Second Street, Paris, France. I don't think that can be right, do you? Do you mind taking it to her and asking what she *does* mean? She's just gone off to bed."

I took it from him and ran off to Mrs. Leidner with it, and she amended the address.

It was the first time I had seen Mrs. Leidner's handwriting, and I wondered idly where I had seen it before, for it was certainly quite familiar to me. It wasn't till the middle of the night that it suddenly came to me. Except that it was bigger and rather more straggling, *it was extraordinarily like the writing on the anonymous letters.*

New ideas flashed through my head. Had Mrs. Leidner conceivably written those letters *herself?* And did Dr. Leidner half suspect the fact?

CHAPTER X

SATURDAY AFTERNOON

Mrs. Leidner told me her story on Friday. On Saturday morning there was a feeling of slight anticlimax in the air.

Mrs. Leidner, in particular, was inclined to be very offhand with me and rather pointedly avoided any possibility of a tête-à-tête. Well, *that* didn't surprise me! I've had the same thing happen to me again and again. Ladies tell their nurses things in a sudden burst of confidence and then afterward they feel uncomfortable about it and wish they hadn't! It's only human nature.

I was very careful not to hint or remind her in any way of what she had told me. I purposely kept my conversation as matter-of-fact as possible.

Mr. Coleman had started in to Hassanieh in the morning, driving himself in the lorry with the letters in a knapsack. He also had one or two commissions to do for the members of the expedition. It was pay day for the men, and he would have to go to the bank and bring out the money in coins of small denominations. All this was a long business and he did not expect to be back until the afternoon. I rather suspected he might be lunching with Sheila Reilly.

Work on the dig was usually not very busy on the afternoon of pay day as at three-thirty the paying-out began.

The little boy, Abdullah, whose business it was to wash pots, was established as usual in the center of the courtyard, and again as usual, kept up his queer nasal chant. Dr. Leidner and Mr. Emmott were going to put in some work on the pottery until Mr. Coleman returned, and Mr. Carey went up to the dig.

Mrs. Leidner went to her room to rest. I settled her as usual and then went to my own room, taking a book with me as I did not feel sleepy. It was then about a quarter to one, and a couple of hours passed quite pleasantly. I was reading *Death in a Nursing Home*—really a most exciting story —though I don't think the author knew much about the way nursing homes are run! At any rate I've never known a nursing home like that! I really felt inclined to write to the author and put him right about a few points.

When I put the book down at last (it was the red-haired parlormaid and I'd never suspected her once!) and looked at my watch I was quite surprised to find it was twenty minutes to three!

I got up, straightened my uniform, and came out into the courtyard.

Abdullah was still scrubbing and still singing his depressing chant, and David Emmott was standing by him sorting the scrubbed pots, and putting the ones that were broken into boxes to await mending. I strolled over toward them just as Dr. Leidner came down the staircase from the roof.

"Not a bad afternoon," he said cheerfully. "I've made a bit of a clearance up there. Louise will be pleased. She's complained lately that there's not room to walk about. I'll go and tell her the good news."

He went over to his wife's door, tapped on it, and went in.

It must, I suppose, have been about a minute and a half later that he came out again. I happened to be looking at the door when he did so. It was like a nightmare. He had gone in a brisk, cheerful man. He came out like a drunken one—reeling a little on his feet, and with a queer dazed expression on his face.

"Nurse—" he called in a queer, hoarse voice. "Nurse—"

I saw at once something was wrong, and I ran across to him. He looked awful—his face was all gray and twitching, and I saw he might collapse any minute.

"My wife—" he said. "My wife— Oh, my God!"

I pushed past him into the room. Then I caught my breath.

Mrs. Leidner was lying in a dreadful huddled heap by the bed.

I bent over her. She was quite dead—must have been dead an hour at least. The cause of death was perfectly plain—a terrific blow on the front of the head just over the right temple. She must have got up from the bed and been struck down where she stood.

I didn't handle her more than I could help.

I glanced round the room to see if there was anything that might give a clue, but nothing seemed out of place or disturbed. The windows were closed and fastened, and there was no place where the murderer could have hidden. Obviously he had been and gone long ago.

I went out, closing the door behind me.

Dr. Leidner had collapsed completely now. David Emmott was with him and turned a white, inquiring face to me.

In a few low words I told him what had happened.

As I had always suspected, he was a first-class person to rely on in trouble. He was perfectly calm and self-possessed. Those blue eyes of his opened very wide, but otherwise he gave no sign at all.

He considered for a moment and then said, "I suppose we must notify the police as soon as possible. Bill ought to be back any minute. What shall we do with Leidner?"

"Help me to get him into his room."

He nodded.

"Better lock this door first, I suppose," he said.

He turned the key in the lock of Mrs. Leidner's door, then drew it out and handed it to me.

"I guess you'd better keep this, nurse. Now, then."

Together we lifted Dr. Leidner and carried him into his own room and laid him on his bed. Mr. Emmott went off in search of brandy. He returned, accompanied by Miss Johnson.

Her face was drawn and anxious, but she was calm and capable, and I felt satisfied to leave Dr. Leidner in her charge.

I hurried out into the courtyard. The station wagon was just coming in through the archway. I think it gave us all a shock to see Bill's pink, cheerful face as he jumped out with his familiar "Hallo, 'allo, 'allo! Here's the oof!" He went on gaily, "No highway robberies—"

He came to a halt suddenly. "I say, is anything up? What's the matter with you all? You look as though the cat had killed your canary."

Mr. Emmott said shortly, "Mrs. Leidner's dead—killed."

"What?" Bill's jolly face changed ludicrously. He stared, his eyes goggling. "Mother Leidner dead! You're pulling my leg."

"Dead?" It was a sharp cry. I turned to see Mrs. Mercado behind me. "Did you say Mrs. Leidner had been *killed?"*

"Yes," I said. "Murdered."

"No!" she gasped. "Oh, no! I won't believe it. Perhaps she's committed suicide."

"Suicides don't hit themselves on the head," I said dryly. "It's murder, all right, Mrs. Mercado."

She sat down suddenly on an upturned packing-case.

She said, "Oh, but this is horrible—*horrible."*

Naturally it was horrible. We didn't need *her* to tell us so! I wondered if perhaps she was feeling a bit remorseful for the harsh feelings she had harbored against the dead woman, and all the spiteful things she had said.

After a minute or two she asked rather breathlessly, "What are you going to do?"

Mr. Emmott took charge in his quiet way.

"Bill, you'd better get in again to Hassanieh as quick as you can. I don't know much about the proper procedure. Better get hold of Captain Maitland, he's in charge of the police here, I think. Get Doctor Reilly first. He'll know what to do."

Mr. Coleman nodded. All the facetiousness was knocked out of him. He just looked young and frightened. Without a word he jumped into the station wagon and drove off.

Mr. Emmott said rather uncertainly, "I suppose we ought to have a hunt round." He raised his voice and called, "Ibrahim!"

"Na'am."

The houseboy came running. Mr. Emmott spoke to him in Arabic. A vigorous colloquy passed between them. The boy seemed to be emphatically denying something.

At last Mr. Emmott said in a perplexed voice, "He says there's not been a soul here this afternoon. No stranger of any kind. I suppose the fellow must have slipped in without their seeing him."

"Of course he did," said Mrs. Mercado. "He slunk in when the boys weren't looking."

"Yes," said Mr. Emmott.

The slight uncertainty in his voice made me look at him inquiringly.

He turned and spoke to the little pot boy, Abdullah, asking him a question.

The boy replied vehemently at length.

The puzzled frown on Mr. Emmott's brow increased.

"I don't understand it," he murmured under his breath. "I don't understand it at all."

But he didn't tell me what he didn't understand.

CHAPTER XI

AN ODD BUSINESS

I'm adhering as far as possible to telling only my personal part in the business. I pass over the events of the next two hours, the arrival of Captain Maitland and the police and Dr. Reilly. There was a good deal of general confusion, questioning, all the routine business, I suppose.

In my opinion we began to get down to brass tacks about five o'clock when Dr. Reilly asked me to come with him into the office.

He shut the door, sat down in Dr. Leidner's chair, motioned me to sit down opposite him, and said briskly, "Now, then, nurse, let's get down to it. There's something damned odd here."

I settled my cuffs and looked at him inquiringly.

He drew out a notebook.

"This is for my own satisfaction. Now, what time was it exactly when Doctor Leidner found his wife's body?"

"I should say it was almost exactly a quarter to three," I said.

"And how do you know that?"

"Well, I looked at my watch when I got up. It was twenty to three then."

"Let's have a look at this watch of yours."

I slipped it off my wrist and held it out to him.

"Right to the minute. Excellent woman. Good, that's *that* fixed. Now did you form any opinion as to how long she'd been dead?"

"Oh, really, doctor," I said, "I shouldn't like to say."

"Don't be so professional. I want to see if your estimate agrees with mine."

"Well, I should say she'd been dead at least an hour."

"Quite so. I examined the body at half past four and I'm inclined to put the time of death between one-fifteen and one forty-five. We'll say half past one at a guess. That's near enough."

He stopped and drummed thoughtfully with his fingers on the table.

"Damned odd, this business," he said. "Can you tell me about it—you were resting, you say? Did you hear anything?"

"At half past one? No, doctor. I didn't hear anything at half past one or at any other time. I lay on my bed from a quarter to one until twenty to three and I didn't hear anything except that droning noise the Arab boy makes, and occasionally Mr. Emmott shouting up to Doctor Leidner on the roof."

"The Arab boy—yes."

He frowned.

At that moment the door opened and Dr. Leidner and Captain Maitland came in. Captain Maitland was a fussy little man with a pair of shrewd gray eyes.

Dr. Reilly rose and pushed Dr. Leidner into his chair.

"Sit down, man. I'm glad you've come. We shall want you. There's something very queer about this business."

Dr. Leidner bowed his head.

"I know." He looked at me. "My wife confided the truth to Nurse Leatheran. We mustn't keep anything back at this juncture, nurse, so please tell Captain Maitland and Doctor Reilly just what passed between you and my wife yesterday."

As nearly as possible I gave our conversation verbatim.

Captain Maitland uttered an occasional ejaculation. When I had finished he turned to Dr. Leidner.

"And this is all true, Leidner—eh?"

"Every word Nurse Leatheran has told you is correct."

"What an extraordinary story," said Dr. Reilly. "You can produce these letters?"

"I have no doubt they will be found among my wife's belongings."

"She took them out of the attaché case on her table," I said.

"Then they are probably still there."

He turned to Captain Maitland and his usually gentle face grew hard and stern.

"There must be no question of hushing this story up, Captain Maitland. The one thing necessary is for this man to be caught and punished."

"You believe it actually is Mrs. Leidner's former husband?" I asked.

"Don't you think so, nurse?" asked Captain Maitland.

"Well, I think it is open to doubt," I said hesitatingly.

"In any case," said Dr. Leidner, "the man is a murderer—and I should say a dangerous lunatic, also. He *must* be found, Captain Maitland. He must. It should not be difficult."

Dr. Reilly said slowly, "It may be more difficult than you think, eh, Maitland?"

Captain Maitland tugged at his mustache without replying.

Suddenly I gave a start.

"Excuse me," I said, "but there's something perhaps I ought to mention."

I told my story of the Iraqi we had seen trying to peer through the window, and of how I had seen him hanging about the place two days ago trying to pump Father Lavigny.

"Good," said Captain Maitland, "we'll make a note of that. It will be something for the police to go on. The man may have some connection with the case."

"Probably paid to act as a spy," I suggested. "To find out when the coast was clear."

Dr. Reilly rubbed his nose with a harassed gesture.

"That's the devil of it," he said. "Supposing the coast wasn't clear—eh?"

I stared at him in a puzzled fashion.

Captain Maitland turned to Dr. Leidner.

"I want you to listen to me very carefully, Leidner. This is a review of the evidence we've got up to date. After lunch, which was served at twelve o'clock and was over by five and twenty to one, your wife went to her room accompanied by Nurse Leatheran, who settled her comfortably. You yourself went up to the roof, where you spent the next two hours, is that right?"

"Yes."

"Did you come down from the roof at all during that time?"

"No."

"Did anyone come up to you?"

"Yes, Emmott did pretty frequently. He went to and fro between me and the boy, who was washing pottery down below."

"Did you yourself look over into the courtyard at all?"

"Once or twice—usually to call to Emmott about something."

"On each occasion the boy was sitting in the middle of the courtyard washing pots?"

"Yes."

"What was the longest period of time when Emmott was with you and absent from the courtyard?"

Dr. Leidner considered.

"It's difficult to say—perhaps ten minutes. Personally I should say two or three minutes, but I know by experience that my sense of time is not very good when I am absorbed and interested in what I am doing."

Captain Maitland looked at Dr. Reilly. The latter nodded. "We'd better get down to it," he said.

Captain Maitland took out a small notebook and opened it.

"Look here, Leidner, I'm going to read to you exactly what every member of your expedition was doing between one and two this afternoon."

"But surely—"

"Wait. You'll see what I'm driving at in a minute. First Mr. and Mrs. Mercado. Mr. Mercado says he was working in his laboratory. Mrs. Mercado says she was in her bedroom shampooing her hair. Miss Johnson says she was in the living-room taking impressions of cylinder seals. Mr. Reiter says he was in the darkroom developing plates. Father Lavigny says he was working in his bedroom. As to the two remaining members of the expedition, Carey and Coleman, the former was up on the dig and Coleman was in Hassanieh. So much for the members of the expedition. Now for the servants. The cook—your Indian chap—was sitting immediately outside the archway chatting to the guard and plucking a couple of fowls. Ibrahim and Mansur, the houseboys, joined him there at about one-fifteen. They both remained there laughing and talking until two-thirty—*by which time your wife was already dead.*"

Dr. Leidner leaned forward.

"I don't understand—you puzzle me. What are you hinting at?"

"Is there any means of access to your wife's room except by the door into the courtyard?"

"No. There are two windows, but they are heavily barred—and besides, I think they were shut."

He looked at me questioningly.

"They were closed and latched on the inside," I said promptly.

"In any case," said Captain Maitland, "even if they had been open, no one could have entered or left the room that way. My fellows and I have assured ourselves of that. It is the same with all the other windows giving on the open country. They all have iron bars and all the bars are in good condition. To have got into your wife's room, a stranger *must* have come through the arched doorway into the courtyard. But we have the united assurances of the guard, the cook, and the houseboys that *nobody did so.*"

Dr. Leidner sprang up.

"What do you mean? What do you mean?"

"Pull yourself together, man," said Dr. Reilly quietly. "I know it's a shock, but it's got to be faced. *The murderer didn't come from outside*—so he must have come from *inside.* It looks as though Mrs. Leidner must have been murdered *by a member of your own expedition.*"

CHAPTER XII

"I DIDN'T BELIEVE . . ."

"No. No!"

Dr. Leidner sprang up and walked up and down in an agitated manner.

"It's impossible what you say, Reilly. Absolutely impossible. One of *us?* Why, every single member of the expedition was devoted to Louise!"

A queer little expression pulled down the corners of Dr. Reilly's mouth. Under the circumstances it was difficult for him to say anything, but if ever a man's silence was eloquent his was at that minute.

"Quite impossible," reiterated Dr. Leidner. "They were all devoted to her. Louise had such wonderful charm. Everyone felt it."

Dr. Reilly coughed.

"Excuse me, Leidner, but after all that's only your opinion. If any member of the expedition had disliked your wife they would naturally not advertise the fact to you."

Dr. Leidner looked distressed.

"True—quite true. But all the same, Reilly, I think you are wrong. I'm sure everyone was fond of Louise." He was silent for a moment or two and then burst out, "This idea of yours is infamous. "It's—it's frankly incredible."

"You can't get away from—er—the facts," said Captain Maitland.

"Facts? Facts? Lies told by an Indian cook and a couple of Arab houseboys. You know these fellows as well as I do, Reilly; so do you, Maitland. Truth as truth means nothing to them. They say what you want them to say as a mere matter of politeness."

"In this case," said Dr. Reilly dryly, "they are saying what we *don't* want them to say. Besides, I know the habits of your household fairly well. Just outside the gate is a kind of social club. Whenever I've been over here in the afternoon I've always found most of your staff there. It's the natural place for them to be."

"All the same I think you are assuming too much. Why shouldn't this man—this devil—have got in earlier and concealed himself somewhere?"

"I agree that that is not actually impossible," said Dr. Reilly coolly. "Let us assume that a stranger *did* somehow gain admission unseen. He would have to remain concealed until the right moment (and he certainly couldn't have done so in Mrs. Leidner's room, there is no cover there) and take the risk of being seen entering the room and leaving it—with Emmott and the boy in the courtyard most of the time."

"The boy. I'd forgotten the boy," said Dr. Leidner. "A sharp little chap. But surely, Maitland, the boy *must* have seen the murderer go into my wife's room?"

"We've elucidated that. The boy was washing pots the whole afternoon with one exception. Somewhere around half past one—Emmott can't put it closer than that—he went up to the roof and was with you for ten minutes —that's right, isn't it?"

"Yes. I couldn't have told you the exact time but it must have been about that."

"Very good. Well, during that ten minutes, the boy, seizing his chance to be idle, strolled out and joined the others outside the gate for a chat. When Emmott came down he found the boy absent and called him angrily, asking him what he meant by leaving his work. As far as I can see, *your wife must have been murdered during that ten minutes."*

With a groan, Dr. Leidner sat down and hid his face in his hands.

Dr. Reilly took up the tale, his voice quiet and matter-of-fact.

"The time fits in with my evidence," he said. "She'd been dead about three hours when I examined her. The only question is—who did it?"

There was a silence. Dr. Leidner sat up in his chair and passed a hand over his forehead.

"I admit the force of your reasoning, Reilly," he said quietly. "It certainly *seems* as though it were what people call 'an inside job.' But I feel convinced that somewhere or other there is a mistake. It's plausible but there must be a flaw in it. To begin with, you are assuming that an amazing coincidence has occurred."

"Odd that you should use that word," said Dr. Reilly.

Without paying any attention Dr. Leidner went on. "My wife receives threatening letters. She has reason to fear a certain person. Then she is—killed. And you ask me to believe that she is killed—not by that person—but by someone entirely different! I say that that is ridiculous."

"It seems so—yes," said Dr. Reilly meditatively.

He looked at Captain Maitland. "Coincidence—eh? What do you say, Maitland? Are you in favor of the idea? Shall we put it up to Leidner?"

Captain Maitland gave a nod.

"Go ahead," he said shortly.

"Have you ever heard of a man called Hercule Poirot, Leidner?"

Dr. Leidner stared at him, puzzled.

"I think I have heard the name, yes," he said vaguely. "I once heard a Mr. Van Aldin speak of him in very high terms. He is a private detective, is he not?"

"That's the man."

"But surely he lives in London, so how will that help us?"

"He lives in London, true," said Dr. Reilly, "but this is where the coincidence comes in. He is now, not in London, but in Syria, and *he will actually pass through Hassanieh on his way to Baghdad tomorrow!*"

"Who told you this?"

"Jean Berat, the French consul. He dined with us last night and was talking about him. It seems he has been disentangling some military scandal in Syria. He's coming through here to visit Baghdad, and afterward returning through Syria to London. How's that for a coincidence?"

Dr. Leidner hesitated a moment and looked apologetically at Captain Maitland.

"What do you think, Captain Maitland?"

"Should welcome co-operation," said Captain Maitland promptly. "My fellows are good scouts at scouring the countryside and investigating Arab blood feuds, but frankly, Leidner, this business of your wife's seems to me rather out of my class. The whole thing looks confoundedly fishy. I'm more than willing to have the fellow take a look at the case."

"You suggest that I should appeal to this man Poirot to help us?" said Dr. Leidner. "And suppose he refuses?"

"He won't refuse," said Dr. Reilly.

"How do you know?"

"Because I'm a professional man myself. If a really intricate case of say—cerebrospinal meningitis came my way and I'm invited to take a hand, I shouldn't be able to refuse. This isn't an ordinary crime, Leidner."

"No," said Dr. Leidner. His lips twitched with sudden pain.

"Will you, then, Reilly, approach this Hercule Poirot on my behalf?"

"I will."

Dr. Leidner made a gesture of thanks.

"Even now," he said slowly, "I can't realize it—that Louise is really dead."

I could bear it no longer.

"Oh! Doctor Leidner," I burst out. "I—I can't tell you how badly I feel about this. I've failed so badly in my duty. It was my job to watch over Mrs. Leidner—to keep her from harm."

Dr. Leidner shook his head gravely.

"No, no, nurse, you've nothing to reproach yourself with," he said slowly. "It's *I,* God forgive me, who am to blame. *I didn't believe*—all along I didn't believe— I didn't dream for one moment that there was any *real* danger." He got up. His face twitched. *"I let her go to her death.* Yes, I let her go to her death—*not believing—"*

He staggered out of the room.

Dr. Reilly looked at me.

"I feel pretty culpable, too," he said. "I thought the good lady was playing on his nerves."

"I didn't take it really seriously, either," I confessed.

"We were all three wrong," said Dr. Reilly gravely.

"So it seems," said Captain Maitland.

CHAPTER XIII

HERCULE POIROT ARRIVES

I don't think I shall ever forget my first sight of Hercule Poirot. Of course, I got used to him later on, but to begin with it was a shock, and I think everyone else must have felt the same!

I don't know what I'd imagined—something rather like Sherlock Holmes—long and lean with a keen, clever face. Of course, I knew he was a foreigner, but I hadn't expected him to be *quite* as foreign as he was, if you know what I mean.

When you saw him you just wanted to laugh! He was like something on the stage or at the pictures. To begin with, he wasn't above five foot five, I should think—an odd, plump little man, quite old, with an enormous mustache, and a head like an egg. He looked like a hairdresser in a comic play!

And this was the man who was going to find out who killed Mrs. Leidner!

I suppose something of my disgust must have shown in my face, for almost straightaway he said to me with a queer kind of twinkle, "You disapprove of me, *ma soeur?* Remember, the pudding proves itself only when you eat it."

The proof of the pudding's in the eating, I *suppose* he meant.

Well, that's a true enough saying, but I couldn't say I felt much confidence myself!

Dr. Reilly brought him out in his car soon after lunch on Sunday, and his first procedure was to ask us all to assemble together.

We did so in the dining-room, all sitting round the table. Mr. Poirot sat at the head of it with Dr. Leidner one side and Dr. Reilly the other.

When we were all assembled, Dr. Leidner cleared his throat and spoke in his gentle, hesitating voice.

"I dare say you have all heard of M. Hercule Poirot. He was passing through Hassanieh today, and has very kindly agreed to break his journey to help us. The Iraq police and Captain Maitland are, I am sure, doing their very best, but—but there are circumstances in the case"—he floundered and shot an appealing glance at Dr. Reilly—"there may, it seems, be difficulties."

"It is not all the square and overboard—no?" said the little man at the top of the table. Why, he couldn't even speak English properly!

"Oh, he *must* be caught!" cried Mrs. Mercado. "It would be unbearable if he got away!"

I noticed the little foreigner's eyes rest on her appraisingly.

"He? Who is *he,* madame?" he asked.

"Why, the murderer, of course."

"Ah! The murderer," said Hercule Poirot.

He spoke as though the murderer was of no consequence at all!

We all stared at him. He looked from one face to another.

"It is likely, I think," he said, "that you have none of you been brought in contact with a case of murder before?"

There was a general murmur of assent.

Hercule Poirot smiled.

"It is clear, therefore, that you do not understand the A.B.C. of the position. There are unpleasantnesses! Yes, there are a lot of unpleasantnesses. To begin with, there is *suspicion."*

"Suspicion?"

It was Miss Johnson who spoke. Mr. Poirot looked at her thoughtfully. I had an idea that he regarded her with approval. He looked as though he were thinking, "Here is a sensible, intelligent person!"

"Yes, mademoiselle," he said. "Suspicion! Let us not make the bones about it. *You are all under suspicion here in this house.* The cook, the houseboy, the scullion, the pot boy—yes, and all the members of the expedition, too."

Mrs. Mercado started up, her face working.

"How *dare* you? How dare you say such a thing! This is odious—unbearable! Doctor Leidner—you can't sit here and let this man—and let this man—"

Dr. Leidner said wearily, "Please try and be calm, Marie."

Mr. Mercado stood up, too. His hands were shaking and his eyes were bloodshot.

"I agree. It is an outrage—an insult—"

"No, no," said Mr. Poirot. "I do not insult you. I merely ask you all to face facts. *In a house where murder has been committed, every inmate comes in for a certain share of suspicion.* I ask you what evidence is there that the murderer came from outside at all?"

Mrs. Mercado cried, "But of course he did! It stands to reason! Why—" She stopped and said more slowly, "Anything else would be incredible!"

"You are doubtless correct, madame," said Poirot with a bow. "I explain to you only how the matter must be approached. First I assure myself of the fact that everyone in this room is innocent. After that I seek the murderer elsewhere."

"Is it not possible that that may be a little late in the day?" asked Father Lavigny suavely.

"The tortoise, *mon père,* overtook the hare."

Father Lavigny shrugged his shoulders.

"We are in your hands," he said resignedly. "Convince yourself as soon as may be of our innocence in this terrible business."

"As rapidly as possible. It was my duty to make the position clear to you, so that you may not resent the impertinence of any questions I may have to ask. Perhaps, *mon père,* the Church will set an example?"

"Ask any questions you please of me," said Father Lavigny gravely.

"This is your first season out here?"

"Yes."

"And you arrived—when?"

"Three weeks ago almost to a day. That is, on the twenty-seventh of February."

"Coming from?"

"The Order of the *Pères Blancs* at Carthage."

"Thank you, *mon père.* Were you at any time acquainted with Mrs. Leidner before coming here?"

"No, I had never seen the lady until I met her here."

"Will you tell me what you were doing at the time of the tragedy?"

"I was working on some cuneiform tablets in my own room."

I noticed that Poirot had at his elbow a rough plan of the building.

"That is the room at the southwest corner corresponding to that of Mrs. Leidner on the opposite side?"

"Yes."

"At what time did you go to your room?"

"Immediately after lunch. I should say at about twenty minutes to one."

"And you remained there until—when?"

"Just before three o'clock. I had heard the station wagon come back—and then I heard it drive off again. I wondered why, and came out to see."

"During the time that you were there did you leave the room at all?"

"No, not once."

"And you heard or saw nothing that might have any bearing on the tragedy?"

"No."

"You have no window giving on the courtyard in your room?"

"No, both the windows give on the countryside."

"Could you hear at all what was happening in the courtyard?"

"Not very much. I heard Mr. Emmott passing my room and going up to the roof. He did so once or twice."

"Can you remember at what time?"

"No, I'm afraid I can't. I was engrossed in my work, you see."

There was a pause and then Poirot said, "Can you say or suggest anything at all that might throw light on this business? Did you, for instance, notice anything in the days preceding the murder?"

Father Lavigny looked slightly uncomfortable. He shot a half-questioning look at Dr. Leidner.

"That is rather a difficult question, monsieur," he said gravely. "If you ask me, I must reply frankly that in my opinion Mrs. Leidner was clearly in dread of someone or something. She was definitely nervous about strangers. I imagine she had a reason for this nervousness of hers—but I *know* nothing. She did not confide in me."

Poirot cleared his throat and consulted some notes that he held in his hand.

"Two nights ago I understand there was a scare of burglary."

Father Lavigny replied in the affirmative and retailed his story of the light seen in the antika room and the subsequent futile search.

"You believe, do you not, that some unauthorized person was on the premises at that time?"

"I don't know what to think," said Father Lavigny frankly. "Nothing was taken or disturbed in any way. It might have been one of the houseboys—"

"Or a member of the expedition?"

"Or a member of the expedition. But in that case there would be no reason for the person not admitting the fact."

"But it *might* equally have been a stranger from outside?"

"I suppose so."

"Supposing a stranger *had* been on the premises, could he have concealed himself successfully during the following day and until the afternoon of the day following that?"

He asked the question half of Father Lavigny and half of Dr. Leidner. Both men considered the question carefully.

"I hardly think it would be possible," said Dr. Leidner at last with some reluctance. "I don't see where he could possibly conceal himself, do you, Father Lavigny?"

"No—no—I don't."

Both men seemed reluctant to put the suggestion aside.

Poirot turned to Miss Johnson.

"And you, mademoiselle? Do you consider such a hypothesis feasible?"

After a moment's thought Miss Johnson shook her head.

"No," she said. "I don't. Where could anyone hide? The bedrooms are all in use and, in any case, are sparsely furnished. The darkroom, the drawing-office, and the laboratory were all in use the next day—so were all these rooms. There are no cupboards or corners. Perhaps, if the servants were in collusion—"

"That is possible, but unlikely," said Poirot.

He turned once more to Father Lavigny.

"There is another point. The other day Nurse Leatheran here noticed you talking to a man outside. She had previously noticed that same man trying to peer in at one of the windows on the outside. It rather looks as though the man were hanging round the place deliberately."

"That is possible, of course," said Father Lavigny thoughtfully.

"Did you speak to this man first, or did he speak to you?"

Father Lavigny considered for a moment or two.

"I believe—yes, I am sure, that he spoke to me."

"What did he say?"

Father Lavigny made an effort of memory.

"He said, I think, something to the effect was this the American expedition house? And then something else about the Americans employing a lot of men on the work. I did not really understand him very well, but I endeavored to keep up a conversation so as to improve my Arabic. I thought, perhaps, that being a townee he would understand me better than the men on the dig do."

"Did you converse about anything else?"

"As far as I remember, I said Hassanieh was a big town—and we then agreed that Baghdad was bigger—and I think he asked whether I was an Armenian or a Syrian Catholic—something of that kind."

Poirot nodded.

"Can you describe him?"

Again Father Lavigny frowned in thought.

"He was rather a short man," he said at last, "and squarely built. He had a very noticeable squint and was of fair complexion."

Mr. Poirot turned to me.

"Does that agree with the way you would describe him?" he asked.

"Not exactly," I said hesitatingly. "I should have said he was tall rather than short, and very dark-complexioned. He seemed to me of a rather slender build. I didn't notice any squint."

Mr. Poirot gave a despairing shrug of the shoulders.

"It is always so! If you were of the police how well you would know it! The description of the same man by two different people—never does it agree. Every detail is contradicted."

"I'm fairly sure about the squint," said Father Lavigny. "Nurse Leatheran may be right about the other points. By the way, when I said *fair,* I only meant fair for an Iraqi. I expect nurse would call that dark."

"Very dark," I said obstinately. "A dirty dark-yellow color."

I saw Dr. Reilly bite his lip and smile. Poirot threw up his hands.

"Passons!" he said. "This stranger hanging about, he may be important—he may not. At any rate he must be found. Let us continue our inquiry."

He hesitated for a minute, studying the faces turned toward him round the table, then, with a quick nod, he singled out Mr. Reiter.

"Come, my friend," he said. "Let us have your account of yesterday afternoon."

Mr. Reiter's pink, plump face flushed scarlet.

"Me?" he said.

"Yes, you. To begin with, your name and your age?"

"Carl Reiter, twenty-eight."

"American—yes?"

"Yes, I come from Chicago."

"This is your first season?"

"Yes. I'm in charge of the photography."

"Ah, yes. And yesterday afternoon, how did you employ yourself?"

"Well—I was in the darkroom most of the time."

"Most of the time—eh?"

"Yes. I developed some plates first. Afterward I was fixing up some objects to photograph."

"Outside?"

"Oh, no, in the photographic room."

"The darkroom opens out of the photographic room?"

"Yes."

"And so you never came outside the photographic room?"

"No."

"Did you notice anything that went on in the courtyard?"

The young man shook his head.

"I wasn't noticing anything," he explained. "I was busy. I heard the car come back, and as soon as I could leave what I was doing I came out to see if there was any mail. It was then that I—heard."

"And you began your work in the photographic room—when?"

"At ten minutes to one."

"Were you acquainted with Mrs. Leidner before you joined this expedition?"

The young man shook his head.

"No, sir. I never saw her till I actually got here."

"Can you think of *anything*—any incident—however small—that might help us?"

Carl Reiter shook his head.

He said helplessly, "I guess I don't know anything at all, sir."

"Mr. Emmott?"

David Emmott spoke clearly and concisely in his pleasant soft American voice. "I was working with the pottery from a quarter to one till a quarter to three—overseeing the boy Abdullah, sorting it, and occasionally going up to the roof to help Doctor Leidner."

"How often did you go up to the roof?"

"Four times, I think."

"For how long?"

"Usually a couple of minutes—not more. But on one occasion after I'd been working a little over half an hour I stayed as long as ten minutes—discussing what to keep and what to fling away."

"And I understand that when you came down you found the boy had left his place?"

"Yes. I called him angrily and he reappeared from outside the archway. He had gone out to gossip with the others."

"That was the only time he left his work?"

"Well, I sent him up once or twice to the roof with pottery."

Poirot said gravely, "It is hardly necessary to ask you, Mr. Emmott, whether you saw anyone enter or leave Mrs. Leidner's room during that time?"

Mr. Emmott replied promptly. "I saw no one at all. Nobody even came out into the courtyard during the two hours I was working."

"And to the best of your belief it was half past one when both you and the boy were absent and the courtyard was empty?"

"It couldn't have been far off that time. Of course, I can't say *exactly.*"

Poirot turned to Dr. Reilly.

"That agrees with your estimate of the time of death, doctor?"

"It does," said Dr. Reilly.

Mr. Poirot stroked his great curled mustaches.

"I think we can take it," he said gravely, "that Mrs. Leidner met her death during that ten minutes."

CHAPTER XIV

ONE OF US?

There was a little pause—and in it a wave of horror seemed to float round the room.

I think it was at that moment that I first believed Dr. Reilly's theory to be right.

I *felt* that the murderer was in the room. Sitting with us—listening. *One of us.*

Perhaps Mrs. Mercado felt it, too. For she suddenly gave a short sharp cry.

"I can't help it," she sobbed. "I—it's so *terrible!*"

"Courage, Marie," said her husband.

He looked at us apologetically.

"She is so sensitive. She feels things so much."

"I—I was so fond of Louise," sobbed Mrs. Mercado.

I don't know whether something of what I felt showed in my face, but I suddenly found that Mr. Poirot was looking at me, and that a slight smile hovered on his lips.

I gave him a cold glance, and at once he resumed his inquiry.

"Tell me, madame," he said, "of the way you spent yesterday afternoon?"

"I was washing my hair," sobbed Mrs. Mercado. "It seems awful not to have known anything about it. I was quite happy and busy."

"You were in your room?"

"Yes."

"And you did not leave it?"

"No. Not till I heard the car. Then I came out and I heard what had happened. Oh, it was *awful!*"

"Did it surprise you?"

Mrs. Mercado stopped crying. Her eyes opened resentfully.

"What do you mean, M. Poirot? Are you suggesting—"

"What should I mean, madame? You have just told us how fond you were of Mrs. Leidner. She might, perhaps, have confided in you."

"Oh, I see. No—no, dear Louise never told me anything—anything *definite,* that is. Of course, I could see she was terribly worried and nervous. And there were those strange occurrences—hands tapping on the window and all that."

"Fancies, I remember you said," I put in, unable to keep silent.

I was glad to see that she looked momentarily disconcerted.

Once again I was conscious of Mr. Poirot's amused eye glancing in my direction.

He summed up in a businesslike way.

"It comes to this, madame, you were washing your hair—you heard nothing and you saw nothing. Is there anything at all you can think of that would be a help to us in any way?"

Mrs. Mercado took no time to think.

"No, indeed there isn't. It's the deepest mystery! But I should say there is no doubt—no doubt *at all* that the murderer came from outside. Why, it stands to reason."

Poirot turned to her husband.

"And you, monsieur, what have you to say?"

Mr. Mercado started nervously. He pulled at his beard in an aimless fashion.

"Must have been. Must have been," he said. "Yet how could anyone wish to harm her? She was so gentle—so kind—" He shook his head. "Whoever killed her must have been a fiend—yes, a fiend!"

"And you yourself, monsieur, how did you pass yesterday afternoon?"

"I?" He stared vaguely.

"You were in the laboratory, Joseph," his wife prompted him.

"Ah, yes, so I was—so I was. My usual tasks."

"At what time did you go there?"

Again he looked helplessly and inquiringly at Mrs. Mercado.

"At ten minutes to one, Joseph."

"Ah, yes, at ten minutes to one."

"Did you come out in the courtyard at all?"

"No—I don't think so." He considered. "No, I am sure I didn't."

"When did you hear of the tragedy?"

"My wife came and told me. It was terrible—shocking. I could hardly believe it. Even now I can hardly believe it is true." Suddenly he began to tremble. "It is horrible—horrible."

Mrs. Mercado came quickly to his side.

"Yes, yes, Joseph, we all feel that. But we mustn't give way. It makes it so much more difficult for poor Doctor Leidner."

I saw a spasm of pain pass across Dr. Leidner's face, and I guessed that this emotional atmosphere was not easy for him. He gave a half-glance at Poirot as though in appeal. Poirot responded quickly.

"Miss Johnson?" he said.

"I'm afraid I can tell you very little," said Miss Johnson. Her cultured, well-bred voice was soothing after Mrs. Mercado's shrill treble. She went on. "I was working in the living-room—taking impressions of some cylinder seals on plasticine."

"And you saw or noticed nothing?"

"No."

Poirot gave her a quick glance. His ear had caught what mine had—a faint note of indecision.

"Are you quite sure, mademoiselle? Is there something that comes back to you vaguely?"

"No—not really—"

"Something you saw, shall we say, out of the corner of your eye hardly knowing you saw it?"

"No, certainly not," she replied positively.

"Something you *heard,* then. Ah, yes, something you are not quite sure whether you heard or not?"

Miss Johnson gave a short vexed laugh.

"You press me very closely, M. Poirot. I'm afraid you are encouraging me to tell you what I am, perhaps, only imagining."

"Then there *was* something you—shall we say—imagined?"

Miss Johnson said slowly, weighing her words in a detached way, "I have imagined—since—that at some time during the afternoon I heard a very faint cry. What I mean is that I dare say I *did* hear a cry. All the windows in the living-room were open and one hears all sorts of sounds from people working in the barley fields. But you see—since—I've got the idea into my head that it was—that it was Mrs. Leidner I heard. And that's made me rather unhappy. Because if I'd jumped up and run along to her room—well, who knows? I might have been in time—"

Dr. Reilly interposed authoritatively.

"Now, don't start getting that into your head," he said. "I've no doubt but that Mrs. Leidner (forgive me, Leidner) was struck down almost as soon as the man entered the room, and it was that blow that killed her. No second blow was struck. Otherwise she would have had time to call for help and make a real outcry."

"Still, I might have caught the murderer," said Miss Johnson.

"What time was this, mademoiselle?" asked Poirot. "In the neighborhood of half past one?"

"It must have been about that time—yes." She reflected a minute.

"That would fit in," said Poirot thoughtfully. "You heard nothing else—the opening or shutting of a door, for instance?"

Miss Johnson shook her head.

"No, I do not remember anything of that kind."

"You were sitting at a table, I presume. Which way were you facing? The courtyard? The antika room? The verandah? Or the open countryside?"

"I was facing the courtyard."

"Could you see the boy Abdullah washing pots from where you were?"

"Oh, yes, if I looked up, but of course, I was very intent on what I was doing. All my attention was on that."

"If anyone had passed the courtyard window, though, you would have noticed it?"

"Oh, yes, I am almost sure of that."

"And nobody did so?"

"No."

"But if anyone had walked, say, across the middle of the courtyard, would you have noticed that?"

"I think—probably not—unless, as I said before, I had happened to look up and out of the window."

"You did not notice the boy Abdullah leave his work and go out to join the other servants?"

"No."

"Ten minutes," mused Poirot. "That fatal ten minutes."

There was a momentary silence.

Miss Johnson lifted her head suddenly and said, "You know, M. Poirot, I think I have unintentionally misled you. On thinking it over, I do not believe that I could possibly have heard any cry uttered in Mrs. Leidner's room from where I was. The antika room lay between me and her—and I understand her windows were found closed."

"In any case, do not distress yourself, mademoiselle," said Poirot kindly. "It is not really of much importance."

"No, of course not. I understand that. But you see, it *is* of importance to me, because I feel I might have done something."

"Don't distress yourself, dear Anne," said Dr. Leidner with affection. "You must be sensible. What you heard was probably one Arab bawling to another some distance away in the fields."

Miss Johnson flushed a little at the kindliness of his tone. I even saw tears spring to her eyes. She turned her head away and spoke even more gruffly than usual.

"Probably was. Usual thing after a tragedy—start imagining things that aren't so at all."

Poirot was once more consulting his notebook.

"I do not suppose there is much more to be said. Mr. Carey?"

Richard Carey spoke slowly—in a wooden, mechanical manner.

"I'm afraid I can add nothing helpful. I was on duty at the dig. The news was brought to me there."

"And you know or can think of nothing helpful that occurred in the days immediately preceding the murder?"

"Nothing at all."

"Mr. Coleman?"

"I was right out of the whole thing," said Mr. Coleman with—was it just a shade of regret?—in his tone. "I went into Hassanieh yesterday morning to get the money for the men's wages. When I came back Emmott told me what had happened and I went back in the bus to get the police and Doctor Reilly."

"And beforehand?"

"Well, sir, things were a bit jumpy—but you know that already. There was the antika-room scare and one or two before that—hands and faces at the window—you remember, sir." He appealed to Dr. Leidner, who bent his head in assent. "I think, you know, that you'll find some Johnny *did* get in from outside. Must have been an artful sort of beggar."

Poirot considered him for a minute or two in silence.

"You are an Englishman, Mr. Coleman?" he asked at last.

"That's right, sir. All British. See the trademark. Guaranteed genuine."

"This is your first season?"

"Quite right."

"And you are passionately keen on archaeology?"

This description of himself seemed to cause Mr. Coleman some embarrassment. He got rather pink and shot the side look of a guilty schoolboy at Dr. Leidner.

"Of course—it's all very interesting," he stammered. "I mean—I'm not exactly a brainy chap—"

He broke off rather lamely. Poirot did not insist.

He tapped thoughtfully on the table with the end of his pencil and carefully straightened an inkpot that stood in front of him.

"It seems, then," he said, "that that is as near as we can get for the moment. If any one of you thinks of something that has for the time being slipped his or her memory do not hesitate to come to me with it. It will be well now, I think, for me to have a few words alone with Doctor Leidner and Doctor Reilly."

It was the signal for a breaking up of the party. We all rose and filed out of the door. When I was halfway out, however, a voice recalled me.

"Perhaps," said Mr. Poirot, "Nurse Leatheran will be so kind as to remain. I think her assistance will be valuable to us."

I came back and resumed my seat at the table.

CHAPTER XV

POIROT MAKES A SUGGESTION

Dr. Reilly had risen from his seat. When everyone had gone out he carefully closed the door. Then, with an inquiring glance at Poirot, he proceeded to shut the window giving on the courtyard. The others were already shut. Then he, too, resumed his seat at the table.

"Bien!" said Poirot. "We are now private and undisturbed. We can speak freely. We have heard what the members of the expedition have to tell us and— But yes, *ma soeur,* what is it that you think?"

I got rather red. There was no denying that the queer little man had sharp eyes. He'd seen the thought passing through my mind—I suppose my face *had* shown a bit too clearly what I was thinking!

"Oh, it's nothing—" I said, hesitating.

"Come on, nurse," said Dr. Reilly. "Don't keep the specialist waiting."

"It's nothing really," I said hurriedly. "It only just passed through my mind, so to speak, that perhaps even if anyone did know or suspect something it wouldn't be easy to bring it out in front of everybody else—or even, perhaps, in front of Doctor Leidner."

Rather to my astonishment, M. Poirot nodded his head in vigorous agreement.

"Precisely. Precisely. It is very just what you say there. But I will explain. That little reunion we have just had—it served a purpose. In England before the races you have a parade of the horses, do you not? They go in front of the grandstand so that everyone may have an opportunity of seeing and judging them. That is the purpose of my little assembly. In the sporting phrase, I run my eye over the possible starters."

Dr. Leidner cried out violently, "I do not believe for one minute that *any* member of my expedition is implicated in this crime!"

Then, turning to me, he said authoritatively, "Nurse, I should be much obliged if you would tell M. Poirot here and now exactly what passed between my wife and you two days ago."

Thus urged, I plunged straightaway into my story, trying as far as possible to recall the exact words and phrases Mrs. Leidner had used.

When I had finished, M. Poirot said, "Very good. Very good. You have the mind neat and orderly. You will be of great service to me here."

He turned to Dr. Leidner.

"You have these letters?"

"I have them here. I thought that you would want to see them first thing."

Poirot took them from him, read them, and scrutinized them carefully as he did so. I was rather disappointed that he didn't dust powder over them or examine them with a microscope or anything like that—but I realized that he wasn't a very young man and that his methods were probably not very up-to-date. He just read them in the way that anyone might read a letter.

Having read them, he put them down and cleared his throat.

"Now," he said, "let us proceed to get our facts clear and in order. The first of these letters was received by your wife shortly after her marriage to you in America. There had been others but these she destroyed. The first letter was followed by a second. A very short time after the second arrived you both had a near escape from coal-gas poisoning. You then came abroad and for nearly two years no further letters were received. They started again at the beginning of your season this year—that is to say, within the last three weeks. That is correct?"

"Absolutely."

"Your wife displayed every sign of panic and, after consulting Doctor Reilly, you engaged Nurse Leatheran here to keep your wife company and allay her fears?"

"Yes."

"Certain incidents occurred—hands tapping at the window—a spectral face—noises in the antika room. You did not witness any of these phenomena yourself?"

"No."

"In fact nobody did except Mrs. Leidner?"

"Father Lavigny saw a light in the antika room."

"Yes, I have not forgotten that." He was silent for a minute or two, then he said, "Had your wife made a will?"

"I do not think so."

"Why was that?"

"It did not seem worth it from her point of view."

"Is she not a wealthy woman?"

"Yes, during her lifetime. Her father left her a considerable sum of money in trust. She could not touch the principal. At her death it was to pass to any children she might have—and, failing children, to the Pittstown Museum."

Poirot drummed thoughtfully on the table.

"Then we can, I think," he said, "eliminate one motive from the case. It is, you comprehend, what I look for first. *Who benefits by the deceased's death?* In this case it is a museum. Had it been otherwise, had Mrs. Leidner died intestate but possessed of a considerable fortune, I should imagine that it would prove an interesting question as to who inherited the money—you—or a former husband. But there would have been this difficulty, the former husband would have had to resurrect himself in order to claim it, and I should imagine that he would then be in danger of arrest, though I hardly fancy that the death penalty would be exacted so long after the war. However, these speculations need not arise. As I say, I settle first the question of money. For the next step I proceed always to suspect the husband or wife of the deceased! In this case, in the first place, you are proved never to have gone near your wife's room yesterday afternoon, in the second place, you lose instead of gain by your wife's death, and in the third place—"

He paused.

"Yes?" said Dr. Leidner.

"In the third place," said Poirot slowly, "I can, I think, appreciate devotion when I see it. I believe, Doctor Leidner, that your love for your wife was the ruling passion of your life. It is so, is it not?"

Dr. Leidner answered quite simply, "Yes."

Poirot nodded.

"Therefore," he said, "we can proceed."

"Hear, hear, let's get down to it," said Dr. Reilly with some impatience.

Poirot gave him a reproving glance.

"My friend, do not be impatient. In a case like this everything must be approached with order and method. In fact, that is my rule in every case. Having disposed of certain possibilities, we now approach a very important point. It is vital that, as you say—all the cards should be on the table—there must be nothing kept back."

"Quite so," said Dr. Reilly.

"That is why I demand the whole truth," went on Poirot.

Dr. Leidner looked at him in surprise.

"I assure you, M. Poirot, that I have kept nothing back. I have told you everything that I know. There have been no reserves."

"Tout de même, you have not told me *everything."*

"Yes, indeed. I cannot think of any detail that has escaped me."

He looked quite distressed.

Poirot shook his head gently.

"No," he said. *"You have not told me, for instance, why you installed Nurse Leatheran in the house."*

Dr. Leidner looked completely bewildered.

"But I have explained that. It is obvious. My wife's nervousness—her fears—"

Poirot leaned forward. Slowly and emphatically he wagged a finger up and down.

"No, no, no. There is something there that is not clear. Your wife is in danger, yes—she is threatened with death, yes. You send—*not for the police*—not for a private detective even—but for a *nurse!* It does not make the sense, that!"

"I—I—" Dr. Leidner stopped. The color rose in his cheeks. "I thought—"

He came to a dead stop.

"Now we are coming to it," Poirot encouraged him. "You thought—what?"

Dr. Leidner remained silent. He looked harassed and unwilling.

"See you," Poirot's tone became winning and appealing, "it all rings true what you have told me, except for that. Why a *nurse?* There is an answer—yes. In fact, there can be only one answer. *You did not believe yourself in your wife's danger."*

And then with a cry Dr. Leidner broke down.

"God help me," he groaned. "I didn't. I didn't."

Poirot watched him with the kind of attention a cat gives a mouse hole—ready to pounce when the mouse shows itself.

"What *did* you think, then?" he asked.

"I don't know. I don't know."

"But you do know. You know perfectly. Perhaps I can help you—with a guess. *Did you, Doctor Leidner, suspect that these letters were all written by your wife herself?"*

There wasn't any need for him to answer. The truth of Poirot's guess was only too apparent. The horrified hand he held up, as though begging for mercy, told its own tale.

I drew a deep breath. So I *had* been right in my half-formed guess! I recalled the curious tone in which Dr. Leidner had asked me what I thought of it all. I nodded my head slowly and thoughtfully, and suddenly awoke to the fact that M. Poirot's eyes were on me.

"Did you think the same, nurse?"

"The idea did cross my mind," I said truthfully.

"For what reason?"

I explained the similarity of the handwriting on the letter that Mr. Coleman had shown me.

Poirot turned to Dr. Leidner.

"Had you, too, noticed that similarity?"

Dr. Leidner bowed his head.

"Yes, I did. The writing was small and cramped—not big and generous like Louise's, but several of the letters were formed the same way. I will show you."

From an inner breast pocket he took out some letters and finally selected a sheet from one which he handed to Poirot. It was part of a letter written to him by his wife. Poirot compared it carefully with the anonymous letters.

"Yes," he murmured. "Yes. There are several similarities—a curious way of forming the letter 's', a distinctive 'e.' I am not a handwriting expert—I cannot pronounce definitely (and, for that matter, I have never found two handwriting experts who agree on any point whatsoever)—but one can at least say this—the similarity between the two handwritings is very marked. It seems highly probable that they were all written by the same person. But it is not *certain.* We must take all contingencies into mind."

He leaned back in his chair and said thoughtfully, "There are three possibilities. First, the similarity of the handwriting is pure coincidence. Second, that these threatening letters were written by Mrs. Leidner herself for some obscure reason. Third, that they were written by someone *who deliberately copied her handwriting.* Why? There seems no sense in it. One of these three possibilities must be the correct one."

He reflected for a minute or two and then, turning to Dr. Leidner, he asked, with a resumal of his brisk manner, "When the possibility that Mrs. Leidner herself was the author of these letters first struck you, what theory did you form?"

Dr. Leidner shook his head.

"I put the idea out of my head as quickly as possible. I felt it was monstrous."

"Did you search for no explanation?"

"Well," he hesitated, "I wondered if worrying and brooding over the past had perhaps affected my wife's brain slightly. I thought she might possibly have written those letters to herself without being conscious of having done so. That is possible, isn't it?" he added, turning to Dr. Reilly.

Dr. Reilly pursed up his lips.

"The human brain is capable of almost anything," he replied vaguely.

But he shot a lightning glance at Poirot, and as if in obedience to it, the latter abandoned the subject.

"The letters are an interesting point," he said. "But we must concentrate on the case as a whole. There are, as I see it, three possible solutions."

"Three?"

"Yes. Solution one: the simplest. Your wife's first husband is still alive. He first threatens her and then proceeds to carry out his threats. If we accept this solution, our problem is to discover how he got in or out without being seen.

"Solution two: Mrs. Leidner, for reasons of her own (reasons probably more easily understood by a medical man than a layman), writes herself threatening letters. The gas business is staged by her (remember, it was she who roused you by telling you she smelled gas). But, *if Mrs. Leidner wrote herself the letters, she cannot be in danger from the supposed writer.* We must, therefore, look elsewhere for the murderer. We must look, in fact, among the members of your staff. Yes," in answer to a murmur of protest from Dr. Leidner, "that is the only logical conclusion. To satisfy a private grudge one of them killed her. That person, I may say, was probably aware of the letters—or was at any rate aware that Mrs. Leidner feared or was pretending to fear someone. That fact, in the murderer's opinion, rendered the murder quite safe for him. He felt sure it would be put down to a mysterious outsider—the writer of the threatening letters.

"A variant of this solution is that the murderer actually wrote the letters himself, being aware of Mrs. Leidner's past history. But in that case it is not quite clear *why* the criminal should have copied Mrs. Leidner's own handwriting since, as far as we can see, it would be more to his or her advantage that they should appear to be written by an outsider.

"The third solution is the most interesting to my mind. I suggest that the letters are genuine. They are written by Mrs. Leidner's first husband (or his younger brother), *who is actually one of the expedition staff.*"

CHAPTER XVI

THE SUSPECTS

Dr. Leidner sprang to his feet.

"Impossible! Absolutely impossible! The idea is absurd!"

Mr. Poirot looked at him quite calmly but said nothing.

"You mean to suggest that my wife's former husband is one of the expedition *and that she didn't recognize him?"*

"Exactly. Reflect a little on the facts. Nearly twenty years ago your wife lived with this man for a few months. Would she know him if she came across him after that lapse of time? I think not. His face will have changed, his build will have changed—his voice may not have changed so much, but that is a detail he can attend to himself. And remember, *she is not looking for him among her own household.* She visualizes him as somewhere *outside*—a stranger. No, I do not think she would recognize him. And there is a second possibility. The young brother—the child of those days who was so passionately devoted to his elder brother. He is now a man. Will she recognize a child of ten or twelve years old in a man nearing thirty? Yes, there is young William Bosner to be reckoned with. Remember, his brother in his eyes may not loom as a traitor but as a patriot, a martyr for his own country—Germany. In his eyes *Mrs. Leidner* is the traitor—the monster who sent his beloved brother to death! A susceptible child is capable of great hero worship, and a young mind can easily be obsessed by an idea which persists into adult life."

"Quite true," said Dr. Reilly. "The popular view that a child forgets easily is not an accurate one. Many people go right through life in the grip of an idea which has been impressed on them in very tender years."

"Bien. You have these two possibilities. Frederick Bosner, a man by now of fifty odd, and William Bosner, whose age would be something short of thirty. Let us examine the members of your staff from these two points of view."

"This is fantastic," murmured Dr. Leidner. *"My* staff! The members of my own expedition."

"And consequently considered above suspicion," said Poirot dryly. "A very useful point of view. *Commencons!* Who could emphatically *not* be Frederick or William?"

"The women."

"Naturally. Miss Johnson and Mrs. Mercado are crossed off. Who else?"

"Carey. He and I have worked together for years before I even met Louise—"

"And also he is the wrong age. He is, I should judge, thirty-eight or nine, too young for Frederick, too old for William. Now for the rest. There is Father Lavigny and Mr. Mercado. Either of them might be Frederick Bosner."

"But, my dear sir," cried Dr. Leidner in a voice of mingled irritation and amusement, "Father Lavigny is known all over the world as an epigraphist, and Mercado has worked for years in a well-known museum in New York. It is *impossible* that either of them should be the man you think!"

Poirot waved an airy hand.

"Impossible—impossible—I take no account of the word! The impossible, always I examine it very closely! But we will pass on for the moment. Who else have you? Carl Reiter, a young man with a German name, David Emmott—"

"He has been with me two seasons, remember."

"He is a young man with the gift of patience. *If* he committed a crime, it would not be in a hurry. All would be very well prepared."

Dr. Leidner made a gesture of despair.

"And lastly, William Coleman," continued Poirot.

"He is an Englishman."

"Pourquoi pas? Did not Mrs. Leidner say that the boy left America and could not be traced? He might easily have been brought up in England."

"You have an answer to everything," said Dr. Leidner.

I was thinking hard. Right from the beginning I had thought Mr. Coleman's manner rather more like a P. G. Wodehouse book than like a real live young man. Had he really been playing a part all the time?

Poirot was writing in a little book.

"Let us proceed with order and method," he said. "On the first count we have two names. Father Lavigny and Mr. Mercado. On the second we have Coleman, Emmott, and Reiter.

"Now let us pass to the opposite aspect of the matter—means and opportunity. *Who among the expedition had the means and the opportunity of committing the crime?* Carey was on the dig, Coleman was in Hassanieh, you yourself were on the roof. That leaves us Father Lavigny, Mr. Mercado, Mrs. Mercado, David Emmott, Carl Reiter, Miss Johnson, and Nurse Leatheran."

"Oh!" I exclaimed, and I bounded in my chair.

Mr. Poirot looked at me with twinkling eyes.

"Yes, I'm afraid, *ma soeur,* that you have got to be included. It would have been quite easy for you to have gone along and killed Mrs. Leidner while the courtyard was empty. You have plenty of muscle and strength, and she would have been quite unsuspicious until the moment the blow was struck."

I was so upset that I couldn't get a word out. Dr. Reilly, I noticed, was looking highly amused.

"Interesting case of a nurse who murdered her patients one by one," he murmured.

Such a look as I gave him!

Dr. Leidner's mind had been running on a different tack.

"Not Emmott, M. Poirot," he objected. "You can't include him. He was on the roof with me, remember, during that ten minutes."

"Nevertheless we cannot exclude him. He could have come down, gone straight to Mrs. Leidner's room, killed her, and *then* called the boy back. Or he might have killed her on one of the occasions when he had *sent the boy up to you."*

Dr. Leidner shook his head, murmuring, "What a nightmare! It's all so —fantastic."

To my surprise Poirot agreed.

"Yes, that is true. *This is a fantastic crime.* One does not often come across them. Usually murder is very sordid—very simple. But this is unusual murder. I suspect, Doctor Leidner, that your wife was an unusual woman."

He had hit the nail on the head with such accuracy that I jumped.

"Is that true, nurse?" he asked.

Dr. Leidner said quietly, "Tell him what Louise was like, nurse. You are unprejudiced."

I spoke quite frankly.

"She was very lovely," I said. "You couldn't help admiring her and wanting to do things for her. I've never met anyone like her before."

"Thank you," said Dr. Leidner and smiled at me.

"That is valuable testimony coming from an outsider," said Poirot politely. "Well, let us proceed. Under the heading of 'means and opportunity' we have seven names. Nurse Leatheran, Miss Johnson, Mrs. Mercado, Mr. Mercado, Mr. Reiter, Mr. Emmott, and Father Lavigny."

Once more he cleared his throat. I've always noticed that foreigners can make the oddest noises.

"Let us for the moment assume that our third theory is correct. That is, that the murderer is Frederick or William Bosner, and that Frederick or William Bosner is a member of the expedition staff. By comparing both lists we can narrow down our suspects on this count to four. Father Lavigny, Mr. Mercado, Carl Reiter, and David Emmott."

"Father Lavigny is out of the question," said Dr. Leidner with decision. "He is one of the *Pères Blancs* in Carthage."

"And his beard's quite real," I put in.

"Ma soeur," said Poirot, "a murderer of the first class *never* wears a false beard!"

"How do you know the murderer is of the first class?" I asked rebelliously.

"Because if he were not, the whole truth would be plain to me at this instant—and it is not."

That's pure conceit, I thought to myself.

"Anyway," I said, reverting to the beard, "it must have taken quite a time to grow."

"That is a practical observation," said Poirot.

Dr. Leidner said irritably, "But it's ridiculous—quite ridiculous. Both he and Mercado are well-known men. They've been known for years."

Poirot turned to him.

"You have not the true vision. You do not appreciate an important point. *If Frederick Bosner is not dead—what has he been doing all these years?* He must have taken a different name. He must have built himself up a career."

"As a *Père Blanc?"* asked Dr. Reilly skeptically.

"It is a little fantastic that, yes," confessed Poirot. "But we cannot put it right out of court. Besides, there are other possibilities."

"The young 'uns?" said Reilly. "If you want my opinion, on the face of it there's only one of your suspects that's even plausible."

"And that is?"

"Young Carl Reiter. There's nothing actually against him, but come down to it and you've got to admit a few things—he's the right age, he's got a German name, he's new this year, and he had the opportunity, all right. He'd only got to pop out of his photographic place, cross the courtyard to do his dirty work, and hare back again while the coast was clear. If anyone were to have dropped into the photographic room while he was out of it, he can always say later that he was in the darkroom. I don't say he's your man but if you are going to suspect someone I say he's by far and away the most likely."

M. Poirot didn't seem very receptive. He nodded gravely but doubtfully.

"Yes," he said. "He is the most plausible, but it may not be so simple as all that." Then he said, "Let us say no more at present. I would like now if I may to examine the room where the crime took place."

"Certainly." Dr. Leidner fumbled in his pockets then looked at Dr. Reilly.

"Captain Maitland took it," he said.

"Maitland gave it to me," said Reilly. "He had to go off on that Kurdish business."

He produced the key.

Dr. Leidner said hesitatingly, "Do you mind—if I don't—Perhaps, nurse—"

"Of course. Of course," said Poirot. "I quite understand. Never do I wish to cause you unnecessary pain. If you will be good enough to accompany me, *ma soeur.*"

"Certainly," I said.

CHAPTER XVII

THE STAIN BY THE WASHSTAND

Mrs. Leidner's body had been taken to Hassanieh for the post-mortem, but otherwise her room had been left exactly as it was. There was so little in it that it had not taken the police long to go over it.

To the right of the door as you entered was the bed. Opposite the door were the two barred windows giving on the countryside. Between them was a plain oak table with two drawers that served Mrs. Leidner as a dressing-table. On the east wall there was a line of hooks with dresses hung up protected by cotton bags and a deal chest of drawers. Immediately to the left of the door was the washstand. In the middle of the room was a good-sized plain oak table with a blotter and inkstand and a small attaché case. It was in the latter that Mrs. Leidner had kept the anonymous letters. The curtains were short strips of native material—white striped with orange. The floor was of stone with some goatskin rugs on it, three narrow ones of brown striped with white in front of the two windows and the washstand, and a larger better quality one of white with brown stripes lying between the bed and the writing-table.

There were no cupboards or alcoves or long curtains—nowhere, in fact, where anyone could have hidden. The bed was a plain iron one with a printed cotton quilt. The only trace of luxury in the room were three pillows all made of the best soft and billowy down. Nobody but Mrs. Leidner had pillows like these.

In a few brief dry words Dr. Reilly explained where Mrs. Leidner's body had been found—in a heap on the rug beside the bed.

To illustrate his account, he beckoned me to come forward.

If you don't mind, nurse?" he said.

I'm not squeamish. I got down on the floor and arranged myself as far as possible in the attitude in which Mrs. Leidner's body had been found.

"Leidner lifted her head when he found her," said the doctor. "But I questioned him closely and it's obvious that he didn't actually change her position."

"It seems quite straightforward," said Poirot. "She was lying on the bed, asleep or resting—someone opens the door, she looks up, rises to her feet—"

"And he struck her down," finished the doctor. "The blow would produce unconsciousness, and death would follow very shortly. You see—"

He explained the injury in technical language.

"Not much blood, then?" said Poirot.

"No, the blood escaped internally into the brain."

"Eh bien," said Poirot, "that seems straightforward enough—except for one thing. *If* the man who entered was a stranger, why did not Mrs. Leidner cry out at once for help? If she had screamed she would have been heard. Nurse Leatheran here would have heard her, and Emmott and the boy."

"That's easily answered," said Dr. Reilly dryly. *"Because it wasn't a stranger."*

Poirot nodded.

"Yes," he said meditatively. "She may have been *surprised* to see the person—but she was not *afraid.* Then, as he struck, she *may* have uttered a half-cry—too late."

"The cry Miss Johnson heard?"

"Yes, if she *did* hear it. But on the whole I doubt it. These mud walls are thick and the windows were closed."

He stepped up to the bed.

"You left her actually lying down?" he asked me. I explained exactly what I had done.

"Did she mean to sleep or was she going to read?"

"I gave her two books—a light one and a volume of memoirs. She usually read for a while and then sometimes dropped off for a short sleep."

"And she was—what shall I say—quite as usual?"

I considered.

"Yes. She seemed quite normal and in good spirits," I said. "Just a shade offhand, perhaps, but I put that down to her having confided in me the day before. It makes people a little uncomfortable sometimes."

Poirot's eyes twinkled.

"Ah, yes, indeed, me, I know that well."

He looked round the room.

"And when you came in here after the murder, was everything as you had seen it before?"

I looked round also.

"Yes, I think so. I don't remember anything being different."

"There was no sign of the weapon with which she was struck?"

"No."

Poirot looked at Dr. Reilly.

"What was it in your opinion?"

The doctor replied promptly.

"Something pretty powerful of a fair size and without any sharp corners or edges. The rounded base of a statue, say—something like that. Mind you, I'm not suggesting that that *was* it. But that type of thing. The blow was delivered with great force."

"Struck by a strong arm? A man's arm?"

"Yes—unless—"

"Unless—what?"

Dr. Reilly said slowly, "It is just possible that Mrs. Leidner might have been on her knees—in which case, the blow being delivered from above with a heavy implement, the force needed would not have been so great."

"On her knees," mused Poirot. "It is an idea—that."

"It's only an idea, mind," the doctor hastened to point out. "There's absolutely nothing to indicate it."

"But it's possible."

"Yes. And after all, in view of the circumstances, it's not fantastic. Her fear might have led her to kneel in supplication rather than to scream when her instinct would tell her it was too late—that nobody could get there in time."

"Yes," said Poirot thoughtfully. "It is an idea."

It was a very poor one, I thought. I couldn't for one moment imagine Mrs. Leidner on her knees to anyone.

Poirot made his way slowly round the room. He opened the windows, tested the bars, passed his head through, and satisfied himself that by no means could his shoulders be made to follow his head.

"The windows were shut when you found her," he said. "Were they also shut when you left her at a quarter to one?"

"Yes, they were always shut in the afternoon. There is no gauze over these windows as there is in the living-room and dining-room. They are kept shut to keep out the flies."

"And in any case no one could get in that way," mused Poirot. "And the walls are of the most solid—mud-brick—and there are no trap doors and no skylights. No, there is only one way into this room—*through the door.* And there is only one way to the door—through the courtyard. And there is only one entrance to the courtyard—*through the archway.* And outside the archway there were five people and they all tell the same story, and I do not think, me, that they are lying. No, they are not lying. They are not bribed to silence. The murderer was *here."*

I didn't say anything. Hadn't I felt the same thing just now when we were all cooped up round that table?

Slowly Poirot prowled round the room. He took up a photograph from the chest of drawers. It was of an elderly man with a white goatee beard. He looked inquiringly at me.

"Mrs. Leidner's father," I said. "She told me so."

He put it down again and glanced over the articles on the dressing-table —all of plain tortoise shell—simple but good. He looked up at a row of books on a shelf, repeating the titles aloud.

"Who Were the Greeks? Introduction to Relativity. Life of Lady Hester Stanhope. Crewe Train. Back to Methuselah. Linda Condon. Yes, they tell us something, perhaps. She was not a fool, your Mrs. Leidner. She had a mind."

"Oh! She was a *very* clever woman," I said eagerly. "Very well read and up in everything. She wasn't a bit ordinary."

He smiled as he looked over at me.

"No," he said. "I've already realized that."

He passed on. He stood for some moments at the washstand where there was a big array of bottles and toilet creams.

Then, suddenly, he dropped on his knees and examined the rug.

Dr. Reilly and I came quickly to join him. He was examining a small dark-brown stain, almost invisible on the brown of the rug. In fact it was only just noticeable where it impinged on one of the white stripes.

"What do you say, doctor?" he said. "Is that blood?"

Dr. Reilly knelt down.

"Might be," he said. "I'll make sure if you like."

"If you would be so amiable."

Mr. Poirot examined the jug and basin. The jug was standing on the side of the washstand. The basin was empty, but beside the washstand there was an old kerosene tin containing slop water.

He turned to me.

"Do you remember, nurse? Was this jug *out* of the basin or *in* it when you left Mrs. Leidner at a quarter to one?"

"I can't be sure," I said after a minute or two. "I rather think it was standing in the basin."

"Ah?"

"But you see," I said hastily, "I only think so because it usually was. The boys leave it like that after lunch. I just feel that if it hadn't been in I should have noticed it."

He nodded quite appreciatively.

"Yes, I understand that. It is your hospital training. If everything had not been just so in the room, you would quite unconsciously have set it to rights hardly noticing what you were doing. And after the murder? Was it like it is now?"

I shook my head.

"I didn't notice then," I said. "All I looked for was whether there was any place anyone could be hidden or if there were anything the murderer had left behind him."

"It's blood, all right," said Dr. Reilly, rising from his knees. "Is it important?"

Poirot was frowning perplexedly. He flung out his hands with petulance.

"I cannot tell. How can I tell? It may mean nothing at all. I can say, if I like, that the murderer touched her—that there was blood on his hands—very little blood, but still blood—and so he came over here and washed them. Yes, it may have been like that. But I cannot jump to conclusions and say that it *was* so. That stain may be of no importance at all."

"There would have been very little blood," said Dr. Reilly dubiously. "None would have spurted out or anything like that. It would have just oozed a little from the wound. Of course, if he'd probed it at all—"

I gave a shiver. A nasty sort of picture came up in my mind. The vision of somebody—perhaps that nice pig-faced photographic boy, striking down that lovely woman and then bending over her probing the wound with his finger in an awful gloating fashion and his face, perhaps, quite different—all fierce and mad.

Dr. Reilly noticed my shiver.

"What's the matter, nurse?" he said.

"Nothing—just goose flesh," I said. "A goose walking over my grave."

Mr. Poirot turned round and looked at me.

"I know what you need," he said. "Presently when we have finished here and I go back with the doctor to Hassanieh we will take you with us. You will give Nurse Leatheran tea, will you not, doctor?"

"Delighted."

"Oh, no, doctor," I protested. "I couldn't think of such a thing."

M. Poirot gave me a little friendly tap on the shoulder. Quite an English tap, not a foreign one.

"You, *ma soeur,* will do as you are told," he said. "Besides, it will be of advantage to me. There is a good deal more that I want to discuss, and I cannot do it here where one must preserve the decencies. The good Doctor Leidner, he worshiped his wife and he is sure—oh, so sure—that everybody else felt the same about her! But that, in my opinion, would not be human nature! No, we want to discuss Mrs. Leidner with—how do you say—the gloves removed? That is settled, then. When we have finished here, we take you with us to Hassanieh."

"I suppose," I said doubtfully, "that I ought to be leaving anyway. It's rather awkward."

"Do nothing for a day or two," said Dr. Reilly. "You can't very well go until after the funeral."

"That's all very well," I said. "And supposing I get murdered, too, doctor?"

I said it half jokingly and Dr. Reilly took it in the same fashion and would, I think, have made some jocular response.

But M. Poirot, to my astonishment, stood stock-still in the middle of the floor and clasped his hands to his head.

"Ah! If that were possible," he murmured. "It is a danger—yes—a great danger—and what can one do? How can one guard against it?"

"Why, M. Poirot," I said, "I was only joking! Who'd want to murder me, I should like to know?"

"You—or another," he said, and I didn't like the way he said it at all. Positively creepy.

"But why?" I persisted.

He looked at me very straight then.

"I joke, mademoiselle," he said, "and I laugh. *But there are some things that are no joke.* There are things that my profession has taught me. And one of these things, the most terrible thing, is this:

"Murder is a habit . . ."

CHAPTER XVIII

TEA AT DR. REILLY'S

Before leaving, Poirot made a round of the expedition house and the outbuildings. He also asked a few questions of the servants at second hand—that is to say, Dr. Reilly translated the questions and answers from English into Arabic and vice versa.

These questions dealt mainly with the appearance of the stranger Mrs. Leidner and I had seen looking through the window and to whom Father Lavigny had been talking on the following day.

"Do you really think that fellow had anything to do with it?" asked Dr. Reilly when we were bumping along in his car on our way to Hassanieh.

"I like all the information there is," was Poirot's reply.

And really, that described his methods very well. I found later that there wasn't anything—no small scrap of insignificant gossip—in which he wasn't interested. Men aren't usually so gossipy.

I must confess I was glad of my cup of tea when we got to Dr. Reilly's house. M. Poirot, I noticed, put five lumps of sugar in his.

Stirring it carefully with his teaspoon he said, "And now we can talk, can we not? We can make up our minds who is likely to have committed the crime."

"Lavigny, Mercado, Emmott, or Reiter?" asked Dr. Reilly.

"No, no—that was theory number three. I wish to concentrate now on theory number two—leaving aside all question of a mysterious husband or brother-in-law turning up from the past. Let us discuss now quite simply which member of the expedition had the means and opportunity to kill Mrs. Leidner, and who is likely to have done so."

"I thought you didn't think much of that theory."

"Not at all. But I have some natural delicacy," said Poirot reproachfully. "Can I discuss in the presence of Dr. Leidner the motives likely to lead to the murder of his wife by a member of the expedition? That would not have been delicate at all. I had to sustain the fiction that his wife was adorable and that everyone adored her!

"But naturally it was not like that at all. Now we can be brutal and impersonal and say what we think. We have no longer to consider people's feelings. And that is where Nurse Leatheran is going to help us. She is, I am sure, a very good observer."

"Oh, I don't know about that," I said.

Dr. Reilly handed me a plate of hot scones—"to fortify yourself," he said. They were very good scones.

"Come, now," said Mr. Poirot in a friendly, chatty way. "You shall tell me, *ma soeur,* exactly what each member of the expedition felt toward Mrs. Leidner."

"I was only there a week, M. Poirot," I said.

"Quite long enough for one of your intelligence. A nurse sums up quickly. She makes her judgments and abides by them. Come, let us make a beginning. Father Lavigny, for instance?"

"Well, there, now, I really couldn't say. He and Mrs. Leidner seemed to like talking together. But they usually spoke French and I'm not very good at French myself though I learned it as a girl at school. I've an idea they talked mainly about books."

"They were, as you might say, companionable together—yes?"

"Well, yes, you might put it that way. But, all the same, I think Father Lavigny was puzzled by her and—well—almost annoyed by being puzzled, if you know what I mean."

And I told him of the conversation I had had with him out on the dig that first day when he had called Mrs. Leidner a "dangerous woman."

"Now that is very interesting," M. Poirot said. "And she—what do you think she thought of him?"

"That's rather difficult to say, too. It wasn't easy to know what Mrs. Leidner thought of people. Sometimes, I fancy, *he* puzzled *her.* I remember her saying to Doctor Leidner that he was unlike any priest she had ever known."

"A length of hemp to be ordered for Father Lavigny," said Dr. Reilly facetiously.

"My dear friend," said Poirot. "Have you not, perhaps, some patients to attend? I would not for the world detain you from your professional duties."

"I've got a whole hospital of them," said Dr. Reilly.

And he got up and said a wink was as good as a nod to a blind horse, and went out laughing.

"That is better," said Poirot. "We will have now an interesting conversation *tête-à-tête.* But you must not forget to eat your tea."

He passed me a plate of sandwiches and suggested my having a second cup of tea. He really had very pleasant, attentive manners.

"And now," he said, "let us continue with your impressions. Who was there who in your opinion did *not* like Mrs. Leidner?"

"Well," I said, "it's only my opinion and I don't want it repeated as coming from me."

"Naturally not."

"But in my opinion little Mrs. Mercado fairly hated her!"

"Ah! And Mr. Mercado?"

"He was a bit soft on her," I said. "I shouldn't think women apart from his wife had ever taken much notice of him. And Mrs. Leidner had a nice kind way of being interested in people and the things they told her. It rather went to the poor man's head, I fancy."

"And Mrs. Mercado—she was not pleased?"

"She was just plain jealous—that's the truth of it. You've got to be very careful when there's a husband and wife about, and that's a fact. I could tell you some surprising things. You've no idea the extraordinary things women get into their heads when it's a question of their husbands."

"I do not doubt the truth of what you say. So Mrs. Mercado was jealous? And she hated Mrs. Leidner?"

"I've seen her look at her as though she'd have liked to kill her—oh, gracious!" I pulled myself up. "Indeed, M. Poirot, I didn't mean to say—I mean that is, not for one moment—"

"No, no. I quite understand. The phrase slipped out. A very convenient one. And Mrs. Leidner, was she worried by this animosity of Mrs. Mercado's?"

"Well," I said, reflecting, "I don't really think she was worried at all. In fact, I don't even know whether she noticed it. I thought once of just giving her a hint—but I didn't like to. Least said soonest mended. That's what I say."

"You are doubtless wise. Can you give me any instances of how Mrs. Mercado showed her feelings?"

I told him about our conversation on the roof.

"So she mentioned Mrs. Leidner's first marriage," said Poirot thoughtfully. "Can you remember—in mentioning it—did she look at you as though she wondered whether you had heard a different version?"

"You think she may have known the truth about it?"

"It is a possibility. She may have written those letters—and engineered a tapping hand and all the rest of it."

"I wondered something of the same kind myself. It seemed the kind of petty revengeful thing she might do."

"Yes. A cruel streak, I should say. But hardly the temperament for cold-blooded brutal murder unless, of course—" He paused and then said, "It is odd, that curious thing she said to you. 'I know why you are here.' What did she mean by it?"

"I can't imagine," I said frankly.

"She thought you were there for some ulterior reason apart from the declared one. What reason? And why should she be so concerned in the matter? Odd, too, the way you tell me she stared at you all through tea the day you arrived."

"Well, she's not a lady, M. Poirot," I said primly.

"That, *ma soeur,* is an excuse but not an explanation."

I wasn't quite sure for the minute what he meant. But he went on quickly.

"And the other members of the staff?"

I considered.

"I don't think Miss Johnson liked Mrs. Leidner either very much. But she was quite open and aboveboard about it. She as good as admitted she was prejudiced. You see, she's very devoted to Doctor Leidner and had worked with him for years. And, of course, marriage does change things—there's no denying it."

"Yes," said Poirot. "And from Miss Johnson's point of view it would be an unsuitable marriage. It would really have been much more suitable if Doctor Leidner had married *her.*"

"It would really," I agreed. "But there, that's a man all over. Not one in a hundred considers suitability. And one can't really blame Doctor Leidner. Miss Johnson, poor soul, isn't so much to look at. Now Mrs. Leidner was really beautiful—not young, of course—but oh! I wish you'd known her. There was something about her— I remember Mr. Coleman saying she was like a thingummyjig that came to lure people into marshes. That wasn't a very good way of putting it but—oh, well—you'll laugh at me but there *was* something about her that was—well—unearthly."

"She could cast a spell—yes, I understand," said Poirot.

"Then I don't think she and Mr. Carey got on very well, either," I went on. "I've an idea *he* was jealous just like Miss Johnson. He was always very stiff with her and so was she with him. You know—she passed him things and was very polite and called him Mr. Carey rather formally. He was an old friend of her husband's, of course, and some women can't stand their husband's old friends. They don't like to think that anyone knew them before they did—at least that's rather a muddled way of putting it—"

"I quite understand. And the three young men? Coleman, you say, was inclined to be poetic about her."

I couldn't help laughing.

"It was funny, M. Poirot," I said. "He's such a matter-of-fact young man."

"And the other two?"

"I don't really know about Mr. Emmott. He's always so quiet and never says much. She was very nice to him always. You know—friendly—called him David and used to tease him about Miss Reilly and things like that."

"Ah, really? And did he enjoy that?"

"I don't quite know," I said doubtfully. "He'd just look at her. Rather funnily. You couldn't tell what he was thinking."

"And Mr. Reiter?"

"She wasn't always very kind to him," I said slowly. "I think he got on her nerves. She used to say quite sarcastic things to him."

"And did he mind?"

"He used to get very pink, poor boy. Of course, she didn't *mean* to be unkind."

And then suddenly, from feeling a little sorry for the boy, it came over me that he was very likely a cold-blooded murderer and had been playing a part all the time.

"Oh, M. Poirot," I exclaimed. "What do you think *really* happened?"

He shook his head slowly and thoughtfully.

"Tell me," he said. "You are not afraid to go back there tonight?"

"Oh, *no,*" I said. "Of course, I remember what you said, but who would want to murder *me?*"

"I do not think that anyone could," he said slowly. "That is partly why I have been so anxious to hear all you could tell me. No, I think—I am sure—you are quite safe."

"If anyone had told me in Baghdad—" I began and stopped.

"Did you hear any gossip about the Leidners and the expedition before you came here?" he asked.

I told him about Mrs. Leidner's nickname and just a little of what Mrs. Kelsey had said about her.

In the middle of it the door opened and Miss Reilly came in. She had been playing tennis and had her racket in her hand.

I gathered Poirot had already met her when he arrived in Hassanieh.

She said how do you do to me in her usual offhand manner and picked up a sandwich.

"Well, M. Poirot," she said. "How are you getting on with our local mystery?"

"Not very fast, mademoiselle."

"I see you've rescued nurse from the wreck."

"Nurse Leatheran has been giving me valuable information about the various members of the expedition. Incidentally I have learned a good deal—about the victim. And the victim, mademoiselle, is very often the clue to the mystery."

Miss Reilly said, "That's rather clever of you, M. Poirot. It's certainly true that if ever a woman deserved to be murdered Mrs. Leidner was that woman!"

"Miss Reilly!" I cried, scandalized.

She laughed, a short, nasty laugh.

"Ah!" she said. "I thought you hadn't been hearing quite the truth. Nurse Leatheran, I'm afraid, was quite taken in, like many other people. Do you know, M. Poirot, I rather hope that this case isn't going to be one of your successes. I'd quite like the murderer of Louise Leidner to get away with it. In fact, I wouldn't much have objected to putting her out of the way myself."

I was simply disgusted with the girl. M. Poirot, I must say, didn't turn a hair. He just bowed and said quite pleasantly, "I hope, then, that you have an alibi for yesterday afternoon?"

There was a moment's silence and Miss Reilly's racket went clattering down onto the floor. She didn't bother to pick it up. Slack and untidy like all her sort! She said in a rather breathless voice, "Oh, yes, I was playing tennis at the club. But, seriously, M. Poirot, I wonder if you know anything at all about Mrs. Leidner and the kind of woman she was?"

Again he made a funny little bow and said, "You shall inform me, mademoiselle."

She hesitated a minute and then spoke with a callousness and lack of decency that really sickened me.

"There's a convention that one doesn't speak ill of the dead. That's stupid, I think. The truth's always the truth. On the whole it's better to keep your mouth shut about living people. You might conceivably injure them. The dead are past that. But the harm they've done lives after them sometimes. Not quite a quotation from Shakespeare but very nearly! Has nurse told you of the queer atmosphere there was at Tell Yarimjah? Has she told you how jumpy they all were? And how they all used to glare at each other like enemies? That was Louise Leidner's doing. When I was a kid out here three years ago they were the happiest, jolliest lot imaginable. Even last year they were pretty well all right. But this year there was a blight over them—and it was *her* doing. She was the kind of woman who won't let anybody else be happy! There *are* women like that and she was one of them! She wanted to break up things always. Just for fun—or for the sense of power—or perhaps just because she was made that way. And she was the kind of woman who had to get hold of every male creature within reach!"

"Miss Reilly," I cried, "I don't think that's true. In fact I *know* it isn't."

She went on without taking the least notice of me.

"It wasn't enough for her to have her husband adore her. She had to make a fool of that long-legged, shambling idiot of a Mercado. Then she got hold of Bill. Bill's a sensible cove, but she was getting him all mazed and bewildered. Carl Reiter she just amused herself by tormenting. It was easy. He's a sensitive boy. And she had a jolly good go at David.

"David was better sport to her because he put up a fight. He felt her charm—but he wasn't having any. I think because he'd got sense enough to know that she didn't really care a damn. And that's why I hate her so. She's not sensual. She doesn't *want* affairs. It's just cold-blooded experiment on her part and the fun of stirring people up and setting them against each other. She dabbled in that, too. She's the sort of woman who's never had a row with anyone in her life—but rows always happen where she is! She *makes* them happen. She's a kind of female Iago. She *must* have drama. But she doesn't want to be involved *herself*. She's always outside pulling strings—looking on—enjoying it. Oh, do you see *at all* what I mean?"

"I see, perhaps, more than you know, mademoiselle," said Poirot.

I couldn't make his voice out. He didn't sound indignant. He sounded—oh, well, I can't explain it.

Sheila Reilly seemed to understand for she flushed all over her face.

"You can think what you choose," she said. "But I'm right about her. She was a clever woman and she was bored and she experimented—with people—like other people experiment with chemicals. She enjoyed working on poor old Johnson's feelings and seeing her bite on the bullet and control herself like the old sport she is. She liked goading little Mercado into a white-hot frenzy. She liked flicking *me* on the raw—and she could do it, too, every time! She liked finding out things about people and holding it over them. Oh, I don't mean crude blackmail—I mean just letting them know that she *knew*—and leaving them uncertain what she meant to do about it. My God, though, that woman was an artist! There was nothing crude about *her* methods!"

"And her husband?" asked Poirot.

"She never wanted to hurt him," said Miss Reilly slowly. "I've never known her anything but sweet to him. I suppose she was fond of him. He's a dear—wrapped up in his own world—his digging and his theories. And he worshiped her and thought her perfection. That might have annoyed some women. It didn't annoy her. In a sense he lived in a fool's paradise—

and yet it wasn't a fool's paradise because to him she was what he thought her. Though it's hard to reconcile that with—"

She stopped.

"Go on, mademoiselle," said Poirot.

She turned suddenly on me.

"What have you said about Richard Carey?"

"About Mr. Carey?" I asked, astonished.

"About her and Carey?"

"Well," I said, "I've mentioned that they didn't hit it off very well—"

To my surprise she broke into a fit of laughter.

"Didn't hit if off very well! You fool! He's head over ears in love with her. And it's tearing him to pieces—because he worships Leidner, too. He's been his friend for years. That would be enough for her, of course. She's made it her business to come between them. But all the same I've fancied—"

"Eh bien?"

She was frowning, absorbed in thought.

"I've fancied that she'd gone too far for once—that she was not only biter but bit! Carey's attractive. He's as attractive as hell. She was a cold devil—but I believe she could have lost her coldness with him."

"I think it's just scandalous what you're saying," I cried. "Why, they hardly spoke to each other!"

"Oh, didn't they?" She turned on me. "A hell of a lot you know about it. It was 'Mr. Carey' and 'Mrs. Leidner' in the house, but they used to meet outside. She'd walk down the path to the river. And he'd leave the dig for an hour at a time. They used to meet among the fruit trees.

"I saw him once just leaving her, striding back to the dig, and she was standing looking after him. I was a female cad, I suppose. I had some glasses with me and I took them out and had a good look at her face. If you ask me I believed she cared like hell for Richard Carey."

She broke off and looked at Poirot.

"Excuse my butting in on your case," she said with a sudden rather twisted grin, "but I thought you'd like to have the local color correct."

And she marched out of the room.

"M. Poirot," I cried. "I don't believe one word of it all!"

He looked at me and he smiled, and he said (very queerly I thought), "You can't deny, nurse, that Miss Reilly has shed a certain—illumination on the case."

CHAPTER XIX

A NEW SUSPICION

We couldn't say any more just then because Dr. Reilly came in, saying jokingly that he'd killed off the most tiresome of his patients.

He and M. Poirot settled down to a more or less medical discussion of the psychology and mental state of an anonymous letter writer. The doctor cited cases that he had known professionally, and M. Poirot told various stories from his own experience.

"It is not so simple as it seems," he ended. "There is the desire for power and very often a strong inferiority complex."

Dr. Reilly nodded.

"That's why you often find that the author of anonymous letters is the last person in the place to be suspected. Some quiet, inoffensive little soul who apparently can't say boo to a goose—all sweetness and Christian meekness on the outside—and seething with all the fury of hell underneath!"

Poirot said thoughtfully, "Should you say Mrs. Leidner had any tendency to an inferiority complex?"

Dr. Reilly scraped out his pipe with a chuckle.

"Last woman on earth I'd describe that way. No repressions about her. Life, life, and more life—that's what she wanted—and got, too!"

"Do you consider it a possibility, psychologically speaking, that she wrote those letters?"

"Yes, I do. But if she did, the reason arose out of her instinct to dramatize herself. Mrs. Leidner was a bit of a film star in private life! She *had* to be the center of things—in the limelight. By the law of opposites she married Leidner who's about the most retiring and modest man I know. He adored her—but adoration by the fireside wasn't enough for her. She had to be the persecuted heroine as well."

"In fact," said Poirot, smiling, "you don't subscribe to his theory that she wrote them and retained no memory of her act?"

"No, I don't. I didn't turn down the idea in front of him. You can't very well say to a man who's just lost a dearly loved wife that that same wife was a shameless exhibitionist, and that she drove him nearly crazy with anxiety to satisfy her sense of the dramatic. As a matter of fact it wouldn't be safe to tell any man the truth about his wife! Funnily enough, I'd trust most women with the truth about their husbands. Women can accept the fact that a man is a rotter, a swindler, a drug taker, a confirmed liar, and a general swine without batting an eyelash and without its impairing their affection for the brute in the least! Women are wonderful realists."

"Frankly, Doctor Reilly, what *was* your exact opinion of Mrs. Leidner?"

Dr. Reilly lay back in his chair and puffed slowly at his pipe.

"Frankly—it's hard to say! I didn't know her well enough. She'd got charm—any amount of it. Brains, sympathy. What else? She hadn't any of the ordinary unpleasant vices. She wasn't sensual or lazy or even particularly vain. She was, I've always thought (but I've no proofs of it), a most accomplished liar. What I don't know (and what I'd like to know) is whether she lied to herself or only to other people. I'm rather partial to liars myself. A woman who doesn't lie is a woman without imagination and without sympathy. I don't think she was really a man hunter—she just liked the sport of bringing them down 'with my bow and arrow.' If you get my daughter on the subject—"

"We have had that pleasure," said Poirot with a slight smile.

"H'm," said Dr. Reilly. "She hasn't wasted much time! Shoved her knife into her pretty thoroughly, I should imagine! The younger generation has no sentiment toward the dead. It's a pity all young people are prigs! They condemn the 'old morality' and then proceed to set up a much more hard and fast code of their own. If Mrs. Leidner had had half a dozen affairs Sheila would probably have approved of her as 'living her life fully'—or 'obeying her blood instincts.' What she doesn't see is that Mrs. Leidner was acting true to type—*her* type. The cat *is* obeying its blood instinct when it plays with the mouse! It's made that way. Men aren't little boys to be shielded and protected. They've got to meet cat women—and faithful spaniel, yours-till-death adoring women, and henpecking nagging bird women—and all the rest of it! Life's a battlefield—not a picnic! I'd like to see Sheila honest enough to come off her high horse and admit that she hated Mrs. Leidner for good old thoroughgoing personal reasons. Sheila's about the only young girl in this place and she naturally assumes that she ought to have it all her own way with the young things in trousers. Naturally it annoys her when a woman, who in her view is middle-aged and who has already two husbands to her credit, comes along and licks her on her own ground. Sheila's a nice child, healthy and reasonably good-looking and attractive to the other sex as she should be. But Mrs. Leidner was something out of the ordinary in that line. She'd got just that sort of calamitous magic that plays the deuce with things—a kind of Belle Dame sans Merci."

I jumped in my chair. What a coincidence his saying that!

"Your daughter—I am not indiscreet—she has perhaps a *tendresse* for one of the young men out there?"

"Oh, I don't suppose so. She's had Emmott and Coleman dancing attendance on her as a matter of course. I don't know that she cares for one more than the other. There are a couple of young Air Force chaps, too. I fancy all's fish that comes to her net at present. No, I think it's age daring to defeat youth that annoys her so much! She doesn't know as much of the world as I do. It's when you get to my age that you really appreciate a schoolgirl complexion and a clear eye and a firmly knit young body. But a woman over thirty can listen with rapt attention and throw in a word here and there to show the talker what a fine fellow he is—and few young men can resist that! Sheila's a pretty girl—but Louise Leidner was beautiful. Glorious eyes and that amazing golden fairness. Yes, she was a beautiful woman."

Yes, I thought to myself, *he's right. Beauty's a wonderful thing.* She *had* been beautiful. It wasn't the kind of looks you were jealous of—you just sat back and admired. I felt that first day I met her that I'd do *anything* for Mrs. Leidner!

All the same, that night as I was being driven back to the Tell Yarimjah (Dr. Reilly made me stay for an early dinner) one or two things came back to my mind and made me rather uncomfortable. At the time I hadn't believed a word of all Sheila Reilly's outpouring. I'd taken it for sheer spite and malice.

But now I suddenly remembered the way Mrs. Leidner had insisted on going for a stroll by herself that afternoon and wouldn't hear of me coming with her. I couldn't help wondering if perhaps, after all, she *had* been going to meet Mr. Carey. And, of course, it *was* a little odd, really, the way he and she spoke to each other so formally. Most of the others she called by their Christian names.

He never seemed to look at her, I remembered. That might be because he disliked her—or it might be just the opposite.

I gave myself a little shake. Here I was fancying and imagining all sorts of things—all because of a girl's spiteful outbursts! It just showed how unkind and dangerous it was to go about saying that kind of thing.

Mrs. Leidner *hadn't* been like that at all.

Of course, *she* hadn't liked Sheila Reilly. She'd really been—almost catty about her that day at lunch to Mr. Emmott.

Funny, the way he'd looked at her. The sort of way that you couldn't possibly tell what he was thinking. You never could tell what Mr. Emmott was thinking. He was so quiet. But very nice. A nice, dependable person.

Now Mr. Coleman was a foolish young man if there ever was one!

I'd got to that point in my meditations when we arrived. It was just on nine o'clock and the big door was closed and barred.

Ibrahim came running with his great key to let me in.

We all went to bed early at Tell Yarimjah. There weren't any lights showing in the living-room. There was a light in the drawing-office and one in Dr. Leidner's office, but nearly all the other windows were dark. Everyone must have gone to bed even earlier than usual.

As I passed the drawing-office to go to my room I looked in. Mr. Carey was in his shirt sleeves working over his big plan.

Terribly ill, he looked, I thought. So strained and worn. It gave me quite a pang. I don't know what there was about Mr. Carey—it wasn't what he *said* because he hardly said anything—and that of the most ordinary nature, and it wasn't what he *did,* for that didn't amount to much, either—and yet you just couldn't help noticing him, and everything about him seemed to matter more than it would have about anyone else. He just *counted,* if you know what I mean.

He turned his head and saw me. He removed his pipe from his mouth and said, "Well, nurse, back from Hassanieh?"

"Yes, Mr. Carey. You're up working late. Everybody else seems to have gone to bed."

"I thought I might as well get on with things," he said. "I was a bit behind-hand. And I shall be out on the dig all tomorrow. We're starting digging again."

"Already?" I asked, shocked.

He looked at me rather queerly.

"It's the best thing, I think. I put it up to Leidner. He'll be in Hassanieh most of tomorrow seeing to things. But the rest of us will carry on here. You know it's not too easy all sitting round and looking at each other as things are."

He was right there, of course. Especially in the nervy, jumpy state everyone was in.

"Well, of course, you're right in a way," I said. "It takes one's mind off if one's got something to do."

The funeral, I knew, was to be the day after tomorrow.

He had bent over his plan again. I don't know why, but my heart just ached for him. I felt certain that he wasn't going to get any sleep.

"If you'd like a sleeping-draught, Mr. Carey?" I said hesitatingly.

He shook his head with a smile.

"I'll carry on, nurse. Bad habit, sleeping-draughts."

"Well, good night, Mr. Carey," I said. "If there's anything I can do—"

"Don't think so, thank you, nurse. Good night."

"I'm terribly sorry," I said, rather too impulsively I suppose.

"Sorry?" He looked surprised.

"For—for everybody. It's all so dreadful. But especially for you."

"For me? Why for me?"

"Well, you're such an old friend of them both."

"I'm an old friend of Liedner's. I wasn't a friend of hers particularly."

He spoke as though he had actually disliked her. Really, I wished Miss Reilly could have heard him!

"Well, good night," I said and hurried along to my room.

I fussed around a bit in my room before undressing. Washed out some handkerchiefs and a pair of wash leather gloves and wrote up my diary. I just looked out of my door again before I really started to get ready for bed. The lights were still on in the drawing-office and in the south building.

I supposed Dr. Leidner was still up and working in his office. I wondered whether I ought to go and say good night to him. I hesitated about it—I didn't want to seem officious. He might be busy and not want to be disturbed. In the end, however, a sort of uneasiness drove me on. After all, it couldn't do any harm. I'd just say good night, ask if there was anything I could do, and come away.

But Dr. Leidner wasn't there. The office itself was lit up but there was no one in it except Miss Johnson. She had her head down on the table and was crying as though her heart would break.

It gave me quite a turn. She was such a quiet, self-controlled woman. It was pitiful to see her.

"Whatever is it, my dear?" I cried. I put my arm round her and patted her. "Now, now, this won't do at all. You mustn't sit here crying all by yourself."

She didn't answer and I felt the dreadful shuddering sobs that were racking her.

"Don't, my dear, don't," I said. "Take a hold on yourself. I'll go and make you a cup of nice hot tea."

She raised her head and said, "No, no, it's all right, nurse. I'm being a fool."

"What's upset you, my dear?" I asked.

She didn't answer at once, then she said, "It's all too awful."

"Now don't start thinking of it," I told her. "What's happened has happened and can't be mended. It's no use fretting."

She sat up straight and began to pat her hair.

"I'm making rather a fool of myself," she said in her gruff voice. "I've been clearing up and tidying the office. Thought it was best to *do* something. And then—it all came over me suddenly—"

"Yes, yes," I said hastily. "I know. A nice strong cup of tea and a hot-water bottle in your bed is what you want," I said.

And she had them, too. I didn't listen to any protests.

"Thank you, nurse," she said when I'd settled her in bed, and she was sipping her tea and the hot-water bottle was in. "You're a nice kind sensible woman. It's not often I make such a fool of myself."

"Oh, anybody's liable to do that at a time like this," I said, "what with one thing and another. The strain and the shock and the police here, there, and everywhere. Why, I'm quite jumpy myself."

She said slowly in rather a queer voice, "What you said in there is true. What's happened has happened and can't be mended." She was silent for a minute or two and then said—rather oddly, I thought, "She was never a nice woman!"

Well, I didn't argue the point. I'd always felt it was quite natural for Miss Johnson and Mrs. Leidner not to hit it off.

I wondered if, perhaps, Miss Johnson had secretly had a feeling that she was pleased Mrs. Leidner was dead, and had then been ashamed of herself for the thought.

I said, "Now you go to sleep and don't worry about anything."

I just picked up a few things and set the room to rights. Stockings over the back of the chair and coat and skirt on a hanger. There was a little ball of crumpled paper on the floor where it must have fallen out of a pocket.

I was just smoothing it out to see whether I could safely throw it away when she quite startled me.

"Give that to me!"

I did so—rather taken aback. She'd called out so peremptorily. She snatched it from me—fairly snatched it—and then held it in the candle flame till it was burned to ashes.

As I say, I was startled—and I just stared at her.

I hadn't had time to see what the paper was—she'd snatched it so quick. But funnily enough, as it burned it curled over toward me and I just saw that there were words written in ink on the paper.

It wasn't till I was getting into bed that I realized why they'd looked sort of familiar to me.

It was the same handwriting as that of the anonymous letters.

Was *that* why Miss Johnson had given way to a fit of remorse? Had it been her all along who had written those anonymous letters?

CHAPTER XX

MISS JOHNSON, MRS. MERCADO, MR. REITER

I don't mind confessing that the idea came as a complete shock to me. I'd never thought of associating *Miss Johnson* with the letters. Mrs. Mercado, perhaps. But Miss Johnson was a real lady, and so self-controlled and sensible.

But I reflected, remembering the conversation I had listened to that evening between M. Poirot and Dr. Reilly, that that might be just *why*.

If it were Miss Johnson who had written the letters it explained a lot. Mind you, I didn't think for a minute Miss Johnson had had anything to do with the murder. But I *did* see that her dislike of Mrs. Leidner might have made her succumb to the temptation of, well—putting the wind up her—to put it vulgarly.

She might have hoped to frighten away Mrs. Leidner from the dig.

But then Mrs. Leidner had been murdered and Miss Johnson had felt terrible pangs of remorse—first for her cruel trick and also, perhaps, because she realized that those letters were acting as a very good shield to the actual murderer. No wonder she had broken down so utterly. She was, I was sure, a decent soul at heart. And it explained, too, why she had caught so eagerly at my consolation of "what's happened's happened and can't be amended."

And then her cryptic remark—her vindication of herself—"She was never a nice woman!"

The question was, what was *I* to do about it?

I tossed and turned for a good while and in the end decided I'd let M. Poirot know about it at the first opportunity.

He came out next day but I didn't get a chance of speaking to him what you might call privately.

We had just a minute alone together and before I could collect myself to know how to begin, he had come close to me and was whispering instructions in my ear.

"Me, I shall talk to Miss Johnson—and others, perhaps, in the living-room. You have the key of Mrs. Leidner's room still?"

"Yes," I said.

"Très bien. Go there, shut the door behind you, and give a cry—not a scream—a cry. You understand what I mean—it is alarm—surprise that I want you to express—not mad terror. As for the excuse if you are heard—I leave that to you—the stepped toe or what you will."

At that moment Miss Johnson came out into the courtyard and there was no time for more.

I understood well enough what M. Poirot was after. As soon as he and Miss Johnson had gone into the living-room I went across to Mrs. Leidner's room and, unlocking the door, went in, and pulled the door to behind me.

I can't say I didn't feel a bit of a fool standing up in an empty room and giving a yelp all for nothing at all. Besides, it wasn't so easy to know just how loud to do it. I gave a pretty loud "Oh" and then tried it a bit higher and a bit lower.

Then I came out again and prepared my excuse of a stepped (stubbed I *suppose* he meant!) toe.

But it soon appeared that no excuse would be needed. Poirot and Miss Johnson were talking together earnestly and there had clearly been no interruption.

Well, I thought, *that settles that. Either Miss Johnson imagined that cry she heard or else it was something quite different.*

I didn't like to go in and interrupt them. There was a deck chair on the porch so I sat down there. Their voices floated out to me.

"The position is delicate, you understand," Poirot was saying. "Doctor Leidner—obviously he adored his wife—"

"He worshiped her," said Miss Johnson.

"He tells me, naturally, how fond all his staff was of her! As for them, what can they say? Naturally they say the same thing. It is politeness. It is decency. It *may* also be the truth! But also it may *not!* And I am convinced, mademoiselle, that the key to this enigma lies in a complete understanding of Mrs. Leidner's character. If I could get the opinion—the honest opinion—of every member of the staff, I might, from the whole, build up a picture. Frankly, that is why I am here today. I knew Doctor Leidner would be in Hassanieh. That makes it easy for me to have an interview with each of you here in turn and beg your help."

"That's all very well," began Miss Johnson and stopped.

"Do not make me the British *clichés,"* Poirot begged. "Do not say it is not the cricket or the football, that to speak anything but well of the dead is not done—that—*enfin*—there is loyalty! Loyalty, it is a pestilential thing in crime. Again and again it obscures the truth."

"I've no particular loyalty to Mrs. Leidner," said Miss Johnson dryly. There was indeed a sharp and acid tone in her voice. "Doctor Leidner's a different matter. And, after all, she was his wife."

"Precisely—precisely. I understand that you would not wish to speak against your chief's wife. But this is not a question of a testimonial. It is a question of sudden and mysterious death. If I am to believe that it is a martyred angel who has been killed it does not add to the easiness of my task."

"I certainly shouldn't call her an angel," said Miss Johnson, and the acid tone was even more in evidence.

"Tell me your opinion, frankly, of Mrs. Leidner—as a woman."

"H'm! To begin with, M. Poirot, I'll give you this warning. I'm prejudiced. I am—we all were—devoted to Doctor Leidner. And, I suppose, when Mrs. Leidner came along, we were jealous. We resented the demands she made on his time and attention. The devotion he showed her irritated us. I'm being truthful, M. Poirot, and it isn't very pleasant for me. I resented her presence here—yes, I did, though, of course, I tried never to show it. It made a difference to us, you see."

"Us? You say us?"

"I mean Mr. Carey and myself. We're the two old-timers, you see. And we didn't much care for the new order of things. I suppose that's natural, though perhaps it was rather petty of us. But it *did* make a difference."

"What kind of a difference?"

"Oh, to everything. We used to have such a happy time. A good deal of fun, you know, and rather silly jokes, like people do who work together. Doctor Leidner was quite lighthearted—just like a boy."

"And when Mrs. Leidner came she changed all that?"

"Well, I suppose it wasn't her *fault*. It wasn't so bad last year. And please believe, M. Poirot, that it wasn't anything she *did*. She's always been charming to me—quite charming. That's why I've felt ashamed sometimes. It wasn't her fault that little things she said and did seemed to rub me up the wrong way. Really nobody could be nicer than she was."

"But nevertheless things were changed this season? There was a different atmosphere?"

"Oh, entirely. Really, I don't know what it was. Everything seemed to go wrong—not with the work—I mean with us—our tempers and our nerves. All on edge. Almost the sort of feeling you get when there is a thunderstorm coming."

"And you put that down to Mrs. Leidner's influence?"

"Well, it was never like that before she came," said Miss Johnson dryly. "Oh! I'm a cross-grained, complaining old dog. Conservative—liking things always the same. You really mustn't take any notice of me, M. Poirot."

"How would you describe to me Mrs. Leidner's character and temperament?"

Miss Johnson hesitated for a moment. Then she said slowly, "Well, of course, she was temperamental. A lot of ups and downs. Nice to people one day and perhaps wouldn't speak to them the next. She was very kind, I think. And very thoughtful for others. All the same you could see she had been thoroughly spoiled all her life. She took Doctor Leidner's waiting on her hand and foot as perfectly natural. And I don't think she ever really appreciated what a very remarkable—what a really great—man she had married. That used to annoy me sometimes. And of course she was terribly highly strung and nervous. The things she used to imagine and the states she used to get into! I was thankful when Doctor Leidner brought Nurse Leatheran here. It was too much for him having to cope both with his work and with his wife's fears."

"What is your own opinion of these anonymous letters she received?"

I had to do it. I leaned forward in my chair till I could just catch sight of Miss Johnson's profile turned to Poirot in answer to his question.

She was looking perfectly cool and collected.

"I think someone in America had a spite against her and was trying to frighten or annoy her."

"Pas plus serieux que ça?"

"That's my opinion. She was a very handsome woman, you know, and might easily have had enemies. I think those letters were written by some spiteful woman. Mrs. Leidner being of a nervous temperament took them seriously."

"She certainly did that," said Poirot. "But remember—the last of them arrived by hand."

"Well, I suppose that *could* have been managed if any one had given their minds to it. Women will take a lot of trouble to gratify their spite, M. Poirot."

They will indeed, I thought to myself!

"Perhaps you are right, mademoiselle. As you say, Mrs. Leidner was handsome. By the way, you know Miss Reilly, the doctor's daughter?"

"Sheila Reilly? Yes, of course."

Poirot adopted a very confidential, gossipy tone.

"I have heard a rumor (naturally I do not like to ask the doctor) that there was a *tendresse* between her and one of the members of Doctor Leidner's staff. Is that so, do you know?"

Miss Johnson appeared rather amused.

"Oh, young Coleman and David Emmott were both inclined to dance attendance. I believe there was some rivalry as to who was to be her partner in some event at the club. Both the boys went in on Saturday evenings to the club as a general rule. But I don't know that there was anything in it on her side. She's the only young creature in the place, you know, and so she's by way of being the belle of it. She's got the Air Force dancing attendance on her as well."

"So you think there is nothing in it?"

"Well—I don't know." Miss Johnson became thoughtful. "It is true that she comes out this way fairly often. Up to the dig and all that. In fact, Mrs. Leidner was chaffing David Emmott about it the other day—saying the girl was running after him. Which was rather a catty thing to say, I thought, and I don't think he liked it. Yes, she was here a good deal. I saw her riding toward the dig on that awful afternoon." She nodded her head toward the open window. "But neither David Emmott nor Coleman was on duty that afternoon. Richard Carey was in charge. Yes, perhaps she *is* attracted to one of the boys—but she's such a modern, unsentimental young woman that one doesn't know quite how seriously to take her. I'm sure I don't know which of them it is. Bill's a nice boy, and not nearly such a fool as he pretends to be. David Emmott is a dear—and there's a lot to him. He is the deep, quiet kind."

Then she looked quizzically at Poirot and said, "But has this any bearing on the crime, M. Poirot?"

M. Poirot threw up his hands in a very French fashion.

"You make me blush, mademoiselle," he said. "You expose me as a mere gossip. But what will you, I am interested always in the love affairs of young people."

"Yes," said Miss Johnson with a little sigh. "It's nice when the course of true love runs smooth."

Poirot gave an answering sigh. I wondered if Miss Johnson was thinking of some love affair of her own when she was a girl. And I wondered if M. Poirot had a wife, and if he went on in the way you always hear foreigners do, with mistresses and things like that. He looks so comic I couldn't imagine it.

"Sheila Reilly has a lot of character," said Miss Johnson. "She's young and she's crude, but she's the right sort."

"I take your word for it, mademoiselle," said Poirot.

He got up and said, "Are there any other members of the staff in the house?"

"Marie Mercado is somewhere about. All the men are up on the dig today. I think they wanted to get out of the house. I don't blame them. If you'd like to go up to the dig—"

She came out on the verandah and said, smiling to me, "Nurse Leatheran won't mind taking you, I dare say."

"Oh, certainly, Miss Johnson," I said.

"And you'll come back to lunch, won't you, M. Poirot?"

"Enchanted, mademoiselle."

Miss Johnson went back into the living-room where she was engaged in cataloguing.

"Mrs. Mercado's on the roof," I said. "Do you want to see her first?"

"It would be as well, I think. Let us go up."

As we went up the stairs I said, "I did what you told me. Did you hear anything?"

"Not a sound."

"That will be a weight off Miss Johnson's mind at any rate," I said. "She's been worrying that she might have done something about it."

Mrs. Mercado was sitting on the parapet, her head bent down, and she was so deep in thought that she never heard us till Poirot halted opposite her and bade her good morning.

Then she looked up with a start.

She looked ill this morning, I thought, her small face pinched and wizened and great dark circles under her eyes.

"Encore moi," said Poirot. "I come today with a special object."

And he went on much in the same way as he had done to Miss Johnson, explaining how necessary it was that he should get a true picture of Mrs. Leidner.

Mrs. Mercado, however, wasn't as honest as Miss Johnson had been. She burst into fulsome praise which, I was pretty sure, was quite far removed from her real feelings.

"Dear, *dear* Louise! It's so hard to explain her to someone who didn't know her. She was such an *exotic* creature. Quite different from anyone else. You felt that, I'm sure, nurse? A martyr to nerves, of course, and full of fancies, but one put up with things in her one wouldn't from anyone else. And she was so *sweet* to us all, wasn't she, nurse? And so *humble* about herself—I mean she didn't know anything about archaeology, and she was so eager to learn. Always asking my husband about the chemical processes for treating the metal objects and helping Miss Johnson to mend pottery. Oh, we were all *devoted* to her."

"Then it is not true, madame, what I have heard, that there was a certain tenseness—an uncomfortable atmosphere—here?"

Mrs. Mercado opened her opaque black eyes very wide.

"Oh! Who *can* have been telling you that? Nurse? Doctor Leidner? I'm sure *he* would never notice anything, poor man."

And she shot a thoroughly unfriendly glance at me.

Poirot smiled easily.

"I have my spies, madame," he declared gaily. And just for a minute I saw her eyelids quiver and blink.

"Don't you think," asked Mrs. Mercado with an air of great sweetness, "that after an event of this kind, every one always pretends a lot of things that never were? You know—tension, atmosphere, a 'feeling that something was going to happen?' I think people just *make up* these things afterward."

"There is a lot in what you say, madame," said Poirot.

"And it really *wasn't* true! We were a thoroughly happy family here."

"That woman is one of the most utter liars I've ever known," I said indignantly when M. Poirot and I were clear of the house and walking along the path to the dig. "I'm sure she simply hated Mrs. Leidner really!"

"She is hardly the type to whom one would go for the truth," Poirot agreed.

"Waste of time talking to her," I snapped.

"Hardly that—hardly that. If a person tells you lies with her lips she is sometimes telling you truth with her eyes. What is she afraid of, little Madame Mercado? I saw fear in her eyes. Yes—decidedly she is afraid of something. It is very interesting."

"I've got something to tell you, M. Poirot," I said.

Then I told him all about my return the night before and my strong belief that Miss Johnson was the writer of the anonymous letters.

"So *she's* a liar, too!" I said. "The cool way she answered you this morning about these same letters!"

"Yes," said Poirot. "It was interesting, that. *For she let out the fact that she knew all about those letters.* So far they have not been spoken of in the presence of the staff. Of course, it is quite possible that Doctor Leidner told her about them yesterday. They are old friends, he and she. But if he did not—well—then it is curious and interesting, is it not?"

My respect for him went up. It was clever the way he had tricked her into mentioning the letters.

"Are you going to tackle her about them?" I asked.

Mr. Poirot seemed quite shocked by the idea.

"No, no, indeed. Always it is unwise to parade one's knowledge. Until the last minute I keep everything here." He tapped his forehead. "At the right moment—I make the spring—like the panther—and, *mon Dieu!* The consternation!"

I couldn't help laughing to myself at little M. Poirot in the role of a panther.

We had just reached the dig. The first person we saw was Mr. Reiter, who was busy photographing some walling.

It's my opinion that the men who were digging just hacked out walls wherever they wanted them. That's what it looked like, anyway. Mr. Carey explained to me that you could feel the difference at once with a pick, and he tried to show me—but I never saw. When the man said *"Libn"*—mud-brick—it was just ordinary dirt and mud as far as I could see.

Mr. Reiter finished his photographs and handed over the camera and the plates to his boy and told him to take them back to the house.

Poirot asked him one or two questions about exposures and film packs and so on which he answered very readily. He seemed pleased to be asked about his work.

He was just tendering his excuses for leaving us when Poirot plunged once more into his set speech. As a matter of fact it wasn't quite a set speech because he varied it a little each time to suit the person he was talking to. But I'm not going to write it all down every time. With sensible people like Miss Johnson he went straight to the point, and with some of the others he had to beat about the bush a bit more. But it came to the same in the end.

"Yes, yes, I see what you mean," said Mr. Reiter. "But indeed, I do not see that I can be much help to you. I am new here this season and I did not speak much with Mrs. Leidner. I regret, but indeed I can tell you nothing."

There was something a little stiff and foreign in the way he spoke, though, of course, he hadn't got any accent—except an American one, I mean.

"You can at least tell me whether you liked or disliked her?" said Poirot with a smile.

Mr. Reiter got quite red and stammered. "She was a charming person—most charming. And intellectual. She had a very fine brain—yes."

"Bien! You liked her. And she liked you?"

Mr. Reiter got redder still.

"Oh, I—I don't know that she noticed me much. And I was unfortunate once or twice. I was always unlucky when I tried to do anything for her. I'm afraid I annoyed her by my clumsiness. It was quite unintentional—I would have done *any*thing—"

Poirot took pity on his flounderings.

"Perfectly—perfectly. Let us pass to another matter. Was it a happy atmosphere in the house?"

"Please?"

"Were you all happy together? Did you laugh and talk?"

"No—no, not exactly that. There was a little—stiffness." He paused, struggling with himself, and then said, "You see, I am not very good in company. I am clumsy. I am shy. Doctor Leidner always he has been most kind to me. But—it is stupid—I cannot overcome my shyness. I say always the wrong thing. I upset water jugs. I am unlucky."

He really looked like a large, awkward child.

"We all do these things when we are young," said Poirot, smiling. "The poise, the *savoir-faire,* it comes later."

Then with a word of farewell we walked on.

He said, "That, *ma soeur,* is either an extremely simple young man or a very remarkable actor."

I didn't answer. I was caught up once more by the fantastic notion that one of these people was a dangerous and cold-blooded murderer. Somehow, on this beautiful still sunny morning, it seemed impossible.

CHAPTER XXI

MR. MERCADO, RICHARD CAREY

"They work in two separate places, I see," said Poirot, halting.

Mr. Reiter had been doing his photography on an outlying portion of the main excavation. A little distance away from us a second swarm of men were coming and going with baskets.

"That's what they call the deep cut," I explained. "They don't find much there, nothing but rubbishy broken pottery, but Doctor Leidner always says it's very interesting, so I suppose it must be."

"Let us go there."

We walked together slowly for the sun was hot.

Mr. Mercado was in command. We saw him below us talking to the foreman, an old man like a tortoise who wore a tweed coat over his long striped cotton gown.

It was a little difficult to get down to them as there was only a narrow path or stair and basket boys were going up and down it constantly, and they always seemed to be as blind as bats and never to think of getting out of the way.

As I followed Poirot down he said suddenly over his shoulder, "Is Mr. Mercado right-handed or left-handed?"

Now that was an extraordinary question if you like!

I thought a minute, then: "Right-handed," I said decisively.

Poirot didn't condescend to explain. He just went on and I followed him.

Mr. Mercado seemed rather pleased to see us.

His long, melancholy face lit up.

M. Poirot pretended to an interest in archaeology that I'm sure he couldn't have really felt, but Mr. Mercado responded at once.

He explained that they had already cut down through twelve levels of house occupation.

"We are now definitely in the fourth millennium," he said with enthusiasm.

I always thought a millennium was in the future—the time when everything comes right.

Mr. Mercado pointed out belts of ashes (How his hand did shake! I wondered if he might possibly have malaria.) and he explained how the pottery changed in character, and about burials—and how they had had one level almost entirely composed of infant burials—poor little things—and about flexed position and orientation which seemed to mean the way the bones were lying.

And then suddenly, just as he was stooping down to pick up a kind of flint knife that was lying with some pots in a corner, he leaped into the air with a wild yell.

He spun round to find me and Poirot staring at him in astonishment. He clapped his hand to his left arm.

"Something stung me—like a red-hot needle."

Immediately Poirot was galvanized into energy.

"Quick, *mon cher,* let us see. Nurse Leatheran!" I came forward.

He seized Mr. Mercado's arm and deftly rolled back the sleeve of his khaki shirt to the shoulder.

"There," said Mr. Mercado, pointing.

About three inches below the shoulder there was a minute prick from which the blood was oozing.

"Curious," said Poirot. He peered into the rolled-up sleeve. "I can see nothing. It was an ant, perhaps?"

"Better put on a little iodine," I said.

I always carry an iodine pencil with me, and I whipped it out and applied it. But I was a little absent-minded as I did so, for my attention had been caught by something quite different. Mr. Mercado's arm, all the way up the forearm to the elbow, was marked all over by tiny punctures. I knew well enough what *they* were—*the marks of a hypodermic needle.*

Mr. Mercado rolled down his sleeve again and recommenced his explanations. Mr. Poirot listened, but didn't try to bring the conversation round to the Leidners. In fact he didn't ask Mr. Mercado anything at all.

Presently we said good-by to Mr. Mercado and climbed up the path again.

"It was neat that, did you not think so?" my companion asked.

"Neat?" I asked.

M. Poirot took something from behind the lapel of his coat and surveyed it affectionately. To my surprise I saw that it was a long sharp darning-needle with a blob of sealing wax making it into a pin.

"M. Poirot," I cried, "did *you* do that?"

"I was the stinging insect—yes. And very neatly I did it, too, do you not think so? You did not see me."

That was true enough. *I* never saw him do it. And I'm sure Mr. Mercado hadn't suspected. He must have been quick as lightning.

"But, M. Poirot, why?" I asked.

He answered me by another question.

"Did you notice anything, sister?" he asked.

I nodded my head slowly.

"Hypodermic marks," I said.

"So now we know something about Mr. Mercado," said Poirot. "I suspected—but I did not *know.* It is always necessary to *know.*"

And you don't care how you set about it! I thought, but didn't say.

Poirot suddenly clapped his hand to his pocket.

"Alas, I have dropped my handkerchief down there. I concealed the pin in it."

"I'll get it for you," I said and hurried back.

I'd got the feeling, you see, by this time, that M. Poirot and I were the doctor and nurse in charge of a case. At least, it was more like an operation and he was the surgeon. Perhaps I oughtn't to say so, but in a queer way I was beginning to enjoy myself.

I remember just after I'd finished my training, I went to a case in a private house and the need for an immediate operation arose, and the patient's husband was cranky about nursing homes. He just wouldn't hear of his wife being taken to one. Said it had to be done in the house.

Well, of course, it was just splendid for me! Nobody else to have a look in! I was in charge of everything. Of course, I was terribly nervous—I thought of everything conceivable that doctor could want, but even then I was afraid I might have forgotten something. You never know with doctors. They ask for absolutely anything sometimes! But everything went splendidly! I had each thing ready as he asked for it, and he actually told me I'd done first rate after it was over—and that's a thing most doctors wouldn't bother to do! The G.P. was very nice, too. And I ran the whole thing myself!

The patient recovered, too, so everybody was happy.

Well, I felt rather the same now. In a way M. Poirot reminded me of that surgeon. *He* was a little man, too. Ugly little man with a face like a monkey, but a wonderful surgeon. He knew instinctively just where to go. I've seen a lot of surgeons and I know what a lot of difference there is.

Gradually I'd been growing a kind of confidence in M. Poirot. I felt that he, too, knew exactly what he was doing. And I was getting to feel that it was my job to help him—as you might say—to have the forceps and the swabs and all handy just when he wanted them. That's why it seemed just as natural for me to run off and look for his handkerchief as it would have been to pick up a towel that a doctor had thrown on the floor.

When I'd found it and got back I couldn't see him at first. But at last I caught sight of him. He was sitting a little way from the mound talking to Mr. Carey. Mr. Carey's boy was standing near with that great big rod thing with meters marked on it, but just at that moment he said something to the boy and the boy took it away. It seemed he had finished with it for the time being.

I'd like to get this next bit quite clear. You see, I wasn't quite sure what M. Poirot did or didn't want me to do. He might, I mean, have sent me back for that handkerchief *on purpose.* To get me out of the way.

It was just like an operation over again. You've got to be careful to hand the doctor just what he wants and not what he *doesn't* want. I mean, suppose you gave him the artery forceps at the wrong moment, and were late with them at the right moment! Thank goodness I know my work in the theater well enough. I'm not likely to make mistakes there. But in this business I was really the rawest of raw little probationers. And so I had to be particularly careful not to make any silly mistakes.

Of course, I didn't for one moment imagine that M. Poirot didn't want me to hear what he and Mr. Carey were saying. But he might have thought he'd get Mr. Carey to talk better if I wasn't there.

Now I don't want anybody to get it into their heads that I'm the kind of woman who goes about eavesdropping on private conversations. I wouldn't do such a thing. Not for a moment. Not however much I wanted to.

And what I mean is if it *had* been a private conversation I wouldn't for a moment have done what, as a matter of fact, I actually did do.

As I looked at it I was in a privileged position. After all, you hear many a thing when a patient's coming round after an anesthetic. The patient wouldn't want you to hear it—and usually has no idea you *have* heard it—but the fact remains you *do* hear it. I just took it that Mr. Carey was the patient. He'd be none the worse for what he didn't know about. And if you think that I was just curious, well, I'll admit that I *was* curious. I didn't want to miss anything I could help.

All this is just leading up to the fact that I turned aside and went by a roundabout way up behind the big dump until I was a foot from where they were, but concealed from them by the corner of the dump. And if anyone says it was dishonorable I just beg to disagree. *Nothing* ought to be hidden from the nurse in charge of the case, though, of course, it's the doctor to say what shall be *done.*

I don't know, of course, what M. Poirot's line of approach had been, but by the time I'd got there he was aiming straight for the bull's eye, so to speak.

"Nobody appreciates Doctor Leidner's devotion to his wife more than I do," he was saying. "But it is often the case that one learns more about a person from their enemies than from their friends."

"You suggest that their faults are more important than their virtues?" said Mr. Carey. His tone was dry and ironic.

"Undoubtedly—when it comes to murder. It seems odd that as far as I know nobody has yet been murdered for having too perfect a character! And yet perfection is undoubtedly an irritating thing."

"I'm afraid I'm hardly the right person to help you," said Mr. Carey. "To be perfectly honest, Mrs. Leidner and I didn't hit it off particularly well. I don't mean that we were in any sense of the word enemies, but we were not exactly friends. Mrs. Leidner was, perhaps, a shade jealous of my old friendship with her husband. I, for my part, although I admired her very much and thought she was an extremely attractive woman, was just a shade resentful of her influence over Leidner. As a result we were quite polite to each other, but not intimate."

"Admirably explained," said Poirot.

I could just see their heads, and I saw Mr. Carey's turn sharply as though something in M. Poirot's detached tone struck him disagreeably.

M. Poirot went on. "Was not Doctor Leidner distressed that you and his wife did not get on together better?"

Carey hesitated a minute before saying, "Really—I'm not sure. He never said anything. I always hoped he didn't notice it. He was very wrapped up in his work, you know."

"So the truth, according to you, is that you did not really like Mrs. Leidner?"

Carey shrugged his shoulders.

"I should probably have liked her very much if she hadn't been Leidner's wife."

He laughed as though amused by his own statement.

Poirot was arranging a little heap of broken potsherds. He said in a dreamy, faraway voice, "I talked to Miss Johnson this morning. She admitted that she was prejudiced against Mrs. Leidner and did not like her very much, although she hastened to add that Mrs. Leidner had always been charming to her."

"All quite true, I should say," said Carey.

"So I believed. Then I had a conversation with Mrs. Mercado. She told me at great length how devoted she had been to Mrs. Leidner and how much she had admired her."

Carey made no answer to this, and after waiting a minute or two Poirot went on.

"That—I did not believe! Then I come to you and that which you tell me—well, again—*I do not believe.*"

Carey stiffened. I could hear the anger—repressed anger—in his voice.

"I really cannot help your beliefs—or your disbeliefs, M. Poirot. You've heard the truth and you can take it or leave it as far as I am concerned."

Poirot did not grow angry. Instead he sounded particularly meek and depressed.

"Is it my fault what I do—or do not believe? I have a sensitive ear, you know. And then—there are always plenty of stories going about—rumors floating in the air. One listens—and perhaps—one learns something! Yes, there *are* stories."

Carey sprang to his feet. I could see clearly a little pulse that beat in his temple. He looked simply splendid! So lean and so brown—and that wonderful jaw, hard and square. I don't wonder women fell for that man.

"What stories?" he asked savagely.

Poirot looked sideways at him.

"Perhaps you can guess. The usual sort of story—about you and Mrs. Leidner."

"What foul minds people have!"

"N'est-ce pas? They are like dogs. However deep you bury an unpleasantness a dog will always root it up again."

"And you believe these stories?"

"I am willing to be convinced—of the truth," said Poirot gravely.

"I doubt if you'd know the truth if you heard it." Carey laughed rudely.

"Try me and see," said Poirot, watching him.

"I will, then! You shall have the truth! I hated Louise Leidner—there's the truth for you! I hated her like hell!"

CHAPTER XXII

DAVID EMMOTT, FATHER LAVIGNY, AND A DISCOVERY

Turning abruptly away, Carey strode off with long angry strides.

Poirot sat looking after him and presently he murmured, "Yes—I see." Without turning his head he said in a slightly louder voice, "Do not come round the corner for a minute, nurse. In case he turns his head. Now it is all right. You have my handkerchief? Many thanks. You are most amiable."

He didn't say anything at all about my having been listening—and how he knew I *was* listening I can't think. He'd never once looked in that direction. I was rather relieved he didn't say anything. I mean, I felt all right with *myself* about it, but it might have been a little awkward explaining to him. So it was a good thing he didn't seem to want explanations.

"Do you think he did hate her, M. Poirot?" I asked.

Nodding his head slowly with a curious expression on his face, Poirot answered.

"Yes—I think he did."

Then he got up briskly and began to walk to where the men were working on the top of the mound. I followed him. We couldn't see anyone but Arabs at first but we finally found Mr. Emmott lying face downward blowing dust off a skeleton that had just been uncovered.

He gave his pleasant, grave smile when he saw us.

"Have you come to see round?" he asked. "I'll be free in a minute."

He sat up, took his knife, and began daintily cutting the earth away from round the bones, stopping every now and then to use either a bellows or his own breath. A very insanitary proceeding, the latter, I thought.

"You'll get all sorts of nasty germs in your mouth, Mr. Emmott," I protested.

"Nasty germs are my daily diet, nurse," he said gravely. "Germs can't do anything to an archaeologist—they just get naturally discouraged trying."

He scraped a little more away round the thigh bone. Then he spoke to the foreman at his side directing him exactly what he wanted done.

"There," he said, rising to his feet. "That's ready for Reiter to photograph after lunch. Rather nice stuff she had in with her."

He showed us a little verdigrisy copper bowl and some pins. And a lot of gold and blue things that had been her necklace of beads.

The bones and all the objects were brushed and cleaned with a knife and kept in position ready to be photographed.

"Who is she?" asked Poirot.

"First millennium. A lady of some consequence perhaps. Skull looks rather odd—I must get Mercado to look at it. It suggests death by foul play."

"A Mrs. Leidner of two thousand odd years ago?" said Poirot.

"Perhaps," said Mr. Emmott.

Bill Coleman was doing something with a pick to a wall face.

David Emmott called something to him which I didn't catch and then started showing M. Poirot round.

When the short explanatory tour was over Emmott looked at his watch.

"We knock off in ten minutes," he said. "Shall we walk back to the house?"

"That will suit me excellently," said Poirot.

We walked slowly along the well-worn path.

"I expect you are all glad to get back to work again," said Poirot.

Emmott replied gravely, "Yes, it's much the best thing. It's not been any too easy loafing about the house and making conversation."

"Knowing all the time *that one of you was a murderer.*"

Emmott did not answer. He made no gesture of dissent. I knew now that he had had a suspicion of the truth from the very first when he had questioned the houseboys.

After a few minutes he asked quietly, "Are you getting anywhere, M. Poirot?"

Poirot said gravely, "Will you help me to get somewhere?"

"Why, naturally."

Watching him closely, Poirot said, "The hub of the case is Mrs. Leidner. I want to know about Mrs. Leidner."

David Emmott said slowly, "What do you mean by knowing about her?"

"I do not mean where she came from and what her maiden name was. I do not mean the shape of her face and the color of her eyes. I mean her—herself."

"You think that counts in the case?"

"I am quite sure of it."

Emmott was silent for a moment or two, then he said, "Maybe you're right."

"And that is where you can help me. You can tell me what sort of a woman she was."

"Can I? I've often wondered about it myself."

"Didn't you make up your mind on the subject?"

"I think I did in the end."

"Eh bien?"

But Mr. Emmott was silent for some minutes, then he said, "What did nurse think of her? Women are said to sum up other women quickly enough, and a nurse has a wide experience of types."

Poirot didn't give me any chance of speaking even if I had wanted to. He said quickly, "What I want to know is what a *man* thought of her?"

Emmott smiled a little.

"I expect they'd all be much the same." He paused and said, "She wasn't young, but I think she was about the most beautiful woman I've ever come across."

"That's hardly an answer, Mr. Emmott."

"It's not so far off one, M. Poirot."

He was silent a minute or two and then he went on. "There used to be a fairy story I read when I was a kid. A Northern fairy story about the Snow Queen and Little Kay. I guess Mrs. Leidner was rather like that—always taking Little Kay for a ride."

"Ah, yes, a tale of Hans Andersen, is it not? And there was a girl in it. Little Gerda, was that her name?"

"Maybe. I don't remember much of it."

"Can't you go a little further, Mr. Emmott?"

David Emmott shook his head.

"I don't even know if I've summed her up correctly. She wasn't easy to read. She'd do a devilish thing one day, and a really fine one the next. But I think you're about right when you say that she's the hub of the case. That's what she always wanted to be—*at the center of things.* And she liked to get *at* other people—I mean, she wasn't just satisfied with being passed the toast and the peanut butter, she wanted you to turn your mind and soul inside out for her to look at it."

"And if one did not give her that satisfaction?" asked Poirot.

"Then she could turn ugly!"

I saw his lips close resolutely and his jaws set.

"I suppose, Mr. Emmott, you would not care to express a plain unofficial opinion as to who murdered her?"

"I don't know," said Emmott. "I really haven't the slightest idea. I rather think that, if I'd been Carl—Carl Reiter, I mean—I would have had a shot at murdering her. She was a pretty fair devil to him. But, of course, he asks for it by being so darned sensitive. Just invites you to give him a kick in the pants."

"And did Mrs. Leidner give him—a kick in the pants?" inquired Poirot.

Emmott gave a sudden grin.

"No. Pretty little jabs with an embroidery needle—that was her method. He *was* irritating, of course. Just like some blubbering, poor-spirited kid. But a needle's a painful weapon."

I stole a glance at Poirot and thought I detected a slight quiver of his lips. "But you don't really believe that Carl Reiter killed her?" he asked.

"No. I don't believe you'd kill a woman because she persistently made you look a fool at every meal."

Poirot shook his head thoughtfully.

Of course, Mr. Emmott made Mrs. Leidner sound quite inhuman. There was something to be said on the other side, too.

There had been something terribly irritating about Mr. Reiter's attitude. He jumped when she spoke to him, and did idiotic things, like passing her the marmalade again and again when he knew she never ate it. I'd have felt inclined to snap at him a bit myself.

Men don't understand how their mannerisms can get on women's nerves so that you feel you just have to snap.

I thought I'd just mention that to Mr. Poirot sometime.

We had arrived back by now and Mr. Emmott offered Poirot a wash and took him into his room.

I hurried across the courtyard to mine.

I came out again about the same time they did and we were all making for the dining-room when Father Lavigny appeared in the doorway of his room and invited Poirot in.

Mr. Emmott came on round and he and I went into the dining-room together. Miss Johnson and Mrs. Mercado were there already, and after a few minutes Mr. Mercado, Mr. Reiter, and Bill Coleman joined us.

We were just sitting down and Mercado had told the Arab boy to tell Father Lavigny lunch was ready when we were all startled by a faint, muffled cry.

I suppose our nerves weren't very good yet, for we all jumped, and Miss Johnson got quite pale and said, *"What was that?* What's happened?"

Mrs. Mercado stared at her and said, "My dear, what *is* the matter with you? It's some noise outside in the fields."

But at that minute Poirot and Father Lavigny came in.

"We thought someone was hurt," Miss Johnson said.

"A thousand pardons, mademoiselle," cried Poirot. "The fault is mine. Father Lavigny, he explains to me some tablets, and I take one to the window to see better—and, *ma foi,* not looking where I was going, I steb the toe, and the pain is sharp for the moment and I cry out."

"We thought it was another murder," said Mrs. Mercado, laughing.

"Marie!" said her husband.

His tone was reproachful, and she flushed and bit her lip.

Miss Johnson hastily turned the conversation to the dig and what objects of interest had turned up that morning. Conversation all through lunch was sternly archaeological.

I think we all felt it was the safest thing.

After we had had coffee we adjourned to the living-room. Then the men, with the exception of Father Lavigny, went off to the dig again.

Father Lavigny took Poirot through into the antika room and I went with them. I was getting to know the things pretty well by now and I felt a thrill of pride—almost as though it were my own property—when Father Lavigny took down the gold cup and I heard Poirot's exclamation of admiration and pleasure.

"How beautiful! What a work of art!"

Father Lavigny agreed eagerly and began to point out its beauties with real enthusiasm and knowledge.

"No wax on it today," I said.

"Wax?" Poirot stared at me.

"Wax?" So did Father Lavigny.

I explained my remark.

"Ah, *je comprends,*" said Father Lavigny. "Yes, yes, candle grease."

That led direct to the subject of the midnight visitor. Forgetting my presence they both dropped into French and I left them together and went back into the living-room.

Mrs. Mercado was darning her husband's socks and Miss Johnson was reading a book. Rather an unusual thing for her. She usually seemed to have something to work at.

After a while Father Lavigny and Poirot came out, and the former excused himself on the score of work. Poirot sat down with us.

"A most interesting man," he said, and asked how much work there had been for Father Lavigny to do so far.

Miss Johnson explained that tablets had been scarce and that there had been very few inscribed bricks or cylinder seals. Father Lavigny, however, had done his share of work on the dig and was picking up colloquial Arabic very fast.

That led the talk to cylinder seals, and presently Miss Johnson fetched from a cupboard a sheet of impressions made by rolling them out on plasticine.

I realized as we bent over them, admiring the spirited designs, that these must be what she had been working at on that fatal afternoon.

As we talked I noticed that Poirot was rolling and kneading a little ball of plasticine between his fingers.

"You use a lot of plasticine, mademoiselle?" he asked.

"A fair amount. We seem to have got through a lot already this year—though I can't imagine how. But half our supply seems to have gone."

"Where is it kept, mademoiselle?"

"Here—in this cupboard."

As she replaced the sheet of impressions she showed him the shelf with rolls of plasticine, Durofix, photographic paste, and other stationery supplies.

Poirot stooped down.

"And this—what is this, mademoiselle?"

He had slipped his hand right to the back and had brought out a curious crumpled object.

As he straightened it out we could see that it was a kind of mask, with eyes and mouth crudely painted on in Indian ink and the whole thing roughly smeared with plasticine.

"How perfectly extraordinary," cried Miss Johnson. "I've never seen it before. How did it get there? And what is it?"

"As to how it got there, well, one hiding-place is as good as another, and I presume that this cupboard would not have been turned out till the end of the season. As to what it *is*—that, too, I think, is not difficult to say. *We have here the face that Mrs. Leidner described.* The ghostly face seen in the semidusk outside her window—without body attached."

Mrs. Mercado gave a little shriek.

Miss Johnson was white to the lips. She murmured, "Then it was *not* fancy. It was a trick—a wicked trick! But who played it?"

"Yes," cried Mrs. Mercado. "Who could have done such a wicked, wicked thing?"

Poirot did not attempt a reply. His face was very grim as he went into the next room, returned with an empty cardboard box in his hand, and put the crumpled mask into it. "The police must see this," he explained.

"It's horrible," said Miss Johnson in a low voice. "Horrible!"

"Do you think everything's hidden here somewhere?" cried Mrs. Mercado shrilly. "Do you think perhaps the weapon—the club she was killed with—all covered with blood still, perhaps— Oh! I'm frightened—I'm frightened!"

Miss Johnson gripped her by the shoulder.

"Be quiet," she said fiercely. "Here's Doctor Leidner. We musn't upset him."

Indeed, at that very moment the car had driven into the courtyard. Dr. Leidner got out of it and came straight across and in at the living-room door. His face was set in lines of fatigue and he looked twice the age he had three days ago.

He said in a quiet voice, "The funeral will be at eleven o'clock tomorrow. Major Deane will read the service."

Mrs. Mercado faltered something, then slipped out of the room.

Dr. Leidner said to Miss Johnson, "You'll come, Anne?"

And she answered, "Of course, my dear, we'll all come. Naturally."

She didn't say anything else, but her face must have expressed what her tongue was powerless to do, for his face lightened up with affection and a momentary ease.

"Dear Anne," he said. "You are such a wonderful comfort and help to me. My dear old friend."

He laid his hand on her arm and I saw the red color creep up in her face as she muttered, gruff as ever, "That's all right."

But I just caught a glimpse of her expression and knew that, for one short moment, Anne Johnson was a perfectly happy woman.

And another idea flashed across my mind. Perhaps soon, in the natural course of things, turning to his old friend for sympathy, a new and happy state of things might come about.

Not that I'm really a matchmaker, and, of course, it was indecent to think of such a thing before the funeral even. But after all, it *would* be a happy solution. He was very fond of her, and there was no doubt she was absolutely devoted to him and would be perfectly happy devoting the rest of her life to him. That is, if she could bear to hear Louise's perfections sung all the time. But women can put up with a lot when they've got what they want.

Dr. Leidner then greeted Poirot, asking him if he had made any progress.

Miss Johnson was standing behind Dr. Leidner and she looked hard at the box in Poirot's hand and shook her head, and I realized that she was pleading with Poirot not to tell him about the mask. She felt, I was sure, that he had enough to bear for one day.

Poirot fell in with her wish.

"These things march slowly, monsieur," he said.

Then, after a few desultory words, he took his leave.

I accompanied him out to his car.

There were half a dozen things I wanted to ask him, but somehow, when he turned and looked at me, I didn't ask anything after all. I'd as soon have asked a surgeon if he thought he'd made a good job of an operation. I just stood meekly waiting for instructions.

Rather to my surprise he said, "Take care of yourself, my child." And then he added, "I wonder if it is well for you to remain here?"

"I must speak to Doctor Leidner about leaving," I said. "But I thought I'd wait until after the funeral."

He nodded in approval.

"In the meantime," he said, "do not try and find out too much. You understand, I do not want you to be clever!" And he added with a smile, "It is for you to hold the swabs and for me to do the operation."

Wasn't it funny, his actually saying that?

Then he said quite irrelevantly, "An interesting man, that Father Lavigny."

"A monk being an archaeologist seems odd to me," I said.

"Ah, yes, you are a Protestant. Me, I am a good Catholic. I know something of priests and monks."

He frowned, seemed to hesitate, then said, "Remember, he is quite clever enough to turn you inside out if he likes."

If he was warning me against gossiping I felt that I didn't need any such warning!

It annoyed me and though I didn't like to ask him any of the things I really wanted to know, I didn't see why I shouldn't at any rate say one thing.

"You'll excuse me, M. Poirot," I said. "But it's *stubbed* your toe, not *stepped* or *stebbed.*"

"Ah? Thank you, *ma soeur.*"

"Don't mention it. But it's just as well to get a phrase right."

"I will remember," he said—quite meekly for him.

And he got in the car and was driven away, and I went slowly back across the courtyard wondering about a lot of things.

About the hypodermic marks on Mr. Mercado's arm, and what drug it was he took. And about that horrid yellow smeared mask. And how odd it was that Poirot and Miss Johnson hadn't heard my cry in the living-room that morning, whereas we had all heard Poirot perfectly well in the dining-room at lunchtime—and yet Father Lavigny's room and Mrs. Leidner's were just the same distance from the living-room and the dining-room respectively.

And then I felt rather pleased that I'd taught *Doctor* Poirot one English phrase correctly!

Even if he *was* a great detective he'd realize he *didn't* know *everything!*

CHAPTER XXIII

I GO PSYCHIC

The funeral was, I thought, a very affecting affair. As well as ourselves, all the English people in Hassanieh attended it. Even Sheila Reilly was there looking quiet and subdued in a dark coat and skirt. I hoped that she was feeling a little remorseful for all the unkind things she had said.

When we got back to the house I followed Dr. Leidner into the office and broached the subject of my departure. He was very nice about it, thanked me for what I had done (Done! I had been worse than useless) and insisted on my accepting an extra week's salary.

I protested because really I felt I'd done nothing to earn it.

"Indeed, Doctor Leidner, I'd rather not have any salary at all. If you'd just refund me my traveling expenses that's all I want."

But he wouldn't hear of that.

"You see," I said, "I don't feel I deserve it, Doctor Leidner. I mean, I've—well, I've failed. She—my coming didn't save her."

"Now don't get that idea into your head, nurse," he said earnestly. "After all, I didn't engage you as a female detective. I never dreamed my wife's life was in danger. I was convinced it was all nerves and that she'd worked herself up into a rather curious mental state. You did all anyone could do. She liked and trusted you. And I think in her last days she felt happier and safer because of your being here. There's nothing for you to reproach yourself with."

His voice quivered a little and I knew what he was thinking. *He* was the one to blame for not having taken Mrs. Leidner's fears seriously.

"Doctor Leidner," I said curiously. "Have you ever come to any conclusion about those anonymous letters?"

He said with a sigh, "I don't know what to believe. Has M. Poirot come to any definite conclusion?"

"He hadn't yesterday," I said, steering rather neatly, I thought, between truth and fiction. After all, he hadn't until I told him about Miss Johnson.

It was on my mind that I'd like to give Dr. Leidner a hint and see if he reacted. In the pleasure of seeing him and Miss Johnson together the day before, and his affection and reliance on her, I'd forgotten all about the letters. Even now I felt it was perhaps rather mean of me to bring it up. Even if she had written them, she had had a bad time after Mrs. Leidner's death. Yet I did want to see whether that particular possibility had ever entered Dr. Leidner's head.

"Anonymous letters are usually the work of a woman," I said. I wanted to see how he'd take it.

"I suppose they are," he said with a sigh. "But you seem to forget, nurse, that these may be genuine. They may actually be written by Frederick Bosner."

"No, I haven't forgotten," I said. "But I can't believe somehow that that's the real explanation."

"I do," he said. "It's all nonsense his being one of the expedition staff. That is just an ingenious theory of M. Poirot's. I believe that the truth is much simpler. The man is a madman, of course. He's been hanging round the place—perhaps in disguise of some kind. And somehow or other he got in on that fatal afternoon. The servants may be lying—they may have been bribed."

"I suppose it's possible," I said doubtfully.

Dr. Leidner went on with a trace of irritability.

"It is all very well for M. Poirot to suspect the members of my expedition. I am perfectly certain *none* of them have anything to do with it! I have worked with them. I *know* them!"

He stopped suddenly, then he said, "Is that your experience, nurse? That anonymous letters are usually written by women?"

"It isn't always the case," I said. "But there's a certain type of feminine spitefulness that finds relief that way."

"I suppose you are thinking of Mrs. Mercado?" he said. Then he shook his head. "Even if she were malicious enough to wish to hurt Louise she would hardly have the necessary knowledge," he said.

I remembered the earlier letters in the attaché case.

If Mrs. Leidner had left that unlocked and Mrs. Mercado had been alone in the house one day pottering about, she might easily have found them and read them. Men never seem to think of the simplest possibilities!

"And apart from her there is only Miss Johnson," I said, watching him.

"That would be quite ridiculous!"

The little smile with which he said it was quite conclusive. The idea of Miss Johnson being the author of the letters had never entered his head! I hesitated just for a minute—but I didn't say anything. One doesn't like giving away a fellow woman, and besides, I had been a witness of Miss

Johnson's genuine and moving remorse. What was done was done. Why expose Dr. Leidner to a fresh disillusion on top of all his other troubles?

It was arranged that I should leave on the following day, and I had arranged through Dr. Reilly to stay for a day or two with the matron of the hospital while I made arrangements for returning to England either via Baghdad or direct via Nissibin by car and train.

Dr. Leidner was kind enough to say that he would like me to choose a memento from among his wife's things.

"Oh, no, really, Doctor Leidner," I said. "I couldn't. It's much too kind of you."

He insisted.

"But I should like you to have something. And Louise, I am sure, would have wished it."

Then he went on to suggest that I should have her tortoise-shell toilet set!

"Oh, no, Doctor Leidner! Why, that's most a *expensive* set. I couldn't, really."

"She had no sisters, you know—no one who wants these things. There is no one else to have them."

I could quite imagine that he wouldn't want them to fall into Mrs. Mercado's greedy little hands. And I didn't think he'd want to offer them to Miss Johnson.

He went on kindly. "You just think it over. By the way, here is the key of Louise's jewel case. Perhaps you will find something there you would rather have. And I should be very grateful if you would pack up—all—all her clothes. I dare say Reilly can find a use for them among some of the poor Christian families in Hassanieh."

I was very glad to be able to do that for him, and I expressed my willingness.

I set about it at once.

Mrs. Leidner had only had a very simple wardrobe with her and it was soon sorted and packed up into a couple of suitcases. All her papers had been in the small attaché case. The jewel case contained a few simple trinkets—a pearl ring, a diamond brooch, a small string of pearls, and one or two plain gold bar brooches of the safety-pin type, and a string of large amber beads.

Naturally I wasn't going to take the pearls or the diamonds, but I hesitated a bit between the amber beads and the toilet set. In the end, however, I didn't see why I shouldn't take the latter. It was a kindly thought on Dr. Leidner's part, and I was sure there wasn't any patronage about it. I'd take it in the spirit it had been offered without any false pride. After all, I *had* been fond of her.

Well, that was all done and finished with. The suitcases packed, the jewel case locked up again and put separate to give to Dr. Leidner with the photograph of Mrs. Leidner's father and one or two other personal little odds and ends.

The room looked bare and forlorn emptied of all its accouterments, when I'd finished. There was nothing more for me to do—and yet somehow or other I shrank from leaving the room. It seemed as though there were something still to do there—something I ought to *see*—or something I ought to have *known.*

I'm not superstitious but the idea *did* pop into my head that perhaps Mrs. Leidner's spirit was hanging about the room and trying to get in touch with me.

I remember once at the hospital some of us girls got a planchette, and really it wrote some very remarkable things.

Perhaps, although I'd never thought of such a thing, I might be mediumistic.

As I say, one gets all worked up to imagine all sorts of foolishness sometimes.

I prowled round the room uneasily, touching this and that. But, of course, there wasn't anything in the room but bare furniture. There was nothing slipped behind drawers or tucked away. I couldn't hope for anything of that kind.

In the end (it sounds rather batty, but as I say, one gets worked up) I did rather a queer thing.

I went and lay down on the bed and closed my eyes.

I deliberately tried to forget who and what I was. I tried to think myself back to that fatal afternoon. I was Mrs. Leidner lying here resting, peaceful and unsuspicious.

It's extraordinary how you can work yourself up.

I'm a perfectly normal matter-of-fact individual—not the least little bit spooky, but I tell you that after I'd lain there about five minutes I began to *feel* spooky.

I didn't try to resist. I deliberately encouraged the feeling.

I said to myself, "I'm Mrs. Leidner. I'm Mrs. Leidner. I'm lying here—half asleep. Presently—very soon now—the door's going to open."

I kept on saying that—as though I were hypnotizing myself.

"It's just about half past one . . . it's just about the time. . . . The door is going to open . . . *the door is going to open.* . . . I shall see who comes in. . . ."

I kept my eyes glued on that door. Presently it was going to open. I should *see* it open. And I should see *the person who opened it.*

I must have been a little overwrought that afternoon to imagine I could solve the mystery that way.

But I did believe it. A sort of chill passed down my back and settled in my legs. They felt numb—paralyzed.

"You're going into a trance," I said. "And in that trance you'll see . . ."

And once again I repeated monotonously again and again, "The door is going to open—the door is going to open. . ."

The cold, numbed feeling grew more intense.

And then, slowly, *I saw the door just beginning to open.*

It was horrible.

I've never known anything so horrible before or since.

I was paralyzed—chilled through and through. I couldn't move. For the life of me I couldn't have moved.

And I was terrified. Sick and blind and dumb with terror.

That slowly opening door.

So noiseless.

In a minute I should see—

Slowly—slowly—wider and wider.

Bill Coleman came quietly in.

He must have had the shock of his life!

I bounded off the bed with a scream of terror and hurled myself across the room.

He stood stock-still, his blunt pink face pinker and his mouth opened wide with surprise.

"Hallo, 'allo, 'allo," he said. "What's up, nurse?"

I came back to reality with a crash.

"Goodness, Mr. Coleman," I said. "How you startled me!"

"Sorry," he said with a momentary grin.

I saw then that he was holding a little bunch of scarlet ranunculus in his hand. They were pretty little flowers and they grew wild on the sides of the Tell. Mrs. Leidner had been very fond of them.

He blushed and got rather red as he said, "One can't get any flowers or things in Hassanieh. Seemed rather rotten not to have any flowers for the grave. I thought I'd just nip in here and put a little posy in that little pot thing she always had flowers in on her table. Sort of show she wasn't forgotten—eh? A bit asinine, I know, but—well—I mean to say—"

I thought it was very nice of him. He was all pink with embarrassment like Englishmen are when they've done anything sentimental. I thought it was a very sweet thought.

"Why, I think that's a very nice idea, Mr. Coleman," I said.

And I picked up the little pot and went and got some water in it and we put the flowers in.

I really thought much more of Mr. Coleman for this idea of his. It showed he had a heart and nice feelings about things.

He didn't ask me again what made me let out such a squeal and I'm thankful he didn't. I should have felt a fool explaining.

Stick to common sense in future, woman, I said to myself as I settled my cuffs and smoothed my apron. *You're not cut out for this psychic stuff.*

I bustled about doing my own packing and kept myself busy for the rest of the day.

Father Lavigny was kind enough to express great distress at my leaving. He said my cheerfulness and common sense had been such a help to everybody. Common sense! I'm glad he didn't know about my idiotic behavior in Mrs. Leidner's room.

"We have not seen M. Poirot today," he remarked.

I told him that Poirot had said he was going to be busy all day sending off telegrams.

Father Lavigny raised his eyebrows.

"Telegrams? To America?"

"I suppose so. He said 'All over the world!' but I think that was rather a foreign exaggeration."

And then I got rather red, remembering that Father Lavigny was a foreigner himself. He didn't seem offended though, just laughed quite pleasantly and asked me if there were any news of the man with the squint.

I said I didn't know but I hadn't heard of any.

Father Lavigny asked me again about the time Mrs. Leidner and I had noticed the man and how he had seemed to be standing on tiptoe and peering through the window.

"It seems clear the man had some overwhelming interest in Mrs. Leidner," he said thoughtfully. "I have wondered since whether the man could possibly have been a European got up to look like an Iraqi?"

That was a new idea to me and I considered it carefully. I had taken it for granted that the man was a native, but of course, when I came to think of it, I was really going by the cut of his clothes and the yellowness of his skin.

Father Lavigny declared his intention of going round outside the house to the place where Mrs. Leidner and I had seen the man standing.

"You never know, he might have dropped something. In the detective stories the criminal always does."

"I expect in real life criminals are more careful," I said.

I fetched some socks I had just finished darning and put them on the table in the living-room for the men to sort out when they came in, and then, as there was nothing much more to do, I went up on the roof.

Miss Johnson was standing there but she didn't hear me. I got right up to her before she noticed me.

But long before that I'd seen that there was something very wrong.

She was standing in the middle of the roof staring straight in front of her, and there was the most awful look on her face. As though she'd seen something she couldn't possibly believe.

It gave me quite a shock. Mind you, I'd seen her upset the other evening, but this was quite different.

"My dear," I said, hurrying to her, "whatever's the matter?"

She turned her head at that and stood looking at me—almost as if she didn't see me.

"What is it?" I persisted.

She made a queer sort of grimace—as though she were trying to swallow but her throat were too dry. She said hoarsely, "I've just seen something."

"What have you seen? Tell me. Whatever can it be? You look all in."

She gave an effort to pull herself together, but she still looked pretty dreadful.

She said, still in that same dreadful choked voice, *"I've seen how someone could come in from outside—and no one would ever guess."*

I followed the direction of her eyes but I couldn't see anything.

Mr. Reiter was standing in the door of the photographic room and Father Lavigny was just crossing the courtyard—but there was nothing else.

I turned back puzzled and found her eyes fixed on mine with the strangest expression in them.

"Really," I said, "I don't see what you mean. Won't you explain?"

But she shook her head.

"Not now. Later. We *ought* to have seen. Oh, we ought to have seen!"

"If you'd only tell me—"

But she shook her head.

"I've got to think it out first."

And, pushing past me, she went stumbling down the stairs.

I didn't follow her as she obviously didn't want me with her. Instead I sat down on the parapet and tried to puzzle things out. But I didn't get anywhere. There was only the one way into the courtyard—through the big arch. Just outside it I could see the water boy and his horse and the Indian cook talking to him. Nobody could have passed them and come in without their seeing him.

I shook my head in perplexity and went downstairs again.

CHAPTER XXIV

MURDER IS A HABIT

We all went to bed early that night. Miss Johnson had appeared at dinner and had behaved more or less as usual. She had, however, a sort of dazed look, and once or twice quite failed to take in what other people said to her.

It wasn't, somehow, a very comfortable sort of meal. You'd say, I suppose, that that was natural enough in a house where there'd been a funeral that day. But I know what I mean.

Lately our meals had been hushed and subdued, but for all that there had been a feeling of comradeship. There had been sympathy with Dr. Leidner in his grief and a fellow feeling of being all in the same boat among the others.

But tonight I was reminded of my first meal there—when Mrs. Mercado had watched me and there had been that curious feeling as though something might snap any minute.

I'd felt the same thing—only very much intensified—when we'd sat round the dining-room table with Poirot at the head of it.

Tonight it was particularly strong. Everyone was on edge—jumpy—on tenterhooks. If anyone had dropped something I'm sure somebody would have screamed.

As I say, we all separated early afterward. I went to bed almost at once. The last thing I heard as I was dropping off to sleep was Mrs. Mercado's voice saying good night to Miss Johnson just outside my door.

I dropped off to sleep at once—tired by my exertions and even more by my silly experience in Mrs. Leidner's room. I slept heavily and dreamlessly for several hours.

I awoke when I did awake with a start and a feeling of impending catastrophe. Some sound had waked me, and as I sat up in bed listening I heard it again.

An awful sort of agonized, choking groan.

I had lit my candle and was out of bed in a twinkling. I snatched up a torch, too, in case the candle should blow out. I came out of my door and stood listening. I knew the sound wasn't far away. It came again—from the room immediately next to mine—Miss Johnson's room.

I hurried in. Miss Johnson was lying in bed, her whole body contorted in agony. As I set down the candle and bent over her, her lips moved and she tried to speak—but only an awful hoarse whisper came. I saw that the corners of her mouth and the skin of her chin were burned a kind of grayish white.

Her eyes went from me to a glass that lay on the floor evidently where it had dropped from her hand. The light rug was stained a bright red where it had fallen. I picked it up and ran a finger over the inside, drawing back my hand with a sharp exclamation. Then I examined the inside of the poor woman's mouth.

There wasn't the least doubt what was the matter. Somehow or other, intentionally or otherwise, she'd swallowed a quantity of corrosive acid—oxalic or hydrochloric, I suspected.

I ran out and called to Dr. Leidner and he woke the others, and we worked over her for all we were worth, but all the time I had an awful feeling it was no good. We tried a strong solution of carbonate of soda—and followed it with olive oil. To ease the pain I gave her a hypodermic of morphine sulphate.

David Emmott had gone off to Hassanieh to fetch Dr. Reilly, but before he came it was over.

I won't dwell on the details. Poisoning by a strong solution of hydrochloric acid (which is what it proved to be) is one of the most painful deaths possible.

It was when I was bending over her to give her the morphia that she made one ghastly effort to speak. It was only a horrible strangled whisper when it came.

"The window—" she said. *"Nurse—the window—"*

But that was all—she couldn't go on. She collapsed completely.

I shall never forget that night. The arrival of Dr. Reilly. The arrival of Captain Maitland. And finally, with the dawn, Hercule Poirot.

He it was who took me gently by the arm and steered me into the dining-room where he made me sit down and have a cup of good strong tea.

"There, *mon enfant,"* he said, "that is better. You are worn out."

Upon that, I burst into tears.

"It's too awful," I sobbed. "It's been like a nightmare. Such awful suffering. And her eyes— Oh, M. Poirot—her eyes—"

He patted me on the shoulder. A woman couldn't have been kinder.

"Yes, yes—do not think of it. You did all you could."

"It was one of the corrosive acids."

"It was a strong solution of hydrochloric acid."

"The stuff they use on the pots?"

"Yes. Miss Johnson probably drank it off before she was fully awake. That is—unless she took it on purpose."

"Oh, M. Poirot, what an awful idea!"

"It is a possibility, after all. What do you think?"

I considered for a moment and then shook my head decisively.

"I don't believe it. No, I don't believe it for a moment." I hesitated and then said, "I think she found out something yesterday afternoon."

"What is that you say? She found out something?"

I repeated to him the curious conversation we had had together.

Poirot gave a low soft whistle.

"La pauvre femme!" he said. "She said she wanted to think it over—eh? That is what signed her death warrant. If she had only spoken out—then—at once."

He said, "Tell me again her exact words?"

I repeated them.

"She saw how someone could have come in from outside without any of you knowing? Come, *ma soeur,* let us go up to the roof and you shall show me just where she was standing."

We went up to the roof together and I showed Poirot the exact spot where Miss Johnson had stood.

"Like this?" said Poirot. "Now what do I see? I see half the courtyard—and the archway—and the doors of the drawing-office and the photographic room and the laboratory. Was there anyone in the courtyard?"

"Father Lavigny was just going toward the archway, and Mr. Reiter was standing in the door of the photographic room."

"And still I do not see in the least how anyone could come in from outside and none of you know about it. But *she* saw—"

He gave it up at last, shaking his head.

"Sacré nom d'un chien—va! What *did* she see?"

The sun was just rising. The whole eastern sky was a riot of rose and orange and pale, pearly gray.

"What a beautiful sunrise," said Poirot gently.

The river wound away to our left and the Tell stood up outlined in gold color. To the south were the blossoming trees and the peaceful cultivation. The water wheel groaned in the distance—a faint, unearthly sound. In the north were the slender minarets and the clustering fairy whiteness of Hassanieh.

It was all incredibly beautiful.

And then, close at my elbow, I heard Poirot give a long, deep sigh.

"Fool that I have been," he murmured. "When the truth is so clear—so clear."

CHAPTER XXV

SUICIDE OR MURDER?

I hadn't time to ask Poirot what he meant, for Captain Maitland was calling up to us and asking us to come down.

We hurried down the stairs.

"Look here, Poirot," he said. "Here's another complication. The monk fellow is missing."

"Father Lavigny?"

"Yes. Nobody noticed it till just now. Then it dawned on somebody that he was the only one of the party not around, and we went to his room. His bed's not been slept in and there's no sign of him."

The whole thing was like a bad dream. First Miss Johnson's death and then the disappearance of Father Lavigny.

The servants were called and questioned, but they couldn't throw any light on the mystery. He had last been seen at about eight o'clock the night before. Then he had said he was going out for a stroll before going to bed.

Nobody had seen him come back from that stroll.

The big doors had been closed and barred at nine o'clock as usual. Nobody, however, remembered unbarring them in the morning. The two houseboys each thought the other one must have done the unfastening.

Had Father Lavigny ever returned the night before? Had he, in the course of his earlier walk, discovered anything of a suspicious nature, gone out to investigate it later, and perhaps fallen a third victim?

Captain Maitland swung round as Dr. Reilly came up with Mr. Mercado behind him.

"Hallo, Reilly. Got anything?"

"Yes. The stuff came from the laboratory here. I've just been checking up the quantities with Mercado. It's H.C.L. from the lab."

"The laboratory—eh? Whas it locked up?"

Mr. Mercado shook his head. His hands were shaking and his face was twitching. He looked a wreck of a man.

"It's never been the custom," he stammered. "You see—just now—we're using it all the time. I—nobody ever dreamed—"

"Is the place locked up at night?"

"Yes—all the rooms are locked. The keys are hung up just inside the living-room."

"So if anyone had a key to that they could get the lot."

"Yes."

"And it's a perfectly ordinary key, I suppose?"

"Oh, yes."

"Nothing to show whether she took it herself from the laboratory?" asked Captain Maitland.

"She didn't," I said loudly and positively.

I felt a warning touch on my arm. Poirot was standing close behind me.

And then something rather ghastly happened.

Not ghastly in itself—in fact it was just the incongruousness that made it seem worse than anything else.

A car drove into the courtyard and a little man jumped out. He was wearing a sun helmet and a short, thick trench coat.

He came straight to Dr. Leidner, who was standing by Dr. Reilly, and shook him warmly by the hand.

"Vous voilà, mon cher," he cried. "Delighted to see you. I passed this way on Saturday afternoon—en route to the Italians at Fugima. I went to the dig but there wasn't a single European about and alas! I cannot speak Arabic. I had not time to come to the house. This morning I leave Fugima at five—two hours here with you—and then I catch the convoy on. *Eh bien,* and how is the season going?"

It was ghastly.

The cheery voice, the matter-of-fact manner, all the pleasant sanity of an everyday world now left far behind. He just bustled in, knowing nothing and noticing nothing—full of cheerful bonhomie.

No wonder Dr. Leidner gave an inarticulate gasp and looked in mute appeal at Dr. Reilly.

The doctor rose to the occasion.

He took the little man (he was a French archaeologist called Verrier who dug in the Greek islands, I heard later) aside and explained to him what had occurred.

Verrier was horrified. He himself had been staying at an Italian dig right away from civilization for the last few days and had heard nothing.

He was profuse in condolences and apologies, finally striding over to Dr. Leidner and clasping him warmly by both hands.

"What a tragedy! My God, what a tragedy! I have no words. *Mon pauvre collègue.*"

And shaking his head in one last ineffectual effort to express his feelings, the little man climbed into his car and left us.

As I say, that momentary introduction of comic relief into tragedy seemed really more gruesome than anything else that had happened.

"The next thing," said Dr. Reilly firmly, "is breakfast. Yes, I insist. Come, Leidner, you must eat."

Poor Dr. Leidner was almost a complete wreck. He came with us to the dining-room and there a funereal meal was served. I think the hot coffee and fried eggs did us all good, though no one actually felt they wanted to eat. Dr. Leidner drank some coffee and sat twiddling his bread. His face was gray, drawn with pain and bewilderment.

After breakfast, Captain Maitland got down to things.

I explained how I had waked up, heard a queer sound, and had gone into Miss Johnson's room.

"You say there was a glass on the floor?"

"Yes. She must have dropped it after drinking."

"Was it broken?"

"No, it had fallen on the rug. (I'm afraid the acid's ruined the rug, by the way.) I picked the glass up and put it back on the table."

"I'm glad you've told us that. There are only two sets of fingerprints on it, and one set is certainly Miss Johnson's own. The other must be yours."

He was silent for a moment, then he said, "Please go on."

I described carefully what I'd done and the methods I had tried, looking rather anxiously at Dr. Reilly for approval. He gave it with a nod.

"You tried everything that could possibly have done any good," he said. And though I was pretty sure I had done so, it was a relief to have my belief confirmed.

"Did you know exactly what she had taken?" Captain Maitland asked.

"No—but I could see, of course, that it was a corrosive acid."

Captain Maitland asked gravely, "Is it your opinion, nurse, that Miss Johnson deliberately administered this stuff to herself?"

"Oh, no," I exclaimed. "I never thought of such a thing!"

I don't know why I was so sure. Partly, I think, because of M. Poirot's hints. His "murder is a habit" had impressed itself on my mind. And then one doesn't readily believe that anyone's going to commit suicide in such a terribly painful way.

I said as much, and Captain Maitland nodded thoughtfully.

"I agree that it isn't what one would choose," he said. "But if anyone were in great distress of mind and this stuff were easily available it might be taken for that reason."

"Was she in great distress of mind?" I asked doubtfully.

"Mrs. Mercado says so. She says that Miss Johnson was quite unlike herself at dinner last night—that she hardly replied to anything that was said to her. Mrs. Mercado is quite sure that Miss Johnson was in terrible distress over something and that the idea of making away with herself had already occurred to her."

"Well, I don't believe it for a moment," I said bluntly.

Mrs. Mercado indeed! Nasty slinking little cat!

"Then what *do* you think?"

"I think she was murdered," I said bluntly.

He rapped out his next question sharply. I felt rather that I was in the orderly room.

"Any reasons?"

"It seems to me by far and away the most possible solution."

"That's just your private opinion. There was no reason why the lady should be murdered?"

"Excuse me," I said, "there was. She found out something."

"Found out something? What did she find out?"

I repeated our conversation on the roof word for word.

"She refused to tell you what her discovery was?"

"Yes. She said she must have time to think it over."

"But she was very excited by it?"

"Yes."

"A way of getting in from outside." Captain Maitland puzzled over it, his brows knit. "Had you no idea at all of what she was driving at?"

"Not in the least. I puzzled and puzzled over it but I couldn't even get a glimmering."

Captain Maitland said, "What do you think, M. Poirot?"

Poirot said, "I think you have there a possible motive."

"For murder?"

"For murder."

Captain Maitland frowned.

"She wasn't able to speak before she died?"

"Yes, she just managed to get out two words."

"What were they?"

"The window."

"The window?" repeated Captain Maitland. "Did you understand to what she was referring?"

I shook my head.

"How many windows were there in her bedroom?"

"Just the one."

"Giving on the courtyard?"

"Yes."

"Was it open or shut? Open, I seem to remember. But perhaps one of you opened it?"

"No, it was open all the time. I wondered—"

I stopped.

"Go on, nurse."

"I examined the window, of course, but I couldn't see anything unusual about it. I wondered whether, perhaps, somebody changed the glasses that way."

"Changed the glasses?"

"Yes. You see, Miss Johnson always takes a glass of water to bed with her. I think that glass must have been tampered with and a glass of acid put there in its place."

"What do you say, Reilly?"

"If it's murder, that was probably the way it was done," said Dr. Reilly promptly. "No ordinary moderately observant human being would drink a glass of acid in mistake for one of water—if they were in full possession of their waking faculties. But if anyone's accustomed to drinking off a glass of water in the middle of the night, that person might easily stretch out an arm, find the glass in the accustomed place, and, still half asleep, toss off enough of the stuff to be fatal before realizing what had happened."

Captain Maitland reflected a minute.

"I'll have to go back and look at that window. How far is it from the head of the bed?"

I thought.

"With a very long stretch you could just reach the little table that stands by the head of the bed."

"The table on which the glass of water was?"

"Yes."

"Was the door locked?"

"No."

"So whoever it was could have come in that way and made the substitution?"

"Oh, yes."

"There would be more risk that way," said Dr. Reilly. "A person who is sleeping quite soundly will often wake up at the sound of a footfall. If the table could be reached from the window it would be the safer way."

"I'm not only thinking of the glass," said Captain Maitland absent-mindedly.

Rousing himself, he addressed me once again.

"It's your opinion that when the poor lady felt she was dying she was anxious to let you know that somebody had substituted acid for water through the open window? Surely the person's *name* would have been more to the point?"

"She mayn't have known the name," I pointed out.

"Or it would have been more to the point if she'd managed to hint what it was that she had discovered the day before?"

Dr. Reilly said, "When you're dying, Maitland, you haven't always got a sense of proportion. One particular fact very likely obsesses your mind. That a murderous hand had come through the window may have been the principal fact obsessing her at the minute. It may have seemed to her important that she should let people know that. In my opinion she wasn't far wrong, either. It *was* important! She probably jumped to the fact that you'd think it was suicide. If she could have used her tongue freely, she'd probably have said, 'It wasn't suicide. I didn't take it myself. Somebody else must have put it near my bed *through the window.*'"

Captain Maitland drummed with his fingers for a minute or two without replying. Then he said, "There are certainly two ways of looking at it. It's either suicide or murder. Which do you think, Doctor Leidner?"

Dr. Leidner was silent for a minute or two, then he said quietly and decisively, "Murder. Anne Johnson wasn't the sort of woman to kill herself."

"No," allowed Captain Maitland. "Not in the normal run of things. But there might be circumstances in which it would be quite a natural thing to do."

"Such as?"

Captain Maitland stooped to a bundle which I had previously noticed him place by the side of his chair. He swung it onto the table with something of an effort.

"There's something here that none of you know about," he said. "We found it under her bed."

He fumbled with the knot of the covering, then threw it back revealing a heavy great quern or grinder.

That was nothing in itself—there were a dozen or so already found in the course of the excavations.

What riveted our attention on this particular specimen was a dull, dark stain and a fragment of something that looked like hair.

"That'll be your job, Reilly," said Captain Maitland. "But I shouldn't say that there's much doubt about this being the instrument with which Mrs. Leidner was killed!"

CHAPTER XXVI

NEXT IT WILL BE ME!

It was rather horrible. Dr. Leidner looked as though he were going to faint and I felt a bit sick myself.

Dr. Reilly examined it with professional gusto.

"No fingerprints, I presume?" he threw out.

"No fingerprints."

Dr. Reilly took out a pair of forceps and investigated delicately.

"H'm—a fragment of human tissue—and hair—fair blond hair. That's the unofficial verdict. Of course, I'll have to make a proper test, blood group, etc., but there's not much doubt. Found under Miss Johnson's bed? Well, well—so *that's* the big idea. She did the murder, and then, God rest her, remorse came to her and she finished herself off. It's a theory—a pretty theory."

Dr. Leidner could only shake his head helplessly.

"Not Anne—not Anne," he murmured.

"I don't know where she hid this to begin with," said Captain Maitland. "Every room was searched after the first crime."

Something jumped into my mind and I thought, *In the stationery cupboard,* but I didn't say anything.

"Wherever it was, she became dissatisfied with its hiding-place and took it into her own room, which had been searched with all the rest. Or perhaps she did that after making up her mind to commit suicide."

"I don't believe it," I said aloud.

And I couldn't somehow believe that kind nice Miss Johnson had battered out Mrs. Leidner's brains. I just couldn't *see* it happening! And yet it *did* fit in with some things—her fit of weeping that night, for instance. After all, I'd said "remorse" myself—only I'd never thought it was remorse for anything but the smaller more insignificant crime.

"I don't know what to believe," said Captain Maitland. "There's the French father's disappearance to be cleared up, too. My men are out hunting around in case he's been knocked on the head and his body rolled into a convenient irrigation ditch."

"Oh! I remember now—" I began.

Everyone looked toward me inquiringly.

"It was yesterday afternoon," I said. "He'd been cross-questioning me about the man with a squint who was looking in at the window that day. He asked me just where he'd stood on the path and then he said he was going out to have a look round. He said in detective stories the criminal always dropped a convenient clue."

"Damned if any of my criminals ever do," said Captain Maitland. "So that's what he was after, was it? By Jove, I wonder if he *did* find anything. A bit of a coincidence if both he and Miss Johnson discovered a clue to the identity of the murderer at practically the same time."

He added irritably, "Man with a squint? Man with a squint? There's more in this tale of that fellow with a squint than meets the eye. I don't know why the devil my fellows can't lay hold of him."

"Probably because he hasn't got a squint," said Poirot quietly.

"Do you mean he faked it? Didn't know you could fake an actual squint."

Poirot merely said, "A squint can be a very useful thing."

"The devil it can! I'd give a lot to know where that fellow is now, squint or no squint!"

"At a guess," said Poirot, "he has already passed the Syrian frontier."

"We've warned Tell Kotchek and Abu Kemal—all the frontier posts, in fact."

"I should imagine that he took the route through the hills. The route lorries sometimes take when running contraband."

Captain Maitland grunted.

"Then we'd better telegraph Deir ez Zor?"

"I did so yesterday—warning them to look out for a car with two men in it whose passports will be in the most impeccable order."

Captain Maitland favored him with a stare.

"*You* did, did you? Two men—eh?"

Poirot nodded.

"There are two men in this."

"It strikes me, M. Poirot, that you've been keeping quite a lot of things up your sleeve."

Poirot shook his head.

"No," he said. "Not really. The truth came to me only this morning when I was watching the sun rise. A very beautiful sunrise."

I don't think that any of us had noticed that Mrs. Mercado was in the room. She must have crept in when we were all taken aback by the production of that horrible great bloodstained stone.

But now, without the least warning, she set up a noise like a pig having its throat cut.

"Oh, my God!" she cried. "I see it all. I see it all now. *It was Father Lavigny.* He's mad—religious mania. He thinks women are sinful. *He's killing them all.* First Mrs. Leidner—then Miss Johnson. And next it will be *me!*"

With a scream of frenzy she flung herself across the room and clutched at Dr. Reilly's coat.

"I won't stay here, I tell you! I won't stay here a day longer. There's danger. There's danger all round. He's hiding somewhere—waiting his time. He'll spring out on me!"

Her mouth opened and she began screaming again.

I hurried over to Dr. Reilly, who had caught her by the wrists. I gave her a sharp slap on each cheek and with Dr. Reilly's help, I sat her down in a chair.

"Nobody's going to kill you," I said. "We'll see to that. Sit down and behave yourself."

She didn't scream any more. Her mouth closed and she sat looking at me with startled, stupid eyes.

Then there was another interruption. The door opened and Sheila Reilly came in.

Her face was pale and serious. She came straight to Poirot.

"I was at the post office early, M. Poirot," she said, "and there was a telegram there for you—so I brought it along."

"Thank you, mademoiselle."

He took it from her and tore it open while she watched his face.

It did not change, that face. He read the telegram, smoothed it out, folded it up neatly, and put it in his pocket.

Mrs. Mercado was watching him. She said in a choked voice, "Is that—from America?"

He shook his head.

"No, madame," he said. "It is from Tunis."

She stared at him for a moment as though she did not understand, then with a long sigh she leaned back in her seat.

"Father Lavigny," she said. "I *was* right. I've always thought there was something queer about him. He said things to me once— I suppose he's mad—" She paused and then said, "I'll be quiet. But I *must* leave this place. Joseph and I can go in and sleep at the Rest House."

"Patience, madame," said Poirot. "I will explain everything."

Captain Maitland was looking at him curiously.

"Do you consider you've definitely got the hang of this business?" he demanded.

Poirot bowed.

It was a most theatrical bow. I think it rather annoyed Captain Maitland.

"Well," he barked. "Out with it, man."

But that wasn't the way Hercule Poirot did things. I saw perfectly well that he meant to make a song and dance of it. I wondered if he really *did* know the truth, or if he was just showing off.

He turned to Dr. Reilly.

"Will you be so good, Doctor Reilly, as to summon the others?"

Dr. Reilly jumped up and went off obligingly. In a minute or two the other members of the expedition began to file into the room. First Reiter and Emmott. Then Bill Colcman. Then Richard Carey, and finally Mr. Mercado.

Poor man, he really looked like death. I suppose he was mortally afraid that he'd get hauled over the coals for carelessness in leaving dangerous chemicals about.

Everyone seated themselves round the table very much as we had done on the day M. Poirot arrived. Both Bill Coleman and David Emmott hesitated before they sat down, glancing toward Sheila Reilly. She had her back to them and was standing looking out of the window.

"Chair, Sheila?" said Bill.

David Emmott said in his low pleasant drawl, "Won't you sit down?"

She turned then and stood for a minute looking at them. Each was indicating a chair, pushing it forward. I wondered whose chair she would accept.

In the end she accepted neither.

"I'll sit here," she said brusquely. And she sat down on the edge of a table quite close to the window.

"That is," she added, "if Captain Maitland doesn't mind my staying?"

I'm not quite sure what Captain Maitland would have said. Poirot forestalled him.

"Stay by all means, mademoiselle," he said. "It is, indeed, necessary that you should."

She raised her eyebrows.

"Necessary?"

"That is the word I used, mademoiselle. There are some questions I shall have to ask you."

Again her eyebrows went up but she said nothing further. She turned her face to the window as though determined to ignore what went on in the room behind her.

"And now," said Captain Maitland, "perhaps we shall get at the truth!"

He spoke rather impatiently. He was essentially a man of action. At this very moment I feel sure that he was fretting to be out and doing things—directing the search for Father Lavigny's body, or alternatively sending out parties for his capture and arrest.

He looked at Poirot with something akin to dislike.

"If the beggar's got anything to say, why doesn't he say it?"

I could see the words on the tip of his tongue.

Poirot gave a slow appraising glance at us all, then rose to his feet.

I don't know what I expected him to say—something dramatic, certainly. He was that kind of person.

But I certainly didn't expect him to start off with a phrase in Arabic.

Yet that is what happened. He said the words slowly and solemnly—and really quite religiously, if you know what I mean.

"Bismillahi ar rahman ar rahim."

And then he gave the translation in English.

"In the name of Allah, the Merciful, the Compassionate."

CHAPTER XXVII

BEGINNING OF A JOURNEY

"Bismillahi ar rahman ar rahim. That is the Arab phrase used before starting out on a journey. *Eh bien,* we, too, start on a journey. A journey into the past. A journey into the strange places of the human soul."

I don't think that up till that moment I'd ever felt any of the so-called "glamour of the East." Frankly, what had struck me was the *mess* everywhere. But suddenly, with M. Poirot's words, a queer sort of vision seemed to grow up before my eyes. I thought of words like Samarkand and Ispahan—and of merchants with long beards—and kneeling camels—and staggering porters carrying great bales on their backs held by a rope round the forehead—and women with henna-stained hair and tatooed faces kneeling by the Tigris and washing clothes, and I heard their queer, wailing chants and the far-off groaning of the water wheel.

They were mostly things I'd seen and heard and thought nothing much of. But now, somehow they seemed *different*—like a piece of fusty old stuff you take into the light and suddenly see the rich colors of an old embroidery.

Then I looked round the room we were sitting in and I got a queer feeling that what M. Poirot said was true—we *were* all starting on a journey. We were here together now, but we were all going our different ways.

And I looked at everyone as though, in a sort of way, I were seeing them for the first time—*and* for the last time—which sounds stupid, but it was what I felt all the same.

Mr. Mercado was twisting his fingers nervously—his queer light eyes with their dilated pupils were staring at Poirot. Mrs. Mercado was looking at her husband. She had a strange, watchful look like a tigress waiting to spring. Dr. Leidner seemed to have shrunk in some curious fashion. This last blow had just crumpled him up. You might almost say he wasn't in the room at all. He was somewhere far away in a place of his own. Mr. Coleman was looking straight at Poirot. His mouth was slightly open and his eyes protruded. He looked almost idiotic. Mr. Emmott was looking down at his feet and I couldn't see his face properly. Mr. Reiter looked bewildered. His mouth was pushed out in a pout and that made him look more like a nice clean pig than ever. Miss Reilly was looking steadily out of the window. I don't know what she was thinking or feeling. Then I looked at Mr. Carey, and somehow his face hurt me and I looked away. There we were, all of us. And somehow I felt that when M. Poirot had finished we'd all be somewhere quite different.

It was a queer feeling.

Poirot's voice went quietly on. It was like a river running evenly between its banks, running to the sea.

"From the very beginning, I have felt that to understand this case one must seek not for external signs or clues, but for the truer clues of the clash of personalities and the secrets of the heart.

"And I may say that though I have now arrived at what I believe to be the true solution of the case, *I have no material proof of it.* I *know* it is so, because it *must* be so, because *in no other way* can every single fact fit into its ordered and recognized place.

"And that, to my mind, is the most satisfying solution there can be."

He paused and then went on.

"I will start my journey at the moment when I myself was brought into the case—when I had it presented to me as an accomplished happening. Now, every case, in my opinion, has a definite *shape* and *form.* The pattern of this case, to my mind, all revolved round the personality of Mrs. Leidner. Until I knew *exactly what kind of a woman Mrs. Leidner was* I should not be able to know why she was murdered and who murdered her.

"That, then, was my starting-point—the personality of Mrs. Leidner.

"There was also one other psychological point of interest—the curious state of tension described as existing among the members of the expedition. This was attested to by several different witnesses—some of them outsiders—and I made a note that although hardly a starting-point, it should nevertheless be borne in mind during my investigations.

"The accepted idea seemed to be that it was directly the result of Mrs. Leidner's influence on the members of the expedition, but for reasons which I will outline to you later this did not seem to me entirely acceptable.

"To start with, as I say, I concentrated solely and entirely on the personality of Mrs. Leidner. I had various means of assessing that personality. There were the reactions she produced in a number of people, all varying widely in character and temperament, and there was what I could glean by my own observation. The scope of the latter was naturally limited. But I *did* learn certain facts.

"Mrs. Leidner's tastes were simple and even on the austere side. She was clearly not a luxurious woman. On the other hand, some embroidery she had been doing was of an extreme fineness and beauty. That indicated a woman of fastidious and artistic taste. From the observation of the books in her bedroom I formed a further estimate. She had brains, and I also fancied that she was, essentially, an egoist.

"It had been suggested to me that Mrs. Leidner was a woman whose main preoccupation was to attract the opposite sex—that she was, in fact, a sensual woman. This I did not believe to be the case.

"In her bedroom I noticed the following books on a shelf: *Who Were the Greeks? Introduction to Relativity, Life of Lady Hester Stanhope, Back to Methuselah, Linda Condon, Crewe Train.*

"She had, to begin with, an interest in culture and in modern science—that is, a distinct intellectual side. Of the novels *Linda Condon,* and in a lesser degree *Crewe Train,* seemed to show that Mrs. Leidner had a sympathy and interest in the independent woman—unencumbered or entrapped by man. She was also obviously interested by the personality of Lady Hester Stanhope. *Linda Condon* is an exquisite study of the worship of her own beauty by a woman. *Crewe Train* is a study of a passionate individualist. *Back to Methuselah* is in sympathy with the intellectual rather than the emotional attitude to life. I felt that I was beginning to understand the dead woman.

"I next studied the reactions of those who had formed Mrs. Leidner's immediate circle—and my picture of the dead woman grew more and more complete.

"It was quite clear to me from the accounts of Doctor Reilly and others that Mrs. Leidner was one of those women who are endowed by Nature not only with beauty but with the kind of calamitous magic which sometimes accompanies beauty and can, indeed, exist independently of it. Such women usually leave a trail of violent happenings behind them. They bring disaster—sometimes on others—sometimes on themselves.

"I was convinced that Mrs. Leidner was a woman who essentially worshiped *herself* and who enjoyed more than anything else the sense of *power.* Wherever she was, she *must* be the center of the universe. And everyone round her, man or woman, had got to acknowledge her sway. With some people that was easy. Nurse Leatheran, for instance, a generous-natured woman with a romantic imagination, was captured instantly and gave in ungrudging manner full appreciation. But there was a second way in which Mrs. Leidner exercised her sway—the way of fear. Where conquest was too easy she indulged a more cruel side to her nature—but I wish to reiterate emphatically that it was not what you might call *conscious* cruelty. It was as natural and unthinking as is the conduct of a cat with a mouse. Where consciousness came in, she was essentially kind and would often go out of her way to do kind and thoughtful actions for other people.

"Now, of course, the first and most important problem to solve was the problem of the anonymous letters. Who had written them and why? I asked myself, had Mrs. Leidner written them *herself?*

"To answer this problem it was necessary to go back a long way—to go back, in fact, to the date of Mrs. Leidner's first marriage. It is here we start on our journey proper. The journey of Mrs. Leidner's life.

"First of all we must realize that the Louise Leidner of all those years ago is essentially the same Louise Leidner of the present time.

"She was young then, of remarkable beauty—that same haunting beauty that affects a man's spirit and senses as no mere material beauty can—and she was already essentially an egoist.

"Such women naturally revolt from the idea of marriage. They may be attracted by men, but they prefer to belong to themselves. They are truly La Belle Dame sans Merci of the legend. Nevertheless Mrs. Leidner *did* marry—and we can assume, I think, that her husband must have been a man of a certain force of character.

"Then the revelation of his traitorous activities occurs, and Mrs. Leidner acts in the way she told Nurse Leatheran. She gave information to the government.

"Now I submit that there was a psychological significance in her action. She told Nurse Leatheran that she was a very patriotic, idealistic girl and that that feeling was the cause of her action. But it is a well-known fact that we all tend to deceive ourselves as to the motives for our own actions. Instinctively we select the best-sounding motive! Mrs. Leidner may have believed herself that it was patriotism that inspired her action, but I believe myself that it was really the outcome of an unacknowledged desire to get rid of her husband! She disliked domination—she disliked the feeling of belonging to someone else—in fact she disliked playing second fiddle. She took a patriotic way of regaining her freedom.

"But underneath her consciousness was a gnawing sense of guilt which was to play its part in her future destiny.

"We now come directly to the question of the letters. Mrs. Leidner was highly attractive to the male sex. On several occasions she was attracted by them—but in each case a threatening letter played its part and the affair came to nothing.

"Who wrote those letters? Frederick Bosner or his brother William or *Mrs. Leidner herself?*

"There is a perfectly good case for either theory. It seems clear to me that Mrs. Leidner was one of those women who do inspire devouring devotions in men, the type of devotion which can become an obsession. I find it quite possible to believe in a Frederick Bosner to whom Louise, his wife, mattered more than anything in the world! She had betrayed him once and he dared not approach her openly, but he was determined at least that she should be his or no one's. He preferred her death to her belonging to another man.

"On the other hand, if Mrs. Leidner had, deep down, a dislike of entering into the marriage bond, it is possible that she took this way of extricating herself from difficult positions. She was a huntress who, the prey once attained, had no further use for it! Craving drama in her life, she invented a highly satisfactory drama—a resurrected husband forbidding the banns! It satisfied her deepest instincts. It made her a romantic figure, a tragic heroine, and it enabled her not to marry again.

"This state of affairs continued over a number of years. Every time there was any likelihood of marriage—a threatening letter arrived.

"But now we come to a really interesting point. Doctor Leidner came upon the scene—and no forbidding letter arrived! Nothing stood in the way of her becoming Mrs. Leidner. Not until *after* her marriage did a letter arrive.

"At once we ask ourselves—why?

"Let us take each theory in turn.

"If Mrs. Leidner wrote the letters herself the problem is easily explained. Mrs. Leidner really *wanted* to marry Doctor Leidner. And so she *did* marry him. But in that case, *why did she write herself a letter afterward?* Was her craving for drama too strong to be suppressed? And why only those two letters? After that no other letter was received until a year and a half later.

"Now take the other theory, that the letters were written by her first husband, Frederick Bosner (or his brother). Why did the threatening letter arrive *after* the marriage? Presumably Frederick could not have *wanted* her to marry Leidner. Why, then, did he not stop the marriage? He had done so successfully on former occasions. And why, *having waited till the marriage had taken place,* did he then resume his threats?

"The answer, an unsatisfactory one, is that he was somehow or other unable to protest sooner. He may have been in prison or he may have been abroad.

"There is next the attempted gas-poisoning to consider. It seems extremely unlikely that it was brought about by an outside agency. The likely persons to have staged it were Doctor and Mrs. Leidner themselves. There seems no conceivable reason why *Doctor* Leidner should do such a thing, so we are brought to the conclusion that *Mrs.* Leidner planned and carried it out herself.

"Why? More drama?

"After that Doctor and Mrs. Leidner go abroad and for eighteen months they lead a happy, peaceful life with no threats of death to disturb it. They put that down to having successfully covered their traces, but such an explanation is quite absurd. In these days going abroad is quite inadequate for that purpose. And especially was that so in the case of the Leidners. He was the director of a museum expedition. By inquiry at the museum, Frederick Bosner could at once have obtained his correct address. Even granting that he was in too reduced circumstances to pursue the couple himself, there would be no bar to his continuing his threatening letters. And it seems to me that a man with his obsession would certainly have done so.

"Instead nothing is heard of him until nearly two years later when the letters are resumed.

"*Why* were the letters resumed?

"A very difficult question—most easily answered by saying that Mrs. Leidner was bored and wanted more drama. But I was not quite satisfied with that. This particular form of drama seemed to me a shade too vulgar and too crude to accord well with her fastidious personality.

"The only thing to do was to keep an open mind on the question.

"There were three definite possibilities. One: the letters were written by Mrs. Leidner herself; two: they were written by Frederick Bosner or young William Bosner; three: they might have been written *originally* by either Mrs. Leidner or her first husband, but they were now *forgeries*—that is, they were being written by a *third* person who was aware of the earlier letters.

"I now come to direct consideration of Mrs. Leidner's entourage.

"I examined first the actual opportunities that each member of the staff had had for committing the murder.

"Roughly, on the face of it, *anyone* might have committed it, as far as opportunity went, with the exception of three persons.

"Doctor Leidner, by overwhelming testimony, had never left the roof. Mr. Carey was on duty at the mound. Mr. Coleman was in Hassanieh.

"But those alibis, my friends, were not *quite* as good as they looked. I except Doctor Leidner's. There is absolutely no doubt that he was on the roof all the time and did not come down until quite an hour and a quarter after the murder had happened.

"But was it *quite* certain that Mr. Carey was on the mound all the time?

"And had Mr. Coleman *actually been in Hassanieh* at the time the murder took place?"

Bill Coleman reddened, opened his mouth, shut it, and looked round uneasily.

Mr. Carey's expression did not change.

Poirot went on smoothly.

"I also considered one other person who, I satisfied myself, would be perfectly capable of committing murder *if she felt strongly enough.* Miss Reilly has courage and brains and a certain quality of ruthlessness. When Miss Reilly was speaking to me on the subject of the dead woman, I said to her, jokingly, that I hoped she had an alibi. I think Miss Reilly was conscious then that she had had in her heart the desire, at least, to kill. At any rate she immediately uttered a very silly and purposeless lie. She said she had been playing tennis on that afternoon. The next day I learned from a casual conversation with Miss Johnson that far from playing tennis, Miss Reilly *had actually been near this house at the time of the murder.* It occurred to me that Miss Reilly, if not guilty of the crime, might be able to tell me something useful."

He stopped and then said quietly, "Will you tell us, Miss Reilly, what you *did* see that afternoon?"

The girl did not answer at once. She still looked out of the window without turning her head, and when she spoke it was in a detached and measured voice.

"I rode out to the dig after lunch. It must have been about a quarter to two when I got there."

"Did you find any of your friends on the dig?"

"No, there seemed to be no one there but the Arab foreman."

"You did not see Mr. Carey?"

"No."

"Curious," said Poirot. "No more did M. Verrier when he went there that same afternoon."

He looked invitingly at Carey, but the latter neither moved nor spoke.

"Have you any explanation, Mr. Carey?"

"I went for a walk. There was nothing of interest turning up."

"In which direction did you go for a walk?"

"Down by the river."

"Not back toward the house?"

"No."

"I suppose," said Miss Reilly, "that you were waiting for someone who didn't come."

He looked at her but didn't answer.

Poirot did not press the point. He spoke once more to the girl.

"Did you see anything else, mademoiselle?"

"Yes. I was not far from the expedition house when I noticed the expedition lorry drawn up in a wadi. I thought it was rather queer. Then I saw Mr. Coleman. He was walking along with his head down as though he were searching for something."

"Look here," burst out Mr. Coleman. "I—"

Poirot stopped him with an authoritative gesture.

"Wait. Did you speak to him, Miss Reilly?"

"No, I didn't."

"Why?"

The girl said slowly, "Because, from time to time, he started and looked round with an extraordinary furtive look. It—gave me an unpleasant feeling. I turned my horse's head and rode away. I don't think he saw me. I was not very near and he was absorbed in what he was doing."

"Look here." Mr. Coleman was not to be hushed any longer. "I've got a perfectly good explanation for what—I admit—looks a bit fishy. As a matter of fact, the day before I had slipped a jolly fine cylinder seal into my coat pocket instead of putting it in the antika room—forgot all about it. And then I discovered I'd been and lost it out of my pocket—dropped it somewhere. I didn't want to get into a row about it so I decided I'd have a jolly good search on the quiet. I was pretty sure I'd dropped it on the way to or from the dig. I rushed over my business in Hassanieh. Sent a *walad* to do some of the shopping and got back early. I stuck the bus where it wouldn't show and had a jolly good hunt for over an hour. And didn't find the damned thing at that! Then I got into the bus and drove on to the house. Naturally, everyone thought I'd just got back."

"And you did not undeceive them?" asked Poirot sweetly.

"Well, that was pretty natural under the circumstances, don't you think?"

"I hardly agree," said Poirot.

"Oh, come now—don't go looking for trouble—that's *my* motto! But you can't fasten anything on me. I never went into the courtyard, and you can't find anyone who'll say I did."

"That, of course, has been the difficulty," said Poirot. "The evidence of the servants that *no one entered the courtyard from outside.* But it occurred to me, upon reflection, that that was really *not* what they had said. They had sworn that *no stranger* had entered the premises. They had not been asked *if a member of the expedition* had done so."

"Well, you ask them," said Coleman. "I'll eat my hat if they saw me or Carey, either."

"Ah! But that raises rather an interesting question. They would notice *a stranger* undoubtedly—but would they have even *noticed* a member of the expedition? The members of the staff are passing in and out all day. The servants would hardly notice their going and coming. It is possible, I think, that either Mr. Carey or Mr. Coleman *might* have entered and the servants' minds would have no remembrance of such an event."

"Bunkum!" said Mr. Coleman.

Poirot went on calmly. "Of the two, I think Mr. Carey was the least likely to be noticed going or coming. Mr. Coleman had started to Hassanieh in the car that morning and he would be expected to return in it. His arrival on foot would therefore be noticeable."

"Of course it would!" said Coleman.

Richard Carey raised his head. His deep-blue eyes looked straight at Poirot.

"Are you accusing me of murder, M. Poirot?" he asked.

His manner was quite quiet but his voice had a dangerous undertone.

Poirot bowed to him.

"As yet I am only taking you all on a journey—my journey toward the truth. I had now established one fact—that all the members of the expedition staff, and also Nurse Leatheran, could in actual *fact* have committed the murder. That there was very little likelihood of some of them having committed it was a secondary matter.

"I had examined *means* and *opportunity.* I next passed to *motive.* I discovered that *one and all of you could be credited with a motive!"*

"Oh! M. Poirot," I cried. "Not *me!* Why, I was a stranger. I'd only just come."

"Eh bien, ma soeur, and was not that *just what Mrs. Leidner had been fearing?* A *stranger* from *outside?"*

"But—but— Why, Doctor Reilly knew all about me! He suggested my coming!"

"How much did he really know about you? *Mostly what you yourself had told him.* Impostors have passed themselves off as hospital nurses before now."

"You can write to St. Christopher's," I began.

"For the moment will you silence yourself? Impossible to proceed while you conduct this argument. I do not say I suspect you *now.* All I say is that, keeping the open mind, you might quite easily be someone other than you pretended to be. There are many successful female impersonators, you know. Young William Bosner might be something of that kind."

I was about to give him a further piece of my mind. Female impersonator indeed! But he raised his voice and hurried on with such an air of determination that I thought better of it.

"I am going now to be frank—brutally so. It is necessary. I am going to lay bare the underlying structure of this place.

"I examined and considered every single soul here. To begin with Doctor Leidner, I soon convinced myself that his love for his wife was the mainspring of his existence. He was a man torn and ravaged with grief. Nurse Leatheran I have already mentioned. If she were a female impersonator she was a most amazingly successful one, and I inclined to the belief that she was exactly what she said she was—a thoroughly competent hospital nurse."

"Thank you for nothing," I interposed.

"My attention was immediately attracted toward Mr. and Mrs. Mercado, who were both of them clearly in a state of great agitation and unrest. I considered first Mrs. Mercado. Was she capable of murder and if so for what reasons?

"Mrs. Mercado's physique was frail. At first sight it did not seem possible that she could have had the physical strength to strike down a woman like Mrs. Leidner with a heavy stone implement. If, however, Mrs. Leidner had been on her knees at the time, the thing would at least be *physically possible.* There are ways in which one woman can induce another to go down on her knees. Oh! Not emotional ways! For instance, a woman might be turning up the hem of a skirt and ask another woman to put in the pins for her. The second woman would kneel on the ground quite unsuspectingly.

"But the motive? Nurse Leatheran had told me of the angry glances she had seen Mrs. Mercado direct at Mrs. Leidner. Mr. Mercado had evidently succumbed easily to Mrs. Leidner's spell. But I did not think the solution was to be found in mere jealousy. I was sure Mrs. Leidner was not in the least interested really in Mr. Mercado—and doubtless Mrs. Mercado was aware of the fact. She might be furious with her for the moment, but for *murder* there would have to be greater provocation. But Mrs. Mercado was essentially a fiercely maternal type. From the way she looked at her husband I realized, not only that she loved him, but that she would fight for him tooth and nail—and more than that—*that she envisaged the possibility of having to do so.* She was constantly on her guard and uneasy. The uneasiness was for him—not for herself. And when I studied Mr. Mercado I could make a fairly easy guess at what the trouble was. I took means to assure myself of the truth of my guess. Mr. Mercado was a drug addict—in an advanced stage of the craving.

"Now I need probably not tell you all that the taking of drugs over a long period has the result of considerably blunting the moral sense.

"Under the influence of drugs a man commits actions that he would not have dreamed of committing a few years earlier before he began the practice. In some cases a man has committed murder—and it has been difficult to say whether he was wholly responsible for his actions or not. The law of different countries varies slightly on that point. The chief characteristic of the drug-fiend criminal is overweening confidence in his own cleverness.

"I thought it possible that there was some discreditable incident, perhaps a criminal incident, in Mr. Mercado's past which his wife had somehow or other succeeded in hushing up. Nevertheless his career hung on a thread. If anything of this past incident were bruited about, Mr. Mercado would be ruined. His wife was always on the watch. But there was Mrs. Leidner to be reckoned with. She had a sharp intelligence and a love of power. She might even induce the wretched man to confide in her. It would just have suited her peculiar temperament to feel she knew a secret which she could reveal at any minute with disastrous effects.

"Here, then, was a possible motive for murder on the part of the Mercados. To protect her mate, Mrs. Mercado, I felt sure, would stick at nothing! Both she and her husband had had the opportunity—during that ten minutes when the courtyard was empty."

Mrs. Mercado cried out, "It's not *true!*"

Poirot paid no attention.

"I next considered Miss Johnson. Was *she* capable of murder?

"I thought she was. She was a person of strong will and iron self-control. Such people are constantly repressing themselves—and one day the dam bursts! But if Miss Johnson had committed the crime it could only be for some reason connected with Dr. Leidner. If in any way she felt convinced that Mrs. Leidner was spoiling her husband's life, then the deep unacknowledged jealousy far down in her would leap at the chance of a plausible motive and give itself full rein.

"Yes, Miss Johnson was distinctly a possibility.

"Then there were the three young men.

"First Carl Reiter. If, by any chance, one of the expedition staff was William Bosner, then Reiter was by far the most likely person. But if he *was* William Bosner, then he was certainly a most accomplished actor! If he was merely *himself,* had he any reason for murder?

"Regarded from Mrs. Leidner's point of view, Carl Reiter was far too easy a victim for good sport. He was prepared to fall on his face and worship immediately. Mrs. Leidner despised undiscriminating adoration—and the doormat attitude nearly always brings out the worst side of a woman. In her treatment of Carl Reiter Mrs. Leidner displayed really deliberate cruelty. She inserted a gibe here—a prick there. She made the poor young man's life a hell to him."

Poirot broke off suddenly and addressed the young man in a personal, highly confidential manner.

"Mon ami, let this be a lesson to you. You are a *man.* Behave, then, like a *man!* It is against Nature for a man to grovel. Women and Nature have almost exactly the same reactions! Remember it is better to take the largest plate within reach and fling it at a woman's head than it is to wriggle like a worm whenever she looks at you!"

He dropped his private manner and reverted to his lecture style.

"Could Carl Reiter have been goaded to such a pitch of torment that he turned on his tormentor and killed her? Suffering does queer things to a man. I could not be *sure* that it was *not* so!

"Next, William Coleman. His behavior, as reported by Miss Reilly, is certainly suspicious. If he was the criminal it could only be because his cheerful personality concealed the hidden one of William Bosner. I do not think William Coleman, as William Coleman, has the temperament of a murderer. His faults might lie in another direction. Ah! perhaps Nurse Leatheran can guess what they would be?"

How *did* the man do it? I'm sure I didn't look as though I was thinking anything at all.

"It's nothing really," I said, hesitating. "Only if it's to be all truth, Mr. Coleman *did* say once himself that he would have made a good forger."

"A good point," said Poirot. "Therefore if he had come across some of the old threatening letters, he could have copied them without difficulty."

"Oy, oy, oy!" called out Mr. Coleman. "This is what they call a frame-up."

Poirot swept on. "As to his being or not being William Bosner such a matter is difficult of verification. But Mr. Coleman has spoken of a *guardian*—not of a father—and there is nothing definitely to veto the idea."

"Tommyrot," said Mr. Coleman. "Why all of you listen to this chap beats me."

"Of the three young men there remains Mr. Emmott," went on Poirot. "He again might be a possible shield for the identity of William Bosner. Whatever *personal* reasons he might have for the removal of Mrs. Leidner I soon realized that I should have no means of learning them from him. He could keep his own counsel remarkably well, and there was not the least chance of provoking him nor of tricking him into betraying himself on any point. Of all the expedition he seemed to be the best and most dispassionate judge of Mrs. Leidner's personality. I think that he always knew her for exactly what she was—but what impression her personality made on him I was unable to discover. I fancy that Mrs. Leidner herself must have been provoked and angered by his attitude.

"I may say that of all the expedition, *as far as character and capability were concerned,* Mr. Emmott seemed to me the most fitted to bring a clever and well-timed crime off satisfactorily."

For the first time Mr. Emmott raised his eyes from the toes of his boots.

"Thank you," he said.

There seemed to be just a trace of amusement in his voice.

"The last two people on my list were Richard Carey and Father Lavigny.

"According to the testimony of Nurse Leatheran and others, Mr. Carey and Mrs. Leidner disliked each other. They were both civil with an effort. Another person, Miss Reilly, propounded a totally different theory to account for their attitude of frigid politeness.

"I soon had very little doubt that Miss Reilly's explanation was the correct one. I acquired my certitude by the simple expedient of provoking Mr. Carey into reckless and unguarded speech. It was not difficult. As I soon saw, he was in a state of high nervous tension. In fact he was—and is—very near a complete nervous breakdown. A man who is suffering up to the limit of his capacity can seldom put up much of a fight.

"Mr. Carey's barriers came down almost immediately. He told me, with a sincerity that I did not for a moment doubt, that he hated Mrs. Leidner.

"And he was undoubtedly speaking the truth. He *did* hate Mrs. Leidner. But *why* did he hate her?

"I have spoken of women who have a calamitous magic. But men have that magic, too. There are men who are able without the least effort to attract women. What they call in these days *le sex appeal!* Mr. Carey had this quality very strongly. He was, to begin with, devoted to his friend and employer, and indifferent to his employer's wife. That did not suit Mrs. Leidner. She *must* dominate—and she set herself out to capture Richard Carey. But here, I believe, something entirely unforeseen took place. She herself, for perhaps the first time in her life, fell a victim to an overmastering passion. She fell in love—really in love—with Richard Carey.

"And he—was unable to resist her. Here is the truth of the terrible state of nervous tension that he has been enduring. He has been a man torn by two opposing passions. He loved Louise Leidner—yes, but he also hated her. He hated her for undermining his loyalty to his friend. There is no hatred so great as that of a man who has been made to love a woman against his will.

"I had here all the motive that I needed. I was convinced that *at certain moments* the most natural thing for Richard Carey to do would have been to strike with all the force of his arm at the beautiful face that had cast a spell over him.

"All along I had felt sure that the murder of Louise Leidner was a *crime passionnel.* In Mr. Carey I had found an ideal murderer for that type of crime.

"There remains one other candidate for the title of murderer—Father Lavigny. My attention was attracted to the good father straightaway by a certain discrepancy between his description of the strange man who had been seen peering in at the window and the one given by Nurse Leatheran. In all accounts given by different witnesses there is usually *some* discrepancy, but this was absolutely glaring. Moreover, Father Lavigny insisted on a certain characteristic—a squint—which ought to make identification much easier.

"But very soon it became apparent that *while Nurse Leatheran's description was substantially accurate,* Father Lavigny's was *nothing of the kind.* It looked almost as though Father Lavigny was deliberately misleading us—as though he did *not want the man caught.*

"But in that case *he must know something about this curious person.* He had been seen talking to the man but we had only his word for what they had been talking about.

"What had the Iraqi been doing when Nurse Leatheran and Mrs. Leidner saw him? Trying to peer through the window—Mrs. Leidner's window, so they thought, but I realized when I went and stood where they had been, that it might equally have been *the antika-room window.*

"The night after that an alarm was given. Someone was in the antika room. Nothing proved to have been taken, however. The interesting point to me is that when Doctor Leidner got there he found *Father Lavigny there before him.* Father Lavigny tells his story of seeing a light. *But again we have only his word for it.*

"I begin to get curious about Father Lavigny. The other day when I make the suggestion that Father Lavigny may be Frederick Bosner Doctor Leidner pooh-poohs the suggestion. He says Father Lavigny is a well-known man. I advance the supposition that Frederick Bosner, who has had nearly twenty years to make a career for himself, under a new name, may very possibly *be* a well-known man by this time! All the same, I do not think that he has spent the intervening time in a religious community. A very much simpler solution presents itself.

"Did anyone at the expedition know Father Lavigny by sight before he came? Apparently not. When then should not it be *someone impersonating the good father?* I found out that a telegram had been sent to Carthage on the sudden illness of Doctor Byrd, who was to have accompanied the expedition. To intercept a telegram, what could be easier? As to the work, there was no other epigraphist attached to the expedition. With a smattering of knowledge a clever man *might* bluff his way through. There had been very few tablets and inscriptions so far, and already I gathered that Father Lavigny's pronouncements had been felt to be somewhat unusual.

"It looked very much as though Father Lavigny were an *impostor.*

"But was he Frederick Bosner?

"Somehow affairs did not seem to be shaping themselves that way. The truth seemed likely to lie in quite a different direction.

"I had a lengthy conversation with Father Lavigny. I am a practicing Catholic and I know many priests and members of religious communities. Father Lavigny struck me as not ringing quite true to his role. But he struck me, on the other hand, as familiar in quite a different capacity. I *had* met men of his type quite frequently—but they were not members of a religious community. Far from it!

"I began to send off telegrams.

"And then, unwittingly, Nurse Leatheran gave me a valuable clue. We were examining the gold ornaments in the antika room and she mentioned a trace of wax having been found adhering to a gold cup. Me, I say, 'Wax?' and Father Lavigny, he said, 'Wax?' and his tone was enough! I knew in a flash exactly what he was doing here."

Poirot paused and addressed himself directly to Dr. Leidner.

"I regret to tell you, monsieur, that the gold cup in the antika room, the gold dagger, the hair ornaments, and several other things *are not the genuine articles found by you.* They are very clever electrotypes. Father Lavigny, I have just learned by this last answer to my telegrams, is none other than Raoul Menier, one of the cleverest thieves known to the French police. He specializes in thefts from museums of *objets d'art* and such like. Associated with him is Ali Yusuf, a semi-Turk, who is a first-class working jeweler. Our first knowledge of Menier was when certain objects in the Louvre were found not to be genuine—in every case it was discovered that a distinguished archaeologist *not known previously by sight to the director* had recently had the handling of the spurious articles when paying a visit to the Louvre. On inquiry all these distinguished gentlemen denied having paid a visit to the Louvre at the times stated!

"I have learned that Menier was in Tunis preparing the way for a theft from the Holy Fathers when your telegram arrived. Father Lavigny, who was in ill health, was forced to refuse, but Menier managed to get hold of the telegram and substitute one of acceptance. He was quite safe in doing so. Even if the monks should read in some paper (in itself an unlikely thing) that Father Lavigny was in Iraq they would only think that the newspapers had got hold of a half-truth as so often happens.

"Menier and his accomplice arrived. The latter is seen when he is reconnoitering the antika room from outside. The plan is for Father Lavigny to take wax impressions. Ali then makes clever duplicates. There are always certain collectors who are willing to pay a good price for genuine antiques and will ask no embarrassing questions. Father Lavigny will effect the substitution of the fake for the genuine article—preferably at night.

"And that is doubtless what he was doing when Mrs. Leidner heard him and gave the alarm. What can he do? He hurriedly makes up a story of having seen a light in the antika room.

"That 'went down,' as you say, very well. But Mrs. Leidner was no fool. She may have remembered the trace of wax she had noticed and then put two and two together. And if she did, what will she do then? Would it not be *dans son caractère* to do nothing at once, but to enjoy herself by letting hints slip to the discomfiture of Father Lavigny? She will let him see that she suspects—but not that she *knows.* It is, perhaps, a dangerous game, but she enjoys a dangerous game.

"And perhaps she plays that game too long. Father Lavigny sees the truth, and strikes before she realizes what he means to do.

"Father Lavigny is Raoul Menier—a thief. Is he also—a *murderer?*"

Poirot paced the room. He took out a handkerchief, wiped his forehead, and went on. "That was my position this morning. There were eight distinct possibilities and I did not know which of these possibilities was the right one. I still did not know *who was the murderer.*

"But murder is a habit. The man or woman who kills once will kill again.

"And by the second murder, the murderer was delivered into my hands.

"All along it was ever present in the back of my mind that some one of these people might have knowledge that they had kept back—knowledge incriminating the murderer.

"If so, that person would be in danger.

"My solicitude was mainly on account of Nurse Leatheran. She had an energetic personality and a brisk, inquisitive mind. I was terrified of her finding out more than it was safe for her to know.

"As you all know, a second murder did take place. But the victim was not Nurse Leatheran—it was Miss Johnson.

"I like to think that I should have reached the correct solution anyway by pure reasoning, but it is certain that Miss Johnson's murder helped me to it much quicker.

"To begin with, one suspect was eliminated—Miss Johnson herself—for I did not for a moment entertain the theory of suicide.

"Let us examine now the facts of this second murder.

"Fact one: On Sunday evening Nurse Leatheran finds Miss Johnson in tears, and that same evening Miss Johnson burns a fragment of a letter which nurse believes to be in the same handwriting as that of the anonymous letters.

"Fact two: The evening before her death Miss Johnson is found by Nurse Leatheran standing on the roof in a state that nurse describes as one of incredulous horror. When nurse questions her she says, 'I've seen how some one could come in from outside—and no one would ever guess.' She won't say any more. Father Lavigny is crossing the courtyard and Mr. Reiter is at the door of the photographic room.

"Fact three: Miss Johnson is found dying. The only words she can manage to articulate are 'the window—the window—'

"Those are the facts, and these are the problems with which we are faced: What is the truth of the letters? What did Miss Johnson see from the roof? What did she mean by 'the window—the window'?

"Eh bien, let us take the second problem first as the easiest of solution. I went up with Nurse Leatheran and I stood where Miss Johnson had stood. From there she could see the courtyard and the archway and the north side of the building and two members of the staff. Had her words anything to do with either Mr. Reiter or Father Lavigny?

"Almost at once a possible explanation leaped to my brain. If a stranger came in from *outside* he could only do so in *disguise.* And there was only *one* person whose general appearance lent itself to such an impersonation. Father Lavigny! With a sun helmet, sunglasses, black beard, and a monk's long woolen robe, a stranger could pass in without the servants *realizing* that a stranger had entered.

"Was *that* Miss Johnson's meaning? Or had she gone further? Did she realize that Father Lavigny's whole *personality* was a disguise? That he was someone other than he pretended to be?

"Knowing what I did know about Father Lavigny I was inclined to call the mystery solved. Raoul Menier was the murderer. He had killed Mrs. Leidner to silence her before she could give him away. Now *another person lets him see that she has penetrated his secret.* She, too, must be removed.

"And so everything is explained! The second murder. Father Lavigny's flight—minus robe and beard. (He and his friend are doubtless careering through Syria with excellent passports as two commercial travelers.) His action in placing the bloodstained quern under Miss Johnson's bed.

"As I say, I was almost satisfied—but not quite. For the perfect solution must explain *everything*—and this does not do so.

"It does not explain, for instance, why Miss Johnson should say 'the window—the window,' as she was dying. It does not explain her fit of weeping over the letter. It does not explain her mental attitude on the roof

—her incredulous horror and her refusal to tell Nurse Leatheran what it was that *she now suspected or knew.*

"It was a solution that fitted the *outer* facts, but it did not satisfy the *psychological* requirements.

"And then, as I stood on the roof, going over in my mind those three points—the letters, the roof, the window, I *saw*—just as Miss Johnson had seen!

"And this time what I saw explained everything!"

CHAPTER XXVIII

JOURNEY'S END

Poirot looked round. Every eye was now fixed upon him. There had been a certain relaxation—a slackening of tension. Now the tension suddenly returned.

There was something coming—something—

Poirot's voice, quiet and unimpassioned, went on. "The letters, the roof, 'the window'— Yes, everything was explained—everything fell into place.

"I said just now that three men had alibis for the time of the crime. Two of those alibis I have shown to be worthless. I saw now my great—my amazing mistake. The third alibi was worthless, too. Not only *could* Doctor Leidner have committed the murder—but I was convinced that he *had* committed it."

There was a silence, a bewildered, uncomprehending silence. Doctor Leidner said nothing. He seemed lost in his faraway world still. David Emmott, however, stirred uneasily and spoke.

"I don't know what you mean to imply, M. Poirot. I told you that Doctor Leidner never left the roof until at least a quarter to three. That is the absolute truth. I swear it solemnly. I am not lying. And it would have been quite impossible for him to have done so without my seeing him."

Poirot nodded.

"Oh, I believe you. *Doctor Leidner did not leave the roof.* That is an undisputed fact. But what I saw—and what Miss Johnson had seen—was *that Doctor Leidner could murder his wife from the roof without leaving it."*

We all stared.

"The *window,"* cried Poirot. *"Her* window! That is what I realized—just as Miss Johnson realized it. Her window was directly underneath, on the side away from the courtyard. And Doctor Leidner was alone up there with no one to witness his action. And those heavy stone querns and grinders were up there all ready to his hand. So simple, so very simple, granted one thing—*that the murderer had the opportunity to move the body before anyone else saw it.* Oh, it is beautiful—of an unbelievable simplicity!

"Listen—it went like this:

"Doctor Leidner is on the roof working with the pottery. He calls you up, Mr. Emmott, and while he holds you in talk he notices that, as usually happens, the small boy takes advantage of your absence to leave his work and go outside the courtyard. He keeps you with him ten minutes, then he lets you go and as soon as you are down below shouting to the boy he sets his plan in operation.

"He takes from his pocket the plasticine-smeared mask with which he has already scared his wife on a former occasion and dangles it over the edge of the parapet till it taps on his wife's window.

"That, remember, is the window giving on the countryside facing the opposite direction to the courtyard.

"Mrs. Leidner is lying on her bed half asleep. She is peaceful and happy. Suddenly the mask begins tapping on the window and attracts her attention. But it is not dusk now—it is broad daylight—there is nothing terrifying about it. She recognizes it for what it is—a crude form of trickery! She is not frightened but indignant. She does what any other woman would do in her place. Jumps off the bed, opens the window, passes her head through the bars, and turns her face upward to see who is playing the trick on her.

"Doctor Leidner is waiting. He has in his hands, poised and ready, a heavy quern. At the psychological moment *he drops it.*

"With a faint cry (heard by Miss Johnson) Mrs. Leidner collapses on the rug underneath the window.

"Now there is a hole in this quern, and through that Doctor Leidner had previously passed a cord. He has now only to haul in the cord and bring up the quern. He replaces the latter neatly, bloodstained side down, among the other objects of that kind on the roof.

"Then he continues his work for an hour or more till he judges the moment has come for the second act. He descends the stairs, speaks to Mr. Emmott and Nurse Leatheran, crosses the courtyard, and enters his wife's room. This is the explanation he himself gives of his movements there.

" *'I saw my wife's body in a heap by the bed. For a moment or two I felt paralyzed as though I couldn't move. Then at last I went and knelt down by her and lifted up her head. I saw she was dead. . . . At last I got up. I felt dazed and as though I were drunk. I managed to get to the door and call out.'*

"A perfectly possible account of the actions of a grief-dazed man. Now listen to what I believe to be the truth. Dr. Leidner enters the room, hurries to the window, and having pulled on a pair of gloves, closes and fastens it, then picks up his wife's body and transports it to a position between the bed and the door. Then he notices a slight stain on the window-side rug. He cannot change it with the other rug, they are a different size, but he does the next best thing. He puts the stained rug in front of the washstand and the rug from the washstand under the window. *If* the stain is noticed, it will be connected with the *washstand*—not with the *window*—a very important point. There must be no suggestion that the window played any part in the business. Then he comes to the door and acts the part of the overcome husband, and that, I imagine, is not difficult. For he *did* love his wife."

"My good man," cried Doctor Reilly impatiently, "if he loved her, why did he kill her? Where's the motive? Can't you speak, Leidner? Tell him he's mad."

Dr. Leidner neither spoke nor moved.

Poirot said, "Did I tell you all along that this was a *crime passionnel?* Why did her first husband, Frederick Bosner, threaten to kill her? Because he loved her. And in the end, you see, he made his boast good.

"Mais oui—mais oui—once I realized that it is Doctor Leidner who did the killing everything falls into place.

"For the second time I recommence my journey from the beginning—Mrs. Leidner's first marriage—the threatening letters—her second marriage. The letters prevented her marrying any other man—but they did not prevent her marrying Doctor Leidner. How simple that is—*if Doctor Leidner is actually Frederick Bosner.*

"Once more let us start our journey—from the point of view this time of young Frederick Bosner.

"To begin with he loves his wife Louise with an overpowering passion such as only a woman of her kind can evoke. She betrays him. He is sentenced to death. He escapes. He is involved in a railway accident but he manages to emerge with a second personality—*that of a young Swedish archaeologist, Eric Leidner,* whose body is badly disfigured and who will be conveniently buried as Frederick Bosner.

"What is the new Eric Leidner's attitude to the woman who was willing to send him to his death? First and most important, *he still loves her.* He sets to work to build up his new life. He is a man of great ability, his profession is congenial to him and he makes a success of it. *But he never forgets the ruling passion of his life.* He keeps himself informed of his wife's movements. Of one thing he is cold-bloodedly determined (remember Mrs. Leidner's own description of him to Nurse Leatheran—gentle and kind but ruthless), *she shall belong to no other man.* Whenever he judges it necessary he dispatches a letter. He imitates some of the peculiarities of her handwriting in case she should think of taking his letters to the police. Women who write sensational anonymous letters to themselves are such a common phenomenon that the police will be sure to jump to that solution given the likeness of the handwriting. At the same time he leaves her in doubt as to whether he is really alive or not.

"At last, after many years, he judges that the time has arrived; he reenters her life. All goes well. His wife never dreams of his real identity. He is a well-known man. The upstanding, good-looking young fellow is now a middle-aged man with a beard and stooping shoulders. And so we see history repeating itself. As before, Frederick is able to dominate Louise. For the second time she consents to marry him. *And no letter comes to forbid the banns.*

"But *afterward* a letter *does* come. Why?

"I think that Doctor Leidner was taking no chances. The intimacy of marriage *might* awaken a memory. He wishes to impress on his wife, once and for all, *that Eric Leidner and Frederick Bosner are two* different people. So much so that a threatening letter comes from the former on account of the latter. The rather puerile gas-poisoning business follows—arranged by Doctor Leidner, of course. Still with the same object in view.

"After that he is satisfied. No more letters need come. They can settle down to happy married life together.

"And then, after nearly two years, *the letters recommence.*

"Why? Eh bien, I think I know. *Because the threat underlying the letters was always a genuine threat.* (That is why Mrs. Leidner has always been frightened. She *knew* her Frederick's gentle but ruthless nature.) *If she belongs to any other man but him he would kill her. And she has given herself to Richard Carey.*

"And so, having discovered this, cold-bloodedly, calmly, Doctor Leidner prepares the scene for murder.

"You see now the important part played by Nurse Leatheran? Doctor Leidner's rather curious conduct (it puzzled me at the very first) in securing her services for his wife is explained. It was vital that a reliable professional witness should be able to state incontrovertibly that Mrs. Leidner had been dead *over an hour* when her body was found—that is, that she had been killed at a time when *everybody could swear her husband was on the roof.* A suspicion *might* have arisen that he had killed her when he entered the room and found the body—but that was out of the question when a trained hospital nurse would assert positively that she had already been dead an hour.

"Another thing that is explained is the curious state of tension and strain that had come over the expedition this year. I never from the first thought that that could be attributed solely to *Mrs.* Leidner's influence. For several years this particular expedition had had a reputation for happy good-fellowship. In my opinion the state of mind of a community is always directly due to the influence of the man at the top. Doctor Leidner, quiet though he was, was a man of great personality. It was due to his tact, to his judgment, to his sympathetic manipulation of human beings that the atmosphere had always been such a happy one.

"If there was a change, therefore, the change must be due to the man at the top—in other words, to Doctor Leidner. It was *Doctor* Leidner, not Mrs. Leidner, who was responsible for the tension and uneasiness. No wonder the staff felt the change without understanding it. The kindly, genial Doctor Leidner, outwardly the same, was only playing the part of himself. The real man was an obsessed fanatic plotting to kill.

"And now we will pass on to the second murder—that of Miss Johnson. In tidying up Doctor Leidner's papers in the office (a job she took on herself unasked, craving for something to do) she must have come on some unfinished draft of one of the anonymous letters.

"It must have been both incomprehensible and extremely upsetting to her! Doctor Leidner has been deliberately terrorizing his wife! She cannot understand it—but it upsets her badly. It is in this mood that Nurse Leatheran discovers her crying.

"I do not think at the moment that she suspected Doctor Leidner of being the murderer, but my experiments with sounds in Mrs. Leidner's and Father Lavigny's rooms are not lost upon her. She realizes that if it *was* Mrs. Leidner's cry she heard, *the window in her room must have been open, not shut.* At the moment that conveys nothing vital to her, *but she remembers it.*

"Her mind goes on working—ferreting its way toward the truth. Perhaps she makes some reference to the letters which Doctor Leidner understands and his manner changes. She may see that he is, suddenly, afraid.

"But Doctor Leidner *cannot* have killed his wife! He was on the *roof* all the time.

"And then, one evening, as she herself is on the roof puzzling about it, the truth comes to her in a flash. Mrs. Leidner has been killed from up *here,* through the open window.

"It was at that minute that Nurse Leatheran found her.

"And immediately, her old affection reasserting itself, she puts up a quick camouflage. Nurse Leatheran must not guess the horrifying discovery she has just made.

"She looks deliberately in the opposite direction (toward the courtyard) and makes a remark suggested to her by Father Lavigny's appearance as he crosses the courtyard.

"She refuses to say more. She has got to 'think things out.'

"And Doctor Leidner, who has been watching her anxiously, *realizes that she knows the truth.* She is not the kind of woman to conceal her horror and distress from him.

"It is true that as yet she has not given him away—but how long can he depend upon her?

"Murder is a habit. That night he substitutes a glass of acid for her glass of water. There is just a chance she may be believed to have deliberately poisoned herself. There is even a chance she may be considered to have done the first murder and has now been overcome with remorse. To strengthen the latter idea he takes the quern from the roof and puts it under her bed.

"No wonder that poor Miss Johnson, in her death agony, could only try desperately to impart her hard-won information. Through 'the window,' *that* is how Mrs. Leidner was killed, *not* through the door—through the *window.*

"And so thus, everything is explained, everything falls into place. Psychologically perfect.

"But there is no proof. No proof at all."

None of us spoke. We were lost in a sea of horror. Yes, and not only horror. Pity, too.

Doctor Leidner had neither moved nor spoken. He sat just as he had done all along. A tired, worn, elderly man.

At last he stirred slightly and looked at Poirot with gentle, tired eyes.

"No," he said, "there is no proof. But that does not matter. You knew that I would not deny truth. I have never denied truth; I think—really—I am rather glad. I'm so tired—"

Then he said simply, "I'm sorry about Anne. That was bad—senseless—it wasn't *me!* And she suffered, too, poor soul. Yes, that wasn't me. It was fear."

A little smile just hovered on his pain-twisted lips.

"You would have made a good archaeologist, M. Poirot. You have the gift of re-creating the past.

"It was all very much as you said.

"I loved Louise and I killed her. If you'd known Louise you'd have understood— No, I think you understand anyway."

CHAPTER XXIX

L'ENVOI

There isn't really any more to say about things.

They got "Father" Lavigny and the other man just as they were going on board a steamer at Beirut.

Sheila Reilly married young Emmott. I think that will be good for her. He's no doormat—he'll keep her in her place. She'd have ridden roughshod over poor Bill Coleman.

I nursed him, by the way, when he had appendicitis a year ago. I got quite fond of him. His guardian was sending him out to farm in South Africa.

I've never been out East again. It's funny—sometimes I wish I could. I think of the noise the water wheel made and the women washing, and that queer haughty look that camels give you—and I get quite a homesick feeling. After all, perhaps dirt isn't really so unhealthy as one is brought up to believe!

Dr. Reilly usually looks me up when he's in England, and as I said, it's he who's got me into this. "Take it or leave it," I said to him. "I know the grammar's all wrong and it's not properly written or anything like that—but there it is."

And he took it. Made no bones about it. It will give me a queer feeling if it's ever printed.

M. Poirot went back to Syria and about a week later he went home on the Orient Express and got himself mixed up in another murder. He was clever, I don't deny it, but I shan't forgive him in a hurry for pulling my leg the way he did. Pretending to think I might be mixed up in the crime and not a real hospital nurse at all!

Doctors are like that sometimes. Will have their joke, some of them will, and never think of *your* feelings!

I've thought and thought about Mrs. Leidner and what she was really like. Sometimes it seems to me she was just a terrible woman—and other times I remember how nice she was to me and how soft her voice was—and her lovely fair hair and everything—and I feel that perhaps, after all, she was more to be pitied than blamed.

And I can't help but pity Dr. Leidner. I know he was a murderer twice over, but it doesn't seem to make any difference. He was so dreadfully fond of her. It's awful to be fond of anyone like that.

Somehow, the more I get older, and the more I see of people and sadness and illness and everything, the sorrier I get for everyone. Sometimes, I declare, I don't know what's become of the good strict principles my aunt brought me up with. A very religious woman she was, and most particular. There wasn't one of our neighbors whose faults she didn't know backward and forward.

Oh, dear, it's quite true what Dr. Reilly said. How does one stop writing? If I could find a really good telling phrase.

I must ask Dr. Reilly for some Arab one.

Like the one M. Poirot used.

In the name of Allah, the Merciful, the Compassionate . . .

Something like that.

APPOINTMENT WITH DEATH

A Hercule Poirot Mystery

To Richard and Myra Mallock
to remind them of their
journey to Petra

PART I

1

"You do see, don't you, that she's got to be killed?"

The question floated out into the still night air, seemed to hang there a moment and then drift away down into the darkness towards the Dead Sea.

Hercule Poirot paused a minute with his hand on the window catch.

Frowning, he shut it decisively, thereby excluding any injurious night air! Hercule Poirot had been brought up to believe that all outside air was best left outside, and that night air was especially dangerous to the health.

As he pulled the curtains neatly over the window and walked to his bed, he smiled tolerantly to himself.

"You do see, don't you, that she's got to be killed?"

Curious words for one Hercule Poirot, detective, to overhear on his first night in Jerusalem.

"Decidedly, wherever I go, there is something to remind me of crime!" he murmured to himself.

His smile continued as he remembered a story he had once heard concerning Anthony Trollope, the novelist. Trollope was crossing the Atlantic at the time and had overheard two fellow passengers discussing the last published instalment of one of his novels.

"Very good," one man had declared. "But he ought to kill off that tiresome old woman."

With a broad smile the novelist had addressed them:

"Gentlemen, I am much obliged to you! I will go and kill her immediately!"

Hercule Poirot wondered what had occasioned the words he had just overheard. A collaboration, perhaps, over a play or a book.

He thought, still smiling:

"Those words might be remembered one day, and be given a more sinister meaning."

There had been, he now recollected, a curious nervous intensity in the voice—a tremor that spoke of some intense emotional strain. A man's voice—or a boy's . . .

Hercule Poirot thought to himself as he turned out the light by his bed: *"I should know that voice again. . . ."*

Their elbows on the window-sill, their heads close together, Raymond and Carol Boynton gazed out into the blue depths of the night. Nervously, Raymond repeated his former words:

"You do see, don't you, that she's got to be killed?"

Carol Boynton stirred slightly. She said, her voice deep and hoarse:

"It's horrible. . . ."

"It's not more horrible than *this!*"

"I suppose not. . . ."

Raymond said violently:

"It can't go on like this—it can't. . . . We *must* do something. . . . And there isn't anything else we *can* do. . . ."

Carol said—but her voice was unconvincing and she knew it—

"If we could get away somehow . . . ?"

"We can't." His voice was empty and hopeless. "Carol, you know we can't . . ."

The girl shivered.

"I know, Ray—I know."

He gave a sudden short bitter laugh.

"People would say we were crazy—not to be able just to walk out—"

Carol said slowly:

"Perhaps we—are crazy!"

"I daresay. Yes, I daresay we are. Anyway we soon shall be . . . I suppose some people would say we are already—here we are calmly planning, in cold blood, to kill our own mother!"

Carol said sharply:

"She isn't our own mother!"

"No, that's true."

There was a pause and then Raymond said, his voice now quietly matter-of-fact:

"You do agree, Carol?"

Carol answered steadily:

"I think she ought to die—yes . . ."

Then she broke out suddenly:

"She's mad . . . I'm quite sure she's mad . . . She—she couldn't torture us like she does if she were sane. For years we've been saying: *'This can't go on!'* and it *has* gone on! We've said, *'She'll die sometime'*—but she hasn't died! I don't think she ever will die unless—"

Raymond said steadily:

"Unless we kill her . . ."

"Yes."

She clenched her hands on the window-sill in front of her.

Her brother went on in a cool matter-of-fact tone, with just a slight tremor denoting his deep underlying excitement:

"You see why it's got to be one of us, don't you? With Lennox, there's Nadine to consider. And we couldn't bring Jinny into it."

Carol shivered.

"Poor Jinny . . . I'm so afraid . . ."

"I know. It's getting pretty bad, isn't it? That's why something's got to be done quickly—before she goes right over the edge."

Carol stood up suddenly, pushing back the tumbled chestnut hair from her forehead.

"Ray," she said. "You don't think it's really *wrong,* do you?"

He answered in that same would-be dispassionate tone:

"No. I think it's just like killing a mad dog—something that's doing harm in the world and must be stopped. This is the only way of stopping it."

Carol murmured:

"But they'd—they'd send us to the chair just the same . . . I mean we couldn't explain what she's like . . . It would sound fantastic . . . In a way, you know, it's all in our own *minds!"*

Raymond said:

"Nobody will ever know. I've got a plan. I've thought it all out. We shall be quite safe."

Carol turned suddenly round on him.

"Ray—somehow or other—you're different. Something's *happened* to you . . . What's put all this into your head?"

"Why should you think anything's 'happened' to me?"

He turned his head away, staring out into the night.

"Because it has . . . Ray, was it that girl on the train?"

"No, of course not—why should it be? Oh, Carol, don't talk nonsense. Let's get back again to—to—"

"To your plan? Are you sure it's a—good plan?"

"Yes. I think so . . . We must wait for the right opportunity, of course. And then—if it goes all right—we shall be free—all of us."

"Free?" Carol gave a little sigh. She looked up at the stars.

Then suddenly she shook from head to foot in a sudden storm of weeping.

"Carol, what's the matter?"

She sobbed out brokenly:

"It's so lovely—the night and the blueness and the stars. If only we could be part of it all . . . If only we could be like other people instead of being as we are—all queer and warped and *wrong.*"

"But we shall be—all right—when she's dead!"

"Are you sure? Isn't it too late? Sha'n't we always be queer and different?"

"No, no, no."

"I wonder—"

"Carol, if you'd rather not—"

She pushed his comforting arm aside.

"No, I'm with you—definitely I'm with you! Because of the others—especially Jinny. We *must* save Jinny!"

Raymond paused a moment.

"Then—we'll go on with it?"

"Yes!"

"Good. I'll tell you my plan . . ."

He bent his head to hers.

2

Miss Sarah King, M.B., stood by the table in the writing-room of the Solomon Hotel in Jerusalem idly turning over the papers and magazines. A frown contracted her brows and she looked preoccupied.

The tall, middle-aged Frenchman who entered the room from the hall watched her for a moment or two before strolling up to the opposite side of the table. When their eyes met, Sarah made a little gesture of smiling recognition. She remembered that this man had come to her help when traveling from Cairo and had carried one of her suitcases at a moment when no porter appeared to be available.

"You like Jerusalem, yes?" asked Dr. Gerard, after they had exchanged greetings.

"It's rather terrible in some ways," said Sarah, and added: "Religion is very odd!"

The Frenchman looked amused.

"I know what you mean." His English was very nearly perfect. "Every imaginable sect squabbling and fighting!"

"And the awful things they've built, too!" said Sarah.

"Yes, indeed."

Sarah sighed.

"They turned me out of one place today because I had on a sleeveless dress," she said ruefully. "Apparently the Almighty doesn't like my arms in spite of having made them."

Dr. Gerard laughed. Then he said:

"I was about to order some coffee. You will join me, Miss—?"

"King, my name is. Sarah King."

"And mine—permit me."

He whipped out a card. Taking it, Sarah's eyes widened in delighted awe.

"Dr. Theodore Gerard? Oh! I *am* excited to meet you. I've read all your works, of course. Your views on schizophrenia are frightfully interesting."

"Of course?" Gerard's eyebrows rose inquisitively.

Sarah explained rather diffidently.

"You see—I'm by way of being a doctor myself. Just got my M.B."

"Ah! I see."

Dr. Gerard ordered coffee and they sat down in a corner of the lounge. The Frenchman was less interested in Sarah's medical achievements than in the black hair that rippled back from her forehead and the beautifully shaped red mouth. He was amused at the obvious awe with which she regarded him.

"You are staying here long?" he asked conversationally.

"A few days. That is all. Then I want to go to Petra."

"Aha? I, too, was thinking of going there if it does not take too long. You see, I have to be back in Paris on the 14th."

"It takes about a week, I believe. Two days to go, two days there and two days back again."

"I must go to the travel bureau in the morning and see what can be arranged."

A party of people entered the lounge and sat down. Sarah watched them with some interest. She lowered her voice:

"Those people who have just come in—did you notice them on the train the other night? They left Cairo the same time as we did."

Dr. Gerard screwed in an eyeglass and directed his glance across the room.

"Americans?"

Sarah nodded.

"Yes. An American family. But—rather an unusual one, I think."

"Unusual? How unusual?"

"Well, look at them. Especially at the old woman."

Dr. Gerard complied. His keen professional glance flitted swiftly from face to face.

He noticed first a tall, rather loose-boned man—age about thirty. The face was pleasant but weak and his manner seemed oddly apathetic. Then there were two good-looking youngsters—the boy had almost a Greek head. "Something the matter with him, too," thought Dr. Gerard. "Yes—a definite state of nervous tension." The girl was clearly his sister, a strong resemblance, and she also was in an excitable condition. There was another girl younger still—with golden red hair that stood out like a halo; her hands were very restless; they were tearing and pulling at the handkerchief in her lap. Yet another woman, young, calm, dark-haired with a creamy pallor, a placid face not unlike a Luini Madonna. Nothing jumpy about *her!* And the center of the group—"Heavens!" thought Dr. Gerard, with a Frenchman's candid repulsion. "What a horror of a woman!" Old, swollen, bloated, sitting there immovable in the midst of them—a distorted old Buddha—a gross spider in the center of a web!

To Sarah he said:

"La Maman, she is not beautiful, eh?"

And he shrugged his shoulders.

"There's something rather—sinister about her, don't you think?" asked Sarah.

Dr. Gerard scrutinized her again. This time his eye was professional, not aesthetic.

"Dropsy—cardiac—" He added a glib medical phrase.

"Oh, yes, *that!*" Sarah dismissed the medical side. "But there is something odd in their attitude to her, don't you think?"

"Who are they, do you know?"

"Their name is Boynton. Mother, married son, his wife, one younger son and two younger daughters."

Dr. Gerard murmured:

"La famille Boynton sees the world."

"Yes, but there's something odd about the *way* they're seeing it. They never speak to anyone else. And none of them can do anything unless the old woman says so!"

"She is of the matriarchal type," said Gerard thoughtfully.

"She's a complete tyrant, I think," said Sarah.

Dr. Gerard shrugged his shoulders and remarked that the American woman ruled the earth—that was well known.

"Yes, but it's more than just that." Sarah was persistent. "She's— Oh, she's got them all so so *cowed*—so positively under her thumb—that it's—it's indecent!"

"To have too much power is bad for women," Gerard agreed, with sudden gravity. He shook his head. "It is difficult for a woman not to abuse power."

He shot a quick sideways glance at Sarah. She was watching the Boynton family—or rather she was watching one particular member of it. Dr. Gerard smiled a quick comprehending Gallic smile. Ah! so it was like that, was it?

He murmured tentatively:

"You have spoken with them—yes?"

"Yes—at least with one of them."

"The young man—the younger son?"

"Yes. On the train coming here from Kantara. He was standing in the corridor. I spoke to him."

There was no self-consciousness in Sarah's manner. There was, indeed, no self-consciousness in her attitude to life. She was interested in humanity and was of a friendly though impatient disposition.

"What made you speak to him?" asked Gerard.

Sarah shrugged her shoulders.

"Why not? I often speak to people traveling. I'm interested in people—in what they do and think and feel."

"You put them under the microscope, that is to say!"

"I suppose you might call it that," the girl admitted.

"And what were your impressions in this case?"

"Well"—she hesitated—"it was rather odd. . . . To begin with, the boy flushed right up to the roots of his hair."

"Is that so remarkable?" asked Gerard drily.

Sarah laughed.

"You mean that he thought I was a shameless hussy making advances to him? Oh, no, I don't think he thought that. Men can always tell, can't they?"

She gave him a frank questioning glance. Dr. Gerard nodded his head.

"I got the impression," said Sarah, speaking slowly and frowning a little, "that he was—how shall I put it?—both excited and appalled. Excited out of all proportion—and quite absurdly apprehensive at the same time. Now that's odd, isn't it, because I've always found Americans unusually self-possessed. An American boy of twenty, say, has infinitely more knowledge of the world and far more *savoir-faire* than an English boy of the same age. And this boy must be over twenty."

"About twenty-three or four, I should say."

"As much as that?"

"I should think so."

"Yes . . . perhaps you're right . . . only, somehow, he seems very young. . . ."

"Maladjustment mentally. The 'child' factor persists."

"Then I *am* right? I mean, there *is* something not quite normal about him?"

Dr. Gerard shrugged his shoulders, smiling a little at her earnestness.

"My dear young lady, are any of us quite normal? But I grant you that there is probably a neurosis of some kind."

"Connected with that horrible old woman, I'm sure!"

"You seem to dislike her very much," said Gerard, looking at her curiously.

"I do. She's got a—oh, a malevolent eye!"

Gerard murmured:

"So have many mothers when their sons are attracted to fascinating young ladies!"

Sarah shrugged an impatient shoulder. Frenchmen were all alike, she thought, obsessed by sex! Though, of course, as a conscientious psychologist she herself was bound to admit that there was always an underlying basis of sex to most phenomena. Sarah's thoughts ran along a familiar psychological track.

She came out of her meditations with a start. Raymond Boynton was crossing the room to the center table. He selected a magazine. As he passed her chair on his return journey she looked up at him and spoke:

"Have you been busy sight-seeing today?"

She selected her words at random; her real interest was to see how they would be received.

Raymond half stopped, flushed, shied like a nervous horse and his eyes went apprehensively to the center of his family group. He muttered:

"Oh—oh, yes—why, yes, certainly. I—"

Then, as suddenly as though he had received the prick of a spur, he hurried back to his family, holding out the magazine.

The grotesque Buddha-like figure held out a fat hand for it, but as she took it her eyes, Dr. Gerard noticed, were on the boy's face. She gave a grunt, certainly no audible thanks. The position of her head shifted very slightly. The doctor saw that she was now looking hard at Sarah. Her face was quite impassive, it had no expression in it. Impossible to tell what was passing in the woman's mind.

Sarah looked at her watch and uttered an exclamation.

"It's much later than I thought." She got up. "Thank you so much, Dr. Gerard, for standing me coffee. I must write some letters now."

He rose and took her hand.

"We shall meet again, I hope," he said.

"Oh, yes! Perhaps you will come to Petra?"

"I shall certainly try to do so."

Sarah smiled at him and turned away. Her way out of the room led her past the Boynton family.

Dr. Gerard, watching, saw Mrs. Boynton's gaze shift to her son's face. He saw the boy's eyes meet hers. As Sarah passed, Raymond Boynton half turned his head—not towards her but away from her. . . . It was a slow unwilling motion and conveyed the idea that old Mrs. Boynton had pulled an invisible string.

Sarah King noticed the avoidance, and was young enough and human enough to be annoyed by it. They had had such a friendly talk together in the swaying corridor of the Wagon-Lit. They had compared notes on Egypt, had laughed at the ridiculous language of the donkey boys and street touts. Sarah had described how a camel man, when he had started hopefully and impudently, "You English lady or American?" had received the answer: "No, Chinese," and her pleasure in seeing the man's complete bewilderment as he stared at her. The boy had been, she thought, like a nice eager schoolboy—there had been, perhaps, something almost pathetic about his eagerness. And now, for no reason at all, he was shy, boorish—positively rude.

"I sha'n't take any more trouble with him," said Sarah indignantly.

For Sarah, without being unduly conceited, had a fairly good opinion of herself. She knew herself to be definitely attractive to the opposite sex, and she was not one to take a snubbing lying down!

She had been, perhaps, a shade over-friendly to this boy because, for some obscure reason, she had felt sorry for him.

But now, it was apparent, he was merely a rude, stuck-up, boorish young American!

Instead of writing the letters she had mentioned, Sarah King sat down in front of her dressing-table, combed the hair back from her forehead, looked into a pair of troubled hazel eyes in the glass, and took stock of her situation in life.

She had just passed through a difficult emotional crisis. A month ago she had broken off her engagement to a young doctor some four years her senior. They had been very much attracted to each other, but had been too much alike in temperament. Disagreements and quarrels had been of common occurrence. Sarah was of too imperious a temperament herself to brook a calm assertion of autocracy. Like many high-spirited women, Sarah believed herself to admire strength. She had always told herself that she wanted to be mastered. When she met a man capable of mastering her she found that she did not like it at all! To break off her engagement had cost her a good deal of heart burning, but she was clear-sighted enough to realize that mere mutual attraction was not a sufficient basis on which to build a lifetime of happiness. She had treated herself deliberately to an interesting holiday abroad in order to help on forgetfulness before she went back to start working in earnest.

Sarah's thoughts came back from the past to the present.

"I wonder," she thought, "if Dr. Gerard will let me talk to him about his work? He's done such marvelous work. If only he'll take me seriously . . . Perhaps—if he comes to Petra—"

Then she thought again of the strange, boorish young American.

She had no doubt that it was the presence of his family which had caused him to react in such a peculiar manner, but she felt slightly scornful of him, nevertheless. To be under the thumb of one's family like that—it was really rather ridiculous—especially for a *man!*

And yet . . .

A queer feeling passed over her. Surely there was something a little *odd* about it all?

She said suddenly out loud:

"That boy wants rescuing! I'm going to see to it!"

3

When Sarah had left the lounge, Dr. Gerard sat where he was for some minutes. Then he walked over to the table, picked up the latest number of *Le Matin* and strolled with it to a chair a few yards away from the Boynton family. His curiosity was aroused.

He had at first been amused by the English girl's interest in this American family, shrewdly diagnosing that it was inspired by interest in one particular member of the group. But now something out of the ordinary about this family party awakened in him the deeper, more impartial interest of the scientist. He sensed that there was something here of definite psychological interest.

Very discreetly, under the cover of his paper, he took stock of them. First, the boy in whom that attractive English girl took such a decided interest. Yes, thought Gerard, definitely the type to appeal to her temperamentally. Sarah King had strength—she possessed well-balanced nerves, cool wits and a resolute will. Dr. Gerard judged the young man to be sensitive, perceptive, diffident and intensely suggestible. He noted with a physician's eye the obvious fact that the boy was at the moment in a state of high nervous tension. Dr. Gerard wondered why. He was puzzled. Why should a young man whose physical health was obviously good, who was abroad ostensibly enjoying himself, be in such a condition that a nervous breakdown was imminent?

The doctor turned his attention to the other members of the party. The girl with the chestnut hair was obviously Raymond's sister. They were of the same racial type, small-boned, well-shaped, aristocratic looking. They had the same slender, well-formed hands, the same clean line of jaw, and the same poise of the head on a long slender neck. And the girl, too, was nervous. . . . She made slight involuntary nervous movements, her eyes were deeply shadowed underneath and over bright. Her voice, when she spoke, was too quick and a shade breathless. She was watchful—alert—unable to relax.

"And she is afraid, too," decided Dr. Gerard. "Yes, she is afraid!"

He overheard scraps of conversation—a very ordinary normal conversation.

"We might go to Solomon's Stables."—"Would that be too much for Mother?"—"The Weeping Wall in the morning?"—"The Temple, of course—the Mosque of Omar they call it—I wonder why?"—"Because it's been made into a Moslem mosque, of course, Lennox."

Ordinary commonplace tourists' talk. And yet, somehow, Dr. Gerard felt a queer conviction that these overheard scraps of dialogue were all singularly unreal. They were a mask—a cover for something that surged and eddied underneath—something too deep and formless for words. . . .

Again he shot a covert glance from behind the shelter of *Le Matin*.

Lennox? That was the elder brother. The same family likeness could be traced, but there was a difference. Lennox was not so highly strung; he was, Gerard decided, of a less nervous temperament. But about him, too, there seemed something odd. There was no sign of muscular tension about him as there was about the other two. He sat relaxed, limp. Puzzling, searching among memories of patients he had seen sitting like that in hospital wards, Gerard thought:

"He is *exhausted*—yes, exhausted with suffering. That look in the eyes—the look you see in a wounded dog or a sick horse—dumb bestial endurance. . . . It is odd, that . . . Physically there seems nothing wrong with him. . . . Yet there is no doubt that lately he has been through much suffering—mental suffering. Now he no longer suffers—he endures dumbly—waiting, I think, for the blow to fall. . . . What blow? Am I fancying all this? No, the man is waiting for something, for the end to come. So cancer patients lie and wait, thankful that an anodyne dulls the pain a little. . . ."

Lennox Boynton got up and retrieved a ball of wool that the old lady had dropped.

"Here you are, Mother."

"Thank you."

What was she knitting, this monumental, impassive old woman? Something thick and coarse. Gerard thought: "Mittens for inhabitants of a workhouse!" and smiled at his own fantasy.

He turned his attention to the youngest member of the party—the girl with the golden red hair. She was, perhaps, seventeen. Her skin had the exquisite clearness that often goes with red hair. Although over thin, it was a beautiful face. She was sitting smiling to herself—smiling into space. There was something a little curious about that smile. It was so far-removed from the Solomon Hotel, from Jerusalem. . . . It reminded Dr. Gerard of something. . . . Presently it came to him in a flash. It was the strange unearthly smile that lifts the lips of the Maidens in the Acropolis at

Athens—something remote and lovely and a little inhuman. . . . The magic of the smile, her exquisite stillness, gave him a little pang.

And then with a shock, Dr. Gerard noticed her hands. They were concealed from the group around her by the table, but he could see them clearly from where he sat. In the shelter of her lap they were picking—picking—tearing a delicate handkerchief into tiny shreds.

It gave him a horrible shock.

The aloof remote smile—the still body—and the busy destructive hands . . .

4

There was a slow asthmatic wheezing cough—then the monumental knitting woman spoke.

"Ginevra, you're tired; you'd better go to bed."

The girl started; her fingers stopped their mechanical action.

"I'm not tired, Mother."

Gerard recognized appreciatively the musical quality of her voice. It had the sweet singing quality that lends enchantment to the most commonplace utterances.

"Yes, you are. I always know. I don't think you'll be able to do any sightseeing tomorrow."

"Oh! But I shall. I'm quite all right."

In a thick hoarse voice, almost a grating voice, her mother said:

"No, you're not. You're going to be ill."

"I'm not! I'm not!"

The girl began trembling violently.

A soft calm voice said:

"I'll come up with you, Jinny."

The quiet young woman with wide, thoughtful grey eyes and neatly coiled dark hair rose to her feet.

Old Mrs. Boynton said:

"No. Let her go up alone."

The girl cried:

"I want Nadine to come!"

"Then of course I will." The young woman moved a step forward.

The old woman said:

"The child prefers to go by herself—don't you, Jinny?"

There was a pause—a pause of a moment—then Ginevra Boynton said, her voice suddenly flat and dull:

"Yes—I'd rather go alone. Thank you, Nadine."

She walked away, a tall angular figure that moved with a surprising grace.

Dr. Gerard lowered his paper and took a full satisfying gaze at old Mrs.

Boynton. She was looking after her daughter and her fat face was creased into a peculiar smile. It was, very faintly, a caricature of the lovely unearthly smile that had transformed the girl's face so short a time before.

Then the old woman transferred her gaze to Nadine. The latter had just sat down again. She raised her eyes and met her mother-in-law's glance. Her face was quite imperturbable. The old woman's glance was malicious.

Dr. Gerard thought:

"What an absurdity of an old tyrant!"

And then, suddenly, the old woman's eyes were full on him, and he drew in his breath sharply. Small, black, smoldering eyes they were, but something came from them—a power, a definite force, a wave of evil malignancy. Dr. Gerard knew something about the power of personality. He realized that here was no spoilt tyrannical invalid indulging petty whims. This old woman was a definite force. In the malignancy of her glare he felt a resemblance to the effect produced by a cobra. Mrs. Boynton might be old, infirm, a prey to disease, but she was not powerless. She was a woman who knew the meaning of power, who had exercised a lifetime of power and who had never once doubted her own force. Dr. Gerard had once met a woman who performed a most dangerous and spectacular act with tigers. The great slinking brutes had crawled to their places and performed their degrading and humiliating tricks. Their eyes and subdued snarls told of hatred, bitter fanatical hatred, but they had obeyed, cringed. That had been a young woman, a woman with an arrogant dark beauty, but the look had been the same.

"Une dompteuse!" said Dr. Gerard to himself.

And he understood now what that undercurrent to the harmless family talk had been. It was hatred—a dark eddying stream of hatred.

He thought:

"How fanciful and absurd most people would think me! Here is a commonplace devoted American family reveling in Palestine—and I weave a story of black magic round it!"

Then he looked with interest at the quiet young woman who was called Nadine. There was a wedding ring on her left hand, and as he watched her, he saw her give one swift betraying glance at the fair-haired, loose-limbed Lennox. He knew, then . . .

They were man and wife, those two. But it was a mother's glance rather than a wife's—a true mother's glance—protecting, anxious. And he knew something more. He knew that out of that group, Nadine Boynton alone was unaffected by her mother-in-law's spell. She may have disliked the old woman, but she was not afraid of her. The power did not touch her.

She was unhappy, deeply concerned about her husband, but she was free.

Dr. Gerard said to himself:

"All this is very interesting."

5

Into these dark imaginings a breath of the commonplace came with almost ludicrous effect.

A man came into the lounge, caught sight of the Boyntons and came across to them.

He was a pleasant middle-aged American of a strictly conventional type. He was carefully dressed, with a long, clean-shaven face and he had a slow, pleasant, somewhat monotonous voice.

"I was looking around for you all," he said.

Meticulously he shook hands with the entire family.

"And how do you find yourself, Mrs. Boynton? Not too tired by the journey?"

Almost graciously, the old lady wheezed out:

"No, thank you. My health's never good, as you know—"

"Why, of course; too bad—too bad."

"But I'm certainly no worse."

Mrs. Boynton added with a slow reptilian smile:

"Nadine, here, takes good care of me; don't you, Nadine?"

"I do my best." Her voice was expressionless.

"Why, I'll bet you do," said the stranger heartily. "Well, Lennox, and what do you think of King David's city?"

"Oh, I don't know."

Lennox spoke apathetically—without interest.

"Find it kind of disappointing, do you? I'll confess it struck me that way at first. But perhaps you haven't been around much yet?"

Carol Boynton said:

"We can't do very much because of Mother."

Mrs. Boynton explained:

"A couple of hours' sight-seeing is about all I can manage every day."

The stranger said heartily:

"I think it's wonderful you manage to do all you do, Mrs. Boynton."

Mrs. Boynton gave a slow wheezy chuckle; it had an almost gloating sound.

"I don't give in to my body! It's the mind that matters! Yes, it's the *mind. . . .*"

Her voice died away. Gerard saw Raymond Boynton give a nervous jerk.

"Have you been to the Weeping Wall yet, Mr. Cope?" he asked.

"Why, yes, that was one of the first places I visited. I hope to have done Jerusalem thoroughly in a couple more days and I'm letting them get me out an itinerary at Cook's so as to do the Holy Land thoroughly—Bethlehem, Nazareth, Tiberias, the Sea of Galilee. It's all going to be mighty interesting. Then there's Jerash; there are some very interesting ruins there—Roman, you know. And I'd very much like to have a look at the Rose Red City of Petra, a most remarkable natural phenomenon, I believe that is, and right off the beaten track; but it takes the best part of a week to get there and back and do it properly."

Carol said:

"I'd love to go there. It sounds marvelous."

"Why, I should say it was definitely worth seeing—yes, definitely worth seeing." Mr. Cope paused, shot a somewhat dubious glance at Mrs. Boynton, and then went on in a voice that to the listening Frenchman was palpably uncertain:

"I wonder now if I couldn't persuade some of you people to come with me? Naturally I know *you* couldn't manage it, Mrs. Boynton, and naturally some of your family would want to remain with you; but if you were to divide forces, so to speak—"

He paused. Gerard heard the even click of Mrs. Boynton's knitting needles. Then she said: "I don't think we'd care to divide up. We're a very homey group." She looked up. "Well, children, what do you say?"

There was a queer ring in her voice. The answers came promptly: "No, Mother."—"Oh, no."—"No, of course not."

Mrs. Boynton said, smiling that very odd smile of hers:

"You see—they won't leave me. What about you, Nadine? You didn't say anything."

"No, thank you, Mother, not unless Lennox cares about it."

Mrs. Boynton turned her head slowly towards her son.

"Well, Lennox, what about it; why don't you and Nadine go? She seems to want to."

He started—looked up.

"I—well—no, I—I think we'd better all stay together."

Mr. Cope said genially:

"Well, you *are* a devoted family!" But something in his geniality rang a little hollow and forced.

"We keep to ourselves," said Mrs. Boynton. She began to wind up her ball of wool. "By the way, Raymond, who was that young woman who spoke to you just now?"

Raymond started nervously. He flushed, then went white.

"I—I don't know her name. She—she was on the train the other night."

Mrs. Boynton began slowly to try and heave herself out of her chair.

"I don't think we'll have much to do with her," she said.

Nadine rose and assisted the old woman to struggle out of her chair. She did it with a professional deftness that attracted Gerard's attention.

"Bedtime," said Mrs. Boynton. "Good-night, Mr. Cope."

"Good-night, Mrs. Boynton. Good-night, Mrs. Lennox."

They went off—a little procession. It did not seem to occur to any of the younger members of the party to stay behind.

Mr. Cope was left looking after them. The expression on his face was an odd one.

As Dr. Gerard knew by experience, Americans are disposed to be a friendly race. They have not the uneasy suspicion of the traveling Briton. To a man of Dr. Gerard's tact, making the acquaintance of Mr. Cope presented few difficulties. The American was lonely and was, like most of his race, disposed to friendliness. Dr. Gerard's cardcase was again to the fore.

Reading the name on it, Mr. Jefferson Cope was duly impressed.

"Why, surely, Dr. Gerard, you were over in the States not very long ago?"

"Last Autumn. I was lecturing at Harvard."

"Of course. Yours, Dr. Gerard, is one of the most distinguished names in your profession. You're pretty well at the head of your subject in Paris."

"My dear sir, you are far too kind! I protest."

"No, no, this is a great privilege—meeting you like this. As a matter of fact, there are several very distinguished people here in Jerusalem just at present. There's yourself and there's Lord Welldon, and Sir Gabriel Steinbaum, the financier. Then there's the veteran English archaeologist, Sir Manders Stone. And there's Lady Westholme who's very prominent in English politics. And there's that famous Belgian detective, Hercule Poirot."

"Little Hercule Poirot? Is he here?"

"I read his name in the local paper as having lately arrived. Seems to me all the world and his wife are at the Solomon Hotel. A mighty fine hotel it is, too. And very tastefully decorated."

Mr. Jefferson Cope was clearly enjoying himself. Dr. Gerard was a man who could display a lot of charm when he chose. Before long the two men had adjourned to the bar.

After a couple of highballs Gerard said:

"Tell me, is that a typical American family to whom you were talking?"

Jefferson Cope sipped his drink thoughtfully. Then he said:

"Why, no, I wouldn't say it was exactly typical."

"No? A very devoted family, though."

Mr. Cope said slowly:

"You mean they all seem to revolve round the old lady? That's true enough. She's a very remarkable old lady, you know."

"Indeed?"

Mr. Cope needed very little encouragement. The gentle invitation was enough.

"I don't mind telling you, Dr. Gerard, I've been having that family a good deal on my mind lately. I've been thinking about them a lot. If I may say so, it would ease my mind to talk to you about the matter. If it won't bore you, that is?"

Dr. Gerard disclaimed boredom. Mr. Jefferson Cope went on slowly, his pleasant clean-shaven face creased with perplexity.

"I'll tell you straight away that I'm just a little worried. Mrs. Boynton, you see, is an old friend of mine. That is to say, not the old Mrs. Boynton, the young one. Mrs. Lennox Boynton."

"Ah, yes, that very charming dark-haired young lady."

"That's right. That's Nadine. Nadine Boynton, Dr. Gerard, is a very lovely character. I knew her before she was married. She was in hospital then, working to be a trained nurse. Then she went for a vacation to stay with the Boyntons and she married Lennox."

"Yes?"

Mr. Jefferson Cope took another sip of highball and went on.

"I'd like to tell you, Dr. Gerard, just a little of the Boynton family history."

"Yes? I should be most interested."

"Well, you see, the late Elmer Boynton—he was quite a well-known man and a very charming personality—was twice married. His first wife died when Carol and Raymond were tiny toddlers. The second Mrs. Boynton, so I've been told, was a handsome woman when he married her, though not very young. Seems odd to think she can ever have been handsome to look at her now, but that's what I've been told on very good authority. Anyway, her husband thought a lot of her and adopted her judgment on almost every point. He was an invalid for some years before he died, and she practically ruled the roost. She's a very capable woman with a fine head for business. A very conscientious woman, too. After Elmer died, she devoted herself absolutely to these children. There's one of her own, too—Ginevra

—pretty red-haired girl but a bit delicate. Well, as I was telling you, Mrs. Boynton devoted herself entirely to her family. She just shut out the outside world entirely. Now, I don't know what you think, Dr. Gerard, but I don't think that's always a very sound thing."

"I agree with you. It is most harmful to developing mentalities."

"Yes, I should say that just about expresses it. Mrs. Boynton shielded these children from the outside world and never let them make any outside contacts. The result of that is that they've grown up—well, kind of nervy. They're jumpy, if you know what I mean. Can't make friends with strangers. It's bad, that."

"It is very bad."

"I've no doubt Mrs. Boynton meant well. It was just over devotion on her part."

"They all live at home?" asked the doctor.

"Yes."

"Do neither of the sons work?"

"Why, no. Elmer Boynton was a rich man. He left all his money to Mrs. Boynton for her lifetime—but it was understood that it was for the family upkeep generally."

"So they are dependent on her financially?"

"That is so. And she's encouraged them to live at home and not go out and look for jobs. Well, maybe that's all right; there's plenty of money. They don't need to take jobs but I think for the male sex, anyway, work's a good tonic. Then there's another thing—they've none of them got any hobbies. They don't play golf. They don't belong to any country club. They don't go around to dances or do anything with the other young people. They live in a great barrack of a house way down in the country, miles from anywhere. I tell you, Dr. Gerard, it seems all wrong to me."

"I agree with you," said Dr. Gerard.

"Not one of them has got the least social sense. The community spirit—that's what's lacking! They may be a very devoted family but they're all bound up in themselves."

"There has never been any question of one or the other of them branching out for him- or herself?"

"Not that I've heard of. They just sit around."

"Do you put the blame for that on them or on Mrs. Boynton?"

Jefferson Cope shifted uneasily.

"Well, in a sense I feel she is more or less responsible. It's bad bringing up on her part. All the same, when a young fellow comes to maturity it's up to him to kick over the traces of his own accord. No boy ought to keep on being tied to his mother's apron strings. He ought to choose to be independent."

Dr. Gerard said thoughtfully:

"That might be impossible."

"Why impossible?"

"There are methods, Mr. Cope, of preventing a tree from growing."

Cope stared.

"They're a fine healthy lot, Dr. Gerard."

"The mind can be stunted and warped as well as the body."

"They're bright mentally too."

Gerard sighed.

Jefferson Cope went on:

"No, Dr. Gerard, take it from me, a man has got the control of his own destiny right there in his own hands. A man who respects himself strikes out on his own and makes something of his life. He doesn't just sit round and twiddle his thumbs. No woman ought to respect a man who does that."

Gerard looked at him curiously for a minute or two. Then he said:

"You refer particularly, I think, to Mr. Lennox Boynton?"

"Why, yes, it was Lennox I was thinking of. Raymond's only a boy still. But Lennox is just on thirty. Time he showed he was made of something."

"It is a difficult life, perhaps, for his wife?"

"Of course it's a difficult life for her! Nadine is a very fine girl. I admire her more than I can say. She's never let drop one word of complaint. *But she's not happy,* Dr. Gerard. She's just as unhappy as she can be."

Gerard nodded his head.

"Yes, I think that well might be."

"I don't know what *you* think about it, Dr. Gerard, but *I* think that there's a limit to what a woman ought to put up with! If I were Nadine I'd put it to young Lennox straight. Either he sets to and proves what he's made of, or else—"

"Or else, you think, she should leave him?"

"She's got her own life to live, Dr. Gerard. If Lennox doesn't appreciate her as she ought to be appreciated, well, there are other men who will."

"There is—yourself, for instance?"

The American flushed. Then he looked straight at the other with a certain simple dignity.

"That's so," he said. "I'm not ashamed of my feelings for that lady. I respect her and I am very, very deeply attached to her. All I want is her happiness. If she were happy with Lennox, I'd sit right back and fade out of the picture."

"But as it is?"

"But as it is, I'm standing by! If she wants me, *I'm here!*"

"You are, in fact, the 'parfait gentil knight,' " murmured Gerard.

"Pardon?"

"My dear sir, chivalry only lives nowadays in the American nation! You are content to serve your lady without hope of reward! It is most admirable, that! What exactly do you hope to be able to do for her?"

"My idea is to be right here at hand if she needs me."

"And what, may I ask, is the older Mrs. Boynton's attitude towards you?"

Jefferson Cope said slowly:

"I'm never quite sure about that old lady. As I've told you, she isn't fond of making outside contacts. But she's been different to me, she's always very gracious and treats me quite like one of the family."

"In fact, she approves of your friendship with Mrs. Lennox?"

"She does."

Dr. Gerard shrugged his shoulders.

"That is, perhaps, a little odd?"

Jefferson Cope said stiffly:

"Let me assure you, Dr. Gerard, there is nothing dishonorable in that friendship. It is purely platonic."

"My dear sir, I am quite sure of that. I repeat, though, that for Mrs. Boynton to encourage that friendship is a curious action on her part. You know, Mr. Cope, Mrs. Boynton interests me—she interests me greatly."

"She is certainly a remarkable woman. She has great force of character—a most prominent personality. As I say. Elmer Boynton had the greatest faith in her judgment."

"So much so that he was content to leave his children completely at her mercy from the financial point of view. In my country, Mr. Cope, it is impossible by law to do such a thing."

Mr. Cope rose.

"In America," he said, "we're great believers in absolute freedom."

Dr. Gerard rose also. He was unimpressed by the remark. He had heard it made before by people of many different nationalities. The illusion that freedom is the prerogative of one's own particular race is fairly widespread.

Dr. Gerard was wiser. He knew that no race, no country and no individual could be described as free. But he also knew that there were different degrees of bondage.

He went up to bed thoughtful and interested.

6

Sarah King stood in the precincts of the Temple—the Haram-esh-Sherif. Her back was to the Dome of the Rock. The plashing of fountains sounded in her ears. Little groups of tourists passed by without disturbing the peace of the oriental atmosphere.

Strange, thought Sarah, that once a Jebusite should have made this rocky summit into a threshing floor and that David should have purchased it for six hundred shekels of gold and made it a Holy Place. And now the loud chattering tongues of sight-seers of all nations could be heard . . .

She turned and looked at the Mosque which now covered the shrine and wondered if Solomon's temple would have looked half as beautiful.

There was a clatter of footsteps and a little party came out from the interior of the Mosque. It was the Boyntons escorted by a voluble dragoman. Mrs. Boynton was supported between Lennox and Raymond. Nadine and Mr. Cope walked behind. Carol came last. As they were moving off, the latter caught sight of Sarah.

She hesitated, then, on a sudden decision, she wheeled around and ran swiftly and noiselessly across the courtyard.

"Excuse me," she said breathlessly. "I must—I—I felt I must speak to you."

"Yes?" said Sarah.

Carol was trembling violently. Her face was quite white.

"It's about—my brother. When you—you spoke to him last night you must have thought him very rude. But he didn't mean to be—he—he couldn't help it. Oh, do please believe me."

Sarah felt that the whole scene was ridiculous. Both her pride and her good taste were offended. Why should a strange girl suddenly rush up and tender a ridiculous apology for a boorish brother?

An offhand reply trembled on her lips—and then, quickly, her mood changed.

There was something out of the ordinary here. This girl was in deadly earnest. That something in Sarah which had led her to adopt a medical career reacted to the girl's need. Her instinct told her there was something badly wrong.

She said encouragingly:

"Tell me about it."

"He spoke to you on the train, didn't he?" began Carol.

Sarah nodded.

"Yes—at least I spoke to him."

"Oh, of course. It would be that way around. But, you see, last night, Ray was afraid—"

She stopped.

"Afraid?"

Carol's white face crimsoned.

"Oh, I know it sounds absurd—mad. You see, my mother—she's—she's not well—and she doesn't like us making friends outside. But—but I know Ray would—would like to be friends with you."

Sarah was interested. Before she could speak, Carol went on.

"I—I know what I'm saying sounds very silly, but we are—rather an odd family." She cast a quick look around—it was a look of fear.

"I—I mustn't stay," she murmured. "They may miss me."

Sarah made up her mind. She spoke.

"Why shouldn't you stay—if you want to? We might walk back together."

"Oh, no." Carol drew back. "I—I couldn't do that."

"Why not?" said Sarah.

"I couldn't really. My mother would be—would be—"

Sarah said clearly and calmly:

"I know it's awfully difficult sometimes for parents to realize that their children are grown up. They will go on trying to run their lives for them. But it's a pity, you know, to give in! One must stand up for one's rights."

Carol murmured:

"You don't understand—you don't understand in the least. . . ."

Her hands twisted together nervously.

Sarah went on:

"One gives in sometimes because one is afraid of rows. Rows are very unpleasant, but I think freedom of action is always worth fighting for."

"Freedom?" Carol stared at her. "None of us have ever been free. We never will be."

"Nonsense!" said Sarah clearly.

Carol leaned forward and touched her arm.

"Listen. I *must* try and make you understand! Before her marriage my mother—she's my step-mother really—was a wardress in a prison. My father was the Governor and he married her. Well, *it's been like that ever since.* She's gone on being a wardress—*to us.* That's why our life is just—being in prison!"

Her head jerked around again.

"They've missed me. I—I must go."

Sarah caught her by the arm as she was darting off.

"One minute. We must meet again and talk."

"I can't. I sha'n't be able to."

"Yes, you can." She spoke authoritatively. "Come to my room after you go to bed. It's 319. Don't forget. 319."

She released her hold. Carol ran off after her family.

Sarah stood staring after her. She awoke from her thoughts to find Dr. Gerard by her side.

"Good-morning, Miss King. So you've been talking to Miss Carol Boynton?"

"Yes, we had the most extraordinary conversation. Let me tell you."

She repeated the substance of her conversation with the girl.

Gerard pounced on one point.

"Wardress in a prison, was she, that old hippopotamus? That is significant, perhaps."

Sarah said:

"You mean that that is the cause of her tyranny? It is the habit of her former profession?"

Gerard shook his head.

"No, that is approaching it from the wrong angle. There is some deep underlying compulsion. She does not love tyranny *because she has been a wardress.* Let us rather say that *she became a wardress because she loved tyranny.* In my theory it was a secret desire for power over other human beings that led her to adopt that profession."

His face was very grave.

"There are such strange things buried down in the unconscious. A lust for power—a lust for cruelty—a savage desire to tear and rend—all the inheritance of our past racial memories . . . They are all there, Miss King, all the cruelty and savagery and lust . . . We shut the door on them and deny them conscious life, but sometimes they are too strong."

Sarah shivered.

"I know."

Gerard continued:

"We see it all around us today—in political creeds, in the conduct of nations. A reaction from humanitarianism—from pity—from brotherly good will. The creeds sound well sometimes—a wise régime—a beneficent government—but imposed by *force*—resting on a basis of cruelty and fear. They are opening the door, these apostles of violence, they are letting out the old savagery, the old delight in cruelty *for its own sake!* Oh, it is difficult. Man is an animal very delicately balanced. He has one prime necessity—to survive. To advance too quickly is as fatal as to lag behind. He must survive! He must, perhaps, retain some of the old savagery, but he must not–no, definitely he must not—*deify* it!"

There was a pause. Then Sarah said:

"You think old Mrs. Boynton is a kind of Sadist?"

"I am almost sure of it. I think she rejoices in the infliction of pain—mental pain, mind you, not physical. That is very much rarer and very much more difficult to deal with. She likes to have control of other human beings and she likes to make them suffer."

"It's pretty beastly," said Sarah.

Gerard told her of his conversation with Jefferson Cope.

"He doesn't realize what is going on?" she said thoughtfully.

"How should he? He is not a psychologist."

"True. He hasn't got our disgusting minds!"

"Exactly. He has a nice, upright, sentimental, normal American mind. He believes in good rather than evil. He sees that the atmosphere of the Boynton family is all wrong, but he credits Mrs. Boynton with misguided devotion rather than active maleficence."

"That must amuse her," said Sarah.

"I should imagine it does!"

Sarah said impatiently:

"But why don't they break away? They could."

Gerard shook his head.

"No, there you are wrong. *They cannot.* Have you ever seen the old experiment with a cock? You chalk a line on the floor and put the cock's beak to it. The cock believes he is tied there. He cannot raise his head. So with these unfortunates. She has worked on them, remember, since they were children. And her dominance has been mental. She has hypnotized them to believe that *they cannot disobey her.* Oh, I know most people would say that was nonsense—but you and I know better. She has made them believe that utter dependence on her is inevitable. They have been in prison so long that if the prison door stood open they would no longer notice! One of them, at least, no longer even wants to be free! And they would all be *afraid* of freedom."

Sarah asked practically:

"What will happen when she dies?"

Gerard shrugged his shoulders.

"It depends on how soon that happens. If it happened *now*—well, I think it might not be too late. The boy and girl—they are still young—impressionable. They would become, I believe, normal human beings. With Lennox, possibly, it has gone too far. He looks to me like a man who has parted company with hope—he lives and endures like a brute beast."

Sarah said impatiently:

"His wife ought to have done something! She ought to have yanked him out of it."

"I wonder. She may have tried—and failed."

"Do you think she's under the spell too?"

Gerard shook his head.

"No. I don't think the old lady has any power over her, and for that reason she hates her with a bitter hatred. Watch her eyes."

Sarah frowned.

"I can't make her out—the young one, I mean. Does she know what is going on?"

"I think she must have a pretty shrewd idea."

"H'm," said Sarah. "That old woman ought to be murdered! Arsenic in her early morning tea would be my prescription."

Then she said abruptly:

"What about the youngest girl—the red-haired one with the rather fascinating vacant smile?"

Gerard frowned.

"I don't know. There is something queer there. Ginevra Boynton is the old woman's own daughter, of course."

"Yes. I suppose that would be different—or wouldn't it?"

Gerard said slowly:

"I do not believe that when once the mania for power (and the lust for cruelty) has taken possession of a human being that it can spare *anybody*—not even its nearest and dearest."

He was silent for a moment then he said:

"Are you a Christian, Mademoiselle?"

Sarah said slowly:

"I don't know. I used to think that I wasn't anything. But now—I'm not sure. I feel—oh, I feel that if I could sweep all this away—" she made a violent gesture—"all the buildings and the sects and the fierce squabbling churches—that—that I might see Christ's quiet figure riding into Jerusalem on a donkey—and believe in him."

Dr. Gerard said gravely:

"I believe at least in one of the chief tenets of the Christian faith—*contentment with a lowly place.* I am a doctor and I know that ambition—

the desire to succeed—to have power—leads to most ills of the human soul. If the desire is realized it leads to arrogance, violence and final satiety; and if it is denied—ah! if it is denied—let all the asylums for the insane rise up and give their testimony! They are filled with human beings who were unable to face being mediocre, insignificant, ineffective and who therefore created for themselves ways of escape from reality so to be shut off from life itself forever."

Sarah said abruptly:

"It's a pity the old Boynton woman isn't in an asylum."

Gerard shook his head.

"No—her place is not there among the failures. It is worse than that. She has succeeded, you see! She has accomplished her dream."

Sarah shuddered.

She cried passionately:

"Such things ought not to be!"

7

Sarah wondered very much whether Carol Boynton would keep her appointment that night.

On the whole, she rather doubted it. She was afraid that Carol would have a sharp reaction after her semi-confidencecs of the morning.

Nevertheless, she made her preparations, slipping on a blue satin dressing-gown and getting out her little spirit lamp and boiling up water.

She was just on the point of giving Carol up (it was after one o'clock) and going to bed, when there was a tap on her door. She opened it and drew quickly back to let Carol come in.

The latter said breathlessly:

"I was afraid you might have gone to bed . . ."

Sarah's manner was carefully matter of fact.

"Oh, no. I was waiting for you. Have some tea, will you? It's real Lapsang Souchong."

She brought over a cup. Carol had been nervous and uncertain of herself. Now she accepted the cup and a biscuit and her manner became calmer.

"This is rather fun," said Sarah, smiling.

Carol looked a little startled.

"Yes," she said doubtfully. "Yes, I suppose it is."

"Rather like the midnight feasts we used to have at school," went on Sarah. "I suppose you didn't go away to school?"

Carol shook her head.

"No, we never left home. We had a governess—different governesses. They never stayed long."

"Did you never go away at all?"

"No. We've lived always in the same house. This coming abroad is the first time I've ever been away."

Sarah said casually:

"It must have been a great adventure."

"Oh, it was. It—it's all been like a dream."

"What made your—your step-mother decide to come abroad?"

At the mention of Mrs. Boynton's name, Carol had flinched. Sarah said quickly:

"You know, I'm by way of being a doctor. I've just taken my M.B. Your mother—or step-mother rather—is very interesting to me—as a case, you know. I should say she was quite definitely a pathological case."

Carol stared. It was clearly a very unexpected point of view to her. Sarah had spoken as she had with deliberate intent. She realized that to her family Mrs. Boynton loomed as a kind of powerful obscene idol. It was Sarah's object to rob her of her more terrifying aspect.

"Yes," she said. "There's a kind of disease of—of grandeur—that gets hold of people. They get very autocratic and insist on everything being done exactly as they say and are altogether very difficult to deal with."

Carol put down her cup.

"Oh," she cried, "I'm so glad to be talking to you. Really, you know, I believe Ray and I have been getting quite—well, quite queer. We'd got terribly worked up about things."

"Talking with an outsider is always a good thing," said Sarah. "Inside a family one is apt to get too intense."

Then she asked casually:

"If you are unhappy, haven't you ever thought of leaving home?"

Carol looked startled.

"Oh, no! How could we? I—I mean, Mother would never allow it."

"But she couldn't stop you," said Sarah gently. "You're over age."

"I'm twenty-three."

"Exactly."

"But still, I don't see how—I mean I wouldn't know where to go and what to do."

Her tone seemed bewildered.

"You see," she said, "we haven't got any money."

"Haven't you any friends you could go to?"

"Friends?" Carol shook her head. "Oh, no, we don't know anyone!"

"Did none of you ever think of leaving home?"

"No—I don't think so. Oh—oh—we couldn't."

Sarah changed the subject. She found the girl's bewilderment pitiful. She said:

"Are you fond of your step-mother?"

Slowly Carol shook her head.

She whispered in a low scared voice:

"I hate her. So does Ray . . . We've—we've often wished she would die."

Again Sarah changed the subject.

"Tell me about your elder brother."

"Lennox? I don't know what's the matter with Lennox. He hardly ever speaks now. He goes about in a kind of day-dream. Nadine's terribly worried about him."

"You are fond of your sister-in-law?"

"Yes, Nadine is different. She's always kind. But she's very unhappy."

"About your brother?"

"Yes."

"Have they been married long?"

"Four years."

"And they've always lived at home?"

"Yes."

Sarah asked:

"Does your sister-in-law like that?"

"No."

There was a pause. Then Carol said:

"There was an awful fuss once about four years ago now. You see, as I told you, none of us ever goes outside the house at home. I mean we go into the grounds, but nowhere else. But Lennox did. He got out at night. He went into Fountain Springs—there was a sort of dance going on. Mother was frightfully angry when she found out. It was terrible. And then, after that, she asked Nadine to come and stay. Nadine was a very distant cousin of father's. She was very poor and was training to be a hospital nurse. She came and stayed with us for a month. I can't tell you how exciting it was to have someone to stay! And she and Lennox fell in love with each other. And Mother said they'd better be married quickly and live on with us."

"And was Nadine willing to do that?"

Carol hesitated.

"I don't think she wanted to do that very much, but she didn't really *mind.* Then, later, she wanted to go away—with Lennox, of course—"

"But they didn't go?" asked Sarah.

"No, Mother wouldn't hear of it."

Carol paused and then said:

"I don't think—she likes Nadine any longer. Nadine is—funny. You never know what she's thinking. She tries to help Jinny and Mother doesn't like it."

"Jinny is your younger sister?"

"Yes. Ginevra is her real name."

"Is she—unhappy too?"

Carol shook her head doubtfully.

"Jinny's been very queer lately. I don't understand her. You see, she's always been rather delicate—and—and Mother fusses about her and—and it makes her worse. And lately Jinny has been very queer indeed. She—she frightens me sometimes. She—she doesn't always know what she's doing."

"Has she seen a doctor?"

"No; Nadine wanted her to, but Mother said no—and Jinny got very hysterical and screamed and said she wouldn't see a doctor. But I'm worried about her."

Suddenly Carol rose.

"I mustn't keep you up. It's—it's very good of you letting me come and talk to you. You must think us very odd as a family."

"Oh, everybody's odd, really," said Sarah lightly. "Come again, will you? And bring your brother, if you like."

"May I really?"

"Yes; we'll do some secret plotting. I'd like you to meet a friend of mine, too; a Dr. Gerard, an awfully nice Frenchman."

The color came into Carol's cheeks.

"Oh, what fun it sounds. If only Mother doesn't find out!"

Sarah suppressed her original retort and said instead, "Why should she? Good-night. Shall we say tomorrow night at the same time?"

"Oh, yes. The day after, you see, we may be going away."

"Then let's have a definite date for tomorrow. Good-night."

"Good-night—and thank you."

Carol went out of the room and slipped noiselessly along the corridor. Her own room was on the floor above. She reached it, opened the door—and stood appalled on the threshold.

Mrs. Boynton was sitting in an armchair by the fireplace in a crimson wool dressing-gown.

A little cry escaped from Carol's lips.

"Oh!"

A pair of black eyes bored into hers.

"Where have you been, Carol?"

"I—I—"

"Where have you been?"

A soft husky voice with that queer menacing undertone in it that always made Carol's heart beat with unreasoning terror.

"To see a Miss King—Sarah King."

"The girl who spoke to Raymond the other evening?"

"Yes, Mother."

"Have you made any plans to see her again?"

Carol's lips moved soundlessly. She nodded assent. Fright—great sickening waves of fright . . .

"When?"

"Tomorrow night."

"You are not to go. You understand?"

"Yes, Mother."

"You promise?"

"Yes—yes."

Mrs. Boynton struggled to get up. Mechanically Carol came forward and helped her. Mrs. Boynton walked slowly across the room supporting herself on her stick. She paused in the doorway and looked back at the cowering girl.

"You are to have nothing more to do with this Miss King. You understand?"

"Yes, Mother."

"Repeat it."

"I am to have nothing more to do with her."

"Good."

Mrs. Boynton went out and shut the door.

Stiffly, Carol moved across the bedroom. She felt sick, her whole body felt wooden and unreal. She dropped onto the bed and suddenly she was shaken by a storm of weeping.

It was as though a vista had opened before her—a vista of sunlight and trees and flowers. . . .

Now the black walls had closed around her once more. . . .

8

"Can I speak to you a minute?"

Nadine Boynton turned in surprise, staring into the dark eager face of an entirely unknown young woman.

"Why, certainly."

But as she spoke, almost unconsciously she threw a quick nervous glance over her shoulder.

"My name is Sarah King," went on the other.

"Oh, yes?"

"Mrs. Boynton, I'm going to say something rather odd to you. I talked to your sister-in-law for quite a long time the other evening."

A faint shadow seemed to ruffle the serenity of Nadine Boynton's face.

"You talked to Ginevra?"

"No, not to Ginevra—to Carol."

The shadow lifted.

"Oh, I see—to Carol."

Nadine Boynton seemed pleased, but very much surprised.

"How did you manage that?"

Sarah said:

"She came to my room—quite late."

She saw the faint raising of the penciled brows on the white forehead. She said, with some embarrassment: "I'm sure this must seem very odd to you."

"No," said Nadine Boynton. "I am very glad. Very glad indeed. It is very nice for Carol to have a friend to talk to."

"We—we got on very well together." Sarah tried to choose her words carefully. "In fact we arranged to—to meet again the following night."

"Yes?"

"But Carol didn't come."

"Didn't she?"

Nadine's voice was cool—reflective. Her face, so quiet and gentle, told Sarah nothing.

"No. Yesterday she was passing through the hall. I spoke to her and she didn't answer. Just looked at me once, and then away again, and hurried on."

"I see."

There was a pause. Sarah found it difficult to go on. Nadine Boynton said presently:

"I'm—very sorry. Carol is—rather a nervous girl."

Again that pause. Sarah took her courage in both hands.

"You know, Mrs. Boynton, I'm by way of being a doctor. I think—I think it would be good for your sister-in-law not to—not to shut herself away too much from people."

Nadine Boynton looked thoughtfully at Sarah.

She said: "I see. You're a doctor. That makes a difference."

"You see what I mean?" Sarah urged.

Nadine bent her head. She was still thoughtful.

"You are quite right, of course," she said after a minute or two. "But there are difficulties. My mother-in-law is in bad health and she has what I can only describe as a morbid dislike of any outsiders penetrating into her family circle."

Sarah said mutinously:

"But Carol is a grown-up woman."

Nadine Boynton shook her head.

"Oh, no," she said. "In body, but not in mind. If you talked to her you must have noticed that. In an emergency she would always behave like a frightened child."

"Do you think that's what happened? Do you think she became—afraid?"

"I should imagine, Miss King, that my mother-in-law insisted on Carol having nothing more to do with you."

"And Carol gave in?"

Nadine Boynton said quietly:

"Can you really imagine her doing anything else?"

The eyes of the two women met. Sarah felt that behind the mask of conventional words, they understood each other. Nadine, she felt, understood the position. But she was clearly not prepared to discuss it in any way.

Sarah felt discouraged. The other evening it had seemed to her as though half the battle were won. By means of secret meetings she would imbue Carol with the spirit of revolt—yes, and Raymond, too. (Be honest, now; wasn't it Raymond really she had had in mind all along?) And now, in the very first round of the battle she had been ignominiously defeated by that hulk of shapeless flesh with her evil gloating eyes. Carol had capitulated without a struggle.

"It's all *wrong!*" cried Sarah.

Nadine did not answer. Something in her silence went home to Sarah like a cold hand laid on her heart. She thought: "This woman knows the hopelessness of it much better than I do. She's *lived* with it!"

The elevator doors opened. The elder Mrs. Boynton emerged. She leaned on a stick and Raymond supported her on the other side.

Sarah gave a slight start. She saw the old woman's eyes sweep from her to Nadine and back again. She had been prepared for dislike in those eyes —for hatred even. She was not prepared for what she saw—a triumphant and malicious enjoyment.

Sarah turned away. Nadine went forward and joined the other two.

"So there you are, Nadine," said Mrs. Boynton. "I'll sit down and rest a little before I go out."

They settled her in a high-backed chair. Nadine sat down beside her.

"Who were you talking to, Nadine?"

"A Miss King."

"Oh, yes. The girl who spoke to Raymond the other night. Well, Ray, why don't you go and speak to her now? She's over there at the writing-table."

The old woman's mouth widened into a malicious smile as she looked at Raymond. His face flushed. He turned his head away and muttered something.

"What's that you say, son?"

"I don't want to speak to her."

"No, I thought not. You won't speak to her. You couldn't, however much you wanted to!"

She coughed suddenly—a wheezing cough.

"I'm enjoying this trip, Nadine," she said. "I wouldn't have missed it for anything."

"No?"

Nadine's voice was expressionless.

"Ray."

"Yes, Mother?"

"Get me a piece of notepaper—from the table over there in the corner."

Raymond went off obediently. Nadine raised her head. She watched, not the boy, but the old woman. Mrs. Boynton was leaning forward, her nostrils dilated as though with pleasure. Ray passed close by Sarah. She looked up, a sudden hope showing in her face. It died down as he brushed past her, took some notepaper from the case and went back across the room.

There were little beads of sweat on his forehead as he rejoined them and his face was dead white.

Very softly Mrs. Boynton murmured:

"Ah . . ." as she watched his face.

Then she saw Nadine's eyes fixed on her. Something in them made her own snap with sudden anger.

"Where's Mr. Cope this morning?" she said.

Nadine's eyes dropped again. She answered in her gentle expressionless voice:

"I don't know. I haven't seen him."

"I like him," said Mrs. Boynton. "I like him very much. We must see a good deal of him. You'll like that, won't you?"

"Yes," said Nadine. "I, too, like him very much."

"What's the matter with Lennox lately? He seems very dull and quiet. Nothing wrong between you, is there?"

"Oh, no. Why should there be?"

"I wondered. Married people don't always hit it off. Perhaps you'd be happier living in a home of your own?"

Nadine did not answer.

"Well, what do you say to the idea? Does it appeal to you?"

Nadine shook her head. She said, smiling:

"I don't think it would appeal to *you,* Mother."

Mrs. Boynton's eyelids flickered. She said sharply and venomously:

"You've always been against me, Nadine."

The younger woman replied evenly:

"I'm sorry you should think that."

The old woman's hand closed on her stick. Her face seemed to get a shade more purple.

She said, with a change of tone:

"I forgot my drops. Get them for me, Nadine."

"Certainly."

Nadine got up and crossed the lounge to the elevator. Mrs. Boynton looked after her. Raymond sat limply in a chair, his eyes glazed with dull misery.

Nadine went upstairs and along the corridor. She entered the sitting-room of their suite. Lennox was sitting by the window. There was a book in his hand, but he was not reading. He roused himself as Nadine came in.

"Hullo, Nadine."

"I've come up for Mother's drops. She forgot them."

She went on into Mrs. Boynton's bedroom. From a bottle on the washstand she carefully measured a dose into a small medicine glass, filling it up with water. As she passed through the sitting-room again she paused.

"Lennox."

It was a moment or two before he answered her. It was as though the message had a long way to travel.

Then he said:

"I beg your pardon. What is it?"

Nadine Boynton set down the glass carefully on the table. Then she went over and stood beside him.

"Lennox, look at the sunshine—out there, through the window. Look at life. It's beautiful. We might be out in it—instead of being here looking through a window."

Again there was a pause. Then he said:

"I'm sorry. Do you want to go out?"

She answered him quickly:

"Yes, I want to go out—*with you*—out into the sunshine—out into life—and live—the two of us together."

He shrank back into his chair. His eyes looked restless, hunted.

"Nadine, my dear—must we go into all this again—"

"Yes, we must. Let us go away and lead our own life somewhere."

"How can we? We've no money."

"We can earn money."

"How could we? What could we do? I'm untrained. Thousands of men—qualified men—trained men—are out of jobs as it is. We couldn't manage it."

"I would earn money for both of us."

"My dear child, you've never even completed your training. It's hopeless—impossible."

"No; what is hopeless and impossible is our present life."

"You don't know what you are talking about. Mother is very good to us. She gives us every luxury."

"Except freedom. Lennox, make an effort. Come with me now—to-day—"

"Nadine, I think you're quite mad."

"No, I'm sane. Absolutely and completely sane. I want a life of my own, with you, in the sunshine—not stifled in the shadow of an old woman who is a tyrant and who delights in making you unhappy."

"Mother may be rather an autocrat—"

"Your mother is mad! She's insane!"

He answered mildly:

"That's not true. She's got a remarkably good head for business."

"Perhaps—yes."

"And you must realize, Nadine, she can't live forever. She's sixty-odd and she's in very bad health. At her death my father's money is to be divided equally among us, share and share alike. You remember, she read us the will?"

"When she dies," said Nadine. "It may be too late."

"Too late?"

"Too late for happiness."

Lennox murmured: "Too late for happiness." He shivered suddenly. Nadine went closer to him. She put her hand on his shoulder.

"Lennox, I love you. It's a battle between me and your mother. Are you going to be on her side or mine?"

"On yours—on yours!"

"Then do what I ask."

"It's impossible!"

"No, it's not impossible. Think, Lennox, we could have children . . ."

"Mother wants us to have children, anyway. She has said so."

"I know, but I won't bring children into the world to live in the shadow you have all been brought up in. Your mother can influence you, but she's no power over me."

Lennox murmured:

"You make her angry sometimes, Nadine; it isn't wise."

"She is only angry because she knows that she can't influence my mind or dictate my thoughts!"

"I know you are always polite and gentle with her. You're wonderful. You're too good for me. You always have been. When you said you would marry me it was like an unbelievable dream."

Nadine said quietly:

"I was wrong to marry you."

Lennox said hopelessly:

"Yes, you were wrong."

"You don't understand. What I mean is that if I had gone away then and asked you to follow me you would have done so. Yes, I really believe you would. . . . I was not clever enough then to understand your mother and what she wanted."

She paused, then she said:

"You refuse to come away? Well, I can't make you. But *I* am free to go! I think—I think I *shall* go. . . ."

He stared up at her incredulously. For the first time his reply came quickly, as though at last the sluggish current of his thoughts was accelerated. He stammered:

"But—but—you can't do that. Mother—Mother would never hear of it."

"She couldn't stop me."

"You've no money."

"I could make, borrow, beg or steal it. Understand. Lennox, your mother has no power over me! I can go or stay at my will. I am beginning to feel that I have borne this life long enough."

"Nadine—don't leave me—don't leave me. . . ."

She looked at him thoughtfully—quietly—with an inscrutable expression.

"Don't leave me, Nadine."

He spoke like a child. She turned her head away, so that he should not see the sudden pain in her eyes.

She knelt down beside him.

"Then come with me. Come with me! You can. Indeed you can if you only will!"

He shrank back from her.

"I can't! I can't! I tell you. I haven't—God help me—*I haven't the courage. . . ."*

9

Dr. Gerard walked into the office of Messrs. Castle, the tourist agents, and found Sarah King at the counter.

She looked up.

"Oh, good-morning. I'm fixing up my tour to Petra. I've just heard you are going after all."

"Yes, I find I can just manage it."

"How nice."

"Shall we be a large party, I wonder?"

"They say just two other women—and you and me. One car load."

"That will be delightful," said Gerard with a little bow.

Then he, in turn, attended to his business.

Presently, holding his mail in his hands, he joined Sarah as she stepped out of the office. It was a crisp sunny day, with a slight cold tang in the air.

"What news of our friends, the Boyntons?" asked Dr. Gerard. "I have been to Bethlehem and Nazareth and other places—a tour of three days."

Slowly and rather unwillingly, Sarah narrated her abortive efforts to establish contact.

"Anyhow I failed," she finished. "And they're leaving today."

"Where are they going?"

"I've no idea."

She went on vexedly:

"I feel, you know, that I've made rather a fool of myself!"

"In what way?"

"Interfering in other people's business."

Gerard shrugged his shoulders.

"That is a matter of opinion."

"You mean whether one should interfere or not?"

"Yes."

"Do you?"

The Frenchman looked amused.

"You mean, is it my habit to concern myself with other people's affairs? I will say to you frankly—no."

"Then you think I'm wrong to have tried butting in?"

"No, no, you misunderstand me." Gerard spoke quickly and energetically. "It is, I think, a moot question. Should one, if one sees a wrong being done, attempt to put it right? One's interference may do good—but it may also do incalculable harm! It is impossible to lay down any ruling on the subject. Some people have a genius for interference—they do it well! Some people do it clumsily and had therefore better leave it alone! Then there is, too, the question of *age.* Young people have the courage of their ideals and convictions—their values are more theoretical than practical. They have not experienced, as yet, that fact contradicts theory! If you have a belief in yourself and in the rightness of what you are doing, you can often accomplish things that are well worth while! (Incidentally you often do a good deal of harm!) On the other hand, the middle-aged person has experience—he has found that harm as well as, and perhaps more often than, good comes of trying to interfere and so—very wisely, he refrains! So the result is even—the earnest young do both harm and good—the prudent middle-aged do neither!"

"All that isn't very helpful," objected Sarah.

"Can one person ever be helpful to another? It is *your* problem not mine."

"You mean *you* are not going to do anything about the Boyntons?"

"No. For me, there would be no chance of success."

"Then there isn't for me either?"

"For you, there might be."

"Why?"

"Because you have special qualifications. The appeal of your youth and sex."

"Sex? Oh, I see."

"One comes always back to sex, does one not? You have failed with the girl. It does not follow that you would fail with her brother. What you have just told me—(what the girl Carol told you) shows very clearly the one menace to Mrs. Boynton's autocracy. The eldest son, Lennox, defied her in the force of his young manhood. He played truant from home, went to local dances. The desire of a man for a mate was stronger than the hypnotic spell. But the old woman was quite aware of the power of sex. (She will have seen something of it in her career.) She dealt with it very cleverly—brought a pretty but penniless girl into the house—encouraged a marriage. And so acquired yet another slave."

Sarah shook her head.

"I don't think young Mrs. Boynton is a slave."

Gerard agreed.

"No, perhaps not. I think that because she was a quiet docile young girl, old Mrs. Boynton underestimated her force of will and character. Nadine Boynton was too young and inexperienced at the time to appreciate the true position. She appreciates it now, but it is too late."

"Do you think she has given up hope?"

Dr. Gerard shook his head doubtfully.

"If she has plans no one would know about them. There are, you know, certain possibilities where Cope is concerned. Man is a naturally jealous animal—and jealousy is a strong force. Lennox Boynton might still be roused from the inertia in which he is sinking."

"And you think"—Sarah purposely made her tone very businesslike and professional—"that there's a chance I might be able to do something about Raymond?"

"I do."

Sarah sighed.

"I suppose I might have tried— Oh, well, it's too late now, anyway. And —and I don't like the idea."

Gerard looked amused.

"That is because you are English! The English have a complex about sex. They think it is 'not quite nice.' "

Sarah's indignant response failed to move him.

"Yes, yes, I know you are very modern—that you use freely in public the most unpleasant words you can find in the dictionary—that you are professional and entirely uninhibited! *Tout de même,* I repeat, you have the same racial characteristics as your mother and your grandmother. You are still the blushing English Miss although you do not blush!"

"I never heard such rubbish!"

Dr. Gerard, a twinkle in his eyes, and quite unperturbed, added:

"And it makes you very charming."

This time Sarah was speechless.

Dr. Gerard hastily raised his hat.

"I take my leave," he said, "before you have time to begin to say all that you think."

He escaped into the hotel.

Sarah followed him more slowly.

There was a good deal of activity going on. Several cars loaded with luggage were in process of departing. Lennox and Nadine Boynton and Mr. Cope were standing by a big saloon car superintending arrangements. A fat dragoman was standing talking to Carol with quite unintelligible fluency.

Sarah passed them and went into the hotel.

Mrs. Boynton, wrapped in a thick coat, was sitting in a chair, waiting to depart.

Looking at her, a queer revulsion of feeling swept over Sarah.

She had felt that Mrs. Boynton was a sinister figure, an incarnation of evil malignancy.

Now, suddenly, she saw the old woman as a pathetic ineffectual figure. To be born with such a lust for power, such a desire for dominion—and to achieve only a petty domestic tyranny! If only her children could see her as Sarah saw her that minute—an object of pity—a stupid, malignant, pathetic, posturing old woman.

On an impulse Sarah went up to her.

"Good-bye, Mrs. Boynton," she said. "I hope you'll have a nice trip."

The old lady looked at her. Malignancy struggled with outrage in those eyes.

"You've wanted to be very rude to me," said Sarah.

(Was she crazy, she wondered? What on earth was urging her on to talk like this?)

"You've tried to prevent your son and daughter making friends with me. Don't you think, really, that that is all very silly and childish? You like to make yourself out a kind of ogre, but really, you know, you're just pathetic and rather ludicrous. If I were you I'd give up all this silly play-acting. I expect you'll hate me for saying this, but I mean it—and some of it may stick. You know you could have a lot of fun still. It's really much better to be—friendly—and kind. You could be if you tried."

There was a pause.

Mrs. Boynton had frozen into a deadly immobility. At last she passed her tongue over her dry lips, her mouth opened. . . . Still for a moment no words came.

"Go on," said Sarah encouragingly. "Say it! It doesn't matter what you say to me. But think over what I've said to you."

The words came at last—in a soft, husky, but penetrating voice. Mrs. Boynton's basilisk eyes looked, not at Sarah, but oddly over her shoulder. She seemed to address, not Sarah, but some familiar spirit.

"I never forget," she said. *"Remember that. I've never forgotten anything—not an action, not a name, not a face. . . ."*

There was nothing in the words themselves, but the venom with which they were spoken made Sarah retreat a step.

And then Mrs. Boynton laughed—it was, definitely, rather a horrible laugh.

Sarah shrugged her shoulders.

"You poor old thing," she said.

She turned away. As she went towards the elevator she almost collided with Raymond Boynton. On an impulse she spoke quickly:

"Good-bye; I hope you'll have a lovely time. Perhaps we'll meet again some day."

She smiled at him, a warm friendly smile, and passed quickly on.

Raymond stood as though turned to stone. So lost in his own thoughts was he that a small man with big moustaches, endeavoring to pass out of the elevator, had to speak several times.

"Pardon."

At last it penetrated. Raymond stepped aside.

"So sorry," he said. "I—I was thinking."

Carol came towards him.

"Ray, get Jinny, will you? She went back to her room. We're going to start."

"Right; I'll tell her she's got to come straight away."

Raymond walked into the elevator.

Hercule Poirot stood for a moment looking after him, his eyebrows raised, his head a little on one side as though he were listening.

Then he nodded his head as though in agreement. Walking through the lounge he took a good look at Carol who had joined her mother.

Then he beckoned the head waiter who was passing.

"Pardon, can you tell me the name of those people over there?"

"The name is Boynton, Monsieur; they are Americans."

"Thank you," said Hercule Poirot.

On the third floor Dr. Gerard, going to his room, passed Raymond Boynton and Ginevra walking towards the waiting elevator. Just as they were about to get into it, Ginevra said:

"Just a minute, Ray; wait for me in the elevator."

She ran back, turned a corner, caught up with the walking man.

"Please—I must speak to you."

Dr. Gerard looked up in astonishment.

The girl came up close to him and caught his arm.

"They're taking me away! They may be going to kill me. . . . I don't really belong to them, you know. My name isn't really Boynton. . . ."

She hurried on, her words coming fast and tumbling over each other.

"I'll trust you with the secret. I'm—I'm *Royal,* really! I'm the heiress to a throne. That's why—there are enemies all around me. They try to poison me—all sorts of things . . . If you could help me—to get away—"

She broke off. Footsteps.

"Jinny—"

Beautiful in her sudden startled gesture, the girl put a finger to her lips, threw Gerard an imploring glance, and ran back.

"I'm coming, Ray."

Dr. Gerard walked on with his eyebrows raised. Slowly, he shook his head and frowned.

10

It was the morning of the start to Petra.

Sarah came down to find a big masterful woman with a rocking-horse nose whom she had already noticed in the hotel, outside the main entrance objecting fiercely to the size of the car.

"A great deal too small! Four passengers? *And* a dragoman? Then of course we must have a much larger saloon. Please take that car away and return with one of an adequate size."

In vain did the representative of Messrs. Castle's raise his voice in explanation. That was the size of car always provided. It was really a most comfortable car. A larger car was not so suitable for desert travel.

The large woman, metaphorically speaking, rolled over him like a large steam roller.

Then she turned her attention to Sarah.

"Miss King? I am Lady Westholme. I am sure you agree with me that that car is grossly inadequate as to size?"

"Well," said Sarah cautiously, "I agree that a larger one *would* be more comfortable!"

The young man from Castle's murmured that a larger car would add to the price.

"The price," said Lady Westholme firmly, "is inclusive and I shall certainly refuse to sanction any addition to it. Your prospectus distinctly states 'in comfortable saloon car.' You will keep to the terms of your agreement."

Recognizing defeat, the young man from Castle's murmured something about seeing what he could do and wilted away from the spot.

Lady Westholme turned to Sarah, a smile of triumph on her weather-beaten countenance, her large red rocking-horse nostrils dilated exultantly.

Lady Westholme was a very well-known figure in the English political world. When Lord Westholme, a middle-aged, simple-minded peer, whose only interests in life were hunting, shooting and fishing, was returning from a trip to the United States, one of his fellow passengers was a Mrs. Vansittart. Shortly afterwards Mrs. Vansittart became Lady Westholme. The match was often cited as one of the examples of the danger of ocean voyages. The new Lady Westholme lived entirely in tweeds and stout brogues, bred dogs, bullied the villagers and forced her husband pitilessly into public life. It being borne in upon her, however, that politics was not Lord Westholme's *métier* in life and never would be, she graciously allowed him to resume his sporting activities and herself stood for Parliament. Being elected with a substantial majority, Lady Westholme threw herself with vigor into political life, being especially active at Question time. Cartoons of her soon began to appear (always a sure sign of success). As a public figure she stood for the old-fashioned values of Family Life, Welfare work amongst Women, and was an ardent supporter of the League of Nations. She had decided views on questions of Agriculture, Housing and Slum Clearance. She was much respected and almost universally disliked! It was highly possible that she would be given an Under Secretaryship when her Party returned to power. At the moment a Liberal Government (owing to a split in the National Government between Labor and Conservatives) was somewhat unexpectedly in power.

Lady Westholme looked with grim satisfaction after the departing car.

"Men always think they can impose upon women," she said.

Sarah thought that it would be a brave man who thought he could impose upon Lady Westholme! She introduced Dr. Gerard who had just come out of the hotel.

"Your name is, of course, familiar to me," said Lady Westholme, shaking hands. "I was talking to Professor Clemenceaux the other day in Paris. I have been taking up the question of the treatment of pauper lunatics very strongly lately. Very strongly, indeed. Shall we come inside while we wait for a better car to be obtained?"

A vague little middle-aged lady with wisps of grey hair who was hovering near by turned out to be Miss Amabel Pierce, the fourth member of the party. She too was swept into the lounge under Lady Westholme's protecting wing.

"You are a professional woman, Miss King?"

"I've just taken my M.B."

"Good," said Lady Westholme with condescending approval. "If anything is to be accomplished, mark my words, it is women who will do it."

Uneasily conscious for the first time of her sex, Sarah followed Lady Westholme meekly to a seat.

There, as they sat waiting, Lady Westholme informed them that she had refused an invitation to stay with the High Commissioner during her stay in Jerusalem.

"I did not want to be hampered by officialdom. I wished to look into things for myself."

"What things?" Sarah wondered.

Lady Westholme went on to explain that she was staying at the Solomon Hotel so as to remain unhampered. She added that she had made several suggestions to the Manager for the more competent running of his hotel.

"Efficiency," said Lady Westholme, "is my Watchword."

It certainly seemed to be! In a quarter of an hour a large and extremely comfortable car arrived and in due course—after advice from Lady Westholme as to how the luggage should be bestowed—the party set off.

Their first halt was the Dead Sea. They had lunch at Jericho. Afterwards when Lady Westholme armed with a Baedeker had gone off with Miss Pierce, the doctor and the fat dragoman to do a tour of old Jericho, Sarah remained in the garden of the hotel.

Her head ached slightly and she wanted to be alone. A deep depression weighed her down—a depression for which she found it hard to account. She felt suddenly listless and uninterested, disinclined for sight-seeing, bored by her companions. She wished at this moment that she had never committed herself to this Petra tour. It was going to be very expensive and she felt quite sure she wasn't going to enjoy it! Lady Westholme's booming voice, Miss Pierce's endless twitterings, and the anti-Zionist lamentation of the dragoman were already fraying her nerves to a frazzle. She disliked almost as much Dr. Gerard's amused air of knowing exactly how she was feeling.

She wondered where the Boyntons were now—perhaps they had gone on to Syria—they might be at Baalbek or Damascus. Raymond—she wondered what Raymond was doing. Strange how clearly she could see his face—its eagerness—its diffidence—its nervous tension. . . .

Oh! hell—why go on thinking of people she would probably never see again? That scene the other day with the old woman—what could have possessed her to march up to the old lady and spurt out a lot of nonsense. Other people must have heard some of it. She fancied that Lady Westholme had been quite close by. Sarah tried to remember exactly what it was she had said. Something that probably sounded quite absurdly hysterical. Goodness, what a fool she had made of herself! But it wasn't her fault really—it was old Mrs. Boynton's. There was something about her that made you lose your sense of proportion.

Dr. Gerard entered and plumped down in a chair, wiping his hot forehead.

"Phew! That woman should be poisoned!" he declared.

Sarah started.

"Mrs. Boynton?"

"Mrs. Boynton! No, I meant that Lady Westholme! It is incredible to me that she has had a husband for many years and that he has not already done so. What can he be made of, that husband?"

Sarah laughed.

"Oh, he's the 'huntin', fishin', shootin' ' kind," she explained.

"Psychologically that is very sound! He appeases his lust to kill on the (so-called) lower creations."

"I believe he is very proud of his wife's activities."

The Frenchman suggested:

"Because they take her a good deal away from home? That is understandable." Then he went on. "What did you say just now? Mrs. Boynton? Undoubtedly it would be a very good idea to poison her, too. Undeniably the simplest solution of that family problem! In fact, a great many women would be better poisoned. All women who have grown old and ugly."

He made an expressive face.

Sarah cried out, laughing:

"Oh, you Frenchmen! You've got no use for any woman who isn't young and attractive."

Gerard shrugged his shoulders.

"We are more honest about it, that is all. Englishmen, they do not get up in tubes and trains for ugly women—no, no."

"How depressing life is," said Sarah with a sigh.

"There is no need for *you* to sigh, Mademoiselle."

"Well, I feel thoroughly disgruntled today."

"Naturally."

"What do you mean—naturally?" snapped Sarah.

"You could find the reason very easily if you examine your state of mind honestly."

"I think it's our fellow travelers who depress me," said Sarah. "It's awful, isn't it, but I do hate women! When they're inefficient and idiotic like Miss Pierce, they infuriate me—and, when they're efficient like Lady Westholme, they annoy me more still."

"It is, I should say, unavoidable that these two people should annoy you. Lady Westholme is exactly fitted to the life she leads and is completely happy and successful. Miss Pierce has worked for years as a nursery governess and has suddenly come into a small legacy which has enabled her to fulfil her lifelong wish and travel. So far, travel has lived up to her expectations. Consequently you, who have just been thwarted in obtaining what you want, naturally resent the existence of people who have been more successful in life than you are."

"I suppose you're right," said Sarah gloomily. "What a horribly accurate mind reader you are. I keep trying to humbug myself and you won't let me."

At this moment the others returned. The guide seemed the most exhausted of the three. He was quite subdued and hardly exuded any information on the way to Amman. He did not even mention the Jews. For which everyone was profoundly grateful. His voluble and frenzied account of their iniquities had done much to try everyone's temper on the journey from Jerusalem.

Now the road wound upward from the Jordan, twisting and turning with clumps of oleanders showing rose-colored flowers.

They reached Amman late in the afternoon and after a short visit to the Graeco-Roman theatre, went to bed early. They were to make an early start the next morning as it was a full day's motor run across the desert to Ma'an.

They left soon after eight o'clock. The party was inclined to be silent. It was a hot airless day and by noon when a halt was made for a picnic lunch to be eaten, it was really, stiflingly hot. The irritation on a hot day of being boxed up closely with four other human beings had got a little on everyone's nerves.

Lady Westholme and Dr. Gerard had a somewhat irritable argument over the League of Nations. Lady Westholme was a fervent supporter of the League. The Frenchman, on the other hand, chose to be witty at the League's expense. From the attitude of the League concerning Abyssinia and Spain they passed to the Litvania boundary dispute of which Sarah had never heard and from there to the activities of the League in suppressing dope gangs.

"You must admit they have done wonderful work. Wonderful!" snapped Lady Westholme.

Dr. Gerard shrugged his shoulders.

"Perhaps. And at wonderful expense, too!"

"The matter is a very serious one. Under the Dangerous Drugs Act—"

The argument waged on.

Miss Pierce twittered to Sarah:

"It is really *most* interesting traveling with Lady Westholme."

Sarah said acidly: "Is it?" but Miss Pierce did not notice the acerbity and twittered happily on:

"I've so *often* seen her name in the papers. So *clever* of women to go into public life and hold their own. I'm always so *glad* when a *woman* accomplishes something!"

"Why?" demanded Sarah ferociously.

Miss Pierce's mouth fell open and she stammered a little.

"Oh, because—I mean—just because—well—it's so nice that women are *able* to do things!"

"I don't agree," said Sarah. "It's nice when *any* human being is able to accomplish something worth while! It doesn't matter a bit whether it's a man or a woman. Why should it?"

"Well, of course—" said Miss Pierce. "Yes—I confess—of course, looking at it in that light—"

But she looked slightly wistful. Sarah said more gently:

"I'm sorry, but I do hate this differentiation between the sexes. 'The modern girl has a thoroughly businesslike attitude to life!' That sort of thing. It's not a bit true! Some girls are businesslike and some aren't. Some men are sentimental and muddle-headed, others are clearheaded and logical. There are just different types of brains. Sex only matters where sex is directly concerned."

Miss Pierce flushed a little at the word sex and adroitly changed the subject.

"One can't help wishing that there were a little shade," she murmured. "But I do think all this emptiness is so wonderful, don't you?"

Sarah nodded.

Yes, she thought, the emptiness was marvelous . . . Healing . . . Peaceful . . . No human beings to agitate one with their tiresome interrelationships . . . No burning personal problems! Now, at last, she felt, she was free of the Boyntons. Free of that strange compelling wish to interfere in the lives of people whose orbit did not remotely touch her own. She felt soothed and at peace.

Here was loneliness, emptiness, spaciousness . . .

In fact, peace . . .

Only, of course, one wasn't alone to enjoy it. Lady Westholme and Dr. Gerard had finished with drugs and were now arguing about guileless young women who were exported in a sinister manner to Argentinian cabarets. Dr. Gerard had displayed throughout the conversation a levity which Lady Westholme, who, being a true politician, had no sense of humor, found definitely deplorable.

"We go on now, yes?" announced the tarbushed dragoman and began to talk about the iniquities of Jews again.

It was about an hour off sunset when they reached Ma'an at last. Strange wild-faced men crowded around the car. After a short halt they went on.

Looking over the flat desert country Sarah was at a loss as to where the rocky stronghold of Petra could be. Surely they could see for miles and miles all around them? There were no mountains, no hills anywhere. Were they then still many miles from their journey's end?

They reached the village of Ain Musa where the cars were to be left. Here horses were waiting for them—sorry-looking thin beasts. The inadequacy of her striped wash frock disturbed Miss Pierce greatly. Lady Westholme was sensibly attired in riding breeches, not perhaps a particularly becoming style to her type of figure, but certainly practical.

The horses were led out of the village along a slippery path with loose stones. The ground fell away and the horses zigzagged down. The sun was close on setting.

Sarah was very tired with the long hot journey in the car. Her senses felt dazed. The ride was like a dream. It seemed to her afterwards that it was like the pit of Hell opening at one's feet. The way wound down—down into the ground. The shapes of rock rose up around them—down, down into the bowels of the earth, through a labyrinth of red cliffs. They towered now on either side. Sarah felt stifled—menaced by the ever narrowing gorge.

She thought confusedly to herself: "Down into the valley of death—down into the valley of death. . . ."

On and on. It grew dark– the vivid red of the walls faded—and still on, winding in and out, imprisoned, lost in the bowels of the earth.

She thought: "It's fantastic and unbelievable . . . a dead city."

And again like a refrain came the words: *"The valley of death. . . ."*

Lanterns were lit now. The horses wound along through the narrow ways. Suddenly they came out into a wide space—the cliffs receded. Far ahead of them was a cluster of lights.

"That is camp!" said the guide.

The horses quickened their pace a little—not very much—they were too starved and dispirited for that, but they showed just a shade of enthusiasm. Now the way ran along a gravelly water bed. The lights grew nearer.

They could see a cluster of tents, a higher row up against the face of a cliff. Caves, too, hollowed out in the rock.

They were arriving. Bedouin servants came running out.

Sarah stared up at one of the caves. It held a sitting figure. What was it? An idol? A gigantic squatting image?

No, that was the flickering lights that made it loom so large. But it *must* be an idol of some kind, sitting there immovable, brooding over the place. . . .

And then, suddenly, her heart gave a leap of recognition.

Gone was the feeling of peace—of escape—that the desert had given her. She had been led from freedom back into captivity. She had ridden down into this dark winding valley and here, like an arch priestess of some forgotten cult, like a monstrous swollen female Buddha, sat Mrs. Boynton. . . .

11

Mrs. Boynton was here, at Petra!

Sarah answered mechanically questions that were addressed to her. Would she have dinner straight away—it was ready—or would she like to wash first? Would she prefer to sleep in a tent or a cave?

Her answer to that came quickly. A tent. She flinched at the thought of a cave; the vision of that monstrous squatting figure recurred to her. (Why was it that something about the woman seemed hardly human?)

Finally she followed one of the native servants. He wore khaki breeches much patched and untidy puttees and a ragged coat very much the worse for wear. On his head the native head-dress, the cheffiyah, its long folds protecting the neck and secured in place with a black silk twist fitting tightly to the crown of his head. Sarah admired the easy swing with which he walked—the careless proud carriage of his head. Only the European part of his costume seemed tawdry and wrong. She thought: "Civilization *is* all wrong—*all* wrong! But for civilization there wouldn't be a Mrs. Boynton! In savage tribes they'd probably have killed and eaten her years ago!"

She realized, half humorously, that she was overtired and on edge. A wash in hot water and a dusting of powder over her face and she felt herself again—cool, poised, and ashamed of her recent panic.

She passed a comb through her thick black hair, squinting sideways at her reflection in the wavering light of a small oil lamp in a very inadequate glass.

Then she pushed aside the tent flap and came out into the night prepared to descend to the big marquee below.

"You—here?"

It was a low cry—dazed, incredulous.

She turned to look straight into Raymond Boynton's eyes. So amazed they were! And something in them held her silent and almost afraid. Such an unbelievable joy. . . . It was as though he had seen a vision of Paradise —wondering, dazed, thankful, humble! Never, in all her life, was Sarah to forget that look. So might the damned look up and see Paradise. . . .

He said again:

"You . . ."

It did something to her—that low vibrant tone. It made her heart turn over in her breast. It made her feel shy, afraid, humble and yet suddenly arrogantly glad.

She said quite simply: "Yes."

He came nearer—still dazed—still only half believing.

Then suddenly he took her hand.

"It *is* you," he said. "You're real. I thought at first you were a ghost—because I'd been thinking about you so much." He paused and then said: "I love you, you know. . . . I have from the moment I saw you in the train. I know that now. And I want you to know it so that—so that you'll know it isn't me—the real me—who—who behaves so caddishly. You see, I can't answer for myself even now. I might do—anything! I might pass you by or cut you—but I do want you to know that it isn't me—the real me—who is responsible for that. It's my nerves. I can't depend on them. . . . When *she* tells me to do things—I do them! My nerves make me! You will understand, won't you? Despise me if you have to—"

She interrupted him. Her voice was low and unexpectedly sweet.

"I won't despise you."

"All the same, I'm pretty despicable! I ought to—to be able to behave like a man."

It was partly an echo of Gerard's advice, but more out of her own knowledge and hope that Sarah answered—and behind the sweetness of her voice there was a ring of certainty and conscious authority.

"You will now."

"Shall I?" His voice was wistful. "Perhaps. . . ."

"You'll have courage now. I'm sure of it."

He drew himself up—flung back his head.

"Courage? Yes—that's all that's needed. Courage!"

Suddenly he bent his head, touched her hand with his lips. A minute later he had left her.

12

Sarah went down to the big marquee. She found her three fellow travelers there. They were sitting at table eating. The guide was explaining that there was another party here.

"They come two days ago. Go day after tomorrow. Americans. The mother very fat, very difficult get here! Carried in chair by bearers—they say very hard work—they get very hot—yes."

Sarah gave a sudden spurt of laughter. Of course, take it properly, the whole thing was funny!

The fat dragoman looked at her gratefully. He was not finding his task too easy. Lady Westholme had contradicted him out of Baedeker three times that day and had now found fault with the type of bed provided. He was grateful to the one member of his party who seemed to be unaccountably in a good temper.

"Ha!" said Lady Westholme. "I think these people were at the Solomon. I recognized the old mother as we arrived here. I think I saw you talking to her at the hotel, Miss King."

Sarah blushed guiltily, hoping Lady Westholme had not overheard much of that conversation.

"Really, what possessed me!" she thought to herself in an agony.

In the meantime Lady Westholme had made a pronouncement.

"Not interesting people at all. Very provincial," she said.

Miss Pierce made eager sycophantish noises and Lady Westholme embarked on a history of various interesting and prominent Americans whom she had met recently.

The weather being so unusually hot for the time of year, an early start was arranged for the morrow.

The four assembled for breakfast at six o'clock. There were no signs of any of the Boynton family. After Lady Westholme had commented unfavorably on the absence of fruit, they consumed tea, tinned milk and fried eggs in a generous allowance of fat, flanked by extremely salty bacon.

Then they started forth, Lady Westholme and Dr. Gerard discussing with animation on the part of the former the exact value of vitamins in diet and the proper nutrition of the working classes.

Then there was a sudden hail from the camp and they halted to allow another person to join the party. It was Mr. Jefferson Cope who hurried after them, his pleasant face flushed with the exertion of running.

"Why, if you don't mind, I'd like to join your party this morning. Good-morning, Miss King. Quite a surprise meeting you and Dr. Gerard here. What do you think of it?"

He made a gesture indicating the fantastic red rocks that stretched in every direction.

"I think it's rather wonderful and just a little horrible," said Sarah. "I always thought of it as romantic and dreamlike—the 'rose red city.' But it's much more *real* than that—it's as real as—as raw beef."

"And very much the color of it," agreed Mr. Cope.

"But it's marvelous, too," admitted Sarah.

The party began to climb. Two Bedouin guides accompanied them. Tall men, with an easy carriage, they swung upward unconcernedly in their hobnailed boots, completely footsure on the slippery slope. Difficulties soon began. Sarah had a good head for heights and so had Dr. Gerard. But both Mr. Cope and Lady Westholme were far from happy, and the unfortunate Miss Pierce had to be almost carried over the precipitous places, her eyes shut, her face green, while her voice rose ceaselessly in a perpetual wail:

"I never could look down places. Never—from a child!"

Once she declared her intention of going back, but on turning to face the descent, her skin assumed an even greener tinge, and she reluctantly decided that to go on was the only thing to be done.

Dr. Gerard was kind and reassuring. He went up behind her, holding his stick between her and the sheer drop like a balustrade, and she confessed that the illusion of a rail did much to conquer the feeling of vertigo.

Sarah, panting a little, asked the dragoman, Mahmoud, who in spite of his ample proportions showed no signs of distress:

"Don't you ever have trouble getting people up here? Elderly ones, I mean."

"Always—always we have trouble," agreed Mahmoud serenely.

"Do you always try and take them?"

Mahmoud shrugged his thick shoulders.

"They like to come. They have paid money to see these things. They wish to see them. The Bedouin guides are very clever—very surefooted—always they manage."

They arrived at last at the summit. Sarah drew a deep breath.

All around and below stretched the blood-red rocks—a strange and unbelievable country unparalleled anywhere. Here in the exquisite pure morning air, they stood like gods, surveying a baser world—a world of flaring violence.

Here was, as the guide told them, the "Place of Sacrifice"—the "High Place."

He showed them the trough cut in the flat rock at their feet.

Sarah strayed away from the rest, from the glib phrases that flowed so readily from the dragoman's tongue. She sat on a rock, pushed her hands through her thick black hair, and gazed down on the world at her feet.

Presently she was aware of someone standing by her side. Dr. Gerard's voice said:

"You appreciate the appositeness of the devil's temptation in the New Testament. Satan took Our Lord up to the summit of a mountain and showed him the world. 'All these things will I give thee, if thou wilt fall down and worship me.' How much greater the temptation up on high to be a God of Material Power."

Sarah assented, but her thoughts were so clearly elsewhere that Gerard observed her in some surprise.

"You are pondering something very deeply," he said.

"Yes, I am." She turned a perplexed face to him. "It's a wonderful idea—to have a place of sacrifice up here. I think, sometimes, don't you, that a sacrifice is *necessary*. . . . I mean, one can have too much regard for life. Death isn't really so important as we make out."

"If you feel that, Miss King, you should not have adopted our profession. To us, death is and must always be—the Enemy."

Sarah shivered.

"Yes, I suppose you're right. And yet, so often, death might solve a problem. It might even mean fuller life. . . ."

" 'It is expedient for us that one man should die for the people!' " quoted Gerard gravely.

Sarah turned a startled face on him.

"I didn't mean—"

She broke off. Jefferson Cope was approaching them.

"Now this is really a most remarkable spot," he declared. "Most remarkable, and I'm only too pleased not to have missed it. I don't mind confessing that though Mrs. Boynton is certainly a most remarkable woman—I greatly admire her pluck in being determined to come here—it does certainly complicate matters traveling with her. Her health is poor, and I suppose it naturally makes her a little inconsiderate of other people's feelings, but it does not seem to occur to her that her family might like occasionally to go on excursions without her. She's just so used to them clustering round her that I suppose she doesn't think—"

Mr. Cope broke off. His nice kindly face looked a little disturbed and uncomfortable.

"You know," he said, "I heard a piece of information about Mrs. Boynton that disturbed me greatly."

Sarah was lost in her own thoughts again—Mr. Cope's voice just flowed pleasantly in her ears like the agreeable murmur of a remote stream, but Dr. Gerard said:

"Indeed? What was it?"

"My informant was a lady I came across in the hotel at Tiberias. It concerned a servant girl who had been in Mrs. Boynton's employ. This girl, I gather, was—had—"

Mr. Cope paused, glanced delicately at Sarah and lowered his voice. "She was going to have a child. The old lady, it seemed, discovered this but was apparently quite kind to the girl. Then a few weeks before the child was born she turned her out of the house."

Dr. Gerard's eyebrows went up.

"Ah," he said reflectively.

"My informant seemed very positive of her facts. I don't know whether you agree with me, but that seems to me a very cruel and heartless thing to do. I cannot understand—"

Dr. Gerard interrupted him.

"You should try to. That incident, I have no doubt, gave Mrs. Boynton a good deal of quiet enjoyment."

Mr. Cope turned a shocked face on him.

"No, sir," he said with emphasis. "That I cannot believe. Such an idea is quite inconceivable."

Softly Dr. Gerard quoted:

" '*So I returned and did consider all the oppressions done beneath the sun. And there was weeping and wailing from those that were oppressed and had no comfort; for with their oppressors there was power, so that no one came to comfort them. Then I did praise the dead which are already dead, yea, more than the living which linger still in life; yea, he that is not is better than dead or living; for he doth not know of the evil that is wrought forever on earth. . . .*' "

He broke off and said:

"My dear sir, I have made a life's study of the strange things that go on in the human mind. It is no good turning one's face only to the fairer side of life. Below the decencies and conventions of everyday life, there lies a vast reservoir of strange things. There is such a thing, for instance, as delight in cruelty for its own sake. But when you have found that, there is something deeper still. The desire, profound and pitiful, to be appreciated. If that is thwarted, if through an unpleasing personality a human being is unable to get the response it needs, it turns to other methods—it must be *felt*—it must *count*—and so to innumerable strange perversions. The habit of cruelty, like any other habit, can be cultivated, can take hold of one—"

Mr. Cope coughed.

"I think, Dr. Gerard, that you are slightly exaggerating— Really, the air up here is too wonderful. . . ."

He edged away. Gerard smiled a little. He looked again at Sarah. She was frowning—her face was set in a youthful sternness. She looked, he thought, like a young judge delivering sentence. . . .

He turned as Miss Pierce tripped unsteadily towards him.

"We are going down now," she fluttered. "Oh, dear! I am sure I shall never manage it, but the guide says the way down is quite a different route and much easier. I do hope so, because from a child I never have been able to look down from heights. . . ."

The descent was down the course of a waterfall. Although there were loose stones which were a possible source of danger to ankles, it presented no dizzy vistas.

The party arrived back at the camp weary but in good spirits and with an excellent appetite for a late lunch. It was past two o'clock.

The Boynton family was sitting around the big table in the marquee. They were just finishing their meal.

Lady Westholme addressed a gracious sentence to them in her most condescending manner.

"Really a most interesting morning," she said. "Petra is a wonderful spot."

Carol, to whom the words seemed addressed, shot a quick look at her mother, and murmured:

"Oh, yes—yes, it is," and relapsed into silence.

Lady Westholme, feeling she had done her duty, addressed herself to her food.

As they ate, the four discussed plans for the afternoon.

"I think I shall rest most of the afternoon," said Miss Pierce. "It is important, I think, not to do too much."

"I shall go for a walk and explore," said Sarah. "What about you, Dr. Gerard?"

"I will go with you."

Mrs. Boynton dropped a spoon with a ringing clatter and everyone jumped.

"I think," said Lady Westholme, "that I shall follow your example, Miss Pierce. Perhaps half an hour with a book, then I shall lie down and take an hour's rest at least. After that, perhaps, a short stroll."

Slowly, with the help of Lennox, old Mrs. Boynton struggled to her feet. She stood for a moment and then spoke.

"You'd better all go for a walk this afternoon," she said with unexpected amiability.

It was, perhaps, slightly ludicrous to see the startled faces of her family.

"But, Mother, what about you?"

"I don't need any of you. I like sitting alone with my book. Jinny had better not go. She'll lie down and have a sleep."

"Mother, I'm not tired. I want to go with the others."

"You *are* tired. You've got a headache! You must be careful of yourself. Go and lie down and sleep. I know what's best for you."

"I—I—"

Her head thrown back, the girl stared rebelliously. Then her eyes dropped—faltered. . . .

"Silly child," said Mrs. Boynton. "Go to your tent."

She stumped out of the marquee—the others followed.

"Dear me," said Miss Pierce. "What very peculiar people. Such a very odd color—the mother. Quite purple. Heart, I should imagine. This heat must be very trying for her."

Sarah thought:

"She's letting them go free this afternoon. She knows Raymond wants to be with me. Why? Is it a trap?"

After lunch, when she had gone to her tent and had changed into a fresh linen dress, the thought still worried her. Since last night, her feeling towards Raymond had swelled into a passion of protective tenderness. This, then, was love—this agony on another's behalf—this desire to avert, at all costs, pain from the beloved. . . . Yes, she loved Raymond Boynton. It was St. George and the Dragon reversed. It was she who was the rescuer and Raymond who was the chained victim.

And Mrs. Boynton was the Dragon. A dragon whose sudden amiability was, to Sarah's suspicious mind, definitely sinister.

It was about a quarter past three when Sarah strolled down to the marquee.

Lady Westholme was sitting on a chair. Despite the heat of the day she was still wearing her serviceable Harris tweed skirt. On her lap was the report of a Royal Commission. Dr. Gerard was talking to Miss Pierce who was standing by her tent holding a book entitled *The Love Quest* and described on its wrapper as a thrilling tale of passion and misunderstanding.

"I don't think it's wise to lie down too soon after lunch," explained Miss Pierce. "One's digestion, you know. Quite cool and pleasant in the shadow of the marquee. Oh, dear, do you think that old lady is wise to sit in the sun up there?"

They all looked at the ridge in front of them. Mrs. Boynton was sitting as she had sat last night, a motionless Buddha in the door of her cave. There was no other human creature in sight. All the camp personnel were asleep. A short distance away, following the line of the valley, a little group of people walked together.

"For once," said Dr. Gerard, "the good Mamma permits them to enjoy themselves without her. A new devilment on her part, perhaps?"

"Do you know," said Sarah, "that's just what I thought."

"What suspicious minds we have. Come, let us join the truants."

Leaving Miss Pierce to her exciting reading, they set off. Once around the bend of the valley, they caught up the other party who were walking slowly. For once, the Boyntons looked happy and carefree.

Lennox and Nadine, Carol and Raymond, Mr. Cope with a broad smile on his face and the last arrivals, Gerard and Sarah, were soon all laughing and talking together.

A sudden wild hilarity was born. In everyone's mind was the feeling that this was a snatched pleasure—a stolen treat to enjoy to the full. Sarah and Raymond did not draw apart. Instead, Sarah walked with Carol and Lennox. Dr. Gerard chatted to Raymond close behind them. Nadine and Jefferson Cope walked a little apart.

It was the Frenchman who broke up the party. His words had been coming spasmodically for some time. Suddenly he stopped.

"A thousand excuses. I fear I must go back."

Sarah looked at him.

"Anything the matter?"

He nodded.

"Yes, fever. It's been coming on ever since lunch."

Sarah scrutinized him.

"Malaria?"

"Yes. I'll go back and take quinine. Hope this won't be a bad attack. It is a legacy from a visit to the Congo."

"Shall I come with you?" asked Sarah.

"No, no. I have my case of drugs with me. A confounded nuisance. Go on, all of you."

He walked quickly back in the direction of the camp.

Sarah looked undecidedly after him for a minute, then she met Raymond's eyes, smiled at him, and the Frenchman was forgotten.

For a time the six of them, Carol, herself, Lennox, Cope, Nadine and Raymond, kept together.

Then, somehow or other, she and Raymond had drifted apart. They walked on, climbing up rocks, turning ledges, and rested at last in a shady spot.

There was a silence—then Raymond said:

"What's your name? It's King, I know. But your other name."

"Sarah."

"Sarah. May I call you that?"

"Of course."

"Sarah, will you tell me something about yourself?"

Leaning back against the rocks she talked, telling him of her life at home in Yorkshire, of her dogs and the aunt who had brought her up.

Then, in his turn, Raymond told her a little, disjointedly, of his own life.

After that, there was a long silence. Their hands strayed together. They sat, like children, hand in hand, strangely content.

Then, as the sun grew lower, Raymond stirred.

"I'm going back now," he said. "No, not with you. I want to go back by myself. There's something I have to say and do. Once that's done, once I've proved to myself that I'm not a coward—then—then—I sha'n't be ashamed to come to you and ask you to help me. I shall need help, you know. I shall probably have to borrow money from you."

Sarah smiled.

"I'm glad you're a realist. You can count on me."

"But first I've got to do this alone."

"Do what?"

The young boyish face grew suddenly stern. Raymond Boynton said:

"I've got to prove my courage. It's now or never."

Then, abruptly, he turned and strode away.

Sarah leaned back against the rock and watched his receding figure. Something in his words had vaguely alarmed her. He had seemed so intense—so terribly in earnest and strung up. For a moment she wished she had gone with him. . . .

But she rebuked herself sternly for that wish. Raymond had desired to stand alone, to test his new-found courage. That was his right.

But she prayed with all her heart that that courage would not fail. . . .

The sun was setting when Sarah came once more in sight of the camp. As she came nearer in the dim light, she could make out the grim figure of

Mrs. Boynton still sitting in the mouth of the cave. Sarah shivered a little at the sight of that grim motionless figure. . . .

She hurried past on the path below and came into the lighted marquee.

Lady Westholme was sitting knitting a navy blue jumper, a skein of wool hung around her neck. Miss Pierce was embroidering a table mat with anaemic blue forget-me-nots, and being instructed on the proper reform of the Divorce Laws.

The servants came in and out preparing for the evening meal. The Boyntons were at the far end of the marquee in deck chairs reading. Mahmoud appeared, fat and dignified, and was plaintively reproachful. Very nice after tea ramble had been arranged to take place but everyone absent from camp. . . . The programme was now entirely thrown out. . . . Very instructive visit to Nabatean architecture.

Sarah said hastily that they had all enjoyed themselves very much.

She went off to her tent to wash for supper. On the way back she paused by Dr. Gerard's tent, calling in a low voice:

"Dr. Gerard!"

There was no answer. She lifted the flap and looked in. The doctor was lying motionless on his bed. Sarah withdrew noiselessly, hoping he was asleep.

A servant came to her and pointed to the marquee. Evidently supper was ready. She strolled down again. Everyone else was assembled there around the table with the exception of Dr. Gerard and Mrs. Boynton. A servant was despatched to tell the old lady dinner was ready. Then there was a sudden commotion outside. Two frightened servants rushed in and spoke excitedly to the dragoman in Arabic.

Mahmoud looked around him in a flustered manner and went outside. On an impulse Sarah joined him.

"What's the matter?" she asked.

Mahmoud replied:

"The old lady. Abdul says she is ill—cannot move."

"I'll come and see."

Sarah quickened her step. Following Mahmoud, she climbed the rock and walked along until she came to the squat figure in the chair, touched the puffy hand, felt for the pulse, bent over her. . . .

When she straightened herself she was paler.

She retraced her steps back to the marquee. In the doorway she paused a minute, looking at the group at the far end of the table.

Her voice when she spoke sounded to herself brusque and unnatural.

"I'm so sorry," she said. She forced herself to address the head of the family, Lennox. *"Your mother is dead, Mr. Boynton."*

And curiously, as though from a great distance, she watched the faces of five people to whom that announcement meant freedom. . . .

PART II

1

Colonel Carbury smiled across the table at his guest and raised his glass.

"Well, here's to crime!"

Hercule Poirot's eyes twinkled in acknowledgment of the aptness of the toast.

He had come to Amman with a letter of introduction to Colonel Carbury from Colonel Race.

Carbury had been interested to see this world-famous person to whose gifts his old friend and ally in the Intelligence had paid such unstinting tribute.

"As neat a bit of psychological deduction as you'll ever find!" Race had written of the solution of the Shaitana murder.

"We must show you all we can of the neighborhood," said Carbury, twisting a somewhat ragged brindled moustache. He was an untidy stocky man of medium height with a semi-bald head and vague mild blue eyes. He did not look in the least like a soldier. He did not look, even, particularly alert. He was not in the least one's idea of a disciplinarian. Yet in Transjordania he was a power.

"There's Jerash," he said. "Care about that sort of thing?"

"I am interested in everything!"

"Yes," said Carbury. "That's the only way to react to life." He paused. "Tell me, d'you ever find your own special job has a way of following you around?"

"Pardon?"

"Well—to put it plainly—do you come to places expecting a holiday from crime—and find instead bodies cropping up?"

"It has happened, yes—more than once."

"H'm," said Colonel Carbury, and looked particularly abstracted.

Then he roused himself with a jerk.

"Got a body now I'm not very happy about," he said.

"Indeed?"

"Yes. Here in Amman. Old American woman. Went to Petra with her family. Trying journey, unusual heat for time of year, old woman suffered from heart trouble, difficulties of the journey a bit harder for her than she imagined, extra strain on heart—she popped off!"

"Here—in Amman?"

"No, down at Petra. They brought the body here today."

"Ah!"

"All quite natural. Perfectly possible. Likeliest thing in the world to happen. Only—"

"Yes? Only—?"

Colonel Carbury scratched his bald head.

"I've got the idea," he said, "that her family did her in!"

"Aha! And what makes you think that?"

Colonel Carbury did not reply to that question directly.

"Unpleasant old woman, it seems. No loss. General feeling all around that her popping off was a good thing. Anyway, very difficult to prove anything so long as the family stick together and if necessary lie like hell. One doesn't want complications—or international unpleasantnesses. Easiest thing to do—let it go! Nothing really to go upon. Knew a doctor chap once. He told me—often had suspicions in cases of his patients—hurried into the next world a little ahead of time! *He* said—best thing to do keep quiet unless you really had something damned good to go upon! Otherwise beastly stink, case not proved, black mark against an earnest hard-working G.P. Something in that. All the same—" He scratched his head again. "I'm a tidy man," he said unexpectedly.

Colonel Carbury's tie was under his left ear, his socks were wrinkled, his coat was stained and torn. Yet Hercule Poirot did not smile. He saw, clearly enough, the inner neatness of Colonel Carbury's mind, his neatly docketed facts, his carefully sorted impressions.

"Yes. I'm a tidy man," said Carbury. He waved a vague hand. "Don't like a mess. When I come across a mess I want to clear it up. See?"

Hercule Poirot nodded gravely. He saw.

"There was no doctor down there?" he asked.

"Yes, two. One of 'em was down with malaria, though. The other's a girl—just out of the medical student stage. Still, she knows her job, I suppose. There wasn't anything odd about the death. Old woman had got a dicky heart. She'd been taking heart medicine for some time. Nothing really surprising about her conking out suddenly like she did."

"Then what, my friend, is worrying you?" asked Poirot gently.

Colonel Carbury turned a harassed blue eye on him.

"Heard of a Frenchman called Gerard? Theodore Gerard?"

"Certainly. A very distinguished man in his own line."

"Loony bins," confirmed Colonel Carbury. "Passion for a charwoman at the age of four makes you insist you're the Archbishop of Canterbury when you're thirty-eight. Can't see why and never have, but these chaps explain it very convincingly."

"Dr. Gerard is certainly an authority on certain forms of deep-seated neurosis," agreed Poirot with a smile. "Is—er—are—er—his views on the happening at Petra based on that line of argument?"

Colonel Carbury shook his head vigorously.

"No, no. Shouldn't have worried about them if they had been! Not, mind you, that I don't believe it's all true. It's just one of those things I don't understand—like one of my Bedouin fellows who can get out of a car in the middle of a flat desert, feel the ground with his hand and tell you to within a mile or two where you are. It isn't magic, but it looks like it. No, Dr. Gerard's story is quite straightforward. Just plain facts. I think, if you're interested—you *are* interested?"

"Yes, yes."

"Good man. Then I think I'll just phone over and get Gerard along here and you can hear his story for yourself."

When the Colonel had despatched an orderly on this quest, Poirot said:

"Of what does this family consist?"

"Name's Boynton. There are two sons, one of 'em married. His wife's a nice-looking girl—the quiet sensible kind. And there are two daughters. Both of 'em quite good-looking in totally different styles. Younger one a bit nervy—but that may be just shock."

"Boynton," said Poirot. His eyebrows rose. "That is curious—very curious."

Carbury cocked an inquiring eye at him. But as Poirot said nothing more, he himself went on:

"Seems pretty obvious mother was a pest! Had to be waited on hand and foot and kept the whole lot of them dancing attendance. And she held the purse strings. None of them had a penny of their own."

"Aha! All very interesting. Is it known how she left her money?"

"I did just slip that question in—casual like, you know. It gets divided equally among the lot of them."

Poirot nodded his head. Then he asked:

"You are of opinion that they are all in it?"

"Don't know. That's where the difficulty's going to lie. Whether it was a concerted effort, or whether it was one bright member's idea—I don't know. Maybe the whole thing's a mare's nest! What it comes to is this: I'd like to have your professional opinion. Ah, here comes Gerard."

2

The Frenchman came in with a quick yet unhurried tread. As he shook hands with Colonel Carbury, he shot a keen interested glance at Poirot.

Carbury said:

"This is M. Hercule Poirot. Staying with me. Been talking to him about this business down at Petra."

"Ah, yes?" Gerard's quick eyes looked Poirot up and down. "You are interested?"

Hercule Poirot threw up his hands.

"Alas! one is always incurably interested in one's own subject."

"True," said Gerard.

"Have a drink?" said Carbury.

He poured out a whisky and soda and placed it by Gerard's elbow. He held up the decanter inquiringly but Poirot shook his head. Colonel Carbury set it down again and drew his chair a little nearer.

"Well," he said. "Where are we?"

"I gather," said Poirot to Gerard, "that Colonel Carbury is not satisfied."

Gerard made an expressive gesture.

"And that," he said, "is my fault! And I may be wrong. Remember that, Colonel Carbury; I may be entirely wrong."

Carbury gave a grunt.

"Give Poirot the facts," he said.

Dr. Gerard began with a brief recapitulation of the events preceding the journey to Petra. He gave a short sketch of the various members of the Boynton family and described the condition of emotional strain under which they were laboring.

Poirot listened with interest.

Then Gerard proceeded to the actual events of their first day at Petra, describing how he had returned to the camp.

"I was in for a bad bout of malaria—cerebral type," he explained. "For that I proposed to treat myself by an intravenous injection of quinine. That is the usual method."

Poirot nodded his comprehension.

"The fever was on me badly. I fairly staggered into my tent. I could not at first find my case of drugs, someone had moved it from where I had originally placed it. Then, when I had found that, I could not find my hypodermic syringe. I hunted for it for some time, then gave it up and took a large dose of quinine by the mouth and flung myself on my bed."

Gerard paused, then went on:

"Mrs. Boynton's death was not discovered until after sunset. Owing to the way in which she was sitting and the support the chair gave to her body no change occurred in her position and it was not until one of the boys went to summon her to dinner at six-thirty that it was noticed that anything was wrong."

He explained in full detail the position of the cave and its distance away from the big marquee.

"Miss King, who is a qualified doctor, examined the body. She did not disturb me, knowing that I had fever. There was, indeed, nothing that could be done. Mrs. Boynton was dead—and had been dead for some little time."

Poirot murmured:

"How long exactly?"

Gerard said slowly·

"I do not think that Miss King paid much attention to that point. She did not, I presume, think it of any importance."

"One can say, at least, when she was last definitely known to be alive?" said Poirot.

Colonel Carbury cleared his throat and referred to an official looking document.

"Mrs. Boynton was spoken to by Lady Westholme and Miss Pierce shortly after four P.M. Lennox Boynton spoke to his mother about four-thirty. Mrs. Lennox Boynton had a long conversation with her about five minutes later. Carol Boynton had a word with her mother at a time she is unable to state precisely—but which, from the evidence of others, would seem to have been about ten minutes past five.

"Jefferson Cope, an American friend of the family, returning to the camp with Lady Westholme and Miss Pierce, saw her asleep. He did not speak to her. That was about twenty to six. Raymond Boynton, the younger son, seems to have been the last person to see her alive. On his return from a walk he went and spoke to her at about ten minutes to six. The discovery of the body was made at six-thirty when a servant went to tell her dinner was ready."

"Between the time that Mr. Raymond Boynton spoke to her and half-past six did no one go near her?" asked Poirot.

"I understand not."

"But someone *might* have done so?" Poirot persisted.

"Don't think so. From close on six and up to six-thirty servants were moving about the camp, people were going to and from their tents. No one can be found who saw anyone approaching the old lady."

"Then Raymond Boynton was definitely the last person to see his mother alive?" said Poirot.

Dr. Gerard and Colonel Carbury interchanged a quick glance.

Colonel Carbury drummed on the table with his fingers.

"This is where we begin to get into deep waters," he said. "Go on, Gerard. This is your pigeon."

Dr. Gerard said:

"As I mentioned just now, Sarah King, when she examined Mrs. Boynton, saw no reason for determining the exact time of death. She merely said that Mrs. Boynton had been dead 'some little time'; but when, on the following day for reasons of my own, I endeavored to narrow things down and happened to mention that Mrs. Boynton was last seen alive by her son, Raymond, at a little before six, Miss King, to my great surprise, said point blank that that was impossible—that at that time Mrs. Boynton must already have been dead."

Poirot's eyebrows rose.

"Odd. Extremely odd. And what does M. Raymond Boynton say to that?"

Colonel Carbury said abruptly:

"He swears that his mother was alive. He went up to her and said: 'I'm back. Hope you have had a nice afternoon?' Something of that kind. He says she just grunted 'quite all right,' and he went on to his tent."

Poirot frowned perplexedly.

"Curious," he said. "Extremely curious. Tell me—it was growing dusk by then?"

"The sun was just setting."

"Curious," said Poirot again. "And you, Dr. Gerard, when did you see the body?"

"Not until the following day. At nine A.M., to be precise."

"And your estimate of the time death had occurred?"

The Frenchman shrugged his shoulders.

"It is difficult to be exact after that length of time. There must necessarily be a margin of several hours. Were I giving evidence on oath I could only say that she had been dead certainly twelve hours and not longer than eighteen. You see, that does not help at all!"

"Go on, Gerard," said Colonel Carbury. "Give him the rest of it."

"On getting up in the morning," said Dr. Gerard, "I found my hypodermic syringe—it was behind a case of bottles on my dressing-table."

He leaned forward.

"You may say, if you like, that I had overlooked it the day before. I was in a miserable state of fever and wretchedness, shaking from head to foot, and how often does one look for a thing that is there all the time and yet be unable to find it! I can only say that I am quite positive the syringe was *not* there then."

"There's something more still," said Carbury.

"Yes, two facts for what they are worth and they mean a great deal. There was a mark on the dead woman's wrist—a mark such as would be caused by the insertion of a hypodermic syringe. Her daughter, I may say, explains it as having been caused by the prick of a pin—"

Poirot stirred.

"Which daughter?"

"Her daughter, Carol."

"Yes, continue, I pray you."

"And there is the last fact. Happening to examine my little case of drugs I noticed that my stock of digitoxin was very much diminished."

"Digitoxin," said Poirot, "is a heart poison, is it not?"

"Yes. It is obtained from *digitalis purpurea*—the common foxglove. There are four active principles—*digitalin*—*digitonin*—*digitalein*—and *digitoxin.* Of these, *digitoxin* is considered the most active poisonous constituent of digitalis leaves. According to Kopp's experiments, it is from six to ten times stronger than *digitalin* or *digitalein.* It is official in France—but not in the British Pharmacopoeia."

"And a large dose of digitoxin?"

Dr. Gerard said gravely:

"A large dose of digitoxin thrown suddenly on the circulation by intravenous injection would cause sudden death by quick palsy of the heart. It has been estimated that four milligrams might prove fatal to an adult man."

"And Mrs. Boynton already suffered with heart trouble?"

"Yes; as a matter of fact, she was actually taking a medicine containing digitalis."

"That," said Poirot, "is extremely interesting."

"D'you mean," asked Colonel Carbury, "that her death might have been attributed to an overdose of her own medicine?"

"That—yes. But I meant more than that."

"In some senses," said Dr. Gerard, "digitalis may be considered a cumulative drug. Moreover, as regards post-mortem appearance, the active principles of the digitalis may destroy life and leave no appreciative sign."

Poirot nodded slow appreciation.

"Yes, that is clever—very clever. Almost impossible to prove satisfactorily to a jury. Ah, but let me tell you, gentlemen, if this is a murder, it is a very clever murder! The hypodermic replaced, the poison employed being one which the victim was already taking—the possibilities of a mistake—or accident—are overwhelming. Oh, yes, there are brains here. There is thought—care—genius."

For a moment he sat in silence, then he raised his head.

"And yet, one thing puzzles me."

"What is that?"

"The theft of the hypodermic syringe."

"It was taken," said Dr. Gerard quickly.

"Taken—and returned?"

"Yes."

"Odd," said Poirot. "Very odd. Otherwise everything fits so well . . ."

Colonel Carbury looked at him curiously.

"Well?" he said. "What's your expert opinion? Was it murder—or wasn't it?"

Poirot held up a hand.

"One moment. We have not yet arrived at that point. There is still some evidence to consider."

"What evidence? You've had it all."

"Ah! But this is evidence *that I, Hercule Poirot, bring to you.*"

He nodded his head and smiled a little at their two astonished faces.

"Yes, it is droll, that! That I, to whom you tell the story, should in return present you with a piece of evidence about which you do not know. It was like this. In the Solomon Hotel, one night, I go to the window to make sure it is closed—"

"Closed—or open?" asked Carbury.

"Closed," said Poirot firmly. "It was open, so naturally, I go to close it. But before I do so, as my hand is on the latch, I hear a voice speaking—an agreeable voice, low and clear with a tremor in it of nervous excitement. I say to myself it is a voice I will know again. And what does it say, this voice? It says these words: *'You do see, don't you, that she's got to be killed?'* "

He paused.

"At the moment, *naturellement,* I do not take those words as referring to a killing of flesh and blood. I think it is an author or perhaps a playwright who speaks. But now—*I am not so sure.* That is to say, I am sure it was nothing of the kind."

Again he paused before saying:

"Messieurs, I will tell you this—*to the best of my knowledge and belief* those words were spoken by a young man whom I saw later in the lounge of the hotel and who was, so they told me on inquiring, a young man of the name of Raymond Boynton."

3

"Raymond Boynton said that!"

The exclamation broke from the Frenchman.

"You think it unlikely—psychologically speaking?" Poirot inquired placidly.

Gerard shook his head.

"No, I should not say that. I was surprised, yes. If you follow me, I was surprised just because Raymond Boynton was so eminently fitted to be a suspect."

Colonel Carbury sighed. "These psychological fellers!" the sigh seemed to say.

"Question is," he murmured, "what are we going to do about it?"

Gerard shrugged his shoulders.

"I do not see what you can do," he confessed. "The evidence is bound to be inconclusive. You may know that murder has been done but it will be difficult to prove it."

"I see," said Colonel Carbury. "We suspect that murder's been done and we just sit back and twiddle our fingers! Don't like it!" He added, as if in extenuation, his former odd plea: "I'm a tidy man."

"I know. I know," Poirot nodded his head sympathetically. "You would like to clear this up. You would like to know definitely exactly what occurred and how it occurred. And you, Dr. Gerard? You have said that there is nothing to be done—that the evidence is bound to be inconclusive? That is probably true. But are you satisfied that the matter should rest so?"

"She was a bad life," said Gerard slowly. "In any case she might have died very shortly—a week—a month—a year."

"So you are satisfied?" persisted Poirot.

Gerard went on:

"There is no doubt that her death was—how shall we put it?—beneficial to the community. It has brought freedom to her family. They will have scope to develop—they are all, I think, people of good character and intelligence. They will be—now—useful members of society! The death of Mrs. Boynton, as I see it, has resulted in nothing but good."

Poirot repeated for the third time:

"So you are satisfied?"

"No." Dr. Gerard pounded a fist suddenly on the table. "I am *not* 'satisfied,' as you put it! It is my instinct to preserve life—not to hasten death. Therefore, though my conscious mind may repeat that this woman's death was a good thing, my unconscious mind rebels against it! *It is not well, gentlemen, that a human being should die before his or her time has come."*

Poirot smiled. He leaned back, contented with the answer he had probed for so patiently.

Colonel Carbury said unemotionally:

"He don't like murder! Quite right! No more do I."

He rose and poured himself out a stiff whisky and soda. His guests' glasses were still full.

"And now," he said, returning to the subject, "let's get down to brass tacks. *Is there anything to be done about it?* We don't like it—no! But we may have to lump it! No good making a fuss if you can't deliver the goods."

Gerard leaned forward.

"What is your professional opinion, M. Poirot? You are the expert."

Poirot took a little time to speak. Methodically he arranged an ashtray or two and make a little heap of used matches. Then he said:

"You desire to know, do you not, Colonel Carbury, *who killed Mrs. Boynton?* (That is, if she *was* killed and did not die a natural death.) Exactly *how* and *when* she was killed—and, in fact, the whole truth of the matter?"

"I should like to know that, yes." Carbury spoke unemotionally.

Hercule Poirot said slowly:

"I see no reason why you should not know it!"

Dr. Gerard looked incredulous. Colonel Carbury looked mildly interested.

"Oh," he said. "So you don't, don't you? That's interestin'. How d'you propose to set about it?"

"By methodical sifting of the evidence, by a process of reasoning."

"Suits me," said Colonel Carbury.

"And by a study of the psychological possibilities."

"Suits Dr. Gerard, I expect," said Carbury. "And after that—after you've sifted the evidence and done some reasoning and paddled in psychology—hey, presto!—you think you can produce the rabbit out of the hat?"

"I should be extremely surprised if I could not do so," said Poirot calmly.

Colonel Carbury stared at him over the rim of his glass. Just for a moment the vague eyes were no longer vague—they measured—and appraised.

He put down his glass with a grunt.

"What do you say to that, Dr. Gerard?"

"I admit that I am sceptical of success . . . yet I know that M. Poirot has great powers."

"I am gifted—yes," said the little man. He smiled modestly.

Colonel Carbury turned away his head and coughed.

Poirot said:

"The first thing to decide is whether this is a composite murder—planned and carried out by the Boynton family as a whole, or whether it is the work of one of them only. If the latter, which is the most likely member of the family to have attempted it."

Dr. Gerard said:

"There is your own evidence. One must, I think, consider first Raymond Boynton."

"I agree," said Poirot. "The words I overheard and the discrepancy between his evidence and that of the young woman doctor puts him definitely in the forefront of the suspects.

"He was the last person to see Mrs. Boynton alive. That is his own story. Sarah King contradicts that. Tell me. Dr. Gerard, is there—eh?—you know what I mean—a little *tendresse,* shall we say—there?"

The Frenchman nodded.

"Emphatically so."

"Aha! Is she, this young lady, a brunette with hair that goes back from her forehead—so—and big hazel eyes and a manner very decided?"

Dr. Gerard looked rather surprised.

"Yes, that describes her very well."

"I think I have seen her—in the Solomon Hotel. She spoke to this Raymond Boynton and afterwards he remained *planté là*—in a dream—blocking the exit from the lift. Three times I had to say *'Pardon'* before he heard me and moved."

Poirot remained in thought for some moments. Then he said:

"So, to begin with, we will accept the medical evidence of Miss Sarah King with certain mental reservations. She is an interested party." He paused—then went on: "Tell me, Dr. Gerard, do you think Raymond Boynton is of the temperament that could commit murder easily?"

Gerard said slowly:

"You mean deliberate, planned murder? Yes, I think it is possible—but only under conditions of intense emotional strain."

"Those conditions were present?"

"Definitely. This journey abroad undoubtedly heightened the nervous and mental strain under which all these people were living. The contrast between their own lives and those of other people was more apparent to them. And in Raymond Boynton's case—"

"Yes?"

"There was the additional complication of being strongly attracted to Sarah King."

"That would give him an additional motive? And an additional stimulus?"

"That is so."

Colonel Carbury coughed.

"Like to butt in a moment. That sentence of his you overheard—*'You do see, don't you, that she's got to be killed?'*—must have been spoken to someone."

"A good point," said Poirot. "I had not forgotten it. Yes; to whom was Raymond Boynton speaking? Undoubtedly, to a member of his family. But which member? Can you tell us something, doctor, of the mental conditions of the other members of the family?"

Gerard replied promptly.

"Carol Boynton was, I should say, in very much the same state as Raymond—a state of rebellion accompanied by severe nervous excitement, but uncomplicated in her case by the introduction of a sex factor. Lennox Boynton had passed the stage of revolt. He was sunk in apathy. He was finding it, I think, difficult to concentrate. His method of reaction to his surroundings was to retire further and further within himself. He was definitely an introvert."

"And his wife?"

"His wife, though tired and unhappy, showed no signs of mental conflict. She was, I believe, hesitating on the brink of a decision."

"Such a decision being?"

"Whether or not to leave her husband."

He repeated the conversation he had held with Jefferson Cope.

Poirot nodded in comprehension.

"And what of the younger girl—Ginevra, her name is, is it not?"

The Frenchman's face was grave. He said:

"I should say that mentally she is in an extremely dangerous condition. She has already begun to display symptoms of schizophrenia. Unable to bear the suppression of her life, she is escaping into a realm of fantasy. She has advanced delusions of persecution—that is to say, she claims to be a

Royal Personage—in danger—enemies surrounding her—all the usual things!"

"And that—is dangerous?"

"Very dangerous. It is the beginning of what is often homicidal mania. The sufferer kills—not for the lust of killing—but *in self-defense.* He or she kills in order not to be killed themselves. From their point of view it is eminently rational."

"So you think that Ginevra Boynton might have killed her mother?"

"Yes. But I doubt if she would have had the knowledge or the constructiveness to do it the way it was done. The cunning of that class of mania is usually very simple and obvious. And I am almost certain she would have chosen a more spectacular method."

"But she is a *possibility?"* Poirot insisted.

"Yes," admitted Gerard.

"And afterwards—when the deed was done? *Do you think the rest of the family knew who had done it?"*

"They know!" said Colonel Carbury unexpectedly. "If ever I came across a bunch of people who had something to hide—these are they! They're putting something over, all right."

"We will make them tell us what it is," said Poirot.

"Third degree?" said Colonel Carbury, raising his eyebrows.

"No." Poirot shook his head. "Just ordinary conversation. On the whole, you know, people tell you the truth. Because it is easier! Because it is less strain on the inventive faculties! You can tell one lie—or two lies—or three lies—or even four lies—*but you cannot lie all the time.* And so—the truth becomes plain."

"Something in that," agreed Carbury.

Then he said bluntly:

"You'll talk to them, you say? That means you're willing to take this on?"

Poirot bowed his head.

"Let us be very clear about this," he said. "What you demand, and what I undertake to supply, is the truth. But mark this, even when we have got the truth, there may be no *proof.* That is to say, no proof that would be accepted in a court of law. You comprehend?"

"Quite," said Carbury. "You satisfy me of what really happened, then it's up to me to decide whether action is possible or not—having regard to the International aspects. Anyway it will be cleared up—no mess. Don't like a mess."

Poirot smiled.

"One more thing," said Carbury. "I can't give you much time. Can't detain these people here indefinitely."

Poirot said quietly:

"You can detain them twenty-four hours. You shall have the truth by tomorrow night."

Colonel Carbury stared hard at him.

"Pretty confident, aren't you?" he asked.

"I know my own ability," murmured Poirot.

Rendered uncomfortable by this un-British attitude, Colonel Carbury looked away and fingered his untidy moustache.

"Well," he mumbled. "It's up to you."

"And if you succeed, my friend," said Dr. Gerard, "you are indeed a marvel!"

4

Sarah King looked long and searchingly at Hercule Poirot. She noted the egg-shaped head, the gigantic moustaches, the dandified appearance and the suspicious blackness of his hair. A look of doubt crept into her eyes.

"Well, Mademoiselle, are you satisfied?"

Sarah flushed as she met the amused ironical glance of his eyes.

"I beg your pardon," she said awkwardly.

"Du tout! To use an expression I have recently learnt, you give me the once over, is it not so?"

Sarah smiled a little.

"Well, at any rate, you can do the same to me," she said.

"Assuredly. I have not neglected to do so."

She glanced at him sharply. Something in his tone—But Poirot was twirling his moustaches complacently and Sarah thought (for the second time), "The man's a mountebank!"

Her self-confidence restored, she sat up a little straighter and said inquiringly:

"I don't think I quite understand the object of this interview?"

"The good Dr. Gerard did not explain?"

Sarah said, frowning:

"I don't understand Dr. Gerard. He seems to think—"

"That there is something rotten in the state of Denmark," quoted Poirot. "You see, I know your Shakespeare."

Sarah waved aside Shakespeare.

"What exactly is all this fuss about?" she demanded.

"Eh bien, one wants, does one not, to get at the truth of this affair?"

"Are you talking about Mrs. Boynton's death?"

"Yes."

"Isn't it rather a fuss about nothing? You, of course, are a specialist, M. Poirot. It is natural for you—"

Poirot finished the sentence for her.

"It is natural for me to suspect crime whenever I can possibly find an excuse for doing so?"

"Well—yes—perhaps."

"You have no doubt yourself as to Mrs. Boynton's death?"

Sarah shrugged her shoulders.

"Really, M. Poirot, if you had been to Petra you would realize that the journey there is a somewhat strenuous business for an old woman whose cardiac condition was unsatisfactory."

"It seems a perfectly straightforward business to you?"

"Certainly. I can't understand Dr. Gerard's attitude. He didn't even know anything about it. He was down with fever. I'd bow to his superior medical knowledge naturally—but in this case he had nothing whatever to go on. I suppose they can have a p.-m. in Jerusalem if they like—if they're not satisfied with my verdict."

Poirot was silent for a moment, then he said:

"There is a fact, Miss King, that you do not yet know. Dr. Gerard has not told you of it."

"What fact?" demanded Sarah.

"A supply of a drug—digitoxin—is missing from Dr. Gerard's traveling medicine case."

"Oh!" Quickly Sarah took in this new aspect of the case. Equally quickly she pounced on the one doubtful point.

"Is Dr. Gerard quite sure of that?"

Poirot shrugged his shoulders.

"A doctor, as you should know, Mademoiselle, is usually fairly careful in making his statements."

"Oh, of course. That goes without saying. But Dr. Gerard had malaria at the time."

"That is so, of course."

"Has he any idea when it could have been taken?"

"He had occasion to go to his case on the night of his arrival in Petra. He wanted some phenacetin as his head was aching badly. When he replaced the phenacetin on the following morning and shut up the case he is almost certain that all the drugs were intact."

"Almost—" said Sarah.

Poirot shrugged.

"Yes, there is a doubt! There is the doubt that any man, *who is honest,* would be likely to feel."

Sarah nodded.

"Yes, I know. One always distrusts those people who are *over* sure. But all the same, M. Poirot, the evidence is very slight. It seems to me—" She paused. Poirot finished the sentence for her.

"It seems to you that an inquiry on my part is ill advised!"

Sarah looked him squarely in the face.

"Frankly, it does. Are you sure, M. Poirot, that this is not a case of Roman Holiday?"

Poirot smiled.

"The private lives of a family upset and disturbed—so that Hercule Poirot can play a little game of detection to amuse himself?"

"I didn't mean to be offensive—but isn't it a little like that?"

"You, then, are on the side of the *Famille Boynton,* Mademoiselle?"

"I think I am. They've suffered a good deal. They—they oughtn't to have to stand any more."

"And *la Maman,* she was unpleasant, tyrannical, disagreeable and decidedly better dead than alive? That also—*hein?"*

"When you put it like that—" Sarah paused, flushed, went on: "One shouldn't, I agree, take that into consideration."

"But all the same—one does! That is, *you* do, Mademoiselle! I—do not! to me, it is all the same. The victim may be one of the good God's saints—or, on the contrary, a monster of infamy. It moves me not. The fact is the same. A life—taken! I say it always—I do not approve of murder."

"Murder!" Sarah drew in her breath sharply. "But what evidence of that is there? The flimsiest imaginable! Dr. Gerard himself cannot be sure!"

Poirot said quietly:

"But there is other evidence, Mademoiselle."

"What evidence?"

Her voice was sharp.

"The mark of a hypodermic puncture upon the dead woman's wrist. And something more still—*some words that I overheard spoken in Jerusalem* on a clear still night when I went to close my bedroom window. Shall I tell you what those words were, Miss King? They were these: I heard Mr. Raymond Boynton say: *'You do see, don't you, that she's got to be killed?'* "

He saw the color drain slowly from Sarah's face.

She said:

"You heard that?"

"Yes."

The girl stared straight ahead of her.

She said at last:

"It would be *you* who heard it!"

He acquiesced.

"Yes, it would be me. These things happen. You see now why I think there should be an investigation?"

Sarah said quietly:

"I think you are quite right."

"Ah! And you will help me?"

"Certainly."

Her tone was matter-of-fact—unemotional. Her eyes met his coolly.

Poirot bowed.

"Thank you, Mademoiselle. Now, I will ask you to tell me in your own words exactly what you can remember of that particular day."

Sarah considered for a moment.

"Let me see. I went on an expedition in the morning. None of the Boyntons were with us. I saw them at lunch. They were finishing as we came in. Mrs. Boynton seemed in an unusually good temper."

"She was not usually amiable, I understand."

"Very far from it," said Sarah with a slight grimace.

She then described how Mrs. Boynton had released her family from attendance on her.

"That, too, was unusual?"

"Yes. She usually kept them around her."

"Do you think, perhaps, that she suddenly felt remorseful—that she had what is called—*un bon moment?*"

"No, I don't," said Sarah bluntly.

"What did you think, then?"

"I was puzzled. I suspected it was something of the cat and mouse order."

"If you would elaborate, Mademoiselle?"

"A cat enjoys letting a mouse away—and then catching it again. Mrs. Boynton had that kind of mentality. I thought she was up to some new deviltry or other."

"What happened next, Mademoiselle?"

"The Boyntons started off—"

"All of them?"

"No; the youngest, Ginevra, was left behind. She was told to go and rest."

"Did she wish to do so?"

"No. But that didn't matter. She did what she was told. The others started off. Dr. Gerard and I joined them—"

"When was this?"

"About half-past three."

"Where was Mrs. Boynton then?"

"Nadine—young Mrs. Boynton—had settled her in her chair outside her cave."

"Proceed."

"When we got around the bend, Dr. Gerard and I caught up with the others. We all walked together. Then, after a while, Dr. Gerard turned back. He had been looking rather queer for some time. I could see he had fever. I wanted to go back with him, but he wouldn't hear of it."

"What time was this?"

"Oh, about four, I suppose."

"And the rest?"

"We went on."

"Were you all together?"

"At first. Then we split up." Sarah hurried on as though foreseeing the next question. "Nadine Boynton and Mr. Cope went one way and Carol, Lennox, Raymond and I went another."

"And you continued like that?"

"Well—no. Raymond Boynton and I separated from the others. We sat down on a slab of rock and admired the wildness of the scenery. Then he went off and I stayed where I was for some time longer. It was about half-past five when I looked at my watch and realized I had better get back. I reached the camp at six o'clock. It was just about sunset."

"You passed Mrs. Boynton on the way?"

"I noticed she was still in her chair up on the ridge."

"That did not strike you as odd—that she had not moved?"

"No, because I had seen her sitting there the night before when we arrived."

"I see. *Continuez.*"

"I went into the marquee. The others were all there—except Dr. Gerard. I washed and then came back. They brought in dinner and one of the servants went to tell Mrs. Boynton. He came running back to say she was ill. I hurried out. She was sitting in her chair just as she had been, but as soon as I touched her I realized she was dead."

"You had no doubt at all as to her death being natural?"

"None whatever. I had heard that she suffered from heart trouble, though no specified disease had been mentioned."

"You simply thought she had died sitting there in her chair?"

"Yes."

"Without calling out for assistance?"

"Yes. It happens that way sometimes. She might even have died in her sleep. She was quite likely to have dozed off. In any case, all the camp was asleep most of the afternoon. No one would have heard her unless she had called very loud."

"Did you form an opinion as to how long she had been dead?"

"Well, I didn't really think very much about it. She had clearly been dead some time."

"What do you call some time?" asked Poirot.

"Well—over an hour. It might have been much longer. The refraction off the rock would keep her body from cooling quickly."

"Over an hour? Are you aware, Mademoiselle King, that Mr. Raymond Boynton spoke to her only a little over half an hour earlier and that she was then alive and well?"

Now her eyes no longer met his. But she shook her head.

"He must have made a mistake. It must have been earlier than that."

"No, Mademoiselle, it was not."

She looked at him point blank. He noticed again the firm set of her mouth.

"Well," said Sarah. "I'm young and I haven't had much experience with dead bodies—but I know enough to be quite sure of one thing—Mrs. Boynton had been dead *at least* an hour when I examined her body!"

"That," said Hercule Poirot unexpectedly, "is your story and you are going to stick to it!"

"It's the truth," said Sarah.

"Then can you explain *why* Mr. Boynton should say his mother was alive when she was, in point of fact, dead?"

"I've no idea," said Sarah. "They're probably rather vague about time, all of them! They're a very nervous family."

"On how many occasions, Mademoiselle, have you spoken with them?"

Sarah was silent a moment, frowning a little.

"I can tell you exactly," she said. "I talked to Raymond Boynton in the Wagon-Lit corridor coming to Jerusalem. I had two conversations with Carol Boynton—one at the Mosque of Omar and one late that evening in my bedroom. I had a conversation with Mrs. Lennox Boynton the following morning. That's all, up to the afternoon of Mrs. Boynton's death, when we all went walking together."

"You did not have any conversation with Mrs. Boynton herself?"

Sarah flushed uncomfortably.

"Yes. I exchanged a few words with her the day she left Jerusalem." She paused and then blurted out: "As a matter of fact, I made a fool of myself."

"Ah?"

The interrogation was so patent that, stiffly and unwillingly, Sarah gave an account of the conversation.

Poirot seemed interested and cross-examined her closely.

"The mentality of Mrs. Boynton—it is very important in this case," he said. "And you are an outsider—an unbiased observer. That is why your account of her is very significant."

Sarah did not reply. She still felt hot and uncomfortable when she thought of that interview.

"Thank you, Mademoiselle," said Poirot. "I will now converse with the other witnesses."

Sarah rose.

"Excuse me, M. Poirot, but if I might make a suggestion—"

"Certainly. Certainly."

"Why not postpone all this until an autopsy can be made and you discover whether or not your suspicions are justified. I think all this is rather like putting the cart before the horse."

Poirot waved a grandiloquent hand.

"This is the method of Hercule Poirot," he announced.

Pressing her lips together, Sarah left the room.

5

Lady Westholme entered the room with the assurance of a transatlantic liner coming into dock.

Miss Amabel Pierce, an indeterminate craft, followed in the liner's wake and sat down in an inferior make of chair slightly in the background.

"Certainly, M. Poirot," boomed Lady Westholme. "I shall be delighted to assist you by any means in my power. I have always considered that in matters of this kind one has a public duty to perform—"

When Lady Westholme's public duty had held the stage for some minutes, Poirot was adroit enough to get in a question.

"I have a perfect recollection of the afternoon in question," replied Lady Westholme. "Miss Pierce and I will do all we can to assist you."

"Oh, yes," sighed Miss Pierce, almost ecstatically. "So tragic, was it not? Dead—just like that—in the twinkle of an eye!"

"If you will tell me exactly what occurred on the afternoon in question?"

"Certainly," said Lady Westholme. "After we had finished lunch I decided to take a brief siesta. The morning excursion had been somewhat fatiguing. Not that I was really tired—I seldom am. I do not really know what fatigue is. One has so often, on public occasions, no matter what one really feels—"

Again an adroit murmur from Poirot.

"As I say, I was in favor of a siesta. Miss Pierce agreed with me."

"Oh, yes," sighed Miss Pierce. "And I was *terribly* tired after the morning. Such a *dangerous* climb—and although interesting, *most* exhausting. I'm afraid I'm not *quite* as strong as Lady Westholme."

"Fatigue," said Lady Westholme, "can be conquered like everything else. I make a point of never giving in to my bodily needs."

Miss Pierce looked at her admiringly.

Poirot said:

"After lunch, then, you two ladies went to your tents?"

"Yes."

"Mrs. Boynton was then sitting at the mouth of her cave?"

"Her daughter-in-law assisted her there before she herself went off."

"You could both see her?"

"Oh yes," said Miss Pierce. "She was opposite, you know—only of course a little way along and up above."

Lady Westholme elucidated the statement.

"The caves opened onto a ledge. Below that ledge were some tents. Then there was a small stream and across that stream was the big marquee and some other tents. Miss Pierce and I had tents near the marquee. She was on the right side of the marquee and I was on the left. The openings of our tents faced the ledge, but of course it was some distance away."

"Nearly two hundred yards, I understand."

"Possibly."

"I have here a plan," said Poirot, "concocted with the help of the dragoman, Mahmoud."

Lady Westholme remarked that in that case it was probably wrong!

"That man is grossly inaccurate. I have checked his statements from my Baedeker. Several times his information was definitely misleading."

"According to my plan," said Poirot, "the cave next to Mrs. Boynton's was occupied by her son, Lennox, and his wife. Raymond, Carol and Ginevra Boynton had tents just below but more to the right—in fact almost opposite the marquee. On the right of Ginevra Boynton's was Dr. Gerard's tent and next to his was that of Miss King. On the other side—next to the marquee on the left—you and Mr. Cope had tents. Miss Pierce's, as you mentioned, was on the right of the marquee. Is that correct?"

Lady Westholme admitted grudgingly that as far as she knew it was.

"I thank you. That is perfectly clear. Pray continue, Lady Westholme."

Lady Westholme smiled graciously on him and went on:

"At about a quarter to four I strolled along to Miss Pierce's tent to see if she were awake yet and felt like a stroll. She was sitting in the doorway of the tent reading. We agreed to start in about half an hour when the sun was less hot. I went back to my tent and read for about twenty-five minutes. Then I went along and joined Miss Pierce. She was ready and we started out. Everyone in the camp seemed asleep; there was no one about and, seeing Mrs. Boynton sitting up there alone, I suggested to Miss Pierce that we should ask her if she wanted anything before we left."

"Yes, you did. *Most* thoughtful of you, I considered it," murmured Miss Pierce.

"I felt it to be my duty," said Lady Westholme with a rich complacency.

"And then for her to be so rude about it!" exclaimed Miss Pierce.

Poirot looked inquiring.

"Our path passed just under the ledge," explained Lady Westholme, "and I called up to her, saying that we were going for a stroll and asking could we do anything for her before we went. Do you know, M. Poirot, absolutely the only answer she gave us was a *grunt!* A grunt! She just looked at us as though we were—as though we were dirt!"

"Disgraceful it was!" said Miss Pierce, flushing.

"I must confess," said Lady Westholme, reddening a little, "that I then made a somewhat uncharitable remark."

"I think you were quite justified," said Miss Pierce. *"Quite*—under the circumstances."

"What was this remark?" asked Poirot.

"I said to Miss Pierce that perhaps she *drank!* Really, her manner was *most* peculiar. It had been all along. I thought it possible that drink might account for it. The evils of alcoholic indulgence, as I very well know—"

Dexterously Poirot steered the conversation away from the drink question.

"Had her manner been very peculiar on this particular day? At lunch time, for instance?"

"N-no," said Lady Westholme, considering. "No, I should say that then her manner had been fairly normal—for an American of that type, that is to say," she added condescendingly.

"She was very abusive to that servant," said Miss Pierce.

"Which one?"

"Not very long before we started out."

"Oh, yes, I remember. She *did* seem extraordinarily annoyed with him! Of course," went on Lady Westholme, "to have servants about who cannot understand a word of English is very trying, but what I say is that when one is traveling one must make allowances."

"What servant was this?" asked Poirot.

"One of the Bedouin servants attached to the camp. He went up to her—I think she must have sent him to fetch her something and I suppose he brought the wrong thing—I don't really know what it was—but she was very angry about it. The poor man slunk away as fast as he could, and she shook her stick at him and called out."

"What did she call out?"

"We were too far away to hear. At least I didn't hear anything distinctly, did you, Miss Pierce?"

"No, I didn't. I think she'd sent him to fetch something from her younger daughter's tent—or perhaps she was angry with him for going into her daughter's tent—I couldn't say exactly."

"What did he look like?"

Miss Pierce, to whom the question was addressed, shook her head vaguely.

"Really, I couldn't say. He was too far away. All these Arabs look alike to me."

"He was a man of more than average height," said Lady Westholme, "and wore the usual native head-dress. He had on a pair of very torn and patched breeches—really disgraceful they were—and his puttees were wound most untidily—all anyhow! These men need *discipline!*"

"You could point the man out among the camp servants?"

"I doubt it. We didn't see his face—it was too far away. And, as Miss Pierce says, really, these Arabs all look alike."

"I wonder," said Poirot thoughtfully, "what it was he did to make Mrs. Boynton so angry?"

"They are very trying to the patience sometimes," said Lady Westholme. "One of them took my shoes away, though I had expressly told him—by pantomime too—that I preferred to clean my shoes myself."

"Always I do that too," said Poirot, diverted for a moment from his interrogation. "I take everywhere my little shoe-cleaning outfit. Also, I take a duster."

"So do I." Lady Westholme sounded quite human.

"Because these Arabs they do not remove the dust from one's belongings—"

"Never! Of course one has to dust one's things three or four times a day—"

"But it is well worth it."

"Yes, indeed. I cannot STAND dirt!"

Lady Westholme looked positively militant.

She added with feeling:

"The flies—in the bazaars—terrible!"

"Well, well," said Poirot, looking slightly guilty. "We can soon inquire from this man what it was that irritated Mrs. Boynton. To continue with your story?"

"We strolled along slowly," said Lady Westholme. "And then we met Dr. Gerard. He was staggering along and looked very ill. I could see at once he had fever."

"He was shaking," put in Miss Pierce. "Shaking all over."

"I saw at once he had an attack of malaria coming on," said Lady Westholme. "I offered to come back with him and get him some quinine but he said he had his own supply with him."

"Poor man," said Miss Pierce. "You know it always seems so dreadful to me to see a doctor ill. It seems all wrong, somehow."

"We strolled on," continued Lady Westholme. "And then we sat down on a rock."

Miss Pierce murmured:

"Really—so tired after the morning's exertion—the climbing—"

"I never feel fatigue," said Lady Westholme firmly. "But there was no point in going further. We had a very good view of all the surrounding scenery."

"Were you out of sight of the camp?"

"No, we were sitting facing towards it."

"So romantic," murmured Miss Pierce. "A camp pitched in the middle of a wilderness of rose-red rocks."

She sighed and shook her head.

"That camp could be much better run than it is," said Lady Westholme. Her rocking-horse nostrils dilated. "I shall take up the matter with Castle's. I am not at all sure that the drinking water is boiled as well as filtered. It should be. I shall point that out to them."

Poirot coughed and led the conversation quickly away from the subject of drinking water.

"Did you see any other members of the party?" he inquired.

"Yes. The elder Mr. Boynton and his wife passed us on their way back to the camp."

"Were they together?"

"No, Mr. Boynton came first. He looked a little as though he had had a touch of the sun. He was walking as though he were slightly dizzy."

"The back of the neck," said Miss Pierce. "One *must* protect the back of the neck! *I* always wear a thick silk handkerchief."

"What did Mr. Lennox Boynton do on his return to the camp?" asked Poirot.

For once Miss Pierce managed to get in first before Lady Westholme could speak.

"He went right up to his mother, but he didn't stay long with her."

"How long?"

"Just a minute or two."

"I should put it at just over a minute myself," said Lady Westholme. "Then he went on into his cave and after that he went down to the marquee."

"And his wife?"

"She came along about a quarter of an hour later. She stopped a minute and spoke to us—quite civilly."

"I think she's very nice," said Miss Pierce. "Very nice indeed."

"She is not so impossible as the rest of the family," allowed Lady Westholme.

"You watched her return to the camp?"

"Yes. She went up and spoke to her mother-in-law. Then she went into her cave and brought out a chair and sat by her talking for some time—about ten minutes, I should say."

"And then?"

"Then she took the chair back to the cave and went down to the marquee where her husband was."

"What happened next?"

"That very peculiar American came along," said Lady Westholme. "Cope, I think his name is. He told us that there was a very good example of the debased architecture of the period just round the bend of the valley. He said we ought not to miss it. Accordingly we walked there. Mr. Cope had with him quite an interesting article on Petra and the Nabateans."

"It was all *most* interesting," declared Miss Pierce fervently.

Lady Westholme continued:

"We strolled back to the camp, it being then about twenty minutes to six. It was growing quite chilly."

"Mrs. Boynton was still sitting where you had left her?"

"Yes."

"Did you speak to her?"

"No. As a matter of fact, I hardly noticed her."

"What did you do next?"

"I went to my tent, changed my shoes and got out my own packet of China tea. I then went to the marquee. The guide person was there and I directed him to make some tea for Miss Pierce and myself with the tea I had brought and to make quite sure that the water with which it was made was boiling. He said that dinner would be ready in about half an hour—the boys were laying the table at the time—but I said that made no difference."

"I always say a cup of tea makes *all* the difference," murmured Miss Pierce vaguely.

"Was there anyone in the marquee?"

"Oh, yes. Mr. and Mrs. Lennox Boynton were sitting at one end reading. And Carol Boynton was there too."

"And Mr. Cope?"

"He joined us at our tea," said Miss Pierce. "Though he said tea drinking wasn't an American habit."

Lady Westholme coughed.

"I became just a little afraid that Mr. Cope was going to be a nuisance—that he might fasten himself upon me. It is a little difficult sometimes to keep people at arm's length when one is traveling. I find they are inclined to presume. Americans, especially, are sometimes rather dense."

Poirot murmured suavely:

"I am sure, Lady Westholme, that you are quite capable of dealing with situations of that kind. When traveling acquaintances are no longer of any use to you, I am sure you are an adept at dropping them."

"I think I am capable of dealing with most situations," said Lady Westholme complacently.

The twinkle in Poirot's eye was quite lost upon her.

"If you will just conclude your recital of the day's happenings?" murmured Poirot.

"Certainly. As far as I can remember, Raymond Boynton and the red-haired Boynton girl came in shortly afterwards. Miss King arrived last. Dinner was then ready to be served. One of the servants was despatched by the dragoman to announce the fact to old Mrs. Boynton. The man came running back with one of his comrades in a state of some agitation and spoke to the dragoman in Arabic. There was some mention of Mrs. Boynton being taken ill. Miss King offered her services. She went out with the dragoman. She came back and broke the news to the members of Mrs. Boynton's family."

"She did it very abruptly," put in Miss Pierce. "Just blurted it out. I think myself it ought to have been done more gradually."

"And how did Mrs. Boynton's family take the news?" asked Poirot.

For once both Lady Westholme and Miss Pierce seemed a little at a loss. The former said at last, in a voice lacking its usual self-assurance:

"Well—really—it is difficult to say. They—they were very quiet about it."

"Stunned," said Miss Pierce.

She offered the word more as a suggestion than as a fact.

"They all went out with Miss King," said Lady Westholme. "Miss Pierce and I very sensibly remained where we were."

A faintly wistful look was observable in Miss Pierce's eye at this point.

"I detest vulgar curiosity!" continued Lady Westholme.

The wistful look became more pronounced. It was clear that Miss Pierce had had perforce to hate vulgar curiosity too!

"Later," concluded Lady Westholme, "the dragoman and Miss King returned. I suggested that dinner should be served immediately to the four of us, so that the Boynton family could dine later in the marquee without the embarrassment of strangers being present. My suggestion was adopted and immediately after the meal I retired to my tent. Miss King and Miss Pierce did the same. Mr. Cope, I believe, remained in the marquee; he is a friend of the family and thought he might be of some assistance to them. That is all I know, M. Poirot."

"When Miss King had broken the news, *all* the Boynton family accompanied her out of the marquee?"

"Yes—no, I believe, now that you come to mention it, that the red-haired girl stayed behind. Perhaps you can remember, Miss Pierce?"

"Yes, I think—I am quite sure she did."

Poirot asked:

"What did she *do?*"

Lady Westholme stared at him.

"What did she *do,* M. Poirot? She did not do anything, as far as I can remember."

"I mean was she sewing—or reading—did she look anxious—did she say anything?"

"Well, really—" Lady Westholme frowned. "She—er—she just sat there, as far as I can remember."

"She twiddled her fingers," said Miss Pierce suddenly. "I remember noticing—poor thing; I thought, it shows what she's feeling! Not that there was anything to show in her *face,* you know—just her hands turning and twisting.

"Once," went on Miss Pierce conversationally, "I remember tearing up a pound note that way—not thinking of what I was doing. 'Shall I catch the first train and go to her?' I thought (it was a great aunt of mine—taken suddenly ill), 'or shall I *not?'* And I couldn't make up my mind one way or the other and then I looked down, and instead of the telegram I was tearing up a pound note—a *pound note*—into tiny pieces!"

Miss Pierce paused dramatically.

Not entirely approving of this sudden bid for the limelight on the part of her satellite, Lady Westholme said coldly:

"Is there anything else, M. Poirot?"

With a start, Poirot seemed to come out of a brown study.

"Nothing—nothing—you have been most clear—most definite."

"I have an exellent memory," said Lady Westholme with satisfaction.

"One last little demand, Lady Westholme," said Poirot. "Please continue to sit as you are sitting—without looking around. Now, would you be so kind as to describe to me just what Miss Pierce is wearing today—that is, if Miss Pierce does not object?"

"Oh, no, not in the least!" twittered Miss Pierce.

"Really, M. Poirot, is there any *object—"*

"Please be so kind as to do as I ask, Madame."

Lady Westholme shrugged her shoulders and then said with a rather bad grace:

"Miss Pierce has on a striped brown and white cotton dress and is wearing with it a Sudanese belt of red, blue and beige leather. She is wearing beige silk stockings and brown glacé strap shoes. There is a ladder in her left stocking. She has a necklace of cornelian beads and one of bright royal blue beads—and is wearing a brooch with a pearl butterfly on it. She has an imitation scarab ring on the third finger of her right hand. On her head she has a double terai of pink and brown felt."

She paused—a pause of quiet competence. Then:

"Is there anything further?" she asked coldly.

Poirot spread out his hands in a wide gesture.

"You have my entire admiration, Madame. Your observation is of the highest order."

"Details rarely escape me."

Lady Westholme rose, made a slight inclination of her head, and left the room. As Miss Pierce was following her, gazing down ruefully at her left leg, Poirot said:

"A little moment, please, Mademoiselle?"

"Yes?" Miss Pierce looked up, a slightly apprehensive look upon her face.

Poirot leaned forward confidentially.

"You see this bunch of wild flowers on the table here?"

"Yes," said Miss Pierce—staring.

"And you noticed that, when you first came into the room, I sneezed once or twice?"

"Yes."

"Did you notice if I had just been sniffing those flowers?"

"Well—really—no—I couldn't say."

"But you remember my sneezing?"

"Oh, yes, I remember *that!*"

"Ah, well—no matter. I wondered, you see, if these flowers might induce the hay fever. No matter!"

"Hay fever!" cried Miss Pierce. "I remember a cousin of mine was a *martyr* to it! She always said that if you sprayed your nose daily with a solution of boracic—"

With some difficulty Poirot shelved the cousin's nasal treatment and got rid of Miss Pierce. He shut the door and came back into the room with his eyebrows raised.

"But I did not sneeze," he murmured. "So much for that. No, I did not sneeze."

6

Lennox Boynton came into the room with a quick resolute step. Had he been there, Dr. Gerard would have been surprised at the change in the man. The apathy was gone. His bearing was alert—although he was plainly nervous. His eyes had a tendency to shift rapidly from point to point about the room.

"Good-morning, M. Boynton." Poirot rose and bowed ceremoniously. Lennox responded somewhat awkwardly. "I much appreciate your giving me this interview."

Lennox Boynton said rather uncertainly:

"Er—Colonel Carbury said it would be a good thing—advised it—some formalities—he said."

"Please sit down, M. Boynton."

Lennox sat down on the chair lately vacated by Lady Westholme.

Poirot went on conversationally:

"This has been a great shock to you, I am afraid."

"Yes, of course. Well, no, perhaps not . . . We always knew that my mother's heart was not strong."

"Was it wise, under those circumstances, to allow her to undertake such an arduous expedition?"

Lennox Boynton raised his head. He spoke not without a certain sad dignity.

"My mother, M.—er, Poirot, made her own decisions. If she had made up her mind to anything it was no good our opposing her."

He drew in his breath sharply as he said the last words. His face suddenly grew rather white.

"I know well," admitted Poirot, "that elderly ladies are sometimes headstrong."

Lennox said irritably:

"What is the purpose of all this? That is what I want to know. Why have all these formalities arisen?"

"Perhaps you do not realize, M. Boynton, that in cases of sudden and unexplained deaths, formalities must necessarily arise."

Lennox said sharply:

"What do you mean by 'unexplained'?"

Poirot shrugged his shoulders.

"There is always the question to be considered: Is a death natural—or might it perhaps be suicide?"

"Suicide?" Lennox Boynton stared.

Poirot said lightly:

"You, of course, would know best about such possibilities. Colonel Carbury, naturally, is in the dark. It is necessary for him to decide whether to order an inquiry—an autopsy—all the rest of it. As I was on the spot and as I have much experience of these matters, he suggested that I should make a few inquiries and advise him upon the matter. Naturally, he does not wish to cause you inconvenience if it can be helped."

Lennox Boynton said angrily:

"I shall wire to our Consul in Jerusalem."

Poirot said noncommittally:

"You are quite within your rights in doing so, of course."

There was a pause. Then Poirot said, spreading out his hands:

"If you object to answering my questions—"

Lennox Boynton said quickly:

"Not at all. Only—it seems—all so unnecessary."

"I comprehend. I comprehend perfectly. But it is all very simple, really. A matter, as they say, of routine. Now, on the afternoon of your mother's death, M. Boynton, I believe you left the camp at Petra and went for a walk?"

"Yes. We all went—with the exception of my mother and my younger sister."

"Your mother was then sitting in the mouth of her cave?"

"Yes, just outside it. She sat there every afternoon."

"Quite so. You started—when?"

"Soon after three, I should say."

"You returned from your walk—when?"

"I really couldn't say what time it was—four o'clock—five o'clock perhaps."

"About an hour to two hours after you set out?"

"Yes—about that, I should think."

"Did you pass anyone on your way back?"

"Did I what?"

"Pass anyone. Two ladies sitting on a rock, for instance?"

"I don't know. Yes, I think I did."

"You were, perhaps, too absorbed in your thoughts to notice?"

"Yes, I was."

"Did you speak to your mother when you got back to the camp?"

"Yes—yes, I did."

"She did not then complain of feeling ill?"

"No—no, she seemed perfectly all right."

"May I ask what exactly passed between you?"

Lennox paused a minute.

"She said I had come back soon. I said, yes, I had." He paused again in an effort of concentration. "I said it was hot. She—she asked me the time—said her wrist watch had stopped. I took it from her, wound it up, set it, and put it back on her wrist."

Poirot interrupted gently:

"And what time was it?"

"Eh?" said Lennox.

"What time was it when you set the hands of the wrist watch?"

"Oh, I see. It—it was twenty-five minutes to five."

"So you do know exactly the time you returned to the camp!" said Poirot gently.

Lennox flushed.

"Yes, what a fool I am! I'm sorry, M. Poirot, my wits are all astray, I'm afraid. All this worry—"

Poirot chimed in quickly:

"Oh! I understand—I understand perfectly! It is all of the most disquieting! And what happened next?"

"I asked my mother if she wanted anything. A drink—tea, coffee, etc. She said no. Then I went to the marquee. None of the servants seemed to be about, but I found some soda water and drank it. I was thirsty. I sat there reading some old numbers of the *Saturday Evening Post.* I think I must have dozed off."

"Your wife joined you in the marquee?"

"Yes, she came in not long after."

"And you did not see your mother again alive?"

"No."

"She did not seem in any way agitated or upset when you were talking to her?"

"No, she was exactly as usual."

"She did not refer to any trouble or annoyance with one of the servants?"

Lennox stared.

"No, nothing at all."

"And that is all you can tell me?"

"I am afraid so—yes."

"Thank you, M. Boynton."

Poirot inclined his head as a sign that the interview was over.

Lennox did not seem very willing to depart. He stood hesitating by the door.

"Er—there's nothing else?"

"Nothing. Perhaps you would be so good as to ask your wife to come here?"

Lennox went slowly out. On the pad beside him Poirot wrote "L.B. 4:35 P.M."

7

Poirot looked with interest at the tall dignified young woman who entered the room.

He rose and bowed to her politely.

"Mrs. Lennox Boynton? Hercule Poirot, at your sevice."

Nadine Boynton sat down. Her thoughtful eyes were on Poirot's face.

"I hope you do not mind, Madame, my intruding on your sorrow in this way?"

Her gaze did not waver.

She did not reply at once. Her eyes remained steady and grave. At last, she gave a sigh and said:

"I think it is best for me to be quite frank with you, M. Poirot."

"I agree with you, Madame."

"You apologized for intruding upon my sorrow. That sorrow, M. Poirot, does not exist and it is idle to pretend that it does. I had no love for my mother-in-law and I cannot honestly say that I regret her death."

"Thank you, Madame, for your plain speaking."

Nadine went on:

"Still, although I cannot pretend sorrow, I can admit to another feeling—remorse."

"Remorse?" Poirot's eyebrows went up.

"Yes. Because, you see, it was I who brought about her death. For that I blame myself bitterly."

"What is this that you are saying, Madame?"

"I am saying that *I* was the cause of my mother-in-law's death. I was acting, as I thought, honestly—but the result was unfortunate. To all intents and purposes, I killed her."

Poirot leaned back in his chair.

"Will you be so kind as to elucidate this statement, Madame?"

Nadine bent her head.

"Yes, that is what I wish to do. My first reaction, naturally, was to keep my private affairs to myself, but I see that the time has come when it would be better to speak out. I have no doubt, M. Poirot, that you have often received confidences of a somewhat intimate nature?"

"That, yes."

"Then I will tell you quite simply what occurred. My married life, M. Poirot, has not been particularly happy. My husband is not entirely to blame for that—his mother's influence over him has been unfortunate—but I have been feeling for some time that my life was becoming intolerable."

She paused and then went on:

"On the afternoon of my mother-in-law's death I came to a decision. I have a friend—a very good friend. He has suggested more than once that I should throw in my lot with his. On that afternoon I accepted his proposal."

"You decided to leave your husband?"

"Yes."

"Continue, Madame."

Nadine said in a lower voice:

"Having once made my decision I wanted to—to establish it as soon as possible. I walked home to the camp by myself. My mother-in-law was sitting alone, there was no one about, and I decided to break the news to her then and there. I got a chair—sat down by her and told her abruptly what I had decided."

"She was surprised?"

"Yes, I am afraid it was a great shock to her. She was both surprised and angry—very angry. She—she worked herself into quite a state about it! Presently I refused to discuss the matter any longer. I got up and walked away." Her voice dropped. "I—I never saw her again alive."

Poirot nodded his head slowly. He said:

"I see."

Then he said:

"You think her death was the result of the shock?"

"It seems to me almost certain. You see, she had already overexerted herself considerably getting to this place. My news, and her anger at it, would do the rest. . . . I feel additionally guilty because I have had a certain amount of training in illness and so I, more than anyone else, ought to have realized the possibility of such a thing happening."

Poirot sat in silence for some minutes, then he said:

"What exactly did you do when you left her?"

"I took the chair I had brought out back into my cave, then I went down to the marquee. My husband was there."

Poirot watched her closely as he said:

"Did you tell *him* of your decision? Or had you already told him?"

There was a pause, an infinitesimal pause, before Nadine said:

"I told him then."

"How did he take it?"

She answered quietly:

"He was very upset."

"Did he urge you to reconsider your decision?"

She shook her head.

"He—he didn't say very much. You see, we had both known for some time that something like this might happen."

Poirot said:

"You will pardon me, but—the other man was, of course, M. Jefferson Cope?"

She bent her head.

"Yes."

There was a long pause, then, without any change of voice, Poirot asked:

"Do you own a hypodermic syringe, Madame?"

"Yes—no."

His eyebrows rose.

She explained.

"I have an old hypodermic amongst other things in a traveling medicine chest, but it is in our big luggage which we left in Jerusalem."

"I see."

There was a pause, then she said with a shiver of uneasiness:

"Why did you ask me that, M. Poirot?"

He did not answer the question. Instead he put one of his own.

"Mrs. Boynton was, I believe, taking a mixture containing digitalis?"

"Yes."

He thought that she was definitely watchful now.

"That was for her heart trouble?"

"Yes."

"Digitalis is, to some extent, a cumulative drug?"

"I believe it is. I do not know very much about it."

"If Mrs. Boynton had taken a big overdose of digitalis—"

She interrupted him quickly but with decision.

"She did not. She was always most careful. So was I, if I measured the dose for her."

"There might have been an overdose in this particular bottle. A mistake of the chemist who made it up?"

"I think that is very unlikely," she replied quietly.

"Ah, well, the analysis will soon tell us."

Nadine said:

"Unfortunately the bottle was broken."

Poirot eyed her with sudden interest.

"Indeed! Who broke it?"

"I'm not quite sure. One of the servants, I think. In carrying my mother-in-law's body into her cave, there was a good deal of confusion and the light was very poor. A table got knocked over."

Poirot eyed her steadily for a minute or two.

"That," he said, "is very interesting."

Nadine Boynton shifted wearily in her chair.

"You are suggesting, I think, that my mother-in-law did not die of shock, but of an overdose of digitalis?" she said and went on: "That seems to me most improbable."

Poirot leaned forward.

"Even when I tell you that Dr. Gerard, the French physician who was staying in the camp, had missed an appreciable quantity of a preparation of digitoxin from his medicine chest?"

Her face grew very pale. He saw the clutch of her hand on the table. Her eyes dropped. She sat very still. She was like a Madonna carved in stone.

"Well, Madame," said Poirot at last. "What have you to say to that?"

The seconds ticked on but she did not speak. It was quite two minutes before she raised her head, and he started a little when he saw the look in her eyes.

"M. Poirot, *I did not kill my mother-in-law.* That you know! She was alive and well when I left her. There are many people who can testify to that! Therefore, being innocent of the crime, I can venture to appeal to you. Why must you mix yourself up in this business? If I swear to you on my honor that justice and only justice has been done, will you not abandon this inquiry? There has been so much suffering—you do not know. Now that at last there is peace and the possibility of happiness, must you destroy it all?"

Poirot sat up very straight. His eyes shone with a green light.

"Let me be clear, Madame. What are you asking me to do?"

"I am telling you that my mother-in-law died a natural death and I am asking you to accept that statement."

"Let us be definite. *You believe that your mother-in-law was deliberately killed,* and you are asking me to condone—*murder!"*

"I am asking you to have pity!"

"Yes—on someone who had no pity!"

"You don't understand—it was not like that."

"Did you commit the crime yourself, Madame, that you know so well?"

Nadine shook her head. She showed no signs of guilt.

"No," she said quietly. "She was alive when I left her."

"And then—what happened? You *know*—or you *suspect?*"

Nadine said passionately:

"I have heard, M. Poirot, that once, in that affair of the Orient Express, you accepted an official verdict of what had happened?"

Poirot looked at her curiously.

"I wonder who told you that."

"Is it true?"

He said slowly:

"That case was—different."

"No. No, it was not different! The man who was killed was evil," her voice dropped, "as *she* was. . . ."

Poirot said:

"The moral character of the victim has nothing to do with it! A human being who has exercised the right of private judgment and taken the life of another human being is not safe to exist amongst the community. *I* tell you that! I, Hercule Poirot!"

"How hard you are!"

"Madame, in some ways I am adamant. I will not condone murder! That is the final word of Hercule Poirot."

She got up. Her dark eyes flashed with sudden fire.

"Then go on! Bring ruin and misery into the lives of innocent people! I have nothing more to say."

"But I—I think, Madame, that you have a lot to say. . . ."

"No, nothing more."

"But yes. What happened, Madame, *after* you left your mother-in-law? Whilst you and your husband were in the marquee together?"

She shrugged her shoulders.

"How should I know?"

"You *do* know—or you suspect."

She looked him straight in the eyes.

"I know nothing, M. Poirot."

Turning, she left the room.

8

After noting on his pad "N.B. 4:40," Poirot opened the door and called to the orderly whom Colonel Carbury had left at his disposal, an intelligent man with a good knowledge of English. He asked him to fetch Miss Carol Boynton.

Poirot looked with some interest at the girl as she entered—at the chestnut hair, the poise of the head on the long neck, the nervous energy of the beautifully shaped hands.

He said:

"Sit down, Mademoiselle."

She sat down obediently. Her face was colorless and expressionless.

Poirot began with a mechanical expression of sympathy to which the girl acquiesced without any change of expression.

"And now, Mademoiselle, will you recount to me how you spent the afternoon of the day in question?"

Her answer came promptly, raising the suspicion that it had already been well rehearsed.

"After luncheon we all went for a stroll. I returned to the camp—"

Poirot interrupted.

"A little minute. Were you all together until then?"

"No, I was with my brother Raymond and Miss King for most of the time. Then I strolled off on my own."

"Thank you. And you were saying you returned to the camp. Do you know the approximate time?"

"I believe it was just about ten minutes past five."

Poirot put down "C.B. 5:10."

"And what then?"

"My mother was still sitting where she had been when we set out. I went up and spoke to her and then went on to my tent."

"Can you remember exactly what passed between you?"

"I just said it was very hot and that I was going to lie down. My mother said she would remain where she was. That was all."

"Did anything in her appearance strike you as out of the ordinary?"

"No. At least—that is—"

She paused doubtfully, staring at Poirot.

"It is not from me that you can get the answer, Mademoiselle," said Poirot quietly.

She flushed and looked away.

"I was just considering. I hardly noticed at the time, but now, looking back—"

"Yes?"

Carol said slowly:

"It is true—she was a funny color—her face was very red—more so than usual."

"She might, perhaps, have had a shock of some kind?" Poirot suggested.

"A shock?" She stared at him.

"Yes, she might have had, let us say, some trouble with one of the Arab servants."

"Oh!" Her face cleared. "Yes—she might."

"She did not mention such a thing having happened?"

"N-o—no, nothing at all."

Poirot went on:

"And what did you do next, Mademoiselle?"

"I went to my tent and lay down for about half an hour. Then I went down to the marquee. My brother and his wife were there reading."

"And what did you do?"

"Oh! I had some sewing to do. And then I picked up a magazine."

"Did you speak to your mother again on your way to the marquee?"

"No, I went straight down. I don't think I even glanced in her direction."

"And then?"

"I remained in the marquee until—until Miss King told us she was dead."

"And that is all you know, Mademoiselle?"

"Yes."

Poirot leaned forward. His tone was the same, light and conversational.

"And what did you *feel,* Mademoiselle?"

"What did I feel?"

"Yes—when you found that your mother—*pardon*—your step-mother was she not?—what did you feel when you learned she was dead?"

She stared at him.

"I don't understand what you mean!"

"I think you understand very well."

Her eyes dropped. She said, uncertainly:

"It was—a great shock."

"Was it?"

The blood rushed to her face. She stared at him helplessly. Now he saw fear in her eyes.

"Was it such a great shock, Mademoiselle? *Remembering a certain conversation you had with your brother Raymond one night in Jerusalem?"*

His shot proved right. He saw it in the way the color drained out of her cheeks again.

"You know about that?" she whispered.

"Yes, I know."

"But how—how?"

"Part of your conversation was overheard."

"Oh!" Carol Boynton buried her face in her hands. Her sobs shook the table.

Hercule Poirot waited a minute, then he said quietly:

"You were planning together to bring about your step-mother's death."

Carol sobbed out brokenly:

"We were mad—mad—that evening!"

"Perhaps."

"It's impossible for you to understand the state we were in!" She sat up, pushing back the hair from her face. "It would sound fantastic. It wasn't so bad in America but traveling brought it home to us so."

"Brought what home to you?" His voice was kind now, sympathetic.

"Our being different from—other people! We—we got desperate about it. And there was Jinny."

"Jinny?"

"My sister. You haven't seen her. She was going—well—queer. And Mother was making her worse. She didn't seem to realize. We were afraid, Ray and I, that Jinny was going quite, quite mad! And we saw Nadine thought so too, and that made us more afraid because Nadine knows about nursing and things like that."

"Yes, yes?"

"That evening in Jerusalem things kind of boiled up! Ray was beside himself. He and I got all strung up and it seemed— Oh, indeed, it did seem *right* to plan as we did! Mother—Mother *wasn't* sane. I don't know what you think, but it *can* seem quite *right*—almost noble—to kill someone!"

Poirot nodded his head slowly.

"Yes, it has seemed so, I know, to many. That is proved by history."

"That's how Ray and I felt—that night. . . ." She beat her hand on the table. "But we didn't really do it. Of course we didn't do it! When daylight came the whole thing seemed absurd, melodramatic— Oh, yes, and wicked too! Indeed, indeed, M. Poirot, Mother died perfectly naturally of heart failure. Ray and I had nothing to do with it."

Poirot said quietly:

"Will you swear to me, Mademoiselle, as you hope for salvation after death, that Mrs. Boynton did not die as the result of any action of yours?"

She lifted her head. Her voice came steady and deep.

"I swear," said Carol, "as I hope for salvation, that I never harmed her." . . .

Poirot leaned back in his chair.

"So," he said, "that is that."

There was silence. Poirot thoughtfully caressed his superb moustache. Then he said:

"What exactly was your plan?"

"Plan?"

"Yes, you and your brother must have had a plan."

In his mind he ticked off the seconds before her answer came. One, two, three.

"We had no plan," said Carol at last. "We never got as far as that."

Hercule Poirot got up.

"That is all, Mademoiselle. Will you be so good as to send your brother to me."

Carol rose. She stood undecidedly for a minute.

"M. Poirot, you do—you do believe me?"

"Have I said," asked Poirot, "that I do not?"

"No, but—"

She stopped.

He said:

"You will ask your brother to come here?"

"Yes."

She went slowly towards the door. She stopped as she got to it, turning around passionately.

"I *have* told you the truth—I have!"

Hercule Poirot did not answer.

Carol Boynton went slowly out of the room.

9

Poirot noted the likeness between brother and sister as Raymond Boynton came into the room.

His face was stern and set. He did not seem nervous or afraid. He dropped into a chair, stared hard at Poirot and said:

"Well?"

Poirot said gently:

"Your sister has spoken with you?"

Raymond nodded.

"Yes, when she told me to come here. Of course I realize that your suspicions are quite justified. If our conversation was overheard that night, the fact that my step-mother died rather suddenly certainly *would* seem suspicious! I can only assure you that that conversation was—the madness of an evening! We were, at the time, under an intolerable strain. This fantastic plan of killing my step-mother did—oh, how shall I put it?—it let off steam somehow!"

Hercule Poirot bent his head slowly.

"That," he said, "is possible."

"In the morning, of course, it all seemed—rather absurd! I swear to you, M. Poirot, that I never thought of the matter again!"

Poirot did not answer.

Raymond said quickly:

"Oh, yes, I know that that is easy enough to *say.* I cannot expect you to believe me on my bare word. But consider the facts. I spoke to my mother just a little before six o'clock. She was certainly alive and well then. I went to my tent, had a wash and joined the others in the marquee. From that time onwards neither Carol nor I moved from the place. We were in full sight of everyone. You must see, M. Poirot, that my mother's death was natural—a case of heart failure—it couldn't be anything else! There were servants about, a lot of coming and going. Any other idea is absurd."

Poirot said quietly:

"Do you know, M. Boynton, that Miss King is of the opinion that when she examined the body—at six-thirty—death had occurred at least an hour and a half and probably *two hours* earlier?"

Raymond stared at him. He looked dumbfounded.

"Sarah said that?" he gasped.

Poirot nodded.

"What have you to say now?"

"But—it's impossible!"

"That is Miss King's testimony. Now *you* come and tell me that your mother was alive and well only forty minutes before Miss King examined the body."

Raymond said:

"But she was!"

"Be careful, M. Boynton."

"Sarah *must* be mistaken! There must be some factor she didn't take into account. Refraction off the rock—something. I can assure you, M. Poirot, that my mother *was* alive at just before six and that I spoke to her."

Poirot's face showed nothing.

Raymond leaned forward earnestly.

"M. Poirot, I know how it must seem to you, but look at the thing fairly. You are a biased person. You are bound to be by the nature of things. You live in an atmosphere of crime. Every sudden death must seem to you a possible crime! Can't you realize that your sense of proportion is not to be relied upon? People die every day—especially people with weak hearts—and there is nothing in the least sinister about such deaths."

Poirot sighed.

"So you would teach me my business, is that it?"

"No, of course not. But I do think that you are prejudiced—because of that unfortunate conversation. There is nothing really about my mother's death to awaken suspicion except that unlucky hysterical conversation between Carol and myself."

Poirot shook his head.

"You are in error," he said. "There is something else. There is the poison taken from Dr. Gerard's medicine chest."

"Poison?" Ray stared at him. *"Poison!"* He pushed his chair back a little. He looked completely stupefied. "Is *that* what you suspect?"

Poirot gave him a minute or two. Then he said quietly, almost indifferently:

"Your plan was different—eh?"

"Oh, yes." Raymond answered mechanically. "That's why—this changes everything. . . . I—I can't think clearly."

"What was *your* plan?"

"Our plan? It was—"

Raymond stopped abruptly. His eyes became alert, suddenly watchful.

"I don't think," he said, "that I'll say any more."

He got up.

"As you please," said Poirot.

He watched the young man out of the room.

He drew his pad towards him and in small neat characters made a final entry. "R.B. 5:55."

Then, taking a large sheet of paper he proceeded to write.

His task completed, he sat back with his head on one side contemplating the result. It ran as follows:

Boyntons and Jefferson Cope leave the camp	3:05 (approx.)
Dr. Gerard and Sarah King leave the camp	3:15 (approx.)
Lady Westholme and Miss Pierce leave the camp	4:15
Dr. Gerard returns to camp	4:20 (approx.)
Lennox Boynton returns to camp	4:35
Nadine Boynton returns to camp and talks to Mrs. Boynton	4:40
Nadine Boynton leaves her mother-in-law and goes to marquee	4:50 (approx.)
Carol Boynton returns to camp	5:10
Lady Westholme, Miss Pierce and M. Jefferson Cope return to camp	5:40
Raymond Boynton returns to camp	5:50
Sarah King returns to camp	6:00
Body discovered	6:30

10

"I wonder," said Hercule Poirot.

He folded up the list, went to the door and ordered Mahmoud to be brought to him.

The stout dragoman was voluble. Words dripped from him in a rising flood.

"Always, always, I am blamed. When anything happens, say always my fault. Always my fault. When Lady Ellen Hunt sprain her ankle coming down from Place of Sacrifice, it my fault, though she would go high-heeled shoes and she sixty at least—perhaps seventy. My life all one misery! Ah! what with miseries and iniquities Jews do to us—"

At last Poirot succeeded in stemming the flood and in getting in his question.

"Half-past five o'clock, you say? No, I not think any of servants were about then. You see, lunch it late—two o'clock. And then to clear it away. After the lunch all afternoon sleep. Yes, Americans, they not take tea. We all settle sleep by half-past three. At five I, who am soul of efficiency—always—always I watch for the comfort of ladies and gentlemen I serving, I come out knowing that time all English ladies want tea. But no one there. They all gone walking. For me, that is very well—better than usual. I can go back sleep. At quarter to six trouble begin—large English lady—very grand lady—come back and want tea although boys are now laying dinner. She makes quite fuss—says water must be boiling—I am to see myself. Ah, my good gentleman! What a life—what a life! I do all I can—always I blamed—I—"

Poirot cut short the recriminations.

"There is another small matter. The dead lady was angry with one of the boys. Do you know which one it was and what it was about?"

Mahmoud's hands rose to heaven.

"Should I know? But naturally not. Old lady did not complain to me."

"Could you find out?"

"No, my good gentleman, that would be impossible. None of the boys admit it for a moment. Old lady angry, you say? Then naturally boys would not tell. Abdul say it Mohammed, and Mohammed say it Aziz, and Aziz say it Aissa, and so on. They are all very stupid Bedouin—understand nothing."

He took a breath and continued:

"Now I, I have advantage of Mission education. I recite to you Keats—Shelley—*Iadadoveandasweedovedied*—"

Poirot flinched. Though English was not his native tongue he knew it well enough to suffer from the strange enunciation of Mahmoud.

"Superb!" he said hastily. "Superb! Definitely I recommend you to all my friends."

He contrived to escape from the dragoman's eloquence. Then he took his list to Colonel Carbury, whom he found in his office.

Carbury pushed his tie a little more askew and asked:

"Got anything?"

Poirot sat down.

"Shall I tell you a theory of mine?"

"If you like," said Colonel Carbury, and sighed. One way and another he had heard a good many theories in the course of his existence.

"My theory is that criminology is the easiest science in the world! One has only to let the criminal talk—sooner or later he will tell you everything."

"I remember you said something of the kind before. Who's been telling you things?"

"Everybody."

Briefly, Poirot retailed the interviews he had had that morning.

"H'm," said Carbury. "Yes, you've got hold of a pointer or two, perhaps. Pity of it is, they all seem to point in opposite directions. Have we got a case, that's what I want to know?"

"No."

Carbury sighed again.

"I was afraid not."

"But before nightfall," said Poirot, "you shall have the truth!"

"Well, that's all you ever promised me," said Colonel Carbury. "And I rather doubted your getting that! Sure of it?"

"I am very sure."

"Must be nice to feel like that," commented the other.

If there was a faint twinkle in his eye, Poirot appeared unaware of it.

He produced his list.

"Neat," said Colonel Carbury approvingly.

He bent over it.

After a minute or two he said:

"Know what I think?"

"I should be delighted if you would tell me."

"Young Raymond Boynton's out of it."

"Ah! you think so?"

"Yes. Clear as a bell what *he* thought. We might have known he'd be out of it. Being, as in detective stories, the most likely person. Since you practically overheard him saying he was going to bump off the old lady—we might have known that meant he was innocent!"

"You read the detective stories, yes?"

"Thousands of them," said Colonel Carbury. He added, and his tone was that of a wistful schoolboy: "I suppose you couldn't do the things the detective does in books? Write a list of significant facts—things that don't seem to mean anything but are really frightfully important—that sort of thing?"

"Ah," said Poirot kindly. "You like that kind of detective story? But certainly, I will do it for you with pleasure."

He drew a sheet of paper towards him and wrote quickly and neatly:

SIGNIFICANT POINTS

1. Mrs. Boynton was taking a mixture containing digitalis.
2. Dr. Gerard missed a hypodermic syringe.
3. Mrs. Boynton took definite pleasure in keeping her family from enjoying themselves with other people.
4. Mrs. Boynton, on the afternoon in question, encouraged her family to go away and leave her.
5. Mrs. Boynton was a mental sadist.
6. The distance from the marquee to the place where Mrs. Boynton was sitting is (roughly) two hundred yards.
7. Mr. Lennox Boynton said at first he did not know what time he returned to the camp, but later he admitted having set his mother's wrist watch to the right time.
8. Dr. Gerard and Miss Ginevra Boynton occupied tents next door to each other.
9. At half-past six, when dinner was ready, a servant was despatched to announce the fact to Mrs. Boynton.

The Colonel perused this with great satisfaction.

"Capital!" he said. "Just the thing! You've made it difficult—and seemingly irrelevant—absolutely the authentic touch! By the way, it seems to me there are one or two rather noticeable omissions. But that, I suppose, is what you tempt the mug with?"

Poirot's eyes twinkled a little but he did not answer.

"Point two, for instance," said Colonel Carbury tentatively. *"Dr. Gerard missed a hypodermic syringe*—yes. He also missed a concentrated solution of digitalis—or something of that kind."

"The latter point," said Poirot, "is not important in the way the absence of his hypodermic syringe is important."

"Splendid!" said Colonel Carbury, his face irradiated with smiles. "I don't get it at all. I should have said the digitalis was much more important than the syringe! And what about that servant motif that keeps cropping up—a servant being sent to tell her dinner was ready—and that story of her shaking her stick at a servant earlier in the afternoon? You're not going to tell me one of my poor desert mutts bumped her off after all? Because," added Colonel Carbury sternly, "if so, that would be *cheating."*

Poirot smiled but did not answer.

As he left the office, he murmured to himself:

"Incredible! The English never grow up!"

11

Sarah King sat on a hilltop absently plucking up wild flowers. Dr. Gerard sat on a rough wall of stones near her.

She said, suddenly and fiercely:

"Why did you start all this? If it hadn't been for *you—"*

Dr. Gerard said slowly:

"You think I should have kept silence?"

"Yes."

"Knowing what I knew?"

"You didn't *know,"* said Sarah.

The Frenchman sighed.

"I did know. But I admit one can never be absolutely sure."

"Yes, one can," said Sarah uncompromisingly.

The Frenchman shrugged his shoulders.

"You, perhaps!"

Sarah said:

"You had fever—a high temperature—you couldn't be clear-headed about the business. The syringe was probably there all the time. And you may have made a mistake about the digitoxin or one of the servants may have meddled with the case."

Gerard said cynically:

"You need not worry! The evidence is almost bound to be inconclusive. You will see, your friends the Boyntons will get away with it!"

Sarah said fiercely:

"I don't want that, either."

He shook his head.

"You are illogical!"

"Wasn't it you"—Sarah demanded—"in Jerusalem—who said a great deal about not interfering? And now look!"

"I have not interfered. I have only told what I know!"

"And I say you don't *know* it—oh, dear, there we are, back again! I'm arguing in a circle."

Gerard said gently:

"I am sorry, Miss King."

Sarah said in a low voice:

"You see, after all, *they haven't escaped*—any of them! *She's* still there! Even from her grave she can still reach out and hold them. There was something—terrible about her—she's just as terrible now she's dead! I feel —I feel she's *enjoying* all this!"

She clenched her hands. Then she said in an entirely different tone, a light everyday voice:

"That little man's coming up the hill."

Dr. Gerard looked over his shoulder.

"Ah! He comes in search of us, I think."

"Is he as much of a fool as he looks?" asked Sarah.

Dr. Gerard said gravely:

"He is not a fool at all."

"I was afraid of that," said Sarah King.

With somber eyes she watched the uphill progress of Hercule Poirot.

He reached them at last, uttered a loud "ouf" and wiped his forehead. Then he looked sadly down at his patent leather shoes.

"Alas," he said. "This stony country! My poor shoes."

"You can borrow Lady Westholme's shoe-cleaning apparatus," said Sarah unkindly. "And her duster. She travels with a kind of patent housemaid's equipment."

"That will not remove the scratches, Mademoiselle." Poirot shook his head sadly.

"Perhaps not. Why on earth do you wear shoes like that in this sort of country?"

Poirot put his head a little on one side.

"I like to have the appearance *soigné,"* he said.

"I should give up trying for that in the desert," said Sarah.

"Women do not look their best in the desert," said Dr. Gerard dreamily. "Miss King here, yes—she always looks neat and well turned out. But that Lady Westholme in her great thick coats and skirts and those terribly unbecoming riding breeches and boots—*quelle horreur de femme!* And the poor Miss Pierce—her clothes so limp, like faded cabbage leaves, and the chains and the beads that clink! Even young Mrs. Boynton, who is a good-looking woman, is not what you call *chic!* Her clothes are uninteresting."

Sarah said restively:

"Well, I don't suppose M. Poirot climbed up here to talk about clothes!"

"True," said Poirot. "I came to consult Dr. Gerard—his opinion should be of value to me—and yours too, Mademoiselle—you are young and up to date in your psychology. I want to know, you see, all that you can tell me of Mrs. Boynton."

"Don't you know all that by heart now?" asked Sarah.

"No. I have a feeling—more than a feeling—a certainty that the mental equipment of Mrs. Boynton is very important in this case. Such types as hers are no doubt familiar to Dr. Gerard."

"From my point of view she was certainly an interesting study," said the doctor.

"Tell me."

Dr. Gerard was nothing loath. He described his own interest in the family group, his conversation with Jefferson Cope, and the latter's complete misreading of the situation.

"He is a sentimentalist, then," said Poirot thoughtfully.

"Oh, essentially! He has ideals—based, really, on a deep instinct of laziness. To take human nature at its best and the world as a pleasant place is undoubtedly the easiest course in life! Jefferson Cope has, consequently, not the least idea what people are really like."

"That might be dangerous sometimes," said Poirot.

Dr. Gerard went on:

"He persisted in regarding what I may describe as 'the Boynton situation' as a case of mistaken devotion. Of the underlying hate, rebellion, slavery and misery he had only the faintest notion."

"It is stupid, that," Poirot commented.

"All the same," went on Dr. Gerard, "even the most wilfully obtuse of sentimental optimists cannot be quite blind. I think, on the journey to Petra, Mr. Jefferson Cope's eyes were being opened."

And he described the conversation he had had with the American on the morning of Mrs. Boynton's death.

"That is an interesting story, that story of a servant girl," said Poirot thoughtfully. "It throws light on the old woman's methods."

Gerard said:

"It was altogether an odd, strange morning, that! You have not been to Petra, M. Poirot? If you go, you must certainly climb to the Place of Sacrifice. It has an—how shall I say?—an atmosphere!" He described the scene in detail, adding: "Mademoiselle here sat like a young judge, speaking of the sacrifice of one to save many. You remember, Miss King?"

Sarah shivered.

"Don't! Don't let's talk of that day."

"No, no," said Poirot. "Let us talk of events further back in the past. I am interested, Dr. Gerard, in your sketch of Mrs. Boynton's mentality. What I do not quite understand is this—having brought her family into absolute subjection, why did she then arrange this trip abroad where surely there was danger of outside contacts and of her authority being weakened?"

Dr. Gerard leaned forward excitedly.

"But, *mon vieux,* that is just it! Old ladies are the same all the world over. They get bored! If their speciality is playing patience, they sicken of the patience they know too well. They want to learn a new patience. And it is just the same with an old lady whose recreation (incredible as it may sound) is the dominating and tormenting of human creatures! Mrs. Boynton—to speak of her as *une dompteuse*—had tamed her tigers. There was perhaps some excitement as they passed through the stage of adolescence. Lennox's marriage to Nadine was an adventure. But then, suddenly, all was stale. Lennox is so sunk in melancholy that it is practically impossible to wound or distress him. Raymond and Carol show no signs of rebellion. Ginevra—ah! *la pauvre Ginevra*—she, from her mother's point of view, gives the poorest sport of all. For Ginevra has found a way of escape! She escapes from reality into fantasy. The more her mother goads her, the more easily she gets a secret thrill out of being a persecuted heroine! From Mrs. Boynton's point of view it is all deadly dull. She seeks, like Alexander, new worlds to conquer. And so she plans the voyage abroad. There will be the danger of her tamed beasts rebelling, there will be opportunities for inflicting fresh pain! It sounds absurd, does it not, but it was so! She wanted a new thrill."

Poirot took a deep breath.

"It is perfect, that. Yes, I see exactly what you mean. *It was so.* It all fits in. She chose to live dangerously, *la Maman* Boynton—and she paid the penalty!"

Sarah leaned forward, her pale intelligent face very serious.

"You mean," she said, "that she drove her victims too far and—and they turned on her—or—or one of them did?"

Poirot bowed his head.

Sarah said, and her voice was a little breathless:

"Which of them?"

Poirot looked at her, at her hands clenched fiercely on the wild flowers, at the pale rigidity of her face.

He did not answer—was indeed saved from answering, for at that moment Gerard touched his shoulder and said:

"Look."

A girl was wandering along the side of the hill. She moved with a strange rhythmic grace that somehow gave the impression that she was not quite real. The gold-red of her hair shone in the sunlight, a strange secretive smile lifted the beautiful corners of her mouth.

Poirot drew in his breath.

He said:

"How beautiful . . . How strangely, movingly beautiful . . . That is how Ophelia should be played—like a young goddess straying from another world, happy because she has escaped out of the bondage of human joys and griefs."

"Yes, yes, you are right," said Gerard. "It is a face to dream of, is it not? *I* dreamt of it. In my fever I opened my eyes and saw that face—with its sweet unearthly smile. . . . It was a good dream. I was sorry to wake. . . ."

Then, with a return to his commonplace manner:

"That is Ginevra Boynton," he said.

12

In another minute the girl had reached them.

Dr. Gerard performed the introduction.

"Miss Boynton, this is M. Hercule Poirot."

"Oh!" She looked at him uncertainly. Her fingers joined together, twined themselves uneasily in and out. The enchanted nymph had come back from the country of enchantment. She was now just an ordinary, awkward girl, slightly nervous and ill at ease.

Poirot said:

"It is a piccc of good fortune meeting you here, Mademoiselle. I tried to see you in the hotel."

"Did you?"

Her smile was vacant. Her fingers began plucking at the belt of her dress.

He said gently:

"Will you walk with me a little way?"

She moved docilely enough, obedient to his whim.

Presently she said, rather unexpectedly, in a queer hurried voice:

"You are—you are a detective, aren't you?"

"Yes, Mademoiselle."

"A very well-known detective?"

"The best detective in the world," said Poirot, stating it as a simple truth, no more, no less.

Ginevra Boynton breathed very softly:

"You have come here to protect me?"

Poirot stroked his moustache thoughtfully. He said:

"Are you then in danger, Mademoiselle?"

"Yes, yes." She looked around with a quick suspicious glance. "I told Dr. Gerard about it in Jerusalem. He was very clever. He gave no sign at the time. But he followed me—to that terrible place with the red rocks." She shivered. "They meant to kill me there. I have to be continually on my guard."

Poirot nodded gently and indulgently.

Ginevra Boynton said:

"He is kind—and good. He is in love with me!"

"Yes?"

"Oh, yes. He says my name in his sleep. . . ." Her face softened—again a kind of trembling, unearthly beauty hovered there—"I saw him lying there turning and tossing—and saying my name. . . . I stole away quietly." She paused. "I thought, perhaps, *he* had sent for you? I have a terrible lot of enemies, you know. They are all around me. Sometimes they are *disguised.*"

"Yes, yes," said Poirot gently. "But you are safe here—with all your family around you."

She drew herself up proudly.

"They are *not* my family! I have nothing to do with them. I cannot tell you who I really am—that is a great secret. It would surprise you if you knew."

He said gently:

"Was your mother's death a great shock to you, Mademoiselle?"

Ginevra stamped her foot.

"I tell you—she *wasn't* my mother! My enemies paid her to pretend she was and to see I did not escape!"

"Where were you on the afternoon of her death?"

She answered readily:

"I was in the tent. . . . It was hot in there, but I didn't dare come out. . . . *They* might have got me. . . ." She gave a little quiver. "One of them—looked into my tent. He was disguised, but I knew him. I pretended to be asleep. The Sheikh had sent him. The Sheikh wanted to kidnap me, of course."

For a few moments Poirot walked in silence, then he said:

"They are very pretty, these histories you recount to yourself."

She stopped. She glared at him.

"They're *true.* They're all *true.*" Again she stamped an angry foot.

"Yes," said Poirot, "they are certainly ingenious."

She cried out:

"They are true—*true—*"

Then, angrily, she turned from him and ran down the hillside.

Poirot stood looking after her. In a minute or two he heard a voice close behind him.

"What did you say to her?"

Poirot turned to where Dr. Gerard, a little out of breath, stood beside him. Sarah was coming towards them both, but she came at a more leisurely pace.

Poirot answered Gerard's question.

"I told her," he said, "that she had imagined to herself some pretty stories."

The doctor nodded his head thoughtfully.

"And she was angry! That is a good sign. It shows, you see, that she has not yet completely passed through the door. She still knows that it is *not* the truth! I shall cure her."

"Ah, you are undertaking a cure?"

"Yes. I have discussed the matter with young Mrs. Boynton and her husband. Ginevra will come to Paris and enter one of my clinics. Afterwards she will have her training for the stage."

"The stage?"

"Yes—there is a possibility there for her, of great success. And that is what she needs—what she *must* have! In many essentials she has the same nature as her mother."

"No!" cried Sarah, revolted.

"It seems impossible to you, but certain fundamental traits are the same. They were both born with a great yearning for importance, they both demand that their personalities shall impress! This poor child has been thwarted and suppressed at every turn, she has been given no outlet for her fierce ambition, for her love of life, for the expressing of her vivid romantic personality." He gave a little laugh. *"Nous allons changer tout ça!"*

Then, with a little bow, he murmured:

"You will excuse me?" And he hurried down the hill after the girl.

Sarah said:

"Dr. Gerard is tremendously keen on his job."

"I perceive his keenness," said Poirot.

Sarah said with a frown:

"All the same, I can't bear his comparing her to that horrible old woman —although, once—I felt sorry for Mrs. Boynton myself."

"When was that, Mademoiselle?"

"That time I told you about in Jerusalem. I suddenly felt as though I'd got the whole business wrong. You know that feeling one has sometimes when just for a short time you see everything the other way round? I got all 'het up' about it and went and made a fool of myself!"

"Oh, no—not that!"

Sarah, as always, when she remembered her conversation with Mrs. Boynton, was blushing acutely.

"I felt all exalted as though I had a mission! And then later, when Lady W. fixed a fishy eye on me and said she had seen me talking to Mrs. Boynton, I thought she had probably overheard, and I felt the *most* complete ass."

Poirot said:

"What exactly was it that old Mrs. Boynton said to you? Can you remember the exact words?"

"I think so. They made rather an impression on me. *'I never forget.'* That's what she said. *'Remember that. I've never forgotten anything—not an action, not a name, not a face.'* " Sarah shivered. "She said it so *malevolently*—not even looking at me. I feel—I feel as if, even now, I can hear her. . . ."

Poirot said gently:

"It impressed you very much?"

"Yes. I'm not easily frightened—but sometimes I dream of her saying just these words and I can see her evil, leering, triumphant face. Ugh!"

She gave a quick shiver.

Then she turned suddenly to him.

"M. Poirot, perhaps I ought not to ask, but have you come to a conclusion about this business? Have you found out anything definite?"

"Yes."

He saw her lips tremble as she asked:

"What?"

"I have found out to whom Raymond Boynton spoke that night in Jerusalem. It was to his sister Carol."

"Carol—of course!"

Then she went on:

"Did you tell him—did you ask him—"

It was no use. She could not go on. Poirot looked at her gravely and compassionately. He said quietly:

"It means—so much to you, Mademoiselle?"

"It means just everything!" said Sarah. Then she squared her shoulders. "But I've got to *know.*"

Poirot said quietly:

"He told me that it was a hysterical outburst—no more! That he and his sister were worked up. He told me that in daylight such an idea appeared fantastic to them both."

"I see. . . ."

Poirot said gently:

"Miss Sarah, will you not tell me what it is you fear?"

Sarah turned a white despairing face upon him.

"That afternoon—we were together. And he left me saying—saying he wanted to do something *now*—while he had the courage. I thought he meant just to—to tell her. But supposing he meant . . ."

Her voice died away. She stood rigid, fighting for control.

13

Nadine Boynton came out of the hotel. As she hesitated uncertainly, a waiting figure sprang forward.

Mr. Jefferson Cope was immediately at his lady's side.

"Shall we walk up this way? I think it's the pleasantest."

She acquiesced.

They walked along and Mr. Cope talked. His words came freely, if a trifle monotonously. It is not certain whether he perceived that Nadine was not listening.

As they turned aside onto the stony flower-covered hillside she interrupted him.

"Jefferson, I'm sorry. I've got to talk to you."

Her face had grown pale.

"Why, certainly, my dear. Anything you like, but don't distress yourself."

She said, "You're cleverer than I thought. You know, don't you, what I'm going to say?"

"It is undoubtedly true," said Mr. Cope, "that circumstances alter cases. I do feel, very profoundly, that in the present circumstances, decisions may have to be reconsidered." He sighed. "You've got to go right ahead, Nadine, and do just what you feel."

She said, with real emotion:

"You're so *good,* Jefferson. So patient! I feel I've treated you very badly. I really have been downright mean to you."

"Now, look here, Nadine, let's get this right. I've always known what my limitations were where you were concerned. I've had the deepest affection and respect for you ever since I've known you. All I want is your happiness. That's all I've ever wanted. Seeing you unhappy has very nearly driven me crazy. And I may say that I've blamed Lennox. I've felt that he didn't deserve to keep you if he didn't value your happiness a little more than he seemed to do."

Mr. Cope took a breath and went on:

"Now I'll admit that after traveling with you to Petra, I felt that perhaps

Lennox wasn't quite so much to blame as I thought. He wasn't so much selfish where you were concerned, as too unselfish where his mother was concerned. I don't want to say anything against the dead, but I do think that your mother-in-law was perhaps an unusually difficult woman."

"Yes, I think you may say that," murmured Nadine.

"Anyway," went on Mr. Cope, "you came to me yesterday and told me that you'd definitely decided to leave Lennox. I applauded your decision. It wasn't right—the life you were leading. You were quite honest with me. You didn't pretend to be more than just mildly fond of me. Well, that was all right with me. All I asked was the chance to look after you and treat you as you should be treated. I may say that afternoon was one of the happiest in my life."

Nadine cried out:

"I'm sorry—I'm sorry."

"No, my dear, because all along I had a kind of feeling that it wasn't real. I felt it was quite on the cards that you would have changed your mind by the next morning. Well, things are different now. You and Lennox can lead a life of your own."

Nadine said quietly:

"Yes. I can't leave Lennox. Please forgive me."

"Nothing to forgive," declared Mr. Cope. "You and I will go back to being old friends. We'll just forget about that afternoon."

Nadine placed a gentle hand on his arm.

"Dear Jefferson, thank you. I'm going to find Lennox now."

She turned and left him. Mr. Cope went on alone.

Nadine found Lennox sitting at the top of the Graeco Roman Theatre. He was in such a brown study that he hardly noticed her till she sank breathless at his side.

"Lennox."

"Nadine." He half turned.

She said:

"We haven't been able to talk until now. But you know, don't you, that I am not leaving you?"

He said gravely:

"Did you ever really mean to, Nadine?"

She nodded.

"Yes. You see, it seemed to be the only possible thing left to do. I hoped—I hoped that you would come after me. Poor Jefferson, how mean I have been to him."

Lennox gave a sudden curt laugh.

"No, you haven't. Anyone who is as unselfish as Cope, ought to be given full scope for his nobility! And you were right, you know, Nadine. When you told me that you were going away with him you gave me the shock of my life! You know, honestly, I think I must have been going queer or something lately. Why the hell didn't I snap my fingers in Mother's face and go off with you when you wanted me to?"

She said gently:

"You couldn't, my dear, you couldn't."

Lennox said musingly:

"Mother was a damned queer character. . . . I believe she'd got us all half hypnotized."

"She had."

Lennox mused a minute or two longer. Then he said:

"When you told me that afternoon—it was just like being hit a crack on the head! I walked back half dazed, and then, suddenly I saw what a damned fool I'd been! I realized that there was only one thing to be done if I didn't want to lose you."

He felt her stiffen. His tone became grimmer.

"I went and—"

"Don't . . ."

He gave her a quick glance.

"I went and—argued with her." He spoke with a complete change of tone—careful and rather toneless. "I told her that I'd got to choose between her and you—and that I chose you."

There was a pause.

He repeated, in a tone of curious self-approval:

"Yes, that's what I said to her."

14

Poirot met two people on his way home. The first was Mr. Jefferson Cope.

"M. Hercule Poirot? My name's Jefferson Cope."

The two men shook hands ceremoniously.

Then, falling into step beside Poirot, Mr. Cope explained:

"It's just got around to me that you're making a kind of routine inquiry into the death of my old friend, Mrs. Boynton. That certainly was a shocking business. Of course, mind you, the old lady ought never to have undertaken such a fatiguing journey. But she was headstrong, M. Poirot. Her family could do nothing with her. She was by way of being a household tyrant—had had her own way too long, I guess. It certainly is true that what she said went! Yes, sir, that certainly was true."

There was a momentary pause.

"I'd just like to tell you, M. Poirot, that I'm an old friend of the Boynton family. Naturally, they're all a good deal upset over this business, they're a trifle nervous and highly strung too, you know, so if there are any arrangements to be made—necessary formalities, arrangements for the funeral—transport of the body to Jerusalem—why, I'll take as much trouble as I can off their hands. Just call upon me for anything that needs doing."

"I am sure the family will appreciate your offer," said Poirot. He added: "You are, I think, a special friend of young Mrs. Boynton's."

Mr. Jefferson Cope went a little pink.

"Well, we won't say much about that, M. Poirot. I hear you had an interview with Mrs. Lennox Boynton this morning and she may have given you a hint how things were between us, but that's all over now. Mrs. Boynton is a very fine woman and she feels that her first duty is to her husband in his sad bereavement."

There was a pause. Poirot received the information by a delicate gesture of the head. Then he murmured:

"It is the desire of Colonel Carbury to have a clear statement concerning the afternoon of Mrs. Boynton's death. Can you give me an account of that afternoon?"

"Why, certainly. After our luncheon and a brief rest we set out for a kind of informal tour around. We escaped, I'm glad to say, without that pestilential dragoman. That man's just crazy on the subject of the Jews. I don't think he's quite sane on that point. Anyway, as I was saying, we set out. It was then that I had my interview with Nadine. Afterwards, she wished to be alone with her husband to discuss matters with him. I went off on my own, working gradually back towards the camp. About half way there I met the two English ladies who had been on the morning expedition —one of them's an English peeress, I understand."

Poirot said that such was the case.

"Ah, she's a fine woman, a very powerful intellect and very well informed. The other seemed to me rather a weak sister—and she looked about dead with fatigue. That expedition in the morning was very strenuous for an elderly lady, especially when she doesn't like heights. Well, as I was saying, I met these two ladies and was able to give them some information on the subject of the Nabateans. We went around a bit and got back to the camp about six. Lady Westholme insisted on having tea and I had the pleasure of having a cup with her—the tea was kind of weak but it had an interesting flavor. Then the boys laid the table for supper and sent out for the old lady, only to find that she was sitting there dead in her chair."

"Did you notice her as you walked home?"

"I did just notice she was there—it was her usual seat in the afternoon and evening, but I didn't pay special attention. I was just explaining to Lady Westholme the conditions of our recent slump. I had to keep an eye on Miss Pierce, too. She was so tired she kept turning her ankles."

"Thank you, Mr. Cope. May I be so indiscreet as to ask if Mrs. Boynton is likely to have left a large fortune?"

"A very considerable one. That is to say, strictly speaking, it was not hers to leave. She had a life interest in it and at her death it is divided among the late Elmer Boynton's children. Yes, they will all be very comfortably off now."

"Money," murmured Poirot, "makes a lot of difference. How many crimes have been committed for it!"

Mr. Cope looked a little startled.

"Why, that's so, I suppose," he admitted.

Poirot smiled sweetly and murmured:

"But there are so many motives for murder, are there not? Thank you, Mr. Cope, for your kind cooperation."

"You're welcome, I'm sure," said Mr. Cope. "Do I see Miss King sitting up there? I think I'll go and have a word with her."

Poirot continued to descend the hill.

He met Miss Pierce fluttering up it.

She greeted him breathlessly.

"Oh, M. Poirot, I'm so glad to meet you. I've been talking to that very odd Boynton girl—the youngest one, you know. She has been saying the strangest things—about enemies and some Sheikh who wanted to kidnap her and how she has spies all around her. Really, it sounded *most* romantic! Lady Westholme says it is all nonsense and that she once had a red-headed kitchen maid who told lies just like that, but I think sometimes that Lady Westholme is rather hard. And after all, it might be true, mightn't it, M. Poirot? I read some years ago that one of the Czar's daughters was not killed in the Revolution in Russia but escaped secretly to America. The Grand Duchess Tatiana, I think it was. If so, this *might* be her daughter, mightn't it? She *did* hint at something Royal—and she has a look, don't you think? Rather Slavic—those cheek bones. How thrilling it would be!"

Miss Pierce looked wistful and excited.

Poirot said, somewhat sententiously:

"It is true that there are many strange things in life."

"I didn't really take in this morning who you are," said Miss Pierce, clasping her hands. "Of course you are that *very* famous detective! I read *all* about the A.B.C. case. It was so *thrilling.* I had actually a post as governess near Doncaster at the time."

Poirot murmured something. Miss Pierce went on with growing agitation:

"That is why I felt that perhaps—I had been wrong—this morning. One must always tell *everything,* must one not? Even the *smallest* detail, however unrelated it may *seem.* Because, of course, if *you* are mixed up in this, poor Mrs. Boynton *must* have been murdered! I see that now! I suppose Mr. Mah Mood—I cannot remember his name—but the dragoman, I mean—I suppose he could not be a *Bolshevik agent?* Or even, perhaps, Miss King? I believe many *quite* well brought up young girls of *good* family belong to these dreadful Communists! That's why I wondered if I *ought* to tell you—because, you see, it was rather *peculiar* when one comes to think of it."

"Precisely," said Poirot. "And therefore you will tell me all about it."

"Well, it's not really anything very *much.* It's only that on the next morning after Mrs. Boynton's death I was up rather early—and I looked out of my tent to see the effect of the sunrise, you know—only of course it wasn't actually sunrise because the sun must have risen quite an hour before. But it was *early—*"

"Yes, yes. And you saw?"

"That's the curious thing—at least at the time it didn't *seem* much. It was only that I saw that Boynton girl come out of her tent and fling something right out into the stream—nothing in *that,* of course, but it *glittered*—in the sunlight! As it went through the air. It *glittered,* you know."

"Which Boynton girl was it?"

"I think it was the one they call Carol—a very nice-looking girl—so like her brother—really they might be *twins.* Or, of course, it *might* have been the youngest one. The sun was in my eyes so I couldn't quite see. But I don't think the hair was red—just bronze. I'm so fond of that coppery bronze hair! Red hair always says *carrots* to me!" She tittered.

"And she threw away a brightly glittering object?" said Poirot.

"Yes. And, of course, as I said, I didn't think much of it *at the time.* But later I had walked along the stream and Miss King was there. And there amongst a lot of other very unsuitable things—even a tin or two—I saw a little bright metal box—not an exact square—a sort of long square if you understand what I mean—"

"But, yes, I understand perfectly. About so long?"

"Yes, how *clever* of you! And I thought to myself, 'I suppose *that's* what the Boynton girl threw away, but it's a nice little box.' And just out of curiosity I picked it up and opened it. It had a kind of syringe inside—the same thing they stuck into my arm when I was being inoculated for typhoid. And I thought how curious to throw it away like that because it didn't seem broken or anything. But just as I was wondering, Miss King spoke behind me. I hadn't heard her come up. And she said, 'Oh, thank you—that's my hypodermic. I was coming to look for it.' So I gave it to her and she went back to the camp with it."

Miss Pierce paused and then went on hurriedly:

"And, of course, I expect there is *nothing in it*—only it *did* seem a little curious that Carol Boynton should throw away Miss King's syringe. I mean, it was odd, if you know what I mean. Though of course I expect there is a very good explanation."

She paused, looking expectantly at Poirot.

His face was grave.

"Thank you, Mademoiselle. What you have told me may not be important in itself, but I will tell you this! It completes my case! Everything is now clear and in order."

"Oh, really?" Miss Pierce looked as flushed and pleased as a child.

Poirot escorted her to the hotel.

Back in his own room he added one line to his memorandum: "Point No. 10. *I never forget. Remember that. I've never forgotten anything. . . .*"

He nodded his head.

"Mais oui," he said. "It is all clear now!"

15

"My preparations are complete," said Hercule Poirot.

With a little sigh, he stepped back a pace or two and contemplated his arrangement of one of the unoccupied hotel bedrooms.

Colonel Carbury, leaning inelegantly against the bed which had been pushed against the wall, smiled as he puffed at his pipe.

"Funny feller, aren't you, Poirot?" he said. "Like to dramatize things."

"Perhaps—that is true," admitted the little detective. "But, indeed, it is not all self-indulgence. If one plays a comedy, one must first set the scene."

"Is this a comedy?"

"Even if it is a tragedy—there, too, the *décor* must be correct."

Colonel Carbury looked at him curiously.

"Well," he said. "It's up to you! I don't know what you're driving at. I gather, though, that you've *got* something."

"I shall have the honor to present to you what you asked me for—the truth!"

"Do you think we can get a conviction?"

"That, my friend, I did not promise you."

"True enough. Maybe I'm glad you haven't. It depends."

"My arguments are mainly psychological," said Poirot.

Colonel Carbury sighed.

"I was afraid they might be."

"But they will convince you," Poirot reassured him. "Oh, yes, they will convince you. The truth, I have always thought, is curious and beautiful."

"Sometimes," said Colonel Carbury, "it's damned unpleasant."

"No, no." Poirot was earnest. "You take there the personal view. Take instead, the abstract, the detached point of vision. Then the absolute logic of events is fascinating and orderly."

"I'll try and look on it that way," said the Colonel.

Poirot glanced at his watch, a large grotesque turnip of a watch.

"Family heirloom?" inquired Carbury interestedly.

"But, yes, indeed, it belonged to my grandfather."

"Thought it might have done."

"It is time to commence our proceedings," said Poirot. "You, *mon Colonel,* will sit here behind this table in an official position."

"Oh, all right," Carbury grunted. "You don't want me to put my uniform on, do you?"

"No, no. If you would permit that I straightened your tie."

He suited the action to the word. Colonel Carbury grinned again, sat down in the chair indicated and a moment later, unconsciously, tweaked his tie around under his left ear again.

"Here," continued Poirot, slightly altering the position of the chairs, "we place *la famille Boynton.* And over here," he went on, "we will place the three outsiders who have a definite stake in the case. Dr. Gerard, on whose evidence the case for the prosecution depends. Miss Sarah King, who has two separate interests in the case, a personal one and that of medical examiner. Also M. Jefferson Cope, who was on intimate terms with the Boyntons and so may be definitely described as an interested party."

He broke off.

"Aha—here they come."

He opened the door to admit the party.

Lennox Boynton and his wife came in first. Raymond and Carol followed. Ginevra walked by herself, a faint faraway smile on her lips. Dr. Gerard and Sarah King brought up the rear. Mr. Jefferson Cope was a few minutes late and came in with an apology.

When he had taken his place, Poirot stepped forward.

"Ladies and gentlemen," he said, "this is an entirely informal gathering. It has come about through the accident of my presence in Amman. Colonel Carbury did me the honor to consult me—"

Poirot was interrupted. The interruption came from what was seemingly the most unlikely quarter. Lennox Boynton said suddenly and pugnaciously:

"Why? Why the devil should he bring you into this business?"

Poirot waved a hand gracefully.

"Me, I am often called in in cases of sudden death."

Lennox Boynton said:

"Doctors send for you whenever there is a case of heart failure?"

Poirot said gently:

"Heart failure is such a very loose and unscientific term."

Colonel Carbury cleared his throat. It was an official noise. He spoke in an official tone:

"Best to make it quite clear. Circumstances of death reported to me. Very natural occurrence. Weather unusually hot—journey a very trying one for an elderly lady in bad health. So far all quite clear. But Dr. Gerard came to me and volunteered a statement—"

He looked inquiringly at Poirot. Poirot nodded.

"Dr. Gerard is a very eminent physician with a worldwide reputation. Any statement he makes is bound to be received with attention. Dr. Gerard's statement was as follows: On the morning after Mrs. Boynton's death, he noticed that a certain quantity of a powerful drug acting on the heart was missing from his medical supplies. On the previous afternoon he had noted the disappearance of a hypodermic syringe. Syringe was returned during the night. Final point—there was a puncture on the dead woman's wrist corresponding to the mark of a hypodermic syringe."

Colonel Carbury paused.

"In these circumstances I considered that it was the duty of those in authority to inquire into the matter. M. Hercule Poirot was my guest and very considerately offered his highly specialized services. I gave him full authority to make any investigations he pleased. We are assembled here now to hear his report on the matter."

There was silence—a silence so acute that you could have heard—as the saying is—a pin drop. Actually, somebody in the next room did drop what was probably a shoe. It sounded like a bomb in the hushed atmosphere.

Poirot cast a quick glance at the little group of three people on his right, then turned his gaze to the five people huddled together on his left—a group of people with frightened eyes.

Poirot said quietly:

"When Colonel Carbury mentioned this business to me, I gave him my opinion as an expert. I told him that it might not be possible to bring proof—such proof as would be admissible in a court of law—but I told him very definitely that I was sure I could arrive at the truth—simply by questioning the people concerned. For let me tell you this, my friends, to investigate a crime it is only necessary to let the guilty party or parties *talk*—always, in the end, they tell you what you want to know!"

He paused.

"So, in this case, although you have lied to me, you have also, unwittingly, told me the truth."

He heard a faint sigh, the scrape of a chair on the floor to his right, but he did not look around. He continued to look at the Boyntons.

"First, I examined the possibility of Mrs. Boynton's having died a natural death—and I decided against it. The missing drug—the hypodermic syringe—and above all, the attitude of the dead lady's family all convinced me that that supposition could not be entertained.

"Not only was Mrs. Boynton killed in cold blood—but every member of her family was aware of the fact! Collectively they reacted as guilty parties.

"But there are degrees in guilt. I examined the evidence carefully with a view to ascertaining whether the murder—yes, it was *murder!*—had been committed by the old lady's family *acting on a concerted plan.*

"There was, I may say, overwhelming motive. One and all stood to gain by her death—both in the financial sense—for they would at once attain financial independence and indeed enjoy very considerable wealth—and also in the sense of being freed from what had become an almost insupportable tyranny.

"To continue: I decided, almost immediately, that the concerted theory would not hold water. The stories of the Boynton family did not dovetail neatly into each other, and no system of workable alibis had been arranged. The facts seemed more to suggest that one—or possibly two—members of the family had acted in collusion and that the others were accessories after the fact.

"I next considered which particular member or members were indicated. Here, I may say, I was inclined to be biased by a certain piece of evidence known only to myself."

Here Poirot recounted his experience in Jerusalem.

"Naturally, that pointed very strongly to M. Raymond Boynton as the prime mover in the affair. Studying the family I came to the conclusion that the most likely recipient of his confidences that night would be his sister Carol. They strongly resembled each other in appearance and temperament, and so would have a keen bond of sympathy and they also possessed the nervous rebellious temperament necessary for the conception of such an act. That their motives were partly unselfish—to free the whole family and particularly their younger sister—only made the planning of the deed more plausible."

Poirot paused a minute.

Raymond Boynton half opened his lips, then shut them again. His eyes looked steadily at Poirot with a kind of dumb agony in them.

"Before I go into the case against Raymond Boynton, I would like to read to you a list of significant points which I drew up and submitted to Colonel Carbury this afternoon:

SIGNIFICANT POINTS

1. Mrs. Boynton was taking a mixture containing digitalis.
2. Dr. Gerard missed a hypodermic syringe.

3. Mrs. Boynton took definite pleasure in keeping her family from enjoying themselves with other people.
4. Mrs. Boynton, on the afternoon in question, encouraged her family to go away and leave her.
5. Mrs. Boynton was a mental sadist.
6. The distance from the marquee to the place where Mrs. Boynton was sitting is (roughly) two hundred yards.
7. M. Lennox Boynton said at first he did not know what time he returned to the camp, but later he admitted having set his mother's wrist watch to the right time.
8. Dr. Gerard and Miss Ginevra Boynton occupied tents next door to each other.
9. At half-past six, when dinner was ready, a servant was despatched to announce the fact to Mrs. Boynton.
10. Mrs. Boynton, in Jerusalem, used these words: *'I never forget. Remember that. I've never forgotten anything.'*

"Although I have numbered the points separately, occasionally they can be bracketed in pairs. That is the case, for instance, with the first two. *Mrs. Boynton was taking a mixture containing digitalis. Dr. Gerard had missed a hypodermic syringe.* Those two points were the first thing that struck me about the case, and I may say to you that I found them most extraordinary—and quite irreconcilable. You do not see what I mean? No matter. I will return to the point presently. Let it suffice that I noted those two points as something that had definitely got to be explained satisfactorily.

"I will conclude now with my study of the possibility of Raymond Boynton's guilt. The following are the facts: He had been heard to discuss the possibility of taking Mrs. Boynton's life. He was in a condition of great nervous excitement. He had—Mademoiselle will forgive me"—he bowed apologetically to Sarah—"just passed through a moment of great emotional crisis. That is, he had fallen in love. The exaltation of his feelings might lead him to act in one of several ways. He might feel mellowed and softened towards the world in general, including his step-mother—he might feel the courage at last to defy her and shake off her influence—or he might find just the additional spur to turn his crime from theory to practice. That is the psychology! Let us now examine the *facts.*

"Raymond Boynton left the camp with the others about three-fifteen. Mrs. Boynton was then alive and well. Before long Raymond and Sarah King had a *tête-à-tête* interview. Then he left her. According to him, he returned to the camp at ten minutes to six. He went up to his mother, exchanged a few words with her, then went to his tent and afterwards down to the marquee. He says that at ten minutes to six *Mrs. Boynton was alive and well.*

"But we now come to a fact which directly contradicts that statement. At half-past six Mrs. Boynton's death was discovered by a servant. Miss King, who holds a medical degree, examined her body and she swears definitely that at that time, though she did not pay any special attention to the time when death had occurred, it had *most certainly and decisively* taken place at least an hour (and probably *a good deal* more) before six o'clock.

"We have here, you see, two conflicting statements. Setting aside the possibility that Miss King may have made a mistake—"

Sarah interrupted him.

"I don't make mistakes. That is, if I had, I would admit to it."

Her tone was hard and clear.

Poirot bowed to her politely.

"Then there are only two possibilities—either Miss King or M. Boynton is lying! Let us examine Raymond Boynton's reasons for so doing. Let us assume that Miss King was *not* mistaken and *not* deliberately lying. What then was the sequence of events? Raymond Boynton returns to the camp, sees his mother sitting at the mouth of her cave, goes up to her and finds she is dead. What does he do? Does he call for help? Does he immediately inform the camp of what has happened? No, he waits a minute or two, then passes on to his tent and joins his family in the marquee and *says nothing.* Such conduct is exceedingly curious, is it not?"

Raymond said, in a nervous sharp voice:

"It would be idiotic, of course. That ought to show you that my mother was alive and well, as I've said. Miss King was flustered and upset and made a mistake."

"One asks oneself," said Poirot, calmly sweeping on, "whether there could possibly be a reason for such conduct? It seems, on the face of it, that Raymond Boynton *cannot be guilty,* since at the only time he was known to approach his step-mother that afternoon, *she had already been dead for some time.* Now, supposing, therefore, that Raymond Boynton is *innocent,* can we explain his conduct?

"And I say, that on the assumption that he is innocent, we can! For I remember that fragment of conversation I overheard. *'You do see, don't you, that she's got to be killed?'* He comes back from his walk and finds her dead and at once his guilty memory envisages a certain possibility. The plan has been carried out—not by him—but by his fellow planner. *Tout simplement*—he suspects that his sister, Carol Boynton, is guilty."

"It's a lie," said Raymond in a low trembling voice.

Poirot went on:

"Let us now take the possibility of Carol Boynton being the murderess. What is the evidence against her? She has the same highly-strung temperament—the kind of temperament that might see such a deed colored with heroism. It was she to whom Raymond Boynton was talking that night in Jerusalem. Carol Boynton returned to the camp at ten minutes past five. According to her own story, she went up and spoke to her mother. No one saw her do so. The camp was deserted—the boys were asleep. Lady Westholme, Miss Pierce and M. Cope were exploring caves out of sight of the camp. There was no witness to Carol Boynton's possible action. The time would agree well enough. The case, then, against Carol Boynton, is a perfectly possible one."

He paused. Carol had raised her head. Her eyes looked steadily and sorrowfully into his.

"There is one other point. The following morning, very early, Carol Boynton was seen to throw something into the stream. There is reason to believe that that 'something' was a hypodermic syringe."

"Comment?" Dr. Gerard looked up surprised, "But my hypodermic was *returned.* Yes, yes, I have it now."

Poirot nodded vigorously.

"Yes, yes. This second hypodermic, it is very curious—very interesting. I have been given to understand that this hypodermic belonged to Miss King. Is that so?"

Sarah paused for a fraction of a second.

Carol spoke quickly:

"It was not Miss King's syringe," she said. "It was mine."

"Then you admit throwing it away, Mademoiselle?"

She hesitated just a second.

"Yes, of course. Why shouldn't I?"

"Carol!" It was Nadine. She leaned forward, her eyes wide and distressed. "Carol . . . Oh, I don't understand. . . ."

Carol turned and looked at her. There was something hostile in her glance.

"There's nothing *to* understand! I threw away an old hypodermic. I never touched the—the poison."

Sarah's voice broke in.

"It is quite true what Miss Pierce told you, M. Poirot. It *was* my syringe."

Poirot smiled.

"It is very confusing, this affair of the hypodermic—and yet, I think, it could be explained. Ah, well, we have now two cases made out—the case for the innocence of Raymond Boynton—the case for the guilt of his sister Carol. But me, I am scrupulously fair. I look always on both sides. Let us examine what occurred if Carol Boynton was innocent.

"She returns to the camp, she goes up to her step-mother, and she finds her—shall we say—dead! What is the first thing she will think? She will suspect that her brother Raymond may have killed her. She does not know what to do. So she says nothing. And presently, about an hour later, Raymond Boynton returns and, having presumably spoken to his mother, *says nothing of anything being amiss.* Do you not think that then her suspicions would become certainties? Perhaps she goes to his tent and finds there a hypodermic syringe. Then, indeed she is *sure!* She takes it quickly and hides it. Early in the morning she flings it as far away as she can.

"There is one more indication that Carol Boynton is innocent. She assures me, when I question her, that she and her brother never seriously intended to carry out their plan. I ask her to swear—and she swears immediately and with the utmost solemnity that she is not guilty of the crime! You see, that is the way she puts it. She does not swear that *they* are not guilty. She swears for *herself,* not her brother—and thinks that I will not pay special attention to the pronoun.

"Eh bien, that is the case for the innocence of Carol Boynton. And now let us go back a step and consider not the innocence but—the possible guilt of Raymond. Let us suppose that Carol is speaking the truth, that Mrs. Boynton was alive at five-ten. Under what circumstances can Raymond be guilty? We can suppose that he killed his mother at ten minutes to six when he went up to speak to her. There were boys about the camp, true, but the light was failing. It might have been managed but it then follows that Miss King lied. Remember, she came back to the camp only five minutes after Raymond. From the distance she would see him go up to his mother. Then, when later she is found dead, Miss King realizes that *Raymond has killed her,* to save him, she lies—knowing that Dr. Gerard is down with fever and cannot expose her lie!"

"I did *not* lie!" said Sarah clearly.

"There is yet another possibility. Miss King, as I have said, reached the camp a few minutes after Raymond. If Raymond Boynton found his mother alive, it may have been *Miss King* who administered the fatal injection. She believed that Mrs. Boynton was fundamentally evil. She may have seen herself as a just executioner. That would equally well explain her lying about the time of death."

Sarah had grown very pale. She spoke in a low steady voice:

"It is true that I spoke of the expediency of one person dying to save many. It was the Place of Sacrifice that suggested the idea to me. But I can swear to you that I never harmed that disgusting old woman—nor would the idea of doing so ever have entered my head!"

"And yet," said Poirot softly, "one of you two *must be lying.*"

Raymond Boynton shifted in his chair. He cried out impetuously:

"You win, M. Poirot! I'm the liar. Mother was dead when I went up to her. It—it quite knocked me out. You see, I'd been going to have it out with her. To tell her that from henceforth I was a free agent. I was—all set, you understand. And there she was—dead! Her hand all cold and flabby. And I thought—just what you said. I thought maybe Carol—you see, there was the mark on her wrist—"

Poirot said quickly:

"That is the one point on which I am not yet completely informed. What was the method you counted on employing? You *had* a method—and it was connected with a hypodermic syringe. That much I know. If you want me to believe you, you must tell me the rest."

Raymond said hurriedly:

"It was a way I read in a book—an English detective story—you stuck an empty hypodermic syringe into someone and it did the trick. It sounded perfectly scientific. I—I thought we'd do it that way."

"Ah," said Poirot. "I comprehend. And you purchased a syringe?"

"No. As a matter of fact, we pinched Nadine's."

Poirot shot a quick look at her.

"The syringe that is in your baggage in Jerusalem?" he murmured.

A faint color showed in the young woman's face.

"I—I wasn't sure what had become of it," she said.

Poirot murmured:

"You are so quick-witted, Madame."

16

There was a pause. Then, clearing his throat with a slightly affected sound, Poirot went on:

"We have now solved the mystery of what I might term *the second hypodermic.* That belonged to Mrs. Lennox Boynton, was taken by Raymond Boynton before leaving Jerusalem, was taken from Raymond by Carol after the discovery of Mrs. Boynton's dead body, was thrown away by her, found by Miss Pierce, and claimed by Miss King as hers. I presume Miss King has it now."

"I have," said Sarah.

"So that when you said it was yours just now, you were doing what you told us you do not do—you told a lie."

Sarah said calmly:

"That's a different kind of lie. It isn't—it isn't a *professional* lie."

Gerard nodded appreciation.

"Yes, it is a point that. I understand you perfectly, Mademoiselle."

"Thanks," said Sarah.

Again Poirot cleared his throat:

"Let us now review our time table: Thus:

Boyntons and Jefferson Cope leave the camp	3:05 (approx.)
Dr. Gerard and Sarah King leave the camp	3:15 (approx.)
Lady Westholme and Miss Pierce leave the camp	4:15
Dr. Gerard returns to camp	4:20 (approx.)
Lennox Boynton returns to camp	4:35
Nadine Boynton returns to camp and talks to Mrs. Boynton	4:40 (approx.)
Nadine Boynton leaves her mother-in-law and goes to marquee	4:50 (approx.)
Carol Boynton returns to camp	5:10
Lady Westholme, Miss Pierce and M. Jefferson Cope return to camp	5:40
Raymond Boynton returns to camp	5:50

Sarah King returns to camp	6:00
Body discovered	6:30

"There is, you will notice, a gap of twenty minutes between four-fifty, when Nadine Boynton left her mother-in-law, and five-ten when Carol returned. Therefore, if Carol is speaking the truth, Mrs. Boynton must have been killed in that twenty minutes.

"Now who could have killed her? At that time Miss King and Raymond Boynton were together. Mr. Cope (not that he had any perceivable motive for killing her) has an alibi. He was with Lady Westholme and Miss Pierce. Lennox Boynton was with his wife in the marquee. Dr. Gerard was groaning with fever in his tent. The camp is deserted, the boys are asleep. It is a suitable moment for a crime! Was there a person who could have committed it?"

His eyes went thoughtfully to Ginevra Boynton.

"There was one person. Ginevra Boynton was in her tent all the afternoon. That is what we have been told—but actually there is evidence that she was *not* in her tent all the time: Ginevra Boynton made a very significant remark. She said that Dr. Gerard spoke her name in his fever. And Dr. Gerard has also told us that he dreamt in his fever of Ginevra Boynton's face. But it was not a dream! It was actually her face he saw, standing there by his bed. He thought it an effect of fever—but it was the truth. Ginevra was in Dr. Gerard's tent. Is it not possible that she had come to put back the hypodermic syringe after using it?"

Ginevra Boynton raised her head with its crown of red-gold hair. Her wide beautiful eyes stared at Poirot. They were singularly expressionless. She looked like a vague saint.

"Ah ça, non!" cried Dr. Gerard.

"Is it then so psychologically impossible?" inquired Poirot.

The Frenchman's eyes dropped.

Nadine Boynton said sharply:

"It's quite impossible!"

Poirot's eyes came quickly round to her.

"Impossible, Madame?"

"Yes." She paused, bit her lip, then went on: "I will not hear of such a disgraceful accusation against my young sister-in-law. We—all of us—know it to be impossible."

Ginevra moved a little on her chair. The lines of her mouth relaxed into a smile—the touching, innocent, half-unconscious smile of a very young girl.

Nadine said again:

"Impossible."

Her gentle face had hardened into lines of determination. The eyes that met Poirot's were hard and unflinching.

Poirot leaned forward in what was half a bow.

"Madame is very intelligent," he said.

Nadine said quietly:

"What do you mean by that, M. Poirot?"

"I mean, Madame, that all along I have realized you have what I believe is called an 'excellent headpiece.' "

"You flatter me."

"I think not. All along you have envisaged the situation calmly and collectedly. You have remained on outwardly good terms with your husband's mother, deeming that the best thing to be done, but inwardly you have judged and condemned her. I think that some time ago you realized that the only chance for your husband's happiness was for him to make an effort to leave home—strike out on his own, no matter how difficult and penurious such a life might be. You were willing to take all risks and you endeavored to influence him to exactly that course of action. But you failed, Madame. Lennox Boynton had no longer *the will to freedom.* He was content to sink into a condition of apathy and melancholy.

"Now, I have no doubt at all, Madame, but that you love your husband. Your decision to leave him was not actuated by a greater love for another man. It was, I think, a desperate venture undertaken as a last hope. A woman in your position could only try three things. She could try appeal. That, as I have said, failed. She could threaten to leave her husband. But it is possible that even that threat would not have moved Lennox Boynton. It would plunge him deeper in misery but it would not cause him to rebel. There was one last desperate throw. *You could go away with another man.* Jealousy and the instinct of possession are two of the most deeply rooted fundamental instincts in man. You showed your wisdom in trying to reach that deep, underground, savage instinct. If Lennox Boynton would let you go to another man without an effort—then he must indeed be beyond human aid, and you might as well then try to make a new life for yourself elsewhere.

"But let us suppose that even that last desperate remedy failed. Your husband was terribly upset at your decision, but in spite of that he did not, as you had hoped, react as a primitive man might have done, with an uprush of the possessive instinct. Was there anything at all that could save your husband from his own rapidly failing mental condition? Only one thing. *If his step-mother were to die,* it might not be too late. He might be able to start life anew as a free man, building up in himself independence and manliness once more."

Poirot paused, then repeated gently:

"If your mother-in-law were to die . . ."

Nadine's eyes were still fixed on his. In an unmoved gentle voice she said:

"You are suggesting that I helped to bring that event about, are you not? But you cannot do so, M. Poirot. After I had broken the news of my impending departure to Mrs. Boynton, I went straight to the marquee and joined Lennox. I did not leave there again until my mother-in-law was found dead. Guilty of her death I may be, in the sense that I gave her a shock—that of course presupposes a natural death. But if, as you say—(though so far you have no direct evidence of it and cannot have until an autopsy has taken place)—she was deliberately killed, then I had no opportunity of doing so."

Poirot said: "You did not leave the marquee again until your mother-in-law was found dead? That is what you have just said. That, Mrs. Boynton, was one of the points I found curious about this case."

"What do you mean?"

"It is here on my list. Point 9. At half-past six, when dinner was ready, a servant was despatched to announce the fact to Mrs. Boynton."

Raymond said:

"I don't understand."

Carol said:

"No more do I."

Poirot looked from one to the other of them.

"You do not, eh? 'A servant was sent'—why a *servant?* Were you not, all of you, most assiduous in your attendance on the old lady as a general rule? Did not one or another of you always escort her to meals? She was infirm. It was difficult for her to rise from a chair without assistance. Always one or another of you was at her elbow. I suggest then, that on dinner being announced, the natural thing would have been for one or another of her family to go out and help her. But not one of you offered to do so. You all sat there, paralyzed, watching each other, wondering perhaps, why no one went."

Nadine said sharply:

"All this is absurd, M. Poirot! We were all tired that evening. We ought to have gone, I admit, but—on that evening—we just didn't!"

"Precisely—precisely—*on that particular evening!* You, Madame, did perhaps more waiting on her than anyone else. It was one of the duties that you accepted mechanically. But that evening you did not offer to go out to help her in. Why? That is what I asked myself—why? And I tell you my answer. *Because you knew quite well that she was dead. . . .*

"No, no, do not interrupt me, Madame." He raised an impassioned hand. "You will now listen to me—Hercule Poirot! There were witnesses to your conversation with your mother-in-law. Witnesses who could *see* but who could not *hear!* Lady Westholme and Miss Pierce were a long way off. They saw you *apparently* having a conversation with your mother-in-law, but what actual evidence is there of what occurred? I will propound to you instead a little theory. You have brains, Madame. If in your quiet, unhurried fashion you have decided on—shall we say the *elimination* of your husband's mother?—you will carry it out with intelligence and with due preparation. You have access to Dr. Gerard's tent during his absence on the morning excursion. You are fairly sure that you will find a suitable drug. Your nursing training helps you there. You choose digitoxin—the same kind of drug that the old lady is taking. You also take his hypodermic syringe since, to your annoyance, your own has disappeared. You hope to replace the latter before the doctor notices its absence.

"Before proceeding to carry out your plan, you make one last attempt to stir your husband into action. You tell him of your intention to marry Jefferson Cope. Though your husband is terribly upset, he does not react as you had hoped—so you are forced to put your plan of murder into action. You return to the camp, exchanging a pleasant natural word with Lady Westholme and Miss Pierce as you pass. You go up to where your mother-in-law is sitting. You have the syringe with the drug in it ready. It is easy to seize her wrist and—proficient as you are with your nurse's training—force home the plunger. It is done before your mother-in-law realizes what you are doing. From far down the valley the others only see you talking to her, bending over her. Then, deliberately, you go and fetch a chair and sit there, apparently engaged in an amicable conversation for some minutes. Death must have been almost instantaneous. It is a dead woman to whom you sit talking, but who shall guess that? Then you put away the chair and go down to the marquee where you find your husband reading a book. And you are careful not to leave that marquee! Mrs. Boynton's death, you are sure, will be put down to heart trouble. (It will, indeed, be *due* to heart trouble.) In only one thing have your plans gone astray. You cannot return the syringe to Dr. Gerard's tent because the doctor is in there shivering with malaria—and although you do not know it, he has *already missed the syringe.* That, Madame, was the flaw in an otherwise perfect crime."

There was silence—a moment's dead silence—then Lennox Boynton sprang to his feet.

"No!" he shouted. "That's a damned lie. Nadine did nothing. She couldn't have done anything. My mother—my mother was already dead."

"Ah!" Poirot's eyes came gently around to him. "So, after all, it was *you* who killed her, M. Boynton?"

Again a moment's pause—then Lennox dropped back into his chair and raised trembling hands to his face.

"Yes—that's right—I killed her."

"You took the digitoxin from Dr. Gerard's tent?"

"Yes."

"When?"

"As—as—you said—in the morning."

"And the syringe?"

"The syringe? Yes."

"Why did you kill her?"

"Can you ask?"

"I *am* asking, M. Boynton!"

"But you *know* my wife was leaving me—with Cope—"

"Yes, but you only learned that in the *afternoon!*"

Lennox stared at him.

"Of course. When we were out—"

"But you took the poison and the syringe in the *morning—before* you knew?"

"Why the hell do you badger me with questions?— He paused and passed a shaking hand across his forehead. "What does it matter, anyway?"

"It matters a great deal. I advise you, M. Lennox Boynton, to tell me the truth."

"The truth?"

Lennox stared at him.

Nadine suddenly turned abruptly in her chair and gazed into her husband's face.

"That is what I said—the truth."

"By God, I will," said Lennox suddenly. "But I don't know whether you will believe me." He drew a deep breath. "That afternoon, when I left Nadine, I was absolutely all to pieces. I'd never dreamed she'd go from me to someone else. I was—I was nearly mad! I felt as though I was drunk or recovering from a bad illness."

Poirot nodded. He said:

"I noted Lady Westholme's description of your gait when you passed her. That is why I knew your wife was not speaking the truth when she said she told you *after* you were both back at the camp. Continue, M. Boynton."

"I hardly knew what I was doing. . . . But as I got near, my brain seemed to clear. It flashed over me that I had only myself to blame! I'd been a miserable worm! I ought to have defied my step-mother and cleared out years ago. And it came to me that it mightn't be too late even now. There she was, the old devil, sitting up like an obscene idol against the red cliffs. I went right up to have it out with her. I meant to tell her just what I thought and to announce that I was clearing out. I had a wild idea I might get away at once that evening—clear out with Nadine and get as far as Ma'an anyway that night."

"Oh, Lennox—my dear—"

It was a long soft sigh.

He went on:

"And then, my God—you could have struck me down with a touch! She was dead. Sitting there—dead. . . . I—I didn't know what to do—I was dumb—dazed. Everything I was going to shout out at her bottled up inside me—turning to lead—I can't explain. . . . Stone—that's what it felt like —being turned to stone. I did something mechanically—I picked up her wrist watch (it was lying in her lap) and put it around her wrist—her horrid, limp, dead wrist." . . .

He shuddered.

"God!—It was awful! Then I stumbled down, went into the marquee. I ought to have called someone, I suppose—but I couldn't. I just sat there, turning the pages—waiting. . . ."

He stopped.

"You won't believe that—you can't. Why didn't I call someone? Tell Nadine? I don't know."

Dr. Gerard cleared his throat.

"Your statement is perfectly plausible, M. Boynton," he said. "You were in a bad nervous condition. Two severe shocks administered in rapid succession would be quite enough to put you in the condition you have described. It is the Weissenhalter reaction—best exemplified in the case of a bird that has dashed its head against a window. Even after its recovery it refrains instinctively from all action—giving itself time to readjust the nerve centers—I do not express myself well in English, but what I mean is this: *You could not have acted any other way.* Any decisive action of any kind would have been quite impossible for you! You passed through a period of mental paralysis."

He turned to Poirot.

"I assure you, my friend, that is so!"

"Oh, I do not doubt it," said Poirot. "There was a little fact I had already noted—the fact that M. Boynton had replaced his mother's wrist watch—that was capable of two explanations—it might have been a cover for the actual deed, or it might have been observed and misinterpreted by young Mrs. Boynton. She returned only five minutes after her husband. She must therefore have seen that action. When she got up to her mother-in-law and found her dead, with the mark of a hypodermic syringe on her wrist, she would naturally jump to the conclusion that her husband had committed the deed—that her announcement of her decision to leave him had produced a reaction in him different from that for which she had hoped. Briefly. Nadine Boynton believed that she had inspired her husband to commit murder."

He looked at Nadine.

"That is so, Madame?"

She bowed her head.

Then she asked:

"Did you *really* suspect me, M. Poirot?"

"I thought you were a possibility, Madame."

She leaned forward.

"And now? *What really happened, M. Poirot?"*

17

"What really happened?" Poirot repeated.

He reached behind him, drew forward a chair and sat down. His manner was now friendly—informal.

"It is a question, is it not? For the digitoxin *was* taken—the syringe *was* missing—there *was* the mark of a hypodermic on Mrs. Boynton's wrist.

"It is true that in a few days' time we shall know definitely—the autopsy will tell us—whether Mrs. Boynton died of an overdose of digitalis or not. But then it may be too late! It would be better to reach the truth tonight—while the murderer is here under our hand."

Nadine raised her head sharply.

"You mean that you still believe—that one of us—here in this room—" Her voice died away.

Poirot was slowly nodding to himself.

"The truth—that is what I promised Colonel Carbury. And so, having cleared our path we are back again where I was earlier in the day, writing down a list of printed facts and being faced straight away with two glaring inconsistencies."

Colonel Carbury spoke for the first time.

"Suppose, now, we hear what they are?" he suggested.

Poirot said with dignity:

"I am about to tell you. We will take once more those first two facts on my list. *Mrs. Boynton was taking a mixture of digitalis* and *Dr. Gerard missed a hypodermic syringe.* Take those facts and set them against the undeniable fact with which I was immediately confronted—that the Boynton family showed unmistakably guilty reactions. It would seem therefore certain that one of the Boynton family *must* have committed the crime! And yet those two facts I mentioned were all *against* that theory. For, see you, to take a concentrated solution of digitalis—that, yes, it is a clever idea, because Mrs. Boynton was already taking the drug. But what would a member of her family do then? *Ah, ma foi!* There was only one sensible thing to do. Put the poison *into her bottle of medicine!* That is what anyone

—anyone with a grain of sense *and who had access to the medicine*—would certainly do!

"Sooner or later Mrs. Boynton takes a dose and dies—and even if the digitoxin is discovered in the bottle it may be set down as a mistake of the chemist who made it up. Certainly nothing can be *proved!*

"Why, then, *the theft of the hypodermic needle?*

"There can be only two explanations of that—either Dr. Gerard overlooked the syringe and it was never stolen, or else the syringe was taken because the murderer had *not* got access to the medicine—that is to say, the murderer was *not* a member of the Boynton family. Those two first facts point overwhelmingly to an *outsider* as having committed the crime!

"I saw that—but I was puzzled, as I say, by the strong evidences of guilt displayed by the Boynton family. Was it possible that, *in spite of that consciousness of guilt,* the Boyntons were *innocent?* I set out to prove—not the guilt—but the *innocence* of those people!

"That is where we stand now. The murder was committed by an outsider —that is, *by someone who was not sufficiently intimate with Mrs. Boynton to enter her tent or to handle her medicine bottle.*"

He paused.

"There are three people in this room who are, technically, outsiders, but who have a definite connection with the case.

"M. Cope whom we will consider first, has been closely associated with the Boynton family for some time. Can we discover motive and opportunity on his part? It seems not. Mrs. Boynton's death has affected him adversely—since it has brought about the frustration of certain hopes. Unless M. Cope's motive was an almost fanatical desire to benefit others, we can find no reason for his desiring Mrs. Boynton's death. Unless, of course, there is a motive about which we are entirely in the dark. We do not know exactly what M. Cope's dealings with the Boynton family have been."

Mr. Cope said, with dignity:

"This seems to me a little far-fetched, M. Poirot. You must remember, I had absolutely no opportunity for committing this deed, and in any case, I hold very strong views as to the sanctity of human life."

"Your position certainly seems impeccable," said Poirot with gravity. "In a work of fiction you would be strongly suspected on that account."

He turned a little in his chair.

"We now come to Miss King. Miss King had a certain amount of motive and she had the necessary medical knowledge and is a person of character and determination, but since she left the camp before three-thirty with the others and did not return to it until six o'clock, it seems difficult to see where she could have had an opportunity.

"Next we must consider Dr. Gerard. Now, here we must take into account the actual time that the murder was committed. According to M. Lennox Boynton's last statement, his mother was dead at four-thirty-five. According to Lady Westholme and Miss Pierce she was alive at four-fifteen, when they started on their walk. That leaves *exactly twenty minutes* unaccounted for. Now, as these two ladies walked *away* from the camp, Dr. Gerard passed them going to it. There is no one to say *what Dr. Gerard's movements were when he reached the camp* because the two ladies' *backs* were towards it. They were walking *away* from it. *Therefore it is perfectly possible for Dr. Gerard to have committed the crime.* Being a doctor, he could easily counterfeit the appearance of malaria. There is, I should say, a possible motive. Dr. Gerard might have wished to save a certain person whose reason (perhaps more vital a loss than loss of life) was in danger and he may have considered the sacrifice of an old and worn out life worth it!"

"Your ideas," said Dr. Gerard, "are fantastic!"

He smiled amiably.

Without taking any notice, Poirot went on.

"But if so, *why did Gerard call attention to the possibility of foul play?* It is quite certain that, but for his statement to Colonel Carbury, Mrs. Boynton's death would have been put down to natural causes. It was *Dr. Gerard* who first pointed out the possibility of murder. That, my friends," said Poirot, "does not make common sense!"

"Doesn't seem to," said Colonel Carbury gruffly.

He looked curiously at Poirot.

"There is one more possibility," said Poirot. "Mrs. Lennox Boynton just now negatived strongly the possibility of her young sister-in-law being guilty. The force of her objection lay in the fact that she knew her mother-in-law to be dead at the time. But remember this: Ginevra Boynton was at the camp all the afternoon. And there was a moment—a moment when Lady Westholme and Miss Pierce were walking away from the camp and before Dr. Gerard had returned to it . . ."

Ginevra stirred. She leaned forward, staring into Poirot's face with a strange, innocent, puzzled stare.

"*I* did it? You think I did it?"

Then suddenly, with a movement of swift, incomparable beauty, she was up from her chair and had flung herself across the room and down on her knees beside Dr. Gerard, clinging to him, gazing up passionately into his face.

"No! no! Don't let them say it! They're making the walls close around me again! It's not true! I never did anything! They are my enemies—they want to put me in prison—to shut me up. You *must* help me! *You* must help me!"

"There, there, my child." Gently the doctor patted her head. Then he addressed Poirot.

"What you say is nonsense—absurd."

"Delusions of persecution?" murmured Poirot.

"Yes—but she could never have done it that way. She would have done it, you must perceive, *dramatically*—a dagger—something flamboyant—spectacular—never this cool, calm logic! I tell you, my friends, it is *so*. This was a reasoned crime—a sane crime."

Poirot smiled. Unexpectedly he bowed.

"Je suis entièrement de votre avis," he said smoothly.

18

"Come," said Hercule Poirot. "We have still a little way to go! Dr. Gerard has invoked the psychology. So let us now examine the psychological side of the case. We have taken the *facts,* we have established a *chronological sequence of events,* we have heard the *evidence.* There remains—the psychology. And the most important psychological evidence concerns the dead woman—it is the psychology of Mrs. Boynton herself that is the most important thing in this case.

"Take from my list of specified facts point three and four. *Mrs. Boynton took definite pleasure in keeping her family from enjoying themselves with other people. Mrs. Boynton, on the afternoon in question, encouraged her family to go away and leave her.*

"These two facts, they contradict each other flatly! Why, on this particular afternoon, should Mrs. Boynton suddenly display a complete reversal of her usual policy? Was it that she felt a sudden warmth of the heart—an instinct of benevolence? That, it seems to me from all I have heard, was extremely unlikely! Yet there must have been a *reason.* What was that reason?

"Let us examine closely the character of Mrs. Boynton. There have been many different accounts of her. She was a tyrannical old martinet—she was a mental sadist—she was an incarnation of evil—she was crazy. Which of these views is the true one?

"I think myself that Sarah King came nearest to the truth when in a flash of inspiration in Jerusalem she saw the old lady as intensely pathetic. But not only pathetic—*futile!*

"Let us, if we can, think ourselves into the mental condition of Mrs. Boynton. A human creature born with immense ambition, with a yearning to dominate and to impress her personality on other people. She neither sublimated that intense craving for power—nor did she seek to master it—no, *mesdames and messieurs—she fed it!* But in the end—listen well to this—in the *end,* what did it amount to? She was not a great power! She was not feared and hated over a wide area! *She was the petty tyrant of one isolated family!* And as Dr. Gerard said to me—she became bored like any other old lady with her hobby and she sought to extend her activities and to amuse herself by making her dominance more precarious! But that led to an entirely different aspect of the case! By coming abroad, she realized for the first time how extremely insignificant she was!

"And now we come directly to point number ten—the words spoken to Sarah King in Jerusalem. Sarah King, you see, had put her finger on the truth. She had revealed fully and uncompromisingly the pitiful futility of Mrs. Boynton's scheme of existence! And now listen very carefully—all of you—to what her exact words to Miss King were. Miss King has said that Mrs. Boynton spoke *'so malevolently—not even looking at me.'* And this is what she actually said: *'I've never forgotten anything—not an action, not a name, not a face.'*

"Those words made a great impression on Miss King. Their extraordinary intensity and the loud hoarse tone in which they were uttered! So strong was the impression they left on her mind I think that she quite failed to realize their extraordinary significance!

"Do you see that significance, any of you?" He waited a minute. "It seems not. . . . But, *mes amis,* does it escape you that those words *were not a reasonable answer at all* to what Miss King had just been saying. *'I've never forgotten anything—not an action, not a name, not a face.'* It does not make *sense!* If she had said: 'I never forget impertinence'—something of that kind—but no—*a face* is what she said. . . .

"Ah!" cried Poirot, beating his hands together. "But it leaps to the eye! Those words, ostensibly spoken to Miss King, *were not meant for Miss King at all!* They were addressed to *someone else* standing *behind* Miss King."

He paused, noting their expressions.

"Yes, it leaps to the eye! That was, I tell you, a psychological moment in Mrs. Boynton's life! She had been *exposed to herself* by an intelligent young woman! She was full of baffled fury—and at that moment she *recognized* someone—a *face* from the past—a victim delivered bound into her hands!

"We are back, you see, to the *outsider!* And *now* the meaning of Mrs. Boynton's unexpected amiability on the afternoon of her death is clear. *She wanted to get rid of her family because*—to use a vulgarity—*she had other fish to fry!* She wanted the field left clear for an interview with a new victim. . . .

"Now, from that new standpoint, let us consider the events of the afternoon! The Boynton family goes off. Mrs. Boynton sits up by her cave. Now, let us consider very carefully the evidence of Lady Westholme and Miss Pierce. The latter is an unreliable witness, she is unobservant and very suggestible. Lady Westholme, on the other hand, is perfectly clear as to her facts and meticulously observant. Both ladies agree on *one* fact! An *Arab, one of the servants, approaches Mrs. Boynton, angers her in some way and retires hastily.* Lady Westholme states definitely that the servant had first been into the tent occupied by Ginevra Boynton but you may remember that *Dr. Gerard's* tent was next door to Ginevra's. It is possible that it was *Dr. Gerard's* tent the Arab entered. . . ."

Colonel Carbury said:

"D'you mean to tell me that one of those Bedouin fellows of mine murdered an old lady by sticking her with a hypodermic? Fantastic!"

"Wait, Colonel Carbury; I have not yet finished. Let us agree that the Arab *might* have come from Dr. Gerard's tent and not Ginevra Boynton's. What is the next thing? Both ladies agree that they could not see his face clearly enough to identify him and that they did not hear what was said. That is understandable. The distance between the marquee and the ledge is about two hundred yards. Lady Westholme gave a clear description of the man otherwise, describing in detail his ragged breeches and the untidiness with which his puttees were rolled."

Poirot leaned forward.

"And that, my friends, *was very odd indeed!* Because, if she *could not see his face* or hear what was said, *she could not possibly have noticed the state of his breeches and puttees!* Not at two hundred yards!

"It was an error, that, you see! It suggested a curious idea to me. *Why* insist so on the ragged breeches and untidy puttees. Could it be because the breeches were *not* torn and the *puttees were non-existent?* Lady Westholme and Miss Pierce both saw the man—but from where they were sitting *they could not see each other.* That is shown by the fact that Lady Westholme *came to see* if Miss Pierce was awake and found her sitting in the entrance of her tent."

"Good Lord," said Colonel Carbury, suddenly sitting up very straight. "Are you suggesting—"

"I am suggesting that having ascertained just what Miss Pierce (the only witness likely to be awake) was doing, Lady Westholme returned to her tent, put on her riding breeches, boots and khaki colored coat, made herself an Arab head-dress with her checked duster and a skein of knitting wool and that, thus attired, she went boldly up to Dr. Gerard's tent, looked in his medicine chest, selected a suitable drug, took the hypodermic, filled it and went boldly up to her victim.

"Mrs. Boynton may have been dozing. Lady Westholme was quick. She caught her by the wrist and injected the stuff. Mrs. Boynton half cried out —tried to rise—then sank back. The 'Arab' hurried away with every evidence of being ashamed and abashed. Mrs. Boynton shook her stick, tried to rise, then fell back into her chair.

"Five minutes later Lady Westholme rejoins Miss Pierce and comments on the scene she has just witnessed, *impressing her own version of it on the other.* Then they go for a walk, pausing below the ledge where Lady Westholme shouts up to the old lady. She receives no answer for Mrs. Boynton is dead—but she remarks to Miss Pierce: *'Very rude just to snort at us like that!"* Miss Pierce accepts the suggestion—she has often heard Mrs. Boynton receive a remark with a snort—she will swear quite sincerely if necessary that she actually *heard* it. Lady Westholme has sat on committees often enough with women of Miss Pierce's type to know exactly how her own eminence and masterful personality can influence them. The only point where her plan went astray was the replacing of the syringe. Dr. Gerard returning so soon upset her scheme. She hoped he might not have noticed its absence, or might think he had overlooked it, and she put it back during the night."

He stopped.

Sarah said:

"But *why?* Why should Lady Westholme want to kill old Mrs. Boynton?"

"Did you not tell me that Lady Westholme had been quite near you in Jerusalem when you spoke to Mrs. Boynton? It was to Lady Westholme that Mrs. Boynton's words were addressed. *'I've never forgotten anything—not an action, not a name, not a face.'* Put that with the fact that Mrs. Boynton *had been a wardress in a prison* and you can get a very shrewd idea of the truth. Lord Westholme met his wife on a voyage back from *America.* Lady Westholme, before her marriage, had been a criminal and had served a prison sentence.

"You see the terrible dilemma she was in? Her career, her ambitions, her social position—all at stake! What the crime was for which she served a sentence in prison we do not yet know (though we soon shall) but it must have been one that would effectually blast her political career if it was made public. And remember this, *Mrs. Boynton was not an ordinary blackmailer.* She did not want money. She wanted the pleasure of torturing her victim for a while and then she would have enjoyed revealing the truth in the most spectacular fashion! No; while Mrs. Boynton lived, Lady Westholme was not safe. She obeyed Mrs. Boynton's instructions to meet her at Petra (I thought it strange all along that a woman with such a sense of her own importance as Lady Westholme should have preferred to travel as a mere tourist), but in her own mind she was doubtless revolving ways and means of murder. She saw her chance and carried it out boldly. She only made two slips. One was to say a little too much—the description of the torn breeches—which first drew my attention to her, and the other was when she mistook Dr. Gerard's tent and looked first into the one where Ginevra was lying half asleep. Hence the girl's story—half make believe, half true—of a Sheikh in disguise. She put it the wrong way around, obeying her instinct to distort the truth by making it more dramatic, but the indication was quite significant enough for me."

He paused.

"But we shall soon know. I obtained Lady Westholme's fingerprints today without her being aware of the fact. If these are sent to the prison where Mrs. Boynton was once a wardress, we shall soon know the truth when they are compared with the files."

He stopped.

In the momentary stillness a sharp sound was heard.

"What's that?" asked Dr. Gerard.

"Sounded like a shot to me," said Colonel Carbury, rising to his feet quickly. "In the next room. Who's got that room, by the way?"

Poirot murmured:

"I have a little idea—it is the room of Lady Westholme. . . ."

EPILOGUE

Extract from the *Evening Shout.*

We regret to announce the death of Lady Westholme, M.P., the result of a tragic accident. Lady Westholme, who was fond of traveling in out of the way countries, always took a small revolver with her. She was cleaning this when it went off accidentally and killed her. Death was instantaneous. The deepest sympathy will be felt for Lord Westholme, etc. etc.

On a warm June evening five years later Sarah Boynton and her husband sat in the stalls of a London theatre. The play was *Hamlet.* Sarah gripped Raymond's arm as Ophelia's words came floating over the footlights:

How should I your true love know
From another one?
By his cockle hat and staff,
And his sandal shoon.

He is dead and gone, lady,
He is dead and gone;
At his head a grass-green turf;
At his heels a stone.

O, ho!

A lump rose in Sarah's throat. That exquisite, witless beauty, that lovely, unearthly smile of one gone beyond trouble and grief to a region where only a floating mirage was truth. . . .

Sarah said to herself: "She's lovely—lovely . . ."

That haunting, lilting voice, always beautiful in tone, but now disciplined and modulated to be the perfect instrument.

Sarah said with decision, as the curtain fell at the end of the act:

"Jinny's a great actress—a great—great actress!"

Later, they sat around a supper table at the Savoy. Ginevra, smiling, remote, turned to the bearded man by her side.

"I was good, wasn't I, Theodore?"

"You were wonderful, *chêrie.*"

A happy smile floated on her lips.

She murmured:

"You always believed in me—you always knew I could do great things—sway multitudes. . . ."

At a table not far away, the Hamlet of the evening was saying gloomily:

"Her mannerisms! Of course people like it *just at first*—but what I say is, it's not *Shakespeare.* Did you see how she ruined my exit? . . ."

Nadine, sitting opposite Ginevra, said:

"How exciting it is, to be here in London with Jinny acting Ophelia and being so famous!"

Ginevra said softly:

"It was nice of you to come over."

"A regular family party," said Nadine, smiling, as she looked around. Then she said to Lennox: "I think the children might go to the matinee, don't you? They're quite old enough, and they *do* so want to see Aunt Jinny on the stage!"

Lennox, a sane, happy-looking Lennox with humorous eyes, lifted his glass.

"To the newly-weds, Mr. and Mrs. Cope!"

Jefferson Cope and Carol acknowledged the toast.

"The unfaithful swain!" said Carol, laughing. "Jeff, you'd better drink to your first love as she's sitting right opposite you."

Raymond said gaily:

"Jeff's blushing. He doesn't like being reminded of the old days."

His face clouded suddenly.

Sarah touched his hand with hers, and the cloud lifted. He looked at her and grinned.

"Seems just like a bad dream!"

A dapper figure stopped by their table. Hercule Poirot, faultlessly and beautifully appareled, his moustaches proudly twisted, bowed regally.

"Mademoiselle," he said to Ginevra, *"mes hommages.* You were superb!"

They greeted him affectionately, made a place for him beside Sarah.

He beamed on them all and when they were all talking, he leaned a little sideways and said softly to Sarah:

"Eh bien, it seems that all marches well now with *la famille Boynton?"*

"Thanks to *you!"* said Sarah.

"He becomes very eminent, your husband. I read today an excellent review of his last book."

"It's really rather good—although I do say it! Did you know that Carol and Jefferson Cope had made a match of it at last? And Lennox and Nadine have got two of the nicest children—cute, Raymond calls them. As for Jinny—well, I rather think Jinny's a genius."

She looked across the table at the lovely face and the red-gold crown of hair, and then she gave a tiny start.

For a moment her face was grave. She raised her glass slowly to her lips.

"You drink a toast, Madame?" asked Poirot.

Sarah said slowly:

"I thought—suddenly—of Her. Looking at Jinny I saw—for the first time—the likeness. The same thing—only Jinny is in light—where She was in darkness. . . ."

And from opposite, Ginevra said unexpectedly:

"Poor Mother . . . She was *queer*. . . . Now—that we're all so happy —I feel kind of sorry for her. She didn't get what she wanted out of life. It must have been tough for her."

Almost without a pause, her voice quivered softly into the lines from *Cymbeline* while the others listened spellbound to the music of them:

Fear no more the heat o' the sun,
Nor the furious winter's rages;
Thou thy worldly task hast done,
Home art gone, and ta'en thy wages . . .